THE SLAVES

Published earlier in the Janus Clan series:

The Defenseless

Next book Birds Flying in the Dark for sale April 30, 2011

Also published by Midnight Fire Media

Your Own Fate

(A few of the) Works to be published:

Night on Earth
The Afterglow trilogy
Season of the Witch
Alarums of Reality
Dreams Belong to the Night
ShadowWalk
Thunder Road: Ice and Fire
Falling
Black Dragon

Poems:

Complete poems 1989 - 2003

For a «complete» list of current and current future Amos Keppler and Midnight Fire Media projects see the back of the book and the Midnight Fire/Midnight Fire Media web pages.

The Janus Clan, Book Two

«The first twenty years - Book Two»
The years 1974 - 1975

The Slaves

By

Amos Keppler

MIDNIGHT FIRE MEDIA
2010

Midnight Fire Media

http://midnight-fire.net/mfm
For more about The Slaves and the Janus Clan:
http://midnight-fire.net/sw

E-Mail:
ak@midnight-fire.net
manofhood@yahoo.com

Cover, text, design, premedia, art and photos Amos Keppler

Crowd picture David Huxley

Also thanks to Obskur

ISBN 978-82-91693-09-5

Prologue: Mark

Chapter One

The body rested there, still and cold. Eyes stared at nothing, as the night ended, as the morning turned to day. There were flowers, flowers of red spread on the rocks surrounding the man. As the Sun passed its highest ascent the body started jerking in violent and sudden spasms. Flashes of reality started penetrating deep within the cold body, growing hot.

He saw several people walk on a broad road in a desert. They fell one by one, striving to reach the fire far ahead. He couldn't see their faces, but he saw bodies stumble and fall. There were mostly indistinct faces, moving forward on shaky legs, sweat pouring from their skin, stumbling through the desert, to the garden of fire ahead. This was the desert, a place no human could survive for long without moisture, without the water of life. And the humans walked, on the road, through the desert, and the road was no longer a road, but the desert itself, encompassing everything.

Eyes still and cold stared straight ahead and saw only sky. Fire lit those eyes. Those eyes blinked. He turned his head, and saw only rock. Eyes started moving, growing alive. Blood, there was blood everywhere. His face was covered in it, a stark mass not covering his eyes. He tore it off the sore skin of his face. He hurt, he knew that. His entire being hurt. It was as if somebody had set his entire body on fire, and he could feel every cell burn.

He turned around, crying out in pain, in rage, looking at all the blood covering the rocks. It looked like five people, at least five people, had bled on those rocks. He would know. He had seen a lot of people bleed. There was a cliff, one sticking out from the mountain wall, a considerable distance from the edge he had fallen off. Sounds penetrated his ears. Sounds of a gun fired, of a knife flying through the air. Images assaulted his eyes. Of battle, about a horror and rage he thought he had put behind him a long time ago. But he had been fooling himself. It wouldn't let him go. He wouldn't let it go. The image of the Cyclops, of One Eye flashed before his inner eye.

He looked dumbfounded around him, saw the image of the man with the staring, dead eyes. Everything around felt… alive. He laughed euphorically, an ugly, shrill sound scaring him to death. He laughed even harder. When looking at his hands it was as if they were glowing, as if he could see more of them like ghost images in the air. Shadows. The air was filled with shadows.

For a moment there, for just a moment he felt as if the Sun had descended and he bathed in its heat. He looked down, at the ravine far below. He looked up, at the edge up there, at the steep wall. The body stretched. He stretched it, felt it, piece-by-piece, limb-by-limb. His clothes… they felt tight, as if they belonged to a completely different person. Died in flames, he thought.

Reborn in fire.

He looked at the wall again. This is hard, he thought, but not impossible. He had been quite the mountaineer in his younger days. There was pain. He moved, stretching arms and legs. The pain turned dull, unimportant. And he started climbing, constantly feeling the sharp pain in his back as the pointed rocks far below penetrated his skin. He died, and was reborn a thousand times.

One hand rose up, finding the next strong or weak hold, holding on to it for his life, moving the heavyset body in the hand's wake. He giggled some more. Another hand reached up, searching for another hold. Not finding it. Seeking again. Gasping in relief when it's suddenly there. Repeat the procedure. Thoughts, actions of younger days returned to his mind on fire. He had been climbing. He and Jean together…

He kept climbing, trying not to think, not to think too much.

There were sounds, sounds of screaming, of screeching, but he saw nothing, saw no other humans awaiting him at the top of the mountain, no vengeful spirit. He was the vengeful spirit, returning from the abyss to wreak havoc on the unsuspecting world and all well planned plans.

Soft skin in his hand, not hard rock, distractions from the world. It had felt so good firing into the crowd that time in San Diego, letting go of all pretense, of all the false aspirations of civilization, and by doing that, embracing his humanity. There was more laughter. He rested on another, smaller cliff, outgrowth of the mountain, hearing the chatter of children and smiling in his stupor, his clarity of vision.

Dust. Dust in his eyes. As if he had been lying there forever. The dry desert sand, tempering his vision to a point of clarity he had never before seen, never before imagined. Dust settled, as the birds of prey, all the birds of prey descended on him. He opened his eyes wide, and stared straight at five eagle chicks gawking at him, seemingly expecting food of him, as if he was their mother. Huge, quite old chicks. Mother had been wise, hidden her chicks far away from where predators could reach them. He grabbed one fairly grown, fat chick, snapped its neck and began devouring it, sinking his teeth, his fangs into its soft flesh, all in one fluid move. A veritable spectacle erupted in the nest. The remaining chicks jumped up and down, as their scream grew louder, cutting through his eardrums like butter. He ignored it and kept digesting the dead, still warm carcass in his hands. The taste of feathers lingered in his mouth. He ignored that, too, everything but the overwhelming sense of Hunger. And as he fed it was as if the food… energized him, in a speed and way he had never before experienced. More distractions; the knowledge of how a full meat dinner usually took four to five hours to digest. One breath, he thought. One breath is a universe.

Blood and feathers slowly settled on the narrow ledge. He started on the second chick, still sensing the Hunger like a bottomless pit inside, hearing the flapping of the wings he had heard his entire life. His father and mother held around him, as they ran through ruins, as they ran for their lives. The flapping of wings turned sharp, distinct. He looked up, and saw the enraged adult golden eagle descend on him. Throwing away his bloody prey he managed to grab the big birds' feet as it descended on him. It attacked him with everything it had, its sharp claws, its beak, and its huge, powerful wings. They struck at him with a force of a hurricane. The claws scratched him. The beak hacked at his eyes and flesh. He threw the bird on the rock, but couldn't hold it down. One powerful flap of the wings and it was free. He grabbed a stick from the nest and began striking his enemy, striking at it with a rage easily comparable to that of the grieving mother. More blood, more feathers danced wildly in the air. Your eyes, he thought wildly. Protect your eyes. He struck again and again, as claws and beak penetrated deep below his skin, and he screamed insanely. He kept striking, striking, striking, until he had nothing but dead weight on his body. Breathing hard and painfully he threw the bird off himself, threw it away like garbage. It fell off the edge and descended slowly, very slowly to the bottom of the ravine, doing a tailspin fall. He looked at the three remaining chicks, shook his head and sat right down in his tracks. The adrenaline in his body made him see stars, red and dancing in his vision. He started breathing, started breathing right, almost automatically, an instinct labored through many years in danger. Hardly a minute had passed when he fought himself back on his feet, and continued climbing. The energy kept raging within him, kept him going. He didn't think, he just *did*.

He was up. He stood on the edge for minutes, as if challenging the mountain, the very wind itself to come and take him. Thinking now, thinking through everything.

Bernie, the dead man remained on the spot where he had killed him.

Nobody had touched the body. Dust had settled on its eyes.

This was a remote, deserted spot. No one would come up here. If anybody, anybody at all would come looking for him, they wouldn't come here. He began walking. First one step in front of the other, the simplest of movement, then faster, more determined. The bird's claws were probably infected. That was not unlikely. He felt the strength course through the body, as if the very poison itself strengthened him.

The fever visions assaulted him. He didn't know how far he had wandered. He didn't care. It was about him. The first time he had experienced death. He had been just a baby. And he, unlike other babies he had heard of, knew what it was. He had felt it, felt its black clouds descend on him, had seen and felt his mother be blown to bits by a German bomb. Then for years, the traveling with the gypsies, actually the happiest time in his life he could recall… until they discovered what he was, and had cast him out.

Then the Gidman family, David and Jean, the first small, cautious, elegant and still bungling burglaries in Anse des Catalans - the old town in Marseille, the city where everything, including human beings was for sale.

A family churchyard by an old English house, people, children and adults staring at him with their burning eyes. He had walked for so long, now, and still no sign of cars, no sign of people. Insane images flared through his inflamed mind.

He still sensed the Hunger, a rumble in his belly, a roar in his mind.

– I'm coming for you, Dave, he shouted. – I'm coming for you, Johnny, coming for you both.

They called to him, as they had always done, and he answered their call, now, finally, without reservations. The dead returned, returned to greet him. He glimpsed Wolf Connors with the usual grin stamped on his face. He saw Nancy. Her face always blocked all the others, eventually, but this time she came almost instantly. She was the eagle coming for him, his angel of death, her wide wings of shadow covering the Earth. Its beak opened. It swallowed him whole, and he was gone.

Shaking with exhaustion and insanity he fell into a deep and large darkness.

2

There was a shed on the edge of the valley, hidden in the bumpy terrain. Francis Caine sat on a rock outside it, smoking, puffing hard on the cigar, something he never did.

The telegram had been short and to the point: I NEED HELP!

Those three words had set in motion a preset pattern. Mark Stewart had showed Caine this shed years ago, in case of this kind of emergency ever happening. And now - it had. Stewart lay delirious on the mattress inside, more alive, deader than ever. Caine couldn't understand how he had been able to walk, far less how he had managed to walk on his feet all this way. Caine was fairly familiar with the Denver area. He knew fully well the approximate distance between here and there, the fateful precipice.

– Clarke, Stewart had gasped, from the mattress.

Caine had nodded, about to confirm that he would indeed be contacting their old fellow gunman as soon as possible.

– *Don't trust Clarke,* Stewart had snarled.

And then, with that horrible, ghostly voice Stewart had rested. Caine still heard the words and felt them to his marrow of being.

3

Stewart sat upright on the bed. Caine had just returned from outside, and couldn't tell how long he had been sitting there.

– There isn't a mark on your body, Caine said lamely. – When you stumbled upon the shed you were more dead than alive. Now you're healthy as a horse.

– I've never felt better, Stewart said.

Caine saw it, too, actually saw it with his two eyes. There was something different about him. Not something easily discernible, but clear and present.

– Do you have any food?

– A month full, as agreed, the man who was called and called himself the Gambler nodded.

Stewart left the bed, completely naked. Caine threw some clothes to him. Stewart dressed, and sat down by the sparse table. He started making sandwiches, feeding while making.

Caine sat down, too, taking his time eating, savoring it, a stark contrast to the wolf at the other side of the table.

– So Clarke is in on it?

Stewart nodded.

– That doesn't really surprise me. The Gambler nodded, too. – He was, after all, in spite of everything always more of a mercenary than the rest of us. I think he, at a certain point, joined us out of convenience, more than anything else.

He grabbed a newspaper from a bag, and threw it on the table. The headline screamed at them:

TWENTY-THREE YOUTHS VANISHED IN LAKE COUNTY

– Has he taken up Gidman's old habit? Perhaps with some of Dave's old friends?

– No. Stewart shook his head, shook it hard. – It's just Dave himself, keeping up his old habits.

Caine paled. His dark skin turned gray and unhealthy.

– But we… you killed him. You filled him with bullets, for God's sake.

– And the day after he rose from the slab and quite simply walked away. You saw the file. You even spotted him in Las Vegas.

– I thought I did. I…

– He and Clarke, and a henchman threw me off the mountain, Frankie. He has returned from death, better than ever. Just like *I* did.

Caine froze then, froze again.

– They did move fast. I wouldn't have thought Ted and the others would even be in Leadville yet.

– You've been in that bed for three weeks, the Gambler stated numbly. – First you were delirious, ranting and raving, but eating everything I put into you, asking for another helping. It was… uncanny. Then… you were absolutely still. Not sweating anymore. Not feverish anymore. Hardly breathing, almost in a coma, and I considered taking you to a hospital, and in the very moment that thought struck me you said:

– *Don't!*

Caine remembered, sensed once again the… presence in the room. That was Stewart, but not, not as he had been.

– I've grown, my friend, Stewart said. – I was in a healing coma, and I've become more than I was.

Caine looked at the table, at the remains of the food Stewart had consumed. It was enough for five men. It had been several days since he had last eaten, but Caine still felt shaken, disturbed in the presence of his old friend, and he realized suddenly, shockingly that he always would. His world had changed, irrevocably.

Caine looked in the mirror. It was an old and dusty mirror. He touched the gray hair at his temples. He was fifty, not really looking the part. But the dust in the mirror seemed to… to touch him, to claim him as its own.

Stewart hadn't changed a bit. He was as young, as vibrant as he had been when Caine had first seen him, his three weeks in bed merely a passing inconvenience. To the Gambler's trained eye he did sway ever so little, but the will to move cursed through him, and he wouldn't be stalled. And he was more, more than he had ever been. There was a kind of impatience there, now, which hadn't been there the last time Caine had seen him. Not before, after, or during the skirmish in San Diego. He had changed.

The two of them left the cabin at dusk. It was just a short walk to the road, and to the car. Stewart accepted Caine's second Luger 1.92 mm with a nod.

Caine took the wheel. Stewart sat down in the other front seat with a distant look in his eyes. They headed towards Denver.

– What's happening, Mark? The Gambler asked.

– I don't know, Francis. Stewart smiled a bit, staring ahead, at the sunset, at the deep red sky. – A vast, terrible tapestry is revealing itself before my eyes, and I can see only bits and pieces.

He turned to his old friend, and it was as if the Sunset turned with him. Frost rattled the experienced fifty-year-old man.

– This isn't something we could have chosen to step away from. It isn't just a matter of Jean and Gidman here. You can go back to Vegas, now, Francis, to your wife and children. Gidman will probably not bother to come for you, not in a few years, anyway, but he will come, and so will… others. There will be no safe place, not on Earth.

Caine looked hard at him. Something hidden and dangerous had awakened in the younger man. It might have been dormant, during times of relative peace, but now it wasn't hiding anymore.

– What are you *talking* about?

– Sorry, old friend, I wasn't aware I was talking…

Denver rose in front of them, the low suburban houses, the tall downtown buildings. Denver was like any major city, dead inside, somewhat less dead outside.

– I need to pick up some stuff, but first we need to take a detour.

He pointed without pointing and Caine turned south.

– I can hear, Stewart sang. – I can hear the roar of the river.

Cain opened his mouth to speak, but there was no sound coming out of it.

South Platte River ran from the south, its rough currents originating somewhere in the mountains.

– So there will be stealth then? Caine finally managed to speak.

– That does seem like the prudent cause of action, Stewart nodded.

– You're dead, Caine pointed out. – We should try to capitalize on that, shouldn't we?

– We should indeed.

– Okay, Caine said. – Let's get moving.

He stopped the car on a dusty, natural parking space where the river made a turn, where there was an old, worn down white-painted house downstream. The remote look in Stewart's eyes intensified as he looked at its gray shape in the approaching dark. He let Caine lead, as they left the car behind.

– There is this nice hideout close by, he said casually.

Caine stopped and let him pass. Stewart led on, on a narrow trail up river, to a natural, secluded spot, where they had a nice view of the nice, old house, to its front side.

And the white foaming river Caine couldn't hear.

– Denver is a great place, he said. – You chose a great place to settle down.

He cursed himself inside. It was a stupid thing to say, but he had to relieve the pressure somehow.

Stewart didn't reply or comment on it. Eyes glowing in fire stared at the house, moving their attention around in its surroundings. And the ears… Caine gasped. The ears moved.

Suddenly, The Gambler was sweating and his heart hammering in his chest.

Stewart listened. He observed the area with his entire self. An uncanny ability Caine had often wondered about. But not like this. Not like this.

– He's coming, Stewart said, his voice hardly audible.

– Who? Caine whispered.

– Chin. I can hear his silent steps on the forest bed, see the leaves bend when he passes them.

Stewart turned to his old friend, eyes black and huge.

– I'm down there with him. Do you understand?

Stewart turned away again.

– Of course you don't. You can't.

A car appeared around the turn down the road. One recently waxed and with six doors. The strong lights crossed the place where the two were hiding, and in one horrible moment Caine imagined they were made, but that was impossible.

The car stopped outside the gate. The driver stepped outside and opened the door for the passenger. The passenger left the car, left the driver behind. Wait here, he said.

– That's Jeff McCabe, Stewart said. – The Chief Commissioner.

The front door of the house opened. Two people stepped out on the stairs. Cindy and Rodney Cousin. From the forest below a figure hardly seen joined the other three, turning visible, turning real. Caine easily recognized him from Stewart's description. The four arrived at the spot at the base of the stairs simultaneously. The Square, the quartet was complete. They… fit together. Even an untrained observer would easily see that, even though he or she probably couldn't have articulated it.

– The Commissioner could be visiting worried parents… Caine said hesitatingly, – but Chin is hardly one to do that, right? He doesn't fit in… but he does.

– They aren't… worried. Stewart concentrated with sweat on his brow. – They're kind of excited, but also calm and relaxed.

He put a finger to his lips, signaling for Caine to be silent.

It was unnecessary, really, or shouldn't have been necessary, but Caine felt shaken, off center.

– How can you hear them? You haven't learned lip reading lately, have you?

Caine strained his hears, but could only hear the wind, the wind blowing towards the two, away from the four.

– I have good hearing. You know that.

The Gambler cursed himself silently, attempting to concentrate, to push beyond the illusion, to set aside unimportant details, what he once had taught Stewart.

Then there was some aggravation down there, as Cousin spoke to McCabe.

– He's giving voice to his discontent, Stewart said. – He wants in on the action. McCabe says: «Your work is done. All you can do now, before returning home is to act out the final scene of your play».

Caine wanted to say something, but he had learned patience in his long life of strife. He just hadn't ever been very good at it.

Suddenly he did hear something, and this was a sound he recognized immediately. It wasn't much. He looked at Stewart's eyes, his stance and knew he, too, had heard it, noticed it. People moving through the forest. There was no smell. There was the smell of metal and oil. Drawn guns. Caine and Stewart drew their own, silently, perhaps not silent enough. Whoever moved through the forest would also be able to hear soundless sounds, smell smells that weren't there, see movements beyond the leaf blowing in the wind. The group charging didn't charge them. They passed the mound and proceeded towards the house, and probably not just from this side, but from every side. Caine turned. He had only looked away for a moment. The four people below the stairs. They vanished rolling on the ground, faded into the general background. He glimpsed Cindy Cousin with a gun in her hand, firing at one of the attackers. There was no sound but the tiny pop the two men on the mound knew so well, that caused by the use of a silencer. She hit him right on the head, and he fell like a wet cloth. Blood and remains of the brain floated in the darkness above the body. There was heard a kind of gurgling sound when one of the attackers was strangled. It was impossible to say who did it. Probably Chin, but they couldn't be certain.

Look at him go, Stewart said silently.

McCabe moved like lightning down there. He fired from both his right and left hand, and killed two adversaries at the precise same moment. Everybody used silencers. There were screams, low and high-pitched, but no thunderous sound of a gun. The attackers were everywhere, but they had no places to go. Rodney Cousin threw knives. Cindy smashed the larynx with swift, deadly kicks. Caine sort of recognized the art form as something resembling Savate, where predominantly feet were used, but this was more elaborate than any Savate he had ever seen. The attackers were massacred. Before they were even aware of it half of them had died, and the second after that four more lay lifeless on the ground. They fled, but didn't get far. Only one got away, and probably just because the four wanted him to. As a message, a warning to whoever had sent the squad. Stewart pointed his gun at the man, as he ran away. It looked as if he debated with himself, whether or not he should kill him.

He fired. The bullet hit the man's head, and he died in an instant. No scream, no sound, as the body hit the ground.

The two looked back at the four. The Square stood there quietly, as relaxed as ever. They hardly even breathed hard. Not McCabe either, a man well over seventy. He looked like he had taken a stroll in the park. The park was dark red. They made no indication they suspected there was anybody else nearby. McCabe said something. Caine could almost make it out.

– He says: Stewart said. – «We have done what we set out to do. We have let loose the beasts of the world, and now we can only wait. Now… it begins».

No more was said. Rodney and Cindy Cousin returned to their house. There were no discernible goodbyes. The scarred oriental man slipped back into the forest. McCabe returned to his luxurious car, a vehicle befitting a Chief.

Silence once more grated the place, and Francis Caine could finally hear the river.

– Let's sneak away from here, Stewart said. – You're right. I'm dead, at least to some people. I want to keep it that way.

They waited a few more minutes, then left, returning to the car. There were mangled and bloody corpses everywhere. Somebody would come and pick them up soon, but no one did yet. For the moment they just lay there, gathering dust and air. The two men moved cautiously, the need for it unnecessary to stress. The four they had spied on had casually and easily executed a number of dangerous people many times their number. Chin was clearly still out here somewhere. They had seen him. And for all they knew the others could be, too. They had learned early in life not to necessarily trust their eyes. Stewart concentrated, constantly moving, moving his eyes, moving his entire self, moving parts of the body almost independently of his body, more astute than Caine had ever seen him.

– Chin isn't here. Stewart said. He started moving a little less sneaky through the terrain.

– But you said you couldn't see him, that he moved like a shadow on the ground.

– I couldn't.

They reached the car. As a part of an old routine they didn't question they looked under the hood, under the car and made a quick search virtually everywhere, before entering the car, before starting it. It took less than a minute. They sat a while in silence.

– So, McCabe is calling the shots, huh?

– It would seem that way. Stewart nodded. – At least he is calling the shots here. I have always thought there was something fishy about him, but exactly what kept eluding me… as if there was nothing there, no cause for alarm or suspicion.

Clarity lit his eyes. Caine shuddered. He could literally see how Stewart's mind worked overtime, how pieces of puzzles moved around in there, how patterns of complexity formed and broke, and formed again.

They returned to downtown, once again taking the circular route.

– Time to pick up my stuff, Stewart stated.

The car was gone. They had put it behind them and they hardly recalled doing so. As they circled in on the little red house Stewart stopped for a moment. Caine imagined he was actually sniffing the air.

– Your ears are *moving*, Caine stated, feeling very foolish.

– So what? It isn't common, but a lot of humans are able to move their ears.

Caine had looked for a word all day, and now it finally dawned on him.

Awkward. Everything felt very awkward. He wondered if he knew this man by his side. If he had ever met him before or just thought he had. He thought perhaps he had encountered the mirror image, and that this was the real person.

The door to the house was closed, locked. Stewart found the keys in his pocket and unlocked, opened it. They walked inside. The air inside was old, decayed. They didn't turn on any lights, but watched it all illuminated by the streetlights outside.

– Someone has cleaned up here, he said. – Aside from that, nothing is missing.

– Not even you or Jean.

– Either Clarke has fixed that, Stewart said drawling, considering, – or… McCabe.

The two looked at each other, at that moment totally in tune.

– Damn, he has been here the whole time. I checked up on him once. He has been here since the fifties… as long as Linda, Mike and Ted have been here.

– And now, Caine said, – now, his time is up.

– Yes… he's leaving. I heard a definite quality of finality in his voice. They're all leaving. Denver is no longer important to them.

The rage returned to Stewart's eyes, the distant look returned. He walked to one corner of the living room, the one farthest from the street, and he grabbed the rug and pulled hard. Furniture fell with a series of cracks. A trapdoor was revealed. Dust rose from the floor, and in such insane amounts that Stewart was momentarily hidden from Caine's prying eyes. The dust turned into fog, into mist.

The trapdoor opened, seemingly by itself. A hole appeared in the floor. Caine coughed and climbed over the turned over furniture, as Stewart reappeared on his way down the ladder. There was a kind of cellar down there, small but big enough for one, even two humans, and supplies.

– Things I've stolen from the police during the years, Stewart grinned, and then once more turning somber: – Waiting for this day to come.

There was ammunition, various assault weapons, the Colt Peacemaker 45", with the inscription.

– This is *his?* Caine wondered, whispered.

– This is one of two. I found this one.

– You… found it?

– Yes. Stewart didn't say more.

He grabbed it and put it inside his coat. There was another thing there, a pouch, he also treated with ambiguity.

– I'm told this belonged to my mother, he said. – She was a witch. She could do magic.

The Gambler was speechless. For the first time in his life he quite simply didn't know what to say. So he said nothing.

Stewart didn't bother closing the trapdoor. He didn't bother closing the door to the house.

Let them wonder, he thought. Let them fear the ghost chasing them.

– So, where do you think old Dave has set up shop this time? Francis Caine hawked and hawked, never really able to clear this throat.

– Somewhere far away, Stewart said distantly, – but I will find him.

– I will kill him.

His voice turned icy and cold. Hatred flared in the large man's eyes. Something long forgotten and dangerous had awakened within him.

– I will kill them.

And in a tree close by a raven flapped its wings, and blood dripped from its beak.

Part one: The Slaves

Chapter Two

Glory Burns stretched her nude body pleasantly in the large, soft bed, lying uncovered in the warm room, the heated air playing with her skin. Linda and Ted Cousin knelt on the bed's edge, their features frozen, their eyes empty. They awaited her command, her slightest whim.

– I and my old parents had to move from the city of Memphis. Glory spoke almost dreamily, like she wasn't there at all. – White «entrepreneurs», developers, chased us off like animals. We had done nothing, nothing to oppose them, nothing to raise their wrath. We were just there, and they didn't want us to be there anymore. So they snapped their fingers and we were gone. Just like that. They chased us off the property the family had owned for generations. It was that easy. Mom and dad had been sick for quite a while. Contaminated water, I guess. Or food or whatever. The thugs beat them both harshly when they threw us out. They just put us on a train afterwards, like cattle. There were many others there, people like ourselves, without hope, without future, without anything worth living for. My parents died shortly after the departure. They shouldn't have, really. Others had taken beatings just as bad and lived in places where the water or something was bad, but my mom and dad had just… lost the will to live. I screamed, begged for a doctor to come and help, for anybody to come, but no one came. I was fifteen. I sat there, fumbling with the scissor in my purse, thinking about ending it. I was so close. I sat there, not dropping a single tear, staring ahead, seeing nothing. A railway representative made sure the bodies were promptly removed, like our remaining money was swiftly removed from dad's wallet. He expressed his sympathies, and then proceeded to drag me into an empty coach, and tear my clothes off. As he pushed me down on the floor and undressed in gasps and furious moves, I pulled the scissor from my purse and stabbed him repeatedly. Blood splashed all over me. I crouched there, with him over me, until the police came and fetched me. Two huge pigs threw me into a patrol car, and were about to join me there when an even bigger man, a giant attacked them. He broke their necks, like other people break twigs. I remember it clearly. I felt no fear for David Gidman that day. The black patch covering one of his eye-sockets just incited trust. He had wounds, too. He wanted to know if I wanted to strike back at the whites, and of course I did. He took me to Denver, and I waited there, waited patiently for this day to come.

She turned and crawled to the end of the bed, to Ted, touching his cheek, caressing his golden bracelets, his humming collar.

– But you're not exactly white, are you. You're not nigger or chink, or anything else either. You're nothing. You belong nowhere, except here, with me. You've got wounds, too. But you're safe here, with me, safe from the big bad world, under my protection.

She touched her own thighs, wet, slippery and supple. Seed flowed from her cunt, Ted Cousin's seed, her property.

– This is the world, she said softly. – The world the masters have created. Most people don't want to face reality, see the world as it truly is. I didn't myself. They just go about their daily chores, and pray the world beyond their cozy, little illusion won't notice them, won't destroy their safe little pocket of reality.

She studied him, the short, clean-cut hair, the dull eyes.

– You're neutered, now. She nodded. – Hardly more dangerous than a doe picking its crumbs. Come to me, picking dove, pick me softly.

Suddenly voice turned hoarse, longing.

He obeyed, of course, like a well-trained animal, knowing fully well how she wanted it, how she liked it. Expectation rose in her, as he crawled up on her increasingly excited body. Her nipples hardened. Excitement turned to desire, desire to need. She sensed his hand in her groin. Skilled like a doll, a robot. Her heat rose, inevitably. She wanted him, wanted him inside of her, hard and thick. A pet did that, satisfied the master or mistress on all levels, at all times. She waited for his hard thing, and later the hot, pleasant flow of seed inside… but it didn't come. He had climbed her, as always, moved on her, as always. His face wasn't quite the same. He looked scared. Weak in her need she felt him below. Everything was just soft and dead.

– Damn you! She shouted, in a fit of rage.

She slapped him on a cheek. It cracked aloud when the hard hand hit his skin, and his head was pushed aside. She kicked him hard, so hard that he practically flew out of bed. He hit the floor hard, hardly preparing for the fall. Even his most primal instincts had been dulled. There was no anger in his eyes, hardly any reaction at all, except subservience. Just like a dog. She laughed out aloud.

– You've failed to please me, slave, she told him, in a strict, patronizing tone. As punishment you will be chained all day. Perhaps then you will have learned to be a good dog.

– As you wish, Mistress, he acknowledged, the pain hardly tangible in his voice, but she did hear it, and it pleased her.

He walked to the post by the wall, and fit an extra collar around his neck, eagerly, unthinkingly doing her bidding. She looked for a reaction in his impassive face, but there was no change there. Suddenly a burst of irritation welled up in her. He was too fucking docile.

She turned to Linda.

– Fill the tub for me, you stupid beast, she ordered.

– At once, Mistress, the ice-blonde beauty responded instantly.

She jumped out of bed and ran to the bathroom, nothing running through her mind but the need, the eagerness to obey, to serve, to please.

Glory burst into laughter.

– A stuck-up white bitch being the eager servant slave of Glory Burns? That, I tell you, would have caused some raised eyebrows in Memphis. In stuck-up, white Memphis.

She walked to Ted, to the pair of dead eyes, grabbing his jaw hard.

– I've always wanted this, she stated. – This is exactly what I've always wanted.

She scorned him with her pose and her words.

– How does it feel to be totally at my mercy? How does it feel to be dirt under someone's heel?

She didn't really expect an answer, and didn't get any. The fine-tuning of his hearing had taught him the nuances in her voice. Rhetoric wasn't supposed to be replied to. And the slaves didn't. Like good slaves. She let go of him. His head hit the wall. She left him and walked to the bathroom. Linda waited for her there, and knelt the moment Glory crossed the threshold.

– The bath is ready, Mistress, Linda, Linda *the slave* reported humbly.

– Excellent, Linda. Glory patted her head.

Like she would a dog.

She looked at the large, luxurious bathroom. The «tub» was a long, broad pool. Soft carpets covered the floor. Decorations on the walls included paintings and more carpets.

– I did it, she said astonished. – I succeeded. My mission succeeded.

She stepped into the pool. It was so big that she could even swim a bit in it. She did. Lazy strokes, enjoying the moment. She sat in a corner. Water was fresh and cooling. Linda soaped her in with those soft hands of her.

– The Mistress is very pleased with you, she intoned. – Very, very pleased.

The slave moaned in pleasure, as she was given her reward.

Did the blue eyes shift somehow, or was it the same unchanging dull expression there? If there had been anything, it was gone now.

Suddenly there was a trickle down her spine. She turned abruptly, looking through the opening, out in the bedroom. She couldn't see Ted, but that wasn't strange. She couldn't see his spot from this position, and it shouldn't have worried her.

Linda rinsed her and washed her with a big, soft sponge. The slave directed her gently, as she was allowed to do in these matters. Glory stood upright in the middle of the pool, while Linda did her hair and body, preparing her for the upcoming tasks, and duties. First the slaves did their Mistress, then they would do each other. Glory felt the slave's hands in her hair, on her body. Glory Burns shivered in the hot water and steam. She imagined Ted out there, chained to the wall. But what she saw wasn't the dull eyes and submissive expression she had come to expect lately. What she saw was a figure shaking in rage, eyes burning in hatred, tears of fire flowing from those eyes, a shadow creature engulfed in dark flames, and she could no longer breathe.

++++++++++++++++++++++++++++++

There was a harbor, there, in the jungle, one very small compared to the enormous structure towering above it. The pyramid was mostly hidden in the jungle, surrounded by tall trees, covered in growth. At a distance, if one spotted the structure at all, it could be confused with one of the many ruins in the area, the remnants of the past. But there were fences around this one, tall, electrified fences. There were guards and growling, four-legged dogs patrolling both inside and outside the estate. The pyramid rose at the night sky, as a revenant. Its surface, beneath the moss and dirt was smooth metal.

Its outer shell was just that, walls covering the vast open space inside.

She pictured it all in her mind, Glory Burns did. She remembered the garden, the storybook midsection of the pyramid, and she remembered the gutter. There was pain, a touch of a hand to the belly, a contraction of the brows. She did the tour in her mind. The tour she had taken along Bob and other valued soldiers to the cause, with a superior and guests, prospective members of the cabal, the inner circle. The superior, the guide, had been Shuen Parker, a young woman with at least part oriental blood. She was tall, taller than Glory. Glory recalled her eyes. More than anything she recalled and constantly re-experienced the eerie light in there somewhere.

The stench was present in her nose, not strong, but always there.

– Welcome, honored guests, young charges, Shuen Parker said proudly, – to the pens.

There was light here, even light even, but there were still shadows everywhere.

This is it, Glory thought. The gutter of the world.

There were cages, hands clutching bars and screams coming from the very walls surrounding them.

– This is the reception area, Shuen Parker said. – The place where the slaves receive their first lessons, and the initial training required for them to later learn their glorious lot in life. In fact, a new batch is coming in right now. I would suggest we stay a while, observing the proceedings.

No one opposed or even commented on her words. Glory observed the guests, the prospectives, the new charges. She saw the apprehension and eagerness in their eyes and stance. They had come to a place where all their dreams, all their nightmares came true.

A new, large group of males and females were brought into the pens, chained hand and feet, chained together, stumbling forward, totally blind by the masks pulled down on their heads.

– What is happening? A boy cried out again and again, in a loud, shrill voice. – What is happening, what is *happening?*

They were being chained to the wall. Their arms stretched high above their heads. Then the whipping started, and the screaming began. The loud cracks when the lash hit the naked skin reverberated in the room. Glory stared at it, unable to look away. She had attempted to close her eyes, but the images echoed in her mind, the sounds mirrored in her ears.

The prisoners, sobbing and howling were separated and thrown into cages. Some lay still, shaking like leaves. Others sought out the bars, and when finding them held onto them as if they were pure gold.

– What's happening? The boy kept saying, his words hardly intelligible, now, after the brutal lashing, and the sobbing made snivel flow from his nose.

There was music somewhere, loud and shrieking, cutting like broken glass. Glory knew there was. She had heard it in her nightmares and slumber.

And beyond, beneath that, and the screams and desolation, she heard the machine, its whirring and turning.

They walked the route, walked the path, of the slaves, the path of suffering. Shuen Parker made no secret of her intentions. She wanted them to see, to experience, to be force-fed it all, so they never forgot.

Dust surrounded them, as they visited the Room of Pain. Their eyes were open.

My eyes are open, Glory thought.

– We are reaching significant numbers already, Parker commented, teaching them. – Even though we're still in test mode, we're having trouble handling all the new arrivals. This place will be full soon. Construction is already well under way on three new facilities, and then we will start in earnest rebuilding the old world, here in this wonderful brave new world. Those who deserve it will continue to rule the world. The rest will continue to serve. It's the way of the world, the way it has always been. Most people won't even realize the subtle changes, the return of the more overt ways of ownership and servitude.

The initiates stopped before the turning pyramids, studied the beasts inside, studied every nuance of muscle, sinew and smile. The quartets within the pyramids performed splendidly and Parker threw candy to them. They caught it with grateful smiles, and pleased moans.

– To call these creatures *slaves* is a bit kind, of course. Slaves have a certain ability to reason, a modicum of independence. These are more like beasts, allowed to bask in the glory of the gods.

Glory shook. She couldn't stop and she couldn't hide it, noticing to her horror that she was wet between her thighs, that the pain down below had suddenly reached an unbearable, previously never before experienced level. She smiled in her fear. She smiled at Ted, not noticing she was doing it.

She remembered touching Ted's cock, and it didn't belong to him anymore, but to her.

Days seemingly passed as they all were tested and prodded. And they passed, they knew they did, even though they couldn't say for sure if they were still all there, when they met again.

They finally reached the elevator, one of four that, except for one single staircase was the only way further up. All five access points were heavily guarded. Ten armed men greeted them with raised guns. Ten more waited inside the room, the large room that was the elevator. Luxury, everything here was the very lap of luxury. They had spared no expenses. None!

The prospective Masters emerged into the large, inner atrium. There was a lot of light here, of daylight. Huge, thick plates of glass revealed the jungle, the sun outside. Parker stopped, and they stopped, too. She studied them, with her merciless eyes.

– You have all been scrutinized and carefully selected for membership, for service. You joined our ranks the moment you accepted our invitation. You may choose to serve in lower stations, but you can never leave us. You will address your superiors either as «My Lady» or «My Lord». The slaves will call you Master. We hold hard with the old ways here.

What an insidious, devious plot, Glory thought. It is fear. Fear is the key.

– We are the guides of guides, the force behind the throne, Shuen Parker said. – We herd the world. On Earth there is a white light, illuminating everything, a garden where no weed is growing, and we are its gardeners. We are the Thousand Feet, the Abraxas Omega, the everything and the all.

Glory observed how the others repeated the Lady's word, and Glory found herself moving her own lips, as well, in something becoming a chant, becoming a litany, a litany of fear.

More days passed, and nights, too, even though she hardly noticed them.

So close are these walls, Glory Burns thought. They're smothering me, like a mother's touch.

She left her quarters, with her two, personal slaves in tow, holding them by thin chains attached to their collars. The corridor outside her home was cold and impersonal. An even, white light made everything the same. It gave her the willies, it did. She recalled Linda's sea blue cold eyes during the bathing and washing, her lilywhite hands, the glimpses of the dark one outside, chained to the wall.

And she heard the hum of the engine, the machine. It surrounded her, embraced, penetrated her skin, until it became a part of her, she became a part of it, until she, too, hummed and whirred, and hardly moved except in stiff, mechanical movements.

She moved exclusively horizontally today. Her two slaves walked behind her, hardly there at all. She was dressed in the prescribed black silk robe. Her hair was done, well done. She felt it dance behind her back, tickle the skin beneath the robe. The breasts clearly showed in the cleft of the robe, the nipples visible through the cloth. She knew she was desirable, knew she needed to be, knew it as she curled and pouted her full lips.

After a few minutes walk she met Bob, Bob Tremblay. She hardly thought of him by his name anymore. He had transformed into something new and strange.

He had Tilla in tow. Glory studied Ted, studied Tilla, but there was not even a hint of recognition in any of their eyes.

But in Bob's eyes she saw a lot, a pleasure, a glee making her uneasy. She knew he had been offered Ted, but he had declined and taken Tilla instead.

He had had the bandages removed by now. Glory saw that the surgery had worked wonders. The face was no longer one single heap of skin and bones and blood. There weren't even any scars to speak of. Quite remarkable. But he would never regain his face as it had been. His skin had an eerie, bluish taint and there wasn't any pronounced facial hair. His smile wasn't a smile, but a sickly grin beyond description. An unbidden thought entered Glory's conscious mind: And that was how he looked inside, as well.

They hardly spoke, except the exchange of pleasantries, and continued on their way together.

There was only one guard at this gate, and it could hardly be called a gate either. It was just a passage really, with a man holding a gun blocking the way.

He stepped aside. No words were spoken. Glory and Bob entered the atrium, the bright hall leading into the center of the pyramid.

– Symmetry, everything here is symmetry. Bob looked elated at her and the surroundings with insane eyes. – Everything fits. Everything has its place.

He shook, shook hard Tilla's chain. She stumbled and almost lost her footing. Her face didn't change expression. There wasn't a single, discernible change in the doll-like face.

– Look at her, he said. – Look at them. Now they're all *fixed.* Now they are as they're supposed to be.

She did look. There was nothing there she hadn't seen before, but she looked still.

They reached the center, the large, luxurious living room. The smell of flowers, long since noticeable, became overwhelming. And there were guards. They weren't seen, they weren't heard, but they were here. There weren't any visible shadows here, but hidden in those shadows were the people ready to shoot and kill her at a moment's notice. The two of them, the five of them, she corrected herself, approached the people around the expensive table, on the couch, in the deep chairs. She looked at them and couldn't stop apprehension from entering her heart, her paper heart. As she looked at Kurt Meinz, David Gidman, Shuen Parker, The Mask, Kurman Al Rashid and Rudolf Verheyen.

These were the people, the masters, who could either condemn or condone her. Her counselor, her teacher, her immediate superior, who tested and guided her, spoke about them as if they were gods.

And they were.

She and her fellow acolyte approached them respectfully. She curtseyed. He bowed. The slaves knelt on the floor behind them.

– My Lords, My Lady, she greeted them. – We were called and we came.

She spoke. She was higher ranked than Bob. He had failed in his mission. She had not. The only reason he was still here, still standing, and not kneeling on the floor was his father and his powerful connections. Connections were everything.

Her eyes fell on Gidman, shyly, apprehensive, interested beyond herself. And the hot, burning place below intensified in strength and power.

– We called you and you came, the Mask said. – We bid you welcome, young charges.

She wondered about his voice, as she attempted to keep her calm, her pretence of indifference. It wasn't distorted. There was an opening for the mouth. And she wondered.

She listened. Everything was so quiet, so very quiet.

The six studied her, studied them, constantly evaluating, judging. Fear was heavy in her gut.

Silent, she thought. Everything is always silent here.

She moved and displayed herself to them, with small gestures, with a smile and an admiring look. They were her superiors, her milk and blood. And her slaves moved with her, attentive to *her* needs, her demands, an extension of her being, like Glory herself was an extension of the six people gauging her.

– My Lords, My Lady, she curtseyed, – we present these slaves to you, present ourselves.

– And what a presentation it is, David Gidman, One Eye stated… eying her.

And the Cyclops eyed her, and she was frozen as ice on a glacier, melting like lava in a volcano.

– Sit with us, Glory. Shuen Parker patted the available seat to her left.

Nobody told Bob to sit and he stood. Glory sat down, feeling the soft velvet cushion of the seat. One Eye didn't look at her. It was as if he didn't even acknowledge her presence, but merely his close proximity made her glow in heat, and she could hardly think.

There was music somewhere, a low rumble making her rattle and shake, making her freeze on her spot.

– I fucking love this, Verheyen rumbled. – A place where everybody knows their place, knows how to behave before their betters.

Verheyen was from South Africa, belonging to the ruling caste there. Glory didn't find his position surprising.

– It's a great relief, My Lord, she replied politely.

She sat there among them, quietly, unmoving, while they, her betters were having their conversation. She didn't really listen, she listened, scared to death to be caught unaware, to be found unworthy.

– You've done well, Glory, Parker said pleasantly. – It will not be forgotten.

– Thank you, My Lady.

A servant arrived with a plate of fruit. Parker took a plum, biting into the juicy flesh. Glory did, too, feeling the cold juice on her lips, on her jaw.

– So, any problems with the slaves?

– No, she replied, pretending to be considering it. – They're so polite, so obedient, so serving and pleasing that I can hardly believe it. I hardly recognize them. They're like puppets, their eyes, their movements, stiff and doll-like. It is like they're not *they,* at all.

– And does this bother you? Gidman asked.

– Hell, no, it exalts me, My Lord. She gave him her best, sensuous smile. While she looked shyly into his eye the smoldering heat below increased even a notch or two more.

– Come to my quarters tomorrow, he commanded.

And she opened and closed her mouth in an inaudible gasp.

She hadn't been asked to visibly or audibly consent, so she didn't. One didn't refuse a Lord's order. One eagerly obeyed it.

Kurt Meinz rose, and she only marginally managed to focus on him.

– Then we're all done here, I gather? He said, to his fellow cabal members. – Time for the doctor's appointment, perhaps?

– We're done, the Mask nodded. – We've seen what we wanted to see. You guys just run along.

Very patronizing, very condescending. Glory saw and practically felt Meinz' reaction, saw beneath his mask of indifference.

She rose, too, and accompanied by Bob and the three slaves, she followed Meinz, followed him closely, with weary eyes, as he left the bright, open space and headed for the shadows. She looked around. At his quarters, his office, an office far superior to the one he used below. She couldn't remember getting here. But she was here, she knew that. Bob was here. And Ted, Linda and Tilla. Nobody was here, except Kurt Meinz. They were all merely extensions of his being. She sensed his power, and shivered and shrank in his presence.

He struck Ted. Ted's head was pushed aside. Aside from that, there was no reaction, not a single visible reaction, neither voiced nor shown. Meinz pushed the boy down on the floor, and started kicking him, started punishing him. There were moans of pain, but the eyes remained glass, glass, glass. Bob looked at it all with wonder in his eyes.

– Isn't this the… wrong choice of treatment, he queried. – If you want the conditioning to last, I mean?

– On the contrary. Meinz breathed heavily. Glory never saw him excited, except when Ted was nearby. – These are tests designed to show if the slaves have reached the required level where further teaching may begin.

When Ted was present Meinz was almost human.

– But won't the bad treatment eventually encourage them to rebel? Glory asked.

– Certainly not. They're getting used to it, more and more convinced this is the natural order of things… Rebel? Against the gods? Don't be silly. They don't know the word, not even in their core of cores.

He stared at her, and his eyes twinkled in green.

– And it is, of course, the natural way of things. It's the way society, civilization itself teaches all of us to react anyway. We're just refining it a bit here.

He signed to Linda. She ran to him. He fondled her breasts, squeezed them, hurting her, humbling her, any way he could.

– The stiffness and blank stare will eventually fade, he said, – And by then they will be truly slaves. Nothing but programs, buttons we may push to our heart's desire. This is the future. This is the glorious destiny of mankind.

Glory felt faint. The need, the horrible need, didn't leave her. Rather it intensified. Sweat broke out all over her body, making the robe cling to her skin. Meinz ignored her as he ignored everybody. She wanted him to notice her, wanted it badly.

I belong to One Eye, she thought. And her need grew to an unbearable level.

But Meinz was a Lord as well. She belonged to him, too. And she wanted him to touch her, touch her as he touched the female slave to acknowledge her presence.

– They're so well trained, she said drowsily, – like dogs.

– Indeed. We're teaching them to serve us in all things. They're assassins, infiltrators, whatever we desire or find useful.

In all things… Glory's lips turned soft and moist. She noticed distantly, the bulge on Bob's pants.

– So, if you haven't realized it by now, feel free to do exactly as you wish with your charges, except damaging them, because everything you do to them, every indignity, every harm you visit upon their souls will only reinforce their thorough programming and making them easier to control. We control everything, control even their perceptions and perception is reality.

– What do you mean? Bob asked hoarsely.

– Exactly what I am saying, my young apprentice. They live in our Universe. We are their gods. We give them their reason to exist. We define their very reality. They see, hear, feel and sense what we want them to do.

He turned.
– Linda, he said softly, casually.
She straightened, looking attentive at the Master, eagerly awaiting his command, the opportunity to obey, serve and please him.
– I'm going to give you a soda, Linda, the Voice said. – It's sweet and tasty, and you'll love it, and it's on the table over there.
The girl lit up like a Christmas tree, eyes filled with joy and gratitude.
– Go to it, slave, and drink it, drink it all.
– Thank you, Master, she cried. – Thank you so much.
She ran to the table and grabbed the bottle. Glory looked closer at it as Linda started drinking, joyfully and enthusiastically, and the black girl wondered if Meinz had grown soft or what point he was making. There was always a point. There had to be.
There was no label on the bottle. It contained a yellowish, brownish fluid, a garish contrast to the slave's pale skin. And then it dawned on Glory. She began a hoarse, uncertain laughter, noticing how Bob shook his head incredulously, noticing how her stomach twisted in cramps, as she met Meinz' dancing green fire.
– Ethanol Acid, he enlightened the two of them. – In non-technical terms, in case you've forgotten your science, called vinegar.

Chapter Three

It went on and on. The inventive torture of the three slaves continued for hours, way beyond anything Glory Burns had ever imagined.

She had never imagined dolls could scream, could feel pain, but the screams were there in their faces, in the very walls surrounding them.

Nothing was revealed, but she shook inside, shook badly and couldn't stop shaking.

She recalled it all. Recalled how she had met up briefly with the Lords in their bright common sanctum, how everything had been alright, how it had appeared to be alright. Then there had been the short walk to Meinz' aerie, and during the critical first minutes everything had changed. At least that was what she thought but couldn't be certain of, certain of anything anymore.

This had been different, she realized, from what she had experienced during the slaves' initial training. It didn't sink in, then, didn't feel like being stepped on by a thousand feet.

And she was just a shaking bundle, unable to hold onto the thinnest thread, the weakest link in her mind.

– You've both done an excellent job, the Lord praised them. – Both your slaves and you are ready to move on, move to the next level. I'll be sure to commend you in my next meeting with the council. Congratulations.

Bob mumbled something. She did, too. Voicing loud and clear their gratitude towards their Lord and Master, for the fact that he found them pleasing, found them useful.

Flow. Thrust. Pull. Movement. Green eyes haunted her. Training, rigorous training in the gym, in the jungle outside. Apprentices and their slaves. They were one flow. They were one. Wet. Her entire being was wet, her skin drowning in sweat, in moisture. Parker trained them, ran them through the jungle, through the hoops and traps. It was hot inside, hot in the gym. And there were those who fainted and were removed from… were removed.

– You don't think, Parker said. – You do. You're an extension of your superiors, of your betters.

Parker was a hurricane. She was Night and Fear personified. They all revered her.

Glory hit the wall. Hit it, until she could no longer remember how many times she had hit it. Her hands hurt. She studied the slaves, how eager, how passionless they performed their training. There was no pain, no joy in their faces, in their eyes, except the joy of serving. Obedience, the teaching of obedience was beaten into them. They were taught to kill, to kill and live for the glory of the Masters.

Glory saw green eyes under red locks. Dead, glassy. The form. Arms, legs, head. A function, a tool. Nothing inside but the need to serve.

Parker beat up on an apprentice. She struck him down. Called him up. Beat him back to the ground.

He stood on shaking legs, stood straight, as she circled him, as she inspected him.

– Is this all you can DO? Parker shouted. – Is this the glory you can bring to the Thousand Feet?

– NO, MY LADY, he responded. – I'll do better. I'll do much better.

It was military discipline, but it was more. Glory couldn't think, only do. She, in turn, like all apprentices, subsequently taught her slaves. She repeated Parker's words as she recalled them. Her moves, her expression, her self.

And the slaves were also taught on other levels, in the laboratory, and by other teachers, educated for the purpose of teaching slaves. Words were hammered into their minds. Glory heard them. Heard them in her feverish brain.

Linda oiled her, oiled her sore body. Her hands were soft. Linda was the geisha, the perfect servant. Glory stretched her body on the table in her bathroom, the bathroom full of steam and moisture, while the geisha's hands moved over her body, softened hardened limbs. Ted gave the massage. She felt the strength in his hands, in both their hands, so controlled, so… mastered.

– You're both such good sheep, she mumbled drowsily. – Such cute beasts. I'll keep you with me forever. I'll never let you go.

She rolled on to her back, revealing herself to Ted, to his dead, non-enquiring eyes.

– Your old friend Kurt is… hiding something, she pondered. – I wonder what it is. He has an agenda, one beyond the organization. I wonder what it is. I get the impression that all this isn't important to him at all. He's waiting, relaxing here, doing other's work, while waiting, and I wonder what he's waiting for, you know. I wonder a lot.

There was no reaction in the boy, no reaction at all, even when she mentioned Meinz' name. There was no break in the routine of his hands moving over her body.

She stood before the mirror. Her two… maids… she giggled… dressed and coddled her, brushed her hair. Linda drowned her in perfume.

Glory coughed. It was a bit too much of it. It itched and burned in her throat. For a moment she considered punishing Linda, but the girl looked at her with such blind trust and worship, so much like a dog, that Glory felt determination fade like dew in the morning. The Mistress returned her attention to the figure in the mirror.

– I'm beautiful, she exclaimed. – Am I not beautiful, am I not desirable, Linda?

– You're beautiful, Mistress, Linda intoned evenly. – You're desirable. The Lord will marvel at the very sight of you.

The Lord… A sting of worry disturbed her peace for a moment, until she dismissed it as the foolishness it was.

The corridors and hallways again. White walls. No thought. She walked, with Linda in tow, holding a chain fastened to the slave's collar. Linda's skin was like marble, pale like death, glowing in desire. Glory felt that glow in herself, as well, tinged with just the slightest apprehension, the most numbing fear. No guards, no patrolling sentries. She saw Linda, without seeing her, as she was now, as she was then.

– We've succeeded with you, haven't we? She mused. – Succeeded with you all. And it was so easy, like snapping fingers. Amazing, so amazing.

Euphoria almost overwhelmed her, and she had to concentrate hard to pull herself together.

She saw no one, until she met the oriental guarding the entrance to David Gidman's quarters. He was taller than the average oriental. She spotted some possible touches of Caucasian blood in his features. He looked poised, like a tiger, ready to jump. Hands held hard on to his weapon, his automatic gun. In his belt he also had a gun she knew shot darts, sedative darts. For some reason this made her more worried. The sentries did have the power over life and death, and she couldn't tell what was worse.

He grinned knowingly to her, as she provided her passport, her proof of citizenship. This was already big enough that not everybody knew or even knew of each other. Glory blinked, once again seeing Kurt Meinz, hearing him speak.

– Behold the future, mankind's golden dawn.

His voice felt so real, so life-like that she had to turn and look to assure herself he wasn't there.

She studied the young oriental. He was about her age, perhaps a bit older. Like her he was dressed in the subscribed black robe, the sign, the proof that he was blessed, that he was favored by the Lords. He wore a chip on his shoulder. She saw that easily. He hated her, hated everybody.

– I've seen many of you go in there… He grinned and turned his and her attention to the giant glass doors at the end of the black carpet. – Everybody has been carried back out.

His snarl cut into her.

– I would worry more about myself, if I were you, she snarled back.

Mostly to hide her apprehension, her rubber knees, but also to rise to the occasion. He had dared challenging her, and he had to pay.

He practically crouched there, before her, averting his eyes and lowering them in deference to her stature, and she felt pride.

– I meant no disrespect, he said humbly, behaving as he was taught in the company of his betters.

– I accept your apology, she said in a crushing blow. – You're an eager servant of the Lord, and might even be commended.

– Thank you, he said humbly, knowing fully well what she implied.

So easy, she thought. How easily we all fall into the new pattern weaving itself.

– I can read your mind, she said casually to him, building on the fears the lower classes felt for their superiors. – I know how you think, know every thought crawling through that slow mind of yours. Remember that.

– I will, he said with shivering lips. – Thank you, My Lady.

Triumph swelled within her. She passed him, without bothering to further acknowledge his presence. Linda, too, aping her Mistress' behavior, scolded him.

– You may visit me tomorrow, she said, as it fit her to show mercy. – We'll talk some more.

She didn't hear his reply, if a reply there was. He was gone, dismissed like a bad memory. The doors opened up to her, welcomed her and closed behind her. The choir welcomed her, the human choir, seemingly from a thousand throats. Glory translated automatically, feeling chilled to the bone. There was insanity here, thinly veiled.

– «Iluso is our Master. Iluso is our God. Beware his wrath. We are the People of Legend, and we are mighty beyond words».

His court, his cohorts, his children, his devoted cult. She had heard about them, but never seen them, never met any, as far she knew. Religious fervor had been their thing even before his death and resurrection in San Diego. After that it had truly taken off…

Her attempt at levity, at irony, folded like the house of cards it was. The pulsing in her loins once again overwhelmed her, as it spread to every piece of her body, every synapse in her brain and soul. Mechanically she stepped further into the shadowy place, with Linda in tow. Her throat was dry, her mind numb, hardly more than a mist believing it was flesh. She was flesh, and she felt its power.

Jean Gidman appeared out of the shadows. She was nude, totally nude, and so sensual that she burned Glory's eyes. Glory stared right through her, and her throat turned paper dry. The mark, the tattooed fist on her thigh glowed like blood.

– A servant… She tried and failed to speak. – A servant and a slave for Lord Gidman.

Jean didn't reply. She merely turned and returned to the inner chambers of the quarters. Glory followed, hesitatingly at first, then eagerly, so eager that it hurt.

There were flashes, soft flashes in shadow, spilling over white skin… and then Glory noticed it.

Jean wore no collar. And there were no signs of her ever wearing any. Her skin was light brown, darkened by the sun. The slaves had spent a long time without much sun on their body. Stabs of jealousy shot through Glory. She wanted to strike the other woman, but fear kept her back.

Jean faded away in the shadows. Glory looked for her, but couldn't see her. The woman had vanished like a ghost. Glory pressed on. There was a light somewhere ahead. She thought she heard breathing, breathing from many people, but couldn't be certain. Everything seemed awry, out of whack. She drew her breath hard. This was David Gidman's consecrated place, his place of power, where he made his world. She imagined she saw a dead man on a slab. She imagined she saw him open his eyes, and rise. Life returned to the body, and it grew bigger and more powerful than it had ever been before.

Her toes touched the carpet, moved and danced on the soft surface. If only the rats from the slum had seen her now, seen the luxurious surroundings, the expensive carpets on the floor.

The two girls emerged into a bright room. Glory stopped, hardly able to catch her breath. He sat in a big chair, nude. His big… thing was very much visible. She curtseyed. Linda knelt.

– You call, my Lord, she said throatily. – And I come.

– Undress, he commanded sternly, cold and distant.

She nodded, swallowing hard, and slipped easily out of her robe. It fell on the floor behind her.

He studied her, impassionate. She turned, letting him see it all. He had seen her before, of course, but that was just a frail, defenseless girl, so long ago.

– What do we have here, Glory? He asked her. – What is this place?

Is this a multiple response question? She wanted to ask. She held her tongue.

She smiled, confident, secure in her world.

– That one is easy, she replied.

She met his stare boldly and not too afraid.

– It's a Hawkworld, where the strong prey on the weak. This is just like in Memphis or any other slum or dive in the world, no matter how rich or poor the owners might be. The world never changes. I know how to turn in the world, My Lord.

He nodded. Wild abandon and hope constricted her throat.

– You think, he said. – That makes you different from others.

She swelled with pride.

He rose, and his cock rose with him, and she couldn't take her eyes off it.

– On the bed, he snarled. – Your bitch as well.

She couldn't even recall moving. Suddenly, in a flash, both she and Linda knelt on the soft, soft, huge, huge bed, knelt before the giant towering over them.

He was such a big man, even bigger than he had been when she first saw him that fateful day on the train from Memphis. She didn't imagine it. He had grown and kept growing, and he truly reminded her of the giants in the old legends, the Cyclops receiving her in his cave. He didn't have muscles. He had logs. Both his arms and thighs were so thick that everything she had seen previously, even on wrestlers looked ridiculously weak. Mist clouded her mind. She moved her hands over sore breasts, pinched them and struck herself, in a vein attempt to master her unbearable need.

– I submit myself to you, My Lord, she breathed. – A god among gods. Please take me into your kingdom, make me yours.

Then he was right by her, in the bed. He grabbed her arms, grabbed hard, and it *hurt*. She cried out in pain. Tears jumped from her eyes. She blinked, imagined that her cry was returned to her, an echo in the haze her life had become. He fondled, squeezed her breasts, and he didn't care about her at all. He touched her weakness, spread her legs, spread them wide. She spread them for him, in an attempt to please him, please, please, please him. Then she heard it, the choir rising from the depths. It was just the choir. She couldn't make out the words, even though she knew what they were. He emptied himself quickly in Linda. It was nothing but a quick snack to him. Glory didn't feel the slightest bit offended. He threw the white girl on the floor, and turned to Glory once more, returning to full power in an instant. The Cyclops pushed inside her, and she screamed, screamed in pain, as lust beyond anything ravaged her. She rested in his arms afterwards, sniffing, smiling, a female cringing before the dominating male. He touched her again. One, two three touches, and she was in full heat again, ready for him again. He dragged her up on his lap. She crouched across his knees, on her belly. Suddenly there was a sharp and horrible pain on her back. She cried out in pain and shock, an incredulity beyond anything she could have imagined. He was… spanking her, beating his huge flat hand on her buttocks. She writhed in his grip, eyes bulging, as he hit her again and again. He held her hard, held her in place without the slightest effort. She cried. Huge, horrible sobs, as the pain became to overwhelm her, dominate her entire perception, and it never stopped. Eventually she just lay there, totally limp, as the flat hard hand kept hitting her sore butt. She lay in bed, on her back, writhing under his touch, crying. Her back hurt, hurt terribly. When he pushed a big, fleshy hand at her groin she pushed back at it, automatically, without thought, without will. She heard the choir again, and this time she could make out the words.

– «Iluso is our Master. Iluso is our God. Beware his wrath. We are the People of Legend, and we are mighty beyond words».

They were all around them, around the bed, Jean… and others, males and females. Shadows, empty faces, empty eyes. They held her. Jean patted her head.

– We have a new sheep in our fold, Jean said, half speaking, half chanting. – Welcome her, welcome her to the Glory of our savior.

– WELCOME, they choired.

Glory smelled smoke, saw fire somewhere, couldn't say where. On a throne sat the giant, sat the Cyclops. Crouched on the ground was the girl, his new devotee, initiate. Around her the creatures of the circle danced, chanting their permeating song. The girl swayed her head from side to side, back and forth, back and forth. Her eyes widened, until they were no longer eyes, but merely pain in her face. Her lips moved, moved as the others moved, as she joined the choir, as she melted into its circle, its creed.

– One Eye, she cried out. – I love you, One Eye. Love you, Iluso.

Her litany of dedication changed into a scream as the terrible heat was pushed against her skin, as it penetrated her very being and transformed her, transformed her into something new, into his creature.

She was taken many times. She was unable to know, to be positive if it was actually Gidman every time, but she saw his face every time, as she cried out his name, his exalted name.

And they were around her, always around her. No matter where she went, they were There, reminding her of who she was, who she belonged to, what she was, a vessel of his Glory. The insistent voices whispered to her in her sleep, in all the hours of the day. Please, please, s-stop, she begged them. Please, please, pretty please tell me, tell me everything I need to want. And they did, and she cried out in joy, as she gave praise to the Lord, to her savior, and she became His vessel, nothing more than an extension of his exalted being, and she cried out in joy and a misery catapulting her to the deepest pits. Her surroundings changed around her, as she moved without moving. It was morning. She knew it was morning. What morning she didn't know.

There was a shadow, a Shadow, and she couldn't understand why this one scared her so much more than all the others. It flapped its wings, shook in rage, and the world shook with it.

She moved, and pain cut through her. The door was open. There was a draft from the corridor, sucking air from her lungs. She kept gasping for air, but there never seemed to be enough. The cold draft froze her sweaty skin. She turned. Linda and Ted were chained to the wall. They didn't acknowledge her movements. They weren't programmed to do that, not until they were freed. It was no use calling to them. She wanted to leave the bed, free the slaves, so they could coddle her, so she could close the door, but she couldn't move. Everything was frozen within her.

A man stood by her bed. She had heard steps, but had been unable to move. The intruder was Tim Croydon, the oriental man she had «invited» yesterday, ages ago.

– You told me to come, and I came, he said.

She didn't reply. She didn't move. Neither limbs nor lips.

– The door was open, he stated. – A serious breach of the security regulations, don't you think?

I don't think. I'm just a shell, a vessel for a man's spirit.

She crouched there on the bed, naked for his eyes. There was desire in those eyes, and slowly she started to smile, smile sweetly to him.

– You bitch, he spat. – You fucking bitch.

He undressed in swift, abrupt moves. She studied the sick grin of expectation as if it wasn't there, curious like a cat on the prowl. He was hard already, pushing against the cloth, standing straight out even before he removed the cover.

– Yeah, come to me, she breathed, inviting him with her moist eyes, her swelling breasts and cunt, her entire desirable heat. – Use me, the vessel, as you see fit.

She turned, and he froze, froze like the dead. He saw it, couldn't avoid seeing it, the brand on her thigh. She looked at him, looked right through him.

– What's the matter? She asked sweetly. – Don't you want me anymore? Don't you want what I have to offer?

He ran. With utter panic carved into his face he ran, not even caring to dress before fleeing through the open door, coincidentally grabbing his robe with the tip of his finger, slamming the door behind him, as he fled, fled, fled.

– I know you do, she said. – You want me to reward you. You want death and destruction at my hands, and you shall have it.

He fled, and she played it back time and time again in her mind.

She rose from the bed, slowly walking to the mirror, turning slightly, so she could study it, study her brand.

It was more of a tattoo, than a brand, really, and it wasn't painted red like the others she had seen, but dark green, and encircling it was a huge, writhing snake. She could actually see it, feel it move, crawl on her skin and in her mind. Her fingers touched it. It hurt, but also tingled. It was beautiful. Her attention wandered, was drawn elsewhere, pouting. She carefully touched her butt, and instantly gasped in pain. The skin was sore and swollen there, the brown skin an unhealthy shade of black, and she imagined she saw the mark of his hands, the many, many marks of ownership, of infinite affection. Her features twisted in her face as tears filled her eyes. She fell to her knees, sobbing, hiding her face in her hands, her quivering hands, and slowly, slowly her entire body started shaking, shaking like a leaf, and it didn't stop.

++++++++++++++++++++++++++++++++++++

He was alone again, left alone, there on the wall again, chained and frozen. His eyes, he was unable to close his eyes. They were open, staring at everything.

Open. I am open.

He gasped, couldn't contain the gasp, couldn't keep it inside.

Open eyes, closed eyes saw the Black Dome, a place sucking all light from the surroundings, a darkness strong enough to keep the day at bay.

It was a tango, a tango in the night, and oddly enough, it comforted and strengthened him.

Ted had never imagined it would be like this not to see.

The first time they had pulled the black mask down on his head he had thought he would still be able to hear, smell and taste. But everything was just darkness and an infinite emptiness slowly devouring everything that remained within him. They had even taken away his dreams. There was nothing there, nothing but the black dome. He saw shapes there, movement. But he didn't dream.

He should be grateful, he knew that, for the Master's favors, for the fact that they, in their grace allowed him to think. Often he couldn't. A heavy fog descended on his mind, and it grew thicker and thicker. There were huge black holes in his memory. Sometimes he couldn't recall what happened from one minute to the next. He could stand here, chained and blinded, and then suddenly be somewhere else, without any recollection of how he got there.

Even now, in one of his clearest moments, he couldn't… couldn't…

I can't remember, remember anything.

He wondered if there was anything else, something more out there, and knew there wasn't. He heard the sound of the shower and didn't know why. He looked right at the shower, the bathroom, right now, and there was no one there. The water wasn't running. He smelled blood, but there was no blood. He heard the sound of a gun, but there was no gunsmoke.

The crouching creature chained to the wall shook and twisted, like in fever, as it muttered and mumbled insanely to itself.

He heard the sound of fire, but there was no smoke, only the smell of fog, a cabin hidden in fog.

– I think, he mumbled. – Thinking is bad

I don't know what, but I think. I am. Master, where is thy whip?

– The city I grew up in… he said aloud, muttered in the dark. – Dennis? Dennis something. I hurt, I shout, I cry.

I hurt, I shout, I cry, I obey, I serve, I please. Please, please, please.

The dark mire wore him down, sucked him into its void. And it hurt. It hurt terribly. And so it should, the Voice said. Thinking is bad. Feel good. Feel nothing. Slave is bad. S-scold the slave, punish the slave, the wicked slave.

It hurt, and he moaned, moaned in anguish, moaned in pain.

Dennis was the name of a boy, a boy he had known. Joy filled him like fire. Terror washed him like ashes. He flapped his wings, his broken wings.

Dennis had died, in the ashes left by the masters.

– Den… Den-ver.

– DENVER, he shouted. He began crying again, crying like the last time he had seen his sister. – I didn't think… didn't think I would remember.

Huge sobs shook him. He had seen his sister, his stepsister take a shower when he was twelve. He had killed his brother with a gun when he was sixteen.

Thinking is bad, action is worse. He sobbed, shaking in fear, in utter, vast numbness.

Footsteps in the hall, the hall of mirrors. Where the fuck was the hall of mirrors? He broke down in hard, uncontrollable sobs.

Depressions are quite common initially among slaves. They have trouble adjusting to their new circumstances, their new life, so we help them, help them adjust, help them conform. Conformity is everything. Conformity is also milk and blood. Fear is the milk and the blood. Fear is the key.

Footsteps. Everything suddenly turned bright, so bright. No, dark, so dark, even darker than before. Close to the total darkness, Death. The living dead.

A hand tore off his mask.

– Fuck, the stud has sniveled today again.

Darkness fell then, pulling him in. He descended slowly towards the black hole. And also this time fear flowed through him, fear of not returning, of never returning.

He sensed cool hands on his skin and the sound of splashing water. Washing time. He felt no relief over being able to think again, only the same, prevailing emptiness.

Washing time. Every day they were led here in groups of ten. It wasn't strictly necessary, he knew that. They could have cleaned themselves in their cubicles, in their master's quarters. This was a ritual, a labor of control. If only he could remember for certain how many times he had been here. Then he would at least be able to count the days.

But he couldn't.

He stared blindly at those sharing his plight today. Some he knew. Others he didn't. The slaves were always regrouped, shuffled in the masters' deck of cards. He didn't even recall the names of those he recognized. Did they, too, have thoughts or was he the only one still glimpsing the light, the… shadow?

Animals think in images, he recalled. I'm an animal.

(inferior)

Please. Not yet. Let me have more time.

A girl suddenly threw a piece of soap at one of the guards. He grabbed it surprisingly easy in the air and her face twisted in rage.

– I can't take it anymore, she cried hysterically. – I'm not a slave. No human being should be treated this way. I am a human being.

Poor little dumb slave, Ted thought. The High Lady will punish her.

– Bring her to me, Lady Parker commanded, from her high dais.
The slaves surrounded the distressed girl.
– Please don't do it. You must fight. Please fight.
Surrounded her in an ever-tighter circle.
– NO! She shouted despairingly.
She threw herself at the circle, and managed, incredibly enough, to break through, and escape the fumbling hands.
But she didn't get very far, before the circle caught up with her. It recaptured her and this time she didn't get free. The slaves' hands grabbed her and held on to her like magnets, pulled her away. The High Lady waited at the top of the stairs. The slaves carried the girl to the pool's edge. She writhed in their grip.
– Let go of me, she screamed. – Let go.
To no avail. Like a sacrificial lamb she was lifted up, into the hands of guards. Then she relented, and an expression of apathy dawned on her face. She willingly allowed herself to be carried up the stairs. They threw her brutally at the feet of the Almighty. She crouched there, shivering like a mouse. It took a while, but she finally lifted her head. She looked up at Lady Par-ker, a mighty among the mighty.
– On your knees, the woman commanded in masterful tone of voice. – Bow down in the dust for me.
After a few seconds the slave obeyed, but only partly. She went up on her knees, but didn't bow her head. Instead she knelt there, obstinate staring into Lady Par-ker's eyes.
One of the guards took one step forward, but a lifted hand stopped him.
– So the slave is resisting is it? Let's see what it is made of, shall we? I'm so excited.
Shuen Parker turned her full attention to the slave.
– Bow your head, slave, and kiss my feet in deference.
The slave held Par-ker's eyes surprisingly long. Fifteen, perhaps twenty seconds. First she blinked once, then twice. She started shaking violently, averted her eyes and her head fell to the floor. She smothered the other woman's feet in kisses, from toes to ankles. Afterwards she lay still on the floor, hiding her face in her hands, gasping for air, feeling no air reach her. Tears flowed from her eyes.
Par-ker bent down and patted and comforted her.
– Don't cry little girl. Everything is well. You might even end up as my private maid. I'm sure you will enjoy that.
– NO! The girl jumped to her feet and backed off, backed off, until she stood with her back to the wall. – I'm not a slave. Do you HEAR ME?

You've kidnapped me, captured me, but you shall not break me. Even if you have transformed those poor suckers in the pool into unthinking animals, you shall never succeed with me.

She looked around her with huge, scared eyes. Par-ker smiled to her.

– What's your name, slave?

– So, you don't think I'll remember, huh? Arrogant bastards.

Her fists opened and closed for every heartbeat. Her lips shook.

– My name is Denise… Denise Thorn… dyke? Yes, Thorndyke, Denise Thorndyke. You see? She looked around some more, before her face once again froze in intense and terrible concentration. – I live… lived in London. My father is Lewis - my mother… I have a brother and sister. They names are…

The scream of pain filled the entire hall. The other slaves watched indifferently the tortured figure collapsing with her hands glued to her neck. She rolled down one step and remained there, twisting in horrible cramps. Long, long. When Par-ker finally turned off the electricity the girl lay still. Not even a hair moved.

The High Lady bent down and patted her belly.

– What's your name, sweetie?

The slave opened her eyes and smiled happily.

– Denise, she stated clearly, distinct, without doubt. – I am Denise and I am a slave.

Ted was once more chained to the wall, with the mask covering his head.

Something had happened, something important. And he couldn't for his life remember what. Another nightmare in a long, long line. He sensed it. Something nasty, an experience without the right of life, hid inside him somewhere.

He felt his hands hit walls, hit flesh, felt it bend and break.

There were flashes, muted in fog. Soft, lukewarm water hitting him on the beach, the beach of nails. He remembered more of the life outside. He had always meant horror and death for the people he knew and who knew him. So many had died in his wake. Coogan, Mike, Stewart and Linda. Linda, who was just as dead as he was.

He grabbed the fog, reached for something to hold on to.

His mask. The Mask. Pain as his hand clutched the nails, dropped the blood, the acid blood. A mask floating in a foggy landscape. Appearing from the ugly cabin, making him cringe in fear. The man with the mask. The most powerful of the High Ones. The High Ones, the slaves' life and death. Alpha and Omega.

My life and my death.

Death is Change.
South Platte River. Water. The pool. He remembered.
Things were different the next time they removed the mask. Reality didn't slip away. Some of it did, but not all. There were lights, sounds and colors. The spot of tears on the floor was gone.
The brother and sister slave nursed and tended Mistress. She moaned and suffered on the table, and they suffered with her.
He remembered: He remembered her return. They carried her, two male Masters. One of them removed the chain from Linda's collar. He looked in disgust at her content, lazy expression and the clotted spots on her thighs.
– Wash yourself,
She smiled and graciously crossed the floor on her way to the bathroom. She was taught to smile, also when she only had thoughts for what was done to her.
(feel how good it is)
I hate it. Ted shook, as he realized he heard what sister thought.
He had to look down when Linda turned on the water and started cleaning herself. To not be overwhelmed by memories, drown in the hot fire washing the beach. He hardly noticed that he was being released from the wall.
– Tend your Mistress well tonight, the Master grinned. – She needs it.
And they did, as they coddled her, coddled her pain.
Water flowed from the ceiling and down in the small pool. Linda was showered in water. The white body seemed almost gray in all the steam. Ted watched Linda. He watched Glory, Glory Burns, heard her writhe in discomfort and horrendous pain. She didn't have a good time, that's for sure. There were often moans of pain, and her forehead was covered in sweat. He realized she had nightmares while still awake. Suddenly Ted felt a boiling devil-may-care feeling swell inside. That the girl had nightmares, nightmares already, wasn't really that strange. He surmised she was probably closer to a state of unconsciousness than actual sleep.
She had been thoroughly fucked.
Laughter bubbled in his throat. He laughed so hard that the walls shook, so hard that he eventually stopped in wonder. He hadn't thought he was still able to laugh. The sound erupting from him was vicious and cruel, but it was laughter.
Suddenly everything turned quiet. The shower had been turned off. Where he hid outside the bathroom, he could hear the sound of birds, the sound of chirping birds. Linda stepped out on the floor. As she was now,

with the long, white hair clinging to her body, she almost took his breath away.

Now he understood better why the older boys at school stared at her all the time.

She was… beautiful.

Afterwards she visited him at his place, in the tree, down by the river.

– You watched me. I saw you.

– Yes, he replied.

He had never lied to her before, and had no intention of starting now.

So strange, he thought, that she isn't angry, and that I don't feel any embarrassment.

The boys at school, red-faced and awkward as they were, suddenly seemed very childish in his eyes. He helped her up on the branch, and they kissed; a hungry lips-to-lips kiss. From that moment on they were no longer children.

She stepped out of the pool and walked to him. Water flowed from the white skin and her feet made marks on the carpet. This time they needed no words. There were eyes to eyes and nothing more was needed. The embrace made Linda release a tiny sob. Now, when he was too weak to resist the most insignificant emotion, he accepted her. And he knew her, knew what she was thinking. He heard her speak in his mind, as they coddled and kissed each other.

They separated, and she dissolved in front of him, dissolved into nothing, into dusk and mist. He was alone, chained to the wall. Name, he had no name, not before, not now. The eternal night embraced him and devoured him, and he wept in gratitude, and stopped flapping his broken wings. He looked at himself in the mirror, the pale skin, the pricking, hurting arm.

He lay down on the floor. Eyes closed. Open eyes closed. Soft carpet. Feel the soft carpet little worm, pathetic little worm. Head drowned in the soft carpet's hair, its waves swallowing him whole. Soft, soft, so very soft. Pleasant dreams, little slave, sleep and be merry.

And he slept and was merry.

The child pulling up his feet, crouching on the floor, waiting for the birth fluid to break, waiting to be born.

Sleeping silently on the carpet.

Chapter Four

The sounds of glasses meeting and loud voices reverberated through the halls and hallways. There was music, muted. There were voices, low, as low as whispers.

Ten slaves left the banquet hall and headed down the broad staircase to the cellar. Doors opened automatically for them as they walked through the various rooms, like the kitchen and more intimate dining rooms, and passed private bedrooms.

The place was dark and chilly. The only light originated from the door they had opened. Just enough that the slaves could spot the long rows of shelves, of shelves filled with dark bottles. Except for the low sound of the fans, there was only that of naked feet walking across the stone floor.

The movements of the five females and five males were fluid, economical, gracious. They grabbed two bottles each and turned back towards the door they had come through. The small drift of light from there made the golden bracelets around their wrists and ankles shine and twinkle and revealed graciously their lightly clad bodies.

If anybody had studied them or passed them on a street, it would have struck those persons how happy they all seemed. They would have noticed the light, effortless walk and the way they held their heads high, especially the boy and the girl leading the procession, how their eyes, their very self seemingly glowed in constant anticipation.

And the others followed their lead.

They moved, returned to the banquet hall, under the watchful eyes of the Lords, the Masters and their hallowed guests. Except for a few posted guards by the exits, everybody sat, in carefully arranged patterns, around the long table. The two and eight knelt down in front of the beloved Lord Masters, the inner circle, in front of the Mask, the High Regarded Leader.

– The champagne, as you requested, Master, the female said huskily.

– Thank you, Iris, the Mask said graciously. – You may now serve the champagne.

Iris rose and using the corkscrew opened the bottle, in one single fluid and lovely motion. It was as if she had done this her entire life, like she was born to do it. There was a crack and the champagne splashed on the skin of her bare belly. She ignored it and started, along with the other two and eight, to fill the empty glasses. Not a drop was spilled. Eyes twinkled at the assembled people around the table, inviting and subservient. Iris noticed the stares of the masters, of course, as she always did, and like everybody could easily see, it affected her profoundly, like it did all the slaves. They stared at her half, hardly concealed breasts and groin. They stared ruthlessly and amazed at all the two and eight.

A man grabbed Iris, grabbed her right wrist.

– So you will do anything for me? He wondered harshly. – No matter how bad it feels for you?

– It won't feel bad for me, Master, she replied politely, softly, glowing in face and skin. – We live to serve, and yes, I am yours. Yours to do with as you please.

– They are programmed to perform a wide range of services, Kurt Meinz said, very smug. – And also to learn further, and interpret, anticipate a Master's… wish.

The man stared at Meinz, and then back at Iris, as if he couldn't believe what he saw and heard.

– Dom Perignon 1967, Ladies and Gentlemen, the Mask said, and bowed while sitting at Shuen Parker.

She obviously ignored his gesture. Those who studied him might suspect that this irritated him, but the mask covering his face and not the least his stoic attitude made it impossible to tell.

His stoic attitude, in spite of the extremely dynamic way he moved and did everything. Every small move he made, made them think of a hurricane, a Storm clothed in flesh.

The champagne had been served and all glasses were full. Kurt Meinz, clearly more of a ceremonial master than any of his peers, took his glass and raised it up.

– To our venture, he cheered, fairly uncharacteristically (they thought). – To our present and future success.

– Hear, hear, Verheyen cheered.

He had clearly had a bit to drink already, speaking a bit indistinct.

Everybody rose and lifted their glasses, and the assembly drank.

– Success, they cried.

– To the thousand feet, Meinz shouted. – May we walk Forever.

– THE THOUSAND FEET, they replied. – *Forever*.

Meinz sat down, and everybody else, too.

Things settled down again fast, but the energy, the worry persisted, at least in some of the invited guests.

– But what do you *do* with them? A woman insisted, staring exasperated, fearful at Meinz.

He shrugged, very deliberately. The other five of the inner circle did as well. At least everybody present imagined that the Mask grinned under the piece of cloth covering his face. They imagined how he looked like under it, and cringed in horror and fascination.

– We're just doing what all governments are doing, Meinz lectured dryly, proudly. – Crowd control has been an issue since before the Roman Empire. In today's more complex world behavioral sciences are more important than ever. We're merely doing what everybody is doing; building on the work of those before us. The Doctors Goebbels and Mengele made major developments in Germany in the thirties and forties. So did others. Since then things have really started to happen. Joseph Goebbels would have been absolutely ecstatic today, if he had been able to see what his current peers in western society and government have accomplished, results beyond his wildest dreams. He pushed the value of propaganda and indoctrination in average values. They, building on his work, have made those two rather frowned at idioms household words. Look at the slaves, at the creatures around you, Ladies and Gentlemen, how eager they are to obey, serve and please. I imagine we, in the future, with a sort of remote-control-mechanisms, will be able to do with people in homes and streets what we have done with these cuties. The tools of television and other forms of mass communication… the possibilities are endless. I see my present work as very crude, compared to what the future holds, Ladies and Gentlemen.

They looked at the slaves, at the happy, shining faces and postures, and marveled.

– Lady Shuen here, and myself were fortunate enough to be able to develop our work further during the Vietnam War, working for the Vietcong, I might add. It was an excellent educational study. They were quite the mean sons and daughters of bitches… having an intuitive understanding of the human mind that is quite staggering.

– I tell you, Parker said. – There are American soldiers in Vietnam today that are absolutely convinced they are Vietnamese, and no one will ever be able to tell them differently.

They looked at her, and shuddered. She looked very young. She was, they knew that. She couldn't have been more than a teenager while doing her «educational study» with Meinz.

– We broke them, she said softly. – And we rebuilt them into whatever was our desire. Some of them have returned to their home, but we control them. One word, one phrase or sign from us, and they will once again become our creatures, revealing the fact that they never stopped. They are our children. We are the valve protecting them from the harsh realities of the world.

– They're out there, awaiting our word, Meinz stated. – In our power. They don't know they are. They think they're back, living happily with their families, that they've put the nightmare behind them. They're even better adapted to a mundane life then many of their fellow colleagues, a fact I am quite proud of, I assure you. But they are in truth our creatures, our buttons to push, even more so, than the other sheep. Think about the power that gives us, the ability to make things happen.

The guests of honor on this gala did, and they shuddered.

The music picked up a bit, turning rougher, penetrating everybody's shell, being force-fed into the soul. And it was as if it originated from Meinz, from his dead eyes.

He turned towards the woman, and she cringed. Up to this point he had looked away, a bit aloof, clearly arrogant, but now he looked at her, and she shrunk under his ruthless scrutiny.

– Have you read the novel 1984, by George Orwell, Madam?

– Of course, I have. She sniffed, her head held high. – I'm quite educated, sir.

– It describes a future society where personal freedom, personal expression is virtually eradicated. He spoke as if she hadn't spoken at all. – Through various reinforcements and measures they, the top dogs, control the minutest parts of human existence. They tell their subjects, their minions that up is down, that right is left, and people believe them, because all their experience, all they see and hear, is telling them that it is true. Humans today are raised to be cattle, to be sheep. From birth we're told we're worthless, that we only have value by serving the greater good, and that we can only find satisfaction, gratification in that fact. Doing what I do is simply taking that fact one tiny step further, to its logical conclusion.

He sniffed, leaning back in his chair, clearly content.

– Orwell, Kafka and Huxley were all great writers, great prophets of what's to come, of the future world.

Glory sat in Lord Gidman's section of the long table. With her sat Bob and Sandra and others of her subordinates from her block. Sandra drank too much. That much was obvious from the speed and nervousness in her speech. Glory looked at her with burning, non-visualized suspicion. There had been… sounds in the hall outside her room lately, *suspicious* sounds. She had attempted to ignore them at first, but when she finally had rushed outside to investigate… there had been no one there.

The two of them sat there talking, sat close, just two girls having a bit of a confidential girl-talk, that's all.

Sandra was tipsy, that's for sure. Glory smiled in humorous amazement, like they were really two young girls, two old childhood friends out celebrating together.

– So, he behaved strangely days before he finally had his glorious breakdown, Sandra giggled. – I don't know what made him snap, though. You never do, right?

Glory let Sandra drone on. She sat there on soft pillows, putting on a stoic mask, attempting to ignore, in vain, the persistent pain in her back. It had been days, and it still hurt, hurt terribly. Small tears formed in her eyes, so small she knew they could be only tricks of the light. She used her small pocket mirror to brush her face, brush it free of the uneven and undesirable. She was the squad leader. The others looked to her, looked to her for… for everything. Appearances were important. Appearances were crucial, were everything.

She looked around, not really in doubt as to what she saw.

They're refining their very own feudal society, she thought, expanding it brick by brick, stone by stone.

– I'm not saying you could just take a look at the guy, and see that he was, in fact, an accident waiting to happen, I'm not saying that at all, but the signs were all there, you know.

Glory had actually witnessed the incident, hidden in the hall, staring with open eyes at the ensuing chaos. She relived it as she closed off Sandra's droning voice.

The boy rose from his breakfast table, abruptly, glaring at his fellows in the dining hall. He struck a fist in the table before him, as he rose from his chair, as the chair tipped over and hit the floor with a sharp, metallic sound. All metals were covered in plastic here, so Glory couldn't understand where the metallic sound was actually coming from.

He was unshaven and had huge black bags below his eyes, like he hadn't been sleeping for days, and he probably hadn't.

– Do you KNOW what we're doing here? He shouted, completely beside himself. – Have you ANY idea of what we're actually DOING?

It looked, for a moment like he was going to attack someone, but then he just started sobbing and sat down on the floor, hiding his face in his hands, sobbing uncontrollably.

The orderlies entered the room and fetched him without further incidents a minute or so later.

Glory blinked, still sitting in the banquet hall with Sandra at her side. It had been so real, the reliving of yesterday's memory that she for one moment there, had believed it happened right now. Slowly, only slowly she re-immersed herself in her surroundings.

The boy had not been seen again.

A… worry riddled Glory, one she couldn't make out, but it was there. Words spoken echoed in her mind, in the air she breathed. You think, they told her, and she did, she couldn't stop thinking.

The slaves danced, entertained the masters, everything very precise and choreographed. The audience applauded, amazement and joy visible in their features, in their body language. Glory studied Meinz, as he studied the others and nodded to himself. This was a confirmation of all their hopes, all their dreams. He had to be pleased, of course he was. This was wish fulfillment, all his hopes and all his dreams.

– How… A young man spoke to Glory, hesitatingly and amazed. – How should we… treat them?

She acknowledged his presence with a slight smile.

– Like slaves, she replied simply. – You know how to do that, don't you?

– Y-yes, he stuttered.

– If they displease you have them whipped or punished. Or whip them, punish them yourself. If you feel for it do it anyway, even if they are as lovely as flowers. Or perhaps you should treat them nicely or ignore them, since they are hardly more than dogs, craving the Master's attention, any attention, and doing that you will truly punish them. Do whatever you want to do with them, whenever you want. It's your prerogative, as one of the exalted Masters of the Earth.

He bowed in his chair, lowering his eyes, in deference and respect.

– Thank you. And then, without hesitation. – My Lady.

Shuen Parker nodded to Glory, and the black girl felt a huge swell of approval and pride inside. Shuen Parker rose. Conversation faded and movement stopped, and they all stared at her, all the underlings and novices, prospectives and guests of honor, waiting for her word.

– You all have questions, Lady Parker said. – You all wonder about this, this new, this old, in your life. This is natural, this is good. You should wonder, wonder what the rest of your life will be about, what life is truly about. You should know, beyond doubt, and you will. As both opportunity and chance, planning and coincidence will have it, we have prepared a demonstration, a show and tell. It should prove both educational and entertaining.

She walked and they followed. Shuen Parker moved like a queen through the hallways. She didn't even glance at the guards of honor marking her route. Glory saw her eyes, saw how conscious the woman was of Power. The thought sent a thrill of fear and desire through Glory.

Parker stopped, addressing the assembly.

– Sandra, my aide, will show you to your designated spots. Enjoy the show, Ladies and Gentlemen.

She departed, and they all turned to Sandra. Glory and the other established members did as well, even though they knew where she would be leading them.

– Good afternoon, ladies and gentlemen, Sandra said in a soft, but yet accentuated speech. – I've been given the task of serving you tonight. If you will follow me, please.

They were led into a hall very much resembling a movie theatre, a Greek setting or perhaps Roman or a mix. It was clearly intended to bring the thoughts to the old Empire. There were seats there, directing their attention to the curtain-covered wall a bit downwards from the upper seats.

People filed in, and were directed by aides, to the designated seats, bearing their name. Wide seats, a lot of room for the legs, befitting that of a citizen of a New Rome. People looked at each other, with fear and pride in their eyes.

It was red. Everything in the room was either red or gray, stone or blood. Glory closed her hands into fists. Long nails buried themselves deep into the flesh of the palms.

I can do this, she told herself in front of the mirror. I can do Power.

Ted and Linda didn't look at her, but she sensed their eyes on her.

She was in the room again, the Empire Theatre. She looked at the big curtain as it split and revealed what was behind. They looked at a window, one to a bedroom, a large bed, matching beige. All colors were pale, faded. Soft light revealed the crouching figure on the bed.

– What you're about to see is an exercise in control, Sandra explained pleasantly, enthusiastically, respectfully.

She clearly read from a script, even though she had learned the words to such a degree that it was hard to tell for people not used to interpreting posture and speech patterns. It wasn't Sandra who spoke. Most of them recognized Kurt Meinz' lecturing and posturing. She stood there in front of the mirror, to what from the other side was a one-way mirror, a confident young female executive.

– It will be demonstrated beyond doubt that the slave you see is in our power, down to the most detailed nuances and depth of Self. Enjoy Ladies and Gentlemen.

She pulled back. Lights in the auditorium were muted. What the audience saw was the window square. Aside from that there was nothing but shadows. Glory shook and couldn't understand why.

Silence dominated the two rooms for a few seconds until they all saw a door open in the beige wall, and saw Shuen Parker enter, approaching the bed. The creature on the bed rose and rushed out on the floor, kneeling graciously before her Mistress.

The beige bedroom… invaded the other, larger hall, invaded the hearts and minds of the spectators. It was as if they were in there, being both women.

– Good morning, Denise, Parker said lightly.

– Good morning, Mistress, the kneeling slave said happily.

– That's a good doggie, Parker praised. – You may eat, now, child.

Denise lit up like christmas, not just the tree, and crawled on all fours to a bowl a few steps away. There was a camera somewhere, recording the moment. The content of the bowl showed on a large screen appearing behind another set of curtains. The audience saw clearly what it was. They smelled the feces as if they were bending over them like Denise, digesting them like Denise. They saw the flies, heard their buzz. Denise chewed and swallowed everything, every bit and fly.

– You have just consumed the waste of a Master, Denise, Parker giggled. – Aren't you honored?

– Very honored, Mistress.

There was a dreamy quality to the girl's voice, as if she wasn't really there, as if she was in her own world, as if she was exactly where she wanted to be.

Suddenly she crouched and she retched. Vomit flew like water and mud from her mouth, decorating the floor in a wide circle. Denise started crying like a small child, as her body shook in cramps.

– Don't be sorry, little pet. Parker walked to her and comforted her, petted her neck. – That's an involuntary reaction we haven't quite mastered yet.

The slave looked up at her with a dog-like gratitude. Her tears slowly dispersed.

– Go to the bed now. It's time for your true reward. Soon, you'll have a large and hard cock right into your juicy cunt.

The slave's eyes turned misty, as she crawled to the bed. She placed herself on all fours there, breathing visible faster, clearly excited, clearly aroused, an arousal increasing for every second she writhed there on the silk. She stared at the ceiling. Sweat wet her brow. Shuen Parker signed and another door opened.

Denise didn't notice anything before the gaping Schaefer placed itself above her. The gape didn't frighten her. What did - and exposed her, was the sight of the dog's growing cock and his back descending.

– No! She screamed. – Noooo!

She attempted to twist her body away, but the Schaefer instantly sat his teeth in her neck and growled a warning.

– No! She screamed again. – Take it off. Please. TAKE IT OFF!

She had the sense of the hard limb in the groin, and the scream turned into a thin and desperate howl. The dog turned even more eager.

– CARL, STOP!

The dog froze and looked up at its Mistress. Then it jumped out of the bed and up on a stool, where it sat down and started grooming itself.

Denise crouched on her side, shaking uncontrollably. Parker grabbed her shoulder and easily turned her back on her back. She didn't resist, but shook a bit more.

– You took that quite hard, didn't you? Strange, I thought you KGB guys were taught everything.

– KGB? What are you talking about? Denise stopped shaking.

– Don't go there, honey, Parker said pleased. – Let's see, you're born in Czechoslovakia in 1954. Twelve years old you were recruited as a sleeper. You were arrested for stealing in a party store in Prague… During the '68 uprising you «escaped» to the West. You were adopted by a British family. Do you want me to continue?

– A damn defector must have snitched on me, Denise said enraged, turning already twisted hands into fists. – I'm going to kill him and I am going to kill you.

Parker slapped her on her cheek. The girl cried sharply. The white mark made by the glove slowly turned red.

– You little bitch. Are you truly so naïve that you believe you can ever get out of here without our consent? You think a defector told us about you? There is no defector. It was you. You told us everything, singing like a bird. You held out longer than the others, but that only served to point you out to us, exposing you. We realized quickly you had had training in resisting brainwashing, and we broke you.

The girl wanted to move away from the Mistress, but Parker grabbed her hair and forced her to look at her.

– On the floor, slave. Display yourself, Denise, so I can teach you once and for all how pathetic you are.

The girl stared defiant and angry at her, and didn't move. Shuen Parker smiled teasingly and moved her hand to the thin chain she wore on her hips. There was a tiny box with a button there. The girl shook, and hurried from the bed. She stepped out on the floor and stood straight, displaying herself.

– Yes, Parker nodded. – You know how to stand. I knew you did, Denise.

– My name is not Denise. It's…

– Your previous name is no more. You are Denise now. We have *named* you. You are our creature.

– I won't reply when you c-call m-me Denise.

– But you will, honey.

The voice was sweet and warm like a breeze. The devil's voice.

It hurt. Somewhere it hurt terribly.

– The electricity hurts. I will obey you because I'm afraid of the pain. But you haven't broken me. I can still think and feel. I'm not a puppet, not a robot without a will of its own. You won't break me.

Denise's voice had turned gradually higher during the last few sentences. She was unable to hide the despair dominating her perception.

– But poor girl, if you're afraid of the bad electricity, we won't use it. We have other means at our disposal to convince you of the righteousness of our cause.

– Are you serious? Denise wondered incredulous.

– Of course, I am, child. If you don't go berserk or something. Then we will have to resort to such… drastic measures, I'm afraid.

Denise stood there, torn between confusion and fear. But she had turned hard since that day in Prague, and hung on to her sense of self by a thread, even though the calm, confident Shuen Parker scared her far more than one enraged would have done. Something was not right, something was wrong, but she couldn't tell what.

– I remember, she said defiant. – My stepfather and stepmother are Lewis and Stella Culverstone. My sister Marsja and my brother Kazimirez.

– Not bad. Parker said. Once again she seemed quite pleased. – It sounds so good, doesn't it? So very good…

She giggled again, but her eyes stayed cold and hard.

– I remember it all, Denise emphasized. – You made us feel hunger, didn't you? You practiced your kind of hypnotherapy on us. You made us behave like a pack of animals at the sight of food.

– That's what I told the others. KGB made a coup when they «recruited» you. They fucked up royally when they sent you here as a slave, though. Infiltrating us through ordinary channels would have been easier.

– Why do you *talk* like that? Denise raised her fists. – You don't have to do that. There's something *wrong* here.

– I knew you were bright. Parker clapped her hands. – The last few sentences weren't even in your programming.
– Programming? But… WHAT ARE YOU DOING?
The shouting didn't affect the woman's calm. She shrugged.
– What I'm doing, honey? I'm playing a game, and you're my toy. She met the girl's eyes, and the girl's eyes wavered. – I'll show you, now, show you Power.
Denise spat on the floor. She wanted to say something, but her voice failed her. Parker walked to her. Parker smiled again, and everything turned horrible.
– On your knees, slave. Kneel for your mistress, Denise.
The voice was so commanding and the woman so confident that Denise almost obeyed out of hand, but she resisted, and stood her ground.
– I'm not a slave or your inferior, and therefore I won't kneel for you. And besides, my name isn't Denise.
She stopped breathing. Her heart stopped beating. Fear was distant butterfly wings raising a storm.
Parker patted her cheek, comforting her.
– Denise is so sweet. She went to the woods and picked raspberries for her old and frail grandmother.
– What…
Something happened to her. She… weakened, not only in her limbs, but in her mind as well. Will drifted away and faded. And what the audience saw in the girl's eyes were absolute bewilderment, a confusion and a horror beyond anything they could imagine.
She opened her eyes again, but now her entire attention was focused on Shuen Parker, she who ruled her, ruled her life and death.
– KNEEL IN THE DUST FOR ME, DENISE. KISS AND LICK MY FEET.
Denise knelt, and she smothered the Mistress' feet in kisses and licking them, and she kept licking them, until Parker kicked her away. The horror and bewilderment no longer manifested in the girl's face, but in the depth of her eyes, it was still visible. Tears rolled off her wide-open wounds to the soul.
– W-what happened? What are you doing to m-me?
– We are showing you, Parker grinned, so very, very pleased. – Showing you beyond doubt your place in life. You know, now, we have already broken you, long since torn you apart, and put you back together, grain by grain. You're like an instrument we can play. The musician is playing a chord, a tone. We play a sound, a word, a sentence, a movement,

anything. We have created you, Denise. We're your mother, your father, and you're an attentive and obedient and pleasing child.

– That's a lie.

But there was no strength behind the words, no conviction. The hand wasn't a fist. It didn't strike the floor, but merely touched it and hardly even that. Pale, dull fear lit the girl's eyes.

– No, she whispered. – Please, no.

She begged the Mistress with her wet eyes.

– Rise, Denise, rise, slave. Attend your Mistress.

And Denise obeyed, misty eyed, eyes like a doe.

– I attend thee, Mistress, she said, – how may I serve thee? Please give me thy word.

They virtually saw all thought, all mind leave the girl, leaving nothing but eager servitude. Murmurs reverberated through the auditorium.

A woman, clearly distressed rose abruptly and spoke up.

– Why is she showing me this? A woman shouted. – Why are you?

His companion attempted to silence her, in vain. Glory watched her, watched her insane eyes, and sweat broke all over her body.

– Come with me, sweet Denise, Parker whispered. – Walk into the forest and meet your mountain king.

And so she did, followed in her mistress' shadow. There was a sound. Glory realized it was the sound of an engine. She saw how the room seemed to move. It was a stage and another set revealed itself. Other sounds reached the audience and they realized it was moans and gasps, the sound of fucking. Glory shifted in the seat. Heat was like a glowing poker in her cunt.

The new set was a hall with ten cages. Parker and Denise walked through the door, as the bedroom vanished behind them. In nine of the cages couples were fucking, constantly touching and mating.

In the tenth cage there was only a single male. He knelt by the bed. His cock rose the moment his eyes fixed on Denise.

– This is Nathan, Denise, the mate we have chosen for you, the father to your children, your perfect match. You are all our parents here, and you will give us many obedient sons and daughters.

The horror was still visible in Denise's eyes, but so weak, oh, so weak. Desire lit those eyes, a need overtaking her completely. She wanted to scream, but nothing reached the surface.

Parker opened the door to the cage, and Denise hurried inside. She knelt down by the male, and kissed him. He grabbed her and started caressing her all over her body. Everything was so pleasant. He touched her belly and she moaned in joy. After just a short while she started returning his affection. Their moans mixed with all the others.

– Feels good, doesn't it? So much better than the bad electricity?

Denise blinked. She wanted to cry, but there were no tears.

– You have a lousy memory, by the way. Your stepparents are Frank and Iris Jones, pretty far from your suggestions. And you didn't give me the names of your stepsister and brother, but those of your brother and sister in Prague, those who died. Isn't that strange?

And now Denise did cry, tears and all. And it was tears of joy as she kissed her mate.

– I guess you get the picture somewhat by now. You thought you became yourself again because of your training. You were being silly. The only reason you had anything resembling independent thoughts, was because we let you. Why, you may wonder? Why all the… fuzz?

Denise did turn her head, briefly towards her Mistress, before once more and forever turning her complete attention to her beloved. Nathan lifted her up and carried her to bed.

– Are you truly the KGB agent? Parker mused. – Or are you, for instance, in truth, the daughter of plain Australian farmers? Are you the name you thought you were or did we build you from scratch, into a creature with no more substance than a mirage? I leave you, now, Denise, with those words, and you won't even remember them.

– You are so warm, so pleasant, Denise cried into Nathan's ear. – Lovely, lovely Nathan.

Consciousness faded. She wanted it to. She wanted for nothing, nothing more.

Parker closed and locked the door. She walked through the room, passing all the cages, and left through another door. There was a short remission as she disappeared before everybody's eyes and they saw her again, as she entered the auditorium.

The buzz faded as she stopped, as she faced them all.

– This is just the beginning, she stated. – It won't be many years before we are self-sufficient, until we have thousands of children we can mold from the moment they draw their first breath. Until eventually, over time, we will be able to breed specific traits, breed desirable qualities. We *will* be the father, be the mother.

Generations, Glory thought. She's talking generations.

The applause started slowly. It slowly filled the room, until hardly anything was heard, but the applause.

– I like power, too, the woman five seats away said to her companion.

Impossibly enough Glory heard her, just for a moment, over the noise. – I can do this. I know I can.

Then the applause drowned everything else in Glory's ears.

Chapter Five

Something scratched on the walls. For the fifth or sixth time that day Glory rushed across the floor and tore open the door. But just as before, there was no one outside. She kept looking up and down the hall, but it was just as empty.

She closed the door with a loud crack, as she had done five or six times before today. But this time she kept close to the door, stood there, waiting, waiting for the scratching sound to reappear. She stood there until her legs started to hurt.

Nothing happened. The scratching sound didn't come again. She finally gave up and returned to the table, to the chair Ted held for her. It happened so slowly that she suspected he did it on purpose. She sat down hard.

– LINDA.

Linda appeared before her eyes, like clockwork, a soft and pleasant maid, so sweet.

– Fix me a drink. And be quick about it.

She cast a suspicious glance at Ted, something she had done several times already.

The sound of a small glass door being opened, of a glass being filled played pleasantly in her ears. She stared straight ahead when the glass was put on the table. This was the first time she had actually considered taking advantage of the wide selection of alcohol at her disposal. She had seen her father drown in it. With a furious move she struck the glass, and it broke against the floor, its content splashing across a wide area. Her arm remained on the table, dead and still. She put her head on it and registered how it slowly cut off the blood supply to her hand. The fingers moved like a fly in a spider's web. She sat like that for a long time watching the pool on the floor, watching fibers of glass caught in its surface, slowly sinking, one by one. Finally, only the big shards were visible from above.

Glory sat there naked, half sat in the chair half lay on the table, rubbing the tattoo with her fingertips, the mark, the sign of ownership, moaning in need, in horror.

The scratching returned. Like birds' claws, cutting her insides. Glory jumped to her feet. She was so enraged, so beside herself by the time she reached the door that she had trouble opening it. She pushed it open, and it hit the wall with a loud crack. Its hinges screamed in pain. She pushed her head outside, hardly caring if anybody saw her naked. Just in time to see another door two rooms further down close. Sandra's door, Sandra's room.

– LINDA, my robe!

Controlled rage seethed below the surface, erupting like a geyser. Linda rushed to her Mistress, who grabbed the black cloth in a furious mode. She dressed while running, not bothering to tie it in front. Twenty steps down. It wouldn't have mattered if there had been hundreds. Her rage would still have burned. She opened the other door and kicked it at the wall inside. Sandra was in bed, enjoying the company of a slave. Glory rushed to her, grabbed her hair, and dragged her out on the floor. Sandra struck out, liberated herself, and snarling attacked in a classic Martial Arts way, but was quickly stopped by a foot hitting her in the face. She hit the floor paralyzed and dizzy, and before she recovered her arms were twisted behind her back and her face pushed at the floor.

– Don't even try, Glory breathed into her ear. – You know I'm better than you.

Sandra attempted to pull free. Glory grinned viciously. She twisted and twisted… At this point Sandra attempted to scream, but the pain paralyzed her. There was only a strangled sound, and she could hardly breathe.

– Listen up. Glory kept breathing into her ear. – One more little nuisance from you the next few years, and I will break every bone in your body. One single caustic remark, and I'll pull out your tongue.

She pulled the other girl's head up, pulled hard.

– Do you understand?

She twisted arms so the creaking of the limbs was clearly audible. Sandra howled.

– Yes, YES! For the love of God, let me go.

Glory let her go, the butchered meat before her feet. Glory kicked her in the ribs.

– One final reminder…

– It hurts, Sandra whined when she attempted to move her arms. – IT HURTS!

– That pleases me, Glory grinned.

She released her captive, and backed off, wondering about the sickly, triumphant smile Sandra sent her.

Glory returned to her apartment, hardly seeing where she was going.

The heavy door closed behind her. She locked it. There were locks here, even though they were hardly used. Sandra hadn't locked her door, hadn't bothered with it.

Glory made sure her door was locked, made sure several times.

She turned. She spotted Ted and Linda, kneeling on the floor. Not in reverence to her, but to another, standing a bit in shadow, sending a chill down her spine. She saw him standing there, hardly there at all, other than an indistinct, fuzzy figure.

Tim Croydon.

– What are you doing here? She wondered dumbfounded.

– You invited me.

– And you came, she said scornfully, – and you ran like a rabbit.

– I've returned, he persisted. – I want what is due me.

She studied him, saw his determination, the dark spots under his eyes. He should be easy to handle.

– Okay. She shrugged. – You'll get your pound of flesh.

She clapped her hands. Ted and Linda jumped to their feet and turned to her, attentive and lovely.

– Prepare today's dinner for two, she commanded. – And you'd better be thorough about it.

– At once, Mistress, Linda replied softly, with the childish smile of happy servitude painted on her face.

Linda curtseyed. Ted bowed. Glory always found it unnerving that only one of them replied verbally, and you could never know who it would be, like they were one person.

They went at it. She turned to Croydon, easily spotting the sign of relief beneath his rough surface. He nodded once, almost in gratitude.

Ted and Linda left the room to fetch more slaves, more workers. They had hardly left at all, before they returned with a lot of busy bees, rearranging the room. Lights were dimmed, the dinner table made. The scent of food filled nostrils, filled the room. Ted stopped before Glory. She nodded.

– Dinner will be ready soon, Mistress. Perhaps you and your guest would care to sit down?

She nodded, as she imagined she saw the candle flame reflected in his dark eyes. There was no way she could actually point to anything obvious, but in ways she couldn't identify… he was… changed.

He was docile, attentive, a perfect slave, as he and the doll sister pulled out the chairs, and Glory and Croydon sat down. Wine was poured in the glasses. The distinct sound of running fluid jarred in the Mistress' ears.

– To your continued good health.
She raised her glass.
– To yours, he replied with a leer.
Her and Croydon's glass met and parted.
Music filled the room. She rose, reaching her hand out to Croydon. He accepted it, and they danced. She pushed herself at him, moved her breasts up and down, back and forth on his chest, kissed him softly on the neck. His large vein… she knew she could bite it, chew it to pieces in one swift move. It wouldn't even take much of an effort. She waited for him to move on her, but he didn't. Disappointment and irritation warred within her. Music was muted. Food was put on the table and they returned to their chairs.
She studied him, worrying about his calm. He had no reason to be this together, this confident. He didn't sweat. His hands were not shaking. But…
Hers were.
The room's colors were soft, romantic. The oriental ate with a great appetite, while she hardly touched the food. She sipped the wine, felt it flow down her throat, burn in her stomach. His face glowed ghostly in the soft darkness. In the emptiness behind his eyes she saw Ted's face.
She sat still, measuring him, realizing she had sensed fear in herself the very first time she had encountered this man. Her world was crumbling before his eyes.
– So, she said lightly, – will you be up for advancement soon?
– If the fates are kind. He shrugged.
It was a typical oriental reply, and it irritated her immensely.
– I can put in a word for you…
She took his hand softly and leaned over the table, allowing her breasts to almost fall out, allowing him to see, to take a good look.
See, but not touch.
– Thank you, My Lady, he said with lowered eyes.
He lifted her hand to his lips and kissed it, and she allowed it.
His lips burned her flesh. His fangs punctured the skin.
Ted and Linda served the desert. There were no more people in the room by now. The other slaves had withdrawn, discreetly, respectfully, like good dogs.
They were not even barking, except in their Masters' service. A thrill shot through Glory Burns. She held her hands hidden under the table. They shook so hard she wouldn't stand a chance of hiding that for the underling across the table. She was in command here. She was Power.

She ate the desert in a daze, ate it without truly tasting it. It was bland, tasteless. She laughed when Croydon made a joke, smiling seductively to him.

The dinner ended. She smiled some more as she rose, as he rose. Triumph rose in her as she walked to bid him farewell. She would ask him to return at a later time. He could be a useful ally, a useful tool.

– Thank you for coming, she said pleasantly. – I had a great time. We must do it again sometime.

He struck her, a hard slap on her left cheek. She stared thunderstruck at him. And before she was able to react he struck her again, on the other side, even harder this time. She fell, and she hit the floor hard. Then he kicked her, kicked the breath out of her. And he kept kicking her until she lay there paralyzed, moving her lips in a coved, useless begging for mercy. Then he grabbed her hair and pulled her to the bed, lifted her up and threw her on it.

– You damn stupid bitch. He laughed short and sharp, a scorn cutting deep. – You thought I would be content with dinner, huh?

He tore off her robe, tore every piece of it off her.

– You've fallen from grace, he snarled. – Everybody knows it. It was merely a matter of who would be the first to take advantage of that fact. It pleases me it turned out to be me. It pleases me greatly.

He exposed himself to her, already in his full power. She whimpered and attempted, terrified, to crawl away from him. He was on her instantly, smacking her on the butt, smacking her hard and repeatedly.

– Stick your ass up, bitch. I won't tolerate more shit from you. I hope for your sake that we're clear on this…

He kept hitting her until she nodded and nodded, and she did what he wanted. And he kept at it. Put his hands on her hips and smiled triumphantly. He panted now, as he stared hungrily at the waiting, helpless prey. She dug her nails into the bed and waited for the inevitable, waited for the piercing pain, didn't dare utter even a word of defiance. She was ready for him. He saw it, sensed it, and he enjoyed it all that much more. He didn't hear the sound of naked feet, didn't see two folded hands curl into one fist. This double fist struck his neck. He fell on the bed, and lay there, unmoving.

– He isn't dead, Ted mumbled. – I should have struck harder.

– Thank you, Glory gasped. – Oh, thank you!

– Don't move! He snarled.

She was shocked and terrified. His voice was firm and clear. She sensed how he removed the chain around her waist, and heard it be thrown away,

hit the wall somewhere. She had no control over him anymore.
– How does it feel, Glory, feel to be totally at my mercy? How does it feel to be dirt under someone's heel?
He looked down at her, at her stuck up ass. She saw the storm in his eyes, in his entire frame. Seething in hatred and wrath he climbed into the bed and continued where Croydon had left off. It was so intoxicating all of it, the hatred and wrath filling him, directed at her. He had never felt so pure, so… fulfilled.
– Now, it's your turn to suffer, your turn to feel pain and scream until you can scream no longer. I'm gonna teach you what we felt, what we endured, at least a tiny part of it.
He grabbed her hips and brutally forced himself inside her, shouted in joy when she started screaming almost instantly. To get away from the horrible, tearing pain she attempted to wrest herself free, but she was caught in his grip and he would never let go. All she achieved was to be pushed down on her belly. He leaned forward and grabbed her breasts and he squeezed. Driven by his boundless hatred he kept going and kept going and kept going…
She fought him and cursed him, to no avail. And she couldn't keep it up for long. He was too strong, and he didn't allow any lasting defiance. He was way too strong and she was so weak. And then she started moving under him, matching his moves with her own. She cried out in misery and fear, as pleasure mingled with the pain. He came as he hit her butt in wild strokes, totally unconcerned with her well being, and he overpowered her completely, and she moaned, as the first stirrings of pleasure rode her. He just kept pumping her up, his cock hardly even shrinking. And the pleasure rose in her and completely overwhelmed the pain. It was so strange. She wasn't afraid anymore, only nonplussed. There was only pleasure now, the pain being nothing but a distant memory. She cried out in joy, as he possessed her entire body, her entire Self. He saw the smile on her lips as he lowered her down on the bed, and as he made himself ready to take her for the third time he hesitated.
– I was so stupid, she whispered, – believing you were my slave.
She still gasped and moaned. Her eyes were glassy, dreamingly. There was no way she could pretend.
– Have you never been taken hard before? He asked her scornfully.
– Not like this. Not even by One Eye. He was merely fucking me. And he had help. You possess me… My Lord. I've always believed I've loved making love, soft hands, kisses and such shit… until now… until you, My Lord.

– You're nuts. He shook his head.

She released herself from his weak grip, turning around on her back.

– Please, My Lord. Do me again. Now!

She grabbed his shoulder and dug her nails deep into his skin. He moaned and fell on her. The hatred was still there, but he couldn't resist the purely beastly invitation made clear by her face and body.

– Okay, he said, teeth gritting. – I'll grant your wish, grant the slave girl's fevered wish.

She moaned, both because of the contempt in his voice, and because he squeezed her breasts again. She came then, and another time just afterwards, the moment he did, as she bit so hard into his shoulder that he bled freely. The blood hurt her, like it hurt everybody. The blood flooded her mouth, flowed down her throat, and with wide-open eyes she no longer saw the room, but mountains and sand, and she once more saw the bird, the bird of prey roaming this desolate landscape at will. And there was fear in her heart.

They both crouched there, enjoying, fearing the aftermath, as desire faded, as hunger faded. Ted felt refreshed, awake, but still memory faded, faded again. Memory had lasted long this time, much longer than last time, but now it was fading. He feared he was once more on his way into darkness, the darkness without awareness. Two hands grabbed his hair and pulled hard. It hurt. It was Linda.

He grabbed her hands and squeezed them quietly.

– Do we kill her now? Linda wondered with perfectly normal voice. Nice weather today.

Glory heard and she grew aware once more as well. Linda, too. The old Linda, but with a face completely changed. The previously open and soft expression was hardened in cold hatred. Clearly not so strange. Slowly it dawned on Glory how wrong she had been, in all things.

– I don't think so, Ted pondered. – She might be useful. Besides, I think she has to help us, that she doesn't have any choice. Am I wrong?

He turned back towards Glory. She thought of Sandra, Sandra's triumphant, expectant expression, and she let her eyes wander through the room. From the unconscious Asian, the mess everywhere, to the sharp knife in Linda's hand.

– You're not wrong, Glory Burns said.

++++++++++++++++++++++++++++

They tied up Croydon, and put him in a closet.

Glory picked up the waistband and refitted it to her body. She searched the two pair of eyes before she did so, for signs of worry. There were none.

– This is a sign of a Master's stature, she said hoarsely. – If I am seen without it, it will raise instant suspicion.

– And there is no way to disable the electrical current in the collars? Linda's voice was sharp as razorblades, cutting to Glory's bones.

– Not without the keys. They are meant to be one with a slave… forever.

– I can still remember, Ted said desperately. – Not everything, but a little bit, enough to know… but it's fading, fading.

He and Linda kept pulling each other's hair, but it was a method clearly lacking in permanence.

– Stay with me, Glory ordered them. – Or are you nothing but slaves pretending to be human?

The harsh tone did work, but it didn't last, not that either.

– Please stay with me, Glory whispered. – Just a little bit longer.

She rushed to a drawer. There were a lot of pills there.

– Amphetamine, she said, with hope beyond hope. – Speed. That will do the trick. I have enough to last for days, long after we're out of here.

The brother and sister were unable to lift their hands.

– Open your mouths, she commanded, and they did.

She put the pills in their mouths, and like good slaves they swallowed.

– I can bury the blade in your heart, Linda said. – I know I can. No matter what.

Glory swallowed. She wasn't angry because they didn't trust her. She wasn't sure she trusted herself. Shame coursed through her like a vice, and she knew it would always be there, like a pain, a curse.

It worked. Linda and Ted's eyes turned foggy and shiny, but they could think again. And as that happened Glory felt like her mind cleared as well.

– I see Gidman's twisted words, she said. – I see myself. I'm sorry, and I know that no matter how many times I say it I can never make it all right. I wasn't misled. I misled *myself*. Fuck me!

She stepped close to the big man in front of her, drowning in his presence. He wasn't as big as Gidman, but he embraced her, embraced her like Shadow. She felt it, felt and relived what she could hardly believe.

– Ted, I… saw something, dreamed something. She spoke hesitatingly, quickly, to get it all out, before it was too late. – Experienced things about myself I've never acknowledged about myself. I saw you and Meinz fight, fight in a desolate future landscape. Like two birds of prey over an abyss. You clinched, tearing each other apart. I saw blood flow. And then you fell, you both fell, descended into the fire and the smoke, into the Abyss.

– The Abyss, Ted said, fear and fascination evident in his voice and expression.

They walked through the hallways, through the many hallways. The Mistress led her slaves in chains.

I have walked this way before, he thought, Many times.

Many times. Naked.

Vulnerable.

And now people stared at him, and he felt nothing. His face eyes remained empty, empty of expression, his mind seemingly empty of thought, another mindless chained creature on his way from a to b, to nowhere. Clothed people stared at him, studying every single point of anatomy on his body.

But he didn't feel embarrassed.

Not once.

He didn't redden.

Not once.

Everything here is so big. So small. Small enough for him to crush it all, them all, under his heel, his hatred, his boundless wrath. He fantasized about having them all at his mercy, about torturing them endlessly until finally putting them out of their misery. He could remember all the faces, even though the names weren't clear to him. And it was as if the very walls shook under the onslaught of his thoughts.

She listened by a door, a door they all knew so very well, and they shivered in the warm, pleasant environment. They didn't hear anything, but that didn't necessarily mean shit. He could be alone in there, doing nothing.

– He isn't here at this time, Glory mumbled.

Determination rushed through her. She pushed down the handle and the door opened. They hurried inside.

A fairly typical doctor's office revealed itself to them. They all remembered. Ted shook, shook in every cell of his body. He remembered. The memories flooded his mind. He relived the dance, the mad dance. Tilla, sweet and treacherous. A revolver covered in blood. A burning cabin covered in so thick a smoke that one could hardly see the flames. The Mask and One Eye charged him through the mist. He remembered the words of the redhaired cat. She spoke from far away, but she spoke to him. He heard her voice clearly.

They looked through the office, Kurt Meinz' office.

The benches were still here. The electric needles were still here. They shook, couldn't stop shaking. Glory's lips shook. She remembered. The needle in her hand pushed once again at Ted's skin. Everything turned black around her. Pain swatted them like flies. Fear swarmed them. They were unable to move for a long time. Fear, fear is the key.

Glory pulled out drawers, searched through them all. Searched through lockers, hands shaking in frustration and fear, fear of failure.

– I can see them, Ted said dreamingly, – all the wax dolls, lines on lines of them, an infinite number. No thought but the need to serve.

– NO! Linda grabbed him. – We can stop it, stop it from happening, from continuing. You can stop it. *Phoenix* can stop it.

He turned to her, looking at her with surprised, distant eyes.

– The keys are not here. Glory walked in circles, forming her hands like claws. – It has to be here. He had them when he…

They all looked at the door, the closed door. Glory ran to it and attempted to open it. It was locked.

– It doesn't matter, she said brightly. – I'm great at this, great with lock-pickets. There wasn't a house in Memphis where I couldn't get inside. My sister brought me, taught me when times were tough. And we survived another day, another night. She taught me to be strong. I'm not weak. It's a long time since I taught myself to be strong. So why are they after me, why have I… fallen from grace? I'm gonna show them, show them how strong I am.

She grabbed a few tools from a table, a table by a bench, tools stained by blood. Ted could see it, see beyond the sterility, the cleaning. The name, the name Linda had used… just by hearing that name reality… opened, opened up to him.

Eyes… he saw eyes in the sky. Dispassionate, detached, looking at humanity from inside their invisible disks. Looking at all the wax dolls.

Just a few moves, and it was done. There was a click. Glory pushed down the handle, and the door slid open.

She giggled, euphorically.

– I knew I could do it, she said. – I knew it!

She hurried inside. The other two followed. Ted stopped, as he looked astounded down on his right foot. It wouldn't move forward, it just wouldn't move.

The three of them stood there, frozen. No, not only frozen, not only like statues. Their paralysis extended far beyond that, beyond such trifles.

They found themselves in a kind of… laboratory, a very advanced one, and what they saw there frightened them beyond anything they had previously experienced. They had experienced a lot, and it was next to nothing compared to this. Glory was unable to keep the scream inside. Panicked she struck her own face and stumbled back. Ted stood still with an unmovable face, but the shock nearly pushed all reason from his mind. The world started spinning again, as memory faded.

I must remember, he thought. I must remember *this*.

Glory crouched and vomit poured in a straight line from her mouth. She was pale, and shook so uncontrollably that she could hardly stand.

– I've waited for you, young lady, but not this early. I guess I shouldn't be surprised at being surprised.

The voice belonged to Kurt Meinz. It was almost cheerful, and that made it even more horrible.

She turned, slowly, painfully. He stood only a few steps away from her. She wondered how she could stand here, this calm. She felt numb, beyond fear.

– How c-can you d-do something like this? She stuttered. – You're a monster, not a human being.

– Soon you will be even less, he said icily. – You'll be nothing.

He took a step forward. She took one back.

– Calm down, child. His laughter shook her further. – I won't touch you, at least not yet. I leave that to the two nice youths in your company.

– Linda, Ted, take her.

She looked astonished at the two when they grabbed her arms and held her in an iron grip.

– Let go, she commanded angrily. – Let go of me, Ted and Linda.

No reaction. When she realized to her horror that they wouldn't obey her command, she acted. She attempted to shake them off, to free herself. Linda struck her in the ribs, keeping her from breathing, in effect paralyzing her. A bigger heavier hand struck her neck, and she was helpless in their grip. She was unable to hide her fear when looking at Meinz through swimming eyes.

– You must truly be naïve, he stated, – if you thought you would have greater power over the slaves than I have. Well, you will pay for your assumption.

Glory hung broken in the slaves' iron grip, staring dully at Meinz as he found a bottle and turned it around, wetting a cloth.

– No one will help you, he said. – Nobody cares.

He grabbed her hair, pulled her head so far back that he almost broke her neck.

Suddenly, inspiration and understanding rocked her.

– You are the priest, the Lord of Order, she gasped. – And Ted is…

– You think, Meinz said, and she stared at him with boundless fear in her eyes.

Tears flooded her eyes. Fear overwhelmed her and she begged him:

– Please let me go. I'll do anything you want.

– Anything? The cloth closed in on her face. She whimpered.

– YES! ANYTHING!

The thought of becoming a part of his horrendous experiments made her shake in nameless fear.

– No, he shook his head, an obviously false gesture. – I don't need your consent, not for anything.

He pressed the cloth at her mouth and nose. She attempted to hold her breath, but it was no use. She had to blink. Eyelids turned heavy. She thought she caught a glimpse of Ted's scornful eyes, but she wasn't certain. She wasn't certain of anything anymore. Her vision blurred. And then she couldn't see anymore, and then she couldn't feel anymore. She knew Meinz pinched her nipple, but she didn't feel it. There was a sense of cold metal at her skin, though, and more dull panic filled her.

– You have another sister, now, Meinz said to the two holding her. – Aren't you pleased?

– Yes, Master, Ted and Linda choired. – So very, very pleased.

The ecstatic smile appeared in the slaves' faces. It spread through Glory's mind until that was the only thing she could see, and she smiled herself, and horror spread with it.

She raised her head from the floor. The laboratory faded around her. She realized she had been left in a hallway, one of the countless permeating the pyramid.

What has happened? Am I free?

– I'm free, she said aloud.

Everything was spinning, and she had to close her eyes again. Head hurt as it said thud, thud, thud.

The poison, she thought dully.

There was a cold draft somewhere, and she was freezing. She put her hands on her shoulders and rubbed them.

Ice, she thought. I'm cold as ice.

Rubbed her naked shoulders. She looked at her body, her naked body.

– Meinz, you BASTARD!

She wanted to cry out her hatred in a loud and powerful voice, but it was just a mumble. Fearful and queasy she realized her precarious situation. Meinz had rid himself of her in a very clean and efficient manner. Everything would proceed smoothly from here on.

A terrible suspicion made her bring a hand to her neck, and it was there, the collar. She couldn't stop the sob from erupting. The sound spread throughout the corridor.

– No! NO! She struck the floor desperately.

Nooonoonoooooo

Sound of steps, of approaching doom. Two pair of legs reached her line of vision. The messengers of bad tidings.

– On your feet, slave, one of the guards commanded.

She rose, fearful, her face wet with tears.

– I'm not a slave, she insisted. – You know me, Carl. You know it's true. I'm the victim of a conspiracy. Help me. Please, *help* me.

And then she felt it, the horrible electricity. Hands sought her neck, as the pain paralyzed mind and body. Her innate strength was slowly reduced to insignificance. Everything happened in a dream, a nightmare. She screamed and fell in a spiral to the floor, writhing in cramps, eventually crouching there without moving.

– Slaves do not speak within being spoken to, without explicit permission from a Master, the female guard told her coldly. – Now, slave, *on your feet!*

She rose again, eager and fearful, blind and dumb. There was no mercy in Carl or the female guard, only cold and ruthless looks. She understood now why she had been disowned. Not because she was weak, but because she wasn't weak enough, because she hadn't submitted properly. She asked questions, questioning her orders. Therefore she was a danger to those above her. She hadn't properly submitted to society's rules and that's why she had to go.

– In *position,* the female snapped. – Submit yourself.

Glory knelt humbly before the two Masters, displaying herself, her inferiority, as she had seen the slaves do countless times. She swallowed hard, as she desperately attempted to smile, to smile sweetly. The only thing on her mind was the horrible electricity and the pain it could bring her.

– Yes, Carl said pleased. – You know the drill.

She looked up at him, her lips quivering like a moth's wings. Then she lowered her eyes again, fearful and timid.

– Repeat the Oath. The female commanded harshly, with a slight smile on her lips.

– I am born inferior, Glory recounted, and it was easy. – Born to serve, born to obey the Abraxas Omega in all things. I am the lowest of the low. I am a slave, and a slave I will remain until the day I die.

– Good slave. The female patted Glory's cheek.

Carl snapped his whip, making Glory turn her entire attention to him.

– Come, slave, he commanded. – We will take you to your fate.
They walked, and she walked behind them.
Bars. I can feel bars in my hands.
And Glory Burns walked the path of a slave.
++++++++++++++++++++++++++++++++

A light breeze filled the air. Aside from that it was dark - and quiet. The silhouette of a ship towered at the night sky. It took up all the space in the fairly large harbor. Suddenly it seemed like the day arrived at the place, arrived with a vengeance. A thousand lights were lit on the large, northern pyramid wall. The lights exposed people, armed, uniformed guards standing in two lines on the long platform leading to the ship's entrance. The deep silence was broken by a low rumble, the sound of an engine. A door opened in the pyramid wall. A procession waited inside, two lines of more people or something resembling people.

A sharp command and the procession started moving forward. The slaves smiled and moved easily between the honor guard lines. The ship where they would start their service in earnest awaited them, like a mother. The teaching was complete, and they rejoiced.

Veronica was there. She walked first. Ted a bit behind. Linda was also there. And Iris, Bruce, John, Tilla… or was it Betty? Glory… and many, many others.

The Lords and the Lady observed it all from high above. Verheyen smoked a big cigar, more than resembling a high placed executive. Shuen Parker was at the Mask's side, her left arm entwined in his right.

– Look at the dolls, he said pleased. – The very profitable dolls.

She nodded exalted and clung to him.

The ship swallowed the slaves one by one, swallowed them whole. None made any attempt to break through the line of guards or even to break formation. Kurt Meinz nodded to himself, and the smile hardly wavered on his thin lips.

– This is the world, David Gidman said, – and it is ours.

– We might need to share it with a few others, Verheyen puffed. – But I can live with that.

There were no more slaves, no more guards on the platform. They had all vanished into the ship. The door in the pyramid wall closed. The door in the ship's hull closed.

The ship blew its whistle for the first time. Soon it would depart this godforsaken harbor and be on its way.

Chapter Six
DISTANT BUTTERFLY WINGS
New York 1935

Virgil Warren and April Powell got married on an ice-cold January day. It was a huge church wedding and the majority of the city and the United States' elite were present on the exclusive benches at the front of the great hall.

– Do you swear to honor and obey the man standing by your side, the priest spoke to April, – as long as you both shall live?

– I do. April smiled enigmatically under the veil.

– Do you swear to honor and protect the woman standing by your side, the priest spoke to Virgil, – as long as you both shall live?

– I do.

And they saw him attempt to smile, to fight off the lethargy that had dominated him his entire adult life.

– Then, by the power vested in me, I declare you married, by the Grace of God and for all the world to see.

You may kiss the bride, now, the priest silently urged him. Virgil smiled and lifted the veil, and kissed her on her lips. She returned the kiss shyly, but also lingering with a promise of future rewards.

Jonas watched Nick. Nick, as the pater familias, in the absence of the father or any close family, had given the bride away. Jonas had seen her hand touch his, squeeze it lightly, full of promise. Nick stood there, unusually, uncharacteristically rigid and reserved, a host of contradicting emotions playing in his face and fireeyes.

James was best man. He and Virgil were close, had always been close, Jonas had been told, since Virgil's sister had died. Rachel and Carla were among the bridesmaids. There were no younger girls in the immediate family. The only one, Trudy, was two years' old, too young for bridesmaid material. A nanny sitting close to Jonas looked after her and her brothers, Jack and Joel. Trudy was very vocal. Joel had seen fit to play with her nose, and she didn't enjoy that, she didn't enjoy that at all. All the three children had difficulties sitting still on the bench. They alternately had yawned loud and raised hell during the entire ceremony and service.

– It is boring, isn't it? A woman on the row behind Jonas whispered to her companion, believing or perhaps not caring if anyone heard her. – But these things have to be done, I suppose.

Jonas looked at the happy couple up there, and was almost overwhelmed by grief. His mask was just as stoic as that of his friend Nick.

His friend... Four years had passed since they had first met that night in Sara Woodward's apartment. Four years passing by like the wind, gone like the wind, always there. Sara had known, like Nick, like Jonas himself, that it had been a special moment. They had taken to each other instantly... Like... like...

The horrible surroundings of the church gave way to the equally horrible surroundings of the Warren Mansion, the seven thousand and five rooms' big house Joe had bought upon his arrival in town with his wife and little son in 1877. And it had bothered the family ever since. Though it didn't seem to bother April. Not April Powell, not April Warren. Jonas could see her, even when he didn't, thriving like fish in the sea. She approached him, and he felt his heart jump a beat or two, couldn't help it. It was like... like a goddess was descending from the sky. And she used that, used it for all it was worth.

She took his arms and kissed him on the cheek.

– Thank you for coming, she said. – Thank you for sharing the happiest day of my life.

– I'm happy to be here, Jonas said.

– And I'm glad you're here, for Nick's sake, too, she said. – You and he hit off right from the start. We all saw that. You're like... like brothers.

Brothers, he thought.

– Look after him for me, will you? I care for him, care for him a lot.

Jonas nodded, didn't trust his voice.

She rushed on, to her brief encounters with the other guests. Later he saw her, they all saw her on the dance floor, as she danced with her husband, a Virgil looking happier than Jonas had ever seen him. In fact he looked almost... cheerful.

Jonas sought out Nick without seeking him out. Perhaps Nick would see right through him as he usually did, but Jonas didn't want to it to be too obvious. And Nick's Clearsight was far from perfect. He didn't see what almost everybody else saw in April. Jonas wondered if it was really true; that love made people blind.

Nicholas Warren was forty-five years old. He still looked like a kid. Time didn't seem to catch him at all, except in the eyes. Those eyes belonged to a man who had already seen far too much of the harsher side of life. He stood by one of the punch bowls, toasting, toasting a lot, with the star-eyed young girls and women surrounding him. He had never remarried, even though there was no lack of prospective mates. Nick saw him, and there was this communication between them, this exchange saying so much more than words. He entertained the girls for a little longer, before he excused himself and joined Jonas at one of the many balconies.

The noise from the city did reach them, but it was distant, muted.

– I've been wondering about something, Jonas finally said.

– Yes? Nick turned to him, and stopped staring at the moon.

– How did you come to meet the rest of them, April, Carla and Rachel, for instance?

When he first met them, Jonas had taken them for being related to Nick and the Warrens, but they evidently weren't.

– I guess they sort of drifted into our spheres. Nick shrugged. – Witches, though certainly not of one mind and heart, tend to drift towards each other and stay together. We do have a lot in common, and there is also the fear of previous centuries, of course, that has never really let go. And then there is the Shadowwalkers. They were a part of that even before we actually met… just like you, Jonas.

The large man was drunk. He never got truly loaded, but he was drunk. Too much punch shared with the star-eyed chicks.

– We haven't told you much of the Warren family history, Have we, now?

– Nancy told me a bit, before she… before she… She told me you were… haunted. By what she couldn't say.

Nick nodded. Again, Jonas sensed the burning impatience inside him, something driving him, at the cost of everything else.

– Come. Let's leave this… this Masquerade.

He emptied another glass of punch. Suddenly it no longer seemed to affect him, not more than drinking a glass of water would. He was still unsteady on his feet, but the eyes were clear. Fire like water moved in there.

They walked to the library. The library was at the opposite side of the house. It was quiet, very quiet, like they walked through a hall of ghosts.

– Joe was seriously warped, Nick commented dryly. – He's one of the few among us who didn't just enjoy normal society, but excelled in it. He thought, like most people, that if you build a fortress big enough, no one can climb its walls. But there will always be those who can.

Nick closed the two heavy doors behind them. They were alone with thousands of books.

Now, sober again, Nick was deep again.

– Don't misunderstand. He had reason to be paranoid. We all have. What Nancy told you is true. We are being haunted and hunted.

He turned and spoke, and it was as if the past turned real as he spoke. Images, sounds, scents and emotions surrounded the words sneaking into Jonas' ears.

– There was a man, Adolph Foster, Karl's father. He married Rebecca, but they found out he never cared for her. She was just a means to an end for him. He was eventually exposed and killed. Trevor, my grandfather… killed him. They fought and died in each other's arms, tearing each other to pieces. But they never found out what Foster's ultimate goal was. If it was to kill them all or something else, but suddenly a lot of previously seemingly unrelated events… made sense.

Nick pulled out a large book and handed to Jonas. Jonas opened it. It contained drawings, lifelike drawings of every family member, their year of birth and death.

– He had green eyes, Jonas said astounded.

– So, he had, and so had also Nancy's «Master» in New Orleans. Our nemesis this century.

You have stumbled into some vast drama, Jonas Bergli, Nancy told him.

Stumbled it is, he nodded to her.

– The first Warren appeared from nowhere on the battlefield in 1756, during the French/English war for dominance over North America. He had no memory of who he was or where he came from, and as far as we know he never regained it. He married and fathered a son, Edward. Edward found his mother dead in the Boston harbor in 1780. Of his father there wasn't a trace. He seemed to have disappeared from the face of the Earth, and he was never found. The body wasn't found, and he was presumed dead, but there was no way of knowing.

Jonas looked at the page of the first drawing in the book.

ADAM WARREN
Born: Unknown
Dead? 1780

– He drew that himself, Nick said. – In an attempt to remember. It's quite impressive, isn't it?

It was. When Jonas looked at it, when he stared at it, it was as if it came alive, the face, the hair, the flames in his eyes.

– Some of us have an artistic talent, some don't. But those of us with it have it in abundance.

– I've noticed. Jonas nodded. – It is as if everything you are, you are much more than most people.

– Edward had three children, Nick continued. – The youngest, Lewis, complained of hearing voices his entire, brief life. He blew himself up using an entire boatload of dynamite when he was only seventeen.

Jonas looked at the drawing. It showed a boy, quite a normal boy. At least it would have been, if it hadn't so splendidly, perfectly depicted the haunted look in his eyes.

– Edward was shot in a seemingly random killing in 1802. Indians kidnapped Marylyn. Ashley had to flee the country because of a murder charge. He returned to United States in 1830. Foster killed him and Marylyn shortly after that. Trevor, Marylyn's son, half Indian, the first Warren we saw born with the fireeyes, witnessed the murders, and lived as a drifter, more than half insane for decades.

Jonas looked at the charts, the drawings, the pictures and the family tree. The tradition with the drawings continued, but was eventually supplemented with photographs. There was one of Nick, and his young bride in front of Titanic. Jonas looked up. Nick was looking at him.

There was one of Susan, Virgil's sister.

– There is one thing…

– Yes? Nick was on him in an instant, eager as a boy.

– With the exception of Lewis and Susan, and a few others you all have children, have children before you die.

– We do believe that is significant. Nick nodded.

– And there are other exceptions. John or Jean, Ashley's son lived to be over a hundred.

– He was killed in North Africa in 1918. Nick nodded again. – He still looked young.

Jonas looked at the drawing of the young man, and at the photograph. They were obviously drawn/taken decades apart. He looked the same.

– As if someone… someone wanted to convey something to you.

Nick smiled then, and Jonas felt that smile, that sense of joy wash over him like a warm wave of water on the shore.

– He was even embarrassed about it, coloring his hair gray and such. I remember the strange feeling I got every time I looked at him. He looked old. He didn't look old. And… more.

He looked out of the window, into the night.

– The brief time we spent in New Orleans was very… educational. I felt something there, felt something deep within myself. Now, these days I feel it virtually everywhere, but it's much stronger there. It's… frustrating. We hardly have any from the older generation to teach us. Before we're old enough to learn much, we're killed off.

They looked at each other, in glimpses of understanding.

– But you're here, now, Jonas pointed out.

– I am, Nick nodded, a film covering his eyes for a moment, almost as if he wasn't there.

They eventually left the library, the place of knowledge, and returned to the party. It felt strange, all this, after the silence of the library.

April and Virgil were on their way out of the door, to the awaiting car, starting on their honeymoon. The happy couple waved to the assembled crowd, and then they were off in a cloud of dust and a roar. Jonas didn't have to look at Nick anymore to look at him.

– I've never liked cars very much, Nick said to the air.

Jonas put a hand on his shoulder, and they stood there, stood in the entrance for a long time.

It was done. The party continued, even without the main attraction, but it slowly disintegrated, as ever more guests politely drifted off and left.

But smoke and dust didn't settle. It kept whirling in the air, and Jonas saw Nick stare at it, as if he could see something in those patterns, the way most people could see forms in clouds.

Jonas didn't know what made him turn. He never did. But he did. They both did. Carla had stopped under the arch leading to the great hall. She stared at them with misty eyes.

– Yes, we're hunted, she said in a hollow voice. – We've always been hunted.

She walked to them, touched Jonas, touched his shoulder, and her fingers were like claws, and her claws were like ice.

– I remember you kneeling before me outside old York, she said. – Or perhaps what would become old York, I can never tell. You were a good warrior then, too. You've always served me. I'm sorry.

– Telling us plainly what's going on would be a good start, Carla, Nick said rigidly.

– It's a Pandora's Box, riddles within riddles within riddles.

She said, smiling in pain and wonder.

– Sometimes I can see it all. Sometimes I can see nothing. Sometimes I was there at the beginning. Sometimes I'm not.

And then she left them, left them to rot. She just faded away in the dust and the mist.

The evening ended. James and Rachel, and the children came to say goodnight. Rachel kissed Jonas on the cheek. She never did that with Nick or even touched him, skin to skin. Jack, blue-eyed Jack jumped up and held on to Jonas's hips. Trudy kicked Joel in the foot. Jonas had learned their peculiarities these four years.

– Does Rachel seem particularly haunted to you? He asked Nick later, on their balcony, their balcony of thought and words.

Nick didn't reply, but stared at the city, the city of poison and dirty lights.

Jonas walked upstairs. The house was quiet. Everybody else had gone to bed. He went to his bedroom, well after midnight, in the deep of the night.

The bed was huge. The room was huge. He found it small. The walls closed in on him, as they always did. He pulled out a drawer, picked up a piece of paper, and sat down on the bed, on the edge of the bed. He unwrapped the paper, the worn paper, and read the words, read the words again.

«Dear, Jonas.

I send this letter from Berlin, Germany, as you can see of the stamp. I won't be here when you receive it. It's getting ugly here. It wasn't at first, but now it is. What I'm saying is this: Don't try to find me. I'm sure you can, if you put your mind to it. I'm fine. I'm seeing the world, learning a lot, about the world, about myself. I'm open, and the wound that opened me is slowly healing, making me even more open. I'm changing, Jonas, changing into what I've always been, and the witch I'm becoming might return to you one day or one night. I don't know, but here is hope. There is always hope.

Nancy
Yours»

++

The Warren Mansion seemed to… come alive during the course of the next months. As April's belly grew bright lights seemed to expand into corners and shadows. Except for the people cleaning the place weekly, there were no servants. April convinced Virgil to hire a personal maid for her, but even she couldn't persuade him to do more than that.

James, Rachel and the children finally moved in, in the late summer, after rejecting Virgil's offer for years. Jonas virtually witnessed how a man was reborn. He saw Virgil watch the three monsters playing and generally turning the house upside down, and almost becoming a different man. The anger and the hatred had frozen his face in a twisted form. Now it softened visibly. Everybody could see it. People passing him on the street saw it.

Nick stayed away. He still lived in his small crawlspace in Brooklyn. He did visit, but never stayed long.

It was Labor Day, September 2, when a hurricane hit the Florida Keys, and left death and destruction in its wake. They were all present in the study, listening to the radio broadcast, to the eyewitness reports in the days to come. The failed rescue operations, the reconstruction and the survivors' accounts.

– I can see it, Carla said. – See its wrath, feel it shake soil and bones.

– Nature will always strike, Nick said. – No matter what humans do or don't do. And… this is just the beginning, the beginning of wrath unparalleled.

Both stood there, frozen, with opaque eyes and rigid features. In many ways it was like the storm had entered the room, entered the house and shaking them all, shaking them to the bone.

– I read a paper from 1895 written by a guy named Arrhenius, Swante Arrhenius recently, James said. – He and others claim that one day storms such as these will be daily occurrences, that the temperature will rise rapidly all over the planet and lead to, cause untold disasters, that the release of civilization's CO2 into the atmosphere will cause it, *is* causing it.

Rachel looked affectionately at him, and he saw that, and returned her smile, but perhaps he didn't spot the flash of worry there, deeper in her eyes.

– What *haven't* you read? She struck her elbow in his ribs. He gasped theatrically.

A strange unrest grabbed them, grabbed them all, one even stronger than they usually felt, and it didn't go away in the days and weeks to come.

Nick stayed in the mansion, and he hardly ever sat still. He kept mostly to himself, as he sometimes did, but he had never shut them out more than he did right now.

Jonas and Carla went to him one day in early October, when the leaves had started to pale on the trees outside. They found him in the library, where he had spent most of his restlessness lately, as if the books there could give him some kind of peace.

But they clearly couldn't. There was clear evidence to the contrary in his haunted eyes. He stood by his desk, what was jokingly referred to as his private desk, looking out of the window. Photographs, pictures, pieces of houses, broken lines and carnage, images of Florida, covered the desk. There was even a heap of them there, a bit to the left of the desk's center. He paced back and forth some more, before stopping and looking at them.

– I… feel something, he said exasperatedly, – but it's random, non-localized. I can't get a grip on it. Every time I attempt to focus on a specific point, it goes away.

– Precognition isn't an exact science, Nicholas, Carla said softly. – Even less so, perhaps, than the other, so-called sciences.

– I look at Florida. Nick kept speaking, as if she hadn't spoken. – And it is gone. But it's clearly there… sort of…

They looked at the images of carnage, calamity and death, and they both understood and didn't understand why it made such an impression on the giant of a man in front of them.

– Perhaps… we should go there, Jonas said hesitatingly, not understanding why he hesitated. – Perhaps you need to see it for yourself?

The other two looked at him and he felt very looked at.

– Yes… Nick nodded slowly. – That might work. They've cleaned up most of the rubble by now, of course, but since Florida is still there, after all, I should get something. I should get more…

He looked at Carla, and she nodded.

– Yes, you should, she said, as enigmatic as ever. – And we were going to the labor meeting in Charleston anyway, so we just extend our trip a bit.

– Just a bit. Nick nodded, too.

The three looked at each other, both relieved and worried, the way they often felt.

They walked to the dining hall. Nick joined them. The family members and other strangers were all pulled together by the smell of food, but also much more than that. Jonas spotted April and her big, big belly. He saw her walk to Nick, and whisper in his ear.

– It's all right, she told him. – My day is early to middle November. I will be okay.

And Jonas heard it, even though he knew there was no way he could hear her across the large room. He had often wondered if Nick… broadcasted to him, consciously or subconsciously, keeping him updated on… matters. Jonas wondered a lot.

James and Virgil brought the food. Many of those gathered could cook, but James was seen as the master.

– Strange, isn't it? Rachel cried out cheerfully, cried out in glee. – We gather around the dinner table, just like a normal family.

They laughed, and they did sit down, and they did eat, and laughter and joy rose in the moist air.

Briefly, all too briefly.

Hours passed. Days passed.

Jonas and Nick walked through Harlem with Charles Burns, one of the fringe associates of the Shadowwalkers.

They crossed the invisible demarcation line marking its borders, and everything changed. Six months or so after the riots, even though there had been some clean up, it looked very much like a storm had passed through here. And it had. A human storm, just as volatile as another force of nature.

The event that had triggered the riots was a black shoplifter who had been beaten senseless by the white owner and aides. But what had turned Harlem into a powder keg waiting to blow was that Roosevelt's New Deal policy had pretty much overlooked unemployed blacks and the Harlem area in general. That and the overt racism among New York police officers.

– This was a great place in the twenties, Nick told Jonas. – A center for «colored» and alternative art, as much, if not more «swinging» than the rest of the city.

Jonas saw it, saw it through Nick's eyes, experienced it as it had been, and as it became, after the start of the depression… and on the days of the riots. People screaming, running and throwing rocks, breaking windows and fighting. Police officers with clubs, clubs dipped in blood. Jonas stopped, suddenly sweating profusely. Nick grabbed his arm gently and led him a few steps, until Jonas once more walked under his own power.

People stared at them. The hatred in their eyes stabbed them, and Jonas couldn't help getting a weird feeling of fear when looking back at the black faces and meeting the pitch black eyes. He detested this feeling, but there it was.

Fear, he thought. Fear is the key.

– Yes, Burns nodded. – We had a great thing going here, but it was crushed in the inception, as usual.

Jonas wanted to forget. He wanted to remember every single piece of detail in this place, this prelude to hell.

– It will get worse, Nick said, suddenly, and Jonas recognized the special, hollow and scary voice. – It will only get worse.

Burns looked curious at him, running scared inside.

– It will probably get worse before it gets better, he reckoned. – But we can't give up.

– You should take your family and move, Nick said dreamingly. – Run away from this place. You will die here.

Burns knew something of Nick and his more unsavory abilities, but he hadn't really experienced it fully, until this moment.

Nick shook his head, pulling himself together.

– Of course, we shouldn't give up, he insisted. – It's too easy to give up.

But the frost stayed in Burns' eyes.

That frost stayed with Jonas, as they penetrated deeper within Harlem.

He looked at Nick, as he often did, and finally… finally Nick also looked at him.

– I always feel down when walking through streets, Nick said. – Not just here, but every street, all over the city, every city. It's so sad. Beyond every other bad feeling it «encourages» I first and foremost feel sadness. Beneath the anger, alienation and hopelessness, I feel *sad*. Everything is so fucked up, and it shouldn't be.

Jonas wanted to say something, but the words stuck in his throat.

And then, there it was, what Jonas had wanted to say, adding Nick's intuitive understanding of life, of shadows.

– Perhaps we're too normal, Nick said. – Perhaps we shouldn't be.

Burns looked at them both, pulling back a little, pulling back even more.

– These people are just trying to get by, he said.

– There's nothing wrong with that, Nick countered angrily, excitedly and not the least passionately. – As long as they're not stuck there, as long as they keep trying to grow out of their own confines.

The frost kept haunting Jonas, as the thrill of Nick's words penetrated deep within him.

In a dark, abandoned warehouse shadows and angry words rose up in the air, into the invisible ceiling far up there somewhere.

– So how can you, who are stinking rich, tell us what to do? A man shouted at Nick.

– You, yourself were reasonably wealthy ten years ago, Nick candidly pointed out to him, to the seething crowd. – Does that make your opinion worthless?

His voice, his passion cut through the crowd, silencing it, making them listen.

– You know the Shadowwalkers, he said. – You know we're a varied lot. Some of us are poor, some not. Those of us who are reasonably wealthy use that wealth, making it work for us. You know we aren't popular in the halls of the rich and mighty, and that we will never be. Wealth can be a trap. This is a trap, your trap. You must look beyond this. Of course, you must fight also within the confines of Harlem, of New York City, but it isn't enough, because the core of what's wrong with this world, with human society isn't only here, but everywhere. You know this. You *know* the truth of my words.

The frost traveled with them, to the Ohio mining town, between the high wires, well armed guards and dirty faces. On a low, wooden platform Nick, Jonas and Carla attempted to be heard in a cauldron of boiling blood and hopelessness and seething rage.

– I can feel it, Nick mumbled, and Jonas heard him. Through all the ruckus Jonas *heard* him. – I can feel everything here. It's strengthening me. It's weakening me. I had never thought… never imagined it could be like this.

He stepped forward, and it was like he grew there and then, as if he suddenly was twice as tall as one second earlier. Carla smiled brightly and Jonas looked at him in awe.

– YOU'RE AFRAID, he shouted.

Everybody stopped talking, stopped shouting, started staring.

– THAT'S OKAY. FEAR IS OKAY. YOU HAVE GOOD REASON TO BE AFRAID. IT MAY EVEN GIVE YOU AN EDGE, STRENGTHEN YOUR ABILITY TO FIGHT, TO FIGHT ON. BUT YOU MUST NOT LET YOURSELF BE CRUSHED BY THAT FEAR. IF YOU'RE SCARED, THEY WILL JUST KEEP SCARING YOU.

The shouts among the miners faded. Even the scorn from the men with guns surrounding the gathering lost its potency. Everybody listened.

– Never forget the reason you do this. He spoke quietly now, almost subdued. – Yes, you need money. Money is needed in this world, this wretched world… But never forget *why* you're doing this, *why* you're opposing the mining companies, and the people lining their own pockets aided by your suffering. Never forget that you're doing this because you want to claim your *dignity,* your right to be treated as a *human being,* not a *sheep*. For you to organize, to start labor unions is one step in the right directions to do that, to *claim* your dignity, your birthright as a human being, as a sentient, living individual and person. Remember that there is strength in numbers. Yes, you are alone, and perhaps you won't get help, but always remember that giving up, believing the lies of your «employers», will only serve to weaken you and return you to the codependent creatures you were before, before you took the crucial step forward and *claimed* your humanity.

He spoke different from the people in the valley. His wording was more «sophisticated», more elaborate, but they understood him.

– Remember that freedom can't be given, but must be taken. You don't kneel before another man and beg him for favors, for elementary, fundamental human rights. The human being is born free, but today, in our fundamentally unjust and dominant society, this… pyramid of fear, chains are shackling us from the moment of our first breath, and freedom must be taken. The chains must be broken, so they can *never* more be used to shackle us, to make us something less than human. This is the message I'm sending to you and to your professed masters.

He stood there afterwards, among jubilant people shaking his hands. Carla kissed his cheek, stars in her eyes.

– They will die, he said on the train later. – Many of them will die.

– People have always died and will always die, Carla told him. – What's important is how they die… and how they live. You've given them a chance to live, never forget that. You've shown them what is beyond fear, beyond subservience, and I love you for it. I love you so very much.

And the stars in her eyes turned hot.

Jonas heard them in the neighboring compartment while he sat there alone. Sounds smothered his ears and mind. He didn't even have to close his eyes to see them.

They returned, holding hands and giving each other still feverish kisses.

The three of them were heading south. The weather turned warmer, like another spring, Leaves turned green and summer bathed them in its heat.

They were the only three in their compartment. It was a little odd, even though there were not many passengers on the train. But the neighboring compartment compartments, even the entire coach was empty, except for the three of them. Jonas checked, walked from one end of the coach to the other, and there was no one, before returning to his two companions with a puzzled look in his face.

– Don't look at me, Nick grinned. – I'm not doing it.

He and Carla sat tight, but they didn't exclude Jonas in any way, and neither did they attempt to include him, in any awkward way. Everything felt very natural, and Jonas didn't feel bad about it, not in any way.

The window was open, of course. All windows were. It was the only way to keep the smoldering heat somewhat away. The wind played with Carla's red brown hair. In this light the first gray hairs were clearly visible. She might not look the part quite yet. Her face was smooth and without major wrinkles. But she was aging, contrary to Nick, who still looked like a twenty-year-old kid.

The train stopped.

– This isn't a station, Jonas stated, totally unnecessary.

– We're having visitors, Nick told the two of them. – Don't worry about it.

The sound of steps slowly grew louder than the sound of the train. Heavy steps, several pairs. They weren't alone anymore. Jonas saw the approach of the three men through Nick's eyes, saw them through a haze

as they appeared in the doorway. And he recognized them.
– Good afternoon, the man greeted them politely.
– Good afternoon, Carla returned the greeting. – What can we help you with?
– My name is Brooks, Jefferson Brooks. You've probably heard of me.
– We have indeed, Mister Brooks, Jonas said casually.
– To get right to the point: I have one brief message for you: You're upsetting my workers, causing trouble for everyone. I want you to stop, stop this second. We, I and my associates in the miner's guild, won't take it anymore. That's all.
He turned to leave.
– Mister Brooks…
He turned back, facing Nick.
– Yes?
– You come here to impress us, Mister Brooks. Nick spoke evenly, without raising his voice the slightest, without doing any threatening moves, remaining in his seat. – You're wrong if you think we're easily impressed or threatened.
– That's too bad, Brooks said. – I…
– I'm warning you, Brooks. Don't try to intimidate us. Don't even think of using your usual strong-arm tactics and intimidation techniques on us. You will fail, and everything you do will be returned to you tenfold.
Jonas felt it, felt the brush of frost from his friend with the ruby eyes. Brooks did, too. Something… *entered* the compartment, something that had always been there, suddenly growing, growing beyond belief. Brooks shook, his entire body shook, and he staggered backwards, shock and horror engraved in his fleshy face.
– W-what…
– This is the only warning you'll ever get, Nick told him. – Stay away from us, turn your life around and stop harassing people who don't agree with your political views. That's all I have to say to you. You, yourself must take responsibility for the cesspool you've made of your life, drag yourself up from the gutter in which you have placed yourself. Am I making myself clear?
– G-gutter?
The man kept staggering, kept fighting to recover from the onslaught he suffered under.
– WHAT DID YOU DO, YOU SON OF A BITCH? WHAT DID YOU DO?
Nick rose, abruptly, terrifyingly.

– I never knew my mother, he said.

And there was still no visible indication that there was anything but a normal man standing there speaking.

His two companions looked uncertain at Brooks, ready to attack Nick, just for the heck of it. Brooks raised an arm, stopping them.

– Be at ease, boys, he grinned. – We didn't come here to argue, just to deliver a message, and we've done so. It wasn't appreciated, but that's often the case, isn't it, and it must be dealt with… in time.

He turned to Nick, also indicating Jonas and Carla.

– You will pay, he swore. – You'll pay for everything.

The three men left. The sound of heavy steps faded as they walked away. A minute or so later the train made another unannounced stop, and Jonas saw the three men enter a car, and the car drive away.

– It's happening, Carla exclaimed weakly, thunderstruck. – It's finally happening.

She looked at Nick, looked at him in fear and affection.

The three kept heading south, and during the days to come it was Carla's excited face Jonas kept seeing.

– A Woman wasn't a person fifty years ago, Carla Wolf said, to a hall of shouting women and men, a meeting discussing women's rights, in Charleston, West Virginia. – After marrying she wasn't legally allowed to handle her own affairs. Not according to the law of United States of America, the land of the free. She was a non-person, one totally without legal influence over her own life. And women are still oppressed, not allowed the freedom and economic power denied them for so long.

Cheers and boos rose at her, at the three of them at the podium, like knifes, like prods stuck in the fire. Carla smiled.

– Let me say one thing: Men aren't the enemy here. They, too, are oppressed by the system, the world pyramid with the many below and the few above. This is a system hostile to all humans, not only to women. But women are a «natural» underclass in this system, because they, in some key places in society are still considered less than human. Fifty percent of humanity, ladies and gentlemen, and we aren't human?

– HARLOT!

A man stood up and screamed at her. Spittle flowed from his mouth.

– Thank you, sir, she grinned. – Always nice to be appreciated.

And the laughter drowned the man's insane glee, and an insane rage was lit in his eyes.

– RETURN TO THE KITCHEN SINK YOU BOLSHEVIK WHORE!

Another man shouted.

– YOU'RE A WITCH, a woman shrieked. – A SERVANT OF SATAN.

– So odd, Jonas shouted back. – To fear the truth…

And it was satisfying to hear a few cries of agreement.

But even among the people they had come here to support there was… hesitation. They probably felt Carla had gone overboard in her speech, probably felt unease over the passion in which she spoke. Jonas nodded to himself. Something had changed, in Carla, and thereby the world. He felt a thrill shoot through his body, his fevered, excited mind.

The Storm raged around them, in Charleston, during their journey south, and in the now still ruins of Florida.

Time. Time is ever subjective on a human mind.

Nicholas Warren stood quiet in the midst of those ruins, and suddenly, briefly it was as if the storm reasserted itself. Jonas felt the wind in his hair, even though it was quiet, even though there was not the slightest physical indication that any wind was blowing. Jonas saw people, ghosts run for their lives, saw them be pulled into the air… and he imagined he felt four hundred people die. Soldiers not having died in the Great War had died here, killed by nature's wrath.

Nick stood still, the fire brightening his eyes, the… Jonas saw it, but couldn't really believe it, not even he could. Jonas Bergli saw small fires, small bursts of shadow, dance around Nick and Carla.

– The Earth is angry, Nick said.

– Yes, angry, Carla nodded. – She has been angry for so very long. And now, finally, the reckoning is here.

They walked through the wasteland for hours, without really reaching an end to it. Repairs and the cleaning up had begun, but it all seemed so insufficient, so useless.

– This is just one storm, Carla said happily. – One of many in the Storm that's coming.

And suddenly, just like that, they were on their way north again.

Did Jonas see doubt in Nick's burning eyes? He couldn't tell.

– I'm… glad we came here, Nick finally said.

– I am, too, Carla said, taking his hand.

Nick turned to Jonas.

– Carla has waited a long time for this, he said gently.

– Waited for the Shadowwalkers, she said passionately, taking Jonas' hand. – *The* Agents of Change

And even though Jonas had trouble wrapping his mind around it all, he did understand. He finally understood what Nancy had attempted to tell him, what she had strived to make him understand.

The train raced north. The world outside the window whirled, as it passed by, turning indistinct. There were other passengers in this compartment, but they didn't care about them. It was just the three of them there, on the entire train.

– This feels so good, Carla said, stretching her arms above her head, stretching her body in delight. – The three of us together, traveling, storming foreign beaches and distant lands.

Other passengers came and left. The three of them stayed in that compartment, making a world of their own.

– You're the Shadowwalkers? A well-dressed man said.

Jonas eyed him, but he eyed Nick as well, and Nick didn't seem the slightest surprised.

– You are Johnny Berg, Carla Wolf and Nicholas Warren?

– Yes, we are. Nick sounded almost amused. – What can we do for you, sir?

– My name is Bertram Caine. This is my wife, Juana, and my son Francis.

He offered his hand to Nick. Nick took it, briefly closing his eyes. Caine also offered his hand to Jonas and Carla. That told them something about him. That Juana was clearly Mexican in origin told them more.

Juana and the child also shook hands with them all. She couldn't hide a relieved expression in her eyes.

The other passengers had looked hard at them all, and they did so even more now.

– I just wanted to tell you I support what you're doing. I was at your meeting in Baltimore, and was thoroughly impressed.

– Thank, you, sir, Carla, said bemused. – It had to be Baltimore, I guess…

It had been one of their livelier meetings… in a series of lively meetings.

The other passengers rose abruptly and left the compartment. The train was full. There were no available seats anywhere on the train, but still they left.

– Baltimore Sun called us Satanists, Carla said aloud and cheerfully.

– And you're not? Juana asked pointedly. – You are rejecting God, aren't you?

– No. Nick shook his head. – That would be quite impossible… since we don't believe in the existence of either Satan or God, or any gods or demons, for that matter. We can't reject anything we don't believe exist, now, can we?

Juana rose.

– Come, she said to the boy, reaching out a hand to him.
– Sit down, Juana, Bertram snapped.
– What…
– You're denigrating people with a different belief than your own, and I won't have it. *Sit down!*
She did, her face stoic as stone.
– My wife will never apologize, Bertram said, to the three. – Therefore, I will do it for her.
– That's quite all right, Bertram, Nick said. – We're used to being attacked for our beliefs. – It's always more encouraging meeting one who won't, instead of one more of the thousands that do.
– You escaped physically from your strict upbringing, Juana, Carla said softly, – but you didn't escape completely, did you?
It wasn't a question. Juana sat there sullenly, holding the boy's hand, and didn't reply.
– I worry you, don't I?
It came suddenly, quiet as a whisper.
Juana looked stunned at the other woman.
– I worry you deeply, Carla said, – because I am free, free from the shackles you feel on your wrists and ankles, the confines in which you were raised. And more. You can feel more. You see me, see me for what I am?
The wind was blowing again. The water flowed, the fire burned and the Earth moved. Jonas drew his breath, in tandem with Juana.
– And you've never learned politeness, Juana flared, with something very close to hatred in her eyes.
– You would leave us, because we spoke our mind, and you speak of being impolite?
This time the woman's voice was like a whisper.
It was as if Juana didn't listen.
– You're making it worse for them, you know, Juana stated, ranting on.
Bertram looked more than a little embarrassed. He wanted to say something.
Carla held up a hand, stopping him.
– No, that's quite okay, Carla said. And to Juana: – Why is that?
– The *workers,* the poor, giving them ideas, notions way past their station, hinting to them about mysticism, about paganism, about a vastly different, distant, future world. It isn't the right way.
– On the contrary, ma'am, Nick said, very decisively. – I think it's one of the very few paths leading the right way. And the future is *now,* isn't it?

– What they need is improved economic conditions, and that is what should be fought for.

– That, too, Carla nodded. – But it isn't enough. They need more. We all need more. We need a world we can live in, not want to escape from.

– There is the illusion that our current society is basically right, Jonas added. – That it just needs to be improved a little here and there, and not more than that. That is the illusion that should be exposed more than anything as the *lie* it is.

– It isn't easy being a catholic, is it? Carla grinned, solemnly, without malice. – The church tells you to obey and serve your husband, but when your husband doesn't have the same ideas and is quite… critical to the church, it gets quite difficult. What do you do? Accuse him of heresy, disown him? You know you're wrong, Juana, and it's tearing you apart.

– You… sound like my confessional father, Juana whispered.

– God, I hope not! Carla shrugged, not giving an inch.

But she did bend forward and took the other woman's hand.

Juana started crying.

Jonas looked at the two of them just then, of course, but suddenly, as surely as night follows day, his eyes were drawn to Nick.

The ruby eyes glowed like fire.

– What?

Nick turned towards Jonas, with confusion riddling his face.

– I hear… screeching, he said.

And there was more than a hint of worry, in his eyes.

And there was fear in Carla's eyes as she turned to him, and grabbed his collar.

– How long, Nick? She said anxiously. – How long?

– Oh, for several minutes, now. I thought the train was stopping, but it… isn't…

– We don't hear it, Nick, she said sharply. – We don't hear it!

And finally, the fear in his face mirrored hers. He realized what was happening, and Jonas did, as well.

She rose.

– The train will crash, he said.

There was a thud, unbalancing her, and then there was a loud, shrieking sound cutting into their minds, all their minds. Everything happened so fast. Screams of panic overwhelmed Jonas' senses as the train turned over, and the ground on the right side suddenly rushed towards them as if they were falling. Then there was a loud thunder, followed by many loud cracks, as the train, in its entire length crashed against the ground. The world turned dark. Screams of pain mingled with those of fear, of blind, unreasoning fear, as the train slid across the ground on its right side, as it was slowly, quickly shaken to pieces. Jonas was thrown across the compartment. He hit the opposite wall, and then he, too, felt the pain as something broke somewhere in his body.

Glimpses, confusing images assaulted him with the loud noises and scents… the scents of blood. He saw Nick stand at the center of the compartment, the upturned compartment, with his arms outstretched, with his eyes glowing. Nothing could move him, it seemed. Not the shaking train, not the shrapnel flying through the air. Jonas felt a tug, a soft pull, and it was like he was pulled towards Nick, like they all were. A huge chunk of the wall loosened, and it was bright in Jonas' eyes again, tears flooded his eyes, and he couldn't see anything but that indistinct world of tears.

Then they all landed softly in the grass. Pain shot through Jonas again, as he landed on his arm, his broken arm. Flames and smoke and heat were all around them, the small group of six, as they landed in the tall yellow grass in the midst of the wreckage and destruction.

Nick rose slowly. Blood flowed from a deep cut in his side. Jonas saw the bare skin there, and as he watched, as he stared, the wound knitted itself, did so in a manner of seconds.

Nick spoke to him, but he couldn't seem to hear what his friend was saying.

– Are you *alright?* Nick shouted for the second time.

– Y-yes. Jonas nodded, not really aware of himself or what he was saying. – Yes!

Carla rose, dirty and bruised, but okay. The bluish green taint was still like a fire in her eyes.

Juana and Bertram knelt down by their son. Jonas didn't see the boy at first, didn't see anything but a wall of mist.

Francis had a huge piece of shrapnel sticking out of his chest. He stared right up at the sky, seemingly unable to see his parents. Loud gasps quickly turned labored, as he clearly was about to stop breathing.

Nick ran to him, knelt down at his side. He grabbed the boy's shoulder with his left hand and the shrapnel with his right. In one, swift move, he pulled the deadly piece of metal out of the boy's small body. Blood flowed like a fountain from the wound. The giant man put both his hands on the narrow chest, and then… then… his hands started glowing.

Bertram Caine said something, but Jonas couldn't hear what, perhaps something about that Nick shouldn't have pulled out the shrapnel. Juana pulled back, her eyes wide and opaque.

The ten-year-old boy shook, as the ghastly wound mended itself, as blood stopped flowing. Suddenly Nick shook as well, shook hard, and he screamed, and then Jonas saw terror in his eyes.

Nicholas Warren rose, drying saliva from his jaw and cheek. Francis Caine sat up with a bewildered expression in his face mirroring that of his father. Jonas could look now, at the rest of it, at the carnage and death surrounding them, at the yellow grass turned red, at the human remains among the wreckage, the distorted metal all over the area. He even imagined he was floating, floating high up, like a bird, and that he could see everything, even see April in the Mansion, and that sight made him more scared than anything else.

He saw her and the maid say goodbye to Rachel, James, the nanny, and the kids, wishing them well on their trip.

Nick grabbed his broken arm, and Jonas felt a heat far more intense than he could ever have imagined. He gasped. First there was pain, but the pain faded and in its stead came bewilderment, as the arm healed, and it was broken no more. He moved it, turned it, and it was like there had never been a broken bone there at all.

Nick ran to Caine, clearly dizzy, almost falling several times, before reaching the man, grabbing his shoulder, holding on to it for dear life, not letting go.

– We need a car, he said. – We need a car, NOW!

– It's strange, Caine said, shaking his head continuously. – I actually have a friend nearby. At least I'm pretty sure it's nearby. There won't be more trains passing by here for days, I gather. My friend owns a car. I guess you can borrow it for a while. It should be okay. I just tell him it's an emergency. He owns me that much. I can even buy him a new car, if so needed.

He kept talking, kept rambling on, unable to stop, stop rambling.

Juana Caine backed off from Nick, from Jonas, from Carla, pulling her son with her.

– You are Satan's Spawn! She spat. – His demon army, come to conquer the Earth in his name.

Nick pulled Carla and Jonas with him. He didn't have to. His panic, his urgency hit them like a Storm, and stirred their insides like a volcano, but he pulled them hard anyway. Caine grabbed his wife and son and dragged them after the three, half stumbling, half running over the hill, down the hill, to the little village below. Jonas would have wondered how Nick could know where they were going, where they were headed. He would have wondered a few days, perhaps only a few minutes ago, but he wondered no more.

April watered the flowers. She spoke with someone on the phone, probably Virgil. The smile on her face got to Jonas somehow, and he felt the tug of fear, of approaching horror, the minor echo of the Storm inside Nick.

They reached the small red house by the road after no more than a ten minutes' walk. Caine's friend was already outside, looking at the smoke from the disaster. Caine explained everything to him in a few sentences, receiving the keys, handing them over to Nick. Nick sat down in the driver's seat. Carla and Jonas jumped into the backseat. The engine started with a roar, and they were on their way, before Jonas had managed to properly close the door.

– During the healing… Nick said, with lips shivering as if they were blue by cold. – I sensed something…

He didn't really need to say anything. Jonas and Carla nodded before he had finished speaking. But he had a strong need to explain himself, to explain the unexplainable.

– We should never have left her. Nick knocked his head on the wheel. – What were we thinking? What the fuck were we thinking?

They grazed another car in an abrupt turn. Nick didn't seem to notice, notice at all.

– The birth is still a week off, Carla said softly, with a distinct tremor in her voice. – We will be there in two days or even tomorrow, if we're lucky.

There was no vocal reply, and no reply in the eerie glow that was Nicholas Warren's face. His hands clutched the wheel and his knuckles had long since whitened around that black material, whitening to the point of resembling cleaned bones.

It was late evening. Halloween. They saw children with horrible masks running around. It was night. They had finally stopped, after almost crashing twice.

– You need a break, Nick, Carla begged him.

– Can you drive? He shouted at her. – Can JONAS drive? Can you at least try to MAKE SENSE HERE?

And he didn't even try to apologize, to soften the hurt evident in Carla's eyes. He acted like a man possessed, like a spirit, benevolent or not had taken possession of him and wouldn't let go.

They parked outside Philadelphia. Nick just turned to one side and stopped by the sidewalk. The outline of the city was evident if one looked at it, but none of the three of them did.

He slept, and he dreamed. Jonas slept, too. At least he thought so, thinking that the chaotic whirl of impressions couldn't be anything but a dream. Carla spoke. Jonas couldn't make out the words, and he realized that she spoke in a foreign tongue, and it was guttural, crude, completely dissimilar to any language Jonas had ever heard. And he had heard a lot.

It was morning, the morning after Halloween, the Day of the Dead. The sky was dark. The sun was dark. Nick peed on the sidewalk. He had been driving well into the night, and now he was driving again. Jonas was hungry. They hadn't eaten in almost twenty-four hours. The hunger had long since passed the time of pain, and turned into a hollowness somewhere, delocalized, dull. His lips were dry, his throat throbbing for lack of moisture. They had refilled gas somewhere, and he seemed to recall the taste of water, of sweet water as well, but that was long ago, as long ago as when Carla had spoken her archaic language.

There was an intersection right ahead. It was early morning and there were quite a few cars passing through, approaching the intersection from all sides. It was hard to believe, but Jonas noticed that Nick was actually slowing down. He didn't proceed recklessly, but looked to the right before the crossing. Jonas heard the roar of an engine and had no idea where that was coming from.

A car hit them from the left. Hit them hard. Seemingly from nowhere. They were pushed several lengths off to the side. Several other cars collided and in seconds everything had turned to chaos. And then, then Jonas saw another car coming right at them from the right. Jonas opened the door and jumped out, pulling Carla with him, just before the second car hit. They landed hard on the ground. Air was pushed from their lungs, and Jonas discovered that he could hardly breathe. Men in suits rushed from a third car nearby, rushed at the wreck where Nick still sat behind the wheel, rushed at him with guns in their hands. Jonas and Carla drew their guns and started firing at the attackers. Nick stumbled out of the wreck, managing to throw himself on the ground with bullets whistling around him. He drew his own gun and fired at the attacking men. Two of them were hit. Carla and Jonas also hit some of them. They retreated behind cover, behind some of the other wrecks covering the smoke-filled intersection. Other men charged Nick. They fired at him with a completely lack of concern for their own safety. They weren't dressed in suits, but in strange, dark clothes. Nick was hit, several times. Jonas rose, and ran to him, firing at the group. Carla was right behind him. She fired, too. The men fell like cones on a bowling field. Jonas felt himself be hit.

Carla grabbed him, and held him, kept him on his feet. They ran to Nick, grabbed him, and pulled him to safety.

– Two groups, Jonas said. – Do they know each other? What a strange thing that they decided to attack us at the same time.

– A strange thing indeed, Nick mumbled.

His palm was filled with bullets, bloody bullets. Only one of his wounds was still bleeding. It was closing fast. And he put his hand on Jonas, and Jonas felt the heat again, the heat that felt so good and worried him so much.

A fourth and a fifth car came at them. Nick saw it and his eyes widened to an uncanny degree. He grabbed both Jonas and Carla hard.

– Stay down, he said. – Whatever you do, stay down.

And then he rose, then he was up, raising his hands. And *then…* one of the cars seemed to shift… sideways, to move in in front of the other approaching car. There was a sharp and loud CRACK as they collided. It happened with such speed and such force that one of the cars rose in the air, rose high in the air, and it almost looked to Jonas as if it was thrown at Nick. He crouched slightly… and the flying car *stopped* in the air above him, stopped like a specter, hung suspended in the air, like a frozen hawk, without even coming close to its target. Jonas saw Nick, saw him like never before. He had thought he had seen him before, but in truth, he hadn't. Nick turned his head, turned his burning eyes to an undetermined point somewhere ahead, waved his hand, and it was like Nick threw the car at one of the group of attackers, those in the strange black clothes, at the car they hid behind, and there was an explosion, a burst of fire and brimstone lighting the entire place. He curled his hands into fists and «grabbed» another car and sent it towards the group of hoodlums. There was another explosion, and most of the men behind what had been their cover were blown to smithereens. The others ran, panic-stricken, totally beside themselves.

– TELL BROOKS TO STAY AWAY FROM US, Nick shouted. – Tell him this is his *final* warning.

The other men ran off as well. In their frozen faces of fear were mixed something else, something like awe.

Nick shouted, a study in rage, in wrath.

– I'M FAR STRONGER, FAR MORE POWERFUL THAN YOU, NOW, POWELL. I'M COMING FOR YOU, POWELL! COUNT YOUR DAYS UNTIL I COME FOR YOU, COME FOR YOU IN THE NIGHT.

Jonas heard his words. They echoed within him like knives.

It was quiet again. Aside from the sounds of burning fire, and still exploding vehicles the intersection was quiet and still as death.

One car, miraculously, was whole, its engine still running.

Carla limped away towards the car, towards Nick.

– Come, she told Jonas.

And he followed her through the smoke and the fire.

Nick pushed the gas pedal through the floor, and they were off. This time Jonas was unable to close the door, and it just fell off, and he sat there, completely exposed, as his friend kept driving, more recklessly, more insane then ever.

– I saw him, Nick mumbled. – Saw his green eyes. He was here, watching us, knowing that we, that I could not follow him could not chase him.

And the cold in Jonas turned another knot.

April watered the flowers. The maid was with her. They talked, but Jonas couldn't hear a word of it. April gasped and touched her belly, the smile spreading further on her face. The maid supported her towards the stairs. April gasped, and pointed at the couch. The maid looked horrified at her.

– She's coming, April gasped. – She's coming, a week early. Damn her! Where's Nick? WHERE ARE YOU, NICK? DAMN YOU!

I'M HERE. HOLD OUT. I'M COMING. I'M *coming*.

She raised her head, as if she heard him, as Jonas didn't hear him, as she fell on the couch, and strived to remove her underwear. The nanny rushed to the kitchen. Jonas pictured her there, boiling water, boiling towels, white, white towels.

Jonas re-experienced the carnage in his head. To an outsider, he supposed, it would be strange and frightening beyond words. They wouldn't even begin to know what had really happened. Nick had never really physically touched the cars. He had done everything with his mind, with his *mind,* and the witnesses would, in the days to come deny that certainty with all their timid minds.

They approached New York, its tall, tall buildings and heavy, poisonous air, racing past the slow, slow cars on their right. Brakes howled as drivers attempted to avoid the madman crossing their path. Something gave this car a… *push,* making it considerably faster than any other car around. Jonas froze constantly in the close proximity to the volcanic human being by his side. He felt Carla's breath in his neck. He saw her rigid features, without even looking at her.

– On the Titanic I saw death for the first time, Nick mumbled. – And I knew what I was. I should have known. I should have *known.*

– I should have as well. Tears fell from Carla's wet cheeks. – I've seen it many times before, too many times. I can't believe I forgot, *forgot*.

And Nick looked at her, and perhaps *he* saw *her* for the first time.

And he shook, suddenly and shocking, and he screamed, screamed in rage and despair. He lost control of the car, finally, utterly, and it slid to the right in a curve, slid for seconds, until it crashed into a tree. Nick pulled them out, pulled them to safety in the midst of gasoline vapors and electric sparks.

April SCREAMED, her face suddenly contorted in pain, in a horrible, twisted pain. Jonas had seen mothers give birth quite a few times, and it was nothing like this.

– She's killing me, she gasped. – Sucking all life from me. Female demons become their mothers. AHHH

– What's wrong? The maid shouted, rushing to her side. – Something is wrong, isn't it? I knew we should have called a doctor, I told the missus, told her.

She touched April's naked skin then, and then she, too, screamed, screamed in the same horrible pain ravaging April Warren.

The maid - Jonas realized he couldn't remember her name - started shaking violently. She attempted to remove her hand from April's skin, but it was like glued to it. No matter how much she pulled, it stayed put.

The woman died there, standing, in the grip of something that seemed like a giant invisible hand. She whimpered, stopped breathing, and fell to the floor, the body already frozen in Rigor Mortis, as if it had been dead for hours. Jonas saw it or imagined he saw it, experienced it, and he was unable to decide which.

And then he saw no more. He ran behind Nick and Carla, keeping up with them somehow, feeling utter disbelief because he could. Nick screamed and stopped, before falling to his knees, shaking in rage and despair, shaking so hard that it was hard to believe. And then - he stopped. He choked, and stopped, and then came the tears, huge, salty tears drowning his face and gathering in a pool beneath him.

They ran, but there was no energy, no spirit behind it anymore. Their faces were drawn, dry. They walked the last stretch to the mansion, in stiff, rigid movements, as if they were walking dead. Jonas had never quite gotten the hang of that expression, never truly realized what it meant, until now. A crowd of people had gathered outside the gate. A few of them turned towards the approaching trio.

– We were called, a man said. – We were called, but we couldn't get inside.

Jonas wondered a bit about that. If they really wanted to get inside, they easily could have gained access, through the windows. Not through the heavily fortified door perhaps, but definitely through the windows. It would have been an effort to remove the bars covering the glass, but they would have made it. He thought that perhaps there had been no time.

Nick walked to the door and before he reached it, it was as if an invisible force of enormous proportions pushed it in, blew it right off the hinges, and it landed silently in the dust, the thick dust inside.

The three walked wide-eyed into the mansion. It looked… old, suggesting that people hadn't lived there for ages. They walked, stumbled into the living room like old people, hardly even able to put one foot in front of another. And what they saw in there would haunt them for eternities.

The dry, wrinkled body of the maid crouched by the couch. It looked like she had been dead for days and even weeks. One could clearly see the skull beneath the rotted skin.

April Warren lay on the couch, dead and still. Her once sparkling green eyes, now turned pale and lifeless, stared at nothing, saw nothing, and her body had also clearly begun decomposing, though not to the degree of the other woman.

On the floor, on the soft carpet, rested the baby girl, vibrant and alive, covered in the placenta. She made small suckling sounds as she breathed, as she greeted them with a solemn, expressionless smile. Her eyes glowed to the point of them heating the air around her. The three halting above her felt them burn their skin. They wanted to grab her, to comfort her, but Carla, and also a bit later Jonas had already stopped in their forward motion well before Nick raised a hand in warning.

Pain was added to the cold, and mingled with it, and the end result stuck inside the shaking forms and never left them.

Intermission:
Mark

Chapter Seven

Chief Jeff McCabe locked the upper drawer on his desk. He didn't care about the rest of them. They contained nothing interesting. He rose and walked to the opposite wall, to the large calendar. It said August fifth. He smiled and tore the upper sheet off. There were very few sheets left, as if the year would end in a few days.

It had turned into a ritual to him, this, the removing of the sheets, very much like with most people, he surmised.

He looked at himself in the mirror, the suit, the tie, and the hat he put on the head, nodded and walked to the outer room, where his secretary, a female police officer sat.

– Only four days left, now, Kelly, he said enthusiastically, – before my greatest and last role is done, and I can go on that fishing trip I'm always talking about.

She giggled. He was weird today, but then again, he had always been a bit off, the way she had heard it.

But today… he was *weird.*

– Are they treating you all right, Kelly? He asked her, clearly wanting to know the answer.

– No, they're not, sir, she replied calmly.

– A shame. He shook his head. – But you should be proud anyway. Remember that not only are you one of the few and proud female officers, but you're one of the few officers making a fuss about things. They don't like that, of course.

– Yes, sir, she said.

– Things will change one day, you'll see, and with that I mean far beyond something as trivial as male police officers' harassment of female officers.

– Yes, sir.

She wanted to ask him if he was on something, but courage failed her.

– I'm leaving now, Kelly, he said. – Will you be so kind to notify people I don't want to be disturbed today or tonight, not under any circumstances.

– Yes, sir, she said hesitatingly. – Just one thing, sir… Lieutenant Clarke wanted to know if you wanted his report today. What do you want me to tell him?
– Tell him to have it ready by tomorrow morning, officer, McCabe replied, a bit less cordial. – And tell him to actually put something in it this time.
He waved and took off, certainly not your usual image of a way past retirement age seventy-five-year-old police Chief. He knew that everybody wondered what he knew, what information he had on key people in the administration, to be able to stay on as long as he had.
And he knew there was a persistent rumor that he had allowed them to retire him. He smiled.
McCabe walked out in the bright light of the afternoon sun. It cast long shadows across town. The parking lot was in darkness. He shook lightly, unable to stop it.
It was completely quiet around him. Far away he could hear the sound of engines, humans.
The car was a Lincoln Continental, the largest model. He opened the door and sat down in the big, pleasant seat. He knew something was wrong the moment his ass hit that pleasant seat, knew he had made a mistake. There was somebody behind him. The instinct gained after a long life living dangerously, told him that. He received the confirmation in the form of cold metal pressed at his neck.
– You should have used that private chauffeur they wanted to hit you with, Jeffrey, a cheerful voice sounded in his ear. – Then you might have avoided this.
– Stewart? He gasped.
He looked at himself in the mirror, at the strangely calm and strange expression.
– You didn't really expect me? McCabe glimpsed exposed fangs in the mirror, and the strange elation and fear didn't leave him. – I know that, and that my presence here may come as a shock to you. I guess you were informed about my little… flight fairly soon after it had happened. That ugly Chinese guy seems like a very thorough scout. Thousand eyes and ears, isn't that how the saying goes?
– Listen, I…
– We're gonna have a nice drive. I want to take another look at those nice, sharp cliffs. I want you to take a look at them as well.
McCabe opened his mouth to speak, but closed it when the gun barrel pushed some more at the skin of his neck.

– Okay, he shrugged. – You got the aces, Frenchman, at least three of them.

Stewart reacted; something about the way the other man said the word «Frenchman». He, too, had a strange expression in his face, as if something wasn't quite right, and it wasn't, of course.

McCabe started the engine, and drove from the parking lot, left the town behind. He drove slowly, but not too slowly. The cold metal rested constantly at the skin of his neck. Streets gave way to mountains. He stopped the car. They were already here. The large car looked tiny compared to the backdrop of the abyss below. Stewart grabbed McCabe and pulled him out of the car, pushed him towards the edge.

Down there… McCabe saw the blood, saw it flow like a river. Red rocks glowed like rubies in the afternoon sun.

– Just a moment. I just want to check something.

He led his hand along the other's neck. It took some doing, but eventually he found what he was looking for, a sharp edge. McCabe wore a mask. He grabbed it and pulled it off.

– Okay, you've got four aces… The strange humor persisted in McCabe's behavior.

Stewart stood there with Jeff McCabe in his hand. The man in front of Stewart didn't look like McCabe at all. If one looked carefully he was just as old, but in many ways it didn't seem that way. The face had less wrinkles, the eyes were sharper, and the features considerably more so.

– You're Jonas Bergli, Stewart said, taken aback, – the theater instructor, the children's instructor.

– Yes, I am. I was.

Bergli was calm, almost serene where he faced Stewart.

– Do I… do I *know* you?

– We met briefly thirty years ago… in London.

Bergli said. Stewart took one step back. Shock was stamped on his face.

– I'm not surprised.

Stewart said, briefly closing his eyes.

He opened them again. They burned, and they burned Bergli, froze him in his tracks. Bergli remained strangely calm, and so did Stewart.

– But you are McCabe. You are the same man who «hired» me, and lorded over me all these years.

– Yes, I am the one who brought you to Denver, Bergli replied. – I gave you the job in the police. I gave you a new life, for as long as it lasted, a temporary calm existence in the eye of the storm.

Stewart laughed out aloud, one sharp, short outburst.

– Sure, you're a true humanitarian. I'm sure Ezra Coogan agrees with that as well.

– I had nothing to do with that. Chin killed Coogan. The reason, as I understand it, as you know, is that he had realized that the Cousins couldn't be the brothers' parents.

– But that… doesn't make sense. Why kill someone to suppress information that the Cousins voluntarily revealed just three years later, anyway?

– It does look rather insane, doesn't it? Bergli said quietly.

There was a brief hesitation, before he continued.

– You do want to ask me more questions, I know that, but you don't really need to, do you…

Stewart threw the mask on the ground, and started pacing back and forth. He lifted the gun, pointing it at Bergli, lowered it once again, several times.

– Let's see… you have worn this thing… He pushed the mask with his foot. – Worn it every day for… how long is it, almost twenty years? Every morning you've painstakingly put it on, like your glasses or a set of clothes, but far more thorough. That suggests quite a bit of dedication, doesn't it? Something far beyond an ordinary call of duty, I'd say. It wasn't like you just put on the mask or a mask. You put on an entire new personality. You're good, Jonas, you're very good. I'll give you that.

The pronunciation, when Stewart said the name, was exactly right.

– Thank you, Bergli said hoarsely.

Stewart turned and walked to the car.

– Just one more thing, Bergli said, just as quietly.

Stewart turned again and stopped.

– When you've freed Jean, will you then have a burning desire to keep up your search, your hunt? If not, I'll give you one last advice: Pull out. Withdraw from the game. The moment you and your wife are safe… *let go*. Fetch your son in New York. Live out your life in peace.

Voice was neither hard nor threatening, only admonishing, like a father would be to a son. Once again it was quiet. They hardly heard the wind.

– A good bit of advice, I gather, Stewart nodded, nodded again. – But I won't heed it. I'm gonna find the man behind all this, and I'm gonna destroy him, destroy him and all his works.

He closed his eyes again, and this time he kept them closed for a long time. Finally he turned his back on the other man and walked the final stretch to the car.

– Do you know what, Jonas? He said with a scornful laughter. – Before we met today I had decided to kill you, but I won't. Do you know why? You don't matter anymore. Chin saw fit to tell you I was dead, but not that I had risen from the «grave». When you retire on Friday, you'll have no more value to your friends. That gives you something to think about, right?

He put away the gun and opened the door to the car. Before he got in and closed the door he said:

– Have a nice walk home, Jonas. You deserve that, considering how much you've lost it the last few years.

He started the car and drove away in a cloud of dust. Jonas Bergli remained. He stood there, stood there for a long time, crouched, with a bowed head, staring at the ground, and no matter how hard he tried, he couldn't hear the wind.

++++++++++++++++

It had turned dark when Mark Stewart and Francis Caine once again approached the Cousin residence. They walked silently through the forest, ready to take cover at the slightest suspicious sound. They hadn't spoken for half an hour. Stewart had willingly related the conversation with «McCabe», but after that he hadn't been very forthcoming.

They had glimpsed Chin, no doubt an encounter not a coincidence, when they had tailed McCabe to the airport. He had left town. Chin had left on the same plane. Caine knew this, because he had actually bluffed his way onto the plane and seen them there. They hadn't been sitting close, but they had been aware of each other. Of course they had. A man with Caine's experience would easily have seen that, even if he hadn't known it.

Everybody was leaving town, everybody somewhat connected to the «case». Thomas Forester had left. Stuart «Hammer» Tremblay as well. Denver had been a focal point for… something for years, and now it wasn't anymore.

– And you want to go in alone? The Gambler tried one more time.

– I said I would, didn't I? Wait here, and be on your guard.

– Are you kidding me?

The Gambler was so surprised that he almost forgot to whisper. Stewart's «admonishing» was virtually equal to an insult in their circles. Caine wanted to say more, but he didn't get the chance. The younger man was already halfway on his way to the house.

Stewart took the stairs in two and two steps, somewhat calm and collected. He shook his ahead in amazement while his ever-inquisitive mind gathered data of his surroundings. The wood of the old house was clearly worn and there were places on the wall without paint. The kitchen window was broken, actually broken. Nobody had kept the place in shape the last three years.

The doors were open. *For me,* he thought. The hall was dark. All lamps but one had broken bulbs. Two suitcases stood fully packed by the kitchen door. He had an idiotic notion of coming home. For some reason he thought about his mother. She had been on his mind since childhood, but even more so the last few years. He shook his head, slightly confused, wondering what made him think about this now, and then he realized how stupid it was to wonder. He didn't wonder. Everything was clear in his mind.

A single lamp burned in the living room. As he left the hall he heard the first chords from Tubular Bells by Mike Oldfield. It floated towards him, assaulted him, as if the music flowed from the very walls around him. There was something fateful about the light piano-like chords, as if the music hid a secret. But it didn't, really, he knew that. It merely provoked notions within himself, which, no doubt, was the purpose of playing it. Stewart felt the trickle down his spine, caused by both fear and expectation. The living room was empty. He stopped at its center, and waited, patiently, with an impatience that had been growing for decades. Time passed. He didn't know how much exactly, but with the first heavy chord he heard steps behind him. He turned. Cindy stood behind him. Rodney to his side. They pointed guns at him.

– You're making this overly dramatic, in my opinion, Stewart said contemptuously. – This is just another stage, another performance, so please spare me.

They put the guns away.

– Accept our apologies, Cousin said, so dryly that he clearly didn't mean it. – As you know one can never be too careful in our profession.

– And you two are undoubtedly outstanding members of «our profession», Stewart said ironically. – You certainly proved that recently…

– They weren't truly worthy of our attention, Cousin shrugged arrogantly.

– You know me, Stewart said. – You know who I am?

– Of course, we know you, Mickey, Cindy said softly. – We know you all.

He felt reality slip around him. The unknown woman had used the name his mother had used, used affectionately, her own, special name for him, the one that wasn't listed anywhere, the one he had last heard his mother speak, during the last few seconds of her life.

– You were only three years old, Mickey, Cousin said. – They looked for you, but couldn't find you, not for years.

– You have a very poetic language, Rodney. Is it learned or are you born with it?

Cousin grinned.

– Oh, that? I'm married to an actress, you know.

– Your English is very distinctive, Rodney. Stewart practically ignored him, even as he was speaking to him. – It took me a while before it dawned on me, but it's an Eastern European accent…

Cousin walked to the record player. He turned it off with such a force that the needle jumped up and down on the record several times before it settled in resting position. The silence abruptly dominated the house. They heard the wind that made the walls quake. Cousin stared at Stewart with a haunted look in his face. He seemed to change completely from one second to the next.

– You were forced to flee the Soviet Union. Stalin and his cohorts didn't exactly appreciate your performances. In fact, you quickly became one of the most unpopular men in the country. So you fled… and they caught up with you. And one man saved you. Not only from torture and a certain death, but more importantly, much more, he saved your self-respect, your pride. He saved the most important thing in a human being. It is self-evident that you were eternally grateful towards this man. In fact, it's safe to say he saved you from despair, from the disintegration of the spirit, the soul and you were and still are willing to do anything for him. *Anything.* He has that affect on people, doesn't he, doesn't he, Cindy?

Stewart had drawn his gun before the hateful Cousin had a chance to react.

– Don't try anything, Rodney. If you do I'll shoot you like the dog you are. For your own sake or that of your Master, you should never challenge me on this.

Cindy stood in the shadows, shaking. The otherwise so proud woman crouched there, shrunken, wasting away by the second.

– What do you want, Markham? She asked weakly. – Why are you speaking to us like this? You…

– I feel sorry for you, Cindy, Stewart interrupted her. – Love can be hard, right? You can be so taken by another person that yourself and your own welfare suddenly doesn't mean a thing anymore. Until you no longer care what happens to your own brother or daughter.

She broke into sobs. Cousin turned red with rage.

– Get out! He screamed at Stewart, wild, but yet pathetic.
The big man ignored him. At the table behind him he spotted an unopened letter.
– Another letter, huh? Those surely get around. Does the person it's addressed to actually get to read it this time? I would very much like to read it, I can tell you that… if I didn't already pretty much know what it says.
The married couple didn't reply. They just stared at him.
– I would follow Peter Clarke around the next few days, if I were you, Markham.
– Thank you, Arturov, Stewart said icily. – You're a thespian for the ages.
He backed off, wanting to turn away from them, unable to do so.
– I'm leaving now. He took a break so they shouldn't note how dry his throat was. – Tell your Master I don't enjoy being used, not even by him, especially not by him, and that I will enjoy it even less in the future. If he keeps up his game he will face the consequences, and he will anyway. Tell him!
He felt more confident when he saw the other man's pale face and put his gun away. He turned his back to the two, and didn't look back.
Once out on the stairs he started gulping air. He kept walking as he fought to regain control over himself before reaching the place where Francis waited for him.
He realized, at this moment, if not before, that he had always had trouble breathing.
+++++++
They followed Peter Clarke as he left Denver. They saw him put a small suitcase in the trunk of his car, sit down behind the wheel and drive off. Stewart sat down behind the wheel, started the car, and drove off, as he, too, was leaving Denver forever.
Hours later. It was raining. Gigantic drops hammering against the windshield. The Gambler had taken over the wheel. Francis Caine felt trapped, the steering wheel slippery as hell in his hands.
They drove up, up, ever higher into the Rocky Mountains. They weren't really that afraid of losing Peter Clarke in the other car. They knew where he was headed.
– So, what happened in there? Caine had asked Stewart.
– Pretty much what I expected, Stewart had replied. – They didn't really say much, and they didn't need to. And all the time I got the feeling it was just another stage, another play set in motion for unfathomable purposes.

And Stewart didn't really volunteer much in the department of information himself. Caine made no attempt to hide his displeasure. He wanted his friend to see it, and felt even more trapped, when Stewart merely shrugged it off.

– Do you remember our old saying, he carefully asked the man by his side. – What I taught you?

– Sure, Stewart grinned, but the grin was contrived, fake. – «Never enter a train at high speed. If you're on a train traveling at top speed, get off as soon as possible, before it derails, even if the result is a few bruises and wounds».

The wipers went back and forth, completely useless. Water covered the windshield, making the world look like a single mist, impossible to see through.

– It's just that sometimes there are steep walls on both sides, Stewart noted, almost philosophically. – You can't get off, not unless you want to take the fall into the deep, deep abyss far below.

Clarke drove fast, through the wall of rain, and so did they. So fast, really, that they suspected he had spotted them or at least suspected something. But no, he was just in a hurry. Many were speeding up the mountains anyway. If they hadn't, that would have raised suspicion.

The three of them drove into Leadville early in the afternoon, this notable August day 1974. It was in the height of summer. It didn't rain anymore. Suddenly there was blue sky everywhere. Where the clouds had gone they couldn't say. And it was hot. They drove with all the windows open, but it did them little good. The humidity and the heat filled the air, just as much as the rain had done. Filled their bodies, their mind.

Clarke's first stop was at the sheriff's office. He stopped right outside, where it was illegal to park. Stewart stopped far down the same street. Caine used binoculars. Stewart did not. He saw Clarke clearly, saw him through a crystal-clear red haze.

I can only dream in red.

None of them said a word. Never during the long wait and not when Clarke finally left the sheriff's office, not when Caine started the engine and followed him.

Clarke crisscrossed the town for quite a while, seemingly without a goal, stopping by the sights, the Tabor opera house and stuff.

– He's playing the tourist, Caine stated.

He wanted to say *something*.

Anything really, to break the silence. He failed. It stayed silent.

Clarke stopped in front of the Silver Dollar as well and he walked inside, like he had done with a lot of the other sights. But this time he stayed longer. Not more than five minutes but much longer than in the other places. He was in a hurry. So much that he didn't take the time to look for traffic when backing out in the road. Brakes screamed when a car stopped only hairbreadths' away from his bumper. The driver jumped out, red-faced in his anger. Clarke ignored him, and drove on. The enraged driver was left in the cloud of smoke, choking and bewildered.

– Let him go, Stewart said. – We'll find him easily.

Poor ordinary people, he thought. So bewildered, so lost. He watched the dust cloud slowly dispersing.

Drive. Travel to the end of the world. I'll find you.

And kill you.

There were no windows open in the Silver Dollar. Caine noticed the dank mood instantly. There weren't many guests at the moment, even if this was said to be a classy haunt. He sat down at the bar, looking briefly at his own reflection in the mirror, the blond hair. It felt weird, but he told himself that others would probably not think so. He and Stewart had decided to «switch» hair color, a simple disguise and precaution he had learned the value of early in life.

– A beer, please.

The barkeeper gave him one. Caine drank. A surprised look showed on his face, one he was unable to hide.

– You know, he said. – I have to tell you, this beer tastes great. And I'm something of an aficionado concerning beer. I have been most of my adult life. My compliments.

It was true. And his duplicity felt somewhat good because it was the truth. He lied by telling the truth, like he had done most of his adult life.

The barkeeper, evidently the owner himself, melted like snow in May.

Caine pulled forth his false press card, and put it on the bar.

– I'm a freelance journalist, he said, very matter of fact. – Currently working on an exposé about the missing kids for the Washington Post.

Now, the man did hesitate. Caine couldn't tell why.

– They were here, as you probably know. We didn't serve them, since they were underage. I did offer them a guide, though, which they declined.

The man spoke and just kept speaking. It seemed like he had a lot he wanted to get off his chest. Caine had learned early in life to be a good listener and observer. So, he just sat there, listening and observing. He did ask a few questions now and then, but merely because it was expected of him, not because it was necessary.

– Something was… wrong, the barkeeper said frowning.
– Wrong? Caine repeated.
– Yes, the barkeeper who was also the owner insisted. – I've been in this job since I was a teenager, and you learn to be a good listener and observer while tending a bar. People come and go all the time, the strangest people, droves of ordinary people, and you learn to read them, to read situations.
A colleague, Caine thought uplifted. How encouraging.
– In hindsight, I would say I sensed it, even before the youths arrived that day. There were other guests that were also wrong, if you know what I mean.
Caine nodded. He did know what the barkeeper meant.
– They looked at the door when the kids entered. No one does that, unless they expect someone. Everyone looked at the kids when they were at the bar, but everybody else was leering at them. The guys in the corner just… looked, without looking, if you know what I mean. I tell ya, something bad has happened to those kids, something truly bad.
Caine drank two glasses of beer, before leaving the Silver Dollar Saloon. He made a point of relating every word of the conversation to Stewart in the car afterwards, far beyond the moment his great listening and observation skills discovered the frown in the other's face.
– The trail to the cabin begins right outside town. The nice barkeeper told me there's a parking lot there.
The parking lot was indeed easy to find, Clarke's car as well.
– We weren't wrong, Stewart said. – We will find him in the cabin.
He turned towards Caine with a feverish look in his eyes.
– I'm looking very much forward to our upcoming conversation.
++
They almost walked right into the cabin before they hastily took cover. They crouched behind the smallest cover with their weapons drawn, jittery and uncharacteristically nervous.
– A fourteen-minute walk, Caine said, after looking at his watch. – Fifteen, tops.
Stewart stayed silent. He studied the cabin.
– If any of the kids succeeded in screaming someone must have heard them, Caine insisted. – Something is indeed wrong, even beyond the obvious.
They closed in on the cabin the way a lifetime of experience had taught them. Even though, except for recently the last decade or less had been somewhat peaceful, they relearned quickly what they had never forgotten.

They felt their feet touch the ground, air move in and out of their lungs. Their bodies hit the wall of the cabin. They stood there, listening to the sounds inside.

And there were none. They kept moving and kept watching for movement in the terrain, signs of a trap.

But there were none.

Stewart marched to the door, grabbed the yellow ribbon marked CRIME SCENE DO NOT ENTER, and broke the seal. Then he kicked, he actually kicked in the door. Caine gaped. He always laughed when he saw that in movies, knew how hard it was, what kind of coordination and strength it took, and Stewart did it as casually as if he should have merely opened it.

They stepped inside, still wary, still with the same extreme, aggressive caution, looking for their old friend Peter Clarke.

But they didn't find him, not in the cabin or its immediate area. They searched for trapdoors, secret passageways and everything, but they didn't find him anywhere. They didn't find anyone.

– I don't understand it, Caine finally said exasperated. – Except for the signs of the police search there is no proof there have ever been people here for ages.

They actually saw cobwebs in the corners and dust piled up several places on the floor.

– And the truly interesting part is that the police should have seen that, as well, Stewart mused. – Unless they believe in magic, they should have cried havoc instantly, but they didn't.

– I've heard about such cases since I was a boy. Caine shook his head. – Places Time forgot, pulled into the shadow world by dream-weavers, sorcerers with powers over Time and Space. My grandfather believed the stories, I know that.

He looked at Stewart.

– I don't, in case you're wondering.

– Let's look for more mundane explanations first, Stewart said lightly.

He looked so calm, almost serene.

It was like a ghost house in here. Furniture, equipment, everything was in place. One could almost see the youths sitting in these chairs, walking these floors.

But there were no teenagers present, anywhere, in or around the cabin.

Darkness descended around them. There was no electricity. They found a few candles and lit them. There was no canned food, no food at all, and they were suddenly happy they had brought their own, prepared themselves for a longer stay in the wilderness. They sensed the confirmation of their instincts and their rise, within, to what they had been.

– Good. Caine nodded, as he chewed on canned fruit.

– Mmm. Stewart hit the edge of the table with his spoon, regularly and monotonously.

He looked at Caine again with his pointed stare.

– I can sense it, you know, the old knife and blood rise from my depths. It's like it has never been gone, even though for a while I imagined it was never there.

– I don't understand it. Caine did the Latin gestures with his hands.

Stewart only looked at him.

– You saw the clippings, Mark. The journalists, both from Denver and Colorado state, and also national and international media got wind of it all right after the police did. When Clarke and the special units headed for Leadville an entire battalion of journalists followed in their tracks.

McCabe, Stewart thought.

– The journalists were posted outside all the time during the search. They would certainly have noted if the police had marched out with rucksacks, a score of light bulbs and tons of mattresses and sheets. They found one item: Tilla Stevens' rucksack.

Tilla, yes. Tilla.

– Everybody seems to have missed the most obvious explanation… Stewart said slowly, – that the children were never here in the first place.

Caine could almost see how Stewart's mind worked, and he felt both awe and fear.

– Frank Forester told the people at the Silver Dollar he didn't need a guide, and in spite of his bravado, he was convincing, or the guys would have insisted on sending a guide with them anyway…

They rushed to the big window, and opened it. They could hear the sounds of Leadville.

– They weren't abducted on their way to the cabin…

They grabbed their flashlights and hurried outside, hurried back to the town. Except for a few seconds here and there, they could actually see Leadville on most of the walk and didn't even have to use the flashlights. They stood at the crossroads just outside the heaviest population center, studying the place. Stewart looked and looked, and Caine felt more of that awe and fear. It was something almost… supernatural about the way Stewart's cognitive and inquisitive mind worked.

Finally he walked to the pole, where there were signs, pointing in all directions. The pole was skewed. Stewart dug a bit in the soil at its base with his hands. The ground around the pole was soft, the pole was loose.

– Somebody turned it? Caine said hoarsely, said it because he knew Stewart never would. – To lead them astray?

– To lead them somewhere, where they could be easily and quietly abducted, Stewart said. – But as we have seen, it's sloppy work, really. They haven't reckoned with anybody putting the obvious clues together. Or they just didn't bother.

– And their cocky behavior is quite understandable. Caine spoke, clearly irritable, frustrated. – We still have no idea what direction they went, where they were herded. What now?

– We sleep, Stewart grinned.

Caine stared astounded at him.

++++++++++++++++++++++

Caine didn't get much sleep that night. They used the kitchen floor in the cabin. Had found some blankets to rest on and as cover, but he still found the bed hard and uncomfortable. In his younger days it wouldn't have mattered, but now it hurt in his tired and stiff limbs.

He heard Stewart sleep, without snoring. Eight years ago, before the fateful trip to San Diego, he had snored. So loud that Jean had reddened in embarrassment. The memory made The Gambler smile, and he closed his eyes once again, in another attempt to fall asleep.

An hour later he gave up. He rose on unsteady legs and walked into the living room.

He thought about David Gidman, saw him before his eyes… before and after, and he couldn't really fault Stewart for being obsessed by him. Caine himself felt a smoldering fear, on so many levels. He saw Gidman dead, dead on the floor, dead on the slab, and he saw the vibrant man he was now.

Caine watched the moon. It was up there, blood red just under the clouds. It really seemed to be under the clouds, hovering just above him, so close he could almost reach out and touch it, and feel its power.

He had been caught by terrifying, unknown powers, forces, forever beyond his control… from the moment he crossed paths with David Gidman, with both Gidman… and Mark Stewart.

Mark Stewart, born in Paris 1937. Father: François Stewart. Mother: Joan Fontaine. Orphaned when he was three. «Adopted» by passing Gypsies. Taken in by the Gidman family. Spent most of his childhood in Marseille, in its «dark alleys and backstreets», as Stewart himself had related to Caine once. Called himself Fontaine when returning to Paris in the late fifties, a powder keg of nascent revolutionary movements and oppression. Charles DeGaulle and his henchmen ruled France with an iron fist.

But there were more, so much more, things Caine didn't know, that he desperately wanted and not wanted to know.

He stood by the window, looking at the moon for a long time, until he felt his eyelids close and he gathered he would fall asleep the moment he lay down. Then he heard sounds, then he heard voices. He drew his gun. Not voices, only one voice. Stewart's. He returned to the kitchen. Stewart wasn't awake, but speaking in his sleep.

– No… no… don't *do* it!

Caine felt both like an idiot and absolutely astonished simultaneously. Stewart had a nightmare. He writhed back and forth on the floor, sweating, moaning. Something Caine would have thought was an impossibility.

Very few words were intelligible. Stewart's voice sounded much higher pitched than it usually did. Caine could move, couldn't decide what to do. Suddenly Stewart sat up. He waved wildly with is arms and his eyes were, shockingly enough, open.

– DON'T LET HIM DO IT MOMMY MOMMY HIT HIM HIT HIM HIM HIM

The twisted face made Caine back off. And the voice. The voice… He shuddered.

The voice belonged to a small child.

++++++++++++++++++++++++++++

They walked the road taken, the path the kids had walked, the way they had to have taken. But within that fact was a wide array of possibilities. They chased from cabin to cabin, up and down steep, muddy hills, every second on guard, every moment ready to react to hostilities. It took its toll on them, inevitably.

They sat down, resting, somewhat close to a top, somewhat hiding behind a cluster of bushes, with a great view of the shadowy valley below. Sweat had soaked Caine's clothes, and he was still breathing hard, several minutes after the stop. Stewart looked just as fresh.

– Look at it. Even in the wilderness, this far from heavy population centers, civilization has left its mark.

He indicated the valley with his hand, the many, many cabins there.

– The next will probably be skyscrapers…

– Humanity has truly come a long way, Caine said cautiously, studying the other man.

Stewart shook his head, shook it hard.

– Humanity is Earth's bastard child, shunned by stream and moor. And we've made it so ourselves. We've fucked up to such a degree that we don't even know ourselves anymore.

Even Stewart's voice had changed compared to how Caine remembered it.

– I can feel it, you know, feel both stream and moor and everything. It's speaking, singing to me.

Caine didn't comment on that. He had nothing to say.

He recalled the night before, and cautiously watched the stranger before him.

– Ready to move on, old man?

Caine stared at him, stared at the condescending stranger.

– It will be a long walk. Do you think you can take it?

Caine's eyes turned dark in anger.

– Let's get this straight, Mark. I don't need either positive or negative encouragement. Not of any kind.

The sun slid behind a cloud just then. Stewart straightened. His face was in shadow. What shadow? It would have to be something in Stewart's face making it appear that way. The dark hair made him look different. Of course it did.

– I'll remember that, Stewart said. – But you should as well. Always.

The stranger moved on, and Francis Caine followed in his tracks.

They walked the last few hills out of the valley, and headed even higher up. They walked in the shade, spared the worst heat from the burning sun, but sweat still poured from Caine's skin. Step by step he fell behind. Stewart seemed to be gaining energy the longer he walked, not losing it. Caine feared his friend was losing it, and tired as he was, he could think of few other things.

The fog descended with the onset of twilight, descending on Caine's mind. In his opinion they hadn't seen any signs of human presence for hours. They walked on a trail, but it might just as well be a natural track resembling something human-made. He felt cut off, estranged from the life he had known. He had two kids in Nevada and wondered why he wasn't with them.

– We're nearly there, Stewart said.

But did he really speak or was it just Caine's imagination?

– How do you know?

– I can smell it.

He sniffed in the air, and Caine, reflexively, did the same, and then he did smell something, smelled food.

At least he thought he did.

Everything was the same up here, in the mist. What was seen was not seen. What was heard was not heard. What was smelled was not smelled. Nature assaulted him on all fronts, but the man ahead of him seemed to embrace it, becoming one with it, with the sound of birds in the air, with the sighs of mist, with the growls in the wilderness.

Stewart stopped and turned.

– Let me guess… You're *worried,* aren't you?

Caine gaped, before pulling himself together, before catching his breath.

– Well, now when you mention it…

– It's just a side of me you haven't seen before, that's all.

Caine laughed, a laughter trite and tired.

– You've acted weird before, but you've never been poetic before.

– I've always been weird…

Stewart turned and kept walking, walking down a short slope. Caine hurried after him, and almost collided with Stewart's back, as the large man stopped again.

There, right above Stewart's head, between two giant rocks, was the cabin. They both saw it, saw it instantly, what was wrong, what was right about it.

– Those bastards, Caine said. – They built a copy.

– Yeah, Stewart nodded. – An exact copy, I gather, a place to fatten the game, before the hunt began.

– No one would look here, Caine gasped. – No one would look here in a million years.

– There's blood on the ground, Stewart said. – They haven't even bothered to remove it.

There was smoke from the chimney. They saw two men relax on the porch. The two men were armed. Stewart and Caine saw that easily, with their experience. But aside from that, there was nothing even remotely… off with this picture. Not without information, without crucial knowledge. Caine still felt like all this was a dream, that this wasn't even real. The pale, faded blood on the ground was just ketchup or red ochre and nothing but.

Dreams were brittle, like China, he knew that. He had always known that.

Peter Clarke walked out on the porch evidently relaxed and confident. They knew this man. He was still the same man they had always known. He had changed. Somewhere along the line, he had changed. Or he had made one, irrevocable decision. It was hard to tell. It always was.

The third guard joined Clarke and the other two men there on the porch, joined them from inside, whispered something in Clarke's ear. These were professionals. They didn't take any chances. Even here, in the middle of nowhere, they whispered important messages.

Clarke didn't. They heard him, clear as day.

– Time to dig that grave, he laughed, almost gagging and almost bending over.

Caine and Stewart looked at each other.

– I don't think he's burying his dog, do you?

Caine said quite unnecessary.

He spoke so low that Stewart heard it like a roar in his ears.

They advanced forward in a wide circle. As they advanced they couldn't avoid hearing the sound of their feet on the ground. It sounded loud and alarming in the silence of the mountains. They knew, from experience, from instinct that nobody further away than a few steps would be able to hear it, but in spite of that experience, that honed instinct, a part of them worried.

Behind another rock. Breathing controlled, not labored. They knew perfectly well they might have been discovered from the cabin already, and that there was a high probability they wouldn't notice until it was… late, very late, but they were prepared for that, for that, too.

The cabin wall. They hit it, without hitting it, crawling under a window, on their way to the back door. For all they knew ten guys waited for them inside, hid, waiting for them, waiting patiently. Caine almost giggled, clutching his gun. For some reason the image in his mind was hysterically funny.

– You've got something to look forward to, boys, they heard Clarke say.
– I've seen the pictures of all the cute and eager girls in chains. I myself look very much forward to playing with that ice princess Linda Cousin.

He sounded like a bragging young boy.

– Wasn't it she who spat in your face, boss? One of the men said, with a bit of challenge present in his voice, but also clearly cautious, afraid of the repercussions if he showed himself too bold.

– It was indeed. But a patient man is a patient man…

And the side of the man Caine had hardly even glimpsed came to light. The Gambler concentrated, concentrated on not being rocked by the chill in his own heart, focusing on the task ahead.

There was a rattling of chains. A slap on a cheek, a moan, coming from the bathroom inside, easily heard through the open window.

– At this moment Ralph is digging your grave quite a distance away from here, Clarke said. – Two agents have been spotted in the area, but they won't find you. They won't find anything but a burned-out cabin. Nobody will ever find out what happened here. Not what happened then, not now. You should have left accounts somewhere, you know.

Stewart and Caine kicked off their shoes and moved inside. Caine almost stepped on a piece of wood, but caught himself in time. He was rusty, so damn rusty. Clarke laughed, with a voice full of scorn at the man, the prisoner inside, as he left him, as he and his two men were on their way out in the hall. Caine and Stewart stepped forward with raised guns. They shot Clarke's companions in their heads. Brain mass decorated the steamy air in the bathroom, lit by the light from outside.

– Freeze, Peter, Stewart snarled at the man in front of them.

They saw it, saw how Peter Clarke froze, how he recognized them, how he crouched there, froze there, as he prepared to explode. Stewart stepped close to him, swift as lightning, and just as he was about to draw his weapon, Stewart struck him in his left temple. He fell on his knees. Stewart bent down and removed his gun in another swift move, so decisive, so rational, so devastating an act.

– How does it feel, Peter, to be the inferior, the underdog?

– A ghost in disguise. Clarke grinned, as he shook his head in amazement and shock, as he tried to look up, as he tried to look at his two old companions through swimming eyes. – I'll be damned. How did you do it, Mark?

– I'm a god of vengeance coming to claim your soul, you shithead. I can't die.

– You're spouting the same routine as One Eye, huh? Can't say I'm surprised. And you two, huh, Frank? Just like the old days, I guess.

Caine stood half in, half out of the room, looking in both directions, and also at the small window, for approaching hostility. So far there were no signs of it. He was sweating.

Stewart bent down shaking the half conscious, half beaten to death bound man.

– Floyd McKenzie, FBI, the man mumbled. – You'll find the ID in my left pocket.

– We know who you are, Stewart said.

– They took my daughter, McKenzie said.

Stewart turned to Clarke again.

– You've always been fond of hearing your own voice, Peter. Time to take advantage of that, if you want my opinion…

He pushed the barrel at the kneeling man's temple.

– You're gonna sing, Peter. You're gonna tell us everything you know. Every name, every hiding place. Everything you know about those damn rats.

Stewart lock-picked McKenzie's chains, and had him free in no time. It was amazing. Caine had some skills in this matter himself, but he had never seen anyone even remotely close to Stewart in skill.

McKenzie fought himself up. It was unbelievable. He looked more like a hamburger than a human being, but he stood on his feet, and when he took two steps forward and kicked Clarke in the ribs, he wasn't even close to loosing his balance. Clarke didn't cry out, but there was blood coming from his mouth. He had bit his tongue.

– Sorry, McKenzie said. – I just a needed to return a small bit of your kindness and hospitality.

– Don't worry. Stewart grinned, grinned horribly. – He will survive it. He will survive a lot worse. *On your feet.*

His voice, when he pulled Clarke up, when he hauled him up by the power of his roar, was chilling, even more chilling. The others saw it, and Clarke did as well, how his fingers trembled on the trigger. Not because of any anxiety on Stewart's part, but pure rage. Clarke was very careful not to make any sudden moves when they pushed him out in the hall, when they surrounded him on all sides.

Suddenly there he was, the third guard, firing from one of the other rooms. A bullet passed right between Stewart and Clarke's heads. Caine and Stewart reacted like one man, and fired at the target. One bullet hit Stewart in the arm, but he kept firing. The enemy's third shot went straight up, making a hole in the ceiling, as he was being filled with bullets. The hits pushed him backwards. The body hit the floor and lay still on the back, while the blood poured from it, and made a pool on the polished floor.

Stewart held onto the gun, held it a bit higher, to keep the blood flowing from his arm from wetting his hand.

– Are you okay? The Gambler inquired.

– It's just a flesh wound. Stewart dismissed it as he would dismiss a wasp bite. – A bit of cleaning and such, and it will be all right.

He did grit his teeth a bit. That fact pleased Caine, as it did make his old friend more human.

They walked into the living room, the huge, bright living room. And they once more got the uncanny feeling of having been here before.

– I'll be damned, Caine exclaimed. – This is indeed a complete replica

of the other cabin.
– Perhaps not down to the last nail, Stewart nodded. – But close, very close. Do you have any idea what kind of «dedication» those assholes needed in order to do that?
The living room embraced them, embraced their hearts and squeezed it. It was the same nice wallpaper, the same furniture, even though some of it was broken beyond recognition. Everything was the same.
– They were here, Stewart said. – They're still here.
He blinked, and as he blinked Caine imagined he could see the room through Stewart's eyes, hear the roar of chaos and horror through his ears. There was still blood on the carpet, still broken furniture. There were moans and desperate, unheeded pleas for mercy. Caine wanted to close his eyes, to block his hearing, but there was no way to do that, to block this sight, this hearing.
Stewart walked a bit. To the others it was like he was sniffing, sniffing like a dog. He walked to a corner, bent down, and picked something up. A knife, a blade, a black blade, smeared in dried blood.
– This is Linda's, he said, putting it away. – Her parents gave it to her as a coming of age present.
Caine looked at him, just looked at him.
Stewart pushed Clarke down on the couch.
– They were here, McKenzie confirmed, picking up one of the few remaining bloodied ropes from the floor.
Stewart undressed his upper body. He did so slowly and methodically, and didn't cry out a single time. Not during the undressing and not when Caine cleaned and bandaged the wound. He kept the gun in his hand the entire time, pointing it steadily at Clarke.
He dressed again, alternately holding the gun in his right and left hand. It *never* did anything but point at Clarke.
– Here, he said to McKenzie, handing him something from his pouch. – Rub this into your skin, and you won't feel absolutely horrible later today and when you wake up tomorrow.
McKenzie accepted the little box hesitantly. He opened it.
– It's herbs and stuff. Stewart shrugged.
McKenzie took some on his fingers and started to apply it on his skin, shaking his head.
And eventually, finally, all three of them turned to Clarke on the couch.
– Go to hell! Clarke snarled.
– Don't be silly, Pete. It will be lot more pleasant for you if you talk, if you start talking now, instead of *later*.

– Do you think I've become stupid lately? Clarke breathed heavily. – Don't underestimate me. I won't give away my only advantage without guarantees. You know that.
– We don't have time to play that game, Pete, Stewart said, cocking his gun. – If you don't start talking, we will kill you now.
His hand did shake. The wound did hurt. At least for now. But he wouldn't miss on this range.
– You've got ten seconds.
He began the countdown.
– Ten!
He didn't speed it up. He thought of Jean and enjoyed it all. Clarke knew that. They all saw it in his eyes.
As he counted down to zero.
– Two!
– NO! NO! Don't shoot, Clarke finally said, very hastily. – I'll talk. I'll tell you everything, everything I know.
Stewart had started putting pressure on the trigger and couldn't stop it. His finger started shaking, and he fired. The bullet hit the wall right by Clarke's left temple.
– You were lucky there, Pete. I don't think the fates will favor you like this again, do you?
Clarke sat there, unmoving, sweating, his eyes moving, obviously straining to hold onto his cool.
He shrugged, but it wasn't very convincing.
– I had enough after San Diego, he began. – I wanted peace and quiet in life, a steady income. Steady and high. So, after being employed in Denver I let it be known that I was on the take. It was amazingly simple. They came to me after two days, before I had managed to even start on my more individually adapted schemes. On occasions I've been tempted to believe they knew about my change of heart even before I did. Perhaps they had several possible candidates «ready», and waited for the right moment. I don't know and I don't care. It was the chance I had been waiting for, and I grabbed it with both hands. An old acquaintance wanted us to meet in San Diego, at Connors' grave… and when I arrived there good ol' new giant Dave waited for me, very friendly, very suggestive. I was in, and I've never regretted it.
– Most people don't, Stewart said. – When they give in to the oppression ruling the world, they lose their ability to think and act for themselves.
– I recruited Mike Cousin. Clarke kept talking, as if he was paid to do it. – They wanted him. Admittedly I couldn't understand why at first, but

I soon realized he was both ruthless and sly. He was in fact a seventeen-year-old boy with an old, old heart. Gidman told me that he knew about that family, about their qualities, and after a while I couldn't do anything but agree.

Stewart shook, but no one noticed.

– When he was killed, it didn't really matter anymore. We were done preparing for what was to come: the enslavement of the selected boys and girls at Denver High. I don't why they chose Denver High instead of New York or elsewhere, but I've come to trust their judgment. I value theirs and they value mine. We work so well together. It was easy, so very, very easy, without anybody suspecting a thing. Everything is coming together nicely.

Caine felt nausea overwhelm him. The man was actually bragging. Bragging.

– And they talked about «the brother», always the brother. They were very nervous about him, about something he might do. I couldn't understand why. I still don't. But I know he's resourceful. I know they all are. But when push came to show he was nothing but a defenseless boy, just like the rest of the boys and girls, the sweet boys and girls…

The brother. Caine looked at Stewart then, too. Saw even more of his haunted Self. It was as if it lived within him, bounced back and forth like a ball.

– Why did you cross the line, Pete? Was it because of Wolf Connors?

Clarke looked up at The Gambler and shrugged.

– I understand why you ask, he replied. – Where you're going with it. Why begin with corruption, murder and enslavement when I could live comfortably on minor money transfers and risk being shot to pieces without the people I would help even bothering to shrug? That is what you're asking, right?

– I've always wondered about the same myself, Stewart said, his voice strange and ghostly. And then he continued in the same voice: – I must warn you, Pete. You're saying a lot without saying anything. That won't do. That won't do at all.

He kicked Clarke in the kneecap and grinned viciously when his old friend cried out.

– In other words, shut the fuck up with your bullshit and delaying tactics, he said contemptuously. – We want places, names and events, and we want a detailed list.

Saliva flowed from Clarke mouth now, caused both by boundless anger or fear?

– Well, except for Gidman and Cousin I dealt with only one man really… Thomas Forester.

– You're a lying shit, Pete, Caine stated. – He wouldn't kidnap his own son. He might be a lot of things, but that ain't one of them.

– But it is, Stewart said. – I saw him, saw him in moonlight and shadow.

And if that was meant to be reassuring to Clarke (and Caine), it clearly wasn't. He looked quite mad at that moment, a voice cutting like silver and glass.

– Great performance there, Stewart. McKenzie shook his head in wonder. He didn't seem fazed or anything. – I think the bureau should incorporate it in future interrogation techniques…

– Aside from that I really don't know that much, Clarke insisted, even before the three others gave him their eye. – I'm not privy to the inner workings yet. If you know anything about them, you know they're doing their freemason shit, and I'm hardly more than an apprentice. I've got my foot inside, that's all.

Stewart looked at him, and he turned even colder.

– I heard some implications of a party when I overheard a conversation between Gidman and Forester… a party on New Years' Eve somewhere, where they're going to parade their work, their newly acquired… servants, showing off, showing how obedient and pleasing those servants have become. Yeah, my superiors are very cocky. They reckon no one will look twice at the slaves, and they're correct… aren't they?

None of them took his challenge or denied his words. Caine swallowed several times in quick succession.

– Anyway, it's a private party, but I do expect an invitation, a part in the future delights, and I will enjoy myself, enjoy the spoils of the world. That's what I know so far, but I do expect to know far more fairly soon when I take my rightful place among the masters of the world.

It turned quiet. A tap was dripping in the kitchen.

– Get up, Stewart snarled icily. – You're gonna walk all the way to your cell, and if it's up to me they'll throw away the key and let you rot like the rat you are. You won't get a deal with this lack of important information, but it will be enough, more than enough, to hang you.

Clarke rose. The relief was visible in his features, to those who knew what to look for. He started walking, and the three followed him, like an honor guard.

– You know… I was never afraid you would kill me, he said scornfully. – You've always been soft. You're living in a fantasy world, where things make sense. The luck that has kept you alive won't last.

What followed Francis Caine would remember, remember vividly, until the moment of his death. Stewart's mouth twisted in a hateful grin defying any description, any fantasy. He raised his gun slightly. And his eyes *burned*. Caine had never seen anything remotely similar. It froze him, made it impossible for him to move, to act. Without truly changing expression Stewart shot Clarke in the back. First once. Clarke was pushed at the wall, at the nice wallpaper. With hands like claws he attempted to stay on his feet.

– You really thought I would let you live so your masters could liberate you? Talk about living in a fantasy world. I'm not playing the game anymore, Pete, not playing others' game.

It wasn't a voice. Only a chain of snarls forming words.

As Clarke started sliding down the wall, Stewart fired two more bullets. The shot to pieces body formed a broad trail of blood on the wall. Caine hoped beyond hope it was over now, but shocked beyond words he heard a moan. Clarke was still alive. Then Stewart fired one final time and Clarke's head broke like an eggshell.

PART TWO:
THE PASSENGER LINER APHRODITE

Chapter Eight

FLORIDA.

The land of sun and dreams. The commercial showed beautiful images. From nature, from crowded beaches, where tanned people smiled into the camera. From the water ski show in Miami, from Cypress Garden and Disneyworld.

Disneyworld…

Aside from Hollywood the dream capital of the world. A place where one could be an astronaut in Space, visiting distant planets. One could be a western hero or be scared in spooky ghost houses.

On its flight over Disneyworld the camera descended in front of a distinguished elder gentleman interviewed by a young, muscular guy in shorts. Both were tanned like nuts. The young muscular guy had a smile and pearly white teeth like in one of those commercials.

– Good morning, people. Welcome to Miami Today. We have a lot for you this morning. First say hello to Charlie. He stands here, right beside me. Charlie has lived here in these parts his entire life. Isn't that right, Charlie?

– Every day since I was born, Charlie confirmed proudly.

– And my question is: How many sunny days have you experienced, Charlie?

Charlie scratched his jaw. The Sleeping Beauty castle towered behind him.

– Hard to tell. It would be easier to count the sad days. There was one day in… forty-eight, I think that wasn't very nice. I had toothache that day, and that didn't feel good.

– There you have it, people, the young man with the pearly white teeth grinned. – Thank you, Charlie. I'm positive everybody agrees with you in your praise of everything down here.

He slapped the old man on his shoulder and moved on, and the camera moved with him.

– Yes, people, this is the land where dreams come true and the sun never sets. I will now present our latest lady for you. I have the honor of giving a warm welcome to another member of our proud, extended family. She's a virgin, and will in a few days set sail for London. Ladies and Gentlemen, I present to you our great new passenger liner… M/S Aphrodite.

During the last sentence the image of the nice young man faded and was supplanted by a large ship at sea. Then that image faded as well and it was cut to a harbor in Miami, an image showing the same ship, showing cheering men, women and children. The harbor was filled with people. There was celebration and music everywhere. The crew on the ship waved to the people on land, and they excitedly returned the waving. Two orchestras, one on land and one on the ship, competed on playing the anthems of Florida and United States simultaneously.

Eric Carr waved as well, playing the tourist, striving to find a better position for the taking of his own pictures. He wanted to include the waving arms, but they tended to get in the way, to get too close to him as he strived to capture tomorrow's front-page picture on the Miami Herald. The editor would crucify him if he didn't get one, reward him handsomely if he did get the one.

The heat made him gasp. Everybody strived to breathe inside the whirling mass of people. The cooling breeze from the sea didn't reach the thousands imprisoned inside the massive crowd.

– It's like this every time, a woman cried weakly. – I think, even though I'm not sure, I'll stay away the next time.

This time of year, late September and later, the tourist season, was often warmer than this, but being caught inside the crowd made any day hot as hell. Carr constantly wiped a sleeve across his brow, to no avail.

He almost collided with a bunch of Seminole Indians, three girls and four boys. One of the girls smiled to him. He pretended not to see it.

A few minutes later, an endless series of pushes and sharp elbows later, he could finally relax in the press lounge nearby, in its cool and shady interior. The air still made it hard to breathe, but the sun and the crowd was a distant memory.

He removed the exposed film from the camera and supplanted it with a new, raw. It was virtually an automatic process, one he did without thinking. He had done it thousands of times during the last few years.

The lounge was full. The stench of cigarette smoke and alcohol never left his nostrils. The place was filled with reporters. His nostrils twisted, and not because of the smoke. That another ship joined the numerous preceding it based in Miami wasn't exactly news. But the room was still filled with reporters. So his interest was aroused, at least for a few seconds.

A man pulled out the chair opposite him. He recognized Andrew Benedict immediately, recognized the stink of burned tobacco and old alcohol.

– Hello, Eric, long time no see, huh?

Carr wanted to say something, but stopped when he finally looked at the other man. He hardly recognized him. Benedict wasn't much older than himself, about twenty-five, but he looked like he was. His hair had turned gray at the temples, and he didn't have much of it left. He had changed dramatically since the last time Carr had seen him, in New York three years earlier.

– Hello, Andy, what are you doing here?

– There are rumors about this particular ship, Benedict grinned, a grin resembling that of a dead man. – They're so persistent that even my editor, and yours apparently, heard them.

He had one glass of beer in each hand. He had already consumed almost everything in one of them.

– Yes, he continued. – I'm employed these days. Investigative journalism is still popular. The general population, with its fickle mind hasn't quite forgotten Watergate yet.

He started on his second glass, and sent for more.

– So, Eric, what are you doing down here? More society news? Do you still bring tidings from the warm south to the frozen north?

– I moved here. Carr shrugged. – I'm working for the Herald.

He swallowed one rather large amount of his own beer. It seemed to be stuck in his throat. He put the glass down.

– It makes sense. Benedict kept grinning. – This is the Sunshine State, after all, the promised land within the promised land. Many people come here from the cold north, a few weeks each year, to forget the real world. But you're lucky enough to live here…

The exchanged words were empty and paper dry. There was no empathy anymore.

– You should have done as I did, Carr said cheerfully. – If you had heeded the advice I and Patrick gave you, you, too, would have enjoyed a well paid, secure employment.

He had just about consumed half of his glass. Benedict had already started on his third, and he constantly asked for more.

– Patrick, yes… I assume he has given even more in to his mother by now, given in to anything.

Carr finally reacted to the more than thin-veiled sarcasm in the other's voice, straightening in the chair.

– Speaking of salary and such… Benedict bent forward, bent closer. – What are you looking for in these auspicious surroundings?

– Looking for auspiciousness, Carr replied lightly, uncaring. – This is, at the very least the social event of the month, perhaps even of the year.

There won't be any lack of juicy stories. The editor values my skills, my ability to get to the heart of things…
– Good old Smitty, Benedict cackled insanely. – What a great way to keep the true journalistic spirit alive. While others are still chasing Gerald Ford because he pardoned Nixon, you're chasing the filthy rich and privileged to see whose dick is stuck in whose cunt. You and your editor are in truth two feet in one shoe.
Carr could no longer hide his irritation. Smitty was the «affectionate» name those claiming to be «true» journalists had given him. Smith was an ordinary name. Mr. Average. One that never had his own opinions, never did anything that had even the most remote chance of danger.
– You're a specialist in increasing sales, Smitty, one «colleague» had told him while drunk once. – But you've got no idea of what true journalism is about.
– I can already see the headline tomorrow, Benedict boasted, and laughed some more. – FLORIDA WELCOMES ITS NEW QUEEN, WELCOMES APHRODITE
He started coughing, and once he started he couldn't stop. The laughter stopped and the entire body shook by the violent coughing.
Carr rose. He hesitatingly reached out a hand, held it there for one second, two, before letting it fall, before pulling back, before turning away, and leaving the table, leaving the room, returning to the heat outside, the heat and bright light only slowly, very slowly melting the ice in his veins, the frost paralyzing his heart.
+++++++++++++++++++++++++++++++
He was still cold. He couldn't even smell the moldy ghost anymore, and he was still cold. In there, with the ghost, with the freshly stirred memories, it was as if the frost from Vietnam had returned, like it had done that day in New York, in Patrick Warren's luxurious Park Avenue apartment.
Yes, Patrick. He had it easy. He was born rich. His path was decided from birth. There had been no need for him to make choices. But he had still done so, at least for a while.
Carr took more pictures. He walked around in a consciously relaxed manner, and he discovered that he could, that he could, at least momentarily, forget the flashes drilling holes in his skull. There were fewer people now, inevitably, as many had been forced to seek shelter in the houses and the shade, easier to pick his targets, his potentials. He took more pictures of the ship for a while, but then, deciding he had enough, enough angles, he started zooming in on specific bodies, on faces, on

smiles, wide smiles and all the beautiful people, some of them even being here to pose, to be seen.

He spotted the girl, the girl who had smiled to him. She was still smiling, a happy smile warming him, doing what the sun couldn't do.

She wasn't Seminole. Neither were her friends. He saw that easily now. They had dark, smooth hair and dark skin, but their features had very little resemblance to American natives in general or the Seminole in particular. Their clothes were just costumes.

So much for your vaunted power of observation, he thought dismayed.

He focused on them, hardly even looking away or capturing anyone else on film, watching the seven through the camera. The girls pulled away from the boys after a while, and went off on their own. Three beautiful dolls. They snickered and pointed at him, evidently having discovered his interest some time ago, and they waved. He waved back. They whispered a bit among themselves, before one of them kissed the others goodbye, and set course towards him. He breathed faster. It was the right one, the smiling one.

– Hello, there, she greeted him, stopping boldly right in front of him. – Who are you?

– Eric, he replied. – Eric Carr.

He and the editor had discussed the use of a false identity, but hadn't really bothered exploring it. It was amazing what people would tell journalists if the circumstances were right, far more than they would tell others.

He reached out a hand. She accepted it, her smile in place, laced with a teasing edge.

– So, what do you do, Eric Carr?

– I'm a journalist, he said. – I'm working for the Miami Herald and I'm here to cover Aphrodite's virgin voyage.

He grinned.

– My father doesn't like journalists much, she said sourly, seemingly pulling back a little.

He tried, tried very hard to keep his long face from growing longer.

– I, on the other hand, just love them.

She grinned widely.

Her full lips glowing like blood close to his.

– And I'll also be traveling with sweet Aphrodite…

– You shall perhaps be working there? He wondered.

– Nope. I have my own cabin. I wanted to travel and I wanted to travel with that ship, and I bugged daddy until he finally caved in. Daddy is rich…

She put her hands on her back and looked coyly at him.

– And I can pay for myself when we go out.

– Out? He gaped. – Tonight?

– No, she stated decisively. – Not, tonight. Now! I won't wait a minute longer. How about it, Eric, are you willing to entertain a spoiled, needy daddy's girl?

She looked at him, and he returned the look, drowning in her eyes, in the lines of her body.

They started out at an expensive restaurant on the harbor coincidently the first they passed. «I'm starving», she announced and looked starving at him.

They walked inside.

After a good look at the menu they had lobster and oyster, very expensive lobster and oyster and wine. Carr was glad he had a fat representation account. He loved this, being a rich man raiding the city.

One day will come, he thought, when it won't be pretend anymore.

Carr slowly started enjoying himself. Time fled in the girl's company. She wasn't an immature girl, but well educated and able to speak well for herself. She had class, and it was a pleasure accompanying her.

They went dancing. He had thought he was a good dancer, but she was truly good. She attracted attention wherever they went, and they went a lot of places. They raided the city, from north to south, from west to east, and back again.

– Do you enjoy displaying me? She whispered in his ear, with her arms on his shoulders. – Do I make you proud?

– Yes, he said hoarsely.

He wanted to say more, but everything just stopped in him.

They walked on a pier, as the sun set in the western seaside, arm in arm, holding hands. The light touch of her hand held untold promises.

They had another light dinner. Red wine twinkled like blood in the dying light of the sun. Glasses met and parted. He drank. She sipped. Her hair changed color, until it had exactly the color of the setting sun.

– To us, she said, very straightforward.

– To us, he said.

And they drank some more.

– Your father hasn't sent big, ugly bruisers with you? He wondered, looking around, slightly worried.

– No. She shook her head. – He isn't worried. I'm a big girl, and I can defend myself. He made me study martial arts from the age of five. He kept telling me that it was the best protection money could buy.

– So you're tough little cookie?

– I am. But I can be sweet, too…

She took his hand, squeezing it lightly. Every time she touched him it sent stings of electricity through him. She kept her eyes on him, kept meeting his eyes, steady, unwavering, inviting. It was as if he was pulled into them, pulled into her lap.

She finally stopped. They had seemingly been walking forever from the restaurant, he thought. It was no more than hundred steps. He had lost count, but he felt confident of that much.

– This is my hotel, she said. – I've had fun. Thank you.

She faced him, holding both his hands.

– No problem, he reddened (he actually reddened). – I enjoyed myself.

He behaved like he had all day, like an inexperienced boy, dating a girl for the first time, and he wondered what was wrong with him.

In an attempt to hide how confused he was, he counterattacked.

– So how about inviting me to your room for another drink to end a perfect day?

She pulled a note from her pocket and handed it to him. He registered that the movement pushed her big breasts at the Indian suit. It was easy to see she wore nothing underneath. He swallowed hard.

– My cabin number, she said, smiling sweetly.

She lifted her arms above her head, displaying herself, and he imagined she was embracing the very air itself.

– It will be a great voyage, won't it? She kissed him shyly on the cheek. – Good night, Eric. Sweet dreams.

She ran up the stairs to the hotel entrance and he thought:

She's not that experienced.

The girl that wasn't a Seminole stopped in the door, and now the teasing expression had returned to her smile.

– Haven't you forgotten something, Eric?

And just then he felt very, very stupid.

– What's your name? He wondered.

– Betty.

– Just Betty?

– Just Betty, she laughed. – Just Betty, Mr. Smith.

And then she was gone.

++++++++++++++++++

It was two days later, on the evening of October first, when M/S Aphrodite left Miami on her maiden voyage. Once more spectators gathered in huge numbers. As had been prominently featured in all local newspapers the owners of the ship had invested quite a bit in Florida, created a lot of new jobs.

The place was bright as day. A thousand lamps were lit in the harbor and onboard Aphrodite. The maiden glowed like a thousand stars as it slowly slipped away. People waved and cried. The passengers waved to the less fortunate people on land, proudly and patronizingly.

Andy Benedict sat down in the bar, starting on his third bottle of red wine. The bar was virtually deserted. There were a few other drunks here and there, accompanying him, but they looked more like a part of the furniture than actual people. He raised his glass to them, but there was no response. They had probably been drinking since the ship had arrived at the harbor.

– Look at them up there, Benedict said aloud to the empty room. – The filthy rich are displaying themselves, displaying their important lack of importance. The others are there for an empty memory they can carry with them for the rest of their wretched lives, something they can brag about, brag about the time when they for one brief moment of time shared space with the powerful, the elite of the world.

A guy mumbled something in the corner, somewhat coherent.

– We tore up our draft notices. Yes, we did. But it didn't help. We were drafted anyway. Yes, we were.

He broke into tears, fell apart there, on the spot. The liquor he consumed opened all his wounds, all his nightmares.

And for a moment there, Benedict imagined he was the drunk, was the man dissolved in alcohol there in the corner. Benedict hadn't been drinking at all before his «tour» in Vietnam. He and Eric and Patrick had ripped their draft notices to pieces, like many other students. In a storm of cheers and heat the entire gathering had done so, one by one on the stage, those who dared doing it up there, and all the others on the campus' parking lot. They had been young then, full of life, and desire to live.

But life…and the war had done something to them all. They had been drafted and sent off to Vietnam like packages, parcels, with no life of their own. The war and the process itself destroyed emotions, ideals, crushing humans' dreams.

– God bless America, the drunk in the corner blubbered. – I wonder what can save the shit, and the rest of the world. I ask, but I get only echoes. No one will answer me. Only the gods know, and they're not telling.

He laughed insanely, as he sat there, drinking himself to death.

His head fell down, and he kept mumbling under his own breath.

Benedict's head hit the wood, the polished wood of the bar. Stars were lit behind his closed eyelids, and he sat there, speaking incoherently to anybody who might listen, and nobody did. And he fell, just fell, into an ever-deeper stupor, a festering well of his own making.

When Aphrodite had sailed a minute or so all lights were put out, on land and at sea. It turned pitch black. For five, ten seconds… until there were cracks and whistles in the night, and fireworks brightened the sky.

– Look, Eric, LOOK! Betty jumped up and down and shouted in her enthusiasm. Her face turned red in excitement.

– It's a great spectacle, Carr admitted. – The people behind this have both money and the style to go with it.

He put his right arm around her, pulling her close. She didn't object. Her excitement and youthful exuberance were contagious, and he kissed her, spontaneously and inevitably. First on the cheek. But when her body turned limp, formed itself after his, he kissed her neck. She returned the kiss shyly, and took one step back. But she smiled, and didn't stop him from catching up, to get close again.

– You're a sight for sore eyes, he said, unable to take his eyes off her.

– I know, she said, in another mix of dread and joy. – I've heard it since I was five.

I've never met anyone like you, he wanted to say, but held back. Such a mix of shyness and experience.

– I'm both whore and Madonna, am I not, Eric?

She wore a dress tonight, very revealing, very honorable. He nodded.

The fireworks ended. The lights from Miami faded, until it was visible as nothing more than a weak glow on the horizon, the horizon they left behind. Laughing and cheerful Carr and Betty followed the others down to the great dance hall, where the festivities continued.

– What a setup. Carr shook his head. – What an insidious setup.

– Isn't it? She grinned. – We've really ended up in the midst of things this time, haven't we?

He nodded, nodded to her and smiled, a silly grin feeling far removed from the person he had thought he was.

There was no staircase, only a slightly curved floor leading to the floor below. The floor was polished wood, so shiny one could see one's mirror image in it.

The hall revealed itself to them, to the guests, the overwhelmed guests. They had been impressed with the festivities before the departure from Miami and the fireworks, but this… this was almost too much.

The extended hall was round. A perfect circle, Carr suspected. A worthy symbol of wealth and power. It was split in three sections. On one side was the restaurant, dark, quiet, secretive, and on the other side the dance floor itself. The floor and the ceiling were made of interconnecting giant mirrors. Between the restaurant and the dance floor was another circle, a large platform, a stage, sticking up from the floor.

– I've heard rumors, a woman cried breathlessly. – But this…

Everybody stood there, out of breath, out of words, admiring the luxury, blinded by it, overwhelmed by it.

A servile, dressed man stopped in front of them and bowed.

– Ladies and Gentlemen, he greeted them. – Welcome to the dance hall. The music will begin shortly, for those of you who want to dance. For those of you who want food dinner will be served at anyone's leisure.

Top service, Carr thought. A floating five star hotel.

He and Betty sat down by the wall. The chairs were deep, comfortable, right in relation to the table. Carr had visited many a rich man's home in the course of his job, but this was as extravagant as any of them.

– This is a great setup, he repeated.

She nodded, her eyes shining. She didn't understand the more… the deeper connotations of his words.

– Something is off, he kept at it.

And now he did see understanding, and also something else in her eyes.

The waiter, a smiling, but still laidback man arrived at their table.

– May I take your order?

His voice was well modulated, his words carefully spoken. He reminded Carr of a Victorian servant, though undoubtedly brought up to date. More perfection.

– Yes. Carr nodded. – I'll have the entrecote with the wine of the kitchen's choosing.

The Victorian or non-Victorian waiter wrote it all down without looking at his notepad.

– That will be all. Carr nodded.

– Thank you, sir.

Said the waiter.

And turned to Betty.

– And the Lady?

– I'll have the same, please. She grinned and put away the menu.

The waiter disappeared and Carr hardly noticed him leave.

– What do you think will happen, now? Betty wondered. – Oh, I'm *so* excited.

Only the guests were present in the room. At least only the guests were *seen*. Carr hardly saw the waiters and crew, even when looking for them. These people were clearly professionals. They didn't stick out. They weren't noticed, until they were close by. Carr shuddered by an association, but kept it together.

He spotted Benedict. The man snooped around, until he found a lonely table. The paranoid shit!

– I don't really know, Carr replied to Betty. – They'll probably serve the food…

– You're really funny, she giggled. – I like funny. I'm so glad I met you.

– There has been too much solemnity in my life so far.

Her eyes penetrated deep within him. They were… firegreen. He was unable to find another or a better description. Burning eyes and thick, black hair.

– You're beautiful, he exclaimed.

– That's so sweet of you to say, she whispered. – Thank you.

It was as if a very long time had passed for Carr when he heard the first drums, slowly growing from the buzz of his own dreams, and the voices around him.

They were rock drums, Carr surmised, played as a march, and flowing from speakers concealed in the wall. He rose and walked around, checking a bit. The sounds were just as strong, no matter where in the hall one was. They came from everywhere and nowhere. Every man and woman's heart beat in conjunction with the drums.

At the deep end of the restaurant a part of the wall slid aside. A long procession made of two rows appeared. One row with males and one with females. A white male and a black female walked in front. They were dressed in a sort of robe, a robe in blinding white. Beneath it they were covered by something looking like one, large stocking. The stocking went from wrist to wrist, to ankles and the collar around their neck and - and this made the guests gasp - it was practically transparent. The stocking was in shadow, but in flashes and shades one could glimpse what were practically their naked bodies.

And in spite of this everything still seemed modest, unassuming, and absolutely not tacky.

Each couple carried elegantly their large plate between them, above their heads. And if one counted carefully, one would realize that the number of couples was exactly the number of tables in the room, the room and tables filled with people.

– They're *so* young, an older lady said scandalized, while applauding with the others.

One of the high-profiled guests on the ship, the duke of something, was served first by the white male and black female. It was obviously meant as an honor, even though the duke didn't exactly appreciate the attention.

Eric Carr swallowed hard when a skinny, short girl served him, and he was unable to take his eyes off the small breasts and the dark triangle between the slender thighs. And when he did, he saw the boy bending over Betty, saw the cock and nuts pressing against the transparent fabric.

Girl? Boy? No, they were both clearly adults. They were experienced. He saw how they acknowledged the stares, how they seemed to thrive on all this, saw the flashes of pride in their eyes. They enjoyed exposing themselves, enjoyed being looked at.

– You should eat. Betty grinned at him. – This is excellent.

She had already eaten a lot, while he had hardly touched the food. He did and surprise lit his face.

– This is delicious, he said, shaking his head. He had some more. – I've been to many a renowned restaurant the last few years, and this is absolutely on par with the best of them.

The duck seemed to melt in his mouth, flow down his throat like fluid. He looked at Betty. He stared at her, and was unable to look away.

– You should see your face right now. She laughed and laughed thrillingly.

Time melted around him, transformed into fluid, dancing in his mind.

An immeasurable moment later Betty took his hands, squeezing them lightly.

– Wasn't that fantastic? Wasn't all of it like that?

Her soft voice, like fluid, rolling off her tongue.

– Was it? He countered rhetorically.

– Yes, it was, she insisted. – And you think so, too. You can't hide yourself, you know. Not from me. It pleased you. All this pleases you. It's written all over your face. To me it is.

– What an exceptional daddy's girl you are, he joked. – But I've also learned to thread carefully around daddy's girls the last few years.

– But you don't want to, she told him. – You don't want to be careful in anything, and I love you for it.

She bent slightly more forward, and her nipples turned even more visible, pushing against the fabric of her dress.

– Your affairs are purely physical. She stated matter of fact. – And you want them to continue that way. You don't want anything deeper. It complicates things. And daddy's girls can cause a lot of grief if they're not handled properly… right?

He sat there, smiling cynically, unable to hide the turmoil her words caused within him.

– And I am pleased to tell you I understand that, she continued softly. – I understand perfectly. I'll be your mistress on this voyage. I'll be your dream fairy, because I want to and because I can. I think you're a very fascinating man, Eric.

– I would love for you to be my mistress, he said, half jokingly, half solemnly, touching her cheek.

And she smiled gratefully, like a girl given candy.

And the mercury of time flowed even further, even further away from what he knew.

– It was truly something, she said dreamingly. – Did you see the golden bracelets they wore around their wrists and ankles?

– I saw it. He nodded. – It fit well with their collar. Funny, you have one quite similar. They must be fashionable these days.

He reached over the table and touched the ring. She started shivering, as if she was frightened. Her forehead was suddenly covered in sweat. He could smell it on her, smell her fear, smell fear itself, like he had always been able to do in the jungle.

– Oh, I'm ahead of them all, she said, with a shadow of a smile. – My friends and I bought ours on our way to Miami.

– What is it? He asked worried. – You look pale.

– I'm okay. I…

He wanted to try something and let go of the ring. And waited.

– It's nothing, she stated, suddenly perfectly calm. – Nothing important.

– Nothing? He wondered. – You looked like you were scared to death.

– Quite an exaggeration, don't you think so, too? She shrugged, very deliberate. – I always get tense at the start of a holiday. Old habit. Long story. Forget it, okay?

– Okay. He shrugged as well.

She smiled sweetly again, playing roguishly with his fingers.

– Sweet Eric, she said softly. – I swear I'll make it up to you.

She moved closer to him, moved close to him, kissing him on the neck.

The music played, kept playing.

She looked at the waiters, the half naked, practically naked waiters, followed them with her green eyes, and he did, too.

– Look at them, she whispered. – Revealing themselves that way. It must be fantastic to be so free, so uninhibited.

– They're getting paid for it, he said dryly. – Besides, I'm not certain I envy them. A person can smile a lot, and still be cold inside.

Her voice, innocent and teasing simultaneously.
– Is this the hidden puritan speaking? If a man or woman wants to reveal their bodies, expose their sensuality, they're automatically whores?
– I didn't say that, he protested. – I…
– What, then, did you mean? She asked sweetly.
– Oh, it's pretty well-known stuff, Carr replied, suddenly quite relaxed. – I know the international scene, scenes like this. It's hard to avoid saying B if you've already said A, if you get my drift. Inexperienced people are easily stuck in the mire.
She smiled to him, her strange smile, taking his hand.
– Don't worry, I'm more than experienced enough. If that's what you mean…
Eric Carr experienced the rest of the time there, at the table as very strange, almost unreal or even surreal. There was the woman and the mood surrounding them. Above the DJ, on the dance floor hung a giant clock from the ceiling. It showed one minute post nine. All lights in the hall were turned off. In the pitch-black darkness they heard the DJ fumble with the microphone. They heard a hissing sound. Then the lights on the stage were lit all the way around, and they could see the smoke rise from the floor. In the matter of seconds, the entire circle had been hidden in the flashing, gray inferno. As the smoke slowly dissolved, six frames ascended from the shadows, three men and three women. Then the music was fired from the giant speakers, and the song filled the room and the minds of those in it.

Dance dance
Dance your anger away
Let all sad thoughts go

Two of them sang. The other four danced around them, moving in their sphere, like an extension of their being. They were all dressed in the brown stocking fabric. It looked incredible in the special lighting. One both saw and didn't see their bodies. One single light shone from the ceiling. Outside the beam there was shadow and suggestion. When the six stepped into the light and bent backwards, eyes pointing at the ceiling, they were revealed in all their glory. Eric blinked. He noticed one of the dancers, a girl with long silver blond hair. It reached her to the hips and flashed, flashed in both the light and the shadow. She was so good and danced with such dedication that everybody's attention was focused on her, and not at the singers. Carr figured she had learned to dance before she could walk.
The dance captivated the audience, pulled them in, pulled them up there,

on the stage. Everything was very pure, very intimate.

It wasn't tacky. It just wasn't.

– Can't you feel it? Betty whispered in his ear, and he could hear her, easily hear her. – How your cynicism is weakened, like a river where the water level is sinking and the river is full of many years' collected poison, how everything is just fading away?

– It's… beautiful, Eric said.

The song lasted for nearly ten minutes. When it approached the end the stage started rising, and turned into a pillar rising towards the ceiling. There was applause. Eric felt his palms connect, felt the sting of skin striking skin, but he didn't hear the sound. He heard the song, the melody. Its end consisted of a heavy, mystical piano section and the singers' sweet choir.

Dance dance
Now it's your turn
Are you ready
Let all thoughts go - ooo

The song ended, the dance ended. The audience applauded, in wild excitement and abandon. The six waved gratefully all the way up, clearly grateful beyond words at the overwhelming reception, red faced and flushed. The pillar stopped by an opening right under the ceiling, and the six vanished through it. The hall was once more flooded in lights, in soft light, and music flowed from the speakers, accompanied by the DJ's voice. Hard pulsing drums hammered veins and limbs. Eric Carr felt his blood boil. He heard the girl by his side breathe. When the majority of those present virtually ran to the dance floor, he and Betty remained.

For a long time.

And they noticed nothing around them, looked only at each other.

He finally spoke.

– I've never been very fond of dancing, he said hoarsely. – How about you?

She shook her head.

– Neither have I.

As if by telepathy they both rose simultaneously.

I hear they're playing music, Carr thought, but I don't hear what they're playing.

They left the table, left the hall, arm in arm. Old habits die hard, and even though his attention was focused on Betty, he kept observing his surroundings, kept hearing the whispers of the Vietnam jungle in his mind. They passed through the bar. It was virtually abandoned. One single bartender tended the place, but he didn't have much to do, except polishing glasses. Even Andrew Benedict wasn't there.

Eric turned back to Betty. She turned to him. They clinched and kissed in a heat of a storm, flustered and sweaty.

– My cabin is on the upper deck, she said sweetly.

– How strange, so is mine…

Yellow globes, casting a soft, flickering light lit the stairs. He hardly noticed. She clung to him, breathing ever faster. The floor had just been cleaned. The heat made tiny dots of mist rise from the floor. Or was it him that didn't see clearly?

Outside the door to her cabin she pulled even closer to him. She kissed him, bit his lips to shreds. He fumbled for the handle, fearing she wouldn't to able to find her keys. Breath was like a storm in his ears.

– Betty…?

Eric heard the male voice as if from far away. They both turned. One of the boys Carr had observed with the girls on the quay waited on the corner by the deck exit. Carr felt the familiar pressure at his temples.

– Please excuse me for a moment, Eric, Betty said quickly. – There is something I must do, something I have forgotten. I won't be long. You can wait inside, if you want. Do you want to?

Carr managed a nod. There was no way he could say no to the soft voice and the wet eyes. He patted her shoulder.

– I'll wait, he said.

The last thing he saw before he closed the door was the boy's hand on her left breast and she who turned away from him.

– No, Ted, not now.

He couldn't recall opening the door, but he noticed when it closed behind him, leaving him alone to the silence inside, when he closed it with his body, standing there with closed eyes for a long time, doing nothing but breathing. The cabin was quite luxurious, as he had expected, quite similar to his own. Carr could see the moon and the stars out there. Quite contrary to how he had experienced it below the skyscrapers in Manhattan, where the tall shrines closed off the moon and the stars, and all the pollution darkened the sky. Or in the Vietnam jungle, where the moonlight too often turned blood red.

Images and far more flooded his mind, screams, smells and the taste of rust.

He was perspiring hard in the moist clothes. He ripped them off, rushing to the window, and to his great relief it was possible to open it, open it wide. The cool sea breeze filled the room. It softly embalmed his naked skin. It did him little good. He was just as hot. And thirsty, very thirsty. He grabbed a wine glass and a bottle, clumsily opening it. The pearly white wine flooded into the glass, down his dry, dry throat. He drank it all. Then he drank the entire bottle. It didn't have any discernible effect. He hurried to the bathroom and filled the glass with water, drank it all, filled it again and drank. Drank until he felt the nausea like a ball in his throat. The unpleasantness slowly faded. Skin was dry. He fell down on the bed, unable to elicit the memory of himself leaving the bathroom, the walk to the bed.

Eric Carr rested there on the bed, alone. He didn't look at his watch, didn't need to do that to know that time passed, had passed since he had bathed in the sight of the black hair, the pale skin. They had taught him to measure time without mechanical aid. They had taught him so much. As always, when he waited like this, alone, the nightmares assaulted him, the images of skulls, clean bones, rotting corpses in mass graves. The corpses slowly turning to jelly, to one single, undistinguishable mass, like mashed potatoes in a boiling kettle. He had seen it all.

And he kept seeing it, reliving it, in every quiet moment.

But tonight, there were only women. And even though the bodies were Vietnamese, they had her face. They turned into Indians, dancing on a large, open spot in the jungle. Clothes melted off them. Flesh melted off them. As they danced, danced their dance of submission and heat. Betty waved to him, but she was dressed. He wanted desperately for her to undress, like the others, to fuck him, like the others.

He felt soft lips against his own. He pushed her away, dizzy and confused.

– I guess it took longer than I expected, she said softly. – You've been sleeping.

She touched him, touched his face, lifted his hand, kissed his hand. He stiffened slightly, unable to hold back.

– I know you don't like kissing and coddling, she said. – That's okay with me.

She writhed out of her dress, her very revealing, very honorable dress. It was left in a heap by her feet. She grabbed her breasts and began squeezing them so the nipples grew large and hard. She swayed before him. The vision of her turned into the vision of the Indian females performing for him, in his honor.

– Stop that! He commanded sharply. – Come here!

She did, she obeyed, slipped close to him. He grabbed her hair and pulled her by it to the middle of the bed. She didn't say anything, just knelt there before him, waiting for him. Then, after the sound of her breath grew intolerable, he grabbed her, touched her. There was a lot to touch. He slapped her butt. She released a shout. He slapped her again, and the shout turned into a moan.

– You enjoy that, don't you? Daddy's girl enjoys a firm hand, just loves a good spanking.

Her response was another moan, and a body softening in his hands.

He turned her over, turning her on her back. She was big, big in all ways. And she was his, his to do with as he pleased. He felt his cock rise, felt it push against her thigh, as he descended on the large body, the readied body of a willing female. When he saw a tear in her eye, he bent his head and kissed it away. It was a long time since he had done anything like that.

– Do it, she mumbled. – Do it!

I love you, he thought, uncertain whether or not he said it aloud.

She embraced him in her powerful arms, soft as a feather. He grabbed her around the waist, seeking down on her, into the moist area between her thighs. She moaned, a sound akin to a cry, and spread her legs.

Take me, she begged him, clearly submissive, but also with a fire that would melt just about anything. He knew that. He felt it.

– Please, Eric, she begged him. – I'm your perfect woman, am I not? You have come home, have you not? Come home, Eric, come home…

He mumbled between her breasts, mumbled his thoughts.

I've searched so long.

She did something to him, something touching him in beyond fundamental ways. He kept moving on her, seeing nothing but her sweet face.

There was a swelling on her arm, right by the shoulder. He had squeezed her arm, squeezed it hard, making her cry out. She smiled to him, smiled radiantly to him.

Chapter Nine

The ship had reached open sea, and the weather that morning wasn't nice anymore. It was storming and the rain was pouring down. But since Aphrodite had powerful stabilizers the passengers didn't notice that much of the rocky waters. The outside decks, however, looked like stormy seas.

Betty left the bed quietly and smoothly. She looked at the man lying there. He hadn't moved a finger. She would have known if he was awake, she knew that. Bare feet moved over the wet carpet and towards the window, closing it firmly. The girl hummed a melody. Her face was without expression, like the eyes were empty and dead. But the melody… the melody was full and alive.

She moved to the door, nude, ignoring the dress left on the floor. With a final look at the man on the bed she opened the door and stuck her head out in the corridor. There was no one there. She slipped out of the room and closed the door behind her, rushing to a closet marked LIFEBELTS, and opened it, hurrying inside. The lifebelts covered the bottom of the compartment like a blanket below her. There was more than sufficient room.

– Clear, she said to the air.

Sitting there in the dark, the dreams came to her. The closet expanded, turned into a large, warm valley. She walked there with a man, a man with burning eyes. He was tall, immensely tall. The little girl looked up at him with admiration and fear in her eyes.

– You will leave, the man told her. – But one day you will return. One day you will all return.

The light dissolved her dream. The elevator had stopped on a lower level. Its door opened. A scarred white-haired man sat by a desk not far away. In front of the desk knelt several other naked girls and boys. She waited respectfully.

– Ah, there you are, Kurt Meinz said. – Come here.

Anger, fear and loathing cursed through her. None of it reached her rigid facial expression. He waved to her. She ran to him and knelt before him with an eager smile, joining her fellow slaves before his exalted presence.

Meinz rose and stepped out in front of his desk, towering over the kneeling boys and girls.

– That's good girls, good boys, he said, clearly pleased, clearly filled with scorn. – You may rise.

They obeyed. They stood there, stood still, awaiting his command.

He walked back and forth, in front of them, behind them, among them. They shivered in excitement and pleasure, even before he started touching them, acknowledging their presence. He was fully aware how they saw him.

– I bathe in you, he mused. – Bath in your energies, and they strengthen me. I, your everything and all.

Meinz smiled, as he turned toward the door, the door ajar.

– You may enter, now, Sandra, he said aloud.

The flustered girl pushed open the door, and entered the room, her eyes directed at the floor, shyly and ashamed, ripe for the taking.

– I'm sorry, Doctor Meinz, she said nervously, excitedly. – I know I'm not supposed to be here, not to intrude while you're… working, but I… I…

– … wanted to, she finished meekly.

He studied her dispassionately, with a smile around the thin lips.

– You wanted indeed to be here, while I was working, he said kindly. – You want to learn, to study under a master, and you were afraid to ask, to give voice to your fears, to your innermost yearnings.

– Yeah, that's it. She nodded eagerly, suddenly much more assertive. – That's what I wanted, that's what I want. I want you to teach me, teach how you *do* it, how you're… putting them in their place, how you're *destroying* them with a snap of your fingers. I want to learn everything.

She stood there, shaking, both in fear and anticipation.

He let her boil for a while, let her tremble in uncertainty.

– Don't worry, he finally said lightly. – I don't find your request unreasonable. And you shouldn't be scared because you've shown determination and exposed your future job preferences. I find your interests… stimulating. We all have a duty to teach the next generation, right?

She took one more step forward, and then one more, taking the remaining crucial steps into his sphere, his domain, as fear was slowly supplanted with bravery and recklessness, and the aching desire that had brought her here.

– Observe, he told her.

He walked to Betty, stopped before her, signing to her to step forward. She obeyed, without thought, without the slightest change in her features.

– Good morning, Betty, he greeted her.

– Good morning, Master, she said evenly.

– How did it go, in your opinion, with your designated target? He wondered lightly.

– I made contact, as ordered, she said, filled with pride, with arrogance. – I achieved contact. I got close to him, made him want me, made him love me. It was easy, Master.

Her pride was an illusion, of course, something they had instilled in her, like they had instilled everything. He enjoyed watching her, enjoyed observing her pride, knowing it was an illusion.

She stood there, slightly curling her toes, totally unaware of her doing anything to attract his attention.

– You may speak.

He permitted her.

– Was I good, Master? Was I really good?

She had the same expectant tone in her voice as a little child speaking to her parents, one revealing blind trust, blind need for acknowledgement, for acceptance, for accolades.

– You were a good little bitch, he said, totally relaxed and indifferent. – You were so fine and red and green and blue and the Masters are so very, very pleased with you.

– Oh, thank you, Master, thank you. She smiled in exalted happiness.

He had seen her, on the monitors, through the cameras placed in «her» cabin. She had been exceptional, just like he had known she would be.

And then the good doctor, the teacher turned to Sandra.

– Ted here is also part of the Duke Von Brandenburg… team, Meinz said. – He's assigned to Frau Ilse. You might want to ask him… questions?

– Yes, I would, Sandra replied. – I would love to.

She stepped close to the boy towering above her.

– So… how goes your mission? She wondered.

– I've made contact, Mistress, he replied. – She's strong, but her will is faltering. Soon, I'll have her eating of my hand, and she will serve the Thousand Feet, serve with all her ingenuity and intellect.

– Good boy, Sandra whispered, as she touched him. – Such a good boy…

And she observed how his cock rose, how it hardened and thickened, and pointed at her, how it wanted to serve her.

She turned to Meinz again, with shining eyes.

– They're so docile, so… sweet, she marveled. – Like well-mannered children.

– And becoming more so, Meinz said pleased, – the longer they're under our care. Finally, when this phase of the treatment is complete, we'll allow them to grow up, to leave childhood behind, and become eager agents of our order.

– The possibilities are… endless, right?

He nodded, studying her with a weird stare. She pulled back a little, unable or unwilling to look at him.

– Come children, she commanded gently. – Follow me.

They did, without changing expression. The same happy smile lit their faces. They followed her to the next room. There was a row of large cages there, cages with beds. There was a hum somewhere. Sandra imagined, when she studied them, that it came from their throats, even though it resembled very much that of the ship's engine, the sound of the machine surrounding them all.

– Two and two in the cages, Meinz told Sandra. – Who's going to bed with whom today?

Now Sandra looked at him.

– You want me to…

– Sure. Why not?

She turned to the six, appraising them carefully.

– John will go with Linda today, she said, in a voice filled with scorn, with viciousness.

The two of them smiled to each other, as they entered the cage together, began caressing each other.

– Helen will go with Bruce, and of course that leaves Ted and Betty.

They all entered their cages. They touched and they fell on the beds. Kisses and movements intensified, and moans and grunts rose from them, hums rose louder at the ceiling. John was already inside Linda, and while Meinz and Sandra watched Ted and Bruce also pushed themselves inside the female beneath them. There was no expression in their faces, except for the twisted joy dominating their entire being.

– You're not much worth, now, princess, Meinz mumbled. – Neither you nor your prince.

Sandra looked curiously at him.

– Look at them, Meinz said. – Look at the human garbage lying there. See how easy it is to reduce life's most important act to a purely automatic function. They've become functions, the function we at any time choose to bestow on them.

Sandra's attention was drawn to the six in the cages. The sight clearly excited her.

– You did good, Meinz told her. – My initial assessment was correct. You do have a talent for this.

She pulled attention away from the boys and girls in the cages and

looked at him with misty eyes.
– I… have?
– No need for false modesty any longer, my dear. You know very well I've read your file. You showed that talent long before you even heard about the Abraxas Omega. Why do you think we recruited you in the first place?
She hesitated, one moment, two… before bursting, bursting with it all.
– I studied as a surgeon, she said, breathlessly. – My parents were both surgeons and they encouraged me to follow in their footsteps… and I did… not just the way they anticipated and hoped for… he he…
She crouched a bit, not bothering to hide her arousal to him anymore, as she looked at him, and at the slaves in the cages.
– I cut and cut, and the more I cut the more I liked it, loved it. They threw me in a deep, deep cage, and there I remained, suffering until you guys saved me.
She sent him a grateful look. She wanted to kiss him, but didn't dare.
– I made two boys fight once, she said solemnly, very matter of act. – In jealousy and rivalry, they went at each other's throats, as if they were mortal enemies. Eventually, when one of them showed himself to be the strongest, to be superior, he beat the loser to a pulp, making him bleed all over the floor. I gave myself to the winner, and we left the house in virtual ruins, and at that point I felt better than I had ever felt in my entire life.
– And it wasn't really the sex that turned you on, was it, now?
He looked at the writhing creatures in the cages, and she did, too, her lips dry as leaves.
– No, not just the sex, she said hoarsely.
– Fascinating, he pondered. – Fascinating.
He grabbed her hair and pushed her head brutally at the bars, forcing her to look closely at what happened inside the cages.
– Look at them, he commanded. – I mean, *look at them…* and tell me exactly what you feel.
Pain tore at her scalp. Her eyes remained huge and shiny.
– Excitement… joy, she gasped. – Heat…
He pulled her back up, and as she rubbed her head, whimpering, he slapped her on a cheek. She cried out loud. She fell and hit the floor hard.
– Now, how did you like that?
She fought her away back up, as the red mark from his hand slowly faded.
– I'm not crazy. She shook. – You know that.
– I know that, he said calmly. – Mental illness is a subjective state of

mind anyway.

– B-because… you're like t-that yourself? You feel like… I d-do?

– Certainly not, he arrogantly rejected her words. – I'm a scientist and you're just another interesting case file, another useful tool, that's all. One I can use to further my ambitions, my goal. The daring scientist won't be stopped by anything, and certainly not moral constraints. And he won't be ruled by crude passions and emotions. Intellectual curiosity is the guiding star of all rational humans.

He smiled, and that smile scared her more than anything. Gooseflesh erupted on her skin, spreading pleasantly all over the body.

– May I ask you something?

– Of course, she replied. – Feel free to ask me anything.

– What's your goal in life? Where do you see yourself in ten years?

– I don't know, she said dreamingly. – I've never really thought it through.

He slapped her again, harder this time.

– Here, she said instantly, out of breath. – Here, I'll always have everything I'll ever want.

She looked at him, with eyes suddenly sharp and skewed.

– And You? What's yours?

He looked downright strange then.

– Look at the trash in there, he said, touching her jaw, turning her head, and just like that he had regained control, ignoring her feeble attempt at it. – They do seem to enjoy what they're doing, don't they? Perhaps they are enjoying this, since pleasure is man's primal need.

And she looked, and she couldn't take her eyes off the writhing, gasping creatures.

He shrugged.

– But can you imagine what they're feeling inside? Over their pain, their utter hopelessness, how an electric needle and prolonged torture and numbing drugs fracture the mind? Can you?

His voice had remained dry and cold during their entire conversation. He grew, grew to an infinitely powerful giant in Sandra's eyes.

– You do remind me a bit of Glory, poor, ill-advised Glory, but you don't have her craven need of independence. You want to learn, want to learn beyond doubt the ways of the masters.

She stood there with half-closed, drowsy eyes, as if she was about to fall asleep.

– Do it, she whispered. – Please, teach me.

– Come, he bade her.

She followed him, eagerly, blindly across the room, through another door. And stopped. She realized that this was a torture chamber, one of the many onboard used to discipline the slaves.

– Undress! He said brusquely, very relaxed, as if he was describing the weather.

She wanted to protest, but she had already been taught, in hard ways the iron hard discipline in the ranks of the Thousand Feet, and obeyed in swift, fluid moves.

– You should have told me to strip, she grinned with shivering lips. – I'm quite the mean stripper.

She stood nude before him. He studied her completely indifferent. He didn't seem interested at all.

– I can see your hard-on, she said triumphantly, nervously. – You want me. I knew you would.

He grabbed her right arm and dragged her to the wall, to a set of chains he slapped around her wrists. He pushed a button on the wall, and the chains were pulled up, and her hands were raised above her head, high above, until she stood on her toes. She faced the wall and couldn't see him, and she didn't dare turn. Her nipples touched the bare wall, the cold wall. Terror gripped her. A tender hand rubbed her neck. She held her breath.

– And now for the mask, he informed her casually. – The mask we use to rob the slaves of their identity, their sense of worth.

She wanted to turn, protest, but he slapped her butt, and it hurt so much that tears jumped from her eyes. She had never before felt such pain.

The mask was pulled down her head, covering it completely to the neck. There was one tiny hole for the mouth, to breathe through, that was all. The tears wet the inside of the mask. The room turned silent, for one moment, two…

Then she heard a sound she recognized, a sound she knew too well, that of a whiplash hitting the floor.

The first lash hit her unprotected back. She cried out in protest. She wanted to scream to him, to call him names. But before she could do that, another lash hit her. She gasped, shaking her head. And another, and another.

And the screams began.

+++++++++++++++++

The day. It was quite different from the night, and also from the morning. The sun had risen high in the sky when Eric Carr woke up with Betty sleeping by his side. The light bathed her body and made her skin glow.

He had left without waking her. He needed time to think.
He hadn't seen her since then.
It was such a fine day. He whistled as he walked outside, on one of the wet lower decks. Curly clouds rested near the horizon. They had long since reached open sea. There was no land in sight anywhere, no matter where he directed his eyes. He smiled.
His feet finally steered him towards her cabin. He was hardly conscious of that fact until he saw the door in front of him. It was a quite common, nondescript door, a nondescript design. He knocked on it, knocked on wood, waited. There was no reply. He produced the key she had given him and unlocked the gate to her place. It felt strange to him, like an intrusion, but she had insisted he could visit «anytime he wanted». The cabin was quiet, empty. She wasn't here. He left, closing and locking the door behind him.
Half an hour later the restlessness got the better of him, and he actually started *looking* for her. He had walked around, enjoying the scenery, enjoyed a lot of it, when he suddenly, as he experienced it, got an irresistible urge to see her again. Half an hour after that he had still not found her, and he started to feel real impatience, so unlike him. He had been all over the ship, or at least he felt that he had been. Finally he pushed himself up on the sundeck, pushing aside a lot of people to get there. They shouted angrily at him. A few bruised male egos were even evidently tempted to pick a fight with him, but he looked at them and they were cordially discouraged.
There she was, and she took his breath away. She lay stretched out on deck on a thin mattress. He walked to her, and didn't say anything before he was almost there.
– Hi, sunbeam, he greeted her.
She turned, wearing a bra, loosely tied. If he had been a poet (which he wasn't), he would have described her black hair as a waterfall flowing down her back. His inner heat rose to a level far stronger than the shivering air on the outside.
– Hi, Eric, she said huskily. – Sooo nice to see you again.
– You, young lady, are almost too good to be true, he said.
– You, good, sir, say the nicest things…
She rose, supple and fluid, and embraced him, the touch of her body lingering on his.
– I knew you had to be up here, he joked. – I've been all over the rest of the ship looking for you.
– Such a sweet man, she whispered in his ear, before pulling back,

letting him look at her, admire her, as she posed for him, posed for his wandering eyes.

She lay down again on the mattress, constantly keeping her eyes on him, very coy.

– I need to apply more ointment. Will you do it for me, please? Will you… rub me?

He grinned and bent down, grabbing the bottle by her side. The fluid was so lukewarm that he hardly felt it on the skin of his palm. But he felt her skin as he begun rubbing it. Smooth, with hardly any resistance at all. Like water, like air, but tangible, real.

– There are quite a few supermodels here, he joked hoarsely. – But no one approaching your stature.

– And I've got something behind all the skin and lotion as well, she marveled.

– I like you, he laughed. – You're funny.

He started on her back, and worked his way from there. Even the bones hardly showed under the skin. He looked at the long row of beauties on the deck, the skinny tramps and swallowed hard while looking down at her.

– Under the bra as well, please, she told him.

She turned slightly and pulled the cloth slightly off her breasts, and two swelling nipples appeared. He knew she was turned on, saw it in her misty eyes, the small moves she made between moves. He kissed her neck. She sighed deeply and that small sound was like music to him. He didn't care about the looks the other passengers sent them, but kept rubbing her, rubbing her some more on one shoulder. She was a bit burned there. He stopped abruptly when she cried out in pain, and he remembered.

– I was a bit rough last night, he said.

– Don't worry about it, she said, looking solemnly at him. – It's okay. I'm not made of china or anything. I can take rough.

Before he could say more she once more transformed into the vamp, daring and self-conscious, teasing him with her smile, and her moves.

A few minutes later, when he had rubbed every little piece of skin she had, it was he who felt her hands on him. It was like resting on the beach and having the waves caress one's body, one's skin. He lay there with his eyes closed, and time and space disappeared. But she didn't. She was there, body and soul.

She finished his belly, the last piece of untouched skin on his body. He wanted to ask her if she had been trained as a Geisha or something, but he was halfway into sleep. She looked at him, a bit sad. He saw that and didn't understand it. She used her hands to keep her long hair away from her face and kissed him hungrily and softly on his lips. He felt the pressure of her lips, the soft, hardly noticeable caress, and the contempt he usually felt in such moments was muted, reduced to a hardly burning ember that didn't matter. He pulled her down and returned the kiss, and with an intensity not less than hers.

After a while she liberated herself gently from his grip, her hair mussed and the bra skewed.

– Aren't you the strong one, she grinned. – What did you use to do for a living, weightlifting?

– I wasn't always an office rat. He shrugged.

– I knew that.

She smacked him on the chest. He hardly felt it.

– It wasn't exactly weightlifting, he said, clearly more somber. – But it did keep me in shape.

– No matter, she said, giving him the eye, – I quite enjoy your hands on me…

Time just passed without notice. He certainly didn't notice it. The wind, the girl and the swollen lips dominated his entire perception.

She stood there, watching him, the enigmatic smile once more crossing her lips.

– I need to cool down, she said. – Let's have a bath.

– A bath. That won't cool us down much, now, will it?

– Silly you, she giggled. – The pool water is chilled. It's colder than on the Miami beaches.

She reached out a hand.

He grabbed it, without thought, without conscious sense. She laughed as she pulled him with her, out in the water.

– First hot bun over is a toad, she shouted.

It was a huge pool. Most people stayed on this side of it and not towards the bow, where the wind was blowing. The two of them threw themselves out in the boiling water. Eric sat on the edge and waited for her when she pulled herself up beside him. She slapped him on the cheek.

– You're a toad! She declared.

– I'm not a hot bun, he stated categorically.

They laughed again, embraced each other.

– I am your dream woman, am I not, Eric? I'm funny, but not silly. I'm solemn, but not serious. You're very pleased with me, are you not?

He nodded, hardly able to move his head. She put her head on his shoulder, shaking a bit.

– I'm glad.

The wind was blowing. Just now they were alone out here, in the wind.

– Can I ask you a question? She whispered in his ear.

– Of course you can. You don't have to ask me that, you know.

– Have you been a soldier?

She put a hand over his mouth, keeping him from speaking out, speaking out loud. For the first time that day she met his eyes without looking away, and it was as if she stared deep into him, deep into his caves.

– You were in Vietnam, weren't you? Special Forces, perhaps?

– Special Forces, he confirmed, not certain how he wanted to react to her inquiry, to her astuteness.

– And you were good, she whispered. – You are good, moving like a panther at night, a tiger during the day.

She surprised him again. Not because she was clever. He knew that. But because she told him things about himself he hadn't thought about or hadn't allowed himself to consider.

He started talking. After having looked away for a moment or two, he finally turned back to her, turned back to himself. Finally, he allowed himself to think.

– We were a bunch of students at the university tearing up our draft notices. We did it as a protest against the war. But when push came to shove, when the time came for us to stand up for our beliefs… we failed. Courage failed us. At least something made us back out, made us relent. We were drafted against our will, but we should have fought harder, fought with everything we possessed. Many ran off to Canada or various mountains, but we didn't. We feared the consequences too much, feared the reaction of friends and family and society, feared public condemnation. When time came for us to fight, to stand up for ourselves… we didn't.

She touched the skin below his eyes with a fingertip. He realized astonished that there was a tear there.

– Then, with impeccable logic, since we were going anyway, we thought we could just as well go all the way, and we enrolled in the special training programs. We were lost anyway, or so we thought. We didn't think we could fall any further. Youthful naiveté, I guess. From our platoon, replenished with «fresh meat» several times only six emerged from the insanity somewhat alive, mental and physical wrecks, injured beyond quick repair, all discharged well before Nixon made his «honorable peace». Two of us remained cripples. The four, including me, who returned somewhat whole, had learned something there in the moist jungle… I guess. In training we learned eighty-four… or is that eighty-five… ways to kill another human being, and I know I used every single one of them, and even a few that weren't in the manual. We weren't taught to be warriors, hardly even soldiers, but killing machines. They pushed our buttons, and we killed, killed wantonly, without remorse or thought.

He hadn't spoken up, hadn't raised his voice once during the long speech. She kissed him softly, comforting him as skillfully as she did everything. He wanted to tell her, tell her in no uncertain terms that he didn't need coddling, but then he discovered to his amazement that he stood there shaking, shaking violently.

– You thought all this was behind you, didn't you? But it never goes away, does it, now? It stays with you forever, the hardship, the fear, the bitterness. Even the bitterness is still there.

– They broke all our illusions about life. He choked. – They made useful citizens of us. None of us returned to the radical groups we had once been a part of. We just… caved in, gave up.

– I'm so sorry, she said.

– Don't be, he said curtly, pulling himself together, somehow. – You were just a child.

– I was never a child, she corrected him, and it would seem that she was kidding, but he didn't think she was.

He touched her cheek, tenderly, surprisingly tenderly. The skin was dry, the water from the pool gone in an instant in the hot, hot wind. But the skin was still moist, and cold, ice-cold. Her eyes burned, as if in fever.

– Is something wrong? He said, attempting to keep his voice light.

– No, Eric. She smiled, smiled enticingly to him. – Nothing is wrong. Everything is right, so very right.

– Something is wrong, he insisted. – I'm a trained observer. I can see such things.

She kissed him, a deep, sultry kiss. He almost stopped breathing.

– I must go, she said. – My friends are waiting for me. We're going to have dinner together, and turn the restaurant upside down. Have patience with me, Eric, *please*.

Upbeat, downbeat simultaneously. He shook his head, in wonder, in apprehension.

He nodded, assuring her of his patience, his commitment, impatiently. He wanted to shake her. It was almost visible in his body language, his veneer. He felt so helpless. She gave him a wet kiss on his cheek.

– I need the soldier, or rather *the warrior,* even the murderer, Eric. We all do!

She touched her collar, fingered with it nervously.

– Eric, she choked. – My name is Betty Morgan. Remember it. Never forget it.

And then she was gone, gone like a ghost in a dark castle. The sun was gone. The sky turned dark.

She walked along the pool, correcting her bra a bit, subconsciously posing. It was obviously second nature to her. She looked like a princess, being looked at by her subjects. She was supposed to be looked at.

Before she left the sun deck she stopped and blew a kiss back to Eric. He returned an encouraging smile.

Poor Eric, she thought, not knowing what she thought.

She stumbled down the stairs, the outer stairs, holding on to the rail for dear life, looking down at the sea, the tempting and contemptible sea.

– Fly, she sang, she hummed. – The bird can fly, fly in fire, fly in shadow.

And it comforted her. It scared her.

Fly
The bird can fly
Fly in fire, fly in shadow
It doesn't need to fear anything
Except perhaps death
The walking death
I see a valley
A circle of fire and shadow
And I dance in its shade
On the edge of its abyss

With her hand pressed at her mouth, dizzy with the sudden nausea, she stumbled out of the sun, into the dark corridor, down the dark hallway, to a door marked LADIES.

The door was open. Or she opened it, she couldn't tell, couldn't remember. The room was small. She felt even worse. The mirror stared back at her, the sick girl. She ran to the closest cubicle. Almost before her knees touched the floor the vomit flowed from her mouth. She threw up endlessly, until there was nothing but green slime left, until her skin was nothing but sweat and acid and fire. She half lay, half sat, her back to the wall, staring at nothing with eyes dull and lifeless.

She heard steps, but there was no visible reaction in her to it. A man entered the toilet. She recognized Master Croy-don. He bent down and touched her wet forehead. It was red hot.

– What happened? He demanded.

She looked up at him with watery eyes.

– I did something bad, Master.

– I know that, he said brusquely. – What was it?

– I don't know, Master. I'm sorry, please Master. I was supposed to meet someone, but I don't know if I did. Please punish me, Master. Please!

– Memory loss, huh? You know you're supposed to seek out a master and report before the vomiting. It's a symptom of your disobedience, a need, a drive coming to you every time you've been bad.

– Yes, Master, she replied, absolutely miserable.

– And if you vomit before reporting you lose everything you've done that day.

He looked sternly down on the shaking creature.

– However, I guess your attack came so sudden that you had to choose between running for the toilet, or embarrass us in front of our guests. Rise, slave! I release you from your woes, from your burden, rise, you eager girl.

It was as if a… change came over the girl that instant, as if the words gave her power, power over limbs, at least. She looked better. Life returned to her eyes. He didn't help her up. He didn't need to. She rose fairly easily on her own, and even if the shaking didn't stop immediately and she was still unsteady on her feet, she recovered literally before his eyes. He saw how she began posing for him, the effect of the smothering sensuality only marginally reduced by the vomit covering her hair and body.

– I want you, he said. – Come with me!

The happy, eager smile transformed her face, almost shockingly, even to him, who had known what to expect.

There was a sound. The sound of the door to the toilet opening. A rather tall wrinkled old lady entered the room.

– Oh, I'm sorry. I must have chosen the wrong door. I get so easily distracted these days, you see.

– You did not, Miss Dalhart. He bowed. – It is I who should be apologizing. Betty, here, had some problems I had to help her with. She's fine now.

The woman looked at the girl, at the cubicle and around the room, the vomit on her and that covering the room.

– I got seasick, Miss Dalhart, Betty explained, with a sweet smile. – That isn't unusual, but this one was a doozy, and struck like lightning from a blue sky.

– You don't look so good, the woman said, worry visible in her eyes. –

Can I do anything to help, my dear?

– No, thanks, Miss Dalhart. The girl sent her a grateful smile. – That's very kind of you, but it isn't necessary. I had forgotten to take my pills, but I just did, and I feel better already. I'm fine now, honest.

She almost put her thumb in her mouth as it touched her lips, but a cautious glance from Croy-don stopped her.

– Our physician should still take a look at you, Croy-don said. – Come with me, please.

– Yes, Ma… A moment her forehead wrinkled in confusion, before she brightened, and once more turned into an energetic and well-balanced young woman. – Sure, Tim, lead on.

She smiled some more, as Miss Dalhart looked skeptically at her.

– I know the names of all employees onboard, she grinned. – My father owns shares in the cruise line.

The lady pulled some paper towels from the wall, and dried the worst of the vomit off Betty's skin and bikini, combed her hair with her hands, quickly, efficiently, in ways that more than suggested a practiced ease.

– Thank you again, Miss Dalhart, Betty said. – I guess I'm still a little woozy. I think I'll go to my cabin and lay down for a while.

– Call me Rachel, my dear. I think that's a very good idea.

The two left the toilet, left Miss Dalhart. The stink of vomit was still on Betty, but once released from the horrible room, she felt better. She smiled to her companion, smiled brightly. The doll face smiled to him.

– Is everything all right, Master? Betty is good, isn't she? Isn't Betty good?

– Betty is very good. He nodded. – And soon she will be even better.

The doll face lit up. With a happy sigh the child's eyes turned moist, and she put her thumb in her mouth. He patted her on her cheek, comforted her. After a quick look around he grabbed her hand and led her further down the hallway.

– And if Betty is very good, Master will take very good care of her, very good care indeed.

++++++++++++

The dark-haired woman walked with her head held high. Her hair was recently washed and done. Her make up was as thoroughly applied as it had been earlier in the day and she wore the same sense of pride and confidence. The black dress was like glued to the supple, female form. She hummed a strange melody, one that stirred emotions, both in herself and the people she passed on her way.

She stopped in front of a door, a specific cabin. For a while, a little while she stood there listening. She smiled in expectation when she heard sounds from within. After a brief hesitation, after several glances both up and down the corridor, she opened the unlocked door and slipped inside. She locked the door behind her, quickly, feverishly. One who had a hair just as black as herself sat on the edge of the bed, staring at her.

– Ted…

Betty rushed to him, and they took each other's hands. He pulled her to him, and she kissed him on the cheek.

– I didn't think you would come today either.

– I came, she said unhappily.

He pulled her down beside him. She yelped happily. They embraced, smelled and tasted and sensed the other.

– We won't be disturbed? He wondered hesitatingly, fearfully. – He who occupies this cabin won't come and discover us… expose us?

– He's in the bar, drinking as usual. She dismissed the thought. – He just comes here to fuck Vernie, and that's all. He hardly even sleeps here.

Fear was always present inside them. Fear was the key.

It faded only slowly, painfully, as they turned to each other, as they stared deeply into each other's eyes.

They sat still for a long time, doing nothing but enjoying the closeness of the other. She hummed the melody. It just came to her, from somewhere within. It gave peace, and evoked unrest and discord and loss, longing and need.

– I've heard that one before, he said. – Heard you hum it, heard you sing it.

– It's an old song, she said thoughtfully. – One I heard as a child, heard an old lady hum. I can't… for the life of me remember where. Every time I try to remember it just slips away from me, every time I attempt to work my way around it, it just slips away like water, like dust.

She grabbed his hands, startled.

– We remember so little, she said in despair.

– We remember that we don't remember, he said, as he strived to speak, as he strived to think. – Surely the Masters didn't want that.

– Surely they don't, she replied dully.

Their language, and the way they spoke it was simplistic, childlike. They had difficulties expressing themselves, expressing anything beyond the programming.

Pain came to them. They crouched and began sweating, and after just a few seconds their bodies stank of it.

They embraced again. She kissed him on his neck, and he responded.

She released a low, satisfied sound and moved eagerly in his arms. They tumbled over on the bed. Slowly, and with happy, expectant smiles they began fondling each other, with lazy, but also clearly curious moves. He sniffed the scent of her hair. She scratched his chest hair with her jaw.

– I feel you, he said mechanically. – I…

She pushed her palm at his lips, stopped the hand moving down to her belly, His hands made concentric circles in the air, those he was supposed to make on her skin. She pulled away from him, jumped out of the bed. Deeply wounded he choked:

– Why?

– You, we were about to slip into the Program, the Master's… design for us, she said empathically, on the verge of crying.

He stared at her, slow and dull understanding sort of brightening his features, fighting with the imposed stupidity for supremacy.

– I'm sorry, he said, his head whirring back and forth, back and forth.

– No! She was there with him in an instant. – Don't be sorry. You're trying, struggling. You should be proud, not ashamed.

She kissed his brow, embracing his head, swallowing hard, a ball stuck in her throat. She had trouble speaking.

– Don't speak the words we're supposed to say. Don't touch where we're supposed to touch. And we will be okay.

– Okay…

He echoed her word, her echo.

And any word was empty, was hollow, as if they hadn't really spoken them, as if they were nothing but tape-recorders passively repeating the words and actions of others.

He pulled her cautiously down again, his face a study in concentration, in focusing.

– I remember, she giggled. – You're so very intense, so astute, as if you notice everything in a room, and the people there.

– I looked at you, he said, – when you entered a room, and you were like a princess taking pity on us lowly mortals.

They were both tense at first, but finally, when they snuggled tight and whispered confidently to each other, it was like they had always done it, like small children with their secrets.

In the soft confines of the bed, in the roar from the waves, the open sea reaching them through the open window, they explored and followed every notion and fancy striking them.

– Cloth is in the way, he said, when removing the upper parts of her dress, exposing her breasts.

– Your cloth is too small, she giggled, upon discovering the bulge on his pants.
– Your fruits taste lovely…
– Do it more, she breathed. – It feels so good.
They touched and sensed each other, without lust, really, but with an intense desire to once more think and live. The two youths exchanged thoughts and moods with eyes suddenly crystal clear.
– Not anymore yet. She shook her head. – I'm… confused. We must… talk.
– Yes… talk, Ted nodded.
– He who stays here. Isn't he… isn't he… She curled hands into fists. – Help me, I can't…
– He's a writer, Ted offered.
– He's a writer. Betty brightened. – For a newspaper. He's a… journalist.
Exhausted she closed her eyes and pulled closer to him.
– He is, Ted nodded. – Journa-list.
– The Masters don't want us to talk to journalists, unless we're assigned to them. Vernie is assigned to… to… Bene-dict, like I'm assigned to Carr, like you're assigned to the duchess, but she isn't writing anything, is she?
– She's a classy whore, Ted grinned, – providing window-dressing for her husband, the duke. He isn't interested in her body, much. When it comes to bodies, I'm told he has quite different tastes.
They danced on the floor, turned slowly arms around shoulders and backs, danced to her hum, to her song. He joined in, hesitatingly, apprehensively. A sense of wonder lit his eyes, and that in turn lit hers.
– You know it, she whispered, and this time it was truly a whisper. – You know it by *heart*. Somehow… I knew you would.
And at that same moment, they both gasped in pain, and fell to the floor, fell to the soft carpet and hit it hard. They could hardly move, hardly do anything but holding on to the other.
– I hurt, she whimpered.
– I hurt, too.
– Help me… She sniffed and suffered.
– But… how? I can't…
Then he got a sudden inspiration, and it felt horrible.
– Who are we?
– That's easy, she said gratefully. – You're Ted and I'm Betty.
He felt the heat from her joy, the cold from her fear. An experience he couldn't remember, other than a dim recollection of another world, another life. He grabbed astonished her black mane, stared at it.

– I'm confused, he said. – Your hair… used to be red.
– What are you talking about, Ted? She laughed scornfully, contemptuously. – My hair has never been red.
He stared shocked at her, as he grabbed her hair tighter, as he bit in it, licked it, as the color didn't change. After a momentary hesitation he lifted her dress, exposed her groin. More black hair appeared.
– This hair was also red… before.
– Yes, she nodded. – Red… Before.
– You remember?
– Yes, Ted, I'm sorry, it was the Program. It tells us what to say and what to do, and we say it, we do it. Sometimes I think everything is the program, and that we're not real, not real at all, that there has never been any «before», that it's just something the Masters place inside us, to taunt us, to test us, test our loyalty, and I know I deserve it, that I'm not loyal, obedient and pleasing, that I'm disloyal and vile.
She put her thumb in her mouth and started sucking on it, sucking hard. Spittle flowed down her jaw, and she locked eyes with Ted. He blinked.
– That's not you speaking, he said helplessly. – That's the Masters speaking.
– What else is there? She cooed. – Let's not speak of such matters anymore. It hurts.
– H-hurts, he echoed horrified, his eyes turning as opaque as hers.
– Make me feel good, she whispered seductively. – Let the Program work. Take me, make me feel good.
For the first time that day she kissed him on the lips. A long, sultry and desperate kiss. He returned it, though he did try to remove her hand from his chest.
– Not there. You didn't want to earlier.
– I'm just a silly girl, a silly, silly slave. I think, I hurt. I want to forget everything unpleasant and uncomfortable.
His eyes glossed over.
– I'm just a silly boy, a silly slave, he intoned, mindlessly repeating her words.
And when she once again put her soft hand on his chest he didn't resist. His hand moved to her belly, and the moment he touched it she moaned in joy. Their bodies moved. They reacted to stimuli, just like robots. Faces writhed in joyless smiles. All movements turned automatic, like that of puppets.
They had resisted for a while, in vain. The Program ruled them, to the point of blocking everything else. Imposed sensibilities were used to keep

them in check. Every time an independent thought was born, a number of old, accepted truths attacked it, crushing any notion of a new birth.
They coupled in a way, heat rising, sounds rising, thought fading, every move closely indoctrinated and machinated.
And it was nothing there, nothing of the human beings they had attempted to be.
+++++++++++
– I knew it. Eric Carr spoke, with a voice filled and fueled with sarcasm. – Less than twenty-four hours after departure, and I «bump» into you.
– You should try the salmon, Eric, the other, Andrew Benedict mused. – I recommend it wholeheartedly.
They dined in Rosomovat, one of the more exclusive restaurants on board. They were relatively early. There weren't that many people here yet, and they found a certain peace there.
Carr looked in contempt down at his plate. Its content resembled that of one giant spice heap, in his opinion.
– Don't even go there, he warned the other man. – You know I don't particularly enjoy what you enjoy, whatever that is.
– It hasn't always been like this, Benedict mused some more, very low-keyed, fingering nervously with the newspaper on the table in front of him. – Once we liked the same things and shared the same thoughts.
Benedict resembled even more than usual a walking corpse, even though he had just been returning from the bar, from having his afternoon drinks, and he actually had some color in his cheeks.
– Don't blame me for that, Carr replied dryly. – You're the one who's stuck in the mud. By the way, have you started reading papers again?
Benedict looked downright weird then, at least for a brief moment.
– Not all of us confuse basic altruism with mud, you know, Benedict pointed out, a bit sharper, now. – Mud, in my vocabulary, defined in human terms is more people working for someone earning money on other's misfortune.
Eric rose abruptly.
– Saint Andrew, he declaimed. – Why don't we all kneel and kiss your feet?
People in the restaurant turned and stared, before turning their back, turning their back to it all.
– I think I should go, Carr said. – This conversation ends the way all our recent attempts have done. No surprise there.
Benedict had risen, too, risen in anger, but he calmed down fairly fast, expressing his regret.

– I didn't mean to be excited or to offend you. Please sit. What I have to say won't take long.
He sounded like he was almost pleading, there, at the end.
– You're *asking* me to sit down, instead of *telling* me? That's a new one. It certainly doesn't *sound* like an introduction to one of your morality speeches.
Carr laughed out loud and sat back down. He began eating again, just for spite, clearly making this clear to his friend.
Benedict looked a bit aghast. Or that was one interpretation of it.
– I've quit working as an investigative reporter, he admitted.
And Carr did react strongly to that. He put his face in careful layers of calm.
– That is certainly a surprise, he admitted.
– One month ago I was hired by Stuart «Hammer» Tremblay to find his son, Robert. You do recall that case, I trust?
Carr nodded, not caring about the sarcasm this time, but not really caring either. But he was interested, in spite of himself. The fact that Benedict was interested made him interested.
– I remember, he said, slightly hoarse. – I remember a series of flashing headlines that dominated the media for a while. Then, as things go, things calmed down, and people forgot… They always forget.
The bitterness in his voice surprised him as well. He had thought he had put all that behind him.
– I don't know why Tremblay chose me, Benedict continued. – Perhaps for my skill as an investigative reporter, perhaps not. But I thought about his offer for a while, and found it more and more irresistible, no matter what his motivation was. Perhaps he has sent out an army of private investigators in a desperate hope that someone, somewhere would come up with something. No one else has, that's for sure. As you rightly pointed out the newspapers and television had stopped reporting about the case. None of the disappeared kids have turned up, and logic suggests that our truth-seeking media should continue digging because of that fact… but they haven't. There's nothing to write about anymore, is there? Nothing to make people buy the paper, nothing to hold on to their short-span attention. There's no money in it anymore.
Carr was distracted. From the corner of his eye, he saw Betty and Ted sit down by a table by the entrance, but he still found himself sitting there nodding. He felt deep, unfamiliar stirrings within himself, and found himself entrenched by Benedict's story. It had been curiosity at first, over the fact that Benedict told it, that his *old* friend… Carr smiled bitterly…

had made this drastic change to his life.

– I didn't really know where to start, so I started with the basics, with information gathering, with what was public knowledge.

Before Betty and Ted had managed to sit down properly a man, an oriental approached them. Betty rose and followed him out of the restaurant. Eric looked, by a coincidence, at the boy's face just then. Never before had he seen a face expressing so much despair. It resembled that of a child, so incredibly naked.

Eric… heard something in Andy's voice, a longing, something unexpected, something new and old, and it made something stir within him as well.

– I initially saw my task as rather hopeless, and I told Tremblay that much, but he insisted that I continue, and insisted paying me as well, and I couldn't say no to that, I just couldn't. The police had had no interest in my previous try-outs as a «private investigator», but this case was way different. Here, the state police was in, the FBI, CIA, Interpol… and… they had yet to turn up anything of consequence. So much had happened, so many small things painting the picture. And a few days later the official investigation was halted, was *scrapped*. And I felt the first smell of rot, of something fishy, of a horror, an excitement I hadn't felt for years, Eric. As I traveled to Denver, to Leadville, I found very few key people in the matter still available. Peter Clarke, the lead investigator had disappeared. Jeff McCabe, former Chief of Denver Police Department had left town. Mark Stewart, a Lieutenant, who had investigated a case involving several of the disappeared youths, was nowhere to be seen. Neither was his wife, for God's sake. And these are merely very few of the suspicious facts pertaining to this.

Eric felt it, felt the excitement of the bloodhound inside, felt the horror.

– So, what do you think? Benedict asked, after a longer break.

– I know I should have brought my tape-recorder, that's for sure, Carr said dryly. – So, Colorado is pretty far away. How did you end up here?

– Many reasons… Benedict hesitated a bit before continuing. – One is the fact that the Vice Sheriff of Leadville sits three tables to our right. He quit his job and bought a ticket here. I tracked him down. It wasn't hard, really.

Carr didn't turn his head, but looked to the side anyway, to a table close to the round stage. He saw a huge, broad-shouldered guy smoking a stinking cigar and digesting a large steak. The silver blonde dancer accompanied him, and they looked very close, a scene strangely worrying to Eric.

– I know what you think about this. Benedict kept talking hesitatingly. – About… conspiracy theories. I confess I have no proof, that I'm not totally convinced myself, but I have enough, far more than a feeling, to justify my suspicions.

He pushed his newspaper across the table. Carr looked at him as if he had taken a leave of his senses. He accepted the paper, touched it… and found that it was far thicker than it should have been.

– See you around, Eric.

– Let's have one thing clear, Carr said, letting out more of his ongoing sense of irritation against the other man. – We're not on a first name mode.

Benedict was off. With a weird smile he rose and left the table.

Carr was freezing where he sat in his chair. So much was broken. So much was lost. He was almost in tears and sat there shaking his head, shaking it hard. He looked in the boy's direction to see if Betty had returned. She hadn't. The dark-haired boy left the table and met another woman. A blonde, a slightly chubby woman had joined him. He seemed to be on good terms with her as well. Carr knew her, knew of Ilse, the Duchess of Brandenburg. She was traveling with her husband, the Duke, an international Tycoon with a number of successful ongoing ventures across the world. Carr knew a lot about them, as it was his job to know such things. He knew, for instance that they didn't share a cabin, but had one each, half the ship away from each other. It was what was called «a suitable arrangement» in their circles.

He rose, grabbed the newspaper as a kind of afterthought, and left the table. The ship rocked a little. He looked outside. The sky was about to turn dark, the winds were picking up. He had heard a storm was on its way, a true storm, not the brush they had had with it this morning, the one he had slept through. The ship rocked some more. Glasses started sliding on tables. People almost fell over. Those already drunk did fall. He sat in the bar for a while, sipping a soda, watching the dark boy and the duchess, but everything looked sickeningly proper, and he finally left in frustration. No big scoop there. Not yet. But there would be. He felt certain of that, and it would bring a fat addition to his already fat bank account. He just had to be patient, and be there when Ilse Von Brandenburg deemed it safe to play with her young stud.

People stumbled through the hallways as nature kicked up the storm and ever-larger waves started to rock the boat, rock it a lot. He half expected, half hoped to meet Betty, but he didn't, even though he took the scenic route to his cabin. It was quiet in there, both before and after he had locked himself in. He dropped down on the bed, sat there for a while… looking at the newspaper in his hand. The gale outside gained momentum. He rose abruptly and walked to his suitcase. After a brief hesitation he threw the newspaper, and its hidden content on top of his clothes and closed the top. Then he grabbed his bag and camera on the table and rushed out of the cabin, back to his chores, back to the Duchess and her boy.

+++

Nobody got to see the sunset that day, and not the sunrise the next morning either. The storm ravaged the Atlantic Ocean and all ships traveling on it. Tall waves struck the ship, and in spite of those powerful stabilizers, the proud seafarer rocked violently, so violently that many passengers stayed in their cabin and even in their beds. Eric Carr had bad dreams. In one of them he saw Betty and the dark boy balance on the rail by the bow. Their eyes glowed in red and green fire, and they were laughing ecstatically. And worst of all, he couldn't tell whether or not he was truly dreaming. He saw shadows walk the hallways of the ship, not certain if they looked more like ghosts than human beings. The ship went up and down waves in a constant rollercoaster ride, seen from a lookout point somewhere outside or above like a tiny toy, at nature's ruthless mercy.

The storm continued the entire Thursday, and one more sunset was lost. Continued through the night to the next morning, where early birds could at least tell themselves they were able to glimpse the bright line of light in the horizon, and no longer were overwhelmed by the incessant gray. Only somewhere during the afternoon one could say with certainty that it had stopped raining and blowing. People appeared on the upper deck, slowly filling it, some fresh as birds, others considerably less so.

Eric Carr took pictures of the Duchess and the dark boy at a fair distance. The sea and sky behind them were still a single soup of whirls and waves. He blinked, and what he saw then was Betty's green eyes. His finger snapped a couple more pictures before he returned the camera to its bag and moved closer. He didn't see Betty anywhere.

The boy stood by the rail. The Duchess a safer distance away. Eric spotted his eyes, his empty eyes, staring into the vast emptiness out there.

– It's both charming and alluring, scary and terrifying, Ilse Von Brandenburg said.

It had turned cold. The wind was cold. Carr was still sweating, a cold trickle from every pore on his body. White dots drifted along the ship. They resembled cotton on a Christmas tree. Aphrodite's lanterns were only visible as indistinct bulbs of light. They could be condemned souls restlessly seeking peace.

– A sensitive remark from the Duchess of Brandenburg, the boy said lightly. – That's new.

– It's not. Ilse struck him. – You're cruel.

The Duke stood a distance away, engaging in a conversation with four other men of good breeding, Englishmen as Carr heard it.

– Friday already, the Duke exclaimed sourly. – Two days of the cruise wasted.

The chaps played golf… sort of. They hit the little white balls and sent them off into the mist and the sea. It seemed they had an inexhaustible supply to work with.

Carr took the picture exactly the moment the Duke struck the ball, as he looked his most ridiculous. Carr giggled aloud, unable to help himself, inevitably drawing attention to himself and his works. The Duke scowled at him. Carr grinned and waved, in a very royal, very noble way.

– Nice shot there, Eric, my boy. Bremner, the «representative» for *Images* commented. – I believe I was a moment too late to catch it.

– You know what they say, Lars. Carr grinned even wider. – A good photographer carries his camera with him everywhere. In the john, in bed, when having sex… wherever it happens. If he happens to have surgery he never let go of his one, true love.

– Spoken like a man with a true love for his work, the other one nodded ironically.

Carr wasn't surprised that Bremner didn't take the jibe as a personal insult. There was no love lost between the a-list of international society reporters, but there was no personal enmity either.

– There's nothing, Carr mumbled.

Bremner had left, and didn't hear him.

– The sea is probably down there, somewhere, the dark boy said.

He didn't even seem to see or even acknowledge the older woman standing by his side for a while. She nipped him in the arm, annoyed, impatiently, to get his attention. He looked at her, as if through walls of mist. Eric saw her shiver, visibly shiver. He couldn't fault her for that, shivering a bit himself.

– There's something here. He spoke into the microphone hidden in his pocket. – Something hidden, and it's strange and interesting beyond words.

– Let's go inside, she insisted. – It isn't getting any warmer out here.

– I thought you liked *nacht und nebel,* the boy said ironically, pointedly.

He shrugged and they walked inside. Carr followed on their heels, not bothering to even hide his intentions. But inside, inside the velvet bright light of the hallway, the shadows where the couple sought to be alone, he held back. There wouldn't be anything to report if the duchess spotted him in here, he knew that. She was far less discreet than her Duke, but not stupid. The Von Brandenburgs usually had flings on trips like this, even a quick succession of them. And it was even public knowledge. They didn't bother to hide it. Even in their circles the seventies offered a certain sexual freedom.

But they didn't want disclosure. Not the absolute, irretrievable version of it.

They sought the depth, the dark depths of the smaller dance hall, where no others visited this time of the day, and especially not today, where the scent of vomit still lingered in the air everywhere.

There was no way Eric could take any viable photos in here, and the snotty Duchess knew that. But he stood hidden behind a corner, pointing his directional microphone at the two in there. The microphone was a technological wonder, enabling him to hear far better than through natural means.

– Jesus, she exclaimed. – I swear this entire wreck is one, giant ghost ship.

– Don't shit me, Duchess. I know you well enough to know that you're thrilled by such little horrors.

– Sweet Ted says he knows me, and still he calls me Duchess. What's wrong with this picture?

– I know everybody should know their *place* in life…

Ted… Carr repeated the name, formed it with his lips. His voice seemed so… open, he thought, so… full of life… just like… just like Betty's.

Carr pushed the microphone a bit closer to the corner, as he strived to see better, to get more than the occasional glimpse of them, in there, in the shadows, inevitable anticipation rising in him, from more sources than one. He felt… excitement building, beyond the moment, clearly beyond petty concerns, and it felt strange and terrifying.

– I don't know what to do with you, she laughed. – You're completely… amoral.

– And you like it. In fact you just *love* it.

His right hand slipped down from her shoulder and stopped by a breast. Carr saw it, in glimpses, in shades of gray. She wanted to say something, but it merely came out as a weak moan. Her arms seemed to move of their own volition and embrace the dark boy. He was much younger than her.

The Duchess was in her early thirties, but looking at them, she looked like the girl.

– Stop, she protested. – It isn't… proper.

There was a dark laughter, and then was heard something easily identified as a slap, a slap in the face, a male hand, hitting a woman's face. Carr imagined he saw it, in a flash, a flash of shadow.

Ted pushed her at the wall, the soft velvet carpet covering the wall. He pushed himself at her, kissing her greedily at her lips. When he released her, briefly, later, she was breathing hard. She stared at him, didn't take her eyes off him.

– It's eerie. Her usual so uppity, patronizing manner was gone, now. – You're exactly like I want you to be, like in a… a dream, a lucid dream, where you can decide yourself what happens.

– So, the spoiled missus has realized she liked to be dominated, huh? He said sarcastically. – The Duchess shall receive her just reward.

– No one even dares say no to me, she cried out passionately. – You don't know how that is, how it is when everybody is eagerly jumping through your hoop.

– So, you're complaining that people are too obedient. That's new…

Carr saw, somehow the tape turn in the recorder. He stood there with his mouth open, hardly able to trust his great, beyond great fortune. The fucking shit of an adolescent had opened up the Duchess, the experienced woman, to the breaking point, gutted her like a pig, and all in a matter of a few minutes.

– Who are you? She whispered. Carr imagined she whispered, anyway. – Tell me how you can do this to me, do this so easily.

– Hush. He put a finger on her lips. – Correct me if I am wrong, but we agreed we shouldn't talk about ourselves, right?

– That was stupid, she pouted. – I want to know. I want to know everything about you.

– Careful, now, my Duchess. You know how they used to treat people breaking promises in the old days, don't you.

She gasped.

– You're joking. Surely, you're joking.

He assaulted her again. Carr exposed his own fangs, subconsciously. He sensed their sharp points.

Time passed. Seconds passed. Wheels turned and spun, spun faster.

Ilse Von Brandenburg gasped continuously, now, her desire awakened to the point of no return. She didn't resist anymore, but surrendered to the need, surrendered completely, more and more for every time Ted touched her intimately.

– Yes, she gasped, hardly aware of what she said. – YES! But not here. In the cabin. In bed. PLEASE!

He let go of her, grinning, grinning wolfishly. Ice and fire kept assaulting her.

– That's okay, little girl, I kinda prefer the bed myself.

She sniffed, kissing him in gratitude, clearly both relieved and disappointed she could still reason with him.

Eric pulled further into the darkness as the two passed him. As they slipped by him, and a few seconds later he slipped after them. The cabin. Damn. But not unexpected. Not unexpected at all. Damn!

And then Eric Carr sensed something… again. There was… movement. He was breathing, and the jungle, the shadows breathed around him. And sweat poured from his wide-open pores. He stepped into the light, and he experienced it as if his body was bathed in brightness.

A creature, a tall woman, whose face was hidden, stopped in front of the two people ahead, stopped in front of Ted, practically ignoring Ilse Von Brandenburg.

– *Who are you? Do you know who you are?*

Her voice was hoarse, deep, but still that of a woman. The face was hidden, even though Eric looked right at her.

And in a flash, she was gone.

Ted didn't seem to react, to react in any way, which of course was a reaction, a very strong reaction. Eric knew of such matters.

– What's the matter, honey? Ilse wondered.

– The oyster, Ted finally said. – That fucking oyster.

– The oyster? Ilse said nonplussed. – Ted, what *is* going on here? Did you know that woman?

– I've never seen her before in my entire life, Ted replied. – Will you excuse me for a few minutes, my dear?

– Of course, she responded automatically, drawing on her teaching in etiquette.

The boy rushed off. Carr rushed off after him, not caring if the Duchess saw him. He turned the corner just a few seconds after the boy, but he was already turning the next one. Carr spotted him just as he disappeared into a toilet. Ted had reached a cubicle, and was about to close the door when Carr caught up with him.

– Excuse me for a second. Carr panted. – Can I ask you a question?

The staring black jewels made him uncomfortable.

– Do you know… do you know where Betty is? I haven't seen her for

almost two days. Is she seasick… or has she eaten bad oysters as well?
– I don't know… where she is.
The boy's fresh color had suddenly turned pale as death. Carr smelled his sour sweat.
– You don't look so good yourself. Are you okay?
– I'm okay.
– Who was that woman? Did you know her? What was she talking about?
Eric felt as if he was running on autopilot, and suddenly he feared the moment the autopilot was turned off, and manual flight resumed.
– I don't know her.
Ted swayed and would have fallen, if Carr hadn't caught him in time.
– Listen, you don't really look so hot. Perhaps, the ship's doctor should take a look at you…
– NO!
The boy tore himself loose, with one strong pull. His hand hit the cubicle wall with a loud crack.
That should have been warning good enough for Eric Carr, the experienced observer, but he was so jacked up that he hardly was able to think.
– Don't be silly. You look like you will faint any time.
Carr grabbed him again, impatiently, patronizingly.
– Let… GO OF ME!
Carr turned towards him with the impatience clearly visible in his face.
Ted pushed four stiff fingers into his abdomen. The attack caught him completely by surprise. He gasped and collapsed on the spot. And while Eric was on his way to the floor, Ted hit him in the neck, a hard-edged strike completely pacifying him. He hit the floor hard, and he still didn't feel any surprise. It dawned on him in a haze of pain and disorientation.
He was on his back. The dark creature hovered above him, and when Ted spoke the sound was like thunder in his ears.
– Betty-doesn't-belong-to-you. And she never *will!*
Carr registered dimly that he was kicked in the belly and the head. Every time he was hit it hurt ever more… to a point. Eventually he didn't feel a thing. Sound and sight mixed to nothing…
And he still saw and heard and sensed.
A man, the oriental from the restaurant, stood in the door.
– Shit, the man exclaimed pleased. – Some job you've done here.
Ted stood there without moving. He stared dully at the newcomer.
Rachel Dalhart stood in the door behind the oriental guy. Carr knew her.

Any journalist doing «society profiles» did.

– Jesus, she murmured, and he couldn't tell if she was shocked or amused. – Things happen in the toilets on this ship…

– Just another wayward soul, a bit out of it, Miss Dalhart, the oriental said pleasantly. – We'll take care of it. We always do.

– I heard the Duchess call him Ted the old lady said. – What's his last name, if I may inquire?

– He has written Smith in the ship's guestbook, the oriental grinned. – There are quite a few Smiths and Browns and Jones there…

Unbelievably enough Carr still heard the voices, saw the faces, even though he knew he was just moments away from unconsciousness. Waves of incredulity still hit him like lukewarm water.

Ted held a hand to his mouth. His eyes burned feverishly.

– You've caused enough upheaval for today, Mister Smith, the oriental said, and Carr had no problem hearing the fake concern in his voice. – Come with me, please.

The boy's eyes turned sort of alive again, as he followed the other man out in the hallway. Carr experienced everything. He watched Rachel Dalhart's face. Ted crouched and kept his hand to his mouth.

– Stop that, Ted, the oriental ordered, like he was talking to an underling, one he was intimately familiar with. – Don't throw up, do you hear me?

Ted straightened. His fact was still pale, but he seemed to have regained his faculties somehow, somewhat.

– There's a reason you got sick. What happened?

– I… don't know, Ted lent his head at the wall. – I felt the queasiness and left.

– What in God's name is going on here? Rachel Dalhart said, clearly quite upset. – Tim…?

The oriental turned impatiently and clearly stressed towards her.

– Tim Croydon, Miss Dalhart… This boy has a history of similar symptoms. We need as much information as we can.

A stage, Carr thought. This is a stage. This is all a stage. In so many ways.

He knew illusions when he saw them. He dealt with them professionally every day, knew acting. Saw it every time he opened his eyes. Sometimes, like now, he didn't even have to do that.

– I can understand that, the woman said patiently. – But why the rush? Isn't the ship doctor better qualified to ask the crucial questions?

– Miss Dalhart, *please*…

The man lifted a hand in exasperation.

Ted pushed his hand harder at his mouth. A smaller amount of bile erupted into his mouth without getting further. Carr smelled it.

– We know about the queasiness, Ted, Croydon said impatiently. – We also know that the journalist followed you to get to the girl. Don't throw up. Why did you attack him? *Why?*

Ted crouched some more, using both hands to clutch his belly. Without further warning he threw up. The bile erupted from his mouth and hit the other right in the face.

Chapter Ten

– Do you want me, Eric? Betty whispered to him, smiling ever so sweetly.

Pain. Horrible pain. He remembered now, what he had long since been taught, in a prison camp in Vietnam, by sadistic guards and the female «physician» in the camp. There had been needles, beatings and the most advanced form of torture. He and Patrick and the others had finally escaped, and upon reaching an American outpost discovered that they had been reported killed six months earlier.

Paralysis slowly let go. He wanted to scream every time he moved. But he had learned to deal with pain, learned to keep it inside. He crouched on his back, waving his arms, desperate for something to grab hold of. Finally his right hand hit the night table, and he was able to use the leverage to rise from the bed. He stumbled to the sink, the sink with the golden handles, and filled it with cold water. Even the sound hurt, not just in his ears, but all over. Then he stuck his head in the water, and held it there, until he could no longer hold his breath. Then he finally dared look at himself in the mirror. He felt relieved. Compared to how it hurt, he looked like a choirboy, and when he surveyed his body the same was the case there. There were swellings and bruises, but he wasn't badly injured.

He had been lucky… for once. As when he had stumbled through the corridor like a drunken man. He recalled dimly encountering the Duke, recalled dimly the man's frown of disapproval.

Everything Eric Carr wanted to do when reaching the bed was to fall down on it and remain there. But all his experience screamed at him, telling him what a bad idea that was. He would wake up, stiff as a corpse, and the bruises would swell to incredible proportions.

His mind reeling, close to being delirious he stumbled around in the cabin, before focusing, before certainty dawned on him, realization hit him. He needed his briefcase. Dimly he recalled throwing it under the bed. Just for him to bend down and reach for it, felt like a momentous effort.

Experience? He thought about it a bit, thought about his field equipment. He had carried it with him since the war, but never truly needed it, until now. This Ted Smith had taken him by surprise, something that should never have happened. Had his instincts been this dulled, too dulled for him to ever regain his former edge?

Gritting his teeth, he started undressing. He undressed completely. It hurt less with the clothes off than with them on, and he breathed a sigh of relief. Then, gritting his teeth, preparing for the pain, he began the process of cleaning and tending his lacerations and wounds. He discovered that this was still second nature to him. Hands knew what to do, even though his mind had to relearn what once had been instinct.

There were no deep cuts, only tears. Child's play. He recalled sewing a hole made by a hand grenade once. That made him grin. Both the memory of it and how lightly it played in his mind. He paid for that grin, paid hard, almost blacking out, as that small movement caused pain to rack his body.

When the wounds had been tended to, he took care of the sore limbs and muscles. He found a bottle of oil, applying it all over his body. This was not a ritual to make his skin safe for the burning sun, but to make sure he woke up somewhat able to move tomorrow.

Somewhat pleased he smiled and put the bottle back in the suitcase. He pulled on his pants. The oil had already begun its work, softening skin and sinew. He walked to the closet, finding a shirt, hesitating a bit before bringing the shirt with him back to the bed. Steady fingers sought a place at the floor of the suitcase, finding a secret compartment, pulling out a big, two-edged knife, partly sheathed. He had made the sheath himself, after the original had been lost. He had made it his own. There was no need for him to unsheathe the knife, in order for him to see it, see it before his eyes. He felt himself wake up, wake up slowly from a dream, the dream where he had spent his recent years.

He fastened the sheath below his left shoulder and tied the leather ropes tight around his body. His right hand pulled the knife slowly from its confine. It worked. Everything stayed in place. He hadn't forgotten. A time passed as he adjusted the sheath and the ropes. He stood there, looking at himself in the mirror. Then he drew the knife in one single, fluid move. After doing that for minutes, working up a sweat, he put on the shirt and a jacket. He looked at himself, had no need to look in the mirror, as he saw himself without seeing himself, as he slowly, slowly smiled his invisible smile. It did feel awkward wearing the sheath on his skin again, but he would just quite simply adjust to that… as he already did, every passing second.

++++++++++++++++++

Everything felt weird that day. What he saw, what he sensed, what he thought. Resignation warred with eagerness in him, as he kept looking for Betty. There was a dull thud somewhere inside him… beside the flame, the ember turning fire. He hardly thought at all, on occasions, as he walked his walk, as he went through the motions. Sometimes the confident man he had been days ago felt far away. Even as he realized that that man had not been very confident at all.

He sat in the bar, drinking, getting drunk, slipping into it without really trying. As he sat there, in the dank, shuttered room, he tried to think back, to remember when he had been drunk the last time before this, and he couldn't do it. That was all right. He hadn't really been doing much or doing much in the sense of thinking lately. As he sat there he spotted Benedict arm in arm with the little frail flower a man remembered so well. He seemed to remember that he threw one of the empty bottles after them, but he couldn't be certain. But aside from that possibly real event, he recalled nothing from his visit to the bar, feeling strongly he had… forgotten something. But he couldn't for his life remember what.

When he sometime later threw up over the rail, as he witnessed how the vomit mixed with the raging sea, bathed in the light of the radiant sunset, he recalled crystal clear everything he had forgotten.

The thoughts and memories came to him at night. As soon as he fell asleep the nightmares began. They came to him every night he was alone, and tonight they were worse than ever.

He walked. In front of him was a tall, dark wall. Not a wall exactly, but a wall of soft mist. He knew that. Somehow, he knew that. It was impossible to walk around it or climb it. It was there, in his path. He didn't want to walk into it, walk into the black mist, but something forced him to do so anyway. It was impossible to resist. He wasn't master of his own body.

It was dark in there, and dank. Cold, impenetrable. He walked on an invisible trail, one going on forever. He thought he had walked forever when he saw lights. And the light grew, turned into people, into his pals, his dead pals, translucent corpses with a sick grin painted on their faces. Everybody marched in tandem towards a large, way too large guillotine. A landscape formed around him. Vietnam - the place he had been a captive.

His pals reached the guillotine. One by one they stepped forward and let themselves be decapitated, all the time with the sick grin on their faces.

No, Don't do it! How can you do this to me?

They ignored his objections, and kept going. He tried to charge them, but he couldn't reach them. Sweat poured. He ran, but never reached them, no matter how much he ran, and he feared he never got a single step closer to his pals. He screamed, but the darkness sucked up the high-pitched sound, until only a weak echo remained.

The dark tightened once more, until he suddenly stood before a huge castle. The wind was blowing, and rain was falling around it, but not on it. It was… It was… He suddenly realized it. It was the center of the Storm. Ravens flew and screeched, screeched around the medieval castle, of bricks and mortar, of spirit and mist. He walked inside, crossing a bridge, where the river below was as black as everything, black and snarling and raging. Inside, in the castle yard, a large fire burned. The rain poured, but the fire kept burning unabated. If anything, the rain seemed to fan the fire, like gasoline. And then there was a dream. A scene from an Indian camp. A circle, a circle of fire, where men and women danced, both outside and inside the circle. Men and women staring. Betty danced, and then, suddenly, he was there, with her. Everybody dancing was nude, he and Betty as well. She swayed before a tent, enticing him. With an enticing smile, she slipped inside. He followed her, with his mouth opened in a stupid grin. Inside he stopped abruptly. Betty stood there, waiting for him. At least he believed it was Betty. Her body lacked a head, but her arms reached for him. He was unable to escape her grasp. She led him to a mirror, and there he saw himself. He knew positively it was his own body. It lacked the head, too. He turned crazy. Screamed and screamed. Charged out of the tent. Now the scene had shifted again. He was back in Vietnam. He rushed frantically back and forth in the jungle, the fields, the killing fields, to find a lake in which he could look at himself. And he ran long and hard. Hair and beard grew long, and he could hardly move of sheer exhaustion. Finally, he stumbled the last few steps to a river, a river calm enough for him to mirror himself. The head was there, back on. Thank God! A sound made him look, look back. A girl walked towards him, across the river, across the lake. It was her, the torturer from the prison camp. He snarled and drew the knife in one fluid move, throwing it at her heart. She made no attempt at evading it, and he quickly realized why. The knife passed right through her. She shook her head, very cross, as if scolding an unruly child. He attempted to run away, but it was no good. She easily caught him and threw him on the ground, threw him on his back. He was a puppet in her hands. She knelt over him with a knife in her hand, and grabbed… on, God… grabbed his blood-filled manhood. He could do nothing but watch, look at her sweet face. She smiled like an angel.

– You're my prey, Eric. A soft, innocent voice. – I have captured you, and you belong to me. Now, I'll claim my price.

She lowered the knife, and he felt the cold edge. HE FELT THE COLD EDGE.

– NOOOOOOOOOOOOOO!

The bed vanished beneath him, and he fell hard on the floor, and he kept screaming. Sunlight flooded the cabin. He looked wildly around. There was no one here, no one but himself, himself and his heaving breath. He looked astonished down on himself, at his softening manhood, at the semen dripping from it.

The nightmare stayed nailed in his soul. Open eyes didn't help. Bright light didn't help. He was soaked in shadow. And he couldn't really remember it, not as anything but as nightmarish glimpses into another reality, one fading by the second, staying buried in his gut.

The knife… It stood buried in the opposite wall. He sighed, both humorous and frosty. Confusion faded slowly, faded in, faded out, uncontrollably. He imagined there was blood on the knife, that it was stuck in a body, and that that body bled to death on the floor, slowly turning cold. There was a nagging feeling of him having forgotten something, something crucial, more important than life and death. There were thoughts, jumbled thoughts that didn't leave him.

He dressed slowly, as if moving under water, making sure all the buttons were buttoned, that the jacket sat right. The sunlight moved on the floor, like a living thing, something tangible, something to touch, to feel against sore skin. He headed for the breakfast room, but sat there without having breakfast. The coffee in front of him turned cold and stopped steaming long ago, its blackness pulling him in, pulling him down. He spent time in the bar, deliberately, without drinking a single drop. People spent a lot of time on the various decks today, bathing in the sunlight, the white-hot sunlight, turning his veins to ice. He had dinner. In the crowded restaurant, during the busiest hour he managed to find himself a table. On his way out he met Benedict and his little friend. He passed them without greeting them or saying anything.

The evening came. He stood at the ship's bow and bathed in the rust and the blood. Body felt light. Muscles still hurt a little, but not enough to care about. It was no bother. He touched them, softened them further, as he began to work out, as he began to stretch legs and muscles that hadn't been stretched for a long time.

There was movement by his side. The person there had moved so quietly, so unnoticed that he hadn't been aware of her until she was close by, regrettably close by.

– It's awkward, isn't it?

He turned towards Rachel Dalhart, keeping his face impassive, knowing fully well he wouldn't fool her.

– It's okay, he replied. – Experience counts for a lot, as I would guess you know. The only thing I can't seem to get rid of is the damn headache.

– Headaches are always hard to get rid off, the old lady nodded.

She was dressed in training gear, more than a bit informally, quite a departure from the working gear she used as «manager» for an exclusive club in Paris. Their paths had briefly crossed in the city of lights, when he had captured one of her girls and a customer in a heated moment.

– Something is wrong, she stated, staring at him. – Something is very wrong.

And just then, he felt very wrong.

He felt it all, like ants crawling under his skin.

She wore sunglasses. He realized he had never seen her without sunglasses. Not inside and not in the darkest night. He imagined he saw her eyes behind those dark glasses, in the red glow of the setting sun.

– You do remember me. She nodded. – I would have been furious at you if you hadn't.

– I'm always on top of things when working on a story, he said gallantly. – And one doesn't forget you easily, after meeting you.

– You're rather rude smiling to me, young man. I lost quite a lot of funds and face because of that nasty looking article of yours.

She's joking, he thought. Is she actually joking?

He grinned, feeling her, her calluses. She remained as unfathomable as ever. He downright stared at her, in an attempt to get a reaction, any reaction from her, but there was none, none he could discern.

– Some stories quite simply write themselves, Madame…

She waved him off. Carr noticed the diamond ring on her ring finger. He realized astonished it was a wedding ring, and a very special one at that, encircled in sapphires and rubies, shimmering in fire. No way in hell she had been wearing that before. He - and everyone else would have noticed.

– Let's not speak about it, about such trifles.

Her accent occasionally heavy, he would guess that she was born English speaking, but had lived very long in France. She was a mystery.

People attempting to dig up her past, before she arrived in Paris, and there had been a few of them, had come up with nothing. It was like she didn't exist before that.

– Something is happening on this ship, Eric, she said, astonishing him with her directness, the familiarity in which she treated him. – I don't need to tell you that. You're an adult, not ignoring life's harsh realities, like almost everyone else. You know when something is… fishy. You might not see the full ramifications of your observations yet, but you will.

What was she *saying?* He looked around him, ridiculously, to see if anybody was listening.

– Earlier on this voyage I observed your green-eyed girlfriend go to the same toilet as our mutual friend Ted Smith, and do the same throwing up routine, albeit not with the same… violent bi-product. The present attendant tried to convince me it was a kind of seasickness, but I have seen a lot of seasickness in my time, Eric, and this wasn't it.

Eric Carr stood there with his eyes closed. He didn't speak.

Her intonations, the way she pronounced certain words. It evoked something inside of him, something…

It was downright weird. And it wasn't strange at all.

– That's all, really. I thought you might be interested. Goodbye.

He saw Betty for his inner eye, when she sat beside him by the pool. She had called his name, and looked at him with begging eyes.

My name is Betty Morgan, she had said. Remember that. Never forget it.

– Wait, he heard himself say. – What's your interest in this? Why the… bother?

– Goodbye, Eric, she said, with finality in her voice.

He heard her, a whisper in the wind. When he opened his eyes the old lady was gone.

– It's personal for you, he said aloud. – This, all this *means* something to you, to you personally.

And the vast abyss he had long since sensed below his feet opened even wider. Everything seemed unreal. He questioned his sanity, whether she had spoken to him, whether she had been there at all. What had she been talking about? She had taken him by surprise. He should have been more active, asked questions, shaking her to her core, and made her spill her guts. She knew about Betty, about Ted, about everything he didn't know, the vast tapestry he saw unfold… and the excitement in his gut.

She could have helped him find Betty. He needed to find her. She meant so much to him. His need was gnawing fangs and claws inside.

I behave like a madman, he thought.

He went through the conversation again and again in his mind, and it just didn't make sense… not when looking at it with his eyes closed, the way he had done. His eyes burned, and he could no longer close them. He walked away, away from there, but he never truly left this place. His feet moved, moved him, all over the vast ship. He moved restlessly, never really stopping anywhere, other than by a glance, by a glimpse. The man who had been vice-sheriff of Leadville passed with his girl in tow, a totally unimportant incident causing infernos of thoughts to rise in him, in his fevered mind. There were more festivities. There were always festivities. He ignored it. He threw himself on the bed, the bed in his cabin, without really knowing how he had ended up there. The door was unclosed, open. He didn't give a damn. Nightmarish images reached him in his wide-awake state.

Eric Carr rested, somewhat, on his back in bed, with his eyes half closed, slumbering, dreaming wide-awake.

Ilse Van Brandenburg writhed on her back in bed, in the adjacent cabin. She was naked. Her hair was mussed, and her skin covered in sweat. Awakening was slow, dreary. She fumbled with a hand for the person beside her, but there was no one there. He wasn't there. She opened her eyes, as she struck the pillow in anger.

– Leaving me, are you? She mumbled. – You are leaving ME? YOU SON OF A BITCH!

Her mind echoed with images and sounds of yesterday, of last night, confusing and frightening imagery, a cacophony of sound. She moaned in despair, in a continuing, feverish need and shame. She hurt. Her entire body hurt.

She sensed a draft on her body, her sweaty body. Panic set in. The door was open, wide-open. Two women dressed in hospital uniforms walked through the door. One of them closed it. That simple act made incredulity mix with fear inside Ilse. Her half-smile faded, and she pulled the blanket up to her neck.

– W-who are you? W-what do you want?

The tallest of them spoke.

– I am Sandra and this is Shuen. We've heard you're sick and are in need of some *serious* readjustment.

Sandra's smile was sinister beyond words.

– Sick? I'm not sick! You're wearing nurses' uniforms. Are you nurses?

– You're full of scratches and bruises, Duchess. Have you fallen and injured yourself?

It was still the tallest that was speaking. The two kept smiling, but it was eerie and frosty smiles.

The smaller, the dark haired mixed Eurasian woman stepped forward and slapped her on the cheek. Ilse gasped and stared petrified at her.

– Enough delays, Shuen snapped. – Your lesson begins now!

– Rise! Sandra commanded.

Ilse obeyed startled, shocked to the bone.

Eric heard the other bed creak. He lay there sweating, only a wall away, able to hear everything that was being said, the word and the voices. Everything was so familiar, so damn familiar.

Sandra produced a small glass and a bottle filled with dark fluid, and after filling the glass to the rim she pushed the glass at Ilse's lips.

– Drink! She snapped.

After a brief hesitation Ilse parted her lips and drank.

– Now, that's a good girl. Sandra patted her cheek. – That wasn't hard, now, was it?

Tears flowed down Ilse's cheeks. She stared at the two strangers with an incredulity and paralysis that just wouldn't go away, no matter how hard she fought to make it go away.

– Time for the doctor's appointment, Shuen said. – Time to take the sick bitch to her just reward.

– Absolutely.

Sandra nodded eagerly, and hurried to the door. She opened it and pulled inside a huge suitcase. Big enough… Ilse swallowed hard. Big enough to contain a human being.

– Don't worry, Duchess. Everything will actually be very pleasant. It will hardly hurt at all.

Ilse started to feel faint. She wanted to protest, to object, but it just wasn't a very strong desire. Fear faded in from somewhere, but strangely weak. When she took a step forward she stumbled, and would have fallen if the two girls hadn't caught her. Sandra kissed her on the cheek, softly and so very, very comforting.

– Please, she whined. – I'm not sick. Don't take me to the doctor.

– Of course, we'll take you to the doctor. Shuen shushed her. – All good girls go to him.

– Can you speak up a little? Ilse's vision started to turn misty, and she grabbed her head. – I can't hear you well.

I began to fade, Eric thought. I had fallen asleep.

– Just lean on us, honey. You're not well. We told you so.

Ilse wanted to scream, but she couldn't even speak anymore, and she would have fallen if they hadn't held her, kept her on her feet. They led her to the suitcase. Sandra opened it with her eager grin. It was big. Ilse felt like she drowned in it. She was still blinking when they put her into the vast, comforting black space, reminding her of a coffin. The two girls ignored her feeble protests. She attempted to lift her arms, but coordination was gone, and they just fell back down. Sandra patted her head, and then she closed and locked the casket.

– Coast is clear, Shuen said.

They lifted up the suitcase, carrying it in tandem out of the room, through the dark hallway.

Eric saw them, and he heard the crack when the door closed, and he couldn't move. He wanted to run after them. He couldn't move. Not a finger. It had turned quiet in the other room, but he kept hearing the voice of one of the «nurses». He would never forget it. He hadn't.

He rose from the bed, unable to tell how long he had been frozen, frozen in place. The shaking body stood there, by the bed, for a long time, until thought returned to it. It was how he had spent years and years of his life, unable to do anything else, anything beyond existing.

Eric Carr stared at the sweating creature in the mirror. No matter the determination, the growing willpower, the powerful conviction that he was waking from a nightmare he sensed fear growing inside, he was unable to stop his hands from shaking.

It hadn't been hard recognizing the voice. It clearly belonged to an adult person. She had grown up, grown up from the teenager he had learned to know and fear. He hated her with a passion, now, one washing away the fear, the paralysis dominating his life for so long. Hated the demon, the very manifestation of Satan.

Hated *Shuen Parker*.

+++++++++++++++

Dance dance
Now it's your turn
Are you ready
Dance and let all thought go

Eric had just spent a few minutes at the bar when he had had enough. He left the hardly touched drink and left the room, the very room. In the restaurant the dancers ended their show. He glimpsed Ted Smith in the crowd. Just a glimpse, and then the boy was gone.

Eric felt he could breathe outside. At least his breathing turned somewhat normal. All electrical lamps had been turned off on the deck, and that, if nothing else created a persistent, eerie mood in the restless figure. The wind didn't blow. Sea was calm. Eric Carr moved, even while standing still. He turned away when finding himself on a collision course with Benedict, ignoring the sting of regret, of remorse. But he didn't get rid of the image in his mind of Benedict and his little girlfriend, walking arm in arm on the deck. He felt an unrest, almost an excitement he hadn't felt for years. The despair didn't leave him, but neither did the driving force making him continue to take that one, crucial step forward.

That was when he spotted the Duke and a woman. It was certainly not the Duchess, but the guy certainly squeezed her hard enough, and in full public view. Eric was ravaged by another shock. The woman's hair was hidden behind a large, white turban, but the moves, the shape of the body convinced him. It was Betty.

They didn't see him. He pulled further into the shadows, feeling more and more at home there.

The good Duke groped her. Groped her good. Eric took one step forward, ready to intervene, not caring anymore who was most the fool, he or the Duke.

There was no need to worry. She pushed him away, kindly but decisive. He wanted to try again, but she shook her head, very decisive, and he relented. It cut Eric to the bone to see her blow the guy a kiss before she left him, left him to rot. Eric followed her. He realized she wasn't on her way to her or his cabin, but on the contrary on her way to the dancing hall, and he quickly increased his pace to catch up with her. He grabbed her arm. Her skin was just as soft and smooth. Without thinking twice about it he dragged her through the nearest open door, which incidentally was to a cabin. He had no idea whose it was, and didn't care.

– Please, let go of my arm, she said. – It hurts.

She stood there, proud and unapproachable. The turban emphasized her features. The radiant eyes. And the strange look she sent him.

– Betty, don't you recognize me? He exclaimed.

– I do know you, she grinned. – Know of you. You see, you've done a bit of a mistake here. I'm not Betty…

Her eyes, they were gray. He tore off the turban. A waterfall of shiny, red hair flowed down her shoulders. He stared stupefied at her.

– Is everything clear to you, now? She asked with a sweet smile. – May I go in peace?

– Uh… of course. He reddened as he returned the turban to her.

– I'll never forgive you, she scolded him. – It took me hours to make it.

He mumbled an unintelligible apology.

– So, honey, perhaps you'll move away from the door so I can walk through it?

He quickly stepped aside. The girl kissed him on the cheek as she passed him.

– Thank you. Perhaps we can get together another time, huh?

He stood there, on the spot, and just turned hotter and hotter and hotter, wondering where his calm had gone, the indifference that had made him famous and infamous in wide circles among colleagues.

The door to the unfamiliar cabin closed behind him. The abrupt sound didn't bring that much of a shock, really. He walked off, set off on a prearranged course. He knew where to go, where he wanted to be. Less than a minute later he reached the door to Betty's cabin. It was locked, but he still had the key she had given him. He could just as well wait here, as any other place. This was the place. He should have thought about that before. He didn't bother to turn on the lights, but sat course directly for the bed. There was nothing to think about anymore, nothing to do, except wait. To this place, to this exact spot Betty would come.

++

It was like seeing night turning to day in a matter of seconds. But in this daylight, there was a number of shimmering bright lights making it hard to see right. When she finally was able to see, the sight before her eyes was so terrifying that she began shaking completely uncontrollable, but in spite of this it was impossible for her to take her eyes off it.

A film was on, and she was in it. The images were horribly clear, she thought. The sound as well. Every word cut into her like knives.

The woman smiled to the boy and walked to him, touching his jaw lightly with the tip of her fingers.

He slapped her. She looked astonished at him. He slapped her, first on one cheek, than the other. The mouth twisted in a sadistic smile. He grabbed her and pushed her down on the bed. She lay there on her belly, with her arms and legs spread out.

– The little Duchess likes it rough. The little Duchess will get her wish.

He pressed her legs together, and pulled the tight pants she wore down her thighs. Then he tightened the belt so hard that she could hardly move her feet. He nodded pleased.

– Stop! She pleaded with him. – Please stop!

– It's you and not I who're making the decisions here, he grinned. – Just ask me to leave… We can still be friends.

She wanted to, God, she wanted to, but the need kept increasing below, and between her feeble protests there were expectant moans, moans of joy. She curled her hands into fists, but she remained on the bed, on her belly. He smiled in contempt and pulled the shorts down his legs.

– I can promise you this, Duchess. You will remember this.

He crawled on top of her body and pushed his to hers. Another ice-cold shock rattled her when she felt his fingers in her… in her ass.

– But you *can't?*

Her voice was only a whimper, and she detested herself.

– Of course, I can, and I do it because I can, and I like this hole better.

The man brushed aside the woman's buttocks. Then he pushed himself into her smallest opening. She cried out. It hurt just a little. The worst about it was the certainty of what he was doing, the humiliation and the shame over what happened. What she allowed to happen.

– Repeat after me! He breathed into her ear. – I'm a horny little bitch.

Her fingers dug into the sheet. Tears flowed from her eyes.

– I… am a… horny, little bitch.

– I love to feel submissive and unimportant.

– I… love to feel submissive and… un… important.

She cried so much by now that she had problems speaking.

He breathed fast. Like a hurricane, she thought, taking everything with it in its way. One had to lay still and hope it would ignore you. But it didn't. It took her away, and reduced her to just another helpless victim. He moved his body in powerful thrusts and pulls, as he ravaged her, as he unmade her. A big rock grinding her to dust.

When he was done, he said casually:

– Perhaps you'll fart a bit less from now on…

– That wasn't funny, she sobbed. – Was that supposed to be *funny?*

It was cruel, so very, very cruel. The only reply was an uncaring laughter. She released another whine when he pulled out, another sound of bitter disappointment and unfulfilled need. He tightened his grip on her left arm and almost twisted it out of its socket when he turned her over on her back. He placed himself on the knees above her, so his manhood hung above her face. It dripped of it. The semen hit her on the cheek and lips. She closed her mouth tight. He slapped her, and she opened it again, sobbing some more.

– That's it, he shouted. – Lick it up. *Lick it up,* I say!

She kept sobbing when she used her tongue and hands to get everything into her mouth. When she swallowed, she expected to feel sick, but she didn't. The sobbing increased.

– That's better, he said viciously. – Now, we know you've got the taste for it.

He bent forward and pushed his half-erected limb into her mouth.

– Now, you're gonna learn another skill, and you'll do it fast. If your teeth make a single dent, I will by God whip the skin from your body.

To her horror she sensed the need build inside, spread from her pulsing cunt and to her entire body. She could hardly breathe. But she still felt the pleasure rise. She moaned helplessly as he grew in her mouth, as he ejaculated, and her mouth was filled with semen. There was a horrible itch in her throat, but she didn't dare cough in fear of hurting him.

When he pushed himself up and once more stood on his knees above her, she looked at him with shiny eyes.

She writhed on the bed, as her need kept rising.

– Now, bitch, you're in heat.

He pinched her hard in both cheeks. She begged him with her eyes, with her entire body, and he looked at her as if she was nothing.

– Take me, she begged him hoarsely, with an unrecognizable voice. – Fuck me!

He waited, waited, patiently, like a predator for the prey to be ready.

And then… he fell on her.

– Yes, she shouted. – Do it! YES!

He covered her, all of her, but occasionally one caught a glimpse of her distorted face, and one heard her moans and howls, and the thoroughly content throaty sound rising from her as he parted from her, and she slipped into sleep with outstretched arms.

The film ended. The screen turned white. The lights were turned on. In front of her stood Sandra and Shuen, and a gray-haired man in a white coat. The girls scared her, but he gave her the willies.

Both her hands and feet were chained to the wall. She stood before the three, completely exposed and vulnerable.

– Ilse, Shuen Parker said. – May I present Doctor Meinz.

– Good afternoon, Duchess.

Meinz' voice was totally neutral, neither sadistic, triumphant nor excited. But still it evoked fear.

– What's this? Ilse cried. – What the fuck is this?

– There you go, Ilse, Shuen said softly. – Everybody would've heard you if we've had this conversation in your cabin, and we don't want that, do we?

Sandra grabbed… grabbed a whip from the table, and struck its shaft at her boots. Ilse's eyes were as locked on to it. What she had wanted to say just faded with the air flowing between her lips.

– That's right, sweet girl, Sandra whispered. – You will shut up. You will pay attention, and if you ever yap away without explicit permission again, you will get severely punished.

Ilse wanted to speak, wanted to tell these people what she thought of them, but her voice failed. All courage just faded away, faded into black and gray.

– You… trust the Duke, don't you? Meinz said. – You trust each other… to not make a splash, to not embarrass you both. What do you think he will say when he sees this film?

Ilse attempted to look away from the sticking green eyes, but couldn't do it.

– Look at her, Sandra said viciously. – How she's still desperately clinging to her dignity, her sense of self.

Meinz laughed a bit.

– Yes, this is extortion, Duchess. But we don't want money. We have enough of those things. What we want, what we demand from you is… information. You'll be our informant, our mole in the Brandenburg-family's industrial ventures. The Brandenburgs are fiercely independent creatures. They are, as you say… rocking the boat, and we can't have that, now, can we? We need a leash, and you shall be that leash, Ilse, a leash we will hold, we will command. You'll be a trained animal jumping through our hoop.

He sounded so certain, so… definite. Ilse felt as if a darkness descended on her, one that strangled and squeezed all life from her. She relived the movie, the events depicted in the movie, her shiny eyes and ecstatic smile, her horrible howls and moans.

– Yes, Sandra told her triumphantly. – We seduced you, we broke you, and now you're our creature, on our leash for the rest of your life. You're ours. You'll never be free of us. Never!

And when she petted the prisoner it was such a sweet, comforting touch.

Meinz held up a needle. He stuck it in her left thigh in a manner that more than suggested a skill beyond simple learning. Ilse hardly felt the sting. She began blinking not long afterwards.

– This is just the beginning, little Ilse. We will teach you the ropes, teach you what you need to survive and thrive in our care, in the care of Abraxas Omega, teach you everything about life, and in turn you will serve us with all your ingenuity and joy.

Her eyes widened. She knew the name, knew what it entailed. Her eyes widened for a second, two… before closing, before falling, falling down.

Kurt Meinz listened to the low, urgent voice through the speakers some time later. It was his own. The room was small. Ilse Van Brandenburg lay on a soft mattress at its center, moaning in her sleep, in her slumber.

– That was… fantastic. Sandra stood panting by his side. – I feel… feel like reborn.

– That does not surprise me, Meinz said bemused. – I knew you had a talent for this.

– It was such an incredible feeling. Sandra released a low, satisfied sound. – To have such power over her, that I personally could and can squash her like a bug, that I'm her everything and nothing. You've done this. You've taught me.

She held on to him, like a shipwrecked to the lifeboat.

– You still have a lot to learn, he said. – A lot to absorb, but I feel confident in your ability to do so.

He squeezed her breasts. She moaned loudly.

– It hurts, doesn't it? He whispered into her ear.

– It hurts *deliciously*.

She shouted it.

– Remember this, my precious girl…

– YES! YES!

– Where there's no pain, there's no pleasure. It's like sex. It hurts the first time, but then it's just exquisite pleasure and pain.

– I'll remember. I'll always remember.

– Always, Kurt Meinz mumbled. – Always…

He moved his eyes to another window, another room. At its center a girl with black hair stood straight, rigid. The green eyes were just as rigid. They looked like glass. Meinz' eyes were the same, but they were filled with hatred.

Sometimes it was very easy to remember.

++++++++++++++++++++++++++++++

Betty felt cold ravage her skin. She was freezing, in the interior heat of the ship, and she didn't understand why.

Well inside the cabin she fumbled for the light switch. As she reached it a hand grabbed hers.

Eric Carr's familiar face filled her vision.

– I thought you were sleeping, she said softly.

– I couldn't sleep.

He roughed up her hair.

– I'm so ashamed, she said weakly. – I've been sick, but should have managed to give word anyway.

– «Managed»?

– The mad doctor… He spoke constantly about me being contagious and everything. I wasn't sick, didn't even have a fever.

With a few words and soft caresses, she calmed his raging insides, and

made him smile.
– I made quite the impact last night, he said. – I met a red-haired revelation in a turban, and thought she was you.
Betty sighed deeply, but then she giggled.
– You've met my sister. She bet she would be able to fool you before we reached Britain, and she won, that bitch…
She kissed him hard on the lips.
– Mmmmmmm
He disengaged himself briefly from her.
– You do look a little pale, he said.
– I've longed for your company.
She said.
– Well, that's good, because I have a surprise for you.
– A surprise. She lit up. – What is it, Eric?
– Come with me to the bed, and I'll show you.
And she did. Of course, she did.
He opened the drawer and a bottle revealed itself.
She looked at him, astounded.
– That's *Champagne*.
– Indeed it is, he grinned.
He opened the bottle. He did so quickly and efficiently, showing his expertise. There was a loud pop, and the bubble-water erupted from the bottle, and hit Betty right in the face.
– Sorry, he said, in badly veiled satisfaction
– You just had to hit me in the face, she gasped. – You're crazy, Eric!
She overwhelmed him with kisses, from the neck to the forehead, clinging to him wild and uninhibited. Then she snapped the bottle from him, and turned it upside down, leaving a lot of its content in his hair. She made an honest attempt to escape from his groping hands, but laughed so much that she lost control completely. After a brief struggle they tumbled down on the bed.
– There's more than enough left, he mumbled. – Glasses, please.
He grabbed the two glasses from the drawer. She attempted to empty the bottle on his head, but he got hold of it, and filled up the glasses.
– Eric, I've never drunk much. I don't really…
He handed her one of the glasses.
– This is the very best quality. It's good for you. Drink!
It was a command, and she was very good at following commands. Glasses met and parted.
– Cheers! He said cheerfully.

She put the glass to her lips and drank. He did as well.

– It's… good.

– I told you that much, didn't I.

Her breasts clearly showed through the wet fabric. He started to pat them, caress them.

– Do you want me, Eric? She wondered, shivering joy in her voice.

– I want you. You're such a lovely creature and I want you again and again and again.

He saw how that excited her, how it made her flush in heat. He swallowed hard, fearing she would notice, but she seemed totally out of it.

– This won't do. Flustered she released herself from his grip. – We're both wet and sticky. Let's have a shower. C'mon, Eric.

Eager and excited like a girl.

– I was about to suggest just that. You must be psychic.

They giggled so hard that they would have fallen if they hadn't supported each other.

– You have a thing about keeping yourself clean, don't you? If you can't shower at least twice a day, you don't feel good about yourself…

Her eyes darkened, her eyes lit up like stars, like dark stars.

– I like clean, she whispered. – I love clean.

She stared at him while undressing, while performing the feat of softly removing the wet clothes. He could swear he could still see her eyes even when she pulled the shirt over her head. She seemed proud like a princess when she removed the last piece of fabric and let it fall to the floor.

His own clothes just fell away. He couldn't say if he actually used his hands to do it or if they just… dissolved… into nothing, and the insistent, cynical voice deep in his mind became harder and harder to acknowledge. A little later, when they stood in the shower, bathed in a cascade of water whipping their skin he feared it was still there, feared it wasn't. The two were only visible as shadows to an eventual observer, through the curtain, he knew that, and felt more than a little guilty about it.

It was a large shower, luxurious and pleasant to use. They could even move around a lot (and they did), without hitting the walls. When they lay down, they could do so in their entire length.

– The water…? He looked hesitatingly at her.

– Let it flow, she said. – Let it whip our bodies. Let it rinse our minds. We deserve it, Eric. We deserve all of it.

The low spoken words drowned in the roar from the water. The two figures began moving faster. The woman's hand struck the wall as she released a low moan, a cry of joy and excitement.

In the small room deep below on the ship, there was an entire wall filled with video screens. On four of them the two watchers saw all parts of Betty's cabin. It was just what happened inside the shower chamber they didn't get a clear picture of.

– She's amazing. Shuen Parker shook her head. – I think it was wise to keep our Betty away from the journalist for a few days. She has him panting like a dog in heat.

The Mask refrained from speaking. He stood behind her with his arms crossed, cold and unreachable.

She turned and looked intently at him, a curious frown in her face.

– It's almost like we've done him a favor, isn't it? He was almost like a walking dead man before this.

The mask covered his entire face, including his eyes and mouth. It was impossible to tell if he was looking at her, except for the general direction the visible nose pointed. It was even difficult to decide if the mouth was indeed moving or if his words were just vibrations in the ether.

– Life is known to throw people such curves.

The sounds and images from the cabin distracted them, made them move restlessly around the room.

– Looks like he intends to keep it up for a while. He's wrong if he thinks he can tire our Betty. Don't you think so, too…

The Mask was close to her in a flash, clutching her neck, her windpipe. He lifted her up, held her easily, as if he lifted a small child. He held her, and didn't let up. Lack of air began to obscure her vision. She felt the first scents of fear.

– You were about to say my name, weren't you? *My name!*

He let up a little. Enough for her speak, to squeak.

– YES! She gasped. – I'm sorry, so sorry. Please let me go. Please!

He did. She could hardly stand, and couldn't help the sense of relief she felt. He caught her as she stumbled. She leaned hard on him, breathing close to his chest, to the huge, shaking form, giving him soft, comforting caresses on his back.

– I'm sorry, she whispered. – Sorry. Forgive me.

He touched her face, and his touch was surprisingly tender.

They heard Betty's voice:

– The bed, please.

– Absolutely not, Carr chuckled. – I go absolutely insane when I see the water hit your lovely form.

Betty sighed, relented, and a few seconds later they were clearly at it again. Moans and growls were mixed with the buzz of the running water.

Parker fumbled a hand across the instrument panel before hitting the right switch and turning off the sound. She pulled close to the man, kissing the mask, the lips beneath the mask.

– Perhaps this isn't the right place for us, she mumbled. – For a while I thought it was. For a while I thought it was everything I ever wanted, but now I'm not so sure anymore. I'm not the same person I was, the person I was before meeting you. Thank you. Thank you.

She tore at his clothes for seconds, for an eternity, before he responded, and she let out a sigh of joy. There was a bed in this room, too, very convenient. They were as pulled towards it. They walked to it, somewhat composed, but with a growing sense of urgency, of unfulfilled need. She saw him naked, except for the mask. He was never truly naked.

– I've noticed something, he said, fairly relaxed. – You get weird on me every time every time you observe the journalist. So, naturally, I wonder if there's a special reason for this.

– Don't be silly, My Lord, she replied sweetly. – What reason should that be?

It moved under the mask. She couldn't see it, but knew he was smiling.

She touched him, touched his naked skin.

– You're cold, she mumbled. – You're always cold. You're so confident, so frightened. I love you. I love you!

And she repeated those words, silently moving her lips, savoring the feel of the fabric covering his face, his lovely face, as they moved on the bed, as they held on to each other for bare life. Even the buzz of the screens faded in the cold heat of the moment.

Carr turned off the water. He bent down and raised one of Betty's eyelids. She was finally unconscious. The poison had finally worked. It had taken its time. She had the constitution of a mule. He fumbled with his right hand down in the niche between the shower and the wall. When he pulled it back up, he held a razorblade between the thumb and index finger. Careful not to chip it he cut off a lock of Betty's hair. He put the razorblade back in place. Then he hid the lock in his palm, in his fist, and stepped out of the shower.

He pretended to look for the towel and put the hair in the shirt's pocket, before conveniently discovering the towel near the bed. He didn't care about drying himself very much. The heat would take care of that soon enough. The sky brightened outside. It was early, but to him it was late, late, late. He dressed without visible hurry, but his movements had turned economic, very methodical and efficient. A way of life he recalled dimly from younger years, finally recalled. His face remained impassive.

Sometimes it would seem like he was sleepwalking, because his tendency to bump into things. He felt like being born, with the coordination of a baby. Less than a minute later he moved through the ship's hallways, clearly goal-oriented. He hoped fervently it wasn't too evident. There were very few people up this early. Those he heard were employees rushing about, preparing the day. And there were also noises and scents and more that others didn't hear, that he, himself would probably not have heard as late as yesterday, that reminded him… reminded him…

It reminded him of his sneaking suspicion of being watched.

He felt an eternity pass until he not that much later found himself in his own cabin, bent over his suitcase. They didn't watch him here or so he surmised. If he was wrong, he would find himself in deadly peril very soon. He unscrewed fervently, impatiently a bottle. He didn't care about saving anything of the fluid in it and just put the entire bundle of hair into the water-like property. Then he sat down, unmoving, waiting.

Ten, perhaps fifteen seconds passed. The black color vanished slowly. The hairs turned violet, then red, shining red, erasing the last remaining doubt in Eric Carr's mind.

He rushed to the suitcase, opened it so quickly that most of the clothes fell out, and grabbed the bundle of papers Andrew Benedict had given him. Images and names and text turned indistinct in his mind, echoed, confirmed by what he read. Names were ordered alphabetically: *Ted Cousin*. And further down: *Betty Morgan*. And even further: *Tilla Stevens*. *Robert Tremblay*.

Everything fit. Benedict had been right. At least he had stumbled on the truth, touched it, touched its acid burn.

And Carr? He hadn't reacted. Not even when he had heard these names.

My name is Betty Morgan. Don't forget it. Never forget it.

He had forgotten.

The shaking man sat down on the bed.

Recalling moments, smiles and kisses and words of affection.

Eric Carr suddenly started to sweat violently. He realized there and then that Betty, the Betty he had come to know was nothing but a façade, a construct.

He ran back to Betty's cabin, not bothering to hide anymore, to hide his anxiety, his beyond anything insane expression.

– Betty…

He said her name the moment he entered the room, somewhat mellow, somewhat fake. But there was no reply. He rushed to the shower, but there was no one there. He turned the cabin upside down before somewhat coming to his senses, before realizing the inevitable: Betty was gone.

++++

Betty stumbled down the corridor, just wearing her soaking wet clothes. She was on her way to something. Didn't really know what, but the goal was clearly defined in her, even though she couldn't define it. On her way she met some of her friends. She pulled herself together, keeping them from realizing that anything was wrong with her, drew on reserves deep within herself, something undefined that had always been more a part of herself than the exterior she presented to the world. She looked behind her with an animal's sly eyes. Usually Croydon followed her wherever she went, but she knew no one followed her now. When she stood before the door she looked back and forth several times. The hallway was empty. She slipped silently and cautiously into the cabin. Vernie and the journalist lay stretched out on the bed, sleeping soundly.

Her wet feet gave away a sucking sound every time she lifted them from the floor, so she didn't, but swept them across the floor, as she held her breath in close to paralyzing fright. But she kept going, kept putting that crucial step ahead of the previous. She fell quietly to the floor and began writhing her body under the bed. The writhing body didn't stop until it reached the wall. There it remained, crouched, shaking like a leaf.

When the bed finally creaked, a long time had passed. She still shook and put her thumb in her mouth. A pair of lean legs appeared. She sucked hard on her thumb. Vernie wriggled her butt, in honor of the man on the bed, and walked humming to the toilet. Betty didn't take her eyes off her.

If she sees me, she will cry out and they will come. They will hurt me, hurt me more. I don't... want that.

Vernie returned to the bed. Betty heard the content sigh when she crawled tight to Benedict.

Like she had pretended with Eric.

Her clothes didn't seem to dry. Water still flowed from her hair, gathering in a pool on the floor close to her left thigh. She neither dared nor was able to move. Her skin was sickeningly pale, and she felt incredibly tired, but didn't dare close her eyes in fear of falling asleep.

Time no longer mattered to her. Her eyes stayed open, but she saw nothing. She heard, smelled. The two had left the bed by now. They stood tight together, in a pleasure-filled, intimate conversation. Betty's mouth was filled with vomit. It flowed down her jaw and down on her chest. The nausea increased tenfold. She wondered how long she could hold out, could prevail in this place, this hell. They hadn't told her it would be like this. Hard, yes, but not like this. Uncle had not mentioned this horror, this destruction of the spirit, where everything was cold and empty.

Vernie stood on the bathroom and sprayed perfume all over her body. Betty knew that. She did the same every morning. The smell of it, the stinking smell made her even sicker than she was. If she could just crawl to Benedict, now, Tell him everything. While she could still think and remember. Wake Vernie, wake herself.

Something knocked into the bed and she shook, shook so hard that she feared she would make the entire ship shake.

– What's that, Andy? Vernie's light, innocent voice. – Too much wine yesterday, even for you?

Betty didn't hear his reply. The roar rising in her mind overwhelmed any sensible sound.

So real we sound. No one realizes how fake it all is.

She recalled other times she had been able to think. She had faced strangers and wanted to tell them everything. About her helplessness, her despair. But it was useless. Everything spilling from her was sweet, euphonious words. She was merely a puppet, a programmed robot, without any saying over her own life.

The two disappeared eventually, and she was alone. She had crouched here for such a long time, so long that it felt like forever, forever alone. Images of him, the boy, the man, filled her mind, rinsed her like a waterfall, ravaged her like a storm. He would have to come soon, so they could talk, while she was still able to. A nightmare arose from her depths. She saw him enter, and she was still under the bed, unable to move, unable to utter a sound, and then, after a brief hesitation, he would turn and leave again. She pushed her hands, her fingers, her claws at the floor and pulled, pulled herself forward, from under the bed and out on the floor, while sweat poured from her. Shaking her head in a sudden rage, she fought herself up on her knees. She remained on all fours, slowly, dully shaking her head. Suddenly she threw up violently. The remaining power in her arms faded and she fell, fell in her own vomit. She remained there, paralyzed, and she kept throwing up in uneven intervals. She began sobbing, sobbing hard. It just flowed out of her, and she was completely unable to stem its tide. People passing by outside would hear her. She knew that, feared that. But she couldn't, just couldn't help herself. And she sobbed harder, even more desperate.

Time passed, and passed again. Everything dissolved around her, formed and dissolved, time and time again. She moaned, the song of despair rising in her like rusty blades. She sobbed and sobbed and sobbed and couldn't stop.

Ted opened the door cautiously. He shook at the sight of the miserable creature on the floor.

– Don't… leave, she whispered. – Help me…

The plea dug deep in him, far beneath the fog and insipidness of his mind. He knelt by her and helped her up in a sitting position.

– I am *Kwaiala,* she said to him. – Your *Kwaiala.*

He looked curiously at her, filled with the same worry and uncertainty she felt herself.

– I knew it was you. Her voice rising and falling like a whisper. – It took so long before I heard your steps, but I knew instantly they were yours. I know you so well. Your walk, your appearance, your inner life. But now you are as reduced as I am, and I feel so bad, so very, very bad. You came. I've waited so long for you. Since early this morning.

– Have you been here the whole day? What if Benedict had returned? He would have seen you.

– Had to… see you.

– Are you sick? Confusion riddled him like a mare. – I'll get someone. You can't stay here. You need help, need a shower perhaps, a place where you can get back in shape.

Back in shape…

– NO, not shower! She dug her long nails so far into his shoulder that he moaned. – Stay! Don't get anybody! Wash me. Dry me. But not shower.

She saw something, something in his eyes, and there was joy, faint, but there. She nodded to him, encouraged him, and felt it, felt the joy.

He washed her face and her body with the sheets. Afterwards he used the blanket to dry her, dry her body and hair. And when her hair was no longer wet, she looked a lot better. He held her hair, touched it, looked at it, inspected it.

– Your hair is black, he said.

She smiled. She heard the important nuances in his voice. She knew him so well.

– Everything here is wrong, she said. – We must make it right, make ourselves right.

She touched his collar, his wristbands.

– This isn't us, she insisted. – It's wrong. *Wrong!*

– Come, he said, dragging her on her feet. – Let me take you to… to help.

– *Listen* to me! She grabbed him, and held on, her eyes no longer dull. – We must get away from here, away from the Masters.

– Aw-way?

– Escape, she nodded feverishly.

And there was silence, there was thunder.

– We have two *names,* she stated. – Like everyone else. Mine is Betty Morgan and yours is Ted Warren.

A door slammed open in his mind. A beam of fire broke the web clouding his memory, and this time it was so strong that the nausea was fought off, as easy as the sun did the morning dew.

– That's the second time, the first time you've called me that, he said, wrinkling his brow, sensing the apparent contradiction in his words. – Where did you… hear it?

– I d-don't k-know. She moved her head back and forth. – It was just there, you see, sudden like lightning.

– A… memory?

She nodded. She tapped the floor beside her, and he sat down.

They bathed in the sun, their faces rigid as masks. In the shimmering light they saw images from the past, the events that had made the strongest impressions on them, but the images were distorted, chaotic. They had no meaning.

– Man is free, Betty said. – Just like the birds in the air. We're human beings. Those who will keep us in cages are bad.

She turned to him, with a direct, penetrating stare.

– Bad, she repeated.

– And strong, Ted said. – And powerful. They're everywhere, no matter where we run.

She caressed his neck, razed his shoulder with her nails.

– If that's true… Freedom is the most important thing in the world… then we've got only one option.

Both pair of eyes sought the window. There were only five or six steps that way, and then straight down, far below, to the frothing waves. The sea would devour them. Down there no one would catch them.

– Only as a last… resort, Ted stated.

Betty nodded with glass-hard eyes.

If they could just remember.

anything

– The Gray is coming, she said dully. – Hurt me. I don't want to feel good. I don't want to.

He grabbed her hair and pulled in it, pulled hard.

– It's… not… enough. I want to *scream.* Pinch me…

He pinched her nipples, pinched them hard. Her eyes opened wide and she screamed. Wailed like a wounded beast.

– Thank you, she sniffed happily, embracing him, – you saved me, saved me, gave me pain. Thank you.

He couldn't speak. He tried, but couldn't do it.

They rocked back and forth on the floor, dancing in the shadows of the sun, and they felt peace leave them, felt it, right as rain.

– You remember Denver, don't you? He wondered, both hope and fear in his voice.

– Have we truly lived there? She wondered.

She touched his face, an expression of ecstasy in her face.

– I remember Denver, she said dreamingly. – I remember so much more.

An angry light lit Ted's eyes.

– You poisoned me, he said accusingly.

Betty's face brightened then. Life brightened it like the moon.

– You remember? She said, a shiver in her voice.

– I remember! He cried. – Damn it, I do!

– You remember. She choked. – It's true. True!

Tears flowed. First from her eyes, then from his. While competing in laughing and crying the loudest they embraced, embraced even harder, and it felt soft as a feather. It felt like a dam burst, a dam that for so long had kept them from expressing their deeper emotions.

– It's true, he sniffed. – We both remember it.

They sat there, enjoying the moment, the moment of pure, unaltered joy, something they had rarely felt, and not for a very long time.

The door's handle was pushed down. The door opened. Andrew Benedict walked in. His eyes narrowed, and he closed the door behind him.

– What the hell…?

It had turned dark when he once more left his cabin. Halfway towards his destination he met Eric Carr.

– Hi, he said surprised. – What a strange coincidence. I was actually on my way to you.

– I was on my way to you, the other said.

++++++++++++++++++++++++++++++++

A tape turned and turned. The only light in the room came from the bedside lamp. It cast many long dark shadows at the four. Carr could just about make out the shapes of Betty Morgan and Ted Cousin in the extended darkness in front of the open window. There was a draft in the air, from the colder northern October night. He couldn't understand how they could avoid freezing, light clad as they were.

He still thought everything seemed unreal. The strange mood in the air.

The two clutching each other by the window. The strange expression in Benedict's face. The voice on the tape. He felt paralyzed.

– This is the essence of four hours of recording, Benedict had told him. – I thought you would fall asleep if you had to listen to everything.

Once again, Carr ignored the sarcasm. It didn't seem important anymore.

– … was Denver. There was a large river there. We used to bathe in it.

The thin voice belonged to the boy, a sound as naked, as desolate as a remote mountaintop.

– How were you… captured?

– We were in a cabin. To enjoy ourselves… I think. Some… among us helped them… capturing us. Then they came and took us… to the darkness.

– Some of your friends… helped them?

– Yes, the bad feeling is still inside me. Is it hate they call it?

Nobody spoke while the player played. A thin mist coalesced just inside the window, graying the shadows. It turned noticeably colder. Carr's sense of horror rose a few more notches.

– You were given your own cabin and were given the task of mingling with the passengers. Why is that?

– My… task was to befriend Eric Carr, to seduce him, make him trust me.

– How did you do that? I mean, wasn't it hard to… to… pretend like that?

Eric could imagine how she had shaken her head and smiled in pride.

– It was easy. We're well trained. And we don't do it for ourselves, but for t-them.

– You've used that word before. What do you mean by it?

– I can't…

There was a choking sound, and the sound of crying.

– Please, don't cry. I didn't mean…

Carr almost grinned by the helplessness in Benedict's voice. Almost.

– It's the High Ones. Ted spoke. *– They with the power, over us, over life and death and everything in Heaven and on Earth…*

The tape was close to the end. Eric felt vomit rise in his throat, wondering how long he had listened to this. Ten minutes? Half an hour? An hour? He looked at his watch. It was twenty-five minutes. It felt like his entire life.

Everything had been fake, her smile, her tears, her everything. The woman he had befriended didn't exist. She was just a mirage «The High Ones» had helped him create. A human robot adapted to his moods and wiles. They had checked him up, peeled him layer by layer… and created his dream woman.

Benedict turned off the player, hesitatingly looking at his old friend.

– It's hard, isn't it, to be exposed this way? I certainly feel very vulnerable right now.

His voice did shake, did betray a man on the brink.

Carr struck him. It happened so fast, so unexpected that it rattled him, shook him, just as much as Benedict on the receiving end.

Betty and Ted looked impassive at it. They hardly reacted at all.

– Sorry man, *sorry*.

Carr walked back and forth to the door once, before reaching out a hand.

– It's all right, the man on the floor said, rubbing his jaw, drying off blood. – You've wanted to do that for a very long time. I understand, okay. I understand.

Hands met and Carr pulled him back up. Eric felt no sense of relief, of catharsis, just more of the same horror he had, except for brief moments of respite, experienced his entire adult life.

He walked to the two shadows.

– Why? He wondered. – What was the reason for your assignment? What was… the point?

– Aside from it being doable, you mean? She shrugged. – Your job. I was supposed to help you write an article about the Duke, one that would never see print. They wanted him, like they wanted you, like they want everyone.

– Ah, he said, clapping his hands once. – Your sister. Blackmail.

She nodded. Her voice, her demeanor was completely different. She wasn't acting anymore. The green eyes still twinkled, but they twinkled differently.

– Not exactly blackmail, Benedict said. – Far beyond that. They're on a recruitment drive.

And it sort-of made sense. And just hurt more because of it.

– I… Ted rubbed his temple and an expression of pain touched his face.

– Yes? Benedict turned to him.

– Nothing, Ted said. – Nothing important.

Carr turned to him as well, turned fast as a hawk.

– No, we would like to hear it, he said. – Please entertain us.

– I…

– So, you don't remember then?

The boy didn't reply. His eyes suggested he was far away, lightyears away. Carr persisted, kept pushing him.

– Is that it? You don't remember? So, you don't remember everything then?

– We remember, the boy and the girl choired, charging him, grabbing him. – We think, we live, we are. Do you hear?

Benedict acted swiftly and managed to part them. He dragged Carr away, to the other side of the room.

– Listen, he said, speaking in a low, but insistent voice. – Those two live through a nightmare right now. They've been through torture, brainwashing and probably worse. They've just begun to regain memories of their previous life. At the moment they're very vulnerable. You should really take it easy on them.

– Sure. I'll nurse them, play the nice nanny and tell them bedtime stories.

– Listen, Benedict said again, seemingly experiencing major breathing problems. – I can understand that you don't feel too good about the girl and the fact that the boy worked you over…

– You know about *that?* Carr shook his head in absolute astonishment. – How the fuck do you know about that?

– Rachel Dalhart told me, the other replied dryly. – That old lady knows more than the devil concerning secrets and hidden corners. The boy, by the way, doesn't remember anything about it. Neither he nor Betty recall much of anything, really, you know that.

He turned on the player, after changing tapes.

– *What's happening here?* He wondered. – *What the fuck is happening?*

– *It seems totally incomprehensible to me, Mister Benedict,* the old lady said.

Rachel Dalhart again. Another mystery, another unsolved puzzle.

– You're so smooth, suddenly so very smooth, Eric snarled at him. – Why's that, Andy?

He didn't expect a reply, and didn't get any, didn't get an answer, except the wounded look from his old friend.

He returned to the two youths, staring at them.

– You want us to write about this, I assume? Want us to expose this?

– Yes, we want that, Betty said in a hollow voice.

– You were kidnapped in… July? That's three months. What did they *do* to you during all that time? Do you have anything… any physical proof for what they did to you?

He hated himself for the wounded look, the hatred in her eyes.

– You stated that they gave you shots, he continued, virtually begging them. – You've got many, according to your testimony. But that must have left marks. It just must have.

A single tear fell from Betty left eye.

– I can't remember, she said, turned to Ted. – Help me.

He suddenly expressed keen interest in her left arm, quickly pulling up her sleeve and he began to rub her skin. Carr and Benedict exchanged looks, but there was life, frost and certainty in the boy's eyes. To the journalists' astonishment he tore off a large piece of the skin on the girl's upper arm. Carr released a gasp. He was unable to hold it back. Beneath there was also skin, real skin. It was pale and in stark contrast to the otherwise tanned body. At the center of the pale area, blood red and swollen, were the marks of needles, many needles.

– Those bastards, Carr mumbled, his mouth full of bile. – Those fucking bastards.

Ted pointed silently at his own arm, at the same, general area.

– I remember, Betty said with her hollow voice. – They covered our arm. No one could know. No one.

Her eyes widened in horror.

– You know.

She wanted to run to the door. Ted held her firmly.

– The darkness. It's coming… Help me.

The body froze and her eyes turned to glass. Ted was wild in the stare he sent the two men.

– She needs something… to clear her head. Something… Something…

He kicked the floor, concentrating so hard that his face almost turned unrecognizable.

– Something stimulating? Benedict suggested.

– Yes, very much so. Pills. Amph… Amphetamine.

– I don't know if we have anything…

– I have, Carr said quickly. – I'll get it.

He ran rather large parts of the way, almost forgot himself, exposing his state of mind to those who might watch.

The suitcase again, ripped open again, the content emptied on the bed again.

To see her like this, the lovely girl, his lovely girl, ripped him apart. She wasn't human. He had to help her. She had to be human again. Then, perhaps, he could forget, forget he had ever met her, what she had awakened in him.

They had to force her mouth open. The pill remained on the tongue, unmovable.

– What the fuck are we supposed to do?

Carr clutched the small glass. Ted turned Betty's face to his.
– Swallow, Betty, he commanded. – Swallow the pill.
She obeyed instantly.
– Remember the name, he said anxiously. – Say the name. Important.
He tore the glass from Carr's hands. Shook out a pill and put it in his own mouth. Carr saw how he had to concentrate to succeed swallowing it.
– She has kept it going since this morning, unaided, the boy said. – She's so strong.
Betty began speaking and she didn't seem to be present at all. Her ghostly voice covered Eric's body in gooseflesh.
– Uncle told me there would be suffering, but not the extent of it, the horror, the cold and dank horror of the world, the wretched, stinking world.
She turned to Ted. Intelligence and sentience suddenly making her appearance glow in their eyes.
– Can't you feel it? She spoke to Ted, hardly audible. – I know you do. The images, memories rising from the dark, from the abyss. It's so fantastic.
They grabbed each other's hands and stared into each other's eyes.
– You know more about me than I know about myself, he said, also hardly audible. Carr had to strain his ears to understand the words. – We must talk.
– Later, she said brightly. – Later we'll talk. We'll do everything. Everything there is to do.
She sounded so confident, so arrogant. Such an… an alien sight. He saw Betty Morgan appear from the shell where others had hidden her.
Betty Morgan turned to Eric Carr, and her eyes torched his skin, setting it on fire. He wanted her, God, he wanted her. And he felt ashamed.
– They run tests, frequent tests, to assure our continued compliance. And the Doctor, he… The tests will *reveal* our rebellion and we will vanish in there, vanish in their hands, never to be seen again, never to regain our Self. We need to escape, *now,* before the ship reaches the port.
– Ten, tomorrow evening, Eric said. – It should go. It must.
He said to Benedict, to Betty, to himself.
– We must, Andy, he repeated.
Benedict stood there, nodding, breathing, as the jungle started breathing around the two men, as they returned to the jungle, as they finally returned, as the astonishing fact that Carr had used his first name without snarling was evidently lost on him.
So much lost, Eric thought. He felt it, felt himself, felt all four of them

awaken from the slumber modern life had put them in, and just now he wanted, desperately wanted this feeling to persist, to grow.

And somewhere far, far ahead the breathing jungle embraced them all. He already ran through the dark hallways of the ship with a hammering heart. Imagination hammered him. He heard the drums, the swaying trees, spotted the shadows move through the underbrush with weapons in their hands.

Chapter Eleven

As he had done every day, Benedict supplemented dinner with four bottles of wine on his final day onboard M/S Aphrodite. Eric Carr and Betty Morgan sat three tables from him. Everything was looking good. To everyone watching there was still a chill between the two men. They hadn't behaved any differently, done anything to raise suspicion.

Ted Cousin was there as well, sliding in and out of Carr's attention, playing the bored, cruel young man the masters wanted him to play.

Tim Croydon had followed Carr and Betty all day, as Carr had been told he would, when he and Betty enjoyed each other's company, as he had done the entire week without Carr spotting him. Now Carr knew, and he wanted to punch the guy's lights out. But Betty held his hand, and she calmed him, not the other way around.

Everything looked okay, but he worried. Ants crawled beneath his skin. The girl looked at him with cold, calculating eyes.

– It's been a long time since I operated behind enemy's lines, he admitted, giving her a confident smile, – and this is it, this is it for sure. It's different from the jungle, but just as deadly. Perhaps more so, because of the pleasant surroundings. But I'm okay. We will get away. You will be free.

She squeezed his hand, as she kept playing the doll, the pleasant shell he had loved.

The worry buzzed in his ears like wasps. He sat on the bed in his cabin, playing with the red lock. Fingers drummed on the door, the unlocked door. The signal. He placed himself along the wall, what would be behind the door, drawing the knife.

– Enter, he said casually.

Betty rushed inside, closely followed by Ted. Two black ravens out of the deepest corner of the imagination. Their faces were a dark mirroring nothing, but that dark, that shadow. But there was still life there - and frost, ice-cold frost. Eric understood, god, how he understood. He had seen the same expression on his own face the last few years - every time he had looked at himself in the mirror.

– You look quite… elegant, both of you, he commented, cursing the insecurity exposed in his voice.

They were, wearing warm, light clothes. It was the first time Carr saw them in what he deemed normal clothes.

He had closed the window. It was cold outside. He had opened the window in the morning, and the wind had felt like a gust from Dante's Seventh Hell.

– I've got something for you, he said to her, to Betty. – Perhaps it will help you somehow, help you remember.

He gave her the red lock. She accepted it with an unfathomable expression locked in her eyes.

– You *are* clever. She nodded. – I knew you would be.

Her hand closed around the red, the shiny red.

– Remember, she said, repeating it. – Remember.

He couldn't help it, couldn't stop the cold trickle down his spine when she looked at him. He realized that she hated him.

– Here, he said, giving them two pills of amphetamine each. – Take both when you need to.

They accepted them without a word. Hands like claws closed around them.

There was another tap on the door, another signal. The three of them moved, moved into position, taking key positions, like one person, as if they had always worked together. Eric feared he was still slow, still rusty, but felt his insides, what hid inside rising from its slumber, slowly, painfully.

Benedict slipped inside, too. His belly rocked beneath the shirt. But he, too, moved like lightning, like there was nothing but mist beneath him, instead of hard ground.

– It's time, Benedict said.

Carr nodded, quite unnecessarily. The lights of London, of its surrounding areas, had, for some time now, shifted in his eyes, in the eyes and faces of those around him.

– Eric, you'll go first, Benedict said. – Then Ted and Betty. I'll be the rear.

Carr nodded. It was a sound marching order. Carr smiled. It was oddly appropriate. He valued what he saw as Benedict's attempt at levity, at self-irony. The rear indeed…

With luck it would even enhance their chances of survival in the insane venture they had set out on.

He moved, and they moved with him. They were on their way. It was too late for second thoughts, for recriminations. He saw others he recognized from missing posters. And he spotted, with an ever-keener eye, the watchers, mingling with the passengers. The jungle moved around him, and he couldn't breathe, the smell of trees, of moist growth, of decay stuck in his nostrils. He pressed on.

«We walk in a storm», Patrick Warren had said once in Vietnam. «We're at its mercy and have no control over our own lives».

Carr had sworn he would never return to the Storm. Now he was back.

He reached the deck. The night and the cold wind blew in his face. He briefly allowed a smile to cross his face and kept moving, moved across mountains and through northern forests. Nothing had changed.

His two charges appeared behind him. He moved up on the ship, and they did, too. He didn't see Benedict, but didn't expect to, either, as he would be too far behind. The wind shook Carr as he moved up the last staircase to the lifeboats. He heard Betty and Ted's step. Aside from that he heard nothing, except the flapping of the plastic covering the lifeboats.

It was dark. The boats could just be seen as a silhouette against the bright skies behind. He could see his breath in the air. Sensed how labored it was. He cursed himself for the lazy life he had been living.

He signaled the boy and the girl, and they approached.

– You'll jump aboard the moment the boat is shipside, he had told them. – If there's time I'll lower the boat slowly. If there isn't, I'll do it fast, very fast.

He walked to the nearest boat. It was easy. One quick pull in a rope, and three boats would loosen simultaneously. Seconds, he needed only…

There were other people on the deck. He froze. There were three of them, three men with guns. He noticed the silencers, the thick, ugly cylinders in the front of the sleek barrel. Thoughts, hardly thoughts at all, raced through his mind, fevered observations of survival, so crucial for that very survival. They stood close to each other, not bothering with caution, those confident bastards.

Carr didn't move. He just stood there, looking at them, the bad taste of defeat in his mouth. He had let himself be caught unaware. His rusty mind had been easily fooled.

– I knew you were a sensible man, Carr, the leader, Tim Croydon, nodded. – You've realized how miniscule your changes of escaping truly are. Too bad it was you up here. We had such great plans for you.

He was talking. The idiot was talking. Carr almost laughed out aloud.

He wondered where the hell Andy had disappeared to, if they had already taken care of him.

Ted and Betty stood shivering a bit to his left. Naked fear dominated their features, their entire pose.

– Ted and Betty, you've been disobedient, you've been bad, and thus you're punished.

Croydon signed, and the man to the leader's right led a hand to his belt, and pushed a button. As long as he lived Eric Carr would never forget the pain he saw in the two faces and the horrible screams he heard from the boy and the girl. He stared blindly at the two caricatures of human beings writhing on the deck. It was the ring, the collar, the Masters' foremost tool of punishment, of retribution. He no longer faulted Betty for being terrified by the very thought of it.

He threw the knife right in the heart of the man pushing the button. The man grabbed the knife's handle. The gun slipped from his weak grip. With a pathetic howl he fell and died. Everything happened so fast. There was no time to think, only do, and Carr did. He threw himself forward, was leaping at them, seemingly before they had even taken their eyes off their departed «comrade». Amateurs, they were amateurs. He placed a foot in one man's face, and before Croydon managed to fire a single shot Carr had wrested the gun from him. He struck out with a hand, but Carr avoided it easily and pushed an elbow in the opponent's abdomen. Croydon fell backwards by the rail. Carr kept moving. He picked up one of the pistols with his right hand and pulled out the knife from the dead man's chest with his left. There was movement behind him, and the sound Carr recognized too well; that of a popping gun. He threw the knife towards the sound. The bullet missed Carr. He imagined he heard it pass by his ear. It didn't faze him. There was just one bullet, compared to the thousands that had previously passed by him. The knife hit the man he had kicked in the face. It buried itself in his throat, cutting the big vein bringing blood to the brain, and killing him virtually instantaneously. Carr fired at Croydon. The bullet grazed the man's head and made him tumble over the inner rail. Carr heard the sound of the enemy hitting the lower deck, as he kept moving, kept going the momentum. He turned, and turned again, pointing the gun in all directions, before he slowly, temporarily allowed himself to slow down. There was no one, no enemy left, not up here. He pulled the knife out of the dead man's throat, breathing hard, breathing easy. It had been so easy. He felt an enormous relief, as he welcomed the ongoing storm within, the preparation for the unending battle.

The boy and the girl crouched unmoving on the deck. For a moment he couldn't tell if they were breathing. They moved. They sat up, as he rushed to their side. He dried the knife by rubbing the blade again his pants. It didn't matter. He was bathed in blood anyway.

He touched Ted as the boy rose to his feet. He couldn't make himself touch Betty. There was shock, still raw in his eyes when he looked carefully at them both, fearing the next moments, the next seconds and years.

– We're okay. Ted spoke in a hard and accentuated way, triumph thick in his voice. – I can still remember.

– Yes, Betty said. – It just hurts. We can think. Those assholes, those fucking assholes!

There was a quality of madness to her voice and demeanor that both excited and frightened Eric. He closed his eyes hard. With relief, but also because of the prevalent impotence he felt.

– You must have told Benedict about this, he raged, grabbing Ted's collar. – You must have!

– We did, they choired blandly.

Ted shook lightly, but his eyes burned. Carr could swear, for a moment there, a tiny moment that he saw true fire in those cold eyes.

– You… *told* him, and he said nothing, did nothing about it… When did you *stop* seeing him behind you?

– He was there, Betty said. – Then he wasn't.

Eric Carr felt a vast abyss open up beneath him, one in which there was no end in sight.

He felt along the collar, and after a second, two, he did find a keyhole. He rushed to the inner rail, moving along it, looking down on the lower decks. There was nothing there, nothing obviously threatening. It was there. He saw it move, saw it gather momentum against them. The ghosts of the jungle moved between the dark trees.

– We're compromised, he told the two, grabbing their shoulders, speaking low and enraged. – We must assume that the opposition, the… enemy knows everything, everything we planned. So we scrap everything and start over, stop planning, start *doing*.

They nodded, nodded fiercely at him.

– Listen… look…

And they listened and they looked.

– The thing around your neck… it's only *pain*. The words they may speak to you, words designed to dull your mind, control you, they're only words. They have no hold over you, no power except what you're allowing them to have. Do you *understand?*

– Yes, they choired.

He picked up the two guns, wresting them from the two men's dead fingers, and then he handed them to his charges, feeling great and reckless and crazy.

– When you see an enemy you fire, he told them. – Fire until he or she is dead. If you see Benedict, and he makes a single suspicious move, fire at will.

The two nodded. He saw them, how they handled the weapons, apprehensive at first, then, after only a few seconds moves turned fluid, turned confident, as if they had never done anything else.

– You're good with the knife. Ted's eyes twinkled in the bad light.

– You ain't seen nothing yet, Eric grinned, feeling strong, feeling alive.

And he remembered, remembered the rush of blood, not only the fear, the numbing fear.

They rushed back down. Croydon moaned aloud somewhere, as he moved, stumbled across an adjacent deck. There were other people moving as well. Carr heard them, sensed them, sensed them close in on the three fugitives. There was fog on the deck, sudden and almost shocking, growing thick in a matter of seconds. Carr smiled. He had never cared much for fog. He grinned to the snarling gap he sensed in there. The famous London fog welcomed them, haunted them, as they breathed it in and out, as the ship was surrounded in it. The trickle down Eric's back was both apprehension and joy. He welcomed that, too. The three of them held their guns in both hands, as they moved, as they rushed forward, as they charged through the breathing jungle. Carr noticed it all, outside himself, almost like an afterthought. Betty, even though there was fear in her eyes, moved very much like Carr himself, like a gunman, like someone who knew what she was doing, like someone who had had… training. Ted simulated more the other two.

He's… learning, Carr thought. Learning as he goes.

And once again, through the danger and the rock-hard focusing… he sensed the vast tapestry unfolding, wondering what he had stumbled on to.

They approached an entrance, one to the inner workings of the ship. It felt like a gust of rotten breath, making his nose flinch. He had sensed something, something… more, since he had seen the flare in Ted's eyes. The fog surrounded them like a white, ethereal wall, and in that sticky white substance there were people, people resembling ghosts more than actual living, breathing flesh. The number of unconcerned men and women started increasing around them, passengers stumbling around, sipping their drinks, some also dragging their suitcases around, ready for arrival, all seeing nothing, hearing nothing, understanding even less. Some saw the red color on Carr's shirt and the gun in his hand for what it was, though, and paled. Most smiled and laughed and cried.

– Excellent party, huh?

A man with a bottle in one hand and a glass in the other slipped by.

Carr turned, made another turn, pointing his gun where his eyes looked. He saw them. Four this time. They moved like one, with a sense of purpose, clearly distinguishing them from the passengers. They didn't cry out, didn't show with one single sign that they had spotted their prey, but Carr knew they had. He saw it in the way they moved, in the squinting of their eyes, their eyes so clear to him that they could just as well be right in front of him. They didn't want trouble, didn't want known trouble. It was bad for business, bad for so much.

This is our advantage then, he thought, our ace in the hole. He fired. Betty and Ted fired a moment later. Two stalkers vanished from sight. He cursed himself for not removing the silencers. This was a dance, a silent dance. A woman screamed, but it was muted. Hardly anyone noticed, noticed anything.

– Go, he told the two. – Go to Benedict's cabin. Hopefully this is still one of the last places they'll look for you. If I don't come, do your best, your very best, your deadliest.

And he knew their best was considerable, and the thought comforted him.

They turned the next corner. He nodded to them, and they ran off. He followed them with his eyes a second or two. There were no words, no twist in their faces. They seemed indifferent, both in terms of what happened to him, and themselves. Perhaps they had lost their ability to feel. If so, he couldn't fault them.

He put the gun away, and charged forward, returned the way he had come, just as the two remaining stalkers turned the corner. Like he had sensed an enemy hide in the bushes in Vietnam he sensed them approach here. For every second he lived in deadly danger this instinct returned to him.

He threw himself at them, attacked with a classic martial arts kick. The foot hit one of the men in the temple and he fell without a sound. Before Carr landed he had already hit the other with a blow to the neck. He found himself in a whirl of bodies. There were more of them. He kept moving, kept extending his movement to the new enemies. He landed a bit wrong, and perhaps that was the reason the third man miss-stepped his attack, and missed with a murderous blow. Carr pushed four stiff fingers into his abdomen, destroying his spleen. The last two were huge. One was almost unmoved by the elbow sent into his ribs, but Carr heard something break, and hit the man again, punching his ribs into his lungs. The big man gasped, and with that gasp pink lung blood flowed from his mouth. Carr narrowly avoided a kick to his groin from the final opponent. He grabbed the big man's head and brutally, with the full mass of his own body behind the move, pushed the shaven head into the hard metal of the ship's wall.

The battle was done, before it had really started. The only one of the five still conscious stood on his knees and kept spitting blood, dying by the second. The passengers, those who hadn't yet run stood there, staring, terrified and gaping.

Carr limped away. The passengers were quite polite and made way for him. He hardly noticed them, rubbing his thigh, concentrating on ignoring the pain, the numbness spreading. These guys had been professionals, and though they hadn't been very good, he had been lucky to end the fight this early. The Abraxas Omega had underestimated him twice. It wouldn't happen again.

He headed towards Benedict's cabin, thoughts racing through his highly intoxicated mind. Hardly identifiable thoughts in the burning his life had become. He passed the stairs leading to the dance hall, passed further into the darkness, the less traveled part of the ship.

He stopped abruptly around the next corner. Four men headed his way from the opposite side. They seemed pretty ordinary, really, but to him they were very, very distinct. He knew them, knew their economic moves, their deadly intent. They didn't change pace when they discovered him, just speeded up slightly, imperceptible to others. He turned and headed back. Seemingly indifferent and calm he turned the corner again, and the moment he had turned the corner he started running, speeding up, without bothering about the finer points of polite behavior. Angry, ignorant passengers cried ugly words after him. He reached the stairs and had run one floor down when he glimpsed opposition on its way up. Damn. Damn! The upper decks. There was cover there and shadow. His element, not theirs.

He rushed outside again, rushed up, towards the higher points of the ship. People were whispering, as they passed the bloodied forms on the deck, whining and worrying and hurrying on. The stairs to the pool level were a metal grid. He realized that if he walked on them it would be heard all over the ship. So he jumped, and reached the rail on the next level with one hand, reaching it with his other hand, and he dragged himself up. It was hard, but he did it. He was hardly breathing harder when he stood on his feet resting a bit, a second our two, before moving on. He wondered if there were only psychological reasons for his previous exhaustion.

The pool had been emptied of water a few hours earlier, but the ladder was still wet and slippery. He descended the ladder a bit, hiding behind the edge of the hole. Down there, down in the wet shade, he started unscrewing the silencer on the gun. He was ready for them. They were experienced thugs, but he wondered if they were used to death. Probably some of them, a bit, but not like he was. They hadn't stared it in the eye, until it was all they could see. They didn't *know*.

Ten seconds… twenty, thirty passed. He saw and heard them. The idiots, the amateurs. They used the stairs. Only two. Something… something was not right here. They carried no weapons. Carr shook his head in dismay. They entered the light at the top of the stairs and their faces were lit… *One was Andrew Benedict*.

– Carr won't come, Ted said.

They looked at each other, at the door, at each other again. They sat side by side at the edge of the bed in Benedict's cabin. Betty nodded her agreement.

– What do you want to do? She wondered.

He looked strangely at her.

– Do you remember anything from Denver?

– Yes. She nodded.

– Do you remember well the time before Denver?

– I do, she replied calmly.

There were no lights lit in the room. The lights from houses in the Greater London area split ever more of the darkness. The ship would reach its destination soon.

– We'll have to get away on our own, Ted said. – I just don't know how.

– If we attempt to disembark with the passengers, they *will* catch us. Betty rocked back and forth. – We won't stand a chance.

– They'll make us look sick, he nodded, – and then they'll take us away.

They heard steps out in the hallway, slowly growing heavier, coming closer and closer. Both choked and wild and shaking in fear they fell on the floor and crawled under the bed. They clawed and scratched until they pushed themselves against the wall. With heaving breath they clutched each other, waiting for the horrible moment when the door would open.

The steps turned to lesser thunder, turned remote once more.

The two remained on that spot under the bed, doing nothing but breathe. The modest light seemed almost psychedelic to them. Once again they heard the commanding voice inside.

– … helpless

(without us you cannot live)

And then came the insane laughter. Kurt Meinz' recorded voice. Through mist Ted could glimpse the square, horrible face. He was behind the voices, whether he spoke the words or not. The voices that should keep them from rebelling, turn them away from rebellion. Ted knew that, now. He knew it well.

– We don't stand a chance… do we?

Betty was on the verge of hysteria, but at the same time there was something of a strange apathy ruling her. She disengaged herself from Ted and began crawling towards the window.

– Just one way out, she frothed.

It took a few, precious moments before he realized what her words signified, to understand their horrible meaning, what she was about to do. He rolled from under the bed and grabbed her ankle, desperately attempting to hold on to her. When he finally managed to stop her forward movement, she had almost reached the handle that opened the window. He lay down beside her.

– Join me, Ted, she whispered. – Let's do it together.

Together… into the waves down there, be led away by the river far away with no one ever hurting them.

– No! The fire in his eyes flared, and she gasped in joy. – *No!*

She relented, joyfully, ashamed. They sat there, as their breath slowly returned to normal.

– I'm sorry, she whispered. – Everything just felt so hopeless for a moment there, but now it doesn't anymore.

– That's the way of the program. It doesn't want us to be alive and free.

– But we *are* alive and free, and much more, she whispered in triumph. – And we're going to drown their world in flames.

Like a cat she writhed in his arms, pushed herself at him, and this time her fire, her sensuality was true. He felt it in every nerve.

She drew something from a pocket. The red lock.

They stared in awe at the hair, as if it was woven gold.

– The gangway door, she said suddenly. – Before… before arrival.

– I remember, he said excitedly. – It's not that high up. We can jump into the water from there.

– But we must get there. Her smile faded. – We must walk all the stairs. They'll be guarded. We don't stand a chance.

They rested there for a while, silent, filled with silent pain, overwhelmed with hopelessness.

– But… we don't need to go that way.

Betty heard his voice as if in a dream. It was challenging, snarling. For the first time in a very long time she saw something of his old self. And the joy was like music inside her.

– We can take the inner route, she said, hesitatingly. – That way we stand a chance at least. We are that bold, that brave.

She kissed him, in gratitude and passion.

– We will make it, he stated. – We will be free!

– We will make it, she stated. – We will be free!

He rose. She remained. And she dreamed. He hesitated a moment, before grabbing her wrist, the golden bracelet, helping her up.

She looked at the four pills in his palm, the Amphetamine.

– One final time, he said. – And nevermore.

– Nevermore, she echoed. – Or we'll destroy ourselves.

They swallowed two pills each. Without water they felt uneasily hard.

– One day, she said to him. – One day I'll give you everything.

And then, as the stimuli spread in their bodies and made their senses infinitely sharp, he almost understood what she meant. Then it was as if a curtain was drawn before his deeper self, and understanding eluded him… again.

There was nothing of the hunter in the two men. Both Benedict and the other spoke low to each other. Eric barely heard them. They glanced around, like kids stealing apples in the neighbor's garden. Eric felt the rage rise within. His hand shook around the gun, and he wanted to kill Benedict outright. He knew who the other was: Bob Tremblay. And he knew what Benedict's motive had been: Pure greed. Benedict had, anonymously revealed the plan he had been a part of developing, to gain an advantage, to easier escape from the boat with his charge.

It was so cynical, so diabolical, that it made Eric shake violently in hatred and shock. His own cynicism resembled that of a nun in comparison. He grinned in cold and heat.

– How about it? Benedict said to Tremblay. – Is the pill working?

– Yes, Tremblay said weakly. – It's like awakening from a bad dream.

– I'll get you back to your family, Benedict assured him. – Trust me on this.

Carr felt sick. Waves of nausea washed over him, drowning him.

He realized now the significance of the fact that he hadn't heard the entire tape, the tape that Benedict had listened to extensively.

And there was this… this murmur somewhere he couldn't quite identify.

The ship sailed, sailed closer to port, while the frown Carr spotted on Benedict's forehead made the wheels turn and turn in Carr's own mind.

And then he had it. It was so obvious that he almost felt ashamed, ashamed over his continued gullibility.

– You don't wear bracelets and collar, Benedict exclaimed, shock written in his swollen face.

– I thought you would never get it. Tremblay chuckled insanely. The Amphetamine probably made him close to delirious. – What a stupid ass you've been.

Four men rose by the lifeboats. Four more rushed up the stairs. Eric Carr could suddenly count every single hair rising on his neck. Awareness flooded him, his razor-sharp mind. He saw movement, movement in the shadows.

– And you, in the pool aren't much better.

Carr shook his head, perhaps in denial, perhaps in anger, he couldn't tell anymore, as he climbed the ladder, as he ascended from the pool. Benedict stared at him in shock, at *him* in shock.

– This must be poetic justice, don't you think? Carr grinned, couldn't help it, help himself.

– I had to do it, Benedict almost shouted. – I had no choice.

Eric Carr stared at a man with no hope left.

– You've given up. Eric looked startled at him.

Benedict didn't really see anything, anything but the nothing in his eyes. He turned to the young man with desperate stubbornness written all over his face.

– You *are* Robert Tremblay. You *have to be*. Your features differ slightly from the photos. But there are other characteristics. The mole…

– You're stupid as an empty sack. You can't possibly be foolish enough to believe that «Hammer» Tremblay's son disappears without wanting to.

Eric realized that he was standing there with the gun in his hand. It pointed down, and the men covered him, as much as they covered the unarmed Benedict, but he still had it in his hand.

There was movement, and there were steps. Heads were turned, and guns were turned, and all of the men stared absolutely astonished as Rachel Dalhart appeared from the shadows. She used a walking stick and it looked like she had major difficulties walking.

– What's going on here? She wondered incredulously.

The men lowered their weapons, their eyes widening.
Carr started laughing, shaking his head.
– What the fuck *is* going on here? Robert Tremblay exclaimed, suddenly totally out of it, his former cock-a-bull confidence suddenly supplanted with a nagging uncertainty.
Eric Carr looked at him, and saw it, saw how his reason took flight there and then, if it hadn't already.
– You don't get it, do you? Eric told him. – You've lived close to the vast tapestry all these years, and you don't get it. Who's the fool now?
Tremblay snarled and raised his gun, directing it at Carr.
Dalhart moved, and as she moved she… *changed.* The old, frail woman grew as they watched, both taller and stronger, young and powerful. It was a wild creature that charged the nine Abraxas Omega men, a whirl of motion that comforted Eric and lit his own fire, and as he sensed the ashes within turn to volcanic heat, he, too, moved, moved fast as lightning.
Benedict stood still, his face frozen in shock, in inaction, his skin covered in cold sweat. Tremblay shot him three times in the chest, and he died quietly.
– We bet on whether or not you would sweat, Tremblay snarled triumphantly, totally beyond sanity. – I won.
The wild creature was among them, poetry in motion, dancing, taking a new step for every new kick or strike. They lifted their guns to fire, but there was nothing to fire at. Their fists and feet struck only air.
Instinct ruled Carr. Hundreds of decisions were made in an instant. He was in the midst of the other group of four. Tremblay fired at Carr, fired at them. He hit one of the four in the head. Brain mass decorated Carr's right arm. Another bullet grazed his side, and he felt a glowing pain like a sizzle. Carr fired point blank at another man and the man fell. The blood flowed through the air, flowed in every move, every blow that was struck.
– Go, Eric. The wild beast spoke, spoke like a ghost. – Live, Eric!
Dalhart, or whoever she was, who the fuck she was was gone. One moment she was there. The next she wasn't. There was just a whisper in the wind, nothing more, to mark her passing. Carr jumped over the rail, feeling lucky, very lucky. So many bullets could accidentally have hit him, and none had.
He landed on the deck below. The opposition had wanted to play this time, too, in their cock-a-bull confidence and arrogance, and they had paid for it. Pain almost overwhelmed him, as he choked, as he saw Andrew Benedict die, time and time again, as he had seen so many of his fellow warriors go down. He choked so hard that he could hardly swallow,

hardly swallow at all. The non-existing tears in his eyes blinded him, a moment, two, before the crystal-clear clarity overwhelmed him again.

Four more men waited for him. He landed on a deck and let himself fall, rolled and rolled while firing his gun. The four were unarmed, and for the thousandth time he wondered what was wrong with these people, what went through their heads, their empty heads. He managed to fire three times before they reached him. They almost stopped when they heard the cracks. Two of them were hit, one in the head and the other in the thigh and in the side. The gun was kicked out of his hand. Carr gave the guy a killing blow in the groin. The poor guy screamed loud enough to wake the dead, as his own light was extinguished. The fourth guy was good, very good. Carr managed only marginally to parry his blows long enough to get on his feet. He finally found an opening and kicked the opponent far away. But this was truly a tough guy, and he got up almost instantly. Carr looked for his gun, but it was nowhere to be seen.

The tough guy advanced, very confident. Carr let himself be driven a bit back. He waited patiently, trading blows, waiting for the moment, the seconds it took for them to arrive outside the doorway to the great hall, when light spilled across the other man's face. Then Carr drew his knife so fast that the other man looked totally unprepared. The blade cut into the exposed neck, virtually beheading the man. Blood from the jugular vein splashed the deck, splashed everywhere, mixed with water and air and mist, coalescing into night, into red night. Everything so clear Carr saw everything, everything around him. Years, it had been years since he had done this, and it felt like he had never stopped. He jumped, diving through the broad doorway. There was a number of pops, as the bullets headed where he had just been standing. He felt a push, right before he landed inside. At the polished floor he just kept moving, sliding down. The passengers cried in panic as the bloodied man rushed towards them.

– Some maniacs are having a shooting contest up there, he cried. – Someone must *do* something!

There was pain. The bullet had passed through his leg. He didn't have to see it to know it. It had avoided the bone and just penetrated the flesh. He could move and he kept moving. Every time he put weight on the injured leg he feared it would give in, and that he would fall, fall down. He kept running. Air wheezed in and out of his lungs.

He made a fist, two fists. And his fists hurt, hurt so much that he hardly felt the leg at all. He limped at first, but after the first, critical seconds the limp was hardly noticeable. Hell, he had been hit in the leg in Vietnam as well, and had run miles and miles through the jungle without breaking stride. These were not thoughts. These were merely flashes, tongues of fire running through his abyss of a mind.

There was a group of party-clad people that stopped as he passed them, and just stared in incredulity.

– Is there anything we can help you with?

One of them spoke out, very politely.

– Go to…

Some people were just slow on the uptake.

He kept limping on. The wound left a trail of blood on the carpet, way too visible. He ripped off his sleeve and spent a few seconds making a provisional bandage. The stairs were hard. It took time climbing them, way too long time. He managed to run now and then, but he slowed down, and he would keep slowing down, he knew that, until he stopped. Sparkles flew before his eyes. He expected them to find him, to wait behind the next corner the next time he exhausted had climbed another set of stairs. But they didn't come. He couldn't think, couldn't think about the haunting and beautiful wild thing, the poetry in motion he had glimpsed up there on the deck. He walked on, stumbled on, to his last resting place.

Bob Tremblay led a rather large group of men down the same hallway not long afterwards. They followed the trail of blood, followed it like a pack of dogs, followed the scent of the prey.

The spots appeared with ever-shorter intervals, until they stopped with one large outside a specific door.

– His own cabin, Tremblay snarled. – The nerve of that guy. Take us in, Truck.

Truck kicked in the door. It struck the wall inside with a loud crack. They drew their guns and rushed inside.

To no avail. The room was empty. The bathroom was empty. There was no one in the shower. Or in the closets or under the bed. Tremblay sent the man looking under the bed a rather angry message.

– They won't get away from the ship, he mumbled. – They won't get away.

The sheets were shredded. The blood trail went as far as the bed. There it stopped. The suitcase was displayed on the bed, open and mostly empty. His essential equipment was gone. Eric Carr wouldn't return here.

Beyond the stairs, across the ship, in the other section a man locked himself inside the cabin that had belonged to Andrew Benedict. It had been closed off to keep curious people from interfering. The man was hardly more than shadow, hardly even that, a creature dressed entirely in black, a curious mask covering his face. If someone had observed him they would have wondered how he could walk without colliding with something. The mask had no eyes, no mouth.

He used the outside of his hand to turn the switch on the night table lamp. There were two marks of bodies on the bed, as he had suspected there would be. None of the idiots had thought about searching here, of course.

The portable tape recorder had been left on the dining table. He rewound the tape. After a while he pushed the play button with his middle knuckle, and the buzz of the tape filled the room. The voices changed something in him. He straightened almost imperceptibly.

– My sister's name was Linda. I saw her shower on our twelfth birthday. Our brother's name was Michael. I killed him when I was sixteen.

The Mask began pacing around the room.

– We were brothers and were tied with far more than blood. Perhaps that's why we hated each other so intensely. The city we lived in was called Denver. There's a river there. We used to bathe in it, to feel its currents. I loved the nature surrounding the city. We could have long walks in the mountains. We fished a lot. Michael was never very good at it. During my last summer there I had a great time.

The Mask grabbed the table and shook it. The recorder hit the floor and expired in a prolonged sound of pain and electronic horror. The Mask snarled and threw the table across the room and through the window. There was a lot of noise as the window broke and the glass hit the floor. He stood unmoving, listening, listening for the non-existing sound as the table hit the water far below. He turned. There was no sound. Not of step, not of breath, but he still knew there was someone behind him. David Gidman stood right inside the door, with his arms crossed, waiting.

– They'll get away, The Mask said. – Somehow, I always knew they would.

He grinned wildly, his teeth clearly visible through the fabric of the mask. Gidman said nothing, only watched as the other man left the room, as he passed him to enter the hallway. He stopped there, for a moment, as if listening. But then he shook his head and moved on.

Ted and Betty hid in the lifebelt closet, the one almost devoid of lifebelts. Ted looked through a crack and watched as the Mask walked by. He felt the blood boil and knew that, now, he could once more hate. The hatred pulsed so hard in his heart that he had to fight to keep himself from attacking the man out there.

Later. If you're not calm now. There will never be a later.

He and Betty held hands, clutched hands, and it was as if their skin was glowing on the spots they touched.

– We're here, he said for the second time.

This time there was a response. The elevator shook as it started descending.

There was a hum in the speakers, a melody they both recognized, words without words echoing in their mind.

The bright light when they approached from the elevator blinded them, but they were used to that and prepared for it. Shuen Parker waited for them behind the desk. The humming stopped. Their eyes stared straight ahead, stared at nothing, and didn't seem to acknowledge her presence at all.

– Ah, Ted and Betty. I've been expecting you. Approach!

They hurried to her and knelt before her exalted presence.

– You're so brave, she mused, as she rose, as she smiled to them. – So innovative. You quite simply took the chance that whoever waited for you here hadn't heard about your little escape attempt.

And she pushed the button at her hip. And pain cut through them. Hands waved helplessly in the air, as they writhed in horrible cramps on the floor. Ted screamed, he knew he did, but he heard nothing. Everything turned silent, turned dead. He saw Shuen Parker's face unbelievably clear. Then suddenly he saw Betty's face, and sound returned, the scream returned. Ted and Betty clasped hands. And there was a discharge of energy. They saw it, saw it through Parker's eyes. Their hands… glowed. And the monstrosity around their necks… its power sputtered and died, as sparks flew. The golden metal darkened like ash, and suddenly felt so very, very hot.

Shuen Parker stood there gaping. The shock painted her face, as Ted and Betty rose, as Ted and Betty moved, fast as lightning. They grabbed her. Betty kicked her in the belly, paralyzing her, and the woman turned limp in their grip.

She gasped, and gasped, incredulity and fear present in her eyes.

– Ted and Betty, stop, she gasped. – I order you to stop.

Ted laughed at her, scornfully and hate-filled.

– We're leaving, he stated. – And neither you nor anyone else will stop us.

– You're such a sweet thing, Parker said sweetly, rubbing his cheek.

– You s-sick… His hand slapped her cheek.

– How DARE you! She shouted. – VILE, DISOBEDIENT CHILD!

She freed herself from their grasp, just like that, easy as pie, and struck him in the abdomen. He fell, like a tree. Betty's eyes flared in rage. She struck Parker in the head. Parker fell halfway on the desk. Betty struck her again, and again. Betty lifted her hand to strike again.

– Don't! Ted told her, and she stopped, instantly obeying his command. – Let her be awake. Let her feel what we do to her.

He rose and walked to her, to them both. He patted Betty on the cheek and she smiled in joy. Parker's head shook back and forth, and she was unable to move it properly. He grabbed her hair and forced her head far back, almost to the breaking point.

– A gag, if you please, Ted told Betty.

– As you wish. Betty curtseyed and obeyed enthusiastically, ripping off her left sleeve.

Ted didn't notice. He drew the knife from his pocket and pushed it at Shuen Parker's jugular.

– One more sound, one more trick, and I'll kill you, he snarled. – I'll gut you.

He had his face close to hers. She shook confronted by the savage hatred in his eyes, in his stance.

– Don't worry, Betty said and smiled viciously. – She knows who you are, whom she's dealing with and what you may do to her, if you choose to.

She had formed the sleeve into a hard ball, and now she pushed it, pushed it hard into Parker's mouth. Then tearing off the other sleeve, she tied that around Parker's head, so hard that the prisoner's lips turned white.

– Is that good? Betty asked for Ted's approval, eager like a kid.

– Very good, he nodded.

He put the knife away. And then, with a slight twist of his wrist he knocked Parker's head at the desk. More than half unconscious she was putty in his hands. He put her down on the floor, on her belly, twisting her arms on her back. And he kept twisting them, twisting them around and around. He stopped with one arm and concentrated on the other. Shuen moaned in pain and fear, inspiring him to continue. The arm eventually broke, broke with a loud crack. The woman shook. A scream formed in her throat, but the gag kept it from manifesting. He returned to the other arm. When that, too broke, she turned rigid in his hands, before it softened like jelly, and her head fell to the floor while tears of pain flowed from her eyes. Her skin was gray like lukewarm water and her face seemed dissolved and ugly.

– Time to go, Ted told Betty. His face was even uglier when he bent down and whispered into Shuen Parker's ear: – I'll let you live. I'll even let you keep your arms. We don't have time to kill you as slowly and painfully as we wish. But one day I'll hunt you all down. Then you will beg me to let you die, do you hear me? *Beg!*

They left the wet spot on the floor. It didn't move. There were weird, tiny sounds coming from it. Even when they could no longer see it, they heard it. Ted felt no remorse. If he felt anything, it was regret… that she was still alive. He wondered if he had taken another step on his preordained path.

– Why didn't you say anything?

– About what? Betty wondered.

– Over the fact that we used too long time in there?

– I left it to you. You know best.

He stared at her, open-mouthed. She spoke humbly, respectfully almost servile.

– You'll understand. She laughed, her voice loud again. – One day you'll understand.

He stopped and grabbed her arm, pushing her at the wall.

– I'm sick and tired of this, he snarled. – I want an explanation, *now*.

There was no time. Three guards, two men and one woman, dressed in black turned the corner.

The guards drew their guns, their dart-guns, firing poison, firing sleep, capture. Ted and Betty stopped in their tracks, paralyzed, unable to move, disheartened, way too far away to charge the grinning trio.

– So, these are the sweet things that have strayed, the woman purred. – Don't worry, children, we'll set you straight again… after we've had some fun, that is.

The men grinned expectantly when her hand sought the belt and the button. She pushed the button, and the slaves cried out and fell to the floor. They crouched, writhing horribly as the three approached, so very confident, secure in their place in the world, in the scheme of things.

– Please, Ted screamed in falsetto, begging them to turn off the horrible discharge. – P-PLEASE

– You're talking? What an amazing strength you have there, my child. That strength will serve us well eventually, once you're once again properly adjusted.

Ted was close enough, now. She was close enough, now. He grabbed her right foot and twisted it with all his vaunted strength. The woman screamed at the point of whining - and fainted on the spot. Betty kicked out and broke both of the closest man's kneecaps. His head hit the floor and he lay still. When both she and Ted jumped on their feet and charged the third, he panicked completely. He turned on his heels and ran off. Ted calmly picked up one of the sedation guns and fired into the man's back. First, he seemed totally unaffected, but after four of five steps he stumbled and fell.

Ted looked absolutely amazed.

– The dreams… it was like they're telling me what to do.

He turned to Betty, filled with triumph and joy. But then ice assaulted him. She stumbled, too. He had to catch her for her not to fall. They both looked at the dart stuck in her arm.

– Leave me, she said. – Leave me behind.

– NO! He clutched her. – I won't! Not you, too.

– Poor Ted, she mumbled, chuckling softly, tenderly touching his head. – You need to toughen up, My Lord. You're way too soft.

– I order you to come with me, he said intensively. – Do you hear me? I *order* you!

– I hear you. Her eyes stayed large. – Thank you, thank you.

She overwhelmed him with wet kisses.

– Your dreams are telling you what to do. We're living in our dreams.

He supported her the first few steps, but then she walked by herself.

They turned the corner, and they began running.

– It's strange, she said, half out of it. – I should have been out already. You saved me, My Lord. Thank you, thank you. I'm your Kwaiala. I live for you. I die for you.

– It's the Amphetamine, he said curtly. – It's interfering with the poison, keeping it from working fully.

– No, it's you. She smiled. – I love you, I love you.

They kept running.

And finally, they arrived at a crossroad, at two identical doors.

– The left? He wondered, as he reached for the handle.

– The left, she confirmed.

They pushed open the door together, and then, a few more steps later, they found themselves in the ship's reception hall. It almost looked like an alien landscape to them, now, when they could feel and think, with its plants and palms, with its mundane look. There were no humans in sight. It was very quiet, and Ted feared the sound of the door slamming behind them was way too loud.

– We made it, Betty giggled. – We fooled them. Thi, hi hi…

Ted shook her, looking harshly at her.

– I don't know what's wrong with me, she shook her head, unable to completely halt her laughter. – I feel like I can fly.

It was the Amphetamine. Ted knew that. It had reached its highest, most potent point. From now on it would fade in potency, until there would be nothing to keep them awake, except their own, downtrodden selves.

She kept giggling like a little girl. He concentrated on operating the door, the door opening up to the night, and the dark waters below.

The door flipped open, so easy, so very easy.

Something behind made him… made him turn. And Betty, too.

A woman stood in the other door, framed by it, not a part of it, not a part of anything here, but she was still one with her surroundings. They looked at her, her long, disheveled hair and her wild, wild eyes, her burning eyes.

– I… know you?

– You know me, Edward, you know me not.

And then she was gone, faded away before their eyes.

– Do you know her? He asked Betty.

– No, she replied wondering. – I've never seen her before in my life… I think.

And he believed her.

– You don't have to worry about me, she giggled happily. – I know I'm not a dickybird anymore.

And that did worry him, a fleeting moment, before action once more overtook him.

– One more step, he said, she said, taking each other's hand, smiling in triumph.

– Can you do it? He asked harshly, deliberately so.

– Of course. Her eyes flared, and her pride echoed in him.

Behind them there was a bedlam of another world. It didn't matter, didn't matter anymore.

They jumped, stepped into open air. Floated, descended. Ted imagined that the floating, descension lasted forever. The reflection of the city lights in the river turned indistinct. He wondered briefly, only briefly if this was just another game the High Ones were playing with him, and he knew, knew beyond belief that no one would ever play him with again.

The cold water closed around him. He felt a sharp pain in his thigh. There was darkness wherever he looked. The cold and the darkness shocked him to the bone.

Another brief thought, leaving him forever: Let yourself sink, end all your problems.

Something beyond consciousness made him fight his way up, aiding the natural process of *survival*. The sight of the stars above made him feel so good, so very good. The mist faded. Everything was clear. He breathed in the polluted air fully and thoroughly.

The ship was already long gone, far away. Betty swam to him.

– Are you okay? He asked her.

– Never felt better, she replied giddily. – I would recommend cold baths as a cure for all fatigue. Everybody should try it…

He realized she was joking. Joking!

They embraced there, in the cold, cold water, kissing each other's lips of fire, embracing far beyond the physical, and she released a yelp of joy, and they both shouted at the heavens, at the depths, as they made their way towards land, the closest shore.

Four dark-clad people stood in the ship's opening and stared into the darkness, shivering in the night.

– We'll be skinned alive for not giving chase, one choked. – Skinned alive.

– Certainly not, another, a woman said. – We have standing orders not to leave the ship, not under any circumstances.

– They can't hide from us, a third stated hotly. – No one can!

Eric Carr heard her. He held on to a rope a bit off, holding on for dear life, dangling along the ship's side. He had lost all his remaining illusions about life. Sore eyes strained, as he strived to follow the ripples of Ted and Betty's powerful strokes in the dark water. They had escaped, and he could hardly believe it. Illusions rinsed him, joy rinsed him. One could drown in the big city, he knew that, drown in the anonymity. People could disappear in cities like London, both because one wanted to and not. Excitement coursed through him. There was everything here, everything modern human life had to offer, and also, hidden in the shadows, the ancient, dark secrets of mankind, and it waited for them, waited for them all. Excitement coursed through him, as his arms slowly turned numb.

Chapter Twelve
DISTANT BUTTERFLY WINGS
The ship that couldn't sink 1912

He saw the woman and the girl by the rail in the bow. It was sunset. The ship sailed the seas and he saw them as clear as day.

It was a bright, sunny day. The White Star pier of the Southampton dock was filled with people and activity, on this day, April 10th 1912. Nicholas Warren and Tanya Orbov, his young bride waved to their families, as they joined the long row of people headed for the Titanic, a ship already going down in history as one of the most distinguished ships ever built. Only John, Nick's Uncle John followed them the last stretch of the way to the gangway. John, ancient John, with just a hint of gray hair at his temples shook Nick's hand and embraced Tanya, embraced the little boy in her arms.

– Better late than never, John cried. – You two should've had all this four years ago. But now, now, your time has finally come.

Nick looked closer at his kin, the great grandfather of Virgil and Susan, not sure what he meant, wondering if there was a hidden message there. There often was.

The two of them, or rather the three of them were alone on the crowded gangway. The boy, James, unruly and active, moved around a lot in Tanya's arms, causing her a bit of trouble. They turned. John and the rest waved to them one, final time from the pier.

– Did John seem somber to you? She asked him lightly, with just a hint of accent.

– So, you noticed it, too, he grinned. – I thought it was only the figment of my imagination…

She gave him the evil eye, clearly joking, but also clearly with a somber look.

He looked up. One of the gangways blocked his line of sight to the sun. The ship was bathed in sunlight, but its enormous shadow was cast almost everywhere he could see.

– Is the sky darkening? He wondered, suddenly overcome with an intense sort of dread.

– No, you silly man, she giggled. – The sky is blue, and the weather is fine. It will be a great journey.

She turned to him, her eyes lit.

– I feel so excited about this, Nick. THANK YOU!

They reached the interior of the ship, the luxurious first-class reception area. The Grand Staircase welcomed them. They looked at it all with wide eyes.

– This isn't a ship, Nick joked. – It's a mansion.

– Man-sion, James said.

The parents looked at him with unmistakable pride.

– He's so bright, Tanya said proudly. – I think he understands everything. He takes after his father, I guess…

Nick had been told he had been quite a bright toddler, too. A sting of sadness crossed his face.

– You're thinking about your parents again, aren't you?

He nodded curtly, forcing himself to smile, to leave out the sting of sadness.

The image of falling snow and mist never left him, even here, on this warm day.

His mother had died giving birth to him. And his father had left after that. He had lived for twelve years, until being killed in a gunfight, but Quentin Warren had really died that winter day in Montana. Nick had never even seen his face, except in old, faded photographs.

Nick was tall, very tall. Tanya, very tall for a woman, hardly reached to his shoulder. He towered over everyone else in the queue, and he was able to see far ahead, at the long, long sea of humans. Even the wealthy had to wait in line. Nick's hair was dark, short, ruffled. Tanya had despaired in her attempt to make it stay glued to his head, but had given it up. Water didn't help. Oil was useless. Wax was no good. Nothing worked. He didn't wear a hat, like most of the other men and women on first class did. She ruffled his hair a bit more, smiling affectionately. He smiled back. James yawned.

She did wear a hat, a broad one with a rather large number of ornaments that was so popular these days. Her smart matching jacket and skirt did follow the form of her body. She looked very much like the American wives. Only the face was clearly different. Not all the make up in the world could hide her exotic beauty.

They finally reached the large and luxurious cabin, and they both felt small in there. But it was quiet and probably not too excessive, at least not compared to the suites used by Astor, Guggenheim, Ismay and lot.

– As I thought, he nodded. – Desmond went totally overboard with this.

– Your uncle just wants to please you. She corrected him. – To give you a gift of beauty in the world.

Her smile, the sound of her voice made him warm in his heart.

He stepped behind her, and removed her jacket. She pushed her arms back in an elegant move, making it easier for him. She looked just the same then, as she had done that day in the theater in St. Petersburg when he had seen her for the first time. They kissed, and the kiss lingered on his lips as never before. He pushed his hands under the blouse behind her back.

– What are you doing? She giggled.

– I want to remove the fucking corset, he said. – I can hardly hear you breathe because of that shit.

She never reproached him for his swearing, and didn't do so now either, but she did stiffen in his arms. Having been brought up in a strict Greek Orthodox family it was hard for her to put that completely behind her.

– It's expected. You know that. No proper Lady goes anywhere without it. Not in Russia or here or in America.

– And are you a proper Lady? He grinned, the laughter back in his eyes. She just loved those eyes.

– Not with you, she whispered. – Not alone with you, My Lord.

And then, shortly thereafter, he could once more hear her breathe.

+++

The ship made several stops before setting the final course west, crossing the channel to Cherbourg and back to Queenstown, before leaving the European continent altogether. More people came aboard, more of the time's aristocracy, its rich and famous. The steerage below was filled with people, with commoners. The Irish coast faded in the east. He saw the woman and the girl by the rail in the bow. It was sunset. The entire western sky was lit in red. It was Friday evening, April 12th.

They moved differently, but it was more than that. They stood out from the crowd in a way that perhaps only he noticed, and he couldn't help but shake his head over his own thoughts.

He realized he could hear them breathe. They didn't wear corsets, and the other women shunned them. And because of that everybody noticed them.

They both had dark brown reddish hair, and they were tall. Taller than Tanya, taller than any other women he had ever seen. They were obviously closely related, so similar in both behavior and features. He joined the people in the bow. There were several other people there, not just the two. They looked at the sky in the west, whispering in each other's ears, and he could almost make out the words. He stared at the sunset, feeling the peace of the moment, unable to explain to himself why he felt that way.

– Good afternoon, the oldest of the women greeted him.

He looked around him, and realized there was no one but the three of them there. The others had left sometime during the last few minutes.

– Good afternoon, he heard himself say.

– It's a wonderful evening, isn't it?

He nodded, not quite capable of speaking.

– You miss them already, don't you, Nick? You've been away from your own kind for such a brief time, and you already miss them.

He kept looking at them. Shock ravaged him, mixed with curiosity and something different, vague, something making a choking ball stick in his throat. He suddenly had trouble swallowing, as if he had just contracted a cold.

– That's an odd way of phrasing it, he heard himself say.

How do you know my name?

– My name is Cynthia. This is Dalila.

They smiled to him and reached out their hands, and he did the same. They took his hands, squeezing them softly, and it was as if there was an electrical current somewhere.

– Nick, he said automatically, unnecessary, – Nick Warren.

– Nice to meet you, Nick, Cynthia said, pulling close to him, kissing him on the cheek, committing a total breach of etiquette.

– Why are you here? He asked in a choking voice.

He heard himself ask, as if from far away. The buzz from the ship plowing the ocean surface didn't come from below, but from his ears.

– We? We're here because you're here, Nick.

– What do you mean?

He felt the first stirring of irritation, of anger. They were playing games with him. He wasn't a complete fool when it came to women. There had been some early experiences before he met Tanya, but they were nothing like these two.

– Everybody else left the bow. He heard Dalila speak for the first time, a melody, a song resonating deep within him. – I can't for the life of me say why. But you, Nick, you stayed. We watched you stand there, all by yourself, all alone.

– That's funny, I thought it was I who saw you by the bow.

They laughed, showing their teeth, another breach of etiquette. Dalila looked at him, shyly, from under lowered eyelashes.

– Can you sense the fire… She whispered, so low that it was hardly audible. – … the fire down below?

– I heard the crew speak about a fire in Boiler Room 6, he said. – It's also the reason why the ship lists to port, by the way. Too much coal is being used on the starboard side, according to Purser McElroy.

– You listen, Nick. Cynthia laughed softly. – How many others do you think have even noticed?

He looked at the other passengers, as if from afar, their carefree exterior, their quibbles and indifference.

She met his eyes.

– Anyway, that wasn't what dear Dalila asked you, dear Nick… You didn't listen this time. She asked you if you *sense* the fire.

Her eyes were huge, dark brown, but for a moment there, it was as if he could actually see fire there. He gasped.

It was as if he was sucked down below, into the boiler rooms, into that particular boiler room, where there were even more sweat, even worse heat, even more steam, mist and shadow…

And the fire, the fire burning his skin, the smoke burning his lungs.

The two of them were gone, faded into the sunset, as if they had never been there. He stood by the rail for a long time, deeply shaken.

He returned inside, entered the ship's interior, the Palm Court Café through sliding doors. Tanya waved to him.

– You're late, she scolded him, grinning, – as usual…

– It's my curse in life, he joked, kissing her on the cheek she offered to him.

He sat there, watching her eat desert.

– Have some ice cream, Nick, she said lightly.

– I'm full, thank you, he replied distracted.

– Have some ice cream, Tanya begged him. – Please, Nick.

He shook his head.

– I heard the crew receive iceberg warnings from other ships. It doesn't exactly make me keener to try out ice cream, you know.

Her features softened.

– You're afraid we'll hit an iceberg, aren't you? She laughed softly. – You, big baby…

He nodded slowly, not certain if she noticed, not sure if he wanted her to notice.

She patted his hand. She was good at comforting him in his darkest moments. She always had been.

The Palm Court Café was really two identical rooms. It was also used as the first-class children's playing room. James laughed with the other children in the other room. The laughter echoed in Nick's mind.

– Is James okay? She wondered, shaking him out of the deep thoughts.

– Yes, he replied, then adding hastily: – Yes, he is. He's having loads of fun.

– You can sense him, wherever he is, she nodded, taking his hand. – Sense his well-being. I've never seen any other father with empathy such as yours.

She pulled his hand closer, kissing it.

– That's good…

The evening passed quickly. Even the night passed as if in a dream.

They walked briefly on the promenade deck.

– I keep having these images in my head, he said, attempting, striving to explain what couldn't really be explained. – It is as if I'm dreaming while being wide-awake.

– That isn't bad, she told him. – Dreaming is good.

They walked inside, to the bedroom.

– Yes, dream, she whispered. – Feel free. This is the ship of dreams, after all.

They were in bed. He undressed her in quick, hurried moves. She gasped as he pushed himself at her. He undressed her completely. She resisted at first, but as he kissed her hard and relentless, she moaned and relented, surrendered completely to his dark embrace.

– My wild beast, she cried. – My wild, wild man.

And she moved, too, moved as never before. Her water drowned him, and he smelled her scent, smelled it as never before.

He sat there in a chair, staring into the wall. He was unable to sleep, and he walked the ship late at night. She found him in the bow.

– The Orbovs are quite colorful, too, you know, she said lightly. – There are stories going back centuries about practitioners of witchcraft. There are whispers of… of… satanic rituals, about unspeakable acts made in the dark of night.

He turned to her.

– Why have you never told me this before?

– It's treated like a dirty secret. The current Orbovs are very modern and they are christians. And my father was very strict about it, very strict indeed.

She sought close to him, resting her head on his shoulder.

– I'm not afraid of you, she whispered. – Come back to bed. Mate with me, Nick, mate with me until the onset of dawn.

And their scandalous cries resonated through the hallways.

She slept soundly, spent, totally spent. He stood in front of a window, bathing in the early morning light. His eyes. The mirror revealed his eyes.

They had always had the strange color. He had been born with them. But they had never sparked before, had never been glowing before.

The hours of the day also passed as quicksilver. Nick Warren and his beautiful wife walked to the dining room. They were dressed in their best clothes. Servants opened the doors. The dinner was a shared affair. Virtually everybody in first class was present at the long tables. He spotted Molly Brown. Colonel Astor, and others. Captain Smith. Thomas Andrews, the ship builder. J. Bruce Ismay from the West Star Line. And others besides.

And for the first time in his young life, Nicholas Warren was aware of the book turning its pages, aware of the passing of history.

And he wondered why he was here.

J. J. Astor spoke to a captive audience.

– This is such an exciting time. New inventions are entering our life so often that it has almost become trite. Some of us are already flying, like the birds. This ship represents this our gilded age. It's a manifestation of all our hopes and dreams.

– And you don't see just a tiny amount of… hubris in all this?

The voice came from a bit down the table. Nick recognized the voice instantly. It was *her*.

– Not at all, Mrs. Christopher. Astor shook his head with a patronizing smile. – When our dear Mr. Ismay here would claim that this is a ship that will never sink, he is not wrong.

Mrs. Christopher, Nick thought. The name seemed so *familiar*. But every time he attempted to recall where he had heard it, in which context it slipped away from him.

– Humanity, Astor continued. – Humanity has reached such a level of engineering that we're able to control our environment. We've become the masters of the Earth, the way God always intended us to be.

– Hear, hear.

Ismay applauded, and the rest of the table applauded with him.

– Large parts of humanity will still have to be dragged from the mud, of course, but they'll get there eventually.

The drinking and eating around the table were strictly organized. Everything had its place and its turn. Nick observed the choosing of spoons, of forks and all with a certain detached humor. He watched Cynthia and Dalila Christopher from the corner of his eyes, as he was burned by Cynthia's sarcastic smile. She took a big piece of meat in her hands and took a big… a big bite of it. He let out a hysterical burst of laughter, catching himself before it turned too embarrassing.

– So how's your uncle these days, Nick? Benjamin Guggenheim, a prevalent industry captain asked.
– Desmond isn't really my uncle, Nick replied. – We're more like distant cousins. But he's fine, thank you.
It was fairly well known in these circles that Desmond's part of the family was the owners of the family fortune, and that the rest could indeed be described as «poor distant cousins».
– There's a special bond between the members of the Warren family, Mr. Guggenheim, Tanya interjected. – We're far tighter than most folks.
– So, what are your plans, Nick? Molly Brown asked.
He looked at her. She was a strange woman, not really set in her ways, at least not compared to most of those present. Her husband had struck gold out in the west, like Desmond's deceased father Joseph. Did he sense an ambiguity in her voice, in her pose?
– I plan on continuing my work for Uncle Desmond, upon our return to New York, he said. – He quite enjoyed my work in Eastern Europe, I'm proud to say.
He realized he was mimicking the way Guggenheim, Ismay and Astor were speaking, and wanted to kick himself. Cynthia's sarcastic smile burned in his gut.
The dinner ended, finally, after thousands of treats and threats, of sipping wine and tasting the cuisine. Nick wasn't really hungry anyway. He felt strangely full.
Tanya stumbled, as she was about to rise. He caught her quickly.
– Are you all right? He asked.
– My feet feel… rubbery, she noted, giggling. – I guess I am a bit fatigued. It might be the commotion or perhaps I'm just coming down with something.
She spoke perfect English, far more perfect than everybody else present, really, but they still stared at her, cocking their ears.
He helped her to bed. She fell asleep in an instant, before her head had really hit the pillow.
– You must leave her, brother.
He whirled around, but there was no one there, no one else in the room besides him and the sleeping beauty.
Her chest was hardly moving as she slept, slept like the dead.
He walked restlessly back and forth on the lower deck, filled with vigor, with the haunting, strange elation. His hands… he rubbed his left hand with the right… when he looked at his hands they seemed to… glow, to shift and pulse every time he crossed into the shadow. He kept to the

places of sunlight, but it seemed muted, as if it didn't truly reach him. He turned, and Cynthia stood there, not ten steps away.

– You must leave her, brother, she said softly, – or you will surely kill her.

Words stopped in his mouth. He wanted to speak, but nothing found its way out.

She smiled, her sarcastic poise returning.

– Look at you, quite the innocent. In some way perhaps even more so than your blushing bride.

She turned and walked away. He followed her. The dark intensified inside, to the point of turning pitch black, and he imagined he could hardly see where he was walking. She walked without looking back. They passed a group of giggling teenage girls.

– Look how they move, how they perch, how they hardly move the upper part of their body at all, obviously dead from the knee up, and they're not even adults yet.

He heard the whisper right there in his ear, as if she walked by his side, and not ten steps ahead. There was a shadow surrounding her, her lovely form. He kept seeing her smile, the invitation in her eyes, and in that moment a feeling of dread worse than he had ever experienced overwhelmed him. He picked up speed, picked it up from the very air surrounding him, and he caught up with the woman as she opened a door, and disappeared through it. He couldn't remember having closed the door behind him or heard the sound of it closing. But it was closed. The bright light from the hallways outside no longer reached them.

The room was dark, truly dark. It didn't just look that way to him. Only one lamp was lit, one lamp hidden behind a curtain of black velvet.

– Welcome, Nick of the Janus Clan, she greeted him, – Nick Shadowwalker, to our humble abode.

Dalila knelt on the bed, nude. She looked at him. Her entire body looked at him. Suddenly he could no longer find any saliva in his mouth to swallow. His cock rose and pushed hard at his pants. He gaped, in astonishment and shame.

– Yes, Cynthia said, as she undressed, too. – Your intense night with your dear Tanya hasn't weakened you, but rather strengthened you in ways you never imagined.

Dalila performed for him, stretching and writhing, sweet and sensual beyond belief. He drowned in her smile, drowned in her pools of molten shadow.

There was a song in his head, drums unheard as his feet walked him to the bed.

– There are no females in your family, now, are there?

– There's Desmond's wife, he said absentmindedly.

– But Kitty isn't kin, is she? She's just another weak-blooded cow Desmond has chosen to take pity on.

Cynthia met him, as he had almost reached Dalila there on the large, large bed, giving him a sultry kiss.

– There's Susan, of course, but she's young, yet, at least by the standards you've chosen to follow. And she's pale and timid to the point of her taking more after her weak-blooded mother than her father.

He tried to think, tried to speak, but it was as if something was keeping him from doing it, blocking his words. He grabbed Cynthia's wrists and held on.

– Who are you? He spat weakly. – How do you know all this? What are your *intentions?*

– Oh, boy, you're strong, Cynthia grinned, a film covering her eyes. – Beloved Nick, I've never encountered anyone such as you. I feel you like a glow, a sun inside.

Dalila pulled the fabric of his clothes while kissing him on the neck. Wet, beyond sensual kisses. He blinked. There was something… When he… when he blinked, he saw something, saw them in a different light, as if a veil was pulled from his eyes. He grabbed Dalila, too, holding them, holding on to them, before pushing them both away. They fell on their backs on the bed, still with their lovely smile in place.

– You two are two seriously fucked up sisters, he gasped.

They laughed, laughed at him, and it hurt.

– Tell me, beloved Nick, Cynthia said, her eyes dwelling on him, – how old do you think I am?

– Eighteen, nineteen. He shrugged, attempting to shrug it off.

– You believe we're sisters, like most people do. We're not. We're mother and daughter.

There was a ringing in his ears.

– That's amazing, he heard himself say.

– I was born in 1872, she said, – and I'm young. I'll always be young.

He left the bed, shock written in his face. He couldn't stop himself from shaking his head.

– So, beloved Nick, have the blinds fallen from your eyes by now? Not yet, I gather. Not quite yet.

He remembered from the dinner. J. J. Astor had called Cynthia Mrs. Christopher. Then sometime later another, he couldn't recall who, had called Dalila Ms. Christopher. He hadn't been very astute, that was certain, and he wanted to kick himself.

– Behold. See how we truly look like.

And he did behold the two sirens. There was no discernible change at first. Just small things, really, all in all unnoticeable, if one didn't *look*. The bodies stayed the same, but the faces changed. The eyes changed, changed from brown to fire, and there was more. Cynthia wasn't that much different. Thicker lips. A darker hue of skin, very much like Nick's own. A bigger body.

But Dalila had Changed. In all things she reminded him of the drawings of a mermaid he had seen on the historic museums. She had kept her legs, didn't have any fins, but there was something resembling scales on her shoulder and hips. Her skin was beyond dark, and a completely different texture than that of a black or any other person he had seen. The area around her eyes seemed to shift and flow in a bluish taint. She reminded him of a young animal female ready for mating.

– This is us, Nicholas Warren. She said sweetly. – We've embraced ourselves, while you haven't even scratched the surface of what you are.

– You're not human, he gasped.

Anger, recrimination flared in those beastly eyes.

– Are you? Is your Uncle John? Or any of you? Was your much talked about Uncle Karl?

Cynthia stared at him, and while there might be warmth in the daughter's eyes, there was no such thing in the mother.

– You've wondered your entire life who and what you are, fearing the answer. Now, you know.

He backed off, all the way to the door, until he crashed into the door. His hands fumbled with the handle, for minutes, hours. The women remained in bed, staring accusingly at him. He backed off, into the hallways and ran away.

The walk back to the place he shared with Tanya felt infinitely long.

An endless walk through ever more narrowing hallways, transforming into alleys and passages, too narrow to pass through. Tanya's face glowed as he stood over the bed, looking down on her.

He fell on the couch, and after a long, painful attempt at closing his eyes, he finally fell asleep.

++++++++++++++

He felt her lips on his cheek, felt her comforting touch as he slowly ascended from his slumber.

She smiled to him, uncertainty plaguing her features.

He rose, rose from the couch and greeted his wife, on this fateful day, April fourteenth, 1912.

– Nick, you're sweating.

He was. It felt as if he wore sweat, instead of clothes.

– That's what you deserve, I guess, for sleeping in your clothes.

– I guess, he grinned back.

– You're so considerate. You didn't have to spend the night on the couch. I wouldn't have awakened if you had joined me in bed, you know.

She considered it.

– At least not last night. I was sleeping like the dead.

He took the wrong direction. They had to walk through the Smoking Room to get to Palm Court Café. He sat there, watching her eat, not touching his own food.

She tried to pretend for a while. He knew she was. But finally, she pushed the plate away, and looked worried at him.

– Something is weighing heavily on you, my husband. What is it?

He didn't reply at first. It actually took close to ten seconds before he finally replied.

– I dreamt that the ship sank, he grinned. – I dreamt that it hit an iceberg and sank.

Her eyes turned a soft light.

– Oh, my poor baby, she cried compassionately. – How, awful.

– It felt so real, he whispered, – so lifelike. People were floating in the ocean, freezing to death, crying desperately for help, but no help came. And all the time the band played on, and I was so angry. I can't stand their fucking boring music.

People at the neighboring tables turned their heads discretely, glanced at the distraught young man without glancing at him, and that made him furious, too.

He saw it still. Passengers and crew on other passing ships and boats, laughing while the choir of dying people quieted under the dark, star bright sky.

The large body sat in the warm sun for a long time, shaking like a leaf. Tanya held him, and rubbed him, rubbing his back, holding his hands.

– It's funny, he choked, – I can smell ice cream. I can taste it in my mouth. How can that be? I've never had ice cream my entire life. So how can I know how it tastes?

– You're a very special man, Nicholas Warren, Tanya whispered, – and I want you to always remember that.

They kissed, and the kiss lingered, and people glanced at them, and he didn't care.

– How many breaches of social rules have we committed today? He wondered.

– This morning? She giggled. – I've lost count. I've heard there are supposed to be several books written on the subject. My aunt made me read several of them, «before going to America».

She lost her footing. It happened so sudden that he pulled a muscle in his shoulder when he grabbed her.

– Are you alright? He asked, with a worry she didn't see painted in his face.

– Just dizzy. I guess I'm finally getting seasick. But if it doesn't get any worse than this, there isn't much to worry about.

– Come. He took her hand and led her to the bow.

As they walked there, yellow bright light turned the first strands of reddish.

– Christ, it's afternoon already.

She turned to him, as excited as ever.

– Time flies when one's having fun.

J. Bruce Ismay and Captain Smith had a conversation as the married couple walked past them on the deck.

– New speed record again, Ismay cried pleased, clearly wanting the passengers to hear him. – 546 miles in twenty-four hours. Excellent, most excellent. This will make our arrival in New York a triumph of considerable magnitude.

Smith nodded and nodded and nodded, and he just kept nodding. At least that was how Nick would always remember him.

Nick and Tanya picked two chairs and pulled them a bit away from the rest. But they remained bathed in sunlight, where there was a pleasant warmth protecting them from the icy draft of the northern Atlantic.

It was dinner again. Tanya ate like a pig, not really caring about what was proper or not. Nick forced himself to eat. He discovered that he could eat a lot, that the food seemed to burn up inside him.

– I'm so hungry, Tanya cried. – I feel like I could eat a horse.

– It's all the fresh air, honey, Molly Brown commented in her more than rough ways.

There was polite laughter.

And then the evening came. The warm glow of the lamps created a soft light inside.

– I don't even feel nausea anymore, Tanya assured her worried husband. – Food was clearly what the doctor ordered.

They walked on the deck again. Nick felt better out here, away from all the noise and crowds.

It was a clear, star-bright night. There was no moon.

Chunks of ice were floating, were clearly visible like shadows in the dark water. He blinked, blinked in pain.

– Is it me, or is the ship speeding up?

– It isn't you, she grinned.

– You shouldn't be overly worried, Mrs. Warren, a crewmember said, very politely, as he approached them. – This proud ship can easily handle a few chunks of ice.

– So, I shouldn't be *overly* worried, huh? She mused. – How worried should I be, then?

– Precisely, Madam, the crewmember coughed. – The Captain did alter the course slightly to the south and west of his usual course, by the way. Better safe than sorry, right?

Nick recalled the slight sense of inertia in the big bulk of a ship as it had turned in the water. His bet would be that most of the passengers hadn't noticed.

– That man is stupid as a loaf, Tanya cried, not too subtle. – He refuses to see the inherent contradictions in his own statement.

– I wouldn't worry about it, my dear.

Tanya turned, half expecting the words to come from Nick. Nick turned as well, turned to Cynthia and Dalila.

– You'll find that most western males are just as stupid as their Russian counterparts, Cynthia said, Cynthia grinned.

Nick hadn't sensed their approach, and usually he did. He never did.

– What a glorious evening, is it not? Cynthia exclaimed. – The cold, crisp air is like a sharp pain in the lungs.

Dalila spoke little, as was her way. She spoke with her body. Nick heard it, heard her.

Their fiery eyes were fully visible now. They didn't hold themselves back anymore.

Nick stiffened, and he also sensed Tanya stiffen by his side.

– It is indeed, Mrs. Christopher, Tanya nodded, a huge smile, perhaps a bit overdone, brightening her face.

She frowned, as if there was something she couldn't quite recall. And Nick felt that way himself. He had felt like that for quite some time.

Haunted.

– Yes, Nick, Dalila said. – We're ghosts in the world, haunting ourselves.

Tanya looked at her, looked at Nick, a chill touching her face.

And then, suddenly Nick felt the chill, felt it like he had never before felt it.

– Let's go inside. Cynthia offered her arm, and Nick took it, walking in a daze.

The warm glow of the lamps bathed them in its heat, Dalila's face in particular, as she spoke in her kinda childish voice.

– So, how has your honeymoon been so far? Has it been to your… expectations?

– Oh, yes, Tanya cried, equally excited, – I love Nick so much, and he has been so kind to me, so loving and considerate.

Nick recalled their nights, and she blushed, as if she shared his vivid memory of it.

They sat there, talking, having a great time, like old friends meeting up after many years of absence.

The band played its dead tunes, but Nick hardly heard any of it, except as part of the infinite background noise.

The cold from the outside night seemed to creep inside him, inside him to stay, forever.

He moved restlessly in the chair. Tanya looked at him.

– Sorry, he said. – It just feels like I have ants… somewhere, that's all. I've never liked ants very much.

Cynthia looked at him.

– Poor baby, Tanya said, said again, – you don't seem to get a break, do you? I mean, first there's the ice cream thing. Then the nightmare…

Cynthia looked at her.

– Nightmare…?

– Yes, Tanya grinned. – My big, fearless baby Nick dreamed that Titanic, unsinkable Titanic would hit an iceberg and sink.

There was a moment, when Nick saw everything clearly, when everything coalesced into one single fluid event.

– When Nick has nightmares, my dear, Cynthia said, – they aren't dreams, but *visions*.

The ship turned. It was still subtle, still difficult to be absolutely certain it was absolutely happening. Nick heard screams, and he saw that the two women on the opposite side of the table also heard them. There was a grinding sound, like metal against metal, but different.

– There's ice on the deck, they heard someone cry.

They all heard it.

– What… Tanya looked at them.

They all rose, even though virtually everybody else remained seated. It was just after 11.40 pm. The minutes ticked away to midnight.

Cynthia rushed to Nick, grabbing his stiff collar.

– You idiot, she yelled. – Don't you understand? You…

She stopped. A sense of absolute clarity lit the fire in her eyes. She calmed down as he watched.

– I *understand,* now, Cynthia said. – I understand everything.

She looked at Tanya, looked at Dalila, before turning back to him.

– This is destiny, Nick. Don't you *feel* it?

– What are you talking about?

He said lamely. As a thousand stars, a thousand images lit the backside of his closed eyelids.

– I don't understand… Tanya looked bewildered at them.

– The ship will sink, Cynthia told her, – and thousands will die. But we will live.

– Really, Madam, second officer Lightoller passed by, – there's no need for such alarmist talk.

– What alarmist talk should there be, then? Cynthia shouted after him.

He didn't turn.

The four of them walked outside in a daze, in a daze very similar to what the others on the ship were plagued with.

They saw Captain Smith run to the Bridge.

– What have we struck? He cried.

– An iceberg, sir, sixth officer Moody replied.

– Are you… are you kin? Tanya asked astonished.

Before Nick managed to speak, to spit out what burned his mind, Cynthia spoke.

– We are indeed, my dear. A long-lost part of the family, so to speak.

– I didn't know, Nick tried to explain to his wife.

Christopher… He finally managed to connect that name to something.

– They did tell you the story, didn't they, Nick? Cynthia spoke even more softly, with even more of an edge in her voice.

– Yes, he heard himself say.

– The story about Delilah Christopher and your father, about how they left each other in anguish and hatred… But not without some spectacular results as you can clearly appreciate…

– Either they didn't know that… or they left it out.

She spat.

– Mother trained me, trained me for the confrontation that would come, but she was only human. She died of typhoid fever, died young. The entire city died, but I left it, left the ghost town, fresh as a mare. I've

never been sick a day in my entire life, and neither has my brood.
She smiled.
– We're brother and sister, Nick, and we're meant to be together.
Tanya gasped.
– And there's more, Nick, Cynthia said, looking at him with a twisted, beyond twisted expression in her lovely face. – There's always more.
They saw Andrews, the ship builder rush to the bridge. The seconds kept ticking away to midnight.
– Dalila here is both your niece, and your sister.
He stared at her.
– Oh, *yes*. I managed to track down our father, and I took him as mine, and once Dalila was born, I told him, told him everything. I didn't take his life that day, but I killed him, as sure as I would have if I had plunged a dagger through his heart.
He struggled to speak.
– Your mother has destroyed you, he said. – Filled you with hatred.
– James, Tanya said.
– No, not hatred, Nick. *Purpose*. Both my father and mother gave me purpose in life, and that's what you missed by not knowing your parents. That's what I'll grant you.
– You're insane, Nick said.
– I thought I was, she smiled. – Now, I know I'm not.
– Look, he spoke hastily, – we'll *deal* with this. I'll take you both to meet our family, make things right.
– JAMES, Tanya screamed.
She ran off towards the Palm Court Café. They hesitated a second or two before following her. Dalila ran ahead, as quick on her feet as a doe.
Some older children were still playing there, four teenage boys making mincemeat of a table, but James was nowhere to be seen.
Aside from the four boys there was no one.
Nick and the other two followed Tanya through room after room. Rockets were fired outside, distress signals sent for ships to come to Titanic's aid.
They saw a bunch of crewmembers run downstairs. Nick attempted to hold back Tanya, but she was like possessed.
There were already many people on their way up, virtually blocking their way. Tanya pushed them back, clearing the way. She hardly needed help from Nick and Cynthia and Dalila at all. They reached the floor. Tanya kept running, audibly out of breath. There were crewmembers knocking on cabin doors.

They recognized Miss Goodman, one of those among the crew supervising the children.

– What's going on? Tanya asked her.

– The captain has ordered us to wake all the passengers…

Tanya grabbed her, shook her.

– WHERE IS HE? She screamed. – WHERE IS JAMES?

– He was sent to bed *hours* ago, Mrs. Warren, the distraught woman replied. – We wouldn't let small children be up at this hour.

– Of course, Tanya mumbled. – Of course.

They went back up. That was easier. People still walked somewhat calm. Nick noted that the doorways to the steerage were still blocked by iron bars.

– Aren't you going to open those? He asked a passing crewmember.

– Of course, sir. We need someone to bring the keys, that's all.

They walked to the Warren cabin, somewhat composed. The crew knocked on all doors, very composed, very calm.

– You need to come out, sir, they heard one say. – The Captain wants everybody to gather on the boat deck. There's an emergency.

Nick unlocked the door to their cabin and Tanya rushed inside. James lay in bed, sleeping soundly. She woke him and lifted him up in her arms in rushed, frantic moves.

– Relax, baby, she said, her voice muffled. – We need to take a walk. Everything is all right. Relax, baby. Relax.

Someone screamed from the outside.

– THEY'RE LOWERING THE LIFEBOATS. THE SHIP IS GOING DOWN.

And with that statement realization hit Nick. He cried out in pain, as the song, the screams from a thousand dying souls rose inside of him.

– Warm clothes, he mumbled. – We need warm clothes.

The immensity of what was happening slowly dawned on them.

He grabbed the suitcases and just shook them as he opened the lock. Clothes fell on the floor. They dressed quickly, and left the cabin, bringing almost nothing with them. Most other passengers carried huge trunks and suitcases. They walked to Cynthia and Dalila's cabin one level down. They, too, dressed casually and warm.

– You're such a take-charge man, brother, Cynthia grinned. – I just love that. I knew you would be.

His brain, his mind… worked that much better… as if every part of it was on fire. The lethargy still haunted him, but it didn't stop him.

– Let me take him, he said to Tanya.

She hesitated, the dark places of her mind still active, but then she smiled and handed James over. Nick hardly felt his son's weight at all.

They walked, moved with increasing speed and worry. One narrow pathway of stairs upwards was filled with people, so they sought another. They found one, seconds, minutes later. Time seemed to dilate, events to be non-sequential. Nick stopped. The three women behind him stopped, too. The stairs down, to the steerage, to the third-class section were filled with desperate people… and the bars were still in place. The gate was still locked. Members of the crew had a shouting contest with those pushing at the gate from the other side.

– Please, remain calm, there's no need to panic, an officer with a gun shouted.

– Are you daft, man? A man clutching the bars screamed hysterically. – There aren't lifeboats for more than half of the people onboard, and you know it, and you want the rich shit to survive, and don't give a shit about us.

– Not enough… lifeboats? Nick said.

Everything turned quiet, strangely quiet.

– Hell, no. The man behind the bars snarled. – It's just a matter of mathematics, man, but no one in charge seems to have done the math.

– Or perhaps they HAVE, a woman shouted angrily.

– Open the gate, Nick said to the crew. – You don't want to be this heartless, do you?

The officer turned and directed his gun at Nick.

– You don't want to fuck with me, sir. You don't *want to*.

Nick took a step forward, and the man fired. The bullet hit Nick in the belly, narrowly missing the child in his arms. The grown man was pushed back at the wall, an expression of utter astonishment crossing his face. The shouting and ruckus started up again. Nick blinked. There was a crack somewhere, and a deeper sound from below. He heard the sound of flowing water, realizing he had heard it for quite a while, now. Tanya rushed to him. Dalila jumped at the officer and kicked the gun from his hand. She hit him in the face, and blood flowed from his mouth. She held him, snarling, terrifying everybody present.

– THE KEYS. GIVE ME THE KEYS, OR I'LL FLAY THE SKIN FROM YOUR BONES.

Absolutely beside himself he stuck a hand in his pocket, the hand shaking so much that he could hardly get a grip on the keys. No one attempted to stop her as she opened the gate. People flooded the hallway. The white paint on the wall drowned in darker hues.

The three women pulled Nick with them, pulled him away to relative safety. He and they held on, held on to James and each other for dear life.

– I'm okay, he gasped. – Okay.

– Yes, you are, Cynthia said brutally. – It's just a fleabite. Nothing more. Not to you.

It hurt. The pain was like a thud inside him. He sensed the blood leave his body.

– We must bandage it, Tanya said weakly. – We must stop the blood.

She tore a slice off her sleeve, curled it to a ball, and pushed it at the wound.

– Hold it there, she shouted to Nick. – Are you listening to me?

– I am, he assured her, giving her a confident smile. – It's okay. I'll be okay.

He heard water flowing. Everybody looking down the stairs saw it, but he heard it. He sensed how the ship tilted. Not much yet, but enough. Some people slipped and fell on the wet floor. He held on to James, still not feeling the weight of the small body.

– We must go up, he said, – no matter what. We must keep away from the water to avoid hypothermia.

– You're afraid of the cold, aren't you Nick? Cynthia said softly.

He stared at her, stared at her through the haze of pain.

– The cold can't really hurt you. Not unless you allow it.

The image of an ice cream came to him again, and his guts lurched inside him.

– You're afraid of the cold, she stated, smiling to him. – Don't worry, it's okay. Be afraid of the cold, if you want, but embrace the *fire*.

He looked at her. She grabbed him, shaking him, a rare look of desperation in her eyes.

– The wound isn't *there,* she cried. – Not for you. Don't you *understand?*

– Follow me, Dalila said. – I'll clear the way.

He looked at her, the confident young girl, the witch in a pleasant hide.

She ascended the stairs. They followed her, just as the water began flooding this floor, too. Pain cut through Nick. He curled his fists around James's clothes, concentrating, focusing on the pain, on taking it, on holding out.

They entered the lower deck, as the boats were on their way down, down to the black, black water.

– Fiends, a woman shouted. – I saw a boat being lowered, and there were only crew members there, and they weren't even that many. Several boats are being lowered half full. Fiends!

– FIENDS, another cried at the heavens. – FIENDS!

One boat fell too fast, and people, both on and off the boat, screamed and shrieked. They continued upwards. Dalila and Cynthia pushed at people, to no avail. They grabbed them and pushed them back down the stairs, clearing way. As they finally reached the boat deck, one boat was lowered from above, lowered way too fast, almost hitting them, and hitting the deck hard, breaking, useless. Nick stretched his already long neck, looking ahead. A sea of a thousand tiny ants barred the path to the few remaining boats. Titanic's bow sank below the surface. There were more screams of terror, more desperate pleas. The orchestra played somewhere, and he wanted to find them and wring their necks, and for the first time in his life he was afraid of himself, as a black, black rage rose from his depths. He knew his eyes glowed. Saw it in the frightened eyes of his wife, the pleased expression in Cynthia's twisted face.

– The ship that can't sink, she chuckled. – Hah! Made of steel, and it can't sink. Heh, heh!

The bridge was flooded. As its windows broke Nick saw without seeing the lonely whitebeard inside be washed away by the currents.

The ship began to tip over in earnest. They began climbing the ever-steeper deck towards the rear, surrounded by the many hundreds who hadn't been lucky enough to «earn» a place in the lifeboats. People began to slip, some of them totally exhausted by fighting their way to the boat deck. Nick saw it all through a red haze. He was freezing. He wasn't wet, but was freezing anyway. The wound, the wound didn't hurt anymore. He wondered if he was having a fever. His feet kept moving, and he felt it every time they touched the deck anew. He ran and he was hardly breathing hard.

Tanya stumbled. He saw it, from afar. He stepped sideways, reaching out a hand, the bloody hand. She did, too. The hands touched, but bloody and slippery as the hands were, there was no way they could hold on to each other. He watched as she slid down the deck with several others. He stumbled and had to grab hold of the rail. Cynthia looked at him. He stared horrified at her, at James, and down the deck, where Tanya was no longer to be seen.

– Let her go, Nick. She did what she was supposed to. She gave you, gave us James, gave us the future. Let her go.

The ship took another dramatic tip. His grip around the rail slipped, and he fell. James's scream resounded in his ears. For a second or two, an eternity Nick fell. He hit something. His head hit something, and everything turned black.

Heat. Everything was so hot. He blinked. He lay on a wall, a wall turned floor. A moan distracted him, distracted the haze in which he bathed.

Cynthia looked at him, pain twisting her face. She struggled to speak. A pole stuck up through her chest. He fought himself to his feet, unable to fathom how he was still able to move, to react, to reason, to live.

– Heal me, you oaf… heal me…

He stood there paralyzed, indecisive. The pole had penetrated her heart, had split it in many pieces. He saw it, felt it, as life left her. He couldn't fathom how she could still be alive. Fireeyes looked around in panic.

– James? He said lamely.

– Sorry, Nick, she choked. – Sorry… for everything.

And she died.

But he felt strong and he couldn't believe it, how strength seemed to fill his body and mind, his entire being. He saw something… It was as if a shadow was leaving her body, melting into the very air itself, fading away in the ether. He gasped. Cold briefly overwhelmed him.

– What were you *talking* about? He shouted, he choked. – What the hell were you talking

There was something. Someone was shouting at him. He straightened, and he listened. And he realized… realized he did so with everything he was.

Shouting…

Daddy.

And then again.

Daddy.

He heard the voice from far away. Not with his ears, but with his *mind.* He saw small hands wave above, below the still water surface.

The ship broke in two. The sound was loud, so very loud. The half on its way up fell again. It hit the ocean hard. He was thrown back on the deck. Pain shot through him. The two pieces held on to each other, like lovers. He tried to rise. Pain shot through him as he put down his right foot. He stumbled to the rail, staring at the icy, black sea. The bow half of the ship kept sinking, pulling its other half with it. The rear part rose in the air again. People began falling again. He climbed over the rail. Without thought, without hesitation he jumped, he dived at the darkness below. He hit the surface, plowing below. The cold hit him like a hammer. The ice cream numbed his limbs. He realized startled that he was reliving his dreams, as he was swimming with wide, powerful strokes through the water. People, a sea of people floated and swam in the sea around him. He saw, without seeing, the rear stand up in the water, stand straight up. For a moment it seemed to balance, to balance perfectly.

– It's going down, someone cried.

The suction, he thought feverishly. The *suction.* He swam, swam until the fire in his muscles burned his arms.

As a nail penetrating wood, the rear part of Titanic pierced the Atlantic Ocean. Everything turned dark, as night once more dominated the tiny pinprick of reality human invention had briefly swayed.

Nick Warren felt the pull, and he was utterly unable to resist it, as the tiny human body was sucked back towards the sinking wreck, the wreck now split in two, as each part was sinking towards the bottom far away from the other. Nick blinked, as he swam, as he kept swimming. And then he spotted it, the tiny, unmoving human form floating below the surface. He swam towards it, approached it with a speed he could hardly believe. Numb hands grabbed the body and pushed, pushed hard at the surface so far away. He gasped up there, in the boiling water, filled with people, drawing lovely, life-giving air into his choking lungs.

He turned to the boy, the lifeless doll in his arms, grief shaking him. Hands sought bare skin, in vain seeking a pulse, a sign of life. Grief shook him, rage and pain and need.

And he sensed something, a heat, a volcanic heat beyond any fire he to this point had imagined existed. His hands began glowing, and then, the instant after that, the child's bare skin glowed as well. *Heal,* he cried. *Live!*

And the boy heard him. Nick knew he did. Heard his mind.

James coughed, coughed up water, a lot of water, as the spark within him grew to an inferno. As Nick's joy overwhelmed him to the point of exhaustion. People waved in the ocean, their movements slowly stopping, dying. He kept swimming, kept moving in the cold, cold sea, as he held on to James, as he kept warming him.

– The boats will return, a voiceless voice cried. – Just be patient.

Nick saw the boats, saw them move away, saw them, as they didn't return.

– Just be patient the voice croaked minutes later.

– Help! A voice cried. – HELP!

And was instantly joined by a deafening multitude of voices.

Nick made James look at him, and James did, with his clear, clear eyes.

– I want you to hold on to me. Can you do that?

– Yes, daddy, the boy nodded. – I'm so thirsty, daddy.

Nick swam, swam hard, occasionally making sure the small form held on and kept breathing. The cold numbed him, numbed everything, except the living furnace within him. He looked up. The Milky Way above him glowed and sparked. It was as if he was up there, as if he was deep below the surface, and the depths were a sea of souls.

There were no longer deafening screams behind him. Just the occasional shout between the deafening silence.

The sounds of oars thundered in his ears. He stopped a bit, looked up, and he cried out, screamed his lungs out. A dark shape moved towards him, as he was moving towards it. He gave way to his grief, to his rage, his joy, his voice shaking the Earth.

He reached the boat. Hands struck the boat's side, its edge.

– Please take the boy, he gasped, holding on to the boat with icy claws. – The boy. Please.

The voice came from far away. But he sensed warmth. And kindness.

– We have more than enough room.

And they lifted them both onboard.

The boat wasn't even half full. He couldn't decide whether or not he wanted to kill the people in front of him or embrace them.

– We must go back, he gasped. – People are freezing to death back there, do you hear me! Freezing to death!

– We were on our way back, one of the men said.

And they headed back, back to the frozen dolls, all the frozen dolls. They found just a few alive. And they were the only ones looking. He could easily hear the quarrel, the useless squabble in the other boats, and wished he couldn't.

He sat there, he and the boy stripped, covered in blankets and the others' dry clothes. The warmth felt almost overwhelming, now, with all the, to him glowing bodies in his close proximity.

And he felt tired, so very tired, as the visions shook him, shook him apart.

A sea of people, a sea of souls. A multitude of voices rising from the depths.

– I can hear them screaming, he mumbled. – *Hear them.*

– We all can, an officer said.

No, you don't understand, he wanted to say. I can *hear* them.

Six out of fifteen hundred were rescued from the cold.

It was daylight when the cunarder Carpathia picked them up. The day was just as cold. The heat from the sun didn't reach them. The only warmth Nick felt was the bottomless well within him. He sat there with his son, both surrounded by blankets, doing his very best to include him in the furnace that he had become.

Voices spoke to him on the deck. They weren't really aimed at him, but he heard them anyway.

– I heard people onboard SS California saw the ship and also received the distress calls, but didn't do anything.

– Several ships received the SOS, but they thought it was a joke.

– The people on Titanic received the warning about ice and icebergs, but ignored it.

– What a mess.

He touched the place where the bullet had hit him. There was no hole there, not anymore, no mark, no indication that it had ever been a wound. He kicked the deck with his foot. There wasn't any pain, not the slightest hint of it. He bathed in the vast, pleasant, joyful, horrible molten sea within.

The daze didn't let up. There was that. But on another level, he was so very, very astute, so much that he noticed everything around him. He wandered restlessly around on the decks, with James in tow, looking at the survivors. There were people asking the survivors for their names, and they replied, but he heard no familiar voices, saw no familiar faces.

It was night. He saw the statue of liberty in the distance, and he felt it as if he saw it for the first time. He didn't mind just then, standing in the rain, the torrential rain, washing everything away, purifying everything in its path.

He shook himself awake, staring at his surroundings, a remote look in his eyes, as if he didn't really see them at all.

– You were dreaming, weren't you? An eager kid spoke to him.

– Yes…

– What was it about? What were you dreaming?

His mother hushed at him, trying to pull him away from the large human frame standing there, looking at nothing.

– I dreamt about a deep forest, Nick said. – I was swimming at first, swimming endlessly through cold water. But then, an eternity later, I walked through the deep forest, and there was no end to it.

And he walked there, now. Walked there, as he smelled the trees and the animals and those who walked beside him, walked through the great and terrible forest without end.

Intermission:
Mark

Chapter Thirteen

The desert spoke to him, spoke its whispers and truths, and half truths and certainty of blood.

The fast Italian car pulled up before the hotel entrance. The valet boy was there immediately, ready to take the car to its designated spot.

– Don't take this the wrong way, kid, the driver grinned, – but I do my own parking.

He drove on, to the parking complex that was part of the hotel. There was a spot on the first level. He disembarked the car and walked down to the lobby, already drawing more than his share of the attention.

The man with bushy blonde hair and an outlandish purple jacket walked to the desk with lots of curious eyes ogling him.

– Good afternoon, sir, the woman behind the desk welcomed him. – Is there anything we can help you with?

– There is indeed, the man said. – My name is Peter Balthazar, and I have a reservation at your excellent hotel.

The clerk got the name right the first time.

– That's right, sir, she said. – Will that be cash or charge?

– Cash, of course, he said pleasantly. – I can't stand those pesky plastic cards, I'm afraid.

It took a while to complete the formalities, but not too long. The guest, at least, didn't turn impatient.

– Here you are, sir, she said. – Room 204. Have a pleasant stay.

– It's pleasant already, Peter Balthazar assured her, accepting the keys.

She was blushing in a deep shade of red.

The next few days and nights Peter Balthazar made his presence known in Downtown Las Vegas, as a fairly modest, but yet extravagant high-roller. He visited the sights, played the games and celebrated his winnings and losses with equal fervor.

Francis Caine walked up and down Fremont Street in Las Vegas, Nevada. Neon lights, glittering lit streets. Slot machines and games wherever you turned. He had come home.

He had been home, at his home, stood in the darkness outside, looking at those inside. He had always kept his family out of his «affairs», in the vain hope that others would do the same.

– This time they won't, Stewart had said, repeated in his ear. – This is too big, too vast to bother with something like «honor» between «gentlemen», about never-existing terms of engagement.

Caine had turned and walked away.

He passed the Four Queens and Golden Nugget casinos and walked through the open doors to Binion's Horseshoe, passing from the smoldering desert heat outside, to the regulated, artificial chill inside. Red dominated in here. Red walls, red carpet. White light was rare, except over the actual various gambling tables. The red color wasn't unusual on these places, but a bit old-fashioned, old school perhaps. It was a symbol of blood, a gambler's need for escapism, the fervent need to challenge both death and life. This was another world, filled with shadows. The sun outside didn't reach the people in here.

There were people here, even quite a few of them, who knew Francis Caine. But now, when his hair had been colored blond, and things had been done to whiten his skin, and the fashionable shades, he doubted even many of his closest friends recognized him, at least not with a casual look.

And those who did would hopefully acknowledge that he was running one of his scams, and keep their mouths shut.

He spotted Stewart and McKenzie. They sat quite a distance away from each other, evidently concentrating on their respective games. They were in disguise as well, perhaps even more than Caine was. Stewart had developed his a bit further lately. Caine studied him, and it was as if his old friend had disappeared beneath the façade the stranger by the Hold'em Poker table projected. His dark shades seemed, in a downright eerie way to cover his entire body.

Then Stewart gave him the sign, the special sign. A wave of excitement rose in Francis Caine. They had found Thomas Forester. After chasing him through most of the South West they finally had him within reach. Caine saw him the moment he passed into the next section of the casino, where the roulette tables were. Actually saw him physically, with his eyes, for the first time. It was a strange thing this, to chase, to shadow dance with a man without knowing him, without never having met him face to face. What had been just a name became a face, became movement and habits, a human being.

During the next hour the three circulated seemingly randomly through the casino, but at least one of them had always Forester in the line of sight. They didn't let him out of sight a second. They never looked directly at each other, never made any connection that could be discerned by a third or fourth party, all in all something approaching a flawless performance. They moved, in relation to each other as if they had been born triplets, and not just met a few weeks ago. Caine realized, without needing to think about it much, that they were indeed triplets. The same processes, a similar set of circumstances had given birth to them all.

They easily saw the two men in Forester's close proximity very fond of looking at each other. These weren't his ordinary bodyguards. They followed constantly on his heels, and didn't even make any attempt of hiding it. These were more cautious, but to people of the Unholy Triplets' caliber, they were nowhere cautious enough.

Caine played the high roller, a fairly wealthy guy with a long-standing dream of going to Las Vegas, and that naturally threatened to go off the rocker when the goal had been realized. He had lived in a three star hotel for four days, now, and left quite a track record. He slipped around in the surroundings he knew so well and grinned back at all the dealers who didn't recognize him, and made fun of «the fool and his money that easily parted company». He had to concentrate not to win. It cut to the bone every time the dealer took his failed bet.

He stayed mostly at the roulette tables. It was the easiest place to lose without raising suspicion, the best place to stay anonymous. Almost excusing himself in advance he placed his bets on five red numbers. It was clumsily done. The numbers were so spread on the wheel that the chances of winning were small indeed. But he won. It was pure luck, and he was so surprised that he almost exposed himself.

He pulled in his win, and grinned his fake smile. With the big beard it was a very good-natured smile.

– Jeez, that was fun, he exclaimed with a distinct Eastern dialect.

– Jeez, he heard as a virtual echo from behind. – Is that a New Yorker I hear?

The fine-tuned voice made him quiver inside, and when he turned around he wasn't disappointed. He looked into a warm, alive face, traced by long, bright hair.

– That was close, he nodded, while admiring her curves.

– Oh, how close, if I may ask?

– I'm from Manhattan, he grinned.

He liked her, he really did. She undoubtedly belonged to the cast of ladies making a living by keeping gentlemen company at the tables, but that didn't make him pull back. He had never been quick to judge.

– Listen… He hesitatingly touched her hand. – You seem to bring me luck. Will you be willing to stand here, to keep me… company, while I try again?

– You're cute, she mused. – And I've always had a weak spot for New Yorkers…

She pushed her left arm in between his right and his body. He knew he wasn't supposed to let this happen, but her bright smile dissolved his objections. He had always had a weak spot for seductresses. Besides, she was an excellent diversion.

He took his time placing the bets this time. In fact he did his utmost to win.

He lost. And couldn't hide his genuine irritation. While striving to keep the ingenuous expression he bet again, on the same numbers, twice as much as he had lost.

– You'll win this time, she said hoarsely. – You'll win…

He won. And relaxed. Now he had sufficient funds to keep it up for a while without drawing attention to himself. He placed one tenth of his win on thirty-five. People stared at him. He jovially returned a smile. They would quickly enough look indulgent at him again.

But they didn't. He won again. The girl excitedly clapped her hands. Almost unnoticeable he squinted his eyes. With shaking hands - no one saw how calm he truly was - he placed half of his stack at the same number. When he won again, he began to feel a slight sting in his temples, a result of his increasingly boiling blood. He had won two, no, three times against improbable odds. Such events didn't happen often in life. And he knew he would continue winning. Perhaps she truly brought luck.

During the next half hour, he cursed Stewart. He cursed fate that had given him this fantastic luck and not given him the opportunity to profit from it.

He was a tourist from New York, god damn it, and not a professional player. When he stopped playing, he had won, between twenty and thirty thousand dollars, but that was just one fiftieth of what he could have won. The sigh released was quite genuine.

– This took its toll, he said. – I think I'll cash in for today.

Cries of disappointment and salutations echoed in the room.

He exchanged his chips for money and put them in the bank, the casino's bank. All gambling houses worth mentioning had an arrangement to take care of the player's money. It was an arrangement serving everybody well, everybody except the robbers that worked in and out of Las Vegas. Caine was pleased that somebody had informed the «tourist» of this, or he might have been forced to carry the money on him not to expose himself.

They sat down, not far from where he had been playing.

– Oh, I almost forgot. He pulled a handful of chips from his pocket. – I saved these for you. You did bring me luck. You can go and play if you want. I'll just sit here and relax.

– Thank you, she said huskily, – but I don't want to play yet. I'm not after your money, believe me.

He did believe her. For many drawn to the casinos, both men and women, the money didn't really matter that much. It was the atmosphere, the excitement that attracted them. It wasn't greed that made her eyes twinkle, but rather the sense, the conviction that she lived - and lived intensively - face to face with destiny.

They talked. Just talked. A long while. And he, too, felt alive, felt more alive than he had in years. He focused on that - and her - to the point of him almost missing the fact that Forester was about to leave. From then on he had to split his attention between him and the girl. He strived hard so she shouldn't notice.

Forester left, followed by his lackeys. Caine's mind worked overtime, sweating a bit, just a bit. He didn't spot any of his «partners», but if he recalled correctly, it was Stewart who was outside right now. Having one outside at all times was a sound tactic. If any of them had left just after Forester, then that would have been like asking to be exposed. He looked at her. It was time for him to leave. Alone. She had suddenly become a liability, just like he had always known she would eventually become. Damn him!

– Why are you looking at the door all the time?

She was sharp.

– I guess I'm just impatient, he said. – I want to leave… with you.

– I'd like that, she said.

She winked to him, and they rose.

Caine smiled without her seeing it. No one would any longer find it strange that they left the premises.

– What do you say to a little *ride?* He said and led her off. – To celebrate the win.

– That would be fun, she said, with blushing cheeks. – You're the one with the fast Italian, right?

She had been paying attention, but so had quite a few others, he presumed.

– That's right, baby. I drove all the way from Manhattan in that wreck. It can dust almost anything on four wheels, so you better hold on good.

– … to you, she purred, clinging to him.

They reached the parking complex. He glimpsed Stewart somewhere ahead, and also glimpsed Forester and pack further ahead of Stewart. She kept clinging to him, as they approached the car, the «wreck of an Italian». He felt how his pulse beat against his skin.

While he searched his pockets for the keys, the girl touched the hood, the black paint, and admired the smooth curves, like he, himself, did.

The keys were not in the pocket he had expected them to be. Waves of panic rolled over him. He frantically, ever more frantically searched the other pockets. She looked at him. He deliberately met her eyes, shrugging, feeling very, very silly.

– You'll have to forgive me, honey, he said lightly, using his lifelong experience with all kinds of situations for all it was worth. – I seem to have a hole in my pocket. The keys have disappeared on me. If the casino can't find them I'll send for another set, but it will take a few hours.

– Oh, that's no big deal, sweetie, she purred, purred some more. – We can walk. Do you live nearby?

– It's quite a stretch away, he said curtly.

– We can go to my place, she offered. – It's less than a block off.

A few blocks in Las Vegas were quite a stretch. A block or less wasn't that bad.

He saw Stewart drive after Forester and pack. There was no way he could follow Stewart or join him, without calling attention to himself. He shrugged. Stewart could take care of himself.

– That sounds great, he replied.

– To me, too, she said excitedly.

Her mood was quite contagious. He returned her bright, bright smile, and after a couple of quick phone calls he followed her back outside.

He wondered what she would say when she discovered he wasn't blond all over his body…

– You're so cool and collected, she said, casting him an admiring look. – Taking all this in stride. I just *love* that.

He pulled her to him, kissing her. She resisted at first, before turning soft and malleable in his hands, moaning softly.

She began walking faster. He was able to sense her impatience, the restlessness in her body and mind, and he smiled in anticipation. They walked through a dark and narrow alley.

– Just a little longer, she whispered.

They walked through the dark and narrow alley. It was chilly in the dark and narrow alley, chilly in Las Vegas in September. Caine felt the heat, he did, felt it all around him. Suddenly the soft draft in the alley changed to an ice-cold northern wind. They entered a children's playground, a large square. He realized in full how exposed they were, how exposed he was.

He noticed her flickering eyes.

– What's wrong? He felt very stupid, asking her such a silly question.

There was a piercing scream, and he heard the word shouted inside he should have heard long ago: DANGER! A man stumbled from the shadows, from his cover, with blood flowing from his chest. Caine drew his gun. But there was nothing for him to shoot at. The wounded man collapsed. From the darkness he saw the flames from a gun. The girl was hit, and she fell without a sound. Caine couldn't move a finger. The eyes staring at him were dead and cold.

– Bang, you're dead.

He easily recognized the voice.

First there was nothing but hollow sounds in the night. Then, as the lights fell on the man in the shadows, Caine miraculously heard the sound of steps.

– You overdid it, McKenzie told him. – You were too rich and too dumb. They figured there was money in a kidnapping.

Caine opened and closed his mouth constantly. For the first time in years, his snappy mouth failed him.

– They were three, McKenzie kept talking. – The third stiff is behind the corner over there.

He wasn't particularly sarcastic, but Caine still felt the humiliation like a physical blow where he stood with his gun hanging from his shaking hand. In just a tiny moment his clothes had turned clammy, and the need to lift his gun and fire and fire and fire his gun overwhelming.

– The girl… why the fuck did you shoot her? She was never a danger. Do you enjoy shooting people?

His own, final, intense exclamation shocked him. He behaved like a kid caught with his pants down. What was *wrong* with him lately?

– If you had bothered to look closer at her, you would have seen how above suspicion she was. *All the time*.

The last sentence had an edge. Caine looked at her, at the small 22' in her hand. More than big enough to kill him, kill anybody.

McKenzie bent down.

– These guys were fairly skilled, he stated. – They could have made serious trouble for us, if given the chance.

He picked the chips from her pocket. They were soaked in blood.

– You were supposed to follow Stewart, Caine said.

– So were you…

The FBI man rose and dropped the chips into a small plastic bag, before putting them in his own pocket.

– Anyway, I figured Stewart could take care of himself. That's one thing he has in common with me.

– Don't go there, Caine snarled. – You were hardly out of the diapers when I begun working.

– You're absolutely correct there, McKenzie grinned.

Time and time again Francis Caine made a fist of his free hand.

Everything felt dead inside him.

He suddenly realized that he disliked McKenzie intensively.

McKenzie bent down over the girl again, sticking his hand in her other pocket. When he pulled the hand back out, he held the car keys in his hand.

– A good thing they're not soaked in blood, or we would've really been in trouble…

One of the gunmen moved, and then he moaned.

– I thought you were a better shot, the gambler told McKenzie. – Please do better the next time.

He emptied his gun in the shaking body.

There were no echoes. It was still quiet there, on the open square. They heard no signs of commotion, no sirens, no sounds of anybody approaching.

Caine looked around as they returned to the dark alley, to the shadows, the comforting and horrible shadows. There was no movement in their surroundings, no sounds but the background noises of the city… and of the desert, the smoldering, whispering desert. The three bodies on the ground stared at the skies with dead eyes.

This was a children's playground. The irony wasn't lost on the Gambler.

The bodies would probably remain here until the morning, when the playful tiny tykes would arrive, and get their first taste of the cold, hard world.

He mumbled something.

– What was that, Caine?

He didn't dignify the other with a reply.

When I remember someone, I remember the dream.

He mumbled to himself.

And that was all. That was all he did.

++++++++++++++++++++++++++++

They returned to the car, returned to the hotel, each to their own rooms. Caine fell on the bed. It took a long time before he fell asleep. He crouched there, brooding. He pictured Stewart's body in the desert sand, shot to pieces, and he pictured himself doing an insane dance as dark fires consumed that body, turning it to sand, whispering sand blowing in the wind.

He «rested» there for a long time without truly sleeping. He seemed to recall the onset of dawn, but kept slumbering, until Stewart shook him awake. He felt tired at first, as if he hadn't slept at all, but as Stewart looked at him with his burning eyes, he imagined that slivers of ice showered his feverish brain, and he was Awake. He tried, he really tried, later to forget that exact moment, but he couldn't. It gave him the shakes every time he recalled it, and he couldn't stop the uncontrolled shakes, no matter how much he feared that his traveling companions would discover it. He remained awake, and he could no longer close his eyes.

Stewart saw everything. His eyes saw through everything, and were able to see all the world's secrets. Nothing was hidden from his piercing eyes. Uncertainty and fear haunted Caine's every aware moment.

They left Las Vegas at the advent of dusk. They drove south and west, to California and the Mojave Desert. A remote, desolate landscape, resembling photographs Caine had seen of the moon's surface. But there was life here. He knew that. There was life, whispering beneath the sand. The image of Stewart and that of the desert mixed in Caine's mind, becoming interchangeable.

The moment Stewart had shot Peter Clarke was etched in Caine's memory, the expression of boundless hatred engraved in Stewart's face. He was unable to let it go, no matter how much he wanted to. There was a black, black shadow sitting next to him, and the Gambler was drowning in its night.

They left the highway, and drove into a shadowy divide. Sunlight cast long shadows everywhere. Stewart stopped the car, stopped the engine. He grabbed his bag with water bottles and supplies and left the car in a cloud of dust, but the Gambler still saw him unbelievably clear.

– Are you alright? Stewart asked him.

I must be sick, Caine told himself. My runaway imagination is finally exerting its toll.

– I'm okay, he assured the other.

The desert bathed in the sun. He had never really gotten used to it, its breathtaking impression. The sand kept whispering in his ears. The living desert moved and breathed around him.

– This is some place you've taken us, McKenzie mused. – I presume Forrester and bunch are hiding in the sand nearby.

– It's quite a walk from here. Stewart shrugged. – We couldn't drive closer without risk being seen.

– We have a long walk in the sun to look forward to, then.

McKenzie again.

– We'll wait until nightfall. We'll move and hunt in the night.

There was a clear warning in his voice, keeping McKenzie from spouting more sarcasm. Caine had been silent all day. He spouted nothing. It turned quiet between the three. They sought the deepest shadow, close to the mountain, to protect themselves from the sun and the wind. The wind was the sand. In a place without wind the sand was still blowing. The grains rubbing against each other created a deeply disturbing sucking sound.

Stewart spoke and he sounded deeply disturbed.

– It's the whispers of the dead, he mumbled.

He was unable to sit still, or even stand without moving for longer periods of time. Ants crawled under his skin. Caine saw it, felt it. Stewart was cracking up. He knew that. He saw that easily. It wasn't difficult, not difficult at all. He would've seen it, easily, even without the power of observation his long years of experience had given him.

– The sand is speaking to me, Stewart said. – It's shouting, too loud for me to hear.

He drew the Peacemaker, stared at it for a long time, before returning it to its designated place inside the jacket. He rose and began walking. There was constant fluid movement, no transition from the rising and the walking, not like seeing most people move at all.

– Where are you going? McKenzie frowned.

This was the first time Caine had heard indications of worry in his voice.

– To the top, Stewart grinned. – To the mountaintop, to watch the desert, to see the world.

He quite enjoyed it, enjoyed yanking their chain. He saw himself through them both, and he enjoyed it. One second he was himself, then he was McKenzie, was Caine. He made his way up the steep mountain wall without much effort. It was as easy as he knew it would be. One moment he was himself, the next the desert, the wind, the sand, the drought, the cold freshwater deep below the ground.

The wind was blowing at the mountaintop, just as he had expected. But when he looked down there was no more sand. When he looked down, he saw nothing but a vast, dark abyss where the sand was supposed to be.

He mumbled, mumbled curses to himself, his lips only a narrow line of bloodless flesh.

Hands like sand pushed at his facial skin. He closed his eyes, closed them hard, closed them for a long time. When he opened them again, slowly, excruciatingly, he could finally see, see the world. He watched as Caine looked up at him from below, watched him do so several times. Just then it was as if he calmed down, turned calm. He put his hands in the jacket's pockets and set down. Sat down and waited.

He had been sitting like that for a long time when Caine began his own ascent. By then the sun had broken through the clouds, and was very close to the horizon shifting from pale blue to red.

The Gambler didn't shake so much anymore. He was unsteady on his feet the last few steps to where Stewart sat, but there was something very aggressive, edgy about him, about his eyes, his attitude.

– They call me The Gambler, he cried, very theatrical.

Stewart sat there, waiting, watching assessing, like a hawk before diving from the sky.

– Have I ever told you how much I detest that name? Caine said, half choked, half spitting. – «The Gambler»... hah! I haven't truly gambled in my entire life, not once. The name is a joke. I've never risked that much, never played the highest stakes. I've played with money, only money.

– Look at it, Francis Caine, Stewart said quietly. – Look at our target.

Caine looked, looked at the small cluster of buildings to the west. It was at the foot of a hill about a mile off. The flying sand almost looked like mist in the twilight.

– A military base, Caine said, challenge distinct in his voice, his attitude. – I figured it would be something like that. With a tall electrical fence, I presume? And you won't tell me it isn't guarded by a pack of two-legged dogs, won't you?

– On the contrary? A disarming smile. – It's quite heavily guarded, more so even, then most other bases out here. Soldiers are constantly patrolling the area, both inside and outside the fence.

As with many a conversation with Stewart lately, Caine couldn't find anything to say.

– There's a flying saucer, a spaceship hidden in one of these bases, Frankie. It looked like the big man closed his eyes, but they were open, wide open. – It crashed close to Roswell, New Mexico in 1947. The military and the power behind the throne in this country, in the world have kept that find and many others from the public the entire time since then.

– You're kidding, Caine exploded. – Tell me you're kidding.

Stewart turned towards the other man, and it was as if he turned indefinitely, as if he would never turn completely.

– You don't see me, old friend. You see a creature of fire and shadow, and you don't realize it's me.

– What the FUCK are you talking about? Caine shouted.

Stewart turned his attention back to the cluster of buildings in the west. But he kept his eyes on Caine, made them burn his hide. Caine felt it, felt the fire singing his skin, and that admission wasn't hard at all.

– That's not a military base, Stewart whispered, Stewart spoke. – It's a gate, a place of transformation, where we'll change our lives, metamorphose into something new and different and never return to what and who we were. That's what that is, Frankie. You're looking at the future. Not theirs, but *ours*. Are you ready? Are you primed? This is who we are.

– It would help if you'll tell me how we're gonna break into that place without being captured or shot to pieces. I can't see how we're gonna do it, without sprouting wings and turn invisible.

Stewart laughed, and Caine felt the laughter's sting.

– You're good, Frankie. I'll never say anything to the contrary. But I don't know if I've told you this before, old friend, but I've always detested your propensity for shadow fighting. Why don't you speak plainly? We both know you know well how we'll do it, how we'll accomplish our task.

Caine hadn't expected this, hadn't expected this either, so straight to the point. He shook. He had wanted to take the initiative between them, hold it between his hands like grains of golden sand, but even that was denied him.

– The Great Gambler is afraid. Stewart scorned him. – Not for me exactly, but for what I am.

Caine struck out with his hand in the air, clearly frustrated.

– I admit I found your enigmatic ways frustrating at first. He scowled. – That was years ago. Now, I find we're long past the moment where you should've leveled with me.

– But I *am* leveling with you, Frankie, Stewart insisted. – That it's not what you want to hear shouldn't be my problem… right?

He had turned the tables again, and Caine felt older than ever.

– I can sense your doubt, your raging open wound.

Stewart stared at the other man, and he looked right through him, right through nothing.

– This is it, then. This is the truth, uncut and to the point. This is what I know:

And Francis Caine, called The Gambler and worse things besides, listened to the words in the wind, the desert wind.

– My parents were killed when I was three. They were taken from me, and I was alone. But long before then my mother and I… spoke. She taught me what she called «the silent language», that of the *mind.* She was what people may call a witch. She used that word herself as well. But not without some ironic distance. We're a tribe, one older than the Jews and the Gypsies and others, older than time. She was a witch, she told me. I was a witch. We belonged to an extended family of witches called The Janus Clan or the *Shadowwalkers.* Her mind told me everything, and it was as if a thousand years passed in a second. I *remember.* She died by my side, and I felt her die, felt her Shadow as it left her body, as it burned me, as it returned to the shadowlands. The gypsy tribe found me and took me in. They even succeeded in tracking down my family, but I was with them only a few fleeting, though revelatory moments. I lost them or they lost me, I don't know, but I've never been able to find them, to track them down. When I remember someone, I remember the dream.

Caine stood there with his mouth open. There was a secret here, vast and terrifying. Caine's feet were locked to the spot he stood. But he still backed off. He was still pushing against a wall, like a cornered animal.

– Mother warned me. Because you're born different, she told me, people will fear you and they will hate you and harm you.

Caine was quite the bastard himself. Not Spanish, not Mexican, not white, never belonging anywhere, going everywhere, seeking every dark corner there is.

– I was in a state of denial for years. I married. I even settled down. I played at being human.

There was hatred here, thinly veiled. Caine froze in the deep abyss the mountaintop had become.

– Mother warned me. She told me that although normal humans may deny the truth, deny their very Self *we* can't. Our nature will surface. Our Self will assert itself. We're the stuff dreams are made of. We make dreams come true.

The sun didn't set. The blood red light permeated the landscape.

– I was alone, and I didn't even look for more, not for years. I didn't find anything. It found me. You see, the thing about sticking your head in the sand is that you don't see what's right in front of you…

– But I did, and to call it a revelation doesn't in any way do it justice.

– But you do have… powers, right? Caine had to speak, had to give voice to his horror. – Why haven't you used it to get rich?

– That's a stupid question. Why aren't you rich? Why did you come running when I finally, after eight years contacted you? It's because ordinary games are too easy. They're boring. Life becomes impossible without challenges. Life turns meaningless…

– I see it, old friend, see it in flashes lasting an eternity, see the tapestry unfolding.

Stewart seemed to be enjoying himself. But his eyes were hard and sharp as knives. And there was more. There was so much *knowledge* in those eyes, so much madness, as if all the horrors of the world were gathered there. Caine realized a truth he had been aware of from the beginning, the fact that Stewart hadn't really told him *anything*, and that he never would.

Caine blinked and realized that he had forgotten. Stewart's smile confirmed it. Caine began sweating.

– I'm very rusty, Frankie, but that wasn't hard to read. I should be angry with you, but how can I? In you I see a mirror, in you I see myself.

– I found one, Frankie. I found all.

– Who? Caine exclaimed.

There was something missing, something he didn't get.

He had sought Stewart up here, sought this place to get clarity, but clarity kept evading him. He strived to clear his mind, find meaning in the meaningless, and find answers to the questions haunting him.

Stewart wanted to tell, and he did. And in doing so he weaved his spell.

– You should've known that. Listen now, this is the whole caboodle.

They burned again, now, Stewart's eyes, like fire. Behind him the sun did set. The clouds formed a specific formation, suddenly turning the evening sky blood, blood red. Not just like blood. It was blood. Caine tasted the iron, the rust in his mouth. He started shaking again, harder than before. He had set out to *know.* He had wanted certainty because he had imagined it would be easier to choose then. He had been wrong. At this very moment his choices narrowed to one. And there was no certainty anywhere.

– Stewart is my father's name, so it became mine. The words were released slowly, as if in sleep. But there was no doubt that Stewart was awake - extremely awake. – But it isn't really me. It's just a sound, a random arrangement of patterns. It doesn't mean anything. My mother and her name, that's what's important, what's crucial. Joan Fontaine was only briefly, very briefly my stepmother. Since I used her name briefly you were convinced that was mother's name. That's just one of your many erroneous presumptions about me. Mother was an American citizen. Her last name was *Warren*.

Francis Caine crouched. So fast that he nearly lost his footing, lost it on flat, solid ground, and he did. Stewart was right. He should have known. Everything rushed him like an avalanche. Stewart didn't need to say anything more. Caine understood now, understood nothing. Perhaps for the first time in his adult life he was truly and utterly terrified. He knew now that it would've been better for him if he had never met Stewart, never stepped in his footsteps or spoken or even known his name.

Chapter Fourteen

– It's a bit risky this, McKenzie pointed out with clear skepticism in his voice. – The place is crawling with guards. If we run into a single one and that person is able to cry out we're done.

– We won't be discovered, won't be caught, Stewart assured him. – I spent hours here last night learning the guard's search and sweep patterns.

Lie, Caine thought.

– I guess we should be okay then, McKenzie shrugged. – I've yet to meet a soldier showing any true initiative.

They sneaked in during the night. When they reached the patrolled area the time was a few minutes past two. They walked between massive dunes and the desert was dark as the inside of a sack.

There wasn't that much of a danger in speaking. The sand kept whistling around their ears. But they preferred to keep quiet anyway. It was part old habit, part preference. They didn't need words to understand each other.

They moved through the ghostly terrain, led by Stewart. The other two went at each other's side, making the three a triangle. They had walked for a while when Stewart slowly stopped and signed for them to do it as well. He stood there, still as a statue. Caine knew his eyes were closed.

– What's he doing? McKenzie asked.

– Listening, Caine replied, which was the factual truth of the matter.

But McKenzie would certainly have been surprised if he had known how Stewart listened.

And this is what Stewart said, what he told his two companions:

– I can sense another place where it's raining, where the sky is gray, and the thousand needles fall on the quiet ocean. I can hear the sound of bugles blowing.

– I didn't know you were interested in poetry, Stewart, McKenzie commented dryly, skepticism and contempt clear in his voice and stance.

When they reached the fence, the time was a few minutes before three. Stewart listened for a second or two more, before bending down and digging under the fence. The soil, the sand was much looser there than elsewhere, and Caine realized that someone had been digging there earlier. Stewart last night.

They stood on the other side, subconsciously brushing sand off their clothes.

– We must hurry, Stewart whispered. – There's a change of guards showing up soon. Just follow me.

They ran. Their feet made virtually no sound on the fine-grained sand, the soft ground. Caine and McKenzie still glanced nervously around them. It was at least hundred steps to the nearest building, and they didn't even run straight forward. Stewart led them in huge circles. They imagined they heard the soldiers pass by, but they never saw them, never saw them close.

And the trio reached the once so distant building. The shadow it cast swallowed them.

– Jeez, McKenzie exclaimed softly. A new quality had entered his voice and stance. He was impressed. – Aren't these soldiers supposed to be Special Forces? What if we had been Russians…

– It was fantastic, Caine said excitedly. – Fantastic!

Stewart sent Caine a warning with those eyes of his. And Caine felt chastised, like a schoolboy.

They entered a near empty hangar. There were a lot of echoes in there, but nothing came from them. The door squeaked a bit when Stewart closed it, but there was no echo. It was an old, almost derelict building. They could see lights between the cracks in the wall. There were no lights in here, and the walls could no longer keep the wind out.

The siren sounded; a penetrating sound cutting through the buzz from the wind and sand. For a while they heard loud shouts of commands and many running feet outside. McKenzie writhed uncomfortably. The two others sat still. Then the loud noises and activities in the camp once again turned less insistent. Once again there was only the wind and the desert.

– We stay here during the night, Stewart told them. – At dawn Forester and bunch are gonna leave with one of the choppers, and we will join them. There are two choppers. We will dismantle the other as we use the one. The army would probably not have involved themselves anyway, but left the problems to their friends, but these friends may be present in force on the base. So we take care of the redundant chopper.

– So what's Forester doing here, anyway? McKenzie wondered.

– He came here to meet his son, Stewart replied. – I heard them speak last night, heard them speak about a lot of things. Forester junior was very confused, and senior had to explain it all to him, one hell of a snow job, if I ever witnessed one.

– So, I guess Frank was «found» around here, somewhere, Caine said, – miraculously appearing from his ordeal. He doesn't remember much, and can't give details about what has happened to the others. And it will all blow over. The media blizzard will fade, as it always does, and the boy's friends will keep rotting under the heels of the Thousand Feet.

– But there's a lot not adding up here, McKenzie said. – Why all the elaborate schemes? They're not truly necessary. The Thousand Feet has the power to do anything they want, so why the pussyfooting?

Stewart looked directly at him, grinning dangerously.

– Because there's more than one force at work here, Stewart elaborated. – Because the Feet themselves are split in several fractions. And even though they're basically cooperating under a common purpose, there's rivalry. I see a lot of delicate negotiations as the set up here was completed to the satisfaction of everybody involved.

– And then, of course, there's the most important reason: They have only limited, far from total control over the society, the garden they're tending. Even though they have the power to do what they want, they can't do so, not without the risk of being compromised, and secrecy has always been one of their most important creeds, since their early days as the nascent power of the Holy Roman Empire. So, they move in silence, act in subterfuge, because they need to uphold the illusion of a free and just society. And because it's tradition. Tradition is everything. We're talking about a rigid system that hasn't changed for millennia, not in its basics.

Nothing more was said. Caine wanted to, wanted to say a lot. Stewart sat down with his back to the wall. He closed his eyes, and, just like that, he slept. The even breathing more than proved the point. Caine didn't look at Stewart then, but at McKenzie, who was staring, staring hard at the sleeping man, visibly upset, at least to a man of Caine's experience.

Caine closed his own eyes, not really sleepy, but still attempting to ignore the frantic pacing of the government official accompanying them. Caine wondered if Stewart had only chided him, as he often did with everybody, or if there was something more behind it this time.

There was always more.

The Tapestry, Francis Caine thought. The Tapestry unfolding.

And the wind and the gray light penetrating the hangar and the men inside it hurt and kept hurting him, his bones and flesh. Caine closed his eyes tight, as the desert and the grains of sand blew through him, blew straight through his mind and soul.

++++++++++++++++++++++++

He felt a deep disappointment when he was shaken awake, even though it was McKenzie who did it, and Stewart stood near the door and looked through one of the cracks in the wall.

The gray morning light shone on his face. Caine touched his head and grimaced. He felt horrible and didn't care about hiding it.

– You better get up and running, McKenzie said coldly. – It's time.

– Time…? Caine fought himself up, as Stewart stepped aside, and let him look outside.

He saw the two choppers, one being cleared for take off.

Saw the soldiers swarming out there, all the soldiers between the three of them and the chopper.

– It all looks even more impossible in daylight, he mumbled. – Such a stretch. How are we supposed to get there without being seen?

– That's not an untimely question, you know… McKenzie squinted his eyes at the outside light.

He didn't seem overly worried.

– We're not going there without being seen, Stewart told them, definitely not worried.

Caine turned to him, a devil-may-care fearful expression in his face.

– What are you gonna do then? Fly us after the chopper on your invisible wings?

Stewart looked harshly at him. Now, you were careless, the eyes said. They bespoke a warning, a more than clear warning. The excitement in Caine rose a few more notches and the sense of horror returned. For good, this time. It would never again leave him.

He realized, as an afterthought that Stewart saw McKenzie as an outsider, and not Caine. The thought made him warm and cold all over. He wasn't sure he would count it as a blessing.

– We will rush them, Stewart said simply. – When the chopper takes off, both we and the Foresters will be onboard.

Something tied itself in knots inside The Gambler. Something froze, never to melt, never to untangle.

– But what about the guards, and the other soldiers? Are we gonna fire at them? We may injure or even kill innocent people, people being in the wrong place at the wrong time.

– Are you serious, Caine? McKenzie wondered scornfully. He spoke low, but in spite of the considerable distance between them they still heard him clearly. – It wasn't in Kindergarten you gained your fearsome reputation, was it? This is no game. Our enemies are everywhere. This includes the military. You can bet your last deck of cards that they'll be first in line to take us out. But if not… If you don't want to be buried at the state's expense, you'll have to defend yourself, pal.

Caine shrugged. Stewart grinned. Hard.

Stewart started undressing. What the… He removed his jacket and pants, and sweater. Below his ordinary clothes he had a full-fletched Lieutenant uniform.

One more triumph, Caine thought, one more ace in the hole, rabbit from a hat.

He felt old.

The three men checked their guns, an old habit, a reflex, an instinct beaten into them through dozens of situations similar to this.

– Follow me, Stewart commanded.

It wasn't necessary, but he did it anyway.

They put their guns away, grabbed their bags with left hands, hardly feeling the weight and walked outside, into the bright, pervasive and beyond hot desert morning. There were voices, voices in the dark, flying out of the night. The Foresters with entourage were on their way towards the chopper. The Foresters in the middle. The two bodyguards from Vegas on each side, and behind them was someone that was almost certainly the base's commander.

The Thousand Feet had, as expected, their powerful representatives on the base. Stewart cursed silently under his breath, a volcano about to burst, and he welcomed it.

– Take it easy, Stewart, McKenzie said coldly. – You'll get an outlet for your aggression soon enough.

You're a sneaky shit, Stewart thought. You know people, a lot about how to control them, to make them dance to your tune, but it won't work with me.

First step. This is only first step… on the stairs to Infinity. His rage was calm, like a low burning flame within. He grinned, and he knew that grin unnerved both Caine and McKenzie.

The boy grabbed his father's arm when the small group was only ten steps or so from the chopper, worried about something. They were clearly in a hurry. Senior didn't even turn or react in any way, as far as the three men observed.

They walked in the same tracks as the other group, surrounded by the early morning activity, by their honor guard of soldiers, some armed, some not. One armed soldier waited by the chopper. One of the bodyguards turned. He nipped the Commander's arm. Caine felt how the hot wind cooled his sweaty body. They walked on, approached the chopper, not that far after the Forester group. Thomas Forester and the others turned towards them, not that worried. Heavy sweating was natural in this place, this smoldering cauldron, Caine told himself.

Close now. The boy and one bodyguard entered the chopper. Forester and the Commander turned towards the approaching men. There was a military honor guard with guns not far away. Nothing new or newly alarming about that. They weren't that close, not close enough to be effective.

Just a few more steps. The Commander stared at them with critical eyes. The bodyguard held a hand inside his jacket.

The three new arrivals put down their gear. Stewart stopped in front of the Commander and saluted him. Caine almost giggled.

– Lieutenant Darnell reporting for duty, sir. I was told you would be out here. I bring a message from the Chief of Staff, sir.

– What the hell are you doing here, Lieutenant? The commander grudgingly returned the salutation. – You don't look like a typical messenger boy to me.

– Everything is explained in the letter, Commander, Stewart replied, very formal.

He reached inside his jacket. Forester's dog stiffened. Stewart pulled out the envelope. It was printed with the Unites States' national seal. Everybody visibly relaxed, sending each other embarrassed glances. The dog's paws re-appeared empty-handed. The other dog appeared from the chopper, also empty-handed.

The Commander scrutinized the two behind Stewart.

– And your companions?

– Everything is explained in the message, Commander.

Stewart handed him the envelope. The Commander reached for it. Stewart let go of it a bit too early. The Commander failed to grab it, and it sailed between his legs. People's attention was locked on the white paper as it hit the ground, and those who didn't look at it, looked at Stewart.

McKenzie tore the gun from the soldier's hands, and struck him with its shaft. And before the soldier had hit the ground McKenzie had directed the weapon against one of the bodyguards. The man had just drawn his weapon when McKenzie shot him in the head. Brain mass stood out in a straight line in the air behind him.

– No more funny stuff, McKenzie snapped to the rest. – You've got your warning.

No one moved, and when Stewart and Caine also drew their guns all resistance evaporated. Everything had happened so fast, so totally paralyzing.

– Everyone inside the chopper, Stewart cried. – And be quick about it.

He jumped inside first and ran to the cockpit, ignoring the stunned boy he passed. The pilot had opened a box below the instrument table and was about to grab a gun. Stewart fired a bullet into the chair, right by his thigh. The hand froze close to the gun.

– We don't really need you, Stewart told him icily. – Grab the gun with two fingers. Slowly. Throw it here. You sit down in the seat and you don't move a muscle. If you do that, you die. It's your choice. It's that simple.

The man obeyed. Stewart put his own gun away and picked up and checked the one the pilot had given up. It was loaded and ready for use. McKenzie pushed Forester senior and junior down in the seats. The Commander sat down without help, a study in anger and astonishment. A professional easily recognizing his peers, though. He sat still.

The remaining bodyguard wanted to follow them inside. Caine struck him on the head.

– Dream on, Caine grinned. –You're very stupid if you think we want you with us.

He jumped inside.

– It's a go, he shouted. – Let's get this show on the road.

The soldiers started to react, to point and gesture. They were too far away. Some of them lifted their arms. Stewart grabbed the Commander and pushed him forward, displaying him in the chopper's opening, putting the barrel of the gun at the man's head. The soldiers didn't fire.

Stewart nodded to the pilot. As they lifted off McKenzie shot the other chopper systematically to pieces. It blew up, and they felt its heat.

McKenzie closed the door. Stewart pushed the Commander back in his seat. Everything was calm. The three hijackers had complete control.

– Where were you headed? Stewart asked the pilot.

A brief hesitation, then:

– Denver.

– Nice try. Try again.

Stewart put the barrel at the man's head.

– Too bad our brief friendship should end like this. I count to three. ONE…

– SAN FRANCISCO. Relax man.

The pressure increased.

– It's true! I SWEAR!

His breathing was uneven, ragged. Stewart removed the barrel. The breathing returned very slowly to normal.

– San Francisco, huh? That sounds better. I think we'll set course there.

He turned, and then he stopped, as if he didn't look at anything.

– What is it? Caine was there instantly.

– Nothing. Stewart shook his head. – Nothing important.

They were already high in the air. When they turned and sat course west people ran back and forth like rabbits down there. Lines of communications probably glowed all over the country.

– Relax, Stewart said. – They won't make it official business but leave it to the Abraxas Omega thugs.

– Relax…? Caine grinned.

– What's the PURPOSE of this? The Commander spoke up, seemingly furious. – I don't know who you are, but you've made cardinal mistake here. You've gone to war against the American army and thereby the American nation. You've…

– Didn't you hear what I just said, Stewart said to him. – We know you're just playacting here, so please shut your mouth, okay.

– NO reason to get excited, Thompson, Forester said soothingly in his usual, confident voice. And then to Stewart: – If it is a matter of money…

– Didn't you hear me? It isn't money…

Stewart's cold unbalanced Forester.

– Not money? But then…

– It seems like you're unable to imagine a situation that can't be solved with money, huh? You never change.

For the first time Stewart spoke with his normal voice. Forester frowned, while his calm permanently disappeared.

– It seems like someone has made a serious mistake somewhere, the Commander stated, suddenly very calm.

– Shut up, Forester snapped. He looked at his son, but Frank just sat there with foggy eyes. He didn't seem to get anything of what happened. – You talk too much.

– Do I? The Commander said, turned to Stewart. – I doubt that.

– I know you, Forester exclaimed hoarsely, also to Stewart. – Who *are* you?

Stewart sheathed his gun. He began to slowly remove his extensive disguise.

First the false moustache. A huge thing almost covering both the mouth *and* the nose. Some of the make-up loosened in the process. Bright, short hairs appeared. Then he removed the nose and the ears. He bent down and blinked. Two colored lenses fell into his palm. He grabbed skin below his jaw. It looked like he was actually pulling off his face. It was a special form of make-up, solidifying into a sort of jelly, a perfect mask. He pulled it off and the wig followed… and then he stood there as himself, a palatable, terrifying presence.

– STEWART! Frank exclaimed happily.

The chubby, but ragged face ruptured in a huge smile. He had been close to apathy. Now, it vanished with a stroke.

– That's impossible, his father shouted. – You're…

He held his tongue, as it dawned on him what he was doing.

– You're *dead?* Was that what you were about to say, Tom? Strange, I thought I was listed as *missing*. Only certain parties know I was supposed to be dead. If you ask me you sound both surprised and shocked. And disappointed…

– What *is* this? What's going on?

Certainty, fear and excitement raged the boy. Then, as he turned to his father, he turned calm as ice and his eyes turned hard:

– You're one of them.

– You're not that stupid, are you, boy? Forester cried. – Do you believe them instead of me? Stewart is wanted in Europe, a criminal…

Frank rose with great difficulty from the seat.

– I heard you and the other rat speak at the base, father. For the first time in years he called him that. – I didn't understand much of it then, but now it's all clear to me, so very clear.

He stood frozen for a moment, unable to proceed.

– Yes, I believe him, he whispered. – I'll rather believe Satan himself than you. Are you aware of what you've… done, what you've contributed to? Have you felt the pain, heard the screams?

The whisper fell, until it was hardly more than silence.

Stewart put his hand on his shoulder, but pulled it back instantly, as if he had burned himself. He backed off in horror, pulling himself together by an act of will, his face remaining naked and open for seconds before slowly regaining that of a stoic mask.

– What do you think our fortune was built on, boy? Forester tried again. – What do you think all the world's fortunes are built on? Charity? By aiding the poor and huddled masses? No, it was by strength, boy, strength to make the right decisions.

– Is there a toilet back there? Frank wondered. – I think I'm going to be sick.

While they heard the sound of the boy throwing up Caine walked to Stewart. He didn't ask. Not with words.

Stewart stared out of the window. Down at the sand, the vast emptiness.
– I looked right into his mind, saw images straight from hell. Stewart shook his head in wonder. – Experienced what he had experienced, stronger than I've ever felt.
Horrors, distractions, Caine felt it, as Stewart shared, deliberately or not, what raged through him. Distractions were death. They knew that. In this game no one got old by being distracted.
There was a thump, the sound of a moan and a body hitting the wall. McKenzie. They whirled around and drew their guns in the same movement, but were still too slow. Thompson and Forester were already over them. Like so many times before in similar situations there was no time to think. Everything went on autopilot, following an instinct millions of years old, honed through decades, countless days and nights. Forester struck Caine's arm, making him lose the gun. But Caine had allowed that. It created an opening. Caine struck Forester on the nose, making tears flow from his eyes. It slowed him down, but didn't stop him. Caine was pushed backwards, and fell. In glimpses he saw McKenzie on the floor. Saw it just before Forester closed his eye with a rock-hard fist.
Stewart had also lost his gun. It was on the floor, between him and Thompson. They circled it and measured each other.
Forester almost reached the gun. Caine felt the strength of a thousand suns swell inside of him, as he desperately counterattacked. Stewart hardly looked at the gun by his feet. Thompson moved in a typical martial arts defense position. Stewart feigned an attempt to grab the gun. Thompson reacted instantly, sending a murderous kick at Stewart's head. He took the brush of the kick on his shoulder and followed the force of it backwards, towards McKenzie. He pulled the man's gun from weak fingers, rolled once and pointed the gun at Thompson. The Commander stood with the Peacemaker in his hand, but the barrel pointed at the floor. Stewart shot him twice in the heart, and he died with his mouth opened in a silent protest. Caine threw Forester off him, and reached for his gun. Forester rose and was about to charge again.
– *Freeze!*
Stewart's icy voice. Forester snarled, but froze. He knew he was covered from two sides.
– You've got me. He shrugged. – You win. You win, now.
– Move aside, Caine told him sharply, suddenly nervous. – *Now!*
The pilot was no longer in his seat. From Stewart's viewpoint, the wall covered him. And Forester blocked Caine's view.
– Why? Forester sighed, almost bored. – I can see no reason…

There was thunder. One, two, three times. One of the bullets whistled past Caine' head. The two others hit Forester in the back. Stewart fired through the wall. It didn't hit the pilot, but evidently distracted him, since he also missed Caine with his fourth shot. A cascade of thunder filled the insides of the chopper. The Gambler saw the man, saw the whirl of motion, and he fired a rain of bullets in the pilot's shaking body. Lines of blood stood horizontally from it as it fell dead to the floor.

Red. The color of air was red.

It turned quiet. Deadly quiet.

Caine rose slowly. He stared hard at the dying Forester.

– He fired at you, too. You were obviously expandable. So you might use the short time you've got left of your rotten life to tell us *something*. It can't be much. You don't have much time. If you care about your son at all, you'll do it.

– Go… fuck yourself.

McKenzie moaned and blinked. Stewart pulled him up in a sitting position. The agent shook his head, clearly ashamed.

Frank's face was white when he stumbled from the toilet. He fell to his knees by his father's side and started shaking him.

– Don't die yet! He choked. – I want to know why you did it. How you could even think about supporting them. The BASTARDS.

Forester moved his lips a few times without producing a sound. But then it came. Poisonous, harsh.

– You're a little shit, boy. You've always been a shit. You're like all ungrateful kids discarding what their parents do for them, endlessly complaining, never content. You'll never amount to anything. You'll come to beg for food. You're a failure… going to the dogs… sniveling child…

– You SATAN! Frank shouted to him. – I hate you. HATE you! Don't die yet. I haven't told you everything I want to tell you… how much I loathe you, how much I curse you… curse you…

The voice decreased into an unintelligible mumble. Forester had stopped breathing. Frank's head fell to his chest. His hand was still clutched around his father's collar. He remained like that, unmoving. There was the occasional choking sound. Aside from that, there was only silence.

Stewart sat down in the pilot seat. The instrumental panel flashed and burned in front of him.

– We didn't hit any vital parts, he said cheerfully. – Always an advantage…

The fight lingered in him, as it always did. Images, pain, death. He rejected it, as he always did.

Careful, with steady moves, he disengaged the autopilot and grabbed the stick. A minor pull, that was all.

– Thank the Lord. Caine breathed.

Just then, there was a loud crack somewhere.

– What the hell…

The black computer screen on the left of the panel was suddenly filled with pulsing white dots. Dots slowly organizing itself into a clock. It showed fifteen minutes past three.

– Whoever programmed this thing didn't have the correct time, Stewart said.

– It goes backwards, Caine said, feeling a strong urge to say it.

– I would say we need to get this wreck down on the ground as soon as possible, McKenzie said. – And then run like hell.

– I see. Caine swallowed hard. – I see…

He saw them go down in flames.

Again.

– That damn pilot, Stewart swore. – He reaches out for us from hell. But we'll cheat him. We'll cheat him of that pleasure.

To confirm that, to deny that the minute hand, slipping backwards, reached the number twelve for the first time. At that moment the screen started flashing red and the hand speeded up significantly.

– We've got three minutes, McKenzie enlightened them. – We're faced with one of the army's self-destruct mechanisms. There won't be enough left of us to sweeten the tea. And don't waste time attempting to reprogram it. The disengaging of the autopilot made the process irreversible.

Stewart had already begun the descent. He sat course for the mountains, for cover.

He flew the machine, flew it as if he had never stopped, never had had years of absence from flying. It turned alive in his hand, and he felt it dying.

– Stand ready, he shouted. – Here we go.

He sat course for a soft dune in the mountain shadow. He felt its softness, its pleasant, dry waves. The hand passed twelve for the final time. All lights inside the chopper began flashing and a klaxon horn hurt their ears. Caine opened the door out. The chopper dove to the ground, evidently without control, but Stewart managed to balance the need for speed and still keep them from losing the last vestige of control. The doomed bird landed and the loose sand gushed in all directions, like water, like water in a sea. McKenzie and Caine jumped out. Frank sat on the floor, totally out of it. Stewart pulled him up, grabbed the boy in both body and mind, in ways he had never before done. The boy's eyes widened in shock and clarity.

Frank jumped, and he ran, ran like the wind. All four of them fought themselves through the dunes, fleeing from the doomed machine behind them.

Caine felt sick. It was as if the sand came alive around them. He saw burned wreckage, bloody and mangled human bodies, and it was all so real, so real that he thought he was already dead, and hadn't quite realized it yet.

Stewart pushed the three of them down, and followed them himself, in the last possible moment. The chopper exploded. Flames blew to all sides and the sand rose in the air, blocking out the sun, blocking out everything, except the frantic beating of hearts. Burning metal pieces fell all over the area, but the humans were not hit. The sand hit them, like a deluge, like a wave of salty blood. They all crouched there gasping, breathing air, breathing life into their lungs.

Seconds passed. Ages passed, as red and beige dust settled around the four people.

Frank raised his head, moving his lips for seconds, in a horrible attempt to speak.

– I saw… saw myself dead in the sand. It was horrible… horrible. I can't describe it, I just can't.

Is this just our imagination? Caine wondered. Is this the dream, and the visions the reality?

He watched Stewart, and also McKenzie. Even McKenzie looked shaken. His eyes flickered back and forth and he didn't understand what had happened.

Stewart pulled them all up, freeing them from the dry sand's moist clutches.

McKenzie brushed the sand off his coat, squinting his eyes, squinting them hard.

– I guess it's a fair estimate that we have a long walk ahead of us?

– A very long walk, Stewart replied distantly.

They all stared at the debris, the many burning pieces. Caine stared at Stewart. He could only see his back. Stewart knew that. He sensed the other's eyes.

Eyes sought the one bag with supplies, the one Stewart had brought.

– Without much food, without much water, McKenzie said. – With the hordes of hell chasing our tail.

– We'll find more water, Stewart stated. – We'll find more food. The hordes of hell won't catch us.

Caine opened his mouth to say something, but changed his mind. Stewart noticed it, and felt the usual bitterness, the usual sense of loneliness.

They walked past the burning wreckage. The dust still hadn't settled, and in Caine's mind it never would. They glimpsed torn off limbs. Frank kept his eyes tightly closed until they were far beyond it all.

It took hours to cross the divide between the mountains. Ages passed until night finally descended on them, delivering them from the searing heat. They looked for planes in the air, hunters on the ground, but there was nothing, only the burning chopper etched into their mind. It faded only slowly, finally merely a pinprick in the horizon. The sun burned, even at night. Everything was quiet. But the wind would start blowing soon. Erase every single proof that there had ever been human beings here. Their persecutors would come, and they would find nothing. They would seek, but they would not find. The desert swallowed everything. Its Storm, like any storm would come and sweep away all things, leaving nothing but dust.

++++++++++++

They rested under a sunshade, one sheltering them from the harsh light cast by the Florida sun. The tourists were sweating and suffering around them. Caine thought there was a slight chill in the air. After the horrible trip through the desert he imagined everything would always seem chilly to him.

– What do you think? Stewart broke into his thoughts. – He's half an hour late. Do you think he has mistaken the day or something?

Caine shook his head decisively.

– He's precision incarnated in everything he does. He'll be here.

– I know he will be here soon, Stewart grinned. – How are your burns by the way? The sun burned you quite hard.

– They're okay, Caine replied automatically. – Okay now. I haven't even itched for days, and I guess I have you to think for that, for all that.

Stewart had *touched* him, and *healed* him, just like that, and with that had followed a sense of well being Caine had a hard time dealing with. Caine felt… touched, both in body and soul.

He could still sense it, sense the desert like an actual presence within. And he could sense Stewart.

Stewart had saved them all. He had led all the time. Every time someone had been close to submit, to surrender to the hardship and the hopelessness, he had given them the little push they needed to keep going, to go on living. With scorn or even with a kind word. He had known what was needed, known every time. Caine recalled one of the times he had fallen, and Stewart had helped him up. Once again, he had felt pure strength flow from Stewart and into himself, like… like the sun had been down there with them, and not far above. Every preconceived notion about life Caine might have had, had been shaken to its foundations. From then on he had been convinced they would survive.

There had been a storm, burying them in sand whirling in the air. And they had heard the sound of engines, but no one had found them. The storm had been eerie, as if Stewart was leading them through the kingdom, the Kingdom of Death. But they had re-emerged on the other side, alive and thriving.

– You know, in the chopper. You actually looked like somebody did walk over your grave or something for a moment there. You looked… scared.

– Somebody did, Stewart burned.

And it was just one more of many ambiguous replies that weren't answers Stewart had given him lately.

– I have a confession to make, Stewart said, making Caine crash and burn again. – I told McKenzie I would need an extra hour before we met today, told him before we parted company. I fixed it so we would be able to talk without being disturbed.

Stewart surprised him again. He always surprised him.

– McKenzie isn't on our side. He… worries me. I believe… I *know* he's hiding something from us. The question is what and how significant it is.

Caine didn't say anything. He wanted to, but couldn't find the words.

– I know the fact that he's on his side, not on ours, isn't anything new. We always knew he was trustworthy and an ally… to a point. But this goes beyond that. He wasn't ashamed. There was no trace of that in his mind. Aboard the chopper he let himself be taken out. He quite simply counted on us to make it, to correct his «mistake». It wasn't us he wanted taken out, but the other people in the chopper. He didn't want them to recognize him… and subsequently reveal something about him he didn't want revealed… and he got his wish.

– He's in this knee-deep, with both feet.

Caine finally managed to speak. And it felt good, so very good.

The Sun hurt. It would always hurt.

– McKenzie is a fake, Stewart nodded. – Not in the sense that he isn't who he says he is, but because who he says he is isn't everything he is. Typical higher placed «civil servant». He will be useful to us, to us all, to a point. We'll just have to be extra aware, and recognize the moment when that will no longer be the case.

Stewart looked dangerous then, downright scary then.

But that wasn't anything new either.

– We're using him, and he's using us, Caine grinned, gooseflesh haunting his skin. – The question is who will stop using who first…

McKenzie arrived on time, not late, not early. They had taken a walk around the block and had just returned when he approached them. They greeted him exactly as he expected, not friendly, not warmly, but as a colleague, an associate in a world of confusion and chaos.

– The information we procured in San Francisco was on the money, he cut to the chase. – Aphrodite sat course here after the construction had been completed on Forester's wharf. After a mysterious detour south after passing through the Panama Canal… I'm told.

– You mean it will come here? Caine wondered. – Where was the detour?

– It did… and left. It set course for Europe ten days ago. No one I spoke to knew where the detour went, but they were very nervous about it. The European destination, however, is no secret.

– London, Stewart said muted.

– London, the other confirmed.

He pulled a newspaper from his coat. It was a two weeks' old edition of the New York Times.

– The ad here was featured in all major newspapers.

This covered the entire page:

REMEMBER THE STORIES
ABOUT THE OLD PASSENGER LINERS?
ABOUT THE GOLDEN AGE OF SEAFARING
WHEN CROSSING THE ATLANTIC
WAS SO MUCH MORE THAN A MERE CROSSING?
EXPERIENCE APHRODITE
THE GODDESS OF LOVE
MAKE YOUR HOLIDAY A VOYAGE TO REMEMBER
BOOK YOUR TICKET NOW

– Diana… my daughter found out about this, about a lot of it. She attempted to tell me, but I wouldn't listen. And subsequently I suspect she didn't tell me everything she knew, what I needed to know to make sense of it all. She has always been headstrong.

He paused a bit, before finishing.
– I guess the joke is on me.
– Don't hit yourself too hard on the head, Stewart commented, sympathy tangible in his voice and stance. – We should all have been more clear-sighted.
And Caine didn't look at him.
– Okay… partner. McKenzie smiled grimly. – Your words are like balsam on a sore consciousness. I see you're no longer in your pleasant disguise. It's time to stop walking around and say boo, huh?
– This is when the booing starts in earnest, Stewart said empathically. – This is when the ghost does more than haunt the intruders of its house.
And Caine saw the ghost, saw it walk through the streets of San Francisco, saw the ghost be haunted itself, saw it look around with haunted eyes, as if the very town was looking at it, as if the house didn't look favorably at its ghost.
– You have some sense of humor, Stewart, McKenzie chuckled. – I'll give you that.
Stewart was virtually boiling with emotion. In McKenzie, if there was any of that inside that cold exterior of his, it was carefully masked and stored away.
– My take on it is slightly different from yours, Stewart grinned. – You know, the guys we managed to get arrested in Frisco? They got out after only a day in custody. The judge didn't feel there was any evidence against them. So I ask: What's the alternative to a humoristic approach?
– Another one on our list.
McKenzie's laughter was cold, accentuated.
– There's a plane leaving for London at ten thirty tonight. Stewart looked at his watch. – Six hours from now. I suggest we use the remaining time well.
The three men showing up at the airport a few hours later didn't have much in common with the three tourists visiting Central Miami earlier in the day. They had all become respected gentlemen and businessmen, carrying briefcases and very correct clothing. They didn't truly speak to each other. Everything concerned business and monetary transactions. They wouldn't speak for a long time, not during the entire boring flight across the Atlantic.
There was one thing no one had mentioned, but that none of them had any trouble realizing.
The shots that had been fired, the losses the Abraxas Omega had suffered had a certain pattern. The three could no longer hope for the leeway they

had enjoyed to this point. Their opponents knew now there were more than ghosts hunting them.

Those arrested in San Francisco, now out on bail had recognized Stewart, or at least thought they had recognized him. The uncertainty could still work in Stewart's favor, he knew that. Certain parties wouldn't be less nervous learning about the ghost that slowly but surely closed in on them.

He hardly heard the voice of the flight attendant telling them to fasten the seatbelts. It seemed so far away. Suddenly the plane was airborne, on route to London, to Europe, where he was wanted for murder. The thought created a quivering expectation in him.

In the dark window he saw his own face. Now, when the hair was once more black, he resembled much more his relative, Ted Warren. In the depth of the eyes burned a low fire. He closed them and the images and sensations came to him. They had never before come so easy as they did just now. He leaned back in his seat, and he slept. But he wasn't on the plane. He was in London. He experienced the streets. He saw the people. Creatures running and hunting. He tasted the blood, saw its river, its sea. Sensed the danger. Felt Death in the coal black darkness.

FINAL PART:
THE CITY OF CITIES

Chapter Fifteen

The wet and slippery riverbank seemed to both push at them in front, pulling them back down from behind, making each move forward a brutal and strenuous hurdle. They had to climb up through dirt and clay. For a long time they imagined they didn't make any progress, any progress at all. They feared they had given up, given in to the forces aligned against them a thousand times, but kept pushing themselves, and at some undetermined point it slowly dawned on them that they could glimpse the end of the climb.

When they finally could rest in the soft grass, the shit covered much of the soaking wet clothes.

They didn't care. Of course, they didn't. They chuckled to each other. And pinched each other hard, to be certain they weren't dreaming, clutching and patting the other warm body. It was no longer a program a mechanism inside making them do it, but them doing it, because they wanted to. They wanted it so badly.

The lights from the big city created a warm glow around them. An eternal twilight they sucked in and grew in. Fear persisted in their eyes, but mixed there was the glow of freedom. They had escaped against all odds. Freedom was a song, a volcanic cauldron within them.

They rose together. In the silence surrounding them, the other's breath was the only sound they could hear. They could only smell, sense and taste each other.

But their ears listened, their eyes looked for movement in the dark, signs of danger, of enemies. Their eyes moved constantly across the riverbed, among the houses further in, on the lookout for shadows carrying sharp blades in their hands and poison in their eyes.

They ran, ran across the field, just a few steps they imagined, before finding themselves among the houses, moving through darkened back alleys, avoiding, without thinking about it, the bright lit streets. The houses were tight, way too tight. They looked for one fairly far away from the others.

They stopped for a brief moment, scouting ahead, taking time, taking time to once more enjoy the closeness. It was more than touch, more than mere contact. He felt her, felt her heart, the fiery buzz of her mind, and it was almost too much.

– That back there, this feels so great, he breathed excited in her ear. – I've never…

– You will, she whispered back. – It isn't new to me. I *know* what it can be. I've been fortunate to know the Glow my entire life. Know that this is merely the nascent beginning.

They hurried on, keeping to the shadows. People passed them, but no one spotted them. They were like ghosts walking the streets of the living, of the dead. The two of them were like the shadows the streetlights cast out in the emptiness, silent and invisible.

It went well for so long, but there were signs, worrying signs, flickering in the girl's radiant eyes. It happened about an hour after they had crawled from the river. Suddenly, from one moment to the next, they were freezing, shaking, in their wet clothes, feeling like they were shaking apart. They had to stop running, and could hardly walk. Stumbling on they tried to jump up and down, to clutch each other, share each other's heat. Nothing helped.

– We need to… she gasped. – We need to…

Exasperated she struck his chest.

I don't understand, he wanted to say, but didn't have the strength.

– Come, she hissed.

He followed her. It took a while before he realized… before he realized what she reminded him of, of a predator hunting its prey. One who had gone hungry for weeks, and was desperate for sustenance.

He saw the man, the lonely man under the streetlight, and astonished he realized saliva flowed into the cavity of his mouth. Betty nodded eagerly, approvingly to him. She knew. Of course, she knew. They jumped the tall, gray-haired man in his fifties in the shadow between streetlights. They struck the first blow simultaneously. Ted in the belly and Betty in the neck. They kept striking him until he lay still on the ground. Blood flowed from his nose and wet the ground. She put a hand on the bare skin of the man's neck. Then she grabbed the boy's hand and put his hand there as well.

– Concentrate, she hissed. – *Take* from him.

– What…

– We need to…

She released a sound, first one of anticipation, then of… of joy.

– … feed.

He felt it. As he saw her eyes lit up. As he saw the glow there turn to a fire, he felt it, felt the distinct quiver in his hand, felt strength, felt power slip from the unconscious man and into himself.

Energy, he thought astounded.

He felt it for a few seconds, before it stopped, so fleeting.

She bent down and found the man's wallet. She pulled bills from it in feverish moves, laughing aloud, as she kicked him in the chest. The shaking stopped. The cold evaporated from their bodies. The boy and the girl kissed each other, before running away.

– That was just a snack, she told him. – Too little contact, too little time. Nothing compared to all the upcoming delights.

He felt worry, mixed with the rising ecstasy, but it was faint and that did worry him.

– Yes, this is who we are, she said, fire dancing in her deep, deep forest eyes.

Taking his hand.

They finally found a remote location, a house fairly distant from all others. One with no lights lit inside. They didn't know the time, but there were still people outside. Rage shrouded them, rage because they needed to hide, like animals. But they whispered to each other, calmed each other, waited patiently, until they neither saw nor heard people nearby.

The boy smashed the glass by the door. It sounded like all hell broke loose as it hit the floor inside. They cringed, expecting people to come charging because of the horrible noise, preparing themselves for the worst. Everything remained quiet. He smiled encouragingly to her and reached through the hole in the window and unlocked and opened the door from the inside.

They hurried inside. Everything stayed quiet. They walked hand in hand through the house, moved like one through the empty rooms. The house was completely robbed of anything even resembling furniture. Walls, ceiling and floor, everything was naked.

There were a few blankets in a corner, old and dusty. That was all. All they possessed in the world, except themselves and their own ingenuity, no one but themselves to trust. They smiled as they undressed, as they pulled the soaked clothes off the other, when they hung them to dry from all the sharp edges there were. There was calm, peace. Fully aware that it wouldn't, couldn't last, they used the sense of belonging for all it was worth. Just now, no one could take that from them, in this place that belonged to them and to them alone. They used one blanket to dry their hair and body. It felt so good. The touch did. They didn't speak. There was no need for that. They crawled under the blankets. Pulled tight together. And then the warmth embraced them, warmth slowly, pleasantly turning to heat.

They mated until morning, on and off the dreaming, the dreamless sleep, looking at each other with the radiant eyes. And as she moved under him, over him, images and impressions came to him, of a valley surrounded by tall mountains. He saw her play there as a little girl, and right there, in the brightest sunlight he saw a human shadow. And everything felt so familiar, as if he had dreamt it many times before. And he knew, beyond doubt that he had.

– Home, she mumbled. – Sanctuary…

They meshed so well, as if they were made for each other, physically, mentally. He flew through the wilderness, flapping his mighty wings, finally finding the place surrounded by the tall mountains. The surroundings, those who hunted them - were unimportant. They were hidden by the mountains, hidden by a vast desert, protected by it, and nothing could touch them. Nothing.

When the cold morning dawned and Ted awakened, Betty didn't wake up with him. He shook her, needed her. She opened her eyes and smiled happily to him.

– Is it morning already? She wondered drowsily. – You should have roused me earlier.

– It's morning and the sun is shining, he said, kissing her. – I just woke up myself. How do you feel?

– Strong, she said, grabbing his hand. – Reborn.

– Free, Ted said. – I never imagined it was possible to feel like this, so clear, so limitless.

She rubbed his cheek. Tenderly.

– Yes, free, she said. – Free like a bird.

They snuggled there, between the blankets, in the warm morning light. They could hear people speak outside, but the voices never reached a threatening level. People just passed by. But they passed by the whole day, making the two of them stay indoors. They pulled on the clothes, still wet and uncomfortable, in the hope of being able to leave unseen, but it was hopeless. And eventually the hunger rose in them, a hunger gnawing on body and soul. And the shaking reappeared. As they suspected, it hadn't been caused by the cold. They tried to pull tight together under the blankets, to no avail.

– We will make it, he stated numbly.

– We will! She nodded, encouraged by the hot rage in his eyes.

– … and we will *get* them.

She silently grabbed one of his hands with both her own, kissing it in acknowledgment and support.

They sat down in silence. Waited patiently. The stomach grumbling finally ended. The shakes as well. For now. He clutched her hands hard, but she didn't cry out. They stared out of the window, at the sun, at the sunset. The moment when the sun vanished was the most peaceful he had ever experienced. There was neither joy nor sorrow, only peace.

It had turned dark. They had just left the house. No one had seen them. They walked the better-lit paths now, wouldn't hide like animals anymore. The first time they encountered people they didn't dare look up. They pretended to be engaging in an intimate conversation. Only after the sound of the steps had faded, they allowed themselves to breathe normally. The second time they managed by sheer willpower to hold their heads high. What had happened to them on their degradation road didn't let go.

They slipped through the streets and alleys. They hunted, but kept looking behind them. Holding hands as they did, people who met them thought they were a couple in love. No one noticed the tense bending of their bodies, the eyes constantly moving back and forth. They passed some kids sitting around a fire, a strange fire seemingly casting its light everywhere, even in its own shadow.

The fire haunted them. Even when they closed their eyes it was there. And the fire inside them inevitably burned even stronger.

– How much money… do we have? He asked her.

– Only ten pounds bills, she replied. – Fifty of them. Five hundred pounds. That's…

– About a thousand dollars, he nodded. – I know.

– It will last for a while, she shrugged. – And we'll have no problems getting more, anyway.

She kissed him on the cheek, strangely laid back. Again, he felt it like an acknowledgement. He caressed her hair, plowed his fingers through it.

– Ah, she sighed content. – It will turn red again eventually. You're looking forward to that, aren't you?

– Yes, he replied. – Yes, I am.

– Me, too. And now she put her head on his chest. – Me, too.

They stopped in front of an old, derelict building, an abandoned gas station. There was no need to break in here. The door was open. Everything was wide open, including the door to the basement. They descended the old, brittle creaking stairs. There were no lights down here, but they saw quite well in the weak reflection from the distant streetlights. There was a couch, placed at the center of the room. Except for that there was nothing. The couch was big, and it was nicely dressed in sheet and blankets. She giggled softly, sending him flashes, sensual grins doing far more than turning him on, penetrating deep inside him.

She let herself fall on the bed, fall on her back. She looked up at him with a direct, shameless stare.

– My man, she called. – Spread out your large wings and embrace me.

He did. There was no hesitation, no holding back.

– Yes, she confirmed, as she met his hungry lips. – This isn't the Ted of old you remember. This is a new creature. The Tapestry of the Dragon has emerged from the chrysalis now. You've undergone trials, slain knights and found truths. The Ted of old no longer exists.

– Who am I, then? He grabbed her arms and held her hard.

She freed herself with hardly any effort. A slight move, one pull and she stood on all fours on the other side of the couch.

– You're the Prime, the fire prophesized, promised for centuries, for millennia, come to set your tribe, your people free.

He was about to comment on that, an angry retort. Suddenly, she was once again right in front of him, placing a finger on his lips. She looked up the stairs, cocking her head slightly, clearly listening, but he didn't hear anything. He strained his ears… and then he heard it. The sound of an approaching car. He realized that she had heard it, an impossible distance away.

The engine died. The car stopped in front of the building. They heard doors be opened and closed, heard giggling and laughing.

– I told you. A boy, breathing hard. – Not in the car. My old man will find out and kill me.

– Where then? The girl said aggrieved. – Not on the ground, right. You're not gonna tell me that, are you…

– Don't worry, the boy assured her confidently. – I have it covered.

– You have, huh? So, you have been here with others. I knew it!

Ted smiled, but it was a strange, bitter smile.

The two entered the building. The two below heard heavy breathing, and the first heavy sigh, the prelude to a needful moan. There was the sound of steps in the stairs.

The young couple stopped abruptly when they spotted the other two on the couch.

– We have visitors, Betty said. – And they're cute enough to eat.

– We didn't know anyone was here, the boy stuttered. – There's n-never anyone here.

– Cross my heart and hope to die, the girl added.

- What are your names? Betty asked softly.

– My name is Gregory, the boy said. – This is Ann.

– Come here, Gregory, come here, Ann, Betty called throatily.

The two kids, probably not much younger than Ted and Betty, if younger at all, exchanged glances, clearly worried.

– We're not the owners, Ted told them. – We came here, just like you, looking for a… a sanctuary.

– You d-did? Ann blurted.

– *Come here,* Gregory, *come here,* Ann! Betty repeated, far more insistent, an… alien quality entering her voice.

Ted sensed it, and he froze down his spine.

– Settle down, Ted said. – Our home is your home.

He looked at them. The girl giggled, and she blushed like a schoolgirl, and she was, that was all she was. He knew what was about to happen, and he felt no regret.

Ted and Betty pulled back to their corner of the couch (*the bed*), and Ann and Gregory hesitatingly picked their own corner.

– Our car broke down, Ted said, never taking his eyes off Ann. – Or so we thought. We finally realized it was empty of gas. We were told to go here with a can. Seems like the locals didn't know their local gas station had packed and gone home years ago. We came here, and realizing the futility of our actions, we stayed. We quite simply didn't bother going any further.

– That's obvious, Gregory blurted.

Then he realized what he had said, and turned red as a tomato.

– Shame on you, Gregory, being ashamed over entertaining such natural thoughts…

Betty crawled to him. She reached out with a hand and touched his cheek.

– Sweet Gregory. She spoke softly, seductively.

And then, just like that, she began undressing, like the most natural thing in the world.

And it is, Ted thought. It *is*.

He undressed, too. A little faster, a bit more impatient. Betty kissed Gregory, undressing him, insistently, seductively, until he abruptly feverishly began removing his own clothes. Ann stared at the growing cock between Ted's thighs, how it struck the left thigh, the right thigh, as he worked his way over to her on his knees. She looked into his eyes, into eternity.

He didn't bother with any foreplay, but touched her right in her groin. She gasped. Hands attempting to push him away fell down. He undressed her, and she writhed in his grip, impatiently aiding him in his task, his fevered task. I don't know this girl. I know her, know her smell, her taste, her burning need. He put her down on her back, just as Betty did the same with Gregory. Both were pushed to the center of the bed. The two couples rose and fell, rose and fell. Ann scratched Ted on his back, eyes momentarily widening as she felt the uneven, hardened surface.

– What's that? She exclaimed. – What have people done to you?

– It used to be far worse, he said. – Nothing they haven't regretted and will regret for eternity.

Ted felt something then. With the sudden burst of rage. With the rage came… He touched the girl, touched her almost on half of her body, and he burned. The girl shook, in joy, in ecstasy. The boy beneath Betty moved harder and faster, and breathing almost stopped as he pumped into her. Ted fell on Ann, as he felt strength leave him, felt it… enter him, felt it fill him up like air swelling a balloon.

Ann smiled beneath him. Gregory smiled in ecstasy beneath him. Ann wanted to touch his cheek, but the hand reaching for him just fell down, drained of strength, of power.

Ted pulled back. He drew breath, and that one breath was like fire.

He stared at Betty, shocked beyond belief. There was pain, and he crouched, he cried out in pain. Suddenly, it was like his skin was on fire, every piece of skin on his body, but there was more.

– It hurts, he gasped. – It hurts everywhere.

– You're being born, Betty told him again. – Being born…

– Being born hurts, he said, staring into her sparkling green eyes.

And the world turned inside out, outside in, and everything was right with the world. He looked at his hand, the fire from his eyes brightening, shadowing the skin.

Ann and Gregory hardly moved there on the bed. They were already well into sleep, the stage just before the closing of eyes. They looked at the man and woman above them with joyful eyes.

– You know what you are, now…

Her soft voice washing over him, a lukewarm wave in summer, an icy avalanche in winter.

– But why, haven't I…

– Why haven't you felt anything like this before?

He stared at her, irritation and gratitude warring within him.

– Because you've been picky, my dear. Except for the Duchess and a few others, I suppose, while being virtually *turned off*, you've only fucked Tilla, and she, like me, being kin, isn't that easy to feed on.

Gregory released one final weak moan before falling asleep. Ann already slept soundly.

– And this wasn't much of a feeding, anyway, Betty went on, a tangible chill present in her voice. – It was just a pale reflection of what it *can* be. We've been taken so far down that it hardly worked at all, and only imperfectly, like lights flickering on and off.

They dressed. It happened quickly, efficiently, strangely without effort.

– Poor sleeping beauties, she grinned, casting one final look at the naked boy and girl.

She was behind him, her lips playing with his neck.

– You know, now, she whispered. – You've taken another step on the long walk.

He turned. He looked at her, but not with anger. With unqualified interest. The difference made her dizzy.

She found the car keys in Gregory's pocket, and they hurried up the stairs.

– I've hardly touched a wheel before, he stated. – What about you?

– Never, she replied, brightly as a bird.

Everything had… opened up again. He wondered how many times he could open, before cracking open like an eggshell.

The London evening greeted them. The air was the same, sharp, and with a strange foreign scent. From the river, they assumed. They had had it in their clothes when reaching shore. People living here probably didn't notice.

– I'll drive, she sniffed.

– All right by me.

He bowed to her and moved to the right side of the vehicle… almost colliding with her.

– The world is so very big, isn't it? She giggled uncontrollably.

He rushed to the left side, sitting down in the passenger's seat. She stumbled and fell, as she was about to open the door on her side. She was up again and in place in her seat, in an instant.

– I'm okay, she assured him, before he could voice his concern.

He saw it, sensed the same ants he felt crawling under his skin, ravaging her. They were on the verge of a drug withdrawal attack, and it was nothing they could do but ride it out.

– I don't want you to *see* me like this. She knocked her head on the wheel. – They told me it would be hard, but not like this, not like this.

Her sweat turned raw just during the next few seconds. He patted her cheek in a hopeless attempt to comfort her. He felt soft hands on both his cheeks. She pulled his head to her and kissed him on his lips.

– I'm so proud of you, she yelped.

Then she turned, turned away, turned the key, and the car started with a roar, one loud enough to wake all neighbors.

– This is insane. She struck the wheel, her temper flaring. – They taught me everything, but not how to drive. How can they've been so stupid? Didn't it occur to them that I might need that particular skill one day?

He realized startled that she wasn't really speaking to him, but through the open window, to the darkness out there.

The drive began with a rocky jump forward, and the engine almost being choked. Before they had even started properly, they almost made contact with one of the streetlight posts. She sat there, breathing in and out. He wondered if he should take over, but looked down at his shaking hands, and rejected the fleeting notion.

– We should just keep walking, he insisted.

– No, she said harshly, staring at him with her hawk's eyes. – We need to move fast, need to get away from here, far away from here… fast. I don't know this city, okay. I know there's supposed to be a Swiss cheese of Underground Stations here, but I don't know where they are.

Unbelievably enough her hands turned steady, turned steady again. He saw how her iron will rose again, how it took control over her flesh, her shaking flesh, how her mind came to dominate her surroundings. He saw her eyes glow in a dull light.

The car moved forward. The first seconds of the drive didn't go well, with a lot of random turns and twists, but she learned. She seemed to learn for every second she clutched that wheel, pushed that gas pedal. He stared at her, and startled didn't even begin to describe how he felt, as he sat there with open mouth, attempting to make sense of it, of it all. She… adapted, for every mistake, every threatening situation they encountered. It was nothing short of amazing, and he could only sit there and shake his head. She drove now, on a clearly bigger road. He saw how her thought processes worked, how she went through countless options, throughout the entire insane ride, picking the most probable option. She didn't drive fast, but fast enough for it not to cause suspicion. The engine was mistreated to the point of continuous risk of instant breakdown, but the car was old. It wasn't that strange.

And even more incredible: It seemed like she knew where she was heading. He realized they were headed for the central parts of the city, feeling as if everything… brightened, how the streets themselves came alive around them.

He wanted to caress her, comfort her. But was unable to, and he felt shame. He had enough with himself and his own shadows.

They stopped for red light, and she dried her sweaty brow. She closed her eyes for a while. For so long that the lights turned green and the monster in the car behind them pushed the horn. She shook, and to Ted it was as if the sun stopped shining. He reached for her again, but she pulled away.

– Not now, My Lord, she said, drying more sweat. – I need to stay sharp, to stay hard. *Please!*

They turned into a broad street. In the much stronger light he saw, also physically, how focused she had to be, how her hair stuck to her skin like glue.

They turned again, and an even bigger street opened up around them. Far ahead Ted noticed the bridge, noticed Tower Bridge. He had seen pictures of it. His neck hurt. The collar tightened around his neck.

– They watch the bridges, he said calmly, not by far calmly enough.

Betty shook, and lost focus, lost concentration, lost everything. She stepped on the brakes, stepped much too hard. Her head hit the wheel. She let up on the brakes and attempted to turn simultaneously, losing the last remnants of control. The car slid on the slippery road, right into a streetlight. The right backdoor was pushed in, and pieces of glass and shrapnel flew everywhere.

The car stopped. Dust and blood whirled in the air. He had had his eyes on Betty all the time. She just collapsed in her seat. There were only minor injuries that his eyes could see, but she was totally burned out. There was nothing but tiny embers left.

– Let's go, he told her.

– You go… she said weakly, hardly able to speak, her eyes half closed. She smiled.

He grabbed her and pulled her out of the car, and held her. She was unable to stand on her own.

– Let's *go!* He shouted. – Damn you!

She nodded, nodded slowly, looking into that endless deep that was his eyes. The first steps she stumbled, but by an act of will, yet another act of will, she ran by his side. He didn't need to hold back anymore. She ran just as fast as him, and yet again he felt that mix of wild hope and despair.

A police car stopped at the other side of the road. The driver stuck his head out, spotted the two rushing on. He jumped out of the car, not even attempting to hide his intentions, hide who were his true employers.

– STOP! You won't get away!

Ted and Betty hardly heard the wild shout. But they realized its significance. They saw the man chase after them, heard the howl of his whistle that almost instantly was answered by a dozen other whistles close by.

Ted ran with Betty by his side, and the policeman just vanished behind them. Ted realized early that the man didn't have a snowball in hell's chance of catching up with them and enjoyed that fact immensely. But he felt rage as well. Because they had to flee, again. There was a need, something savage deep in his mind, telling him to stop and *fight*.

More joined the hunt. For a fleeting, long second, they imagined there were enemies all around them.

They dived into a narrow alley, into the darkness. Kept running. Until they no longer heard the sound of the hunters. They crouched behind a garbage container. Ted hardly strained with his breathing, while Betty's was labored and desperate.

– Are they coming? Betty whispered with a weakness she could no longer conceal from him.

They listened for a long time, but heard no running feet, no one with labored breathing, just people passing by in more or less friendly conversation. They relaxed, as much as they dared.

– No one is coming, he replied. – That isn't bad, running that easy from a local cop.

She nodded, managed a weak smile.

– It's funny, he said. – For a moment there I thought I heard the sounds of chasing dogs…

He still saw it, like ghosts behind closed eyes.

– You did, she stated, closing her eyes for a moment. – We've always been hunted and the experience of it will always be with us.

He wanted to ask her about that, ask her about so much, but there wasn't time. Hands seeking each other clasped and clutched. He made himself hard, rising, pulling her on her feet. It was just fair. She had done it so many times with him.

– I'll be all right, she said, sending him another grateful smile.

– They will come, he said. – Come soon, and they'll know who and what to look for.

They moved, holding hands, walking, and attempting to look inconspicuous, not that much different from most people. They stepped into the light, mixed with the crowd, another couple in love, on a night out in town. They didn't allow themselves to be fazed by a patrol car filled with gloomy policemen. There was no sense of recognition, no sense of discovery there. This was just a set of cops cruising for trouble.

– We need to reach the Underground, Betty said anxiously. – Once we've entered the system, the Swiss cheese, we can be far away in a matter of minutes. The Underground stations are marked with a blue, oblong sign and a round white with…

– I know, he said, calming her.

– *Yes!* She kissed him. – Come.

Excitement spurred her on and made her stronger again. She led on, now.

We will make it, Ted thought.

They walked for long minutes, stretching into hours, looking for a station. They walked and walked, and it all seemed so futile. The fatigue returned to their long-time weary bones, sneaky, like cancer.

– The city is so big, she said in frustration. – It might look like the stations are tight as hail on a map, but we'll be plain lucky to encounter one, unfamiliar as we are with the territory.

Ted had entertained similar thoughts himself, but he hadn't wanted to express them, wanting to encourage, not discourage his companion.

Betty stumbled. Ted managed to catch her before she fell. They kept moving. Ted began turning his head, not consciously aware of it at first, not until Betty looked at him with those observant, astute eyes of hers.

– We're being followed, he said.

Her reaction surprised him. She was smiling, smiling radiantly. She wasn't afraid.

– You felt him, she said. – You're growing, growing at an unprecedented rate.

Her words didn't really surprise him. He had long since realized that she knew far more about him than he did.

They turned a corner and the radiant blue sign with white writing lit their faces, their eyes: LONDON BRIDGE.

They rushed inside and bought a ticket to a random station they had no intention of traveling to. The guy behind the window stared at them, but then they would always be stared at, Ted surmised. They descended the stairs, pushed aside those who were ahead of them in the line. Ted fell when they were almost down. He hit the rail and just felt it as if his feet vanished beneath him. Crouching on the floor, shaking his head he saw Betty a few steps away, staring intensely at him. They ran again, but he couldn't remember climbing back on his feet. Everything seemed disjointed, and he feared he kept losing moments to the growing Nothing within. They reached a train a moment before the doors closed. The train moved before they reached the seats. They sat there for a while, with their eyes closed, feeling the pulse of the train as it raced over the rails. Betty opened her swollen eyes just a bit, sensing more than seeing the looks people sent them, an attention failing both to surprise and disappoint her. Even the most unaware individual couldn't help noticing their disheveled hair, dirty faces and the ruined, expensive clothes. The London locals were used to quite a bit, but this was beyond even their average day. There was something about the two youths going beyond their appearance and it made people turn cold in their seats.

Let them stare. They don't matter.

The train slowed down, and they arrived at the next station. It took time until the train slowed down sufficiently for Ted to read the text on the round signs on the wall, but just before they stopped, he did: BOROUGH.

They were on their way south, on the black line, on Northern Line. Ted saw that easily, now, as he studied the map on the wall.

Not here, he thought. Next stop.

A pull, and they were moving again. Betty touched her temples, touched her temples again. Dizziness overwhelmed her and she fell over, practically in the lap of the woman to her left. Ted grabbed her and pulled the limp body to him. Her eyes remained dull, but she straightened, managed to sit straight without him holding or supporting her.

– I… think you must continue… alone, she whispered into his ear.

– Next station, he said, almost begging. – It's an intersection. We can jump on another train, and then, shortly after that we'll reach another intersection, with a lot of possible directions. We'll be next to impossible to… track.

She grabbed his hand and nodded slowly.

– I will make it.

He had to support her off the train, on the shaky ground, but outside, on the solid floor, she walked without aid. They rushed to the other train, heading north in another direction, on The Bakerloo Line. The train was practically empty, something he was grateful for, at least. Betty's condition worsened by the second, now. When he helped her down in her seat she was visibly shaking, and her skin was cold and wet.

At the next stop he rushed outside and grabbed the first person he could get hold of.

– The closest hospital, he snarled. – Quickly!

– Next station, the man said, very quickly. – Waterloo.

No one followed the boy inside the coach. Where he and the girl sat there were no other passengers, but no one went there. A red gleam in the boy's eyes discouraged all brave souls. They shuddered there on the platform, and didn't even choose another coach on that train.

Betty was close to delirious now. He took her hand.

– Take from me, he insisted.

– Impossible. She grinned sickly, fading in and out of consciousness. – I can't take from you more than you can take from me. And at this point it won't help to bring me… others either. It will just speed up the process, the process we must both endure.

He used his jacket to dry her forehead. She threw up, waited a bit, and threw up again. Without it resulting in other than slime. He realized they hadn't eaten in over a day. They had quite simply forgotten. Betty began mumbling incoherently. She waved her arms wildly, and nearly scratched him with her long nails.

Waterloo Station. Ted, carrying Betty cleared their path of people, pushing aside everybody slow to react, reaching the street surprisingly easy and fast. He heard no protests, but glimpsed a few scared glances.

Fear is the key.

It didn't occur to him to ask for directions anymore. He just ran. Betty was unconscious now, or so delirious that she could just as well be unconscious. He had no idea whether or not that was a good sign. He just ran. Wondering how long he had run, what the time was. He had no idea.

Breathing was labored and his arms hurt. He didn't stop. Legs were like lead, his brain on fire. He didn't stop. Pain didn't seem to faze him anymore. He moved like a machine, without emotion, without thought. Only when he spotted the hospital building, he stopped. He slipped into the shadows and lowered Betty carefully to the ground. He had to rest a bit… now. Later, he might not be allowed to.

He opened the doors with his foot, and carried Betty the last few steps into the reception hall. The lights were muted in there. That pleased him. They still made his eyes flow with tears. The nurse behind the desk looked up from her writing. She rose abruptly and rushed to the two youths.

– We were… together, Ted said. – Suddenly, she… fell. When I touched her she was covered in sweat and she was shaking hard. I don't know what to do. I…

– It's all right, the nurse said softly. – Calm down. It will be all right. Just put her on the couch and sit down there with her. Help will be here in a minute.

She sat down again and grabbed the com-phone.

– We have a situation here, she cried. – Possibly overdose.

She had seen it a thousand times before, rich kids playing with fire and getting burned. She began filling out the admission forms, somewhat calm and collected.

– Come over here, please, so we can have all formalities in order in good time.

There was no reply. She looked up, suddenly worried, scanning the hall feverishly. The girl was still there, but not her friend. The boy was gone, nothing but a faint memory in her mind.

Ted had to smile, observing the nurse's confusion. He cast one last look at Betty. There was no choice. He had to leave her. In the city, with him, she might have died. There was no way of knowing.

One of the large elevator doors opened and five men in white coats appeared. Ted left the hospital area with quick steps, slipping away, into the darkness.

He passed the underground entrance several blocks away. The sidewalk was filled with people. He remained alert, but hardly noticed them. He thought about Betty, about everything she had said, she had told him, about him. He strived desperately to hold on to it, to remember.

She was proud of him, she had said. And she had meant it. That wasn't some game from her side. It was more than gratitude. He wondered what she meant when she called herself *Kwaiala,* wondered about that a lot, heard her speak the word and saw her lips move. She knew a lot about him, about his thoughts and feelings and inner yearnings. But she knew more than that. She knew who he was, what he was. Way too much. She had told him to embrace her with his large wings. Her sensual smile once again warmed him. She saw him as a bird, a large bird… and he wondered what kind. He imagined he heard the flapping of wings in the night.

He was alone again, now, as he had always been.

London was a large city, one of the largest on Earth.

He knew what to do. Excitement filled him, mixed with his eternal despair. He raised his fist up, into the night, to those who hunted him, to those who were his enemies.

I'm alone.

The thought didn't sadden him, didn't please him. It just was. And nothing more.

Filled with certainty, filled with doubt, he rushed on, into the eternal night.

++++

Ted stared at the dark Thames River below. He stood high above street level, by the concrete fence outside the National Film Theatre. He could easily discern that, because of the posters everywhere.

I'm not familiar with this place, he thought.

It didn't matter.
He was a chrysalis, being born anew into the world, born in pain, in joy, in the rainbow of thought and passion.
The evening was cold and moist. It didn't matter. It had never truly bothered him. Not even during Mike's worst days of terror. There had never been any lasting bodily pain. Whatever it was... bothering him hid in the... the soul. He realized then, realized with a start... that he remembered, remembered everything. The veil of forgetting was gone. Triumph swelled in him. They had done their *utmost* to break him, and they had *failed.*
The ticking in the temples returned. He hit the concrete hard. The skin on his knuckles cracked and blood flowed. The ticking stopped.
He heard someone running. More than one. It was quite a distance away, but he heard it, and the sound grew closer. It didn't really concern him, he knew that. When the frightened girl ran past him, he stood with his back turned. That he also did when the large and strong bruiser passed him, heading in the same direction a few seconds later.
Unexplainably clear he heard the girl stumble. He heard the wheezing of her breath. The gasp when the man captured her, the sound of the man's flat hand against her cheek. Several times he heard it. His feet moved, practically by themselves. He spotted them a fair stretch off. They stood by a wall a few steps from the stairs. The man pushed the girl's face at the wall. He had a knife in his left hand. He waved it every time she showed sign of moving.
– So, you choose to be impertinent, huh? He snarled. – Fucking bitch. Thought you would get away, huh? Know that my patience has come to an end.
– Get away? She choked. – I don't understand. You can't force me to do something I don't... something I absolutely don't want to d-do.
– You'll see what I can force you to, the man grinned. – You won't believe what I can do with you, what I can make you do.
He cut through her sweater and to her arm.
– This is just a remained. A cut means nothing... there.
She gasped terrified at the sight of the blood flowing from the wound and wetting the cloth. He kicked her legs away from her. She fell and crouched shaking by his feet. He forced the boot point into her mouth.
– This is just a taste... he chuckled, – ... of upcoming delights.
Something... snapped within Ted.
The man pulled out a stick from inside his coat. It was long and thin, and looked like a police club. With a move more than suggesting practiced

ease, he struck her in the belly. Her face twisted in horrendous pain, and she clearly attempted to scream, but the foot in the mouth kept her from uttering more than a weak, pitiful sound. Blood colored the boot.

– Your beautiful teeth might have gone to the pits there, princess. Do you want me to keep going? Are you that stupid?

He pulled his foot out of her mouth.

She shook her head.

– Then you'll return willingly with me?

She hesitated, before fearfully shaking her head.

– Ah, you've yet to learn your lesson, then. Take off your clothes. I want to do a quality control. Better safe than sorry.

He taunted her, played with her. She made a final attempt to get away, but he caught her easily, pushing the blade at her neck.

– I'm out of *patience,* little girl. From now on, you do as I say, *when* I say it. Or I'll make an example of you, one making all the rest of my birds *know* what will happen to insolent bitches.

Ted approached silently. They, at least, had heard nothing. But he stepped hard on the last step. The man with the knife turned slowly. The girl remained still on the ground.

– Don't you know that you're scaring good little girls when you do that?

The man stared at the boy, stared hard, more than a bit incredulous.

– Listen, kid, the man said harshly. – I can tell you aren't a native. Therefore, I've decided to be generous. If you vanish before I've counted to ten, we'll forget this.

He was about to start the countdown when Ted stopped him by lifting a hand.

– Your offer is very generous, sir. Therefore, I won't be any less so. I'll count to fifteen. If you're sensible, you're gone well before then.

The boy's voice had a strange quality. It sounded hollow and like it came from far away. The man pulled himself together and made a face.

– It's a good thing you showed up, kid. I can make an example of you and not the girl, thereby making it unnecessary to damage my merchandise.

The confidence he had gained through many similar situations returned. Ted was irritated because of that, felt almost wronged.

– You may not have heard the name Turner Maxwell before, kid, but I assure you, you won't forget it…

The man charged the boy, who still looked paralyzed. He made a pass with the knife, wanted to cut him in his arm. That would teach him. Ted saw the man's arrogant posture. It screamed out to him. The knife missed by a mile. Ted grabbed his arm with both hands. He held it, and then he kicked his opponent right in the groin. Maxwell screamed, shrieking. The knife fell from a weak hand and hit the ground. Ted held him up with his left hand and gave him several hard blows with his right. The fight was over before it had even begun. Maxwell was helpless, and at Ted's mercy. The boy lifted the sack of bones up and carried him to the wall. There he threw the beaten-up body away in contempt. He charged forward and gave the other several brutal kicks in the ribs. There was no more resistance, nothing even remotely resembling it. Maxwell blinked weakly, disoriented. He was still conscious, but just hardly so.

– Listen carefully, Turner Maxwell. Ted bent down above the swollen face. While he spoke, his voice changed. It turned darker and cold. It sounded like the wind an icy winter night. It cracked open the soul. – You're very lucky tonight. You get to live. If I see you again, I will kill you. And you will pray for death, Turner Maxwell.

The man's beaten to a pulp face turned white and his eyes opened wide. He was clearly scared shitless and virtually turned completely around from the seemingly ruthless bully he had appeared to be. Ted felt so great when he saw himself reflected in the other's eyes. With a snort of utter contempt he knocked the beaten, *broken* man's head into the wall and the eyes closed. Easy as pie.

Thoughts, ideas and inspiration churned through his mind. He could hardly believe where those thoughts led him.

His eyes caught the special belt the unconscious man wore. After briefly considering the matter he removed it and put it around his own waist. The knife twinkled in the darkness. He picked it up and put it away inside his jacket, before returning his attention to the girl.

She sat up, confused, anxious. Ted helped her to her feet. The confusion was mixed with awe and fear.

– You took him out, she said. – As if it was nothing, as if he was nothing.

– It was easy. He underestimated me, and he met an enemy he can't even begin to comprehend. I showed him that he was indeed nothing.

That was right. He had terrified the man, scared him out of his wits. And it had been easy as pie. He hadn't even needed to…

To do more. More.

He looked at her. She was a head lower than him, had bright hair and sharp blue gray eyes. Her face was kind of broad, her features diluted, but her body was supple and neat. She wasn't beautiful, but she was indeed pretty. That was the word. Pretty.

– What's your name? He asked her.

She didn't redden. This was clearly a girl of the world. But she didn't meet his eyes when she reached out her hand.

– Cathy, she replied. – Cathy Randolph.

– Let's get away from this sordid place, Cathy Randolph, he said.

He grabbed her arm and led her away from the stairs and the unconscious man on the ground.

– B-but. She resisted. – Shouldn't we call the police?

He stopped and sought her eyes, made her meet his.

– This guy bothered you for quite some time, right?

– Yes. She nodded solemnly. – A long time.

– And you've filed countless complains. The police haven't reacted at all… right?

This time she was silent. She merely nodded, and followed him without protests.

– Tell me… do you have your own apartment or something in the city?

– I live alone, yes, she replied, a bit edgy.

– Good, he said cheerfully. – Then we'll go there.

A shadow passed her face.

– But we can't go there, can't go back there. She looked at him in despair. – We just can't.

Her voice was more than edgy. Gooseflesh rose all over her bare arms.

– Why do you say that? He asked lightly.

Her only reply was a glance behind her.

– You won't ever see him again.

I sound so cold, he thought. And so confident, so infinitely confident. What's happening to me?

A few minutes later, when they sat on the train Cathy couldn't keep back the reaction anymore. She looked down at her hands. They shook uncontrollably. No matter how much she tried, she was unable to keep them steady.

– I'm not scared easily, she said. – I've grown up in this town. But Maxwell made me strangely… weak. He made me *weak!*

– Forget him.

He exposed his teeth in an encouraging smile.

And she was encouraged. She shook as the burning eyes stared at her.

– You are human, she joked nervously. – You are sweating.

The train hurried on. He felt like they had been sitting on the train forever. She touched his face. Cold sweat wet her hand.

– It looked so easy when you did it, she whispered. – But it had to have been a huge expenditure of power, both physically and mentally. Thank you. Thank you.

They left the train at Leicester Square Station. This is our stop, she told him shyly. Ted turned, on their way up the escalators. There had been a shadow, an itch in his back. A shadow that was now gone. He knew it in every nerve. The sense of having been tagged had just vanished. He didn't know exactly where, perhaps already when they walked into Waterloo Station. It didn't matter. Relief and shame warred within him.

As they appeared from the Underground, he felt it, the smell of spices in the air, assaulting his senses, the mood of the people walking up and down Charing Cross Road.

She sees it, he realized. Sees my reaction. And she smiles.

– Welcome to the City of Cities, she said proudly. – This is Cibola, the golden place in the desert. There's no one quite like it in the world.

She brought him to Leicester Square, to the one spot where they could see five movie theaters with just a slight turn of the head. It was late at night and the Square was filled with people. There were performers and street musicians on several spots, crying out to the world. The music and singing echoed within him.

– Is it always like this? He wondered.

– This is nothing, she grinned. – You should see it during weekends…

He stood still, taking it all in, or attempting to take in as much as possible.

– I feel life here, he said, not certain he had said it aloud.

On this night, in October 1974 the Sixties' fashions were still prevalent. Most people had long hair and wore outlandish clothes. He felt it, felt it all, the despair and the joy and the stubbornness, in those refusing to give in, like most of their brethren had already done.

Everything moved within him. There was something, right outside his awareness, something to reach for, something to grab and touch. It…

Then he felt it, the undeniable pain in his gut. He crouched there, in the middle of the crowd. And the pain felt as if it had been a part of him forever.

– Are you sick? She wondered anxiously.

– Sick? Far from it. I'm *styling*.

He knew he went through the same as Betty, didn't need anyone to tell him that.

Everything swam before his eyes. He grabbed her and kissed her. She laughed and expertly freed herself from his hard grip.

– I need to eat, he said, wondering if she could see how it was with him.

– No problem, she said. – There are a zillion restaurants within walking distance.

– Listen, he said. – I'm in a bit of trouble and need a place to unwind, to eat and rest in calm surroundings.

– Okay, she shrugged, grinning. – I guess I can make something. I can't recall the last time I cooked, but I can do it. Very few Londoners cook, that's all.

She led him further through West End. She lived in a rather quiet neighborhood, as he had hoped, a place to vanish safely for a time.

There were three locks on the door. She cast nervous glances around her, as she had done throughout the courtyard and neighborhood. Maxwell hadn't acted alone. He knew that. Knew it well.

The apartment was *huge*. It had five bedrooms, one kitchen, bathroom and a large living room.

– Tell me, are you in the movie business or something.

– Or something, she admitted. – You're *so* good at guessing. I'm an assistant executive for a guy, Richard Gallagher, who chooses what films to buy for the Classic Cinema chain, one of the largest in the country. I bought the apartment cheap, through his connections.

The stench of food filled the apartment. It ripped into his nostrils and made him crouch on the stool. Plates and pans not used for so long came to life again. The room felt strange to him, but then he would guess that all places felt that way, now.

It was as if… he was here… as if he had become part of the room, as if he was the air he breathed, the walls he felt, the food boiling on the oven. His sense of smell was… It was like he smelled everything. The girl's perfume tore at his nostrils. And her scent beneath that. Her real scent. Her hormones, her juices. It was eerie. It was disconcerting. It felt great.

He ate slowly, chewed the tender meat thoroughly before swallowing it. His stomach kept rumbling, kept making trouble. He kept to the vain hope that he would be able to stomach the food if he digested it slowly. Cathy took it as a sign of delight on his part.

– I kinda thought I had forgotten how to cook, she jested. – It's been years since I ate here.

– You've made a mistake there, he nodded, in a very flattering way, sending her a hot stare.

She didn't notice, or deliberately didn't notice. She had already completed her own, modest meal.

Ted squinted his eyes. She had been grateful for what he had done, of course, and shown that. And she was nice, acting as if she had known him for ages. But there was still something reserved in her eyes and behavior.

She strived to keep him at arm's length, both physically and mentally. When he grabbed her, as they did the dishes, she freed herself from his grip, excusing herself with a cute smile. Every time he attempted to kiss her, she slipped away.

– The dinner was great, he insisted. – You're a great cook.

– Thank you, she replied neutrally.

A few minutes later he walked to the window. The curtain covered most of it, as it had done when they entered the place. Keeping to his somewhat pulled-back position he looked at the crowds on the streets below. This was one of the world's biggest cities, both in terms of size and population numbers. He saw it, experienced it, as it reached far out at the countryside.

This is the place I'll hide and prepare, he thought. It will take time before they find me, and when they do, I'll be ready for them. I'll be ready tomorrow, if tomorrow comes.

This was already a fortress, ideal for his purposes.

He saw it, not as it looked right now, but the way it would be.

– It's strange that you should enjoy my cooking, she said brightly.

– Oh, how so?

He turned towards her, and it was merely a slight movement, so easy, so effortless.

– My father always insisted I was and would be a lousy wife. I wouldn't be a wife anyway, and I told him so.

– And you've kept telling that to him and everybody else all the time since.

She nodded.

– And very few have liked that very much, have they?

– No, she whispered.

– Society does everything in its power to halt inappropriate behavior, Ted said.

– What do you mean? She stared uncomprehending at him.

Disappointment burned within him. She didn't get it. In spite of what she had experienced, everything she had endured, and her bright mind she didn't understand what he was talking about, at least not on a conscious level.

No one did.

Suddenly he was overwhelmed by pain, and he realized that he experienced another seizure. Skin was covered in cold sweat. Everything turned indistinct before his eyes. Bile flowed into his mouth. His vision cleared somewhat, but he wasn't getting any better. He felt the ants crawl

beneath the skin, eating him up from the inside.
– Where's the fucking toilet? He asked her hoarsely.
– You know that, she said, clearly frightened. – You've been there.
He pushed her aside, pretty roughly, and stumbled the few steps to the bathroom. The stretch seemed infinite. The shaking body halted in the door, turning its head, locking on to her eyes. It was as if the entire body looked at her. She looked into the dark behind the swollen eyelids and was unable to move a single muscle.
– No doctor, he growled. – Not a single one.
– You *are* sick, she said anxiously. – Why didn't you say anything? Let me…
The rest just faded for him. He fell on his knees in front of the toilet bowl, his thoughts burning beneath the icy skin, burning, as they were fading, fading.
Then he threw up, and he recalled no more.
++++++++++++++++++++++++++++++++
It was raining in London that night. Wind rushed in from the west. Water flowed in the streets. This type of weather was rare in these parts of the world. The lights from the big city didn't reach far in the virtually supernatural darkness. It fell easy to believe that all the sluices of heaven - and hell - were open tonight.
In Cathy Randolph's apartment Ted had a tiny lucid moment in his feverish dreams. He sat on the bed and stared at the darkness. A pair of glowing, red-brown eyes stared back.
Turner Maxwell vanished completely. None of those who had known him ever saw or heard of him again, either in London or other places.
In an elegant villa in Kings Cross Robert Tremblay paced back and forth. The building was silent. The only sounds he heard were from the Storm outside. Heavy curtains covered the windows.
Tremblay grouched a while longer, attempting to postpone the inevitable. Then he swore and grabbed a pile of papers from the desk, and after a few more rounds of pacing, he left the room. Big, heavy doors opened and closed. This house was old money, something he was intimately familiar with.
He walked upstairs, up a broad old staircase, one covered by a soft red carpet. The Power resided upstairs, something he was also intimately familiar with.
The room he entered was filled with various forms of electronic surveillance equipment. Screens covered two of the walls. Lamps blinked and buzzed, creating a psychedelic landscape, creating the illusion that the

room was even bigger than it, in truth was.

Two men waited for him. To get to them he had to cross something resembling a field of flickering shadows. Tremblay shivered, unable to help himself. The two sat in the only two chairs in the room. He stopped before them, standing straight like a schoolboy, another thing on his list of intimate familiarities. His very long list.

The two didn't greet him, in any way. They didn't acknowledge his presence in any way he could discern. They didn't need to. They were two bigwigs within the organization. They were The Mask and David Gidman. A single word, one small sign from them, and he was dead.

– Stewart is alive, he said.

The mask showed no discernible reaction. But Gidman, uncharacteristically, shook.

– That's impossible, he cried.

The Mask laughed, and his laughter sent chills upon chills down Tremblay's spine.

– «I've become immortal», The Mask quoted, clear scorn in his voice, – «Kill me again, and I will come back stronger and better than before. Kill me a thousand times, and I will rise again. Will you return from Death, as I did?»

Tremblay stared blankly at him, but the voice.... The voice made him so cold that he had major problems keeping himself from openly shaking.

Gidman stared at his fellow council member with hatred in his face.

– All the information is here, Tremblay said, and put the pile of papers on the desk before the two men. He was unable to keep the scorn he inevitably felt out of his voice. – Our man from the United States wrote it all down in my presence. He arrived here, directly from Heathrow.

The Mask grabbed the pile and began reading.

– Tell us, Gidman commanded.

Tremblay took a deep breath.

– Stewart was recognized by two of our operatives in California, while he, Floyd McKenzie and Francis Caine cleared an office there. The fact that he's alive explains a lot of the other difficulties we've experienced in the United States the last few months, the Forester incident included.

He also felt it had been a major mistake, failure of leadership to not make sure that Stewart was dead, but he kept his mouth shut about that, about that, too.

The Mask looked up from the pile of papers, and looked at him again, most certainly looked at him. He felt... unwell again.

– That's not a bad retelling, the man with the mask said. – But we know that Stewart isn't behind all our recent troubles… right?

Tremblay froze.

– I haven't made a report on that yet, he said.

– You may do so, now. The voiceless voice hardened. – Why did Carr and the subjects get away?

– We… I underestimated him completely, Tremblay began. – I know he had been Special Forces, but he was better than any of us anticipated. He fought our best, and conquered them easily. They seemed like children in comparison. And then there was the woman, the woman in question not showing up on any passenger lists… I will point out that Croydon also had his shot at him, but when that is said, I take full responsibility for the fiasco afterwards. Still… I doubt anyone on my level could have stopped him, even if he hadn't had… help. The way he fooled me… He was quite simply too good.

Tremblay laughed a bit.

– And he was even rusty at the time. I shudder to think how good he is now, after being back in the game for a time...

There was silence. They waited. He realized that. He wasn't stupid, and not insensitive.

– And then there's Ted and Betty. They shouldn't have been able to get away, but they did. Do you realize, realize what we've set off?

Dull fear bordering on panic tied his gut in knots.

He knew he looked and sounded insane. He didn't care.

The Mask stared even harder at him. Tremblay imagined he could actually see the eyes behind the fabric.

– So, what have you done to deal with Stewart's… huh, resurrection, Bobby?

– I assume… I take for granted that he will come here, Tremblay said. – I've made sure we have double guard on all airports, ports, and major train and bus stations in the Greater London area. That was already under way, anyway, though, because of our other problem…

– You may go. It was Gidman.

Tremblay nodded and hurried to the door. A flash of relief passed his face. It was done. It always was, when Gidman began speaking again.

– Bobby…

The cold surrounded him. He turned again towards the two. No, to him, only to *him*…

– You've shown yourself quite capable, Bobby. But you've also failed us, failed us twice. One more such failure and the scales will no longer balance for you. Understand?

Bobby nodded.
– That won't happen.
The Mask pushed a button on the control panel in front of him, and locked the door behind Tremblay.
– Fuck! He tore off the mask and threw it on the floor.
Silence descended heavily on the large room. It was as if all the buzz from all the electronic equipment just… faded.
– It's the fucking mask. It itches.
– You know very well it isn't the mask, Gidman said calmly. – You were told it would take its time, that you needed to be patient.
– Read this, The Mask growled, – and let's see how patient you are.
He handed Gidman one sheet of the pile Tremblay had brought. It was Stewart's file. He cast a casual look at Stewart's personal information and was about to move on when his attention caught a name. He stiffened.
– His mother's name, he stuttered and actual turned pale, pale.
The sight was almost comical. Comical.
– *Warren!*
The name lingered between them, cutting and shredding.
– You didn't know who he was? Not during all those years?
– I knew *what* he was. I thought that was enough. He called himself Fontaine, when he didn't use Stewart. I thought, I assumed…
– We've got two of them against us now. The Mask shook his head in wonder. – At least two. God knows how many of them will descend on London and the international stage in the months and years to come.
He chuckled, his voice filled with scorn.
– Everything is unraveling, even before it has properly begun, just like I told you it would. This is just another masquerade, even sillier than all the rest of it. It's not your scene, and it's certainly not mine.
Gidman tried to read, tried to pretend the report mattered to him. The words just turned into an unreadable jumble.
– McKenzie… We figured he would be a bit vengeful if he escaped our clutches. And Caine. What about them?
The other leaned back in the chair. The voiceless voice seemed to come from far away.
– They don't matter.
Gidman looked at him, at the mask that seemed to cover his face even when it wasn't. Gidman attempted to pretend the shadows in the room were responsible for him only seeing a shadow where the face should have been.
– So what do we *do?*

– They'll come here. The man not wearing a mask was completely calm, now. – We don't need to do anything except wait for them.
He reached out with his right hand towards the black fabric on the floor, seemingly well out of reach. There was something overly dramatic about it all, as if it was just an act.
A moment later it was as if the mask… rose from the floor of its own accord, and flew into the waiting hand.
Gidman stared at the both familiar and unfamiliar sight, both calming and unsettling him. He nodded slowly, as the two men rose from the chairs and left the room.
The mask was once more in place.

Chapter Sixteen

The hospital slowly emerged from the night's slumber. Empty halls were filled with people. The staff prepared their rounds. The buzz in the girl's head rose from a pleasant sound to a roar.
Betty Morgan had been placed in the trauma ward. She relaxed in the bed farthest from the window, bathing in white sheets. The rising sun smiled to her. She had her face turned towards it, feeling great. It had taken her four days to recover.
She knew that the girls she shared room with looked strangely at her, the staff even more so. They knew she had been very sick, sicker than everybody else when she arrived here, broken by the drug withdrawal symptoms. Now, she was practically recovered. She rocked them at their core, whatever that was, the hysterical confidence they had in their reality.
The doctors and the nurses rode in on their morning round. Betty sensed the fake confidence in them all and hated it. As expected, they came straight for her.
– So, how are we today? The chief medical doctor, Sturgess, asked her rhetorically, sweetly.
She looked exasperated at him, feeling like she was in the chorus line of a divine, ridiculous comedy.
– I feel great, she replied. – I don't know about «we», though…
He looked at her with his fisheyes, and she shrank, she couldn't help it.
– Are you sure you don't want a shot, just a small shot today?
His vanity stood out to her like a sore thumb, or more like a sore *hand*. And by now it was so obvious that she couldn't fathom how the others could fail to notice it.

– No, why would I want that? I'm fully recovered, thanks to your excellent treatment, doctor. I haven't been better since I arrived here.

She enjoyed herself, but added the sweet girl routine as a matter of instinct, of self-preservation. If she had treated him with the ridicule and contempt he deserved, he would have felt even more threatened, and he would have made any possible effort to get his will through. And she couldn't handle that, not as she was now, brought low and weak.

Sturgess signed for his team to withdraw. They walked to the door and began speaking, practically whispering. Betty heard them, and shocked herself, shamed herself by wishing she couldn't. She felt cold and lonely, and a ball stuck constantly in her throat.

– What do you say? Sturgess more than suggested to the team. – It's more than probable that something is hidden below the surface here. How about giving her an injection, just to be on the safe side?

That «safe side» thing seemed to be more than accepted hospital jargon. Betty had heard it several times these few days.

– There might be something to that, an older colleague nodded. – For the sake of me I can't fathom how she could have recovered so fast. It's… *monstrous*. It's absolutely…

Sturgess sent him an admonishing stare. The other man caught himself. Sturgess turned to his team to get their usual silent approval.

– I think we should wait a bit, see how it goes, a young, newly hired doctor said nervously. – Who knows? She might have a well-developed resistance to drugs? If there are no signs of relapse in the next few days, that's probably the case.

Sturgess gave him the evil eye. Betty saw it and shuddered. She felt his seething emotions, boiling beneath his calm surface. He was ready to explode, and just because the young man had the audacity to express his own opinions.

There was dissent in the ranks, and Sturgess couldn't force the issue, without risking damaging his reputation. Betty felt a sickening gratitude towards the brave young man.

Sturgess marched out, followed by his not so loyal court. The door closed with a crack behind them.

Betty sensed the rage return. She knew she needed to wait, until she got out of here, until her strength returned… Exhausted she closed her eyes.

– You handled them well.

A voice seemed to come from far away. She forced herself to raise her eyelids. The girl with the long red hair stood over her. Her name was Marlene and she occupied the adjacent bed.

– W-what?
– The stuck-up assholes. I never could stomach doctors. They think they're above everybody else.
– Oh, that. Betty relaxed. – I think the good Stur-gess felt wronged, just because I didn't behave like a typical drug abuser. Medicine is his religion, and no deviation from the norm is accepted.
– You're so cool, Marlene said. – I'm glad you're better. Before you arrived, I had no one to talk to. Except for us there are only silly gooses here.
She stared contemptuously at them. They turned away, timid and anxious.
– I want to grab a bite. Do you want to join me?
A rumble rose from Betty's belly. She looked guiltily at it and quickly made up her mind.
– Okay, she nodded and sent the other girl a blinding smile.
It would always be advantageous to have an ally, no matter how shaky, here and elsewhere. Pride, in the sense that she could manage on her own, in every possible situation Betty had long since put behind her. It had been plucked from her in her early childhood. Her pride was on another level.
She wanted to sit up, but had hardly raised her head from the pillow before the pain cut through her. She fell back on the bed.
– That doesn't look good, Melanie said compassionately. – You're quite sore, aren't you? Your limbs are quite stiff?
She nodded, hardly able to. It was just this soreness, this stiffness keeping her here, now. The body hadn't recovered as fast as the mind.
– I know. Melanie nodded. – It can be hard. But I can help you.
Betty looked suspiciously at the other girl.
– I'm trained as a masseuse, Melanie grinned softly.
So am I, Betty thought, but kept silent, and let the other girl turn her over on her belly.
And the other's hands started on their walkabout over her skin and sinew, through the rough fabric of the hospital gown. From the neck, down her back, and up again. On her thighs and legs, and up again. Betty started to relax. Marlene touched her, and Betty whimpered, unable to stop herself from opening up, from being exposed. It was as if the other girl had worked her mind, too, not just her body.
– So, Marlene said pleased, when Betty rested on her back again. – Let's see if there's any improvement.
Betty sat up. It was not yet easy, but a world of difference from her

previous attempt, just a few, short minutes earlier. She glowed at Marlene, couldn't help the sense of gratitude swelling in her.

– It feels so good. She brightened visibly. – Thank you. Thank you.

– C'mon, Marlene said. – Let's grab something to eat.

Betty let her lead her, to the dining hall. They ate together, breakfast, dinner and evening meal.

She sat there, amidst a score of skinny girls with a lot of needle marks on their arms, and caught herself being glad her empathic power hadn't completely returned.

Marlene was among those without needle marks, though, and she seemed a lot more upbeat than the others. Some of the other girls hugged and touched each other a lot. They seemed to need it, to hunger for contact, any human contact. Betty was kind of glad Marlene didn't have that problem.

– Look at them, the big girl said in contempt, not bothering if the others heard her or not, a pleasure that also echoed favorably within Betty. – They act as if they belong here.

– And you don't?

– I'm not gonna pretend I don't have a problem, but I am solving it. Marlene bent forward. – But these chicks will all return here or end up at the cemetery within the next six months.

Betty sensed the despair in the room, as the girls' despair increased a few more notches. She couldn't avoid that. And she wouldn't.

– You're so right, she cried. – The wise and strong prepare for the world. They don't run from it.

– Bright girl, Marlene nodded pleased.

Betty Morgan, the valley girl, stood by the window. She looked through it, at the distant moon. Its silver slivers pricked her skin and the ugly buildings and cityscape in front of her seemed to dissolve, to be exposed as the illusion it was.

She woke in the middle of the night from a deep sleep. The moonlight still flooded the room. A hand rubbed her cheek.

– Marlene…

– You have fantastic eyes. You could do a lot with them.

Marlene lifted the blanket and lay down beside her. Betty, hating herself, cast worried looks at the other girls. They didn't move.

– You don't need to worry about them. The injections will make them sleep until morning.

Marlene pulled close to her, giving her the first kiss.

– I couldn't sleep…

She began unbuttoning Betty's gown, down and up.
– Are you hitting on me, Marlene?
The final button was gone, and the fabric was pulled aside.
– That's not a very poetic way of expressing it, but yeah. Marlene grinned and started squeezing one of the exposed breasts. – I'll teach you poetry…
Touch. Marlene's naked skin touched her for the first time, and revelation assaulted her, instantly, undeniably. Betty grabbed her hand, and revelation flooded her.
– You're a fake, Betty said, somewhat calmly, hating the wounded underbrush in her voice.
– W-what…
– You don't need to teach me poetry. I've known that since I was a little girl, and you're just a pretender. You've come here to take advantage of others' weakness. What a contemptible excuse for a human being you are.
– Don't be like that, honey. The voice remained slick and soft. – You feel a bit of apprehension, but you shouldn't let it worry you.
– I don't actually. The truth of the matter is that I have no interest in you, except for the need to brush you off my shoes.
Betty felt it, felt the Beast awaken within, a song, a dance of life.
Marlene just smiled and kept up her soft caresses.
– Get out of my bed!
The voice wasn't loud, but it still cut, cut deep, like a sword. Marlene froze, frowning at first, before fear transformed her face into a pale, unmovable mask.
– What is it? She cried frosty. – What are you doing to me?
– Remove your presence from my vision, you damn fake. Crawl beneath your blanket and stay there.
Marlene crawled backwards away from Betty. In just a moment she was out on the floor. She stopped there, briefly, desperately attempting to grasp her worry, to understand the paralyzing fear gripping her. But it was just there, a bolt of lightning from nowhere, and she kept backing off, until her legs hit the edge of her bed, and she fell back on it. She covered herself, totally unable to feel anything but the numb, paralyzing terror. Betty wasn't there anymore, only the two points of green ice above her, staring at her through the thick, thick wall.
– You sleep well, now, precious. Pleasant dreams!
Marlene shook. Merely the sound of the voice made her shake that much harder.
Betty stood above the other's bed, triumphantly curling her hands into

fists, looking down at the shivering creature under the blanket. Joy mixed with worry as she left the room and entered the dark hall. It had been easy and her powers were returning, but it should have been even easier, and she should have been able to do more. She wanted to.

She had been forced to exhaust herself. Sweat covered her skin again. And the walk to the bathroom felt abysmally long.

Finally, she was able to close the bathroom door behind her. She locked it, locked it twice, just to be sure. The room kept spinning. Her feet felt like jelly. She fell on her knees before the toilet bowl and the partly consumed supper erupted from her mouth. Her body shook violently, until the waterfall of vomit stopped. Seconds, minutes passed by as she fought to regain a semblance of strength. She grabbed the edge of the sink and hauled herself on her feet. It was a hard and painful process. She grabbed toilet paper and started drying herself. The mirror hung there, seemingly in the air before her, taunting her. She wasn't thin anymore, she was skinny. The vomit wouldn't go away. She rubbed her skin hard, used soap and fingers and everything, but the spots remained. Her skin was swollen, both in the face and elsewhere. Her eyelashes quivered. Sick fear gripped her. The key fell out of the keyhole. Another key was put in from the other side. She tried to move, and the pain instantly overwhelmed her.

The door opened. A tall oriental man with a bandaged head appeared in the door. She knew he wanted her. She strived with a name.

Croydon.

Rage filled her. Strength filled her. As he advanced towards her, she sent the hard edge of her hand at his neck. He parried and grabbed it, way too easily. She was slow, way too slow. He struck her, and she was practically thrown at the opposite wall. Blood filled her mouth.

She screamed, screamed for help, screamed in boundless fear, just like any young, innocent and helpless girl in jeopardy would have done. There was no other way. Shame mixed with the boundless hysteria inside. She stopped, choking, choking hard.

– This is fun, little Betty. I would have loved to play, but I'm on a schedule.

There was no sound of anybody approaching, of running feet.

– Just scream some more. See if it benefits you in any way.

She wanted to scream more. But nothing worked. She opened her mouth, but not even the smallest of sounds came.

Croydon pulled a rope from his coat. Her vivid imagination worked overtime. She saw herself on the floor, tightly bound, completely at his mercy, ready to be shipped back to the pens, back to slavery.

There was movement behind the hated man, so fast that she hardly saw it, a fact further decreasing her already low self-esteem. She heard the sound when the heavy hand hit Croydon's neck, the crack when the neck broke, and the sound when the body hit the floor. The silence after that seemed to last an eternity, as another man appeared in the doorframe.

– Princess…

– Chin, she greeted him dully, unsuccessfully attempting to hide her joy, her sickening joy.

She attempted to move, to step forward, but that little effort almost made her faint on the spot.

– You're exhausted, Chin nodded. – That's completely understandable and excusable.

– I'll be okay, she brushed him off.

He looked at the vomit covering the toilet and floor around it.

– That doesn't matter. You know that. As I am now, nausea is fucking me up with the slightest contemptible situation or person I encounter. It was far worse yesterday, when the doc hit on me. Tonight, it was the fucking whore. I think she's working as a recruitment agent for her pimp, but she didn't get me in her net, the bitch.

– I know, he said, mildly reproaching, smiling at her pride.

She stared at him, waiting, unable to move her lips.

– Elizabeth Stevens, princess of princes, he said formally. – It's time for you to go home.

– Do you know where he is? She asked.

– In an apartment off Leicester Square, Chin nodded. – This guy…

He nodded towards the body on the floor.

– … and his crew lost him, at the same time I almost did. He's safe, as safe as he can ever be. He's good, and is getting better.

– He's awakening. Betty sucked her thumb. – Awakening already. He got us off the ship practically on his own. He did it. Even Uncle Jack wasn't certain he would.

– Time to go, princess, time to wait and prepare. And then, ten years hence, you might meet him again.

He reached out a hand. She stepped forward and took it, stumbled into his arms. He supported her out in the hall. There were several other bodies there, both hospital employees and Croydon's goons.

– I know I'll meet him again, she said passionately. – He's the Prime.

– That's not for you to decide. Don't forget who you are.

– I don't. She drew her breath deep. – And neither should the lot of you. The One chooses himself. He won't be dictated. He won't be governed by anybody or anything.

– Spoken like a true Kwaiala, he nodded. – You've grown obstinate in your years in exile, but not more than expected, not more than what will be quite easy to undo. When the Prime appears, you'll be ready to greet him, to serve him, unconditionally, beyond loyalty, beyond Self.

– Yes, she whispered. – Yes.

A van waited for them outside the hospital. She didn't see who the driver was. Chin put her in the back of the van and joined her there. They drove off, the engine running soft and quiet. The vehicle vanished from the light, vanished from the shadows, until it faded from the city's sight.

And then, finally, away from the prying eyes of outsiders, she allowed herself to collapse. She broke into tears. Senseless she leaned back in the seat. Salty water flowed down her cheeks. It felt so good, so very good to cry, she thought, after fifteen years of hardship, harsh lessons and longing.

++++++

He was downed, sometimes in water, sometimes in sand. A walk through the desert turned into a swim in a lake. He swam in a lake, and it changed into sand beneath him, a vast desert with no end in sight. Sand turning into water, into sand, into water, into desert, grains of sand slipping through his fingers, a torrent, a river leading him through a torn, remote landscape, until he reached the lake, the valley far away. He saw the girl with the green eyes. But not the way he was used to see her. This time she was filled with respect and also humility, and she reserved that for the dark shadow walking behind her.

And then… then there was a shadow walking on an endless desert road, a robed, hooded figure without eyes, blood and soul. In its left hand it held a wand, in its right a sword. At the top of the wand was a skull, one of metal, one of flesh.

He strived to make sense of this, but his thoughts just drifted off. The fever tortured him, and he bathed in the sweat flowing from his suffering body.

And then he and the girl stood on a mountaintop. It was during a storm. Rain and wind battered their bodies, but they held out against the raging currents. Their eyes glowed, and they snarled, snarled at the large disk hovering above them.

The feverish visions only confused him. They came in flashes, overlapping each other, flipping back and forth. A river, an image of a large bird rising from the desert, the burning desert. The bird itself was burning, was enclosed in flames, dark and terrible flames.

He woke up with wide-open eyes.

– Be calm. Relax.

A soft voice. Hands on his shoulders. Warmth, mixed with worry. Cathy Randolph.

A hand of his, moving of its own volition, touched the sheet beneath him. It turned soaking wet. He tried, but didn't have the strength to remain upright. He fell back in the warm, wet softness and hated it. The memories of the time of slavery, the fear and hatred returned with a vengeance, way too real.

Still, eventually the dreams faded, even the dreams. His sleep, though never restful, turned somewhat calm. Cathy didn't have to guard him in fear of more anxiety attacks anymore. There was a quiet darkness where he could go, where he could rest.

He had no sense of time, or of time passing. But when he once again opened his eyes, he didn't close them for a while. He wasn't wet anymore, and he felt fine. The setting sun shone in his face. He didn't blink, but instantly locked his eyes on to Cathy's face. She rose nervously from a chair and walked to him.

– I feared you would die, she said frostily.

– But I didn't, he said. – Instead I'm reborn. I feel great.

She sat down on the bed, hesitating a bit before grabbing his arm… his discolored arm.

– You scratched off… the extra skin, she said timidly. – During one of your many episodes.

– It can't have been that many, he said lightly. – I mean, how many are possible during a single day?

– It has been days, she said serious-minded. – Today is Sunday.

He turned cold. Suddenly, it seemed like he had been unconscious forever.

– Sunday, huh? Well, I guess some rest did me good.

– I think it's safe to say so, she nodded.

– I'm clean now, he told her. – Clean as a whistle.

He considered it, sought within himself, considered his reactions. There was no craving, no sweating, no sign of the horrible withdrawal process still happening in his body. He looked at himself through her, and in the mirror. His skin was no longer pale. There were no bags under his eyes. And he felt good. There was no sense of nausea or fatigue. Even seeking deep within himself he sensed no risk of the sickness returning. He had… purified himself. Pride and incredulity surged through him.

He felt the strength of his body as he moved, as he naked left the bed. Her eyes clearly widened. There was no rage now, only the calm of a dormant volcano.

– I'm hungry, he stated.

And she felt the poignant hunger in his eyes, felt it like a sledgehammer in her mind.

– Dinner is still warm. She reddened. – I thought you might recover.

– Thank you, he said.

He kissed her on her lips. She returned the kiss, without thought, without sense.

A few minutes later he started on his second helping of Asparagus soup. He ate, but he never took his eyes off her. When she moved and shifted uncomfortably, he moved his eyes with her. He studied her, gave her far more than a casual look, while feeling the pleasure of slow, inevitable arousal.

She was dressed in no more than panties and a sweaty and transparent t-shirt.

– You're beautiful, he told her.

She blushed. Her entire body turned deep, deep red.

– I should get dressed, she said, uncertainty painted on her face.

– Don't bother.

The cold, measured stare stabbed her, freezing her to the spot.

– What's your name? She whispered. – Please tell me.

– My name is Ted Warren, he said, and he felt something swell within.

– You saved me, she said. – Thank you. Thank you.

She squinted her left eye slightly.

– Your eyes, she said, wondering. – There's something strange about them… You have one black and one brown.

He chuckled aloud. And she didn't have a clue why.

– Which one is it? The left or the right?

– Which is what? She was totally confused.

He laughed even louder.

– Your confusion is certainly not your fault, he grinned. – Which eye is black?

– The right… no, the left.

He bent forward and led both hands towards the eye. Shortly after, unexpectedly to her, a dark colored, transparent plastic lens fell down in the empty plate. She shook.

– I'm so stupid, she said embarrassed. – It's just a contact lens.

Silence descended some more, as she carried the plates to the sink, and they did the dishes. He felt every move, felt every drop of water on his skin. Every time he moved his bare feet and touched the floor anew, he felt it, felt the texture at his skin. And he moved so casual, so easy, unlike how he could ever remember doing. There was no stiffness in his limbs. On the contrary. They felt so supple and strong. It intoxicated him.

– Ted, she began hesitatingly, – are you wanted by the law or something?

She glanced anxiously at him.

– No, he replied. – Not by the law. My difficulties are of a more… private kind.

– Not that it would have made any difference, she added quickly. – I wouldn't have ratted on you anyway.

– You're just curious, he grinned. – That's okay. I like that.

He slipped behind her, putting his arms around her, sniffing her neck, pushing hungry lips at her earlobe.

– And you shouldn't apologize, he added. – No matter what. Do what you want, say what you want, but never apologize.

She slipped out of his hands, and quickly took two steps away from him, sending him an indignant look.

He grinned. It didn't matter. Let her play hard to get. Let her have more time.

– Maxwell was a pimp, right?

A cup dangled from her little finger. He knew he had had shaken her without looking, without checking her out in any way.

– Yes, how…

– C'mon, it doesn't exactly take an Einstein to figure that out, and he wanted you in his stable.

She put the cup down, hard. Her meticulous self-control unraveled.

– He and his crew had a stable of eager hens earning their keep for them. I met him six months ago, without any idea… what he did for a living. We had an affair. He was… cautious. I've been told he's patient, and he was. The first few months he was very nice… But the pretense eventually ended, and he revealed his true intentions for me, that *shit*. I've had him and his gang of thugs after me, bothering me, terrorizing me every day the last month. I fought, but he was… winning. I was waning and he was waxing. I tried to get help, I did. But either people didn't care, or they were scared off. I was alone, so alone.

She fell into Ted's arms, shaking badly, tears filling her eyes.

– He was so confident, so certain of his own strength, his power to find weakness in others… ruling with an iron fist…

Then she shook her head, drying her tears, staring blindly at Ted.

– And then you came, taking him out like he was nothing. Who *are* you?

– Are you sure you really want an answer to that question? He said quietly.

She froze in his arms, liberating herself from him once again.

– You're just a kid, she snarled, – Nothing but a sniveling *boy*.

The patronizing tone in her voice told him that she at least had some acting experience, either on or off the camera. Power struggles weren't unknown to her.

– «I have more memories than if I had lived a thousand years».

– Baudelaire, huh? She smiled sickly. – Throwing quotes at me, now, *boy?*

– Listen, he said, attempting to calm down, calm the raging storm within himself. – You resisted an inhuman pressure for weeks. You're evidently very strong-willed. You should be proud, not keep lashing out at people.

– And I guess you're an expert on such matters, she replied, her voice filled with scorn.

– Yes, *I am!*

She gasped. And he knew his eyes burned. And he didn't need her to tell him that anyway. He felt it, felt the Burning within, felt the fire rise like a tidal wave.

He turned, displaying the lash marks. And he held out his arm.

She looked at him, he knew she did, looked at the scars, some old, some not that old.

– I didn't do this to myself, he pointed out. – It was done to me, by a man, by people making your Maxwell look like an innocent baby. I learned, just like you learned, to return the favor, I learned, like you, about the world.

And then, for a moment, stretching into a second, he imagined he saw a glimmer of understanding in her eyes… before it faded, before it died.

– He isn't «my» Maxwell, she snorted angrily.

– You're not *listening,* he cried, the wrath in his voice far more than in hers.

She stared at him, couldn't help the shivering, the light elephant feet crawling down her spine.

– You have stumbled onto a vast and terrible tapestry, Cathy Randolph, he told her, his voice a dark whisper. – You better be prepared for it, or it will swallow you whole. Any tapestry will swallow you, as long as you keep denying reality, keep denying yourself.

I don't anymore. God help me.

– Fuck you! She spat.

There was no tangible reaction in him to her outburst.

– You're pretty when you're angry, Catherine. I like angry. There are countless good reasons for being angry.

– I'm not called Catherine, she said automatically.

– Do you know what I want to do, now? I want to fuck.

She couldn't stop herself from gasping. She felt she was pretty liberated. In her circle of friends, they used the word as easy as breathing, but to hear him say it… was something different entirely.

– Don't let me stop you, she said sarcastically. – You go out in the street and pick up some tramp, I certainly won't stop you.

He pushed out the chair. She watched him, couldn't help herself. His cock twitched… and rose.

She stood with her back to him. He could easily see how curled her neck was.

– Come here, Catherine, he called softly.

– No.

– Come here and *sit down,* he commanded, frost and fire in his voice.

She obeyed, after a brief hesitation. It irritated him. He grabbed her as she reached him, and pulled her down in his lap. She stopped resisting, just sat there with her arms hanging down. He pushed a hand up under her shirt. Her eyes widened. She had beautiful wide eyes.

– I'll c-cry for help.

He pulled her head to him and kissed her, kissed her hard on sore lips. She had beautiful sore lips. It was like tasting strawberries. The taste was real, and he couldn't believe it.

Her bra blocked his path. It was a D-cup monster, an old fashioned one and a powerful defense grid for sure. It would be difficult to tear it off, without risking injuring her.

– Remove this armor this minute, he said irritatingly.

– No! She replied. – No way!

She straightened, defiantly. He disregarded it completely. With both hands under the shirt, now, he grabbed the grid, tightening his grip around solid fabric and concentrated. In one single violent pull, he ripped the bra to pieces. There was no pain. If she felt anything, anything at all, it was only the sense that the pressure against her skin, against her nipples vanished.

– What did you do? WHAT DID YOU DO? You can't possibly have done it. You're not strong enough. Even if you had fully recovered. You…

He loosened her hair, her rigid arrangement of hair. It fell on her shoulders, loose and free. A hand remained under the shirt, rubbing her breasts, squeezing them slowly, deliberately. She shifted her position uncomfortably, biting her lower lip. His hands sought down to her belly, rubbing that for a moment, before continuing further down. She tried to get away, but he held her, held her in place.

– I can smell you, Catherine, he whispered. – Smell your need. Stop denying yourself.

– You beast, she cried. – You disgusting beast.

– Thank you, he grinned. – You say the nicest things…

She leaned on him, her cheek on his shoulder.

– I like you, she whined. – I like you, I like you, I like you, but I won't fuck you.

– Lift your arms, he commanded.

She obeyed. He pulled off her shirt, revealing her entire enticing, upper body.

– You're just another lying bitch, Catherine, wagging your tail for the strongest. But a very attractive lying bitch and you can be certain I want to fuck you.

– I won't let you. Her voice was choked with desperation.

– You can't stop me, even if you wanted to and you don't want to.

He played with the fabric of the panties for several, unbearable seconds, as he had played with words, until he finally reached her cunt. She stiffened in his arms, and released a loud moan, as all resistance left her.

– Please, I don't know you well enough yet, she pleaded. – I won't make the same mistake as with Turner. Please. You must wait. I don't want to. Not yet.

– What you've done before doesn't matter, Catherine. Your opinion doesn't matter. You don't matter. Do you hear me, Catherine?

She stared at him, shocked and hurt.

She attempted to say something, but her lips hardly moved. Shaking, like the legs of a dying fly. He touched her hard. She released a cry. Her head whirred from side to side, her lips seeking his. He removed her panties, slipping them down her moist thighs, and then he pushed the wet fabric at her nose.

– Smell, he hissed. – Smell yourself!

– No, she moaned. – Please, no.

She breathed deeply, and smelled it, smelled her own scent. There was no more denial. She met his eyes, as she moaned again, as he felt the last remaining resistance fade. He felt so alive. Her eagerness and willingness slowly revealed itself, unquestioningly. The initially tense body softened in his grip. Breathing turned loud. She began moving in his lap, up and down, up and down. He pushed himself between her thighs, and then he pushed himself deep within her.

Her eyes, shiny, shiny, shiny twinkled and flowed, her breath was merely tiny gasps. She released sounds, unintelligible, bending down, finding his lips, with her spicy lips, her spice of life. Everything melted away, faded away. They were in bed. He moved on her, as she writhed and moaned beneath him. She cried out, filled with pain and savage desire, everything she had always denied, everything he had hardly dared acknowledge.

– Your hands, your body, your touch burn, she wailed. – Burn me, burn me, burn me, burn deep inside me.

She pulled him closer, pulled so hard that her nails were buried deep in his back. He felt her, felt the Burning. It was as if she was a sponge and he was squeezing her dry. And he hurt. He burned.

He kissed her, and his lips burned, as he hardened inside her, hardened enough to blow her apart. He grinned wolfishly as he buried his face between her breasts, as he experienced fully what Betty had whispered about, as he filled the girl, filled the room, filled everything in it, and he was a storm ravaging the world.

Chapter Seventeen

It was still dark outside. In the apartment only the light on the kitchen was lit. Or perhaps it wasn't the kitchen, but a hole in reality itself, a sight impossible to fully experience and endure. Ted Warren slipped out of the bed. The floor felt cool beneath his feet. It didn't faze him. His eyes sought the sleeping girl. She slept on her belly, totally spent. Her hands kept clutching the pillow. She seemed small and defenseless.

Before me, she is, Ted thought triumphantly.

To this point he had been afraid, afraid they had done something irreparable to him, to his brain, but they hadn't been able to do anything... except laying bare the volcano in its depths. He wasn't afraid anymore. He curled his hands into fists and raised them above his head, to the ceiling.

His eyes...

He placed himself in front of the large wall mirror opposite the bed, able to watch his entire body in it, a weak mirror image, strong as fire. It wasn't as well muscled as before, but strong and supple. His face appeared far more clearly. All its details appeared to him undiluted, and clearer than anything else... was the eyes. No longer just a flash or flicker, but boiling and burning. He felt himself grow and joy was a wild song within him.

The girl slept. Feet thundered against the floor, and she didn't move, didn't stir. She would sleep a very long time.

It was at this border between sleep and consciousness. Cathy certainly had some conscious thoughts, but they were random, unfocused, and just slipped away. She had been like this for a while, straining in vain to gain a semblance of coherence, straining so hard. How long she couldn't say. And it didn't matter, not like she was, in her present state. It didn't matter. Only putting words to her thoughts mattered.

Eyes finally opened, painfully, slowly, slowly, like pushing open rusty windows. She was awake. Her eyes opened, directed at the white ceiling, so bright. She blinked several times. The entire room was bright, way too bright. She saw the sun's ray on the wall, and realized it was day outside, probably afternoon. The alarm clock on the night table showed half past twelve. It had called four hours ago. Christ, she never slept this long. And that she hadn't awakened by the infernal noise the monster of a clock made was practically unthinkable.

She reached up with her arms, writhed her body to get as high as possible. The movements were slow, as if they were made under water. She let her arms fall, and turned her head over to the side, glanced cautiously at *him*. He was there. It had been no dream. The dream became reality. Her eyes wandered, wandered by themselves, down his body. She suddenly had problems swallowing the saliva filling her mouth. She glanced down her own body, her exposed body, weakly wondering where the blanket was. She sat up, abruptly. There it was, in the dusty corner. She dimly recalled he had thrown it there, before falling on her.

The man by her side. The pleasure he had given her still lingered in her, in her entire body, not letting go. The very thought of what he had done with her made her body heavy once more. Lingering, pervasive desire itched in her nipples and her… her cunt. An itch increasing again at the very thought of it. An itch so sweet that it made her dizzy. She had never felt like this before. It was everywhere, to her toenails and hair, conquering her soul, its farthest corners.

Without really being conscious of it, she started fondling her breasts, aware of them, aware of their need, their itching need. This new, violent thing terrified her, attracted her beyond anything she had previously experienced. There was worry, but compared to the pleasure, the freedom it was like nothing. A hand slipped off a breast. As if had a will of its own it sought the lower parts of her body. She felt hot skin burn beneath the fingertips. It reached down below, where everything was unbearable, was unbearably pleasant.

The doorbell rang. The sound was like ice water falling on her head. The blanket. Her clothes…She had no idea where they had hidden themselves.

She sensed a touch on her arm. His hand. She smiled to him, recalled the ecstasy and then, suddenly, it returned to her. He pushed himself at her, and she pushed back.

She attempted, weakly, to disengage herself.

– It's Chloe, she gasped. – A friend of mine. We had an appointment.

– Forget it, he told her. – Forget her.

The ringing continued. It seemed distant, and was so very, very unimportant. She laughed giddily in his arms.

– She will enter anyway, she grinned. – Enter and see us.

– No, she won't, he said. – The door is locked.

Cathy remembered now. She had started locking the door after Maxwell had turned threatening.

– I'm so silly, she giggled.

– You're worried. He kissed her brow. – That's very normal.

The patronizing tone in his voice cut into her. It made her feel angry, briefly, before he possessed her, filled her space again. Again and again. It felt horrible. It felt so good.

– It could be your father as well, of course…

– My f-father?

– Yes, the message he left on your answering machine suggested he would come over, didn't it?

– He never comes, she said distantly.

– Your father… was quite the possessive one, wasn't he? And he strives to… keep it up?

She nodded, staring at him, shuddering at his perspicacity, his way of cutting to the bone.

The ringing stopped, and she forgot about it, forgot about everything, except the unbearable need rising from below. She moved her head across his chest, sensing the hair on her skin, almost able to count each hair.

He began touching her again, touching not only her body, but deep, deep inside.

– You're learning, now, aren't you? He inquired. – Learning what a freedom it is not to be normal.

She nodded, nodded eagerly.

– And how does it feel?

– It feels so good, she mumbled. – It feels so good, so good, so good.

He touched the writhing body with both hands, methodically, thoroughly. She moaned.

The heat returned. Unbearable. He felt it happen, experienced it in a blinding flash of shadow. When her juices began flowing, when her nipples hardened and the smooth softness, the need pulsed in her. Her eyes begged him, a single tear running down her cheek. She could see nothing but his eyes. Everything around them turned black. Nipples felt like rocks, pulling her down, down to the well of joy below. He turned her around. She writhed with her back to him, pushing her butt at his hardness. She moaned and screamed at him. Screamed. He grabbed her hair, pulled in it, pulled himself tight to her back and pushed himself inside her.

He moved brutally in her lovely tightness. She screamed, in infinite pain and pleasure. Sweat and juices flowed. Ted knew she didn't think, didn't reason anymore. She was just passion, desires. Instincts. A wild beast in the wilderness. Ted knew, because he reached deep down in her. He saw what was exposed. And he dived, dived into it, into the smoldering cauldron deep within her, but most of all deep within himself, into the nether regions of life. He growled, as his fangs and claws turned sharp and pointed. As he became one with her, with what lurked within himself. His claws tore into the mattress, cutting the sheet to ribbons. The glow inside grew even stronger. A river of fire flowed into her. A pungent stench, released from her, in the moment of joining, tore at his nostrils, the proof that she was conquered, that she belonged to him.

Cotton from the mattress floated in the air, all over the room. He rose, lazy and content. She lay there like dead, her chest hardly moving. Shiny eyes looked at him, as she writhed in bed, as she displayed herself to him, displayed her pride. Her strawberries pointed at him.

– I'm *so* exhausted…

She smiled to him, radiantly, openly. Her entire body smiled to him. He smiled, too, but his smile wasn't for her, but for himself. It was as if his entire being was… electrified. He felt enormously stimulated, refreshed like after a cold shower. And that didn't really cover it at all. He had never felt better. Never! She was content. Full. He sensed that. But he also sensed her lethargy, her fatigue. He saw that she had trouble moving. Even the slightest use of her muscles was an effort. He reached out a hand. She had to try twice before she managed to lift one of hers. He grabbed her outstretched hand and pulled her up. She embraced him. Her weak arms fell around his neck.

He kissed her. There was no burning this time, no energy flow, but he knew he could make it come, if he wanted to. She gasped by his mere touch. He felt the Power.

– I love you, Ted, she mumbled. – It feels so good. I love you, love you, love you.

He had devoured her, and she loved it. She wanted him to.

She stumbled and almost fell. He kept her on her feet.

– I must be coming down with something, she giggled. – I can hardly stand.

– You need to eat, he said. – Eat a lot. I've seen many girls overdo their *diet*.

– I didn't eat much yesterday, she nodded, sniffing, blushing some more. She blushed all the time. – Diets shouldn't be overdone, I know that. And I'll bet you like your girls a bit overdone…

She gave him another hot, seductive stare.

– We'll eat here first, he said. – Then we'll go out afterwards.

– I only have some eggs and bacon left, she said uncertain. – Just enough for two, I guess.

– That will do for now, he said, patting her cheek. – It will be a nice filler, until we can feed you a full meal.

He nodded mercifully, and she shrunk under his merciless glare. He slapped her on the butt and pushed her towards the kitchen.

She reached for the bundle of clothes on the chair, setting out to clothe herself, when she heard him cough. His eyes flared in warning.

– Don't! He told her. – I want to look at you.

Deep blushes ravaged her in seemingly endless succession.

The smell of egg and bacon filled the apartment. She looked at him through half-closed lids, feeling horribly naked where she stood. He had undressed her to her bones, to her very soul. She was a castle of sand on the beach. He was the tidal wave.

She served the food as he searched through her drawers and closet. He did so thoroughly, from up to down, left to right.

– I see you have up to date dresses and skirts, he nodded pleased. – That's good.

– I don't understand, she whimpered. – What do you mean?

– You're a smart girl, he stated. – I think you understand perfectly.

He turned. She looked into the strong face. Stronger than that of her father or Turner Maxwell or anyone she knew, stronger than she would have believed possible.

There was his skin, and what was beneath her skin, and everything made her breathless.

– Here, between these walls, as long as we're alone, you'll always be uncovered. Outside, you'll always dress so you're easily accessible to me.

She could hardly breathe. It was as if all her air had gone. He used it all.

While she stood like that, hauled up like that, he tore with meticulous thoroughness her bras and panties to pieces. She didn't take his eyes off him, while he was doing it, horrified and attracted simultaneously.

– You won't need these anymore, he said, as he threw the remaining pieces in the wastebasket.

She crouched, paralyzed, blinded.

– You… you… tore them apart as if they were paper, she said. – How can you do something like that? You don't seem anywhere close to being strong enough.

– Such lack of imagination may have served you well in the past, he chastised her. – No more!

And she felt chastised, and corrected and all.

He sat down, wolfing down the food. She did, too, so horribly hungry.

They were through. She looked astounded at the empty plate before her.

For quite a while, neither of them spoke. Then there was a whisper, so low, that even he had trouble hearing it:

– Take me again.

It was evening. The sun had just set. They walked on Trafalgar Square. The pigeons flew up in front of them. They had just eaten again. He had bought new clothes. She had helped him with that, helped him to choose wisely. He saw flashes of himself in windows they passed. It felt strange. Clothes were a mask as well. He felt like a stranger, felt like himself, whoever that was.

Expectation riddled him, mixed with a bitter herb. Why, he couldn't say. He had taken his time. They had walked around, breathing the very special mood of the city, the City of Cities. It wasn't just the big city he breathed, but the scent of another land, even another land than United Kingdom. In another time, another age, he could have enjoyed it, but now he couldn't.

The lions below the Nelson statue stared at him. He returned the stare, wondering why they were painted black. A strand quivered within him, but didn't bring forth any conscious thought. He let it go and continued onto the sidewalk.

They walked through Admirality Arch. He smiled. She led the way, but he still knew where they were going. They entered the beginning of London's «green» area, the enormous green area starting with St. James's Park, and ending in the distant west, in Kensington Gardens. It wasn't very green now. It was fall… or autumn. He grinned. Ted had never liked this time of year. That was one thing he had had in common with

Mike. When the leaves began falling, he had always had this melancholic pull around his mouth. He turned harder, more desperate. But there was also more, that Ted hadn't realized until now: Eagerness. A longing, undetermined and eerie. Ted had never liked this time of year very much, but he was still attracted to it. The naked cold, the barren beauty.

The park *revealed* itself to him, the same way he had experienced the room, without walls, without boundaries. He saw the group they sought, heard them speak, long before Cathy pointed them out to him. They walked on The Mall for a short while, before turning left, before entering the actual park area. He felt his feet hit the ground. He was… where he was, but he was also… elsewhere, by the castle far ahead, in the air above the park, seeing it stretch out like a river, like a lake. He flapped his wings, and he was down by the water, where people fed the birds, the myriad of birds.

A group of people, boys and girls stood by themselves. They didn't feed the birds, but were engaged in nervous conversation. He heard them speak, and easily noticed the nervous flickering of eyes. And he didn't have to hear them to know what they were talking about anyway.

There were no tents this time. No bikes. It wasn't winter. But there was the icy draft in the air, the confusion and the fear. Ted smelled the stench of smoke and motor oil. It was as if he relived Mike's walk into the bikers' camp, even though he hadn't actually seen it happen.

– I'm telling you he will be back soon. A big and tall redhead spoke. – So, he's gone somewhere without telling us. So what? Will you be the one to tell him that he has to file a report card before taking a vacation?

This should have calmed them down, but for some reason it didn't. One of them took one step towards the girl, a black-haired man. Not really that large, but lithe and hard. Dangerous.

– It isn't that easy, Marlene. There's a rumor, a very persistent rumor that Turner is at the bottom of the river, and if we don't act on that rumor soon, there will be hell to pay.

– He was going after Cathy, right? Marlene smiled, cocky, and very confident.

The others murmured, pulling back a little.

– And you're not gonna tell me that she put him at the bottom of the river, are you?

The murmur increased, as they all shook their head.

There was a clearing of a throat. They, the number of them almost jumped out of their skin. They turned towards the sound, and then they saw the stranger and the familiar girl stand there.

– Catherine didn't put Turner Maxwell at the bottom of the river, Ted Warren said. – I did. So, you're gonna need a new leader, and I am *it!*

They just stood there, frozen, silent, looking at him, casting feverish looks at the surroundings, studying everybody venturing somewhat close by.

Mike was known to the bikers, Ted thought.

– You will all submit to my authority, obey my orders instantly and without question or hesitation. You will do as I say when I say it. You will not attempt to split up, or start for yourselves, because if you do, I will find you. If you try to run, I'll find you, and you'll regret that you were ever born.

Ice. My voice is ice.

– An American, Marlene cried in contempt. – And alone to boot. You must be nuts if you think you can just come here and take over.

– If you know what's good for you, you should run fast as hell, another said. – Or you'll end up on the slab somewhere.

The laughter made them cringe. Sudden, loud and cold. It shocked them all, shocked them to the bone.

– You guys think you're tough, huh? The voice, initially so soft, hardened, turned rough and filled with contempt. And this was contempt, not Marlene's feeble attempt at it. – You don't know shit!

He walked into their midst, stopped in front of he who had spoken last, with a smile filled with scorn. The fangs flashed like blades in the cold sun's light.

They surrounded him. Usually a situation they enjoyed, enjoyed immensely. A victim always felt small surrounded by the threatening circle. But he had let himself be surrounded. He who stood closest to him took one step back, then another. And then, after a heartbeat or two, so did the rest. He stood there, looking each and every one of them in the eyes, even those standing behind him.

– Now, does anyone have any objections? Anyone at all?

Marlene blinked, wondering where all the birds and the people feeding them had gone. There was no one. Usually the riverside crawled with birds and people. She knew that. They met often here. He looked at her. She knew he did. Looked at her with his burning eyes. And she had to pull herself together by an act of will not to reveal her terror, not to shrink to a dwarf in his presence.

– No objections, she replied, straightening, swallowing hard. – We… we're yours to command.

She smiled to him, posed for him.

– Good girl. He patted her cheek. – Clever. Quite useful, I imagine.
– Yes, she whispered. – Very useful.

He studied her, the long red hair, the tall, muscular body. He seemed to consider something, before speaking again.

– I like redheads…

She looked at him. They all did, attentive and fearful.

Another girl caught his attention, one fairly ordinary. She rubbed his calluses, and he couldn't tell why.

– What's your name, sweetie? He asked her, striving to keep his cool.

– S-sandy, she replied.

He studied her in a way he hoped was casual. There was nothing there, nothing he could identify revealing why she, and not the other girls, had caught his interest.

The moment ended. He disregarded her, like he did them all.

– There will be new instructions in a few days. Until then you will continue as usual, as if nothing has changed… even though everything has.

With those words he left them. He was like a breath of wind. Suddenly there. Suddenly gone. And so was the girl. She hadn't spoken a word, and now she was gone. They looked bewildered at each other, wondering if the couple had ever been here, been here at all.

Ted looked back at them from afar. At the frozen, inactive bodies. No one moved or spoke. It had been so easy. They had been eleven, a group to be feared. Now they were merely individuals, shivering beneath his horrific attention.

So easy…

He sought them out the day after, noticing how the darkness faded in as the light faded out. The sensation pleased him. His newfound love of the darkness pleased him.

They were just three, but the three he had figured would be there, Maxwell's lieutenants. Marlene, Ralph and Pete. They emerged from a hole of a pub, a close to derelict building that had so many broken bulbs that Ted couldn't even read its name.

He followed them down the street, slipped in and out of the shadows. Like a demon. Soundlessly and invisible. Never taking his eyes off them. He concentrated, and then he could easily hear what they were saying. He only had to want it, and his senses turned so much sharper. Sharper than dreams. He heard them, heard them breathe. It was as if they were right in front of him. He moved with them. Sometimes he moved in a parallel street, losing sight of them, but never losing them.

Suddenly, in a dark alley, he met them face to face.

They stopped abruptly, all three with their hands on their weapons, before they realized who it was. And then they took their hands off their weapons, as if the metal burned them.

– Christ, man, Pete exclaimed. – Where did you come from?

There was no reply.

– You've collected money today, Ted said to Marlene. – Give them to me.

She fumbled a bit in her pocket, before handing him a thick wallet. He put it away without looking through it.

– We'll have a meeting tonight, he told them. – And everything will be clear.

– Everything? Marlene sent him a sweet smile, one filled with promises. – And what, pray tell, will that be?

– Tonight, he snarled.

The smile froze on her lips.

– You'll come with me, he told her. – You two will gather everybody, and then you will pick up Catherine by the Eros statue, and she will lead you to the meeting. Go!

He spoke as if they weren't there at all, exactly as they expected.

They left, and Marlene was left alone with the stranger. She didn't see them go. She hardly saw anything but the eyes burning her, devouring her, those eyes, quite similar to those she had met recently. Her thoughts tumbled in her mind, making no sense, no matter how much she strived to make sense of them, and of the situation and the horror her life had become. She wasn't herself anymore, as she felt something very unfamiliar to her, a creepy fear, an unfamiliar worry festering inside, gnawing at her bones.

+++++++++++++++

The London Fog formed with the cold draft from the east. Official spokesmen claimed that the Smog, the demonic mix of fog and pollution, was a thing of the past, but still it came, especially on dank autumn evenings such as these. It was so thick that visibility was only a few steps, so poisonous that one breath could cause healthy people to cough for hours, and sick people to die in one whiff.

In an old storage building in Soho, those who had known and feared Turner Maxwell met. They gathered outside, and Cathy Randolph led them inside, up a noisy old staircase, into the part that had been used as office and relaxation space. Into a room filled with furniture and dust. There was an open area at its center, and Cathy led them there, before she stopped, and they stopped, too.

They gathered in a circle around her, out of habit, but also because they wanted to gauge her reaction, to probe for the fear they had sensed in her earlier, in the weeks they had hounded and harassed her. There wasn't any. She calmly returned their stares.

Ralph stepped forward.

– You're among us, now, he spat, towering above her. – Are you our whore now?

The fact that he asked her the question, instead of telling her, told the others something.

– No! She shook her head. – I'm his whore. Only his.

She stepped closer to him, drawing a gasp from the audience, as she looked at them all.

– Yes, that's right, she said proudly, shivering like a leaf. – I've met a monster making all of you look like children in a sandbox.

Those who hadn't been in the park looked at those who had. They easily spotted the jittery nerves, the nervous glances, and it didn't take long before they looked the same.

Ralph wasn't satisfied with the answer. He grabbed the girl and pulled her to him, started fondling her. She didn't resist, not even when he squeezed a breast.

– Do you know what, Ralphie, she said just as relaxed. – I almost feel sorry for you, now…

He let go of her, as if he had burned himself. There was an insane taint in his eyes as he addressed the others.

– What's wrong with you guys, he cried. – Are you willing to let a guy, just one guy, a stranger, just take over, without lifting a finger to stop it?

They didn't reply. There was no need for that.

Ralph kept breathing hard, kept scowling silently at the rest.

– Who is he? Another girl wondered, turned to Cathy. – What does he want?

A deluge of questions assaulted Cathy. She just stood there, silent, until the ruckus died, and silence once more reigned in the old office.

– His name is Ted Warren, she said.

The name echoed within the gathering. Understanding kept eluding them, and they kept looking bewildered at each other.

– He will explain his intentions, Cathy stressed. – He will make everything clear.

And she felt the warm, fuzzy feeling inside grow and multiply.

They all stood there, waiting, as minutes stretched into hours.

It was *cold,* and their legs started to hurt. Some glanced at the couches and chairs, the couches and chairs covered in dust, but that was all they did.

Finally, when they heard sounds from a door opening and closing, and the sound of steps in the noisy staircase, they felt a palatable relief.

There was a brief silence, when they no longer heard the steps…

Then the door was kicked open, kicked off the hinges. It flew across the floor. They had seen this in movies, but never actually experienced it in real life. Some of them jumped backwards, terrified. Ted entered the room. Marlene walked behind him. The first they noticed about her was her hair. It was untangled and messy, unlike how she usually presented herself. She was always very thorough with her looks. He stopped in front of the group. She walked past him, before she, too, stopped, clearly displaying herself before them all. They noticed the mark on her cheek, then the dull eyes. She also seemed strangely lethargic. As if she wasn't there at all. And she clearly wasn't, not the spirited, dangerous girl they had learned to know.

– Yes, look at her, the young, old man said evenly. – Take a *good,* hard look. She attempted to cheat me, the cunt did, and even had the audacity to deny it. But she learned, learned her lesson well.

He turned slightly, slightly in her direction. It was enough.

She knelt, fell on her knees before him, bowing her head. Many of those present gasped horrified.

– I confess, she sniffed, her lips shivering so much that she could hardly speak. – I took more money than I was supposed to. I *stole*, stole from T-ted. I'm sorry. I'm SORRY!

– On your feet, cunt! He bid her calmly.

And she instantly obeyed.

He grabbed her blouse then. And then, in a few, powerful pulls, he ripped the clothes off her, every piece and shred.

They looked at her, looked at her tear-wet face, the exposed body, her humble posture, shocked beyond belief. It was like they were standing there, that their pride had been ripped out of them, and they were exposed to ruthless strangers.

– She confesses, he said. – That's good. Confession is good for the soul. Everyone knows that. She knows she would have been punished, punished *severely* if she hadn't confessed.

They looked at him, stared at him, unable to take their eyes off the creature in front of them. It was like the fog and cold and night had entered the building with him. When they looked at him, they saw a shadow. They saw a giant, far taller than the distance between the floor and the ceiling, and they crouched in fear, shrank in horror. His eyes glowed like two dark suns. Lips were pulled back, and the fangs flashed wildly in the glow from the eyes. The fingers touching Marlene's bare skin resembled claws. She writhed in *pain*. Among them there were killers, also cold-blooded murderers. They killed in the same indifferent way others might swap a fly.

Now they felt fear, felt it like something tangible moving through their blood, cutting the veins. The heat from the monster's eyes made their sweat flow freely. And they froze and burned alternately. They knew beyond certainty that they had encountered a predator they could never measure up to. Never ever!

He pushed the girl down over the back of a chair. She lay there with her butt up. He pulled out his belt. It was a very distinct belt, with initials inscribed both in the leather and the metal buckle. They recognized it easily. There wasn't any doubt in their mind as to whom it had belonged.

– Don't look at this as punishment, he told her, told everybody, instructed them in his doctrine. – This is merely guidance, a tool to avoid further unpleasantness.

She shook. She didn't move, but she shook, to the point of paralysis.

He began the beating. The leather hit Marlene's butt with a snap, a crack of thunder. Cathy shook. They all did. Marlene screamed. After the tenth stroke she screamed to the point of wailing. And by the fifteenth stroke she hardly had any voice left. He stopped by the twentieth, and Marlene fell apart there, as she hung like butchered meat over the chair. She turned completely limp. Huge, tearful sobs erupted from her sore throat.

The monster standing there pulled his belt back on. He knew how he looked to them, how they perceived him. Felt like the pounding of each heartbeat how he terrified, dominated them all. He wondered if he was for real.

– You're not worth much, now, are you, Marlene? I can do whatever I want with you. No one will stop me. No one can stop me. I can do what I want with you, without even touching you. I can kill you all without moving a muscle.

And he turned towards them, and they pulled back, frozen in fear.

It was true, and they knew it. He had no idea where these thoughts originated. Suddenly they were just there. The certainty made his eyes glow even stronger. He had difficulties controlling himself, controlling it. A part of him didn't want to hold back, hold back *it*. He wanted to let go, without reservations. What had always been a part of him, what he now

was aware of with every shred of his being.
He touched the shaking girl's cheek, slapping her. She raised her head, once more attentive and astute.
– There will be no scars. These were merely twenty gentle taps. For all your sakes you should never attempt to discover how true punishment is like.
He drew a knife. They recognized that, too. Recognized the shaft, the blade and the way it flashed a certain way in the light, as it cut through the air.
– I have a few things to say to you, to you all. It pleases me that everybody is present tonight, so I won't have to *repeat* myself.
The blade flashed, flashed darker. He stroked its edge along her thigh. The others didn't see it, but it was never near the skin. A long wound appeared from the kneecap to the hip. Marlene screamed, or rather whispered her scream. That was all she was able to do.
– Still no scar. I know how to avoid that.
An ecstasy, a sense of total freedom coursed through him.
He nodded to the girls crouching just a few steps away.
– You have a three-way system: The leader, the protectors and the protected. I see no reason to change that. But I will say this, I will emphasize that I do mean this, that I mean what I'm saying, and I want you to take this to heart: I wouldn't dream of forcing anybody to be a whore. If you want to withdraw, it's perfectly okay. But if you want to do it, you do it under my supervision. I won't tolerate any disobedience.
He crouched slightly and cut off a lock of the girl's hair.
– I will carry a part of you, a part of each of you with me. Always. Until the end of time.
The shrieking laughter echoed through the room.
He walked to them, to each and every one of them, stopping in front of them, waiting. They bent forward. A couple of the girls curtsied. He cut a lock from their hair. Pete bent his head slightly, clearly signing that he accepted the procedure. Ralph glared at him. Ted glared back. Ralph's lips started shivering, and he bent his neck, bared his neck for the strongest. The triumphant fire burned Ted, as he cut the man's hair. He pulled hard and brutally on it before cutting it. For every new acolyte he cut, Cathy stepped forward with a small plastic bag, filing it all away in her bag.
– You're not into Voodoo, are ya? Ralph yelped.
Ted just grinned to him.
It was done. Ted straightened, once more directing his attention to them all, and they couldn't avoid his attention, his full attention. He held them

in his grip and wouldn't let go.

– I've heard about your wealth-distribution system, he said. – Half to the leader, one third to the protectors and what little remains to the rest. It's a bad cut.

He smiled softly, and that made Cathy shake even more.

He looked like a tiger right before leaping to her. Except that she felt that if a tiger had encountered this… human being, it would have turned tail, and fled as fast as it could.

– From now on all parties get one third each.

Those gathered exchanged glances, not clear what he had just said, what it signified to them.

– I've never been much for injustice, he added.

He turned his attention back to Marlene, deliberating ignoring the shocked but happy smiles of gratitude the girls sent him, mixed with the fear that would always be there. They would never forget this night. He knew that, sensed it in every one of them, knew it without the added certainty.

As he returned to Marlene, the last piece of resistance broke in her. She choked constantly, unable to hold back. She begged him with her red eyes, vulnerable, broken.

– *Sing, little bird.*

– I'm… yours to command. She choked hoarsely, with a voice hardly more than a whisper. – I'm Yours! Whatever you command, Ted, I will do.

– Don't worry, little bird. He petted her hair. – You will soon enough be flapping your wings again. Just be patient. With patience everything comes to you.

The world's biggest lie. The impatience burned in him. Pushed at his insides…

He straightened. He seemed to… to shrink before their eyes, slowly turning human again. The glow in his eyes faded. His features turned smooth once more. The fangs didn't show anymore. He was a completely different person, also compared to whom they had met in the park, totally relaxed. So attractive, Cathy thought. The intensity about him didn't disappear.

– You're used to being treated callously and arbitrarily, he told the girls. – That ends tonight. You will no longer be touched against your will. Not without my explicit permission.

A sign to Cathy, and she appeared eagerly before him.

– This is your new clothing, he said, lifting up the skirt back and front, revealing more of her bare skin. – It makes you attractive and easily accessible.

The girls looked at the dress, looked at him, and nodded, doing their utmost to display their agreement and eagerness.

– You may go! He told them.

They followed the command without hesitation, without question. Cathy did as well. She walked with the others with lowered eyes, unable to face them.

Ted rushed forward, drawing gasps from everyone. He grabbed Ralph, and pushed him at the wall, shaking him like he would a rag doll.

– I accept *one* mistake from you… You will all be allowed one mistake, and no more.

Marlene remained, as the rest filed away. Ralph lurked behind the others, terror visible in his entire being.

She was given the signal, given permission to rise, to *be* again.

And she rose and walked to him, stopped before him.

I've learned, her eyes, her body told him. What is it you want me to do? What is your will? What hoop do you want me to jump?

His smile was just as cold. He fondled her breasts, clearly motivated by desire, not exactly careful. But she was used to that. In truth she didn't expect anything else. And it was also different, now. She reacted to his touch, his uncompromising touch, biting her lip as the first stings of arousal rose in her.

– I've got blood all over me, she said sweetly, clearly ambiguous. – You will, too.

– Don't worry about it, sweetie, he said. – Don't worry.

– May I ask you a question? She spoke humbly, reverently.

– Of course, he granted. – Know that you can always ask me about anything.

– Is it your wish that I will still be helping out with the leadership?

– It certainly is, he granted again.

– Perhaps you should have schooled me while we were alone and demonstrated on another girl, then? No one will respect me, or take orders from me, now.

– They will take orders from you, obey you, because the orders come from me, he told her sternly. – When you speak, it won't be you speaking, but me. You're my vessel, my deputy. That's all they know. That's all they need to know.

She took his hand and kissed it, looking at him with shiny eyes.

– Yes, she mumbled. – Yes!

Cathy reentered the room, quietly through the open door, but Ted heard her.

– Cathy will clothe you, wash you, make you a new woman, he said. – You will obey her because you obey me.

Marlene didn't have to look at the bundle of clothes in Cathy's arms to see that they were a larger copy of those Cathy was wearing.

– After that task you go with her to our apartment. You're moving in with us. Rest assured we will find a use for your old apartment.

The pride of ownership was thick in his voice. She felt the dull, possessive heat rise within again, and her mouth just turned dry, dry as sand.

He looked around, a pleased look in his eyes.

– This place isn't much yet, but in a few weeks it will be.

Marlene tailed Cathy out of there. Cathy guided the bigger girl through the dark and dank corridors in the derelict building. She hoped her shivering wasn't visible to the other girl. Ted's treatment of Marlene had shaken her more than she had believed possible. She had believed she had known him. She had been so wrong.

He had taken the strongest among them. And broken her like a twig.

– There's electricity here, Marlene said wondering. – That's strange.

The sound of the thin, vulnerable voice calmed Cathy's shaking somewhat. She took the other's hand and squeezed it tenderly, comfortingly. They were two now. She had someone to share him with.

– Turner… disciplined me as well, Marlene whispered aloud, choking, – but Ted does it so much better. Turner cared about what others thought about him, and he needed that, needed others' approval, their consent. Ted doesn't. To Turner there were considerations to be made before acting. To Ted it isn't. He's like a storm, a hurricane. I *want* to serve him, serve him for all time.

– Poor girl, Cathy said, not unkindly.

They entered what had clearly been an old, dusty dressing room and adjacent shower room. The shower was recently, very recently refurbished.

– Yes, Cathy said. – He made someone do this. He knew he would need it.

Marlene showered, and Cathy showered with her. And they both shivered, shivered in tandem, bathed in the hot water, unable to hold back anymore.

Civilization had dulled humans' instinct, but not theirs, not anymore.

Ted sensed it, sensed their awakening, as he walked down the squeaking staircase from the «office».

The door to the street outside was open. More mist, more shadow drifted inside. The light from the single bulb seemed to have turned that much weaker during the time he had spent upstairs. He saw Pete, saw him crouch in those shadows, saw him clear as day.

– What a mood, he cried. – What a terrific painting. And I who used to be afraid of the dark.

And now he loved it, loved the mist, the dank and unknown places. Where understanding before had eluded him, understanding now filled him, glowed with the Burning inside.

– I can't imagine, Pete said politely.

He was, like most of the crew, about Ted's age. Ted sensed a sort of ambiguity in him, enough to arise curiosity.

– You decided to hang around here a bit longer, Ted said, non-committal.

– I decided to familiarize myself with our future headquarters, Pete said dryly.

– An eagerness to be commended, Ted nodded.

The place was silent. Ted imagined he could hear the sound of the shower, of the distant city, but he wasn't sure.

Pete turned to him, and there was a tangible shift in his mind, something Ted sensed, that others would never get.

– You… paint?

Pete's voice probably didn't have that eerie quality of curiosity, but Ted sensed it in it anyway.

Ted shook his head, dismissive.

– I've never painted anything in my entire life. Our family is quite special and has quite the artistic streak common to us… but we don't paint.

A car passed by, a few blocks from their position. Ted listened to the sound of it, as it faded away.

– My family also has a story of being… out of the ordinary, Pete said abruptly.

Ted looked at him, stared straight through him.

– We're Celts *and* Gypsies, he added. – A synthesis of both, belonging to neither.

– I can sympathize with that, Ted nodded. – I really can.

– Especially my grandmother was quite the eccentric. She told me many things, things I have remembered to this day. You won't believe the stories she told.

– What are you doing here, Pete? Ted countered sharply, cutting off the game at its inception.

He didn't move, didn't lift his arms and grab Pete in his throat, but he knew the other felt it that way, that he felt Ted Warren's claws buried in his flesh.

Pete pulled himself together, attempting in vain to stop his hands from shaking. Fear did shadow this tough guy's features.

– I look at this stranger, this newcomer, he began hesitatingly, his voice slowly turning confident, turning potent. – I wonder about him. What motivates this man? What does he want? What is he *chasing?*

– I'm «chasing» something, all right, Ted snarled, his eyes flaring. – More than you can ever imagine.

Pete backed off, not with his feet, but his mind stepped a mile back.

– Are you *with* me, Peter Fallon? That's all I need to know, Peter Fallon, if you are *with me*.

– I'm with you, the other man assured the monster hoarsely, fear and hatred blossoming inside of him.

I can break you, Peter Fallon. Break you like a twig. I want to.

– I can even say I might have waited for someone like you, Pete persisted. – During that time I've seen many like Turner Maxwell, seen them come and go. You will come and never go, I know that.

The charged air lingered, and didn't let up. Something happened here. Ted sensed it, and he wanted to ask Pete if he sensed it as well, if he sensed the turning of the wheel, the unfolding of the tapestry.

– What function did Marlene have before? He asked lightly, deliberately casual. – I mean, beside that of being Maxwell's right hand girl?

– She did many things… Pete grinned uncertain, thrown for a loop again, thrown off balance again. – One pleasure she had was to play drug victim, and recruit girls from the hospitals. She's a natural.

Ted threw his head back and laughed hard. Another thing bewildering Pete, unscrewing his already rocked boat. He kept the uncertain grin, but he didn't understand. How could he? Ted dried his eyes, but there wasn't even a glimpse of humor in them, only cold cynicism.

– One thing…

– Name it, Pete said quickly.

– I want you to use one of your set of contacts, for one purpose exclusively, extremely discreet. If anything out of the ordinary happens in our backyard, I want to be notified immediately. And there are other people with my kind of eyes in London and the world. If they're spotted, I want to know about it.

He had looked. He had done nothing but look, but so far, there had been nothing.

– I understand. Pete nodded. – It will be done. They aren't necessarily friendly, huh?

Ted nodded slowly, staring into the mist.

Everything had happened so fast, as it always did. There had been no time to think. Not that it mattered much. There had been no need for thinking. There had been no hesitation. He knew what to do. Period! He lived in his dreams.

He thinks I know about them, about my blood, about myself, where I come from, my kin.

– Get lost, he said icily. – Don't look back!

Pete left quickly, very quickly. He didn't look back. Not once.

Ted looked down at his hands. It was as if they were sparking. The sparking grew as the hands curled into fists. Something resembling a smile lit his face, but it was as far from a smile as it was possible to come.

He returned to the apartment, his apartment, with Cathy and Marlene. They clung to him, warm and willing. There were two of them, two to share him, share his Hunger.

They smiled at him in expectation, whined as he approached them on the bed, melted at his touch.

It was morning again. Earlier today. He awoke earlier every day, slept less every night. It wasn't that long since the sun had first shown its sour smile over the rooftops. Ted stretched in bed, enjoying every move. He woke up without passing through the daze. Eyes weren't sticky, and his vision was clear the instant they opened. He felt strong and ready for what he was about to do. He curled his body and practically jumped out of bed. He stood in front of the mirror, in the shadow the sun didn't reach.

The girls slept hard, unmoving. He could hardly see their nostrils vibrate. Cathy would arrive many hours late at work today. Today, too. He smiled to the mirror, to himself, having taken his first steps. They were his. They were all his, to do with as he pleased. He would take the two out to dinner today. They needed to eat, needed to replenish themselves.

His hands sparked again, even stronger. He smiled.

Hatred, what was that? What was it truly? He didn't know, but it was part of this new in him, what had filled what had been emptiness.

Pity those he hated.

Chapter Eighteen

A dust cloud whirled in the air before him. He coughed, coughed hard.

Eric Carr stumbled down King's Road in Chelsea, disheveled and dirty. His eyes moved constantly from side to side, his head turned back and forth in ever more frenzied movements. The once so bright hair was covered in shit and had darkened considerably. The thing covering the lower part of his face looked like dust, not a beard. The clothes were actually less dirty, but so creased that they looked shredded. It wasn't much left of the elegant man from Aphrodite. He was practically unrecognizable.

He walked down King's Road in Chelsea, and for the first time in two weeks he stood out from the crowd. The Chelsea area wasn't exactly known for its disheveled population.

The two weeks had done something to him. He had spent them in an abandoned building in Battersea, writing down his article on a wreck of a typewriter he had found in a wastebasket. He had the article, with the pile of papers he had inherited from Benedict sewn into the back of his jacket. The food he had gathered from a number of wastebaskets late at night. Every second he spent indoors, he spent outdoors, he had seen the shadows of his enemies, fearing they would turn real, jump at him from behind a bush, the moment he blinked, the moment he allowed himself to blink a single time. It had done something to him. The beyond patient waiting, and the lurking in shadows. The hands always near his weapons… It had told him far clearer than what had happened onboard the ship that he had returned. To the Storm, where life was no more than candles flickering in the wind.

He rushed into a phone booth, glancing around several times before somewhat settling down. Just to use one hand to dial the number made him nauseous. He saw himself using the nose tip, and laughed hysterically.

There was a click, and a cold, distant female voice came on.

– This call cannot be completed because no coins were deposited. Please deposit a coin and try again.

The other hand searched in a pocket, finding a heap of pound coins. He threw them on the small shelf below the phone, picking one and put it at the top of the box. Then he redialed the number.

It took time and a lot of aggravation while he waited for someone to reply. The calling tone made him crazy. Finally, someone bothered to pick up the receiver at the other end. A low, guarded voice.

– Hallo…

– Hallo, Mel. This is Eric.

There was a prolonged silence.

– *Eric?* Where the *hell* have you been? The editor is furious. We didn't think you would show up.

I'll bet, Carr nodded.

– I've had some *trouble,* but now the article is complete. Listen, it's dynamite, true Nitro, actually. The Chief will love it.

– He doesn't want it, the man in the other end said dryly.

– What the fuck do you mean? He doesn't want it? He doesn't even know what it's about…or does he?

– Are you kidding? You damn insane… I guess you still want us to believe your lies, even after what you did onboard Aphrodite.

– I know about you, the editor and the magazine, Eric said evenly. – That part is actually a part of the article.

– I d-don't unders-stand…

– I have witnesses, depositions, the works, on how you wanted me to expose the Duke of Brandenburg. I've traced your membership in the Feet back to its humble beginnings. I have everything.

– Then… WHY DID YOU… The other guy shouted desperately, before realizing something and stopping himself.

– I just wanted the pleasure of hearing your sniveling voice, Mel. Have a nice day!

– YOU'RE FIRED, Mel Pritchard shouted. – FIRED!

Carr began laughing, with a chilling, tearing scorn.

– I'm coming for you, Mel. I'm coming for you all. I just wanted you to know that.

He hung up, and hurried out of the booth, very aware of how he had exposed himself. He knew they had traced him. The question was how fast they would be able to get here.

A London Cab pulled to the sidewalk for another man. Eric pushed him aside and jumped into the black car.

– Drive, he said calmly, pointing a gun at the driver. – Fleet Street. Pronto!

The newspaper street. He had postponed this for a week. A week too long.

Two young girls passed by as the cab stopped for a red light. His thoughts just drifted off. It was as if the car rocked beneath him.

Betty… He saw her all the time. It didn't matter if his eyes were closed or open. She was always there.

– You assholes, he said aloud. – You opened me up. And you used the most wonderful instrument to do it. YOU GUTTED ME LIKE A PIG.

Sweat poured from Eric's forehead. He attempted to dry it, but to no avail. His eyes, he knew, had a more than crazy look.

The driver's hands started shaking as he made a turn. Eric noticed, and frowned. He leaned forward, sticking his head through the inside window, between the driver's place in front and the passenger part in the back.

– Sorry about the gun, he grinned. – I'm in a kinda desperate situation, you see, and drastic situations demands desperate solutions. I'm sure you agree.

Carr had really intended to stop after that, but something ugly and dangerous was suddenly, explicably liberated from its confines.

– You see, he said, scratching his temple with the barrel. – The world is ruled… pretty much, by tyrants and criminals. In the sense that the word «criminal» has any justification, it is the criminals that rule. And I've recently found evidence of this, evidence that the tyranny is far more overt than people would like to believe. You, like most people won't believe that, of course. You wouldn't want to believe it… because it rocks the illusion you've all surrounded yourselves with, the denial you're in, over the way the world works.

– P-please, sir, the driver stuttered.

– So, I guess my question, my challenge to you is this: What have you done to fight the tyranny lately? Or perhaps that is the wrong question. Perhaps I should ask how little you've done? Because you're just a bug, aren't you? A bug among bugs, easily *crushed* under the heel of the mighty. You know mister cab driver… If I were you I would give this very careful thought, because it's you and all your fellow common people out there who are legitimizing the tyranny with your inaction and eager servitude. In other words: You're as GUILTY as the tyrants themselves. I would start thinking hard about this, very hard indeed… Because I will be watching you…

He fumbled in the man's pocket, and found his wallet.

– … Ronald Armitage, and you can bet your last puppet string that I will never stop watching you.

Eric thought about the boat people, the people here, the slaves living the illusion of freedom. The only thing different from the slavery in previous centuries was the setting. Almost everything else was the same. It was a matter of economics, of fulfilling a need.

He left the cab, putting his gun back inside his jacket. The polluted air, the exhaust from the long, long queue of cars suddenly felt clear and crisp like on the highest mountain.

Eric Carr made his visit to the first of his three randomly chosen major newspapers. As it turned out it was no pleasant experience. He knew the editor, knew of him, after a fleeting encounter a few years back. Three weeks earlier he had admired him, but a lot had happened in those three weeks. But Carr had reasoned that it, in this instance, would be an advantage that the guy was a ruthless newshound. As it turned out, he was like many of his colleagues, a newshound only when it came to selected news. Carr noticed that fairly quickly, and he noticed something else, too: The man never met his eyes. The «conversation» lasted for about half an hour, but the poor guy never stopped staring at the floor. Carr was allowed to speak his piece, but the moment he had done so, he was guided out of the office, and the editor himself did the honors.

– Thanks for stopping by, Mister Carr, the man said formally. – You may be hearing from us soon.

– But you don't think so? It was said in precisely the same tone layer.

– You don't expect us to take secondhand material, do you?

The man actually looked embarrassed, more than anyone had ever seen him. That saved him from a fist in the face. Carr wanted to showcase his foot, and ask if that, too, was second hand, but let it go. It wouldn't be of any use. The worry he had felt inside the phone booth in King's Road intensified.

– I understand, he said calmly.

The man reddened, and turned even more eager in his effort to make him leave.

The next editor told him to sit down and relax for a few minutes. There was a meeting to be ended… Carr had hardly sat down before he heard a number being dialed in the adjacent room. He was into the elevator before the dialing was completed. In the third paper the editor and everybody else refused to talk to him about his superarticle or anything else. He knew too well what little good it did to say anything, to speak up and he left without vocal protests.

Out in the streets he had to keep himself in check not to turn his head too many times. And then it wasn't paranoia anymore. He knew they had caught up with him. In the crowd, a stretch behind, four characteristic men slowly but surely advanced. Unnoticeable to others, but not to him.

He increased his speed slightly. Not so much that they noticed. He looked for more of them, but there weren't more. Not yet. Bank of England towered above him, a terrifying example of the resources he fought. There, there was the Underground. Light on his feet he crossed the street. Set course for the oblong sign without looking back. He walked calmly, until he was inside, and was certain that the people chasing him didn't have him in their direct line of sight. Then he ran, jumped over the ticket controlling machines and rushed down the escalators. He pushed people brutally aside, imagining he heard bones break. He pushed on.

Night, he dived into night, even more than he had already done. The silver moonlight surrounded him and the light from the electricity in the modern facilities waned to nothing. A train was just arriving. He heard it, heard the breathing of an engine in the jungle. In a horrible moment he imagined that all the people around him were carrying arms, and he had to concentrate, to focus on what was real, and not a result of his feverish mind. He jumped on the train just as the doors were closing. It moved. He looked back, and caught a glimpse of the four just before the dark twilight tunnel devoured the train.

Heart hammered in his chest. He wasn't really out of breath. The run had been like a walk in a park, a Sunday walk. But his vision turned foggy and he saw two people where there should be only one. Sounds hurt his ears and he had to double over in his seat. The pain cut into him, and it seemed to come from everywhere, from both outside and inside.

He took Northern Line to Moorgate and Metropolitan east to Aldgate East. From there he took District Line west again. Then he was fairly certain they had no idea where he was anymore. Ten minutes, half an hour on the Underground and their prey, any prey could be anywhere within the Greater London area. He leaned back in the seat, leaned his head at the window, staring into the nothing, the wasteland of modern and not so modern engineering. Eyes were half closed. He relaxed as much as possible, conserving his energy or trying to. Everyone on the train was a potential hostile. He knew that, prepared for that. Thoughts were a single jumble, an assault of images, impressions, impossible to organize, slippery like water, impossible to hold on to. Pain somewhere rode him, cut him with a dull knife. The fools, those fucking chickens… Three major papers, randomly chosen, all gagged by the fear and terror and imposed sensibilities.

Alone, I'm alone.

Sweat he wasn't sure wasn't tears flowed down his cheeks. A choke rose in his throat, never reaching the world far up there.

To satisfy his own paranoia more than anything else, he stepped off the train at Westminster. When he passed Parliament Square and turned into Victoria Street he already regretted that decision, knowing fully well he should have waited one more station before hitting the streets. The pain in his foot increased to the point of becoming a bother again. It had never truly healed, and his time holed up in the dank apartment and a lot of moving around hadn't improved anything.

He gritted his teeth in the effort of not limping, but it was hopeless. The body's involuntary reactions made it impossible to impose one's will on it to such a degree.

New Scotland Yard… the police headquarters. He figured he could just as well go straight to the top… or the bottom. The old Scotland Yard had been on a completely different site. This building was modern, raised less than ten years ago, state of the art facilities, a place of glass and steel. He had been visiting during a social event a year ago, in a different world. That contempt for his own, previous self fueled him, kept driving him forward.

The door was closed. It was a heavy door he had to push hard to push open. He walked to the desk sergeant inside the dusty reception hall. The slightly fat man looked sourly up from a pile of papers. The building was strangely silent and there were no other people in the room.

– Greetings to you, good, sir. Carr mobilized what he had learned of worm-like English civility. – Believe it or not, but I actually have some crucial information I would like to share and discuss with your Superintendent.

– Crucial information, huh? The copper seemed, if possible, even more sourly. – Why should I believe you? There are virtually dozens of crackpots every day lined up to talk to him.

– It…

– Crackpots that either belong in a nuthouse, or have lost their dog and want the Super to guarantee its safe return.

– Listen, my good man. Carr tried hard to keep his frustration from surfacing. The polite tone disappeared. – I understand you've had a hard day, that you're sick and tired of everything, but my day hasn't been that good either. What I have to say will sooner or later find its way to your boss, and it better do so before I'm sick and tired of repeating my story, repeating it all the way to the top.

The copper was about to reply, but then he was unable to hold on to the mask anymore, and it cracked in a triumphant smile. The game was done. Carr heard steps behind him, and the anger faded, and was replaced by deadly, deadly calm.

Three coppers stopped behind him. They weren't exactly the christmas card of the helpful, kind policeman.

– So the man will go straight to the top, huh. He doesn't trust us lowly mortals, I gather.

– Perhaps it isn't quite like that, another commented compassionately. – He looks scruffy, if you ask me. A bit confused, perhaps.

– *Very* confused.

The discomfort, the unpleasant buzz in Carr's mind increased a few more notches.

– I lived the life of an ordinary man, he said distantly, not really speaking to the people around him. – With his illusions and false sense of security. But now I'm awake, and you better watch out.

They ignored his outburst, probably not even hearing him, not truly, so far from their reality that it was.

– Tell me, lads, isn't this the madman behind the bloodbath on Aphrodite?

– It certainly is, the desk sergeant exclaimed. – I knew there was something familiar about him.

He grinned and held up two mug shots of Carr, one with beard and one without. The cold invaded Carr and calmed him further, until there was nothing but deadly calm left. They still played the game, believing it gave them an advantage. More the fools them.

– I'm leaving, he told them. – Don't try to stop me.

They let him. He backed off, knowing the precise position of his gun and knife. If they moved two of them would be dead in an instant. He was a weapon, laid bare and hardened in the world's forge. They better fear him.

They didn't move. He smiled to them, teasingly before pulling the door open, opening it easily, as if it was a feather. He rushed outside, taking the first few steps, seeing the movement beyond the movement in the street image before him, throwing himself flat on the sidewalk, rushing behind the rotating Yard sign, as the machine guns played their music and the door was pulverized behind him. He rolled his body fast as a spin, drawing his gun, but there was nothing to shoot at. People ran screaming, terrified past him, back and forth, like hens. Total chaos ruled outside the headquarters of Law and Order. He grinned. The gunmen kept firing. They fired indiscriminately into the crowd. Carr jumped on his feet. Another salvo was fired. Someone close by screamed, and he felt several hits in his right arm. The gun dropped from his hand. He was already moving and couldn't pick it up. Cursing he turned the corner and ran down Broadway with a score of others. Several other people screamed and dropped. Blood pumped through his veins, flowed from his arm. He felt exhilaration. Those who hunted him had dropped all caution, all pretense of concern. The surge of adrenaline made him ignore the pain. The next salvo came from a completely different angle. More people screamed and fell, but he wasn't hit. He saw where the shots were fired from, from two windows across the street.

Thoughts burned in his mind, and now the jumble of thoughts made sense, now he could think. The concrete jungle surrounding him turned into just another battlefield.

Two quick steps, and he was close by a police car about to stop by the sidewalk. He saw it from other angles, that of his possible adversaries. The images hammered him. He was the men with the guns in the window, the pedestrians that might fire at him at any time. The world was a whirl of motion.

He used his right hand to open the door, forcing himself to ignore the pain, using his left to pull the amazed, single copper out. Eric jumped into the seat and returned the car to the road, not bothering to close the door. The windows at the back and left were shot to pieces by another rain of bullets, missing him again. He barked his insane laughter at the world.

The front of the car hit several other cars, several pedestrians crossing the street. He drove ruthlessly outside the queue. The open door was torn off when it hit a pole on the sidewalk. He half-expected bullets to be fired in front of him. He drove a jigsaw route, half on the sidewalk, and half in the road. But no bullets came. But cars. They just had to have cars available. They came, on screaming tires. He grinned, and turned on the sirens. His laughter penetrated the insane noise. Those running off, beyond terrified, beyond reason, ran even faster. He pushed the gas pedal to the floor and raced around the next corner on two tires, repeating the maneuver in the next turn. The dogs chasing him couldn't keep up. A meeting car slid uncontrollably against him, and missed by only a hair's breadth, but couldn't avoid the car behind him. What followed was a grand head-on collision. And chaos erupted everywhere. Several cars crashed into the two wrecks. Three of the dogs' cars hit a huge truck entering from the left. The street suddenly looked like a German Autobahn after a mass collision. The path behind him was blocked. The people in the fourth chase car could do nothing but watch as Carr drove off. He vanished in a growing cloud of smoke from broken engines and burned tires.

– I AM THE LIZARD KING, Eric shouted, – I CAN DO ANYTHING

He struck a hand, the wrong hand at the wheel, and screamed in rage and pain. It hurt, but he could take it, could take anything after this. He had escaped from a well-prepared trap, an iron ring of people and weapons, and couldn't quite believe it. They had had all the advantages, but he had still escaped, made fools of them again, and he could hardly believe it. Fantastic! He choked and laughed alternately, as tears of joy and relief filled his eyes, and he desperately attempted to clear his vision.

His foot eased up on the pedal. He slowed down and turned off the sirens. His eyes kept moving, on both sidewalks, on the road, at his back and front, every intersection he reached.

He drove a few more blocks, and then the car suddenly… stopped roaring. The engine died. He looked incredulous at the fuel indicator, showing no more fuel. The car rolled a bit longer, before it stopped. The engine was dead, and no matter how much he tried to restart it, in the few seconds he tried, it was to no avail.

There was no hesitation. He left the car and began running. There were muscles moving and air moving in and out of his lungs, and that was all there was. He sensed people's stares and heard church bells toll somewhere nearby, but it was all faint, meaningless. He kept moving his eyes, looking out for those who would hurt him.

Water. He smelled water, heard it flow in spite of its smooth surface. Flowing, ice-cold water, for his foot, his burning foot… He hadn't run much more than hundred steps before he realized that his foot wouldn't hold out much longer. The jumping and running, and the humid apartment he had been holed up in… he was now thoroughly convinced it hadn't been good for his poor foot, not good at all. And his arm… His arm hung straight down, totally useless, its fingers numb and dead. The intoxication faded slowly, overrated as it had also been. Because he had really lost. He had escaped this confrontation, too, but as the pain forced his thoughts through to the surface, he knew he had failed. They had shown him their power over established society, how useless his resistance truly was.

Insane images jumbled his vision. After moments resembling an eternity he finally reached St. James's Park. His vision filled up with red spots. The birds resembled vultures and the humans had horribly distorted features. He didn't run anymore, merely stumbled forward without any conscious direction. Church bells kept tolling… far away. The foot didn't obey his commands. He had to drag it along. Birds flapped their wings on all sides of him. Ravens cried out to him. Funny! That was so funny. He had never seen Ravens here before. Water. He smelled water, life-giving water. The wounded beast crawled now, with one foot and one hand, crawled towards the tropical trees with its branches touching the ground and the water. Finally, he found a place, a place to hide, right by the water's shore, where no one could see him, but where he could see everybody. There were no people close on this side of the water, and they were even further away on the other side, where they sat and fed the birds, fed them crumbs of bread, of life. He didn't have the strength to wash the blood off. His arm just fell into the cold fluid and descended below its surface, into its chilling depth. His mind fell, too, into the red haze of fever it had resisted for so long.

He saw them, the three men approaching from far away, fully aware of the fact that he couldn't move, couldn't move a muscle, knowing beyond knowing that when the moment of need came, when he truly needed to *move,* he would be able to. His hand, his untrained left hand sought inside the jacket, found the shaft of the knife, sensing how it kept slipping through his weak fingers. The men had stopped, at a safe distance. They were close compared to all others, but far enough off to be safe, safe from whatever he could throw at them. Professionals. The biggest, the youngest among them spoke, his voice strangely calm, strangely reassuring.

– Can you hear me, Eric? He heard the echo, unsure if there had ever been any casting of that echo. – My name is Mark Stewart. With me are Francis Caine and Floyd McKenzie. We have sort of expected you to show up, to resurface in these parts, so to speak. We've been looking very much forward to it.

The jumble of words finally made sense to him, and he rejoiced. The sense of triumph, of happiness rising within him, made at least a semblance of strength return to his limbs.

They held him, turned him around. Every touch hurt and burned. He gasped, attempting to speak.

– And we can safely say you did, The Gambler told him. – And what a performance that was…

Carr looked at two people he had heard about since childhood.

– Yes, Stewart told him. – The game has changed irrevocably. You aren't alone anymore. There's a gathering of forces, forces strong enough to rock the Earth itself.

And the words warmed him, chilled him.

He looked astonished at Stewart's eyes. They were… glowing, glowing on a clouded, dark day.

Stewart set down on his heels and began to check out the bloodied body. It felt weird. Mixed with the pain was a strangely pleasant sensation.

– You aren't a doctor as well are you? Carr said weakly. – Among the many things I've heard said about you, I've never heard… that…

– I'm far better than any doctor, medical doctor, Stewart replied. – The medicine of nature is far superior to that of civilization.

The big man looked at him, and the eyes suddenly seemed to burn that much stronger.

– You've been more than lucky, kid. Having run through a gauntlet for several weeks, with just one bullet stuck in your body, is downright impressive.

He picked in the torn flesh in the arm. Carr had to grit his teeth not to scream. Through half closed eyes he saw the twisted metal piece in Stewart's hand.

– Your arm is basically okay. It looks worse than it is. Your foot is worse off. Fortunately, I have something that will help, and it will be good as new again. But you're lucky you met me, or you would soon have had one foot less. You've treated it badly, very badly.

Eric didn't understand why he suddenly froze so hard. If he hadn't known better, he would have been tempted to believe that Stewart was attempting to scare him.

– I presume you were watching Scotland Yard, then. But how did you manage to follow me, when no one else could do it?

– Let's say we had the advantage of foresight, Caine grinned. – It's safe to say we used a bit of a different tactic compared to the others.

Stewart pulled a box from his coat and opened it on the ground. He found a bottle there with a fine powder of tiny seeds lined at the bottom, and filled a bit of water on it. A few seconds passed, and then the mixture began swelling.

– Hocus Pocus, huh? Eric stared suspiciously at the porridge-like mass that kept growing bigger and bigger. – I don't know if I… OUCH!

Stewart meticulously smeared the mass on the wounded arm. The easy way he did it more than suggested that he had long practice. The mass grew out of the bottle and he used a new supply in even intervals, keeping it from overflowing. Eric felt the pain as Stewart touched the wounds, but not as much as feared, far less than before. As for the foot it only felt numb, and that he knew was far worse.

– Don't worry, Stewart assured him. – You'll soon be on your feet again. You have a bit of fever, but that will be gone by tomorrow.

– You sound so sure, Carr commented. – I have great difficulties believing how I can believe you… but I do. Damn if I don't…

He giggled, and it sounded like sand in his ears.

– We'll put you in a safe place, McKenzie, said. – We do have access to some of those.

– NO way, Eric said weakly. – Not for long, anyway. I want to join you. You need me.

– You're not useless to us, Stewart nodded dryly.
And it felt so strange to describe anything that man said, in such a way. He was anything but dry.
Stewart closed the box, and put it back inside his coat.
– Truth to tell, kid... we've been looking for you. You have a lot of interesting stuff to convey.
– It's great that you... have found me... interesting.
Damn, why did he suddenly become so sleepy? He had major trouble keeping his eyes open.
– *I can take him*. Caine far away.
– *I'll take him*. Stewart, seemingly even further off.
He felt how he was grabbed and lifted up, put on the big man's shoulder, and he felt the heat from the other body, and he couldn't help but wonder.
They moved, moved fast.
– You asshole. You drugged me!
Stewart merely smiled, and Eric saw it.
– Your eyes... didn't they use to be blue?
Suddenly it dawned on him. They were like Ted's and Betty's. Shock and anger riddled him, as he kicked himself for not seeing the connection immediately.
He strived to say more, as everything slowly stopped working
– Yes, Eric?
There was a long silence. Then it came, well into sleep.
– The Duke...
The small group, larger by one, once more briefly exposed to daylight, returned into night.
+++++++++++++
Darkness and cold... The snow that was nothing but brown slush in the streets did nothing for the weak light. From Birmingham was heard an explosion echoing through the seventies' Europe. Twenty-one people were killed and many more were injured right in the middle of the christmas shopping spree. Two pubs, Mulberry Bush and Tavern in the Town, were blown to smithereens. On November 21st Europe's last colonial power awoke abruptly from the long sleep.
But the christmas shopping spree continued, unstoppable. At least in London, far enough from Birmingham for people not to really care about provincial events. In Portobello Road, Oxford Street, Tottenham Court Road and all over the city, the shopping-hungry gathered to empty their wallets and their hearts. Main streets were filled with advertising, with shallow christmas decorations.

In a dark alley, off Oxford Street people rushed through the darkness in hushed whispers. A girl's long bright hair flashed in the glow from the cold streetlights. It was cold, and she didn't wear that many clothes. She pulled the large scarf tighter around her neck and upper body. The tall, ripe body shook in the moist, chilly weather.

– She's here.

Stewart stood outside the house where the girl was headed. He smiled when he easily noted the eagerness in Carr's voice, even through the electronic buzz of the radio.

– Noted. How are things at your end?

– Not bad. McKenzie fixed the last of the opposition a few minutes ago. He's returning here, now. Uh… I think you actually fixed my foot a little too well. You know the guy that was supposed to live… Well, he didn't. I hit him a bit too hard, I guess.

– Don't worry about it. It isn't that important. You've done a good job. Stay put until the signal is given.

He turned off the radio before Carr managed to say more, grinning to Caine.

– Some kid, that one, but he's talking too much…

Stewart looked very young himself, far younger than his thirty-seven years.

– She's coming, Stewart said.

Caine realized that he heard her steps.

Caine heard nothing, no matter how he strained his ears.

The two of them sought into the shadows, to the places in the street where they would be even less visible. The girl arrived. She crossed the street just a few steps away from them. There was no sense of her having noticed them or of her noticing anything around her. Caine sensed that, too, sensed the emptiness in her. He saw it in her every move, the way she carried herself. She seemed light on her feet, good-humored and fresh, but it was just a façade, a shell walking there. He felt the icy wind overwhelm him, felt it paralyze him, beyond the physical, beyond the senses.

Rage filled him. He knew, and he could never forget.

She rushed up the stairs to the apartment, a smile brightening her face. The door wasn't closed, and she walked straight inside. Stewart and Caine rose and followed her. Stewart ascended the stairs in two steps, as silent as the shadows. Through the glass door he could see the girl kick the shoes off her bare feet. If she had looked outside, she would guaranteed have seen him, but she walked further inside, without looking back. While Stewart grabbed the handle, Caine drew his gun. One look from Stewart and he put it back inside the coat.

They were inside. The door closed silently behind them. Most of the apartment was dark. The only exception was the room ahead of them. From the narrow line through the half open door slipped light and sounds no one could mistake.

Stewart pushed open the door. The room revealed itself to them. The round, large bed at its center. The three enormous mirrors on all sides and in the ceiling. The three in bed. The Duke, a skinny boy, and a girl with sparking red hair. The newly arrived blonde crawled to them, smiling seductively. The Duke was on top of the boy, the older man's face red with excitement. The girls teased him, spurred him on.

It took time before anyone noticed the two men. The redhead spotted them first. She cried out a warning. The boy threw the heavier man off him as if he was a dwarf. The Duke hit the floor. He crouched there, half on his knees, shaking his head to clear it.

– Franz Von Brandenburg? Stewart inquired, with an unmistakably irony in his voice.

The Duke just looked at them. He opened his mouth to speak, but there was no sound forthcoming.

– Scotland Yard, sir, Caine said with his thickest British accent, and pushed one of his special cards at the kneeling man's face.

The Duke kept looking incredulously at them, unable to find the words.

– You've truly *done* it this time… sir.

Caine made no attempt to keep the contempt from his voice and was very pleased when he saw the rage and uncertainty in the Duke's eyes.

– What the hell are you men doing here? What d-do you m-mean?

Caine cast a Stewart a challenging look. Then he drew his gun quick as lightning. He fired four times, so fast that it was impossible to distinguish between each crack. The wall mirrors broke in a thousand pieces. Dust of broken glass fell slowly to the floor and revealed dark rooms behind, revealed the recording devices that still hummed and clicked without human aid.

– Thorough, quite thorough, Caine commented. – There's the same setup in the ceiling, but I didn't want to risk harming your toys.

The Duke opened and closed his mouth continuously without a single sound coming out.

– You're an influential man, sir, Stewart explained, as if to a child, keeping his eyes on the three on the bed. – Both in Germany and here, and in the world at large. Your industrial power, your clandestine service connections… That makes all this quite worthwhile for somebody, as I'm certain you're aware of.

– How do you know about…

– We *know*. And they know, too.

– This is quite a setup, Caine said, the admiration thick in his voice. – Very deliberate and well thought of. Do you know there are six bodies out there? If we hadn't come and they had still been alive, you would've been presented for quite an extensive *invoice,* now, sir.

– This is a *disaster,* the Duke whined. – If this was to be public knowledge…

– We'll take care of this. You can just keep sitting on your fat ass and relax. You'll get away with this like you've gotten away with so much else.

The Duke turned even redder, in anger, now.

– This is an OUTRAGE. I'm going to report you at the first possible opportunity, you can be sure of that. And what about this scum? He pointed, theatrically at the three in the bed. – There's severe punishment for extortion.

– Get the hell out, Stewart snarled, unable and unwilling to keep up the pretence. – Or we'll kick you out, and I can guarantee you it will all be revealed in tomorrow's main pages.

The Duke stumbled, literally, as he fought himself on his feet, grabbed his clothes from the chair and backed out of the room. He slammed the entrance door hard behind him. With closed eyes Stewart heard the sound of his steps as he practically fell down the stairs, as he almost tore his clothes apart as he strived to dress and not stop. Stewart smiled.

The redhead started shifting uncomfortably on the bed and looked at the two with a skeptical look in her eyes, her stone-gray eyes.

– You're not…

– We're not! Caine confirmed.

– Tilla, Linda and John, Stewart whispered intense and loud. – You know who I am. You remember me.

They kept shifting uncomfortably, but didn't move their eyes. Their eyes were hard as glass.

Love dolls, Stewart thought. And murder machines. Twice dangerous, twice deadly.

Sweat poured on his forehead. Eyes narrowed in concentration.

– Francis, go. Slowly.

Caine returned the gun to its place inside the coat. He closed in on the bed in a wide circle.

The girl shook. He stopped advancing.

Let them get used to us, Stewart had told him. It shouldn't be much of a problem. But watch out, they can be deadly. Like cornered animals.

That didn't seem very probable to Caine. Not as he watched the begging, inviting eyes. The sweaty, sensual bodies…

The redhead had suddenly, unexplainably moved close to him. She kicked him in the belly with a naked foot. It felt like a shoe laced with steel. He fell to his knees. When she struck him, he just about managed to avoid that the fist hit his temple with deadly force. It merely scratched it. But he still saw the floor rise up and meet him, as if in a fog, a haze of red.

By God, she almost killed me there.

Stewart reached her in one leap. He grabbed her wrists and forced her arms on her back. As he held them there with the left hand, he grabbed her hair and pulled her head backwards. She attempted to twist loose and kick him, but he had her under control.

He shook her. She moaned as he hardened his grip, as he squeezed her wrists.

– *Listen to me, Tilla,* he said, as he looked intensely at her, as he met her eyes, as his eyes and mind burned into her. – Who am I? Say it. Say my *name!*

It was truly as if a veil was lifted from her eyes. That was no longer just an expression. Not to Caine it was.

– s-stewart? STEWART!

She cried out.

And there was an instant smile. A child's smile, but true.

Linda straightened.

– You're a ghost, she said ghostly. – They said so, promised us so, taunted us with it.

– Touch the ghost, Stewart bid her, bid them all. – See for yourself what's real.

Caine rose, still with major difficulties. He saw them directed towards himself, Stewart's staring eyes.

– I told you to be careful. What if she had gotten hold of your gun?

Mark held on to Tilla with one hand, and with the other he reached out to the other youths, a soft look in his eyes.

Linda smiled radiantly to him. He saw her, saw her memory rise from the ashes. John looked at him with open hostility, but he, too, acted independently of his own, conscious thought.

– Enemy! John snarled.

– No, Linda told him. – Feel. Touch.

She pulled him with her.
– Don't grope, she cried.
The three grabbed Stewart's hands, holding on for dear life, and so, in the final analysis, did he. Mark felt the intended intense joy when he looked into his kin's eyes. Slowly the dull expression faded there, and life returned in its stead. And Hunger. As he had wanted, as he had craved, as he had feared. A tear fell from her eye. The unknown, the horror, the glow rose from his depths, rose from his depths once and for all, stayed there, at his surface, burning, like a lake of fire, dark flames playing with his skin. The others let go, as they regained cognizance, as they grew aware of the dragon blowing its fire, but she didn't. She held on and she wanted more. He had to tear himself free from her. He screamed and fell on the bed.
Francis saw it, experienced it as a dream. The warm glow emanating from Stewart's hands, the visible energy field around his body, the nightmarish images. Caine closed his eyes, but the images remained. He saw them for just a moment, they would never go away. He knew that.
Stewart fought himself up. He suddenly looked very tired. Caine knew what was expected of him. He stepped forward and took Stewart's hand. It was like touching ice. But there was no humidity. Caine felt the cold all over his body, and he briefly blackened out. A few black spots. Then his vision returned to normal. He saw Stewart straighten again, towering above them all.
The three youths swayed on the bed, their attention focused on Stewart, as his attention kept focusing on them. They swayed for a few seconds between sanity and insanity, life and death, until their eyes cleared, the shadows of intelligence and memory and will returning. They recalled all the joy and pain. Triumph and horror filled their being. Caine would have deemed it a miracle… if he didn't know better.
– Free, Linda spat, Linda cried. – F-free?
– Freer than you have ever been, Stewart told her.
He added casually:
– Ted and Betty managed to escape on their own. They're waiting for you, waiting for us all.
– Betty, Tilla said darkly.
– Life is returning to you, Stewart said. – You won't be coddled anymore, not be fed and «cared» for. You're free from the prison of the soul. The rest you must do on your own.
– Time grows short, Caine said uncomfortably, feeling like an intruder.
It was impossible. *Impossible*. The three of them had been more

automatons than people, drugged, brainwashed so thoroughly that they were as easily programmable as a computer. It had seemed like an impossibility for Caine to see any other future for them than a padded cell. Stewart had touched them, snapped his fingers, and voila, they were like reborn, were human again. He choked when bathing in their crystal-clear eyes.

– Not «voila», Francis. They still have a long way to go, but now they have a chance.

Caine choked again, harder this time, very hard. He had carried for some time, now, the sneaking suspicion that Stewart was able to read his mind, but had written it off, in his hopeless simpleton hope as intuitive guesswork. But now he was awake. Now, there was no doubt anymore. He had not lived in the world before. Now… he did.

– We don't have much time. Stewart spoke to the three of them. – There will be more men here, with new clothes for you. They're with us, but not truly with us, do you understand? You must never tell them about or even imply what happened here, when I brought you back, when I freed you.

For your sake and mine, Tilla thought feverishly. She knew, now. The brief contact had freed more than her mind. She was more, now, even more than she had been in Denver. Why didn't you say anything, Mark? Why did you let us fumble in the dark?

Stewart smiled inside, so very proud of himself, over what he could do. He had slept. For thirty-four years he had slept, and only dreamed. Now, he was awake.

Caine knew that there would be a knocking on the door soon, the prearranged signal. And he saw in the redhead's eyes that she knew as well.

Shortly thereafter, five minutes before schedule, there was that knocking on the door.

++++++++

There was a gathering, a gathering of forces that would eventually grow to engulf the Earth.

The building hid in a dark, quiet street. Lights were turned off in all the apartments. Caine approached it by Stewart's side. There were just the two of them. They walked casually, but it still felt to Caine as if they closed in on the place, attacked it… with military precision. Everything, the careful approach, the snipers hidden behind corners and covers, more than suggested danger.

Stewart let Caine knock on the door, another fact that didn't exactly contribute to the Gambler's calm. Stewart was tense, as if ready to explode… or expecting an explosion to hit him… from inside.

– I felt you, a voice said from behind. – Felt your storm.

You will not fire, Stewart had told the others. No matter what, do you hear me? Not until I do.

We hear you, Carr had said through numb lips.

Caine had to pull himself hard not to panic, to not draw his weapon. Stewart turned, somewhat calmly, and Caine did, too. There was a shadow there, under another staircase, on the opposite side of the yard, slowly appearing from the shadows, the deep shadows in the dark alley. The creature was dressed completely in black. Only the face was clearly visible in the weak light. Oddly enough he used sunglasses in the middle of the night. There were just two black spots where his eyes were supposed to be.

– Hello, kid. Stewart greeted Ted with a clear brush of excitement in his voice.

– I felt a ghost in my mind, Mark. I wasn't sure if you were dead or not. The bastards think you are.

And Caine felt the storm in the boy's voice, the ironic snap when he mentioned Stewart's given name.

– Not anymore, Stewart said lightly.

Caine touched his right hand with his left. It was as if it wasn't there. He certainly couldn't feel it.

– You're fully dressed. He heard Stewart's voice again. – Any particular occasion?

Reason, Caine thought. Reason.

– I've had quite the troubled sleep lately.

– I can imagine.

Stewart said.

– There are more of you.

Ted said.

– Yes.

Stewart gave the signal.

– We're quite the diverse bunch, he said.

The six walked out in the open. There was a thrilling laughter, patronizing but full of life. Ted embraced John first. Linda embraced Ted very hard. He kissed her on the cheek. He and Tilla met, body to body. They kissed, and they stood there, holding on, for a long time.

– I've looked for you, he said, removing his shades, revealing his eyes, further stirred by her reaction to seeing them. – I've had others look for you, but London is so damn big.

– I know, she said, touching his cheek.
– There's one here you haven't met before, Stewart said, coughing a bit.
Ted turned, reluctantly from Tilla and to the man by Stewart's side.
– Have we met? He frowned at McKenzie.
– It's not strange that you think so, the man said. – I'm Diana's father.
Ted turned to Stewart.
– She disappeared in Washington the night you left, Stewart told him.
Ted looked down, an expression of pain crossing his face.
– We thought she was just…
He held back.
– Sulking, Tilla said.
He grabbed her and Linda, suddenly very determined.
– Come, let's get inside, he said.
The three did. And the rest followed. He led them straight into the apartment, into the bedroom, where Cathy and Marlene slept soundly. They lay naked and uncovered on the bed. Semen covered their thighs and was also spread unevenly on other places of the body.
– This is where I have kept house lately.
– Good old Ted, Linda said ironically. – As faithful as ever.
There was a chuckle from Tilla. Everybody looked incredulous at her.
– You don't get rid of me this easily, she said, kissing him again, kissing him hard. – I told you. I don't mind sharing you.
The two girls on the bed woke up, first smiling happily, but upon discovering the rather large group of people in the room, they showed clear signs of anxiety.
– It's all right, Ted told them. – These are old and new friends and allies. Say hello.
– HALLO! The girls choired, suddenly quite happy again. – Nice to meet you.
– Nice to meet you, Stewart replied.
The other mumbled a greeting, more or less articulate.
The two rose from the bed, clearly used to displaying themselves, mild curiosity painted in their eyes.
Marlene grabbed a sweater from a stool, and pulled it over her head, slowly, deliberately, more than overtly staring at Tilla. There was well-masked anxiety there, and more.
– Is this a private party, dear Ted? Perhaps I and sweet Catherine should make ourselves absent for the night?
– No! He shook his head. – You may stay.
– How about making dinner, then? Cathy asked softly. – Your friends are

surely hungry.

– That is a great suggestion. Ted nodded. – Do that.

He turned to the others, raising his arms as if embracing them all.

– Let's have a *feast,* he cried. – What do you say?

– A feast sounds great, Carr said hoarsely, when no one else replied.

– I'm looking forward to it, Tilla said, pulling close to him.

He turned his attention, his complete attention to her, finally.

– You look good.

– I feel good, she said hotly. – And you don't look so bad yourself.

They moved. The entire room, everybody else stood still, even those who didn't, but they moved.

Ted walked to Stewart and stopped in front of him.

– Nice eyes, Mark, he said

– Yes, nice eyes, Mark, Tilla said pointedly, spurring Ted on, adding to his rage and frustration.

– Yours are not so bad either, Stewart replied lightly.

– Now, this very moment, Ted began, Ted spat, – is the time for you to stop playing your games. It's about high time for you to *level* with us.

The room, with the bright light in the ceiling, suddenly seemed that much darker. The dark boy darkened, until the other hardly could see more than the fiery eyes. He seemed to tower above Stewart, to grow to a giant in their mind.

– Yes, Stewart pondered, seemingly totally unfazed by the presence breathing down on him, – perhaps it's time.

And Ted pulled back a little. The angry pose remained, but he did calm down, and the light reentered the room, and everybody breathed a sigh of relief.

The four youths from Denver walked to a far corner of the large living room, speaking together in hushed and enraged whispers.

– We will get them, the others heard John's voice.

– Yes, we will, Ted cried darkly. – We'll take what they did to us, and pay them back tenfold.

The scent of heated food and spices slowly filled the place. The gathering sat down by the table. Ted and Tilla lit candles, and turned off all the electric lights. They moved awkwardly in relation to each other, desperation and longing clear in their pointed stares, as they slowly focused their entire attention on Mark Stewart.

They dined, almost all of those present, wolfing down the food, so filled with Hunger that they hardly managed to eat at all.

The fireplace burned hot, now. Its dark flames and those of the candles looked as if they reached for each other, as if they danced in ruby eyes. Stewart sat down by the fireplace, sat there for a while, but he remained frosty. The fire, at least the outward fire didn't seem to warm him at all.

Tilla took Ted's hand, a bit apprehensive, still a bundle of nerves, of excitement. She took his hand, perhaps to share her warmth, for him to share his warmth with her, or to counteract the solemn mood, shared among them all. There had been a digestion of food, a sipping of wine, but there had never been more than that. Ted had been surprised by the pleasant burning of the wine, but he, like the rest of them was too anxious to actually enjoy anything fully. There were too many scars, too much tension and distrust in the room. The dinner was no more than a preparation for the inevitable that followed.

Stewart spoke and everybody listened. Everyone present had been touched by the horrors, the secrets lingering behind the unfolding events, and they knew it, they all acknowledged that, knew it beyond words, and they eagerly awaited some sort of disclosure, but no disclosure came.

– I turned seven that year, that month. It was the fall of 1944… on a cemetery. We were nine. Seven above the ground and two below.

His words instantly evoked emotions of dread and sorrow and longing, images of rain and shadow. A cold drizzle fell over the six figures surrounding Mark the boy at the gloomy cemetery. Flames danced on his unmoving face, as if he wasn't truly in this room, but on that very cemetery thirty years back in time.

– It was the Warren family crypt. We were all below ground, among the dead. The dead were Virgil and James, their mutilated, *rotting* bodies. With them was no one except us. No priest, fortunately not. The happy and strange thing is that none of us believe in god or that shit. Just us. Two adults and five children. Nick, Jack, Joel, Trudy, Ethel and myself. And a friend of the family, a man named Jonas Bergli. I was the youngest. I recall Nick saying something about the dead, before the coffins were pushed into their designated places, to *rot* forever.

Ted couldn't keep the stoic mask. His eyes widened until it hurt.

– That's right, Mark told him calmly. – It is the Trudy you've met. Elizabeth's mother. And Linsey's and June's. And presumably your aunt.

– I knew it. Ted nodded and was just as distant. – She got weird every time she looked at me.

– And Bergli *is* the same man that was your «theater instructor» later in life, he who was also Jeff McCabe.

– He was weird, too, Tilla said. – He was always weird. They… both were!

– Something happened, Stewart continued. – I'm not sure what. It's all sketchy, but they lost me, or I lost them, and I remember traveling with the gypsies again. I was taken in, adopted by the Gidman family, and I kinda got *sidetracked* after that, even though I never stopped looking. Many years later I tracked down Ethel and her son Patrick in New York…

– Patrick? Eric Carr said sharply, crestfallen. – Patrick Warren?

– Yes, Stewart confirmed. – Do you know him?

– I… «served» with him in Vietnam. We've been friends since childhood.

And then quickly, slowly:

– My god, we *are* all involved. This is indeed some tapestry. I rather thought it was, but I had no idea…

He cast his attention on Stewart again, that much more astute and motivated.

And Stewart, showing them the past, kept stirring what lurked in the corners.

– I spoke with them at some length. But Patrick didn't know what had happened and Ethel, if she knew anything, kept it to herself. And then, not long after that, I came to Denver. Yes, I knew who you were when I first met you. I had studied Michael at a distance for quite a while… I found Trudy, but she wasn't volunteering more information with me than she did with you.

– And this is all I *know*. He closed and opened his eyes. – The rest is second-hand information, hearsay or speculation.

He returned to the table, and from then on, words were just words and a voice just a voice.

– Whatever happened in 1944, the other five in the family also lived through it. I've spoken to Nick's friends, the few who are still alive. According to them he searched all over Europe for me. The children traveled with him. He wouldn't let them out of his sight, and he was paranoid as a loon, though after what I hear with more than quite a few good reasons. The family returned weary and close to exhaustion to New York after the war. In 1948 Ethel gave birth to Patrick, only thirteen years old. Nobody knows exactly what happened there either, but there was talk of rape. In 1952 Jack was charged with murder, but was acquitted. It was proven that the dead man was a member of a mafia family, and that Jack had acted in self-defense.

– I remember hearing about both Jack and Joel, Caine said. – There were headlines about their skirmishes, and they were both young, so very young.

– And that's all, Stewart said. – They all vanished in late 1952 and Nick, Jack and Joel have never been seen or heard from again. No one I've spoken to can or will tell why or how or where.

There was silence. Even the burning wood sounded silent. Ted rose abruptly, shaking himself loose from Tilla's comforting touch, and the silence rose to a roar.

– And this you saw fit to keep from me, he said enraged to Stewart. – You're some piece of work, Mark, so fucking clever. You lied to me by telling the truth.

Stewart just sat there, offering no comments or explanation.

Ted rushed outside, slamming the door behind him. The building shook.

He rushed through the streets, blindly, but still he looked, still his eyes moved back and forth, searching the surroundings for potential hostiles. The rage was a song in him, and he welcomed it, welcomed the song, the song of life. He left footprints in the slush, he knew he did, but when he looked back to confirm that, there was nothing there. Everything just faded in the slush.

There was an old construction site nearby. He jumped over the fence surrounding the property. It wasn't hard. Just a jump and a swing of the body. Like taking a step forward. The stairs were already completed inside. He ran upstairs, all the way to the roof. It was far down after merely a few floors. He felt like he was flying.

He stood on the roof, the city stretching out before him, a mist rising in the air. It was the city. It wasn't the city. Emotion raged through him, there on the calm lake. The fire swelled within him. He felt it. And as he gasped, as he closed his eyes he saw it, saw a lake, and through the mist he saw a castle.

There was a sound behind him. He relaxed and spoke without turning.

– I don't know where she is.

– I wanted to ask you… where is…

Eric spoke, before the other's words had really registered in his conscious mind.

– I left her at a hospital. She vanished after four days, leaving a trail of dead bodies in her wake. I don't know where she went, whether or not she was recaptured or what. But she's gone. She is, too.

There was silence. Ted easily sensed Eric's raging emotions, his uncontrolled, chaotic insides.

– You seem to have done… okay for yourself, Eric finally said.

– Don't worry about it, Ted said. – She has just left. She will return one day, when the time is right, when the time has come.

– What time? Eric asked.

But there was no reply.

Ted remained there for while, until he sensed that Carr had left. He turned and stared down the stairs, stared into the dark mass down there, descended the stairs, descended the soft darkness below. The sound of the traffic had been sharp, loud up there. Now, on street level, it turned muted again. He circled a bit before returning to the building in the dark alley.

He passed the door to the apartment, and walked downstairs instead, to the basement, to the laundry room. There was a large wall mirror there, too. He could see his entire body, but he looked only at the eyes.

He had put this off, really. Not consciously, perhaps, but he had postponed it, for days, perhaps weeks. He hadn't truly looked. And now he did. Looked. He had to. Know. He was calm, completely calm. There was nothing exciting him, nothing making his eyes flare. He didn't use his power in any way. But his eyes were no longer brown, not even close.

They were *fire*. Or at the very least the color of it, of dark fire. He couldn't explain it better, describe it in any other way. During the course of these weeks they had changed. They were a predator's eyes. And now they were his - forever.

A pair of extra eyes appeared in the mirror. Paler, not so distinct, but unmistakably similar to his own. He turned, deliberately in a whirl of motion, silently snarling at the other man.

– As you know, mine were blue before I left Denver, Stewart, the new Stewart said. – As you can see they're not anymore.

– What is it with us, Mark? What are we?

– Why do you ask questions when you already know the answer? Stewart replied softly.

Ted stared sullenly at him.

– Does a name, a designation mean anything? Do words change the facts? Can they change the course of mighty rivers?

– If they're sufficiently *slick,* the boy snarled silently at him.

The anger rose in him, and he welcomed it, and he grew to a steaming giant in Stewart's presence, an illusion so terrifying that it threatened to become real.

– We've always existed, Stewart said, standing his ground, attempting to stay unfazed. – We've always been here, and because we're born different, people will fear us, and hate and hunt us. I don't think I need to paint a picture for you, kid. In spite of it all, the extreme circumstances, your ignorance and inexperience… you've kept the secret. You've protected it with every little trick you can think of.

There was a slight pause, before he continued, before he did his own spitting, his own words:

– But you've also started on a very dangerous path, one that will ultimately lead to untold revelation and untold harm.

Another pause. Longer.

– The one walked by your brother… and also your *father*.

And then, there it was, the hatred, a living thing, finally vibrating in open air, thinly veiled. It shook between the two, and grew and multiplied.

Mark felt the shock inside the creature, but nothing was openly revealed except a devious grin.

– Are we talking about «evil» here, Mark?

– No. Stewart shook his head, irritated, frustrated. – It's just a word.

– There is no good or evil, no right or wrong.

Ted said, emphasizing every word.

– Very correct, but the fact remains: You will gain, amass enormous power, if you're not killed first. But to gain that power you'll have to systematically eradicate all your human weaknesses, such as warmth, compassion and the ability to see others' viewpoint. You'll have quite an empty life. I don't think you'll enjoy it much. There's a soft spot in you that you'll have to work hard to get rid of.

The impression of the creature faded slowly. Stewart could breathe normally again. The boy he looked at didn't look that different from any boy in his late teens.

– I think… I think I know what you're getting at, Ted said, with his voice approaching normal. – If I'm not careful I run the risk of turning into what I despise, right? «What does it serve a man if he wins the whole world, but then loses his soul». That is what you're getting at, *right?*

– It's a fair interpretation, Stewart shrugged.

He wasn't pleased. There was… something about the other's… wording that unnerved him. He didn't receive even a tiny bit of impression from Ted, now. The boy was completely calm. Stewart felt the stench of his own sweat.

– There's something you're not telling me, Ted said quietly. – There's something going on. I know that. Eric is right. There's a vast Tapestry involving us all, a puzzle moving us all forward. You have an *agenda,* just like Mike did.

– Perhaps you should grow up, and get one yourself, Stewart countered.

Ted stepped forward, and attempted to grab Stewart's hand. Stewart pulled back, pulled his hand away, elegant like a dancer. Ted stepped close to him, but made no further attempts to touch him, skin to skin.

– Do you know what, Mark? If I decide to do that, to take your cue, walk the *Path of Power*… then there's nothing you can do. I'm far beyond you already, and this is just the beginning. This is just *the Phoenix* basking in its ashes.

A sickly, triumphant, clearly fake smile crossed Stewart's face.

There was no love lost between them. They knew that, now, if they had ever believed differently.

They parted. They simultaneously ascended the stairs to the floor above. There was no mirror they could see on that road, but they still saw the reflection of their eyes as they moved, as they kept their attention at the other beast prowling by their side.

The others welcomed them upstairs. Of course, they did. Ted rushed to Tilla as she rushed to him. They held hands, held bodies. Ted heard the laughter again, patronizing, full of life. Through his inner eye he saw a small red-painted house between green trees. A pond in the wilderness with the clearest water he could think of. There was a catching in his throat, and he had trouble swallowing.

Stewart looked at the apartment, walked through it as if he was a real estate agent.

– This is big and useful, but probably not completely suitable to our needs. We need more room.

– Don't worry, Ted shrugged, very deliberate. – I have thousand eyes and ears in this city, and I have a place for all of them, a war cabinet, a place where we can plan and execute our conquest.

Linda looked at him. Then she looked at Stewart. Something passed between the four, as it always did. Stewart walked to the ice-blonde girl. He drew something from his coat and handed it to her. There was a flash of metal, one of black and red. Her eyes turned wide and dark.

– Here, he said simply.

Mark Stewart returned the ebony blade to her.

Chapter Nineteen

The building that had been derelict and abandoned only a month earlier was now totally changed. Not that much on the outside, but most of the rooms and areas inside had indeed been refurbished to the point of everything looking different. There were many rooms, ideally suited for many people to live under one roof.

Ted and Tilla were alone. Colors shifted around them, hot, gray and cold, and everything between.

– I can feel their hands on me, she hissed.

She shook in his arms, in frustration and rage and vulnerability.

– He healed me, she sniveled. – Restored my memory, opened all the wounds. I'm so grateful, and I want to kill him, roast him over open fire.

– I can sympathize, he said, in a feeble attempt at joking.

– It lingers, she said. – You had nightmares last night. You shook like a baby in the crib.

They had gone to bed together the previous night, but fully dressed. They had crouched there, shaking and suffering together, and their sleep could hardly be called a slumber.

– I remind you, she choked. – Remind you of all you had forgotten, strived to put behind you.

– I can't deny that, he said, fearing the sound of his own voice, fearing she would break in his arms. – But that's just a small part of it, really. There's so much more.

– Far more giving us reason to… shake? She wondered softly.

He nodded, not trusting his voice.

– I know, she said. – I felt it, felt it rage inside Stewart. It scared me, and I wanted more, so much more.

They moved, moved tight to the music from an almost broken cassette player. The sound was set so low that they could hardly hear it.

It was peaceful, as they moved, as they touched and breathed in close proximity. Very slowly a smile transformed her face.

– You've learned, she said incredulously, half grinning, half choking. – You've actually learned to dance.

– HEY, I resent that remark…

– No more stepping on toes, she said dreamingly. – No more blue nails.

– It wasn't that hard, actually, he said distantly. – I just decided to do it, and I did.

– You always had it easy when it came to learning, but now it seems that

that has been increased beyond belief.

She was joking. She wasn't joking. He felt a thrill shoot through him, a sensation part expectation, part fear.

They danced, tighter and tighter, until there was hardly any air between them at all.

She kissed him. The kiss lingered on his lips. She took one step back and began undressing.

– Are you sure? He asked.

– I'm sure.

He undressed faster, to catch up with her. But when she let her last piece of fabric fall to the floor he stopped, and stared. He couldn't help it. She had always had this effect on him.

– Your eyes are glowing, she whispered.

– I know. I hope it doesn't… bother you.

– Are you kidding? It's like my body and mind are bathed in the pleasant rays of the evening sun, like needles pricking my skin. I feel so sensual, so wanted.

They did advance hesitatingly, did take their time. She helped him off with the last few items. They kissed again. They touched. He fondled her breasts. She pushed them into his hands. Everything felt different, but the same. She threw her head back, her hair flowing like embers in the air. Her hands, he felt them on his hips, playing with him, and he hardened. He couldn't help but gasping. His cock pointed straight at her groin as he bent forward. They were in bed, moving against each other, gasping in need and longing and lust.

– Yes… She writhed, pushing herself at him, as if in pain. – YES! I can feel the glow and it feels so good.

Time passed. No time passed.

– I'm so horny, she whispered in his ear. – So terribly horny. NOW, do it NOW, before I go CRAZY.

She tore at his thigh with her long nails, screaming at him, making blood flow. That was the moment he lost it completely, he pushed her back and threw himself on top of her. A roar was thrust between his lips, the very moment he pushed himself deep within her, driven mad by her curves, her smile, her desire. They kissed and kept kissing, sharing air. She stared into his twin suns and shouted in joy. There was something very physical about it all, almost an absence of thought, far beyond a momentary lapse of reason. They were closer to each other than ever before. They heard, far away, the sound of fabric tearing. Time turned insignificant. Far away lurked the unpleasant dreams. The dreams they had had for as long as they had existed. Now it was the heat, the cold, the cold and warmth, death and life, the dark and the shade. The twin suns turned into a reign of stars.

Heaving chests heaved less. Less sweat poured from heated skin. They rested in bed afterwards, touching each other. Tenderness waxed as passion temporarily waned. He studied her cautiously.

– You thought I would be quite… exhausted, huh? She said sweetly. – Like the bitches you've played with lately?

– I've never really let go with them. I didn't dare. But now… I did, and nothing happened.

Like with Betty.

– I'm kin, you know, she said cheerfully. – Besides, I won't accept that *nothing* happened…

They broke in laughter. They made the entire bed shake, until they exhausted and hurting began caressing the other again.

A single tear loosened from his eye. He tried to pull back, to pull himself together, but he couldn't

She touched his cheek, tenderly.

– We're together again, she choked. – Together, for all time. I can feel you, my love, feel you as never before, like you feel me. We'll never more be apart.

Slowly, only slowly, the outside world manifested itself again. The first they noticed, as always, was the wind, the wind in the quiet room. Then it was the sheet, torn to pieces and distributed unevenly throughout the bed and the room.

– We are kin, she repeated, – and Mark knew, knew all the time, and he said nothing.

– Mark wants something, Ted said, clearly frustrated. – He's playing a game, either for his own pleasure's sake… or against someone. He reveals information at his own pace, what he wants us to know. But he doesn't *know* himself. Not truly. Or he wouldn't need us. And he does. He knows a bit about what's coming, enough to scare the living shit out of him.

– I didn't sleep much last night, she whispered. – Just enough to dream, and shake in terror, like you.

– About Gidman, he nodded frosty. – About the man with the green eyes, about Bob. I don't recall everything they did to us, but I recall more than enough.

– We're going after them, right? They're at the top… of the list?

– We *will* get them, he snarled. – They're gonna regret that they were ever conceived.

They held hands, held hard.

– And I dream of the dragon, he said. – Spitting fire, it's roasting the Earth. Flapping its wings, it is the very Storm ravaging land and sea.

She shivered, unable to stop herself.

Outside were sounds of engines and people passing by, faint sounds, hardly real at all.

She moved closer to him, rubbing her skin against his, looking at him, clearly fascinated.

– You have such pretty eyes, she said, in a mumbling voice, her lips pushed at his shoulder. – I wish mine were just as pretty.

– They will be, he said. – In time.

She bent forward, to his bloody thigh. She licked off all the red. Blood flowed from her mouth as she straightened again.

– They're glowing again…

Her lips were redder than any lipstick could make them.

He licked her jaw clean. Then he kissed her.

He could see the mirror image of his eyes in hers. They mated again, not in such a hurry this time. It had been like a storm carrying her with him. The unbearable need had assaulted her, suddenly and irresistibly. Now she was able to notice how it grew in her, just as irresistible, just as much a storm in human form.

The Storm incarnated.

– We may actually be siblings…

– That doesn't bother me, he said, without the slightest hesitation. – The fear of short-term inbreeding is just as stupid as the rest of civilization's rules.

– It's all such hogwash, she grinned.

They felt it both, not just their own reactions, but that of the partner, felt the quickening pulse, the thundering heartbeat, the swelling of the shadow within.

They swallowed the blood-mixed saliva simultaneously.

++

Russel Kramer, the former vice-sheriff of Leadville lived in Bloombury. It wasn't far, but they took their time, circling in on the target, reaching its turf during early twilight. The very modern apartment building was situated close to Russel Square, not far from Tottenham Court Road and Oxford Street.

High up, high up, where the wind was blowing, on a roof nearby, Ted and Eric waited, on their second watch. Ted sensed the wind, moment by moment, as it moved, as it moved the air. Concrete dust itched in his nostrils. And it made him more astute, not less. It didn't distract him, didn't divert his attention from the target ahead. He saw the building and its surroundings clearly. Kramer was in 5b. That apartment's windows, like all the rest were covered by curtains, keeping them from seeing what went on inside. But Ted imagined he could still do so, see the shadows in there move, and speak and breathe.

When he looked through the binoculars, he felt like he was there, just outside the window, floating high above the ground, a sensation completely different from how he had felt when he had used binoculars earlier in his life. It wasn't only that. Everything. Everything felt different, felt new.

And when he concentrated, when he focused, he didn't really need help, didn't need the crutches.

He was there.

Carr rubbed his back, pain crossing his face.

– Jesus. He uttered. – As a guy with a lot of bread to burn he sure is staying put a lot.

Kramer had taken the walk around the corner to the grocery store once in the two days they had kept him under surveillance. Except for that, and the restless pacing inside, he had hardly moved.

– I think the bread might be burning holes in his pockets, Ted mused. – Perhaps he's indeed hearing the screams of his victims. One never knows.

There had been numerous phone calls. Some so loudmouthed that they had almost been able to make out the words.

Ted listened, with his head half tilted, knowing fully his way of listening resembled that of an animal, and he didn't care. He sensed the heat of Carr's eyes on his neck, his more than burning curiosity, and that did distract him, and irritated him and enraged him.

– Nothing to report, Carr spoke in the radio.

– *Nothing here, either,* they heard Caine's tired voice.

Caine always sounded tired.

Ted shifted his attention, to the streets, to Caine and McKenzie. He couldn't see them, but he could feel their presence, feel them in his deep, like flapping butterfly wings. He felt Stewart, like he always did. Stewart had left the scene after his and Tilla's shift were done, «to go home and sleep». He hadn't looked tired though, even though she had. She was there, inside Ted, as well, but she, like Stewart, was an eagle, creating a storm every time the wings flapped.

– There's a new guy in the street, Carr reported laconically.

Ted saw him. A blind beggar with long white hair and beard. Ted felt nothing from him. To his extrasensory senses, his ESP, it was as if the man wasn't there at all.

What's *wrong* with me?

I lie, Stewart told him. That's what I do. I lie by telling the truth.

A lot of people were passing back and forth down there. This was a fairly busy area. He felt them, felt them all.

– I stare into the darkness and see the fire…

– What was that? The curiosity in Carr's eyes intensified.

– Nothing, Ted mumbled. – Nothing important.

– You're impatient, kid, Carr grinned. – Like a young lion before its first hunt. It's perfectly normal, and nothing to worry about. Not as long as you eagerly study the older lions, how they can wait, rest in hiding for hours, before they strike.

Ted looked at him, stared at him.

– My drill sergeant at boot camp always used such analogies, Carr said apologetically, grinning some more.

It was as if his eyes turned darker then, somber.

– And I remembered his words, as I, Patrick, Andrew and our platoon hid outside a Vietcong camp, hid there for hours, sweating and freezing, while our limbs stiffened and our minds turned numb, until the attack order was finally given.

Ted felt that, too, as if he was there, as if he was drowning in Eric's story, his memories, and then there was more…

Caine's voice buzzed loudly through the radio:

– He's outside. I repeat: He's outside, and he's heading your way.

Ten seconds passed, fifteen, more… and then they saw him. The moment he appeared it was as if a burning pike was thrust through Ted's head.

– You don't look good, Carr said, shaking his head. – What is it?

– Killer headache, Ted gasped.

And it wasn't bullshit either. Just then, it felt as if it was actually going to kill him. Images assaulted him that he couldn't possibly make sense of.

– I'm okay, he stated.

Blinking, desperately attempting to clear his vision.

Kramer's walk down there was like a dance, one that resonated in his head.

– He will walk past the grocery store, Carr said. – I'm willing to wager on it. Look at that fat slob. It is as if someone has put a rocket in his ass.

Ted giggled and pain like a lawnmower cut into his head.

It felt like the worst of hangovers, when you writhed on the bed and you feared that the excruciating pain would never go away.

Something… pushed at the insides of his brain. Soldiers marched down there, and they fired their guns, as death and carnage unfolded.

Kramer passed the entrance of the grocery store. Carr grabbed the radio.

– Don't…

– He's past his Sunday trip point. Eric spoke into the radio. – I repeat: he's past his Sunday trip. The weather is good and the course is clear…

– *Don't!*

Ted pulled the radio from Carr's hands, but lost it and it smashed against the concrete.

– Damn it, it's a fucking trap. *I told you!*

Eric shuddered. Of what he saw up there, and what he saw down there.

Ted Warren's demonic face burned at him.

Carr looked down at the street. Kramer left quickly. Suddenly, he walked that much faster, almost to the point of running. Caine and McKenzie walked a bit behind him, one at the left sidewalk and the other on the right. Carr shook his head, not certain what to believe. Ted poked him in the side, making his attention turn further down the street. And then Carr saw it, a pattern in which he was intimately familiar: Eight men, in groups of four chasing the two chasing Kramer.

– There are eight more ahead of Kramer, Ted pointed out.

Indecision rode Carr, making him stay put, making him deaf and mute.

Ted grabbed his arm, grabbed his eyes, held them, held them in a vice. And Eric Carr feared he was caught in a forge hotter than that of any blacksmith.

– You stay here. *Don't* warn them. Give me some time and then, on my signal, you warn them and start jumping up and down and scream, cause so much havoc that you possibly can.

This wasn't a request, but a command, and Eric had learned very early to distinguish between the two, and disobedience didn't even occur to him.

Cold sweat broke all over his skin.

Ted ran to the other end of the roof. There was a ladder there. He walked down it, practically slid down it, without a solid grip. The friction burned his palms. Fly, a voice not a voice told him. Use the airways. But he didn't dare, not even in his present fervor. He landed hard, but didn't fall.

He walked, to the point of running after the eight slowly advancing on the two chasing Kramer. The eight in front of Kramer had slowed down so much that he had almost caught up with them. The trap was about to spring. Caine and McKenzie didn't seem worried, didn't seem worried at all.

One of the men in the back row wore a scarf around his neck. It was red, and to Ted it was glowing in fire. The dreams spoke to him, and the river inside him turned into a waterfall. He shortened the distance to one of the quartets in front to ten steps or so. The sound of their steps thundered in his ears. His feet touched the ground, but there was no sound. He imagined the neck clothed in the red, suddenly *blood red* scarf, imagined a snake twining the thick neck, the muscular body, and *squeezed.*

The man grabbed his neck in front and fell on the sidewalk. The snake stopped squeezing. It took a bite, a big bite. The man screamed in despair and pain, a scream so heartbreaking that it cut into everybody hearing it, into the most hardened of men and mice. Ted felt the pure joy like acid in his veins.

Everybody, far and close turned towards the man writhing on the ground, horror written in their faces. And then Carr began to jump up and down and scream, and perform the greatest of shows up on the roof. The eight were further distracted. Ted registered that McKenzie and Caine drew their guns as he attacked the three closest enemies, as they, too, reached for their guns. Faster than thought, than dream he jumped them, kicked one in the chest. The enemy coughed and fell backwards. He took the two others' heads and smashed them together, heads cracking like eggshells, leaving hardly more than soft brain tissue spread across the sidewalk. He heard shots be fired and more screams. People began desperately to run in all possible directions. The other four lay dead on the sidewalk, their skin cracked open by numerous bullet holes. McKenzie and Caine put their guns back inside the coats. They were unhurt. Ted scanned the area. Kramer and the other eight were nowhere to be seen. The streets were practically empty. It was over, before it had even begun.

Eric came running. Not breathing hard, but still out of breath.

Question marks dominated his face. The other two were too experienced to reveal their confusion and bewilderment openly, but Ted sensed it. It pulsed and waxed within him, and it made him stronger.

– What happened? Carr wondered. – I saw that guy fall, and figured that was as good a sign as any I had ever seen…

– I figured it was a great opportunity to attack, Ted replied, sort of. – I don't know what the fuck happened. I guess he got sick. It was a great distraction. We got lucky…

– He's covered in blood, Eric mumbled. – Dead like a doornail. Looks like his veins just cracked open.

– Where's Kramer? Ted asked him sharply.

– He ran off, Carr reported, – covered by the eight men. I heard one of them scream «fall back, fall back». The cowards looked seriously spooked. I think they picked up on our valued tactic, using the Underground to lose those who would pursue them.

He grinned, pleased beyond words.

– Nine hardened, dangerous men, Caine said. – Scared to such a degree that they were running like rats.

McKenzie bent down over the three other men.

– This one is practically done for. All his ribs are broken. The other two are… well… removed from consideration. You're some piece of work, kid.

He doesn't know, Ted thought. He doesn't have the imagination necessary to conceive of what happened. I'm not so sure about Eric. He sees everything, but Caine…

Caine stared at the remains of the heads on the two bodies before him, stared at them with open terror, unable to even look at the dark figure in their midst.

Ted Warren looked down at the dead men, feeling nothing, feeling nothing but joy.

They pulled away. McKenzie pulled Ted with him. Warren shook his hand off, but kept walking. They turned two corners before increasing the speed slightly as they entered Russel Square Station. They took the tube to Green Park, before leaving the underground and calmly walking back on Piccadilly. There were the sounds of sirens, and police cars constantly passing them, but no one stopped. They returned to the headquarters, their base of operations, without further incidents of any kind.

Returned to the fortress, guarded by a thousand eyes and ears, nothing of it apparent.

– The… help you have acquired? Eric said lightly.

– Yes?

– They're good. There are a few who do expose themselves fairly easily, but some are really undetectable, even if you know they're there. I certainly won't claim the capability to spot everybody.

– Neither will I, McKenzie said. – They're prime recruitment material, that's for sure.

They waited, waited until long after the government man had left them.

– The question is for what, Caine said, also looking at Ted when he said that.

That didn't bother Ted. He was in such an exalted mood that he almost took off completely.

Tilla was in the hall. She ran to him. They embraced. There were others there. The two of them left, sought solitude. He could still sense the others, but they were nowhere near the two of them. She looked at him, immediately knowing something had happened. He told her what had happened, what he had experienced.

– I feel joy, he said.

– Good. She kissed him fiercely, even fiercer than she usually did.

– Aren't you worried?

– No, she stressed. – We need to be powerful, need to be ruthless, to survive in this world.

Her kiss lingered, as it always did. She kissed him again. Her lips pushed against his. He could feel it as each part of her skin met and parted with his. She was so good at it, so very good.

– You're not Mike, she assured him. – You will never be Mike.

And then she added, ambiguously, perhaps deliberately so:

– You've surpassed him in all ways, and would have crushed him like a bug if he was here, now. You're far more than he ever was…

– Yes, he said, kissing her on the cheek. – And a lot of it is probably due to the push our benefactors have given us.

– Mike pushed you and kept you down, she said. – And to fight yourself free from his tyranny you had to grow beyond him. They pushed you, suppressed your growth. And in order to free yourself from their beyond cruel machinations you had to dig deeper into yourself than ever before.

– And I'm gonna show them my appreciation, he said. – I'm gonna show them how grateful I am.

She looked calmly, exalted at him, at the beast in all its power, and she wasn't afraid.

They walked to the living room, to the upper living room, which was somewhat more private. Linda and John were there, and Sandy and Pete, McKenzie, Caine and Carr.

– Stewart left, Linda said, before Ted could speak up. – Right after you, without telling us anything about where he was going or what his errand was.

– He took one of his suitcases, Tilla said, frowning. – The small one.

Ted began laughing. The others stared at him, as if he wasn't right in the head, except Tilla and Caine.

– We need to laugh a bit, McKenzie said pointedly. – Why don't you share the fun with us?

– The graybeard, the blind beggar… was Stewart, Ted said.

They stared incredulous at him, before slowly nodding.

– He did disappear sometimes during the skirmish, Carr nodded slowly. – He probably went after Kramer, right? And totally undetected to boot.

I've seen him in disguise before, but never this thorough. That son of a bitch…

He shook his head in admiration.

– I agree. Caine shook his head. – It's almost uncanny.

And Caine looked as lost as ever.

Ted boiled within, but nothing of it revealed itself.

It was a message, a signal, to them, but most of all to me, showing off. He realized, knew more than the rest of us fools did that Kramer would have an escort, a heavy guard. Well, he got some worth of performance, that patronizing…

He looked out of the window in the bedroom. The gray fog outside merely intensified the pressure within. He heard the door open and close. Felt soft hands across his chest, a wet kiss in the neck.

– Get the HELL out! He snarled.

She gasped. The red mane was pulled off his shoulder. She ran away. Not even closing the door behind her. Damn cunt!

It lasted four hours before Stewart returned. They waited for him.

– The Lone Ranger returns, Carr applauded.

– Is there any food left, Tilla? Stewart wondered.

– We left something for you, she said quickly. – I'll get it.

She wouldn't have been able to identify the feeling she sensed in him before, but now she did. Pent up aggression like in Ted in the bedroom. Like in Ted still.

– So, you decided to go at it alone? Ted asked, calm as ice.

– I did what I had to do, to get a breakthrough, Cousin, Stewart replied with the same, eerie calm. – You of all people should understand that.

– But you got a bit more than you bargained for, didn't you, *Fontaine?*

There was laughter, uncertain and brittle, among the others.

– I feel that you should at least have given us a hint, Stewart, McKenzie said sourly. – Being prepared is always an advantage when one is attempting to survive deadly encounters.

– I figured, as always you didn't need me to hold your hand, Stewart said ironically. – It wasn't that much of a risk, was it? I'm not speaking to ghosts here, am I?

– But we did what we were supposed to do? Caine said, a clear edge in his voice. – You, on the other hand…

– … lost him, Ted completed.

– I followed him to a seedy apartment hotel off Kings Cross, Stewart said. – And yeah, I lost him. They did the classic «man through the lock» maneuver. There was nothing I could do. You would have lost him,

anyway, if I hadn't been there, and far sooner.
He felt he had to explain himself, and his insides lit up one more notch.
– I'll have someone keep an eye on the place. Ted nodded. – Did it have a name?
Mark said the name.
Watch it, kid. Watch it…
He remained in the chair. It had turned dark outside and his plate was cleaned of food. Suddenly he was alone in the room. The others didn't merely turn to ghosts, but they vanished completely. When he was still there, hours later, and Caine returned it was as if no time at all had passed.
Caine kept his distance, cautious, like a scared underling.
– So, did you notice anything else, something… beyond a normal range of things? Something you would like to talk about?
– Not, now, Frankie. No more games. I'm not in the mood.
– Okay, then. The Gambler drew breath. – Did you *see* the boy, what he *did?*
– It's very interesting. Stewart smiled. – He's surpassing my wildest expectations.
– Is that allallall you've got to saysaySAaayyyyyy
The moment Caine raised his voice everything turned haywire. Cold sweat flowed all over his body. He imagined that the walls bulged and pushed at him, to crush him. *I'm not in the mood.*
He had been warned. He walked out of the room in a more or less dignified departure. The walls in the kitchen bulged, too. He increased his speed, panic scratching at his insides.
Stewart hardly noticed that he left. Memories constantly haunted him, like they had always done. He saw Ted. He saw himself.
He had followed Kramer to the whorehouse, but inside the guy had vanished completely. Stewart had removed the disguise before entering and blamed himself for that. A lot of blind, dirty beggars visited whorehouses.
– Hello, sir, the beautiful slender and blond bitch behind the reception desk welcomed him. – Is there anything I can do for you?
– There is, actually, he had heard himself say. – I want a horny bitch, a whore, and I want the best you've got.
– That's me, she said calmly. – But if you want me, you'll have to wait until I can get a replacement here.
He walked to her, throwing a fifty-pound bill on the desk.
– Is this sufficient for you to get moving?
– You're very handsome and everything, she smiled sweetly, still

convinced she could handle this adequately. – There are a lot of others available…

– You're not listening. He didn't raise his voice, but it still changed, turned different and scary. – Get a move on, bitch, before I get angry. *Don't touch that button.*

She pulled her hand away from the desk as if she had burned herself.

– *You'll come with me,* to the best room. I'm not paying. You had that option and let it go, stupid cunt.

She rose and pushed the chair back with her legs. He reached for her. She took his hand, a distant look forming in her face.

– It isn't important, she said while they were ascending the stairs. – There aren't many customers here tonight, anyway. You're so handsome.

He hit her.

– *Listen, I'll do the talking. You will only talk when I tell you to talk.*

She nodded with huge eyes. He had to lead her. She was hardly able to move on her own, a child in his hands.

He opened the door to the room. She stumbled inside. The luxurious room embraced them. The silken sheet covering all the furniture moved under his fingers. She fell on the bed, writhing there, in her thin, transparent dress.

– He who entered the building before me, where did he go?

– He's still here, of course. She smiled enticingly. – Enjoying what the house has to offer.

He slapped her, and kept slapping her. It hurt, but she was unable to scream.

– You'll get no more chances with me, he said, in a crushing blow.

– He walked right through here, she whimpered. – Many people do that, many of the bosses. I speak the truth. I swear. Please. I swear. P-please.

Mark undressed while she spoke. He patted her on the wet, warm cheek. She writhed in ecstasy and fear.

– I believe you, little cunt. I believe you…

And he kept up the pressure, didn't think about letting up.

– There are slaves, here, right? He spat. – Both boys and girls. But you're not. You're a Keeper?

– Yes, she said, unresisting now.

He was now the totality of her will and thoughts. And he felt joy beyond belief. He fucked her, didn't bother with removing her dress. She had an orgasm instantly, but he didn't. She moaned deliriously, constantly.

– *Listen.* The horrible voice. The moaning desisted, but not the writhing. *– You will forget all this. You've never seen me or heard me. You fell* *asleep. If the police ever ask you about what's going on here, you'll confess and tell everything you know.*

A thin, sleepy, joy-filled voice:

– … not seen nor heard… fell asleep… tell…

His face was ruthless in his total insensitivity. She was a big girl, but now she felt tiny. He squeezed her arms, and she moaned louder, in joy, not pain. He dived into her, dived deep inside, deep into himself, until all control slipped away. What did she matter to him? Nothing. Less than a grain of sand, existing only for his pleasure. He stared into her eyes all the time, to better see his own. They had never burned brighter, more intense. He bit her in the shoulder, drawing blood. In that moment she came for the second time, and he came, too. Then he didn't remember anything anymore.

++++++

She had survived. But when he was once more capable of thinking somewhat normally, he saw that it had been a close shave. She was pale and her breath was beyond labored. More than half an hour had passed. How many times he had taken her during that time he couldn't say. He could only recall dreams, confused dreams. Tall flames. People in a circle, ghosts in a world of matter. The jungle, the hunter and his prey. He smiled as he dressed. Everything was warmth inside him. He clapped his hands before her face. She didn't move a muscle.

A few days later, early on a frost-cold morning, that warmth was still there. He crossed the bridge inside St. James's Park with Ted by his side. Caine and Tilla, Linda and John walked thirty steps or so in front of them. On his right was a wastebasket. Fog drifted over the pond. The trees were clothed in gray. The many streetlights couldn't light the shimmering dark. And he saw it all, felt it all, down to the last molecule.

They had caps on their heads and scarves covering most of their faces. It didn't raise suspicion, not today, in this cold.

– So, what are we *doing* here?

The sharp, impatient voice behind the scarf cut through all his armor, impossible to ignore.

– The man between us and the others is Burke Adams, a Sergeant with Scotland Yard, he explained. – We're going to recruit him, win him over to our cause. We need numbers on our side, and he will provide that. We're going to turn his world upside down, and he will never be the same.

Ted turned his attention to the man about twenty steps ahead of them. He felt ready, like a predator catching up with the prey. They had followed the fairly young man in a bowler hat from the other side of the park. Stewart had pointed him out without really needing to do so. The six of them had become so finely tuned by now that they knew what the others were about to do before they did it. As Ted and Stewart closed in on the man from behind, the four others slowed their pace, so they were almost exactly at the man's side the moment Ted and Stewart caught up with him. They grabbed Adams, pushed two guns into his back.

– Will you please follow us, sir? Stewart grinned. – Don't worry. We won't harm you. We desire nothing but a brief conversation. You'll probably not even be late for work…

The man stiffened in their grip, but let himself be led off.

– He just has to worry, John giggled. – Or he's a fool.

– What are you? Adams spoke nervously. – IRA?

– Everything will be explained, sir.

– You're really some piece of work, Mark, Ted said. – A true expert at misdirection. As usual you didn't even try to answer the question.

This didn't exactly calm their prisoner.

– We're not IRA, Ted told Adams. – We're far more dangerous than they can ever be.

– You're not exactly *helping* here, Stewart said exasperated.

– Why don't you kind people take your argument elsewhere, Adams joked. – You can always seek me out again after you're done.

– I knew you had a great sense of humor…

Adams shook in fear. They didn't have to hold him to notice that.

Stewart pushed him on.

They took him to one of the populated houses within the park, empty now. Tilla ran ahead and opened the door, opened it right before they walked through it, in such elegant timing. They pushed him inside, and Tilla closed and locked the door behind them.

Adams' heart-rate slowed down. He turned less pale, calmer. There was no reason for this to happen as far as Ted was concerned, but it still happened. Stewart stood close to him all the time, clearly concentrating, focusing on keeping the sergeant calm.

Stewart removed the scarf and headgear, and the others did the same. Adams frowned, as he stared at Stewart, then at the others, and back to Stewart again.

– Again, allow me to apologize for the way we contacted you, Caine said. – But we didn't have much of a choice.

– Do you know who we are? Stewart asked Adams.

– He knows. Ted said. – You were right, Mark. This is a man who's actually reading incoming bulletins.

They saw, easily enough, a deep sense of unreality assault the policeman.

– I do recognize some of you… And then, exasperated, almost aggressively: – What's *going on* here?

– But you don't think we fit in the same picture, Burke? Stewart inquired. – You're wrong. We do!

Adams couldn't quite find the words.

– So, tell me who I am?

– You're Elmont Fontaine, Adams exclaimed. – You've changed. The eye color is different. So is the hair and face, but it is you. You're wanted by Interpol for the murder of the police Prefect of Paris.

– I was Elmont Fontaine for a brief period of my life, the other man corrected him. – My «real» name is Mark Stewart. I've always had this eye and hair color. Information to the contrary is erroneous.

– *Stewart…*

That name was also clearly familiar to him.

– And to make it clear once again: We have no intention of killing you or harming you. The reason for this is that we need your help, your urgent help.

– I don't think I can actually help *you* much, Adams said. – Unless you're going to turn yourself in.

Everybody laughed. That clearly unnerved him. He had no idea what was happening. and it confused and worried him.

– What we want you to do is to sample my fingerprints, get yourself to work in time, and return here during lunch break.

– Your *fingerprints?* But… why?

– They've never been taken by anybody. I want to emphasize that my case isn't the most important here. But convincing you of my innocence is the first step towards all the improbable events we'll tell you about later.

Stewart pulled a white sheet and an inkpad from his pocket, and put it on the table in front of them.

– Now?

Adams surveyed Stewart's fingers one by one. He nodded to himself, confident that they were not faked.

– You should feel honored… being the first to see my fingerprints close up.

– But that can't be right, Adams protested with strains of desperation in his voice. – I've read quite a bit about you and the case. It's a classic. According to the reports your prints were on the knife.

– They're not mine, Stewart replied. – I never touched the knife, never even got near it.

He reached out his hands again, and Adams took them, hesitatingly, as if they were hot, a hot stove. It was done quickly, almost in a rush.

Adams was held back as he carefully folded the sheet and put it away in the plastic bag provided, as he was about to leave.

– Just a little more of your time, Stewart said. – We need a promise from you, an oath. That you will return alone, and that you won't tell of this to anyone.

– Not even to your parrot, Tilla said cheerfully.

Adams felt even worse then, even more detached from himself and reality.

– Yes, Ted said. – We know about your parrot.

– How do you know you can trust me on my word? What happens if I refuse, if I may ask?

– You're honesty incarnated, Linda snorted. – A true boy scout.

– Why did you choose me? Why the hell did you?

– You don't take orders easily. You're not exactly the run of the mill obedient civil servant.

– You'll be too late for work for the first time since you suffered through the mumps last year, Caine pointed out. – What we can tell you is that we had to overcome your initial, inevitable distrust.

– For what purpose.

– During lunch break… everything will be made clear.

Adam stood there, hesitating a moment or two longer, before nodding.

– You have my word.

It seemed easy to utter those words. They sensed no deception in him.

– Don't even think of implying anything to George Bowers, Stewart cautioned him.

– That won't be easy. He's my superior.

– He's corrupt, Ted snarled. – Rotten like a dead tree.

Adams clearly shook assaulted by the contempt in the young voice.

They saw him leave.

Daylight broke slowly outside. They sat there in the twilight dawn, waiting and pacing. John played with his gun. It was similar to a type he had used for years as a promising sports shooter. Ted knew that. He remembered. And John could handle the weapon so much better, now. Ted saw that, too, both seeing and feeling the ease his hands handled the deadly weapon. John looked at him, clearly ill at ease.

John had the cold, too, the same numbness Ted felt like a knife inside himself. Linda played with her knife, with the black blade. She looked constantly at Ted, and her insides were burning ice. He felt that, felt the black blade being twisted in his guts. In her eyes he saw undying devotion and love.

There was music, as he and Tilla danced, as they spent time. They danced in the other part of the room from where the others sat, in a room of their own.

– Linda is exactly like us, Tilla whispered. – She needs someone to kill.

The phone rang. The music played on. Stewart took the phone, and said a single word. He listened for a while before hanging up.

– Eric says everything looks normal. None of our stations have anything unusual to report.

– So, he isn't sure, Ted nodded to Tilla.

Time passed, slowly, so torturously slow. Francis and John went to the windows every ten second or so. The others never did. Linda walked to Ted and Tilla, and joined their dance. Her face was impassive, stoic, and so were her insides, her volcanic iceberg. She kissed Tilla on the lips. Tilla responded, impulsively, automatically. Linda played with the knife. It was as if it was a part of her, extending her reach.

All of them sat quietly in the chairs, on the couch, waiting, no longer physically pacing. But the unrest was visible in every tiny move they made.

Adams finally returned, during his lunch break. John saw him approach through the dark winter day, and signaled the others. They took their positions.

– He's alone, Stewart said calmly, with just a hint of excitement in his voice.

Linda opened the door for Adams, pulling him inside. He stopped right there. The look of incredulity in his face hadn't lessened any. He surveyed all of them, kept his eyes on Stewart.

– I don't understand… why did you flee?

– I was young… and scared, Stewart replied, his voice a bland nothing. – And I didn't trust the government that much. I still don't.

– Fifteen years on the run, and you come to me, now, after all this time… *Why?*

– We will get to that, get back to all the questions you might have about me, about the others here, about everything. But first we need to know that you're convinced, Burke Adams, that you're convinced beyond words about my innocence, so that you may never have doubts later. Why don't you go through it all, in your own words?

Adams drew his breath, straightening subconsciously.

– I went through everything we had on you, on both of your names… You've done a lot of questionable things through the years, both before and after the incident in question, but you've never been charged with anything except for that. You were seen entering the police headquarters, the Prefect's office. To the desk you claimed you had an appointment. The Prefect confirmed that. You and the Prefect spent several minutes together, alone in his office, or so was believed. The Prefect fired one shot and then he screamed. He was found dead in his chair, a knife buried deeply in his chest, his own knife, from the drawer. You were found on the couch, at the other side of the room, in a catatonic state. At least that was what was believed, until the ambulance stopped for red light, and you vanished like a ghost.

That word again, Ted thought.

Stewart nodded.

– That was another reason it all turned into a matter of face lost. But they never caught me.

– The autopsy revealed that the knife had been used to stab at close range. But there was no blood on you or your clothes. But you were still charged. The fingerprints on the knife were claimed to be yours… but they are not. Studying it carefully makes it a dodgy case from the start, but knowing what I know, now, makes it all absolutely clear: You are innocent. Beyond doubt. Even a hatchet court will find it hard to convict you. It's more than clear that there was a third person present that day.

He cried out the last few words.

– We weren't wrong about you, Burke.

Stewart smiled.

– A pleasure meeting you, Burke, The Gambler said. – I'm Francis Caine. Say hello to John Jackson, Linda Cousin, Tilla Stevens and Ted Cousin.

Close to paralyzed Adams accepted the hands reaching out to his.

– I did research in the other matter, too, he said astonished. – I wasn't wrong. This is unbelievable. What have you kids been doing? What in gods name happened to you? I…

They told him everything, including Eric's part of the story, everything he needed to know. They showed and tell, and made a believer of him.

He just kept shaking his head, even long after he had stopped doing it physically.

– You must understand that our opponents are not «criminals», as you perceive them, Stewart said to him, as if speaking to a child, deliberately patronizing. – They're your employers, your masters, and their servants are present in all levels of society. One word to a man you think you can trust, and you're dead… or worse. The old slogan that if you can't trust anybody you know, trust a stranger, truly applies here.

– Then, I can't see how I can be of much help to you.

– We're like killer whales against the huge whale. We're enough to give it small wounds, but not enough to kill it. You're ideally placed in the hierarchy to supply us with a considerable number of policemen, a reserve, if you will, one that will be there the day we'll need it.

Adams' world had been turned upside down, and he still reeled from it, was still shaken, and it didn't let up. He still strived to pull himself together, as he was about to leave.

– Strive to behave normally, Caine cautioned him some more, and he did feel cautioned. – In fact, it's paramount that you do. We'll be in touch.

Ted stopped him, as he was about to leave.

– I need a favor, he said. – It concerns a certain Van Hoffa. He's hardly more than a nuisance to us, but if he gets eager, he might cause a stir, and we can't afford that right now.

– I know that, Adams nodded. – I'll get him off your back, at least for a while… off Ted Warren's back.

– He's more than we could ever hope for, Caine whistled, as the sergeant hurried away from the house, as they, too, left.

– In a limited, useful way, Tilla nodded.

Stewart turned to Ted, clearly agitated.

– What was that about? Do you want to jeopardize everything?

– On the contrary, Ted said, very patronizing. – That was added insurance, not further jeopardizing…

And they stared at each other for a long time, before finally calming down, after a fashion.

– Killer Whales *are* predators, Tilla said to Ted later that day. – They tear their prey apart, and then they devour it.

– And the whale isn't, Ted nodded.

– We're so far away from home, she said, tears in her eyes. – So very far from the life we're born to live.

– We, all of us, not only us here, but all humans, all over the world are damaged goods, he said, hesitatingly at first, before his voice rose to a higher pitch. – Society has screwed us all up.

– Society is screwed up, she said. – Not so strange, then that its population is screwed up, too.

They parted. They kissed and parted, never really apart, not anymore, both happy and sad.

Ted met Pete and Sandy in the hall. They approached, smiling, but a bit irresolute. Ted didn't care. He was used to that.

– I heard Hoffa is out of *circulation* for a while, Pete grinned. – That will give us some room, at least for a limited time.

– We need it. Ted said.

– And we have it, Pete said, – thanks to you. You did it. You took care of Van Hoffa. Turner never did, no matter how badly he treated his own girls and «ours», or threatened our territory, all the atrocities he committed that Turner never dared himself. I think he saw that shit as a kindred soul. One to aspire to, or something.

– Don't worry about Van Hoffa, Ted said. – If he should be stupid enough to persist in his ways, in spite of the warning he has been given, I'll send him back to the hell he came from. You can bet on that.

And you? What hell do you come from?

Pete walked off, with a smile, and even more respect and admiration in his eyes.

Sandy remained. She blushed and looked shyly up at him, looking at him, studying him with those big eyes of hers. That did throw him off a bit. She wasn't exactly the shyest of persons.

– I want to thank you, she said.

– For what? He wondered, nonplussed.

– You've given us a lot, she said solemnly. – I feared you at first, we all did. But that changed, slowly, imperceptibly. I don't know exactly when. Many small drops made a pond, I guess. Most of us respect you now, no longer fearing you… too much.

He saw it, saw how she grew there on the spot, how she stood up for herself, and he felt joy, kicking himself for caring.

– Above anything else, you've given us *dignity,* a belief in ourselves. We're all birds with damaged wings, but you've taught us that that shouldn't keep us from flying.

There was something strangely, dizzyingly familiar about her, something he had noticed the very first time he saw her, that day in St. James's Park, even though he was positive he had never met her before that. She had entered his dreams, and in his dreams, he did know her. He had to strain himself to not give himself away.

Stewart had also looked strangely at her, noticing it, whatever it was.

She kissed him on the cheek, shyly, before rushing off, flying, as if a great burden had been lifted from her heart.

– Another poet. Another poet in rags. Another bitch in heat. You certainly know how to pick them.

Linda. Linda's voice. When he turned and looked, she was there no longer.

Rage rose in him, as sudden and uncontrolled and ravaging as it always did. He took a shower. It didn't help any. It was as if the water turned to vapor the moment it hit his skin.

Confusion accompanied the rage, as it often did.

He walked through the hallway, towards the shimmering dark light ahead. Thoughts, concepts raced through his mind as never before.

Something had always… bothered him about the scene in the classroom outside Trinidad. And now he knew why. He had been too far away, even too far away for anyone to suspect him of anything, at least not in the heat of the moment. There had never been a chance for him to reach the stumbling boy's foot using… conventional means. So, he had reached out with his mind, subconsciously, knowing in his deeper parts what had not been evident, not until now, in his conscious mind.

Confusion faded, at least in part, and clarity took its place. The rage remained.

Stewart and Caine sat alone in the living room. The television was on. They didn't really watch it or hear the words coming from it. It was just a distraction, one more in a long line.

– The detectives investigating the shootout near Russel Square said, at the press conference that one of the men found dead on the scene may not have taken part in the hostilities at all, may not even have been an intended victim. The autopsy suggests that the man had a rare disease, causing his blood vessels to burst.

– He caused the man's blood vessel to burst, Stewart stated and calmly turned off the TV. – Very careless. I've told him not to worry, though. As you can witness first hand, modern society always strives to find the least worrying explanation to everything.

The Gambler wasn't particularly happy about this topic of conversation. He was relieved that he didn't need to listen more to the news.

– Some performance you entertained us with today, he noted. – The stage has missed a great talent in you. Unless you told the truth and the truth and nothing but the truth… Are you truly Not Guilty of murdering the dear Prefect?

– Did I say that? Stewart asked mildly. – Did you ever hear me claim that I didn't do it?

– But then…

– I most certainly killed him. There was just a snarl. – That rat deserved to die.

He drew a knife from his jacket, pushing its point at the thumb. Then he left it at the table and let it spin. Caine stared as if hypnotized at him.

– I used the knife on him, and it slid into his chest, and punctured his heart. All the green blood flowed.

– But how? Caine asked anxiously.

The knife stopped. Suddenly it stopped. Its point pointed right at him.

– It was pretty spontaneous, done in haste and affect. I've done it just that one time. I've never been able to repeat it, even though I've tried often.

– *He did it like this.*

First a tiny vibration. Then the blade rose up in the air without anybody getting close to it, stopping a brief moment right before the wall, before there was another tug, and the tip of the blade hit the wall at the other side of the room with a loud crack.

Ted Warren stood in a relaxed pose in the doorway. Caine stared at him, blind and deaf and mute.

The knife vibrated hard in the wall.

Chapter Twenty

The Twilight Storm began, as small wisps of clouds in the horizon.

A handkerchief floated in the air in a dark room. Mark Stewart danced with the piece of cloth. His face was sometimes calm, sometimes serene, sometimes marked by intense concentration.

He tried knives, too, but even though they vibrated on the floor, they stayed put.

– One of our guys was harassed today, Pete said, facing the half moon circle of people in the upper living room. – Van Hoffa was released from his holding cell this morning, awaiting his trial, but these were strangers, not his people. And they didn't seem… territorial at all, but wanted to know things. They were… curious.

The eight sat there without speaking, a good while after Pete had left.

– They're on to us, John said nervously. – And the rumors are flying.

– You're right, Stewart said. – Even if they aren't on to us, they will be soon. The time to act is now. A man named Verheyen, a South African, is holding a charity ball on New Year's Eve. That's it. That is our chance, our window of opportunity.

– It *is* him, Ted said, – one of the High Ones, one of the exalted masters.

His voice was thick with sarcasm and hatred.

Impatience ravaged both him and Stewart. Tilla and Caine observed that in big and small ways. She found Ted in the attic one day, a large room covering the entire floor. He sat on his ass, with his back to her, with his feet crossed.

– The walls are shaking, he said, very distinct, very clear. – I recognized you by the sound of your steps. Every person has distinct, easily recognizable steps, did you know that?

– I heard Mark say that to Francis, too, she said. – Both about the walls and the steps.

– I see ruins, Ted said. – And I hear quiet and raging winds. The Shadow speaks to me, speaks to me about the world.

Dust whirled in the air around him, turning into mist.

His voice had the strange, ghoulish quality, making her cold, making her warm.

She sat down on her ass, too, before him, crossing her legs. His eyes cleared, spotted the knife in her hand.

– Give me your hand, she said. – Give me your arm.

He brushed his sleeve away from his wrist, from his lower left arm, and gave her his arm, the one with discolored skin, where the many needle marks were still visible.

She grabbed it, and then she stabbed it, stabbed it right through. The point of the blade appeared on the other side, a deep, ghastly cut.

He yelped in pain, stared at it, strangely detached.

– Concentrate, she whispered. – Concentrate on closing the wound, on *healing* yourself.

He did, as he watched the blood flow. The worst of the flow stopped almost immediately, but the wound was still open. As the fluid hit the floor it hissed and burned. They stared at it, as it seemed to increase in volume, to spread beyond reasonable confines.

Then he felt it, a heat rising from his depths, something that he had experienced before, but that he now was fully aware of. The flood of blood stopped. The wound closed. They both stared at it, and stared even more, as the needle marks faded as well. He made a fist, and it hurt. He made another fist five, ten seconds later, and it hurt less. They stared amazed at the wound as it cauterized itself, as even the mark of the wound faded, and nothing but unblemished skin remained.

Tilla stabbed herself, quickly, hesitatingly, a smaller wound, and then she sat there, concentrating, closing her eyes, opening her eyes. Minutes passed by. Nothing happened, except that the initial small flow of blood finally stopped.

– You heal it, she said.
He took the arm, concentrating, concentrating hard.
– I'm taking from you, he said, shaking his head in desperation. – Not giving.
– Try to… reverse the flow.
He tried. She could see it, feel it.
– I can't do it, he choked. – I can't.
They sat there for minutes, embracing, rocking back and forth.
– It's all right, she whispered. – It's all right.
The wind was blowing. Time was flying.
– No one goes outside alone, Stewart told Ted.
– No one goes anywhere alone, Ted told the assembly of about thirty people in the great hall. – Not on big errands, not on small, not during any circumstances.
He sensed their doubt, their distrust, so he left behind any detached approach.
And he told them the entire story. He felt Stewart's hostility as he did so, but that made him only more determined.
– In my more despairing moments I feel regret because I involved you, he said somberly, before his voice turned ragged, turned forceful, turned hard. – But then I remind myself you're involved anyway, because you may at any time be the victims of any machinations set in motion by those in power, and you are, every second of your life. Don't make the mistake of thinking this has nothing to do with you. You can run, but you can't hide.
One night, Caine was roused from troubled sleep by loud voices, scary voices. He fumbled for seconds, eternities, before finding the light switch on the wall. And then he realized that the voice, the voices came from the bed beside him, from this very room. The different voices came from Stewart. Caine recognized the childish voice from the cabin in Colorado.
– No… no… Not again… not-one-more-time.
Then everything turned indistinct again. The large body threw itself back and forth on the bed, sweating, moaning.
A tape recorder, Caine thought. A kingdom for a tape recorder.
Stewart's eyes were open, but what he saw had nothing to do with this room. The eyes began glowing and the blanket was as if torn off his body and landed in a corner. The bright bulb exploded.
– MOTHERRR
It was close to christmas. They didn't participate in it, not even remotely, but they couldn't help but notice it. They saw it, of course, the

advertising, people rushing in and out of stores, even more stressed out than they usually were.

– Look at them all, Tilla snarled. – Running around like rabbits, hoping for an extra carrot or two.

– More false joy, hypocrisy and compassion, Linda spat in contempt, equally aggravated.

It affected them all, alienated them even more from mundane life, and that pleased them.

– Today is December 21st, Ted emphasized in front of the assembly in the great hall. – This is the shortest day, the longest night celebrated in ancient times, before christianity mucked it up by moving it and then splitting it in two. This is the day and night of renewal, the true New Year's Eve.

– Come, join the circle, Tilla called. – The circle of fire.

Everybody did, even McKenzie, very hesitatingly.

They sat there, in the presence of candles, in the fire of shadows, holding hands. Ted and Tilla touched all hands, as they parted the circle, as they left for its center, its depth.

– We've got tonight, Tilla said. – No matter what may happen later. We've got tonight.

– Sandy, Ted called. – Approach.

And Sandy approached, tentatively, hardly able to look up at first.

She looked up, and turned, turned to look at them all, as she stood at the center of the circle, the circle of fire, looking down at Tilla and Ted sitting by her feet.

Tilla hummed, roughly at first, searching for the sound, the melody. Tilla sang, and they heard it, and it resonated in them all.

Fly
The bird can fly
Fly in fire, fly in shadow
It doesn't need to fear anything
Except perhaps death
The walking death
I see a valley
A circle of fire and shadow
And I dance in its shade
On the edge of its abyss

She and Ted had painfully pieced it together, practiced for hours and hours, as they pulled it from memory, as they remembered Betty, remembered the fire in her eyes.

– I remember, Tilla had said with tears in her eyes. – I *remember!*

And even now there were glimpses of tears in her eyes.

– There's no contradiction in what we're doing now, and what we'll do in the next days and weeks, Ted said. – This is quite simply a time of reflection and contemplation, one where we're seeking a different side of our inner *fire*. Humanity has always done this, before hunting, before going to war.

Sandy rose, a pride, a dignity visible in her they had merely glimpsed before.

– Voices speak to me, she said. – They've always done so. For a long time, I thought I was insane. Mommy and daddy, and everybody else convinced me I was. But I slowly realized that the voices spoke secrets, that they spoke truths.

There was a thump somewhere. Everybody shook. A loud crack. And they couldn't tell from where.

– There's something here, Ted whispered silently into Tilla's ear, and she smiled in wonder.

He felt it. There was a presence. He *felt* it. And he saw that Mark did, too. And Tilla, even if she didn't know she did.

– I saw a ghost once, another girl told them. – I passed by an old house supposed to be haunted, and I saw her clear as day, the transparent woman on the road before me. She smiled to me, and then she faded away, like a dream. But I wasn't dreaming. I know I wasn't.

– In my family line there are both Celts and Gypsies, Pete said. – It's not exactly advertised these days, but my great grandmother had no such compunctions. She spoke about an ancient, wandering tribe with fire in their eyes, The Janus Clan, encompassing all traits of humanity. They wandered this world and the other world, in equal measure. Nothing was beyond their grasp.

Stewart writhed where he sat, holding hands in the circle, an expression of pain clearly visible in his face.

Pete continued.

– She ended her days in a nuthouse, hopelessly mad they said, but I don't think she was. I know she wasn't. She was a witch. She knew more than most folks, and they hated her for it.

– There's an old legend, Sandy said. – About the Giftbringer. We're not talking physical gifts here, but that of the spirit. He or she or It came to human dwellings, asking questions, telling truths, giving them gifts of clarity… and *Magick…*

There was dance and music and song, anger, rage and joy. The four youths from Denver allowed themselves to be submerged into it, to draw strength from it, and to forget for a brief moment.

Sweaty and happy Tilla sought Ted after a dance, and couldn't find him. He wasn't in the great hall. She sought through it twice.

– Have you seen Ted? She finally asked Linda.

– No, I haven't, Linda grinned, with just a hint of hostility. – Haven't you?

He stood by a candle, holding his arm above it. His hand vanished into the shadow. Tilla approached him from behind. She saw his eyes. He knew she was approaching.

She spotted him standing between two rooms upstairs. It was as if he stood before a mirror, as if she could see his mirror image in the doorway, and she gasped, as she saw the eyes, the eyes burning in empty air.

– I can see myself in the shadow, he said.

– I can see you, too, she said. And then jokingly: – You're not seeing things…

She grabbed his hand, grabbed it hard, and spoke, a clear need present in her voice.

– I want to see me, too.

– Come, he said.

They walked upstairs. Tilla wasn't exactly surprised when she discovered that Stewart sat there, alone.

– So, you finally disengaged yourself from all the bonding and sharing, he noted neutrally, very neutral.

– Van Hoffa is out, Ted said.

Stewart wrinkled a brow, shrugging.

– Yes? And so?

Stewart noticed something, something approaching. Tilla sensed it, and expectation filled her up like water in the desert.

– The dreams tell us what to do, Ted said. – You waited for us to come here. You sought this place because you knew we would come here.

– Van Hoffa is out of prison, Tilla heard herself say, – and into our hair.

– He's small fry, Ted said, – and not really important. That's why he is ideally suited for us… for us to… test ourselves.

– You want that, too, Tilla said softly. – Don't you, Mark?

They stared at him, at his nagging doubt.

– It's dangerous, Stewart said hoarsely. – It would have been dangerous even if we weren't untrained, even if we did know what we were doing.

The other two didn't say anything more. Within Mark there was a longing, a need he hadn't truly known was there, until now. Tilla was right. He wanted to.

Candles in their hands, they walked further up the stairs, further up than they had ever ventured at night, to the attic. There was no electricity up here. There never had been. They knew that, of course. But it was different now. Everything changed, as their perception changed. The curiosity they felt about this place increased tenfold.

The moment they closed the door behind them they were met by whispers, by insistent voices they couldn't deny were real.

Then there was a draft, a wind and the candles were out, like a snapping of fingers.

It was pitch black everywhere.

Ted heard the click as Stewart cocked his gun, heard the familiar sound of the peacemaker, Ted's revolver.

– There's nothing here, Ted said sleepily, detached. – Nothing but what we bring with us.

– But that's a lot, Tilla said, with both laughter and fear in her voice.

Ted sensed how his perception… changed, changed *again*. Details emerged. The floor by his feet, the ceiling above his head, and eventually the wall at the far end of the room.

– I can see, he exclaimed dumbfounded, excited.

He wasn't certain whether or not he saw the vast room with his eyes or something else.

– There's nothing here, Mark. You don't need your gun.

– I know, Stewart finally said. – I can see, too. Not as good as you probably, but well enough.

– I can't, Tilla complained. – I can't see shit.

Stewart and Ted saw well enough. Tilla needed to be led.

Ted used a piece of chalk, and drew a circle in the dust on the floor. He had to try twice to get it somewhat right. It wasn't a perfect circle.

– It will do, he said.

– It will do, Tilla replied.

He grabbed her hands. She saw his eyes. She always did.

– My powers, he said. – My powers are *ascending*. I've been sleeping most of my life. Now I'm awake, and I'm constantly waking up…

– I can feel it, he insisted, – *feel* the birth fluid break.

They gathered inside the circle, gathered around the smaller circle within the circle.

– We undress, Ted said. – Remove everything, including watches, rings and jewelry.

They did. Denuded they sat down. The free-floating dust set on their skin. They felt it, felt it attach itself. It spoke to them and burned their skin and mind.

Mark had brought his box. He put it by Ted's left hand, where Ted had put the chalk and a photo of Van Hoffa, taken with a telescopic lens on Leicester Square.

– You're the vessel, Ted told Tilla. – Our gate to the other world.

And she froze at the cold in his voice.

– We share, Ted said, with the hollow voice. – We mix, we ssseek.

Gooseflesh broke on their skin.

He put the photo inside the smaller circle. Then he grabbed the chalk and held over the photo. He crushed the chalk to fine powder and it fell and covered the image.

Tilla felt his eyes on her, fully aware that he had turned to her, that his full attention was on her.

– Are you *sure?*

– Remember what I said, she replied. – I want this. Just as much as you, guys.

Ted and Mark nodded to each other. All three of them reached out with their left hands. Mark held out a small bottle, one of those with a powder at the bottom. A knife appeared in Ted's right. He cut the three wrists in swift, confident moves. They held hands and blood fell on the chalk, on the photo and bathed the powder in the bottle. A pool of blood covered the photo and all the dusty chalk, all the powder, before it stopped flowing. The blood mixed, on the floor, in the bottle, and in the veins connected by the entwined hands. It moved, dust to dust, vein to vein, as they watched it transfixed, watched it crawl, in the dust, on the skin, as ointment began pushing itself out of the bottle. They stared at the glow coming from the connected skin. The wounds closed, but their kin's blood moved under the skin. They felt it, physically, like a tangible force. Suddenly Tilla could see as well. What lit the room wasn't light, but something else entirely. There was a sound, a sound of falling dust, and they heard it.

– Ointment of blood, Ted said, – of life and death, bring out the Shadow. You're our vessel, taking us to the Other World.

He smeared it on Tilla's skin, indiscriminately, on one breast, on her belly, on her lips. She licked her lips. The ointment burned her lips, in her mouth. She swallowed it, and did so with great difficulties, as it kept swelling inside her mouth. Froth covered her jaw.

– I'm the vessel, she mumbled.

Ted and Mark smeared each other. They, too, licked the ointment from their lips. Mark coughed, as it pushed itself from his lips, pushed itself down his throat.

– It swells, he mumbled. – Feel how it swells.

It filled them up, until they were heavy in body, heavy in mind.

– Ssssleepy, Tilla moaned.

– We ssssleep, Ted said. – Our bodies ssssleep, but we don't.

The three arms separated from each other and fell down, hit the sedated bodies. Tilla's face changed, to that of a stranger. They could see their own faces, their own hands, see their hands move in the air, transparent ghosts in the dusty, crimson air. And then Tilla's eyes glowed in green, just as strong as theirs glowed in red.

Concentrate, Ted thought, Ted said, and they heard him, heard him loud and clear. Focus. We are not the body. The body is a vessel of sorts, a home for the traveling Shadow that has no home. This is who we are.

Jumbled, chaotic images assaulted them, brutal, inescapable images of blood and night. They saw Van Hoffa, saw his fear, saw him die a horrible death, his face frozen in paralyzing fear.

Move out of the body. Roam free. We fly over the rooftops, flap our wings in the shadow world, touch all worlds. Roam free. Roam free. Roam

There was a tear, a pain, non-localized, everywhere, as their perception suddenly changed, changed yet again, irrevocably. There was a cry, dark and rumbling, as something that was not matter rose from the paralyzed bodies.

You will fly, obey, fly us on your wings of eagles. Fly wherever we want, until worlds' end.

There was light, darkness, and then light again.

– A nightmare. We're a nightmare haunting the infinite world.

The city was down there, far and close. Distance was no more, non-existing. Time was no more. Non-existing. There was nothing, except the will, the Self.

She flew above the city/the village. Size didn't matter. She spread her wings. Their feathers cut holes in the very air, tears in the fabric of reality. The scenery shifted and changed. She spread her wings in joy, knew she could fly wherever she wanted, because she wasn't only Tilla, but Mark and Ted as well. She sensed their feathers in her gut. They steered her. She had become a new creature, carrying them where they wanted to go. She had to. Still, they let her have a certain freedom. To play, to enjoy what she had become.

A plane in the air. She wanted to take a closer look, and she was there. No delay. No distortion. She «sat» on a wing, laughing aloud. No wind, no resistance, even though she was still form, though not matter. She slipped easily inside the plane. No ordinary walls could stop her. The mortals sat there. The cockpit revealed itself to her. The pilots didn't turn. But she could see herself, the legs, the arms, the wings. She put her feet on the floor, noticing the pressure on the naked soles. Now, she was solid, now she was «matter», now she had a quantifiable existence. She concentrated lightly and the door to the passengers' cabin swung open. Smiling she walked down the aisle. There were horrified stares, people pushing themselves away from her. Then she knew they could see her. She proudly flapped her wings, outside, inside the plane. Let them see. Let them hear. She was there, she was here, simultaneously.

– Behold, mortals, you who claim there are no gods.

She patted a little boy on his head, one of the few who weren't afraid. The strongest thing she sensed in him was an unending curiosity.

They'll tell you this has never happened, that you've imagined it all. Don't listen to them.

She noticed she was being pulled away, before she really wanted to. What she was created for, her mission couldn't be denied. What she had become, what they had become gave her gooseflesh. They were rougher, more dominating, less caring. That was what dominated the metamorphosis, what ruled her.

A brief stop in a room. She couldn't hold herself back, shameless as she was. A male and a female sat on a bed, touching each other. A cry of disappointment rose from the female and the male blushed in shame.

– I don't understand. This has never happened to me before…

She laughed for a long time after she had shut off the female's shrieking voice.

The creature that was Mark/Ted/Tilla descended between the low houses, but what they/it arrived at weren't the city they/it had left. There were ruins, running, terrified people. She/it saw herself/itself in a window that was still whole. A human female with wings. A woman, but still with distinct male properties. An esthetically beautiful and thoroughly terrifying figure.

Explosions everywhere. Death rained from the sky. It was a small boy, now. It was carried through rubble by a dark-haired woman with fiery eyes. There was another glimpse, another shift in perspective, and it saw itself as a small blond and blue-eyed girl, and Death didn't come from the sky, but from the very air itself.

Mother, don't leave me, mother. The mother, blond and blue eyed like the daughter hushed her up.

Wind, violent wind in circles. Bricks and wood in wide circles. Forces of nature ravaged the town around the little girl. The creature was itself again. It levitated in front of the woman and the girl, leading them right. The sense of kinship was strong, unmistakable. All this, both the first destroyed city and this one, seemed familiar - and so very unfamiliar. There - a safe haven in the storm. The angry air wouldn't reach the two females there. Mark/Ted/Tilla left them there, a strange illogical worry haunting them.

It sought its prey, now. In what was and wasn't London Soho. The raging wind was here as well. And not here. The Storm was here. It raged within it, and nature was its friend.

It found the enemy in a room where violent gusts cracked open the walls. He tried repeatedly to rise from a shaking nest, but failed. He stared incredulous at the creature that walked through the wall towards him. It smiled at him, the most terrifying smile he had ever seen. He would die. Die soon. It knew that, and howled in triumph, howled like a giant wolf in the forest. Tilla spread her wings in joy.

It saw the little girl again. She was alone.

Alone in the storm. Fires rose everywhere. They/it knew that they/it changed its appearance. Turned horrible, turned into a monster without peer. Albert Van Hoffa screamed in nameless, infinite fear. He pushed himself at the wall, in a desperate attempt to escape the monster's claws. Escape a vision that was the worst imagination could create. Flames, a snake-like reptile, tall flames. The little girl screamed.

– Mommy, mommy, MOMMYYYYYYY

Mark screamed as well, completely beside himself, in an attempt to escape from the horror, but it was all around him, inside him. The fear stuck in the enemy like a cancer. They/it sensed it flow. The man screamed. Humans would call the sound heartbreaking, but the monster had no heart. It was content with observing with its evil, curious eyes as the pathetic man died.

Van Hoffa kept screaming as he threw himself through the non-existing wall and fell towards the ruins far below. He landed headfirst in the street, his body mashed like a potato.

To Ted it was like awakening from a deep sleep. Ages passed, as he slowly was able to move.

He saw a woman sit by a fire. Many fires, many fields, many forests. She was many. She was the same.

One blink was an eternity, and he feared his very identity was slipping away, like the peeling of an onion.

He was with Stewart an unspecified place. He put his hand on his forehead, became the young Mark Stewart. There was a man there, a presence changing into a fire-breathing monster, burning little Mark to a crisp. And the scream… THE SCREAM REACHED THE HEAVENS

Mark moaned. He fell on his side and managed just about to keep his head from hitting the floor. Tilla moaned. She crawled to Ted, pulled tight to him. He held her. The chalk-circles on the floor… they were gone. The floor was clean. The photo was where he had left it, no longer covered by chalk or dust. The blood had vanished, the image of Van Hoffa as well. The part of the image that had had him sharply represented now showed only the indistinct background.

– Fantastic, Ted whispered in awe. – Absolutely fantastic.

Caine, Pete, and Sandy rushed up the stairs, the sound of their feet distinguishing themselves from the ruckus down below. The flashlights in their hands hurt sensitive eyes. They stared at the three on the floor, at the large, torn hole in the ceiling, one of broken planks and even thick, thick beams.

– Good Lord, The Gambler whispered.

Sandy attempted to speak, but her lips shivered so hard that she couldn't utter a sound.

Ted shook as well. Whether or not it was because of fear, excitement, joy or triumph, or all of the above he didn't know. He charged Mark with an obsessed expression in his face. Mark was still reeling from the experience, his eyes still foggy. Ted squeezed his shoulder.

– That little boy, that was you, *right?*

– Yes, Mark replied hoarsely.

Mark wasn't quite himself yet. Ted sensed the weakness, moved in on it, realized that now was the time, the chance he had been waiting for, the opportunity to squeeze his relative, to get answers to the questions burning in Ted's forge.

– I felt your hatred, strong and potent, approaching pathological. Not for Van Hoffa. Who are you hating, Mark? *Who?* I got to know so much about you, but not that. You're still holding out on me. I won't have it. What are you hiding better than anything else? *What?*

He shook the large, weak body. Mark opened his mouth.

– Hi, boss, Pete said hesitatingly, – we've got a situation here. Everybody heard…

– Shut up. SHUT UP!

Ted's eyes cut into him. Pete wanted to say more, but realized he couldn't. His throat was like squeezed shut. He was even unable to swallow all the saliva gathering in the cavity of his mouth.

Ted turned back to Mark in an instant. Mark smiled, his eyes clear again.

– Too bad, kid, you missed your chance.

– NO, YOU WILL TELL ME. YOU SHALL!

And before their eyes entered the monster, the dark shape, the mist and the cold. Ted struck Mark, struck him so hard that he practically rolled across the floor, blood flowing from his mouth. Ted was about to charge him, to attack him… when he… stopped. Shoulders sagged and once again there was only a human being standing there.

Another eternity, many eternities. Tilla said his name. He couldn't hear it, but he saw her lips move.

– Get your clothes, he told her.

They dressed slowly, fog still in their eyes, clarity still filling their being, their cup to the brim.

He said nothing to Mark. It was if the big man wasn't there at all.

It was cold, as the outside air flowed into the room through the ragged hole. His entire body felt frozen. But he had no trouble moving. He took Tilla's hand, pulling her with him down the stairs, catching a glimpse of Stewart as he fought himself on his feet, and stumbled after them.

They met the many people on their way up, on their way down. Nothing was said. Pete said something about a caved in roof, or he might have. Ted wasn't sure, and he didn't care.

It turned quiet again. It turned dark again, in the final hours before dawn.

The night ended, ended too soon, as most nights did, even the longest night.

It was early next morning. The man that found it necessary to hide his face behind a mask read a newspaper. On the radio a station played Waterloo, performed by ABBA. He turned off the radio, had heard the tune often enough the last few months.

The news was filled with news about Darwin, a city on the northern coast of Australia. A hurricane had practically flattened the entire city. No one knew for sure how many people who had been killed yet. It was one of the worst disasters in human history.

Tilla was awake when Ted returned, carrying a pile of newspapers in his arms.

– That's quite something…

She stretched on the bed, performing for him, but stopped when she noticed it didn't make him smile as it usually did.

– So, what's new? She wondered.

– It's mostly about the failed bomb inside Harrods, he said laconically, –

but not all of it.

She stiffened as she saw the front pages, as he threw the papers on the floor. There were images of the storm, so real to them, so easy to recall.

– Everything happened, she said. – As we experienced it. The woman, the Storm, the little girl, our kin…

She hesitated a bit, before speaking again.

– Did we do this? She asked him. – Did we cause it?

There was no reply.

– The girl is alone, he said. – Her mother died. Someone killed her and took the girl. She's alone.

– We sought her, Tilla said softly. – Were pulled to her.

– Yes, he nodded. – Her power is a lot like Mark's.

– She's alone, Tilla said. – What's gonna happen to her? Will she be forced to grow up like us? Without understanding why she feels so alone, even when she isn't?

– And she is alone, he said. – We weren't. In spite of it all, we weren't alone.

– Can we find her again?

– I can't see how. I think it was pure chance that we did find her once. And we did what we did when she was in mortal danger. We won't be able to recreate the circumstances, not without knowing more about her.

The familiar pain could still hurt them. They parted without touching, and the pain grew.

Ted revisited the attic. He stood there looking at the hole and hardly anything else.

He heard Pete approach. His senses didn't fail him.

– That was a great work of art, Boss, Pete said, at a safe distance.

– I'm hardly even a novice in this. It's still so new to me…

– I'm positive Van Hoffa would disagree, Pete commented. – It's said that he died in his sleep, terrified beyond belief.

– I heard, Ted nodded.

I knew.

The other boy's admiration haunted him, followed him into night, into the new night, coming just as abruptly as all nights before.

He remained there, as sparks of rain lit up the floor beneath the hole.

Darkness. A tall, dark man with shiny black hair stopped in front of the fireplace. He carried a small suitcase. Everything he owned in the world. In the other hand he held an elaborate mask of black velvet. Somebody entered the room behind him. He knew who it was without turning to look, recognized easily Shuen Parker.

– You're… leaving?

– Tonight, I dreamed about the eagle and the serpent again, he said quietly. – And as always, the eagle tore the serpent apart. It's been a long time since I doubted my powers.

He threw the mask into the fire. It was devoured in one single burst of heat.

– If you're wise, you'll join me.

She nodded.

– I need to get dressed. Will you grant me five minutes?

– There are clothes on the couch, he said. – You won't need anything else.

– You knew, she exclaimed theatrically. – Knew I would come.

He was silent a long time, before he sort-of spoke.

– I know so very much.

She had trouble moving her arms properly, and pain painted her face, but she still dressed in quick, flowing moves. After less than a minute she walked to him and allowed him to take her hand. They seemed to be fading away before the fireplace, even as their feet still moved across the floor.

Ted awakened. It wasn't just that morning. It was all days, all nights. He knew the moment he opened his eyes that Tilla was also awake. In the twilight dark he saw chairs float in the air. Tilla's gray eyes were extraordinarily clear.

– This is so fun, she cried.

– It's only a loan, he said softly. – You borrowed a bit from Stewart, a bit from me.

– Don't you think I know that? She complained bitterly. – I can feel it slipping away by the minute. Tomorrow it will be gone.

Like he had borrowed her enhanced empathy, what had served her «well» all her life.

– You've probably been bad in your previous lives, he grinned cruelly.

– Oh, you…

Then it was light and darkness again, warmth and cold.

She and Carr and Linda returned from the outside later that week. He met her in the hall, as she removed her blond wig, and false glasses. She stared at him. Linda stared at him. He felt something had happened, felt it with his own empathy.

– I saw Iris, Tilla said, her voice naked. – She stared at me.

– We saw a bunch of them, Carr said. – They were being «unloaded» from a truck at the Verheyen Mansion by Kings Cross.

Eric's voice was also thick with emotion. He was quite the emotional guy.

It was so strange seeing Linda with the black wig.

– Eric is correct. Tilla grabbed his hands, stared into his eyes. – They're being treated like cordwood, like commodities. I knew that. It was just so *bad* being reminded of that fact.

She screamed at him, her hatred screamed at him.

– Soon, he told her. – *Soon.*

They were in bed again, just enjoying the closeness of the other. They could hardly get enough of that, so hungry, so needy.

They didn't sleep much these days. Days passed as preparation for the attack. The nights were like this, endless touch, joy and pain.

She played with his hair, rubbing herself at him, so enticing, so loving.

– Why not go, now? She wondered.

– Mark is running the show, Ted said frustrated. – There's no denying it. He's got the experience, the cunning for this. And we would be inferior, both in numbers and all. We would be slaughtered. But Mark has something up his sleeve. I know he has. He has a *lot* of that. We must trust him… for now…

– You had him, she cried passionately. – He would have told us everything. Before Pete distracted you. Damn him, too.

They kissed softly, in a hopeless attempt to mute the raging energies within them both.

It was like they were alone in the big building. They felt it like that, anyway, with the silence, with the background buzz. That didn't bother them, because they were alone together.

– We will get them, he assured her. – They will pay.

She brushed her lips against his, smiling.

– And afterwards? If there is an afterwards, what shall we do then?

He kissed her hard, pushing his tongue deep into her mouth, almost strangling her.

– Then we will do whatever we want and take whatever we desire.

++

On Christmas Day Stewart finally told them his plan, and it made them gape in wonder, in incredulity.

– Will this… work? Carr articulated everybody's fears, their nagging doubt.

– It will!

Stewart assured them, and they believed him, believed every word he said. Confidence flowed from the man standing there, before them.

They had been drinking last night, intending for it to be a modest feast, but most had sipped more than what was good for them in their anxiety and impatience.

The next day many walked around with a pained expression in twisted faces. Ted, Tilla and Stewart didn't.

– Someone must have slipped water in our drinks, Ted grinned. – We drank at least as much as everybody else.

There had been a kind of desperation to it, a notion that this could be the last time.

Ted had been drinking as well, feeling a strange lack of worry, lack of contempt. It was the first time he had been drinking voluntarily his entire life, at least anything approaching such quantities, and he felt good about it. His nightmare had been no nightmare at all.

– I've always drunk more than others, in an attempt to get drunk. Stewart shrugged. – Eventually I gave it up.

He looked at the two. And it was that very familiar look that just cut into them, making them feel shaken and vulnerable.

– It just burns up inside of us, you know. Stewart lifted another glass in a mock greeting and emptied it. – Burns to ashes.

It was the official New Year's Eve, December 31st when they made their final move.

The London New Year's Eve celebration was infamous. People met on Trafalgar Square and generally drowned the place in several tons of garbage.

– It will look like a disaster area tomorrow, Sandy giggled, before turning somber, before tuning in on the somber mood of the rest.

– Frank says it will be okay, she added nervously.

– Frank is her spirit guide. Pete enlightened the unenlightened. – He's from outer space, and has come here from the Andromeda Galaxy to bring peace and love to mankind.

Nervous laughter.

Most of them knew about Frank. Sandy hardly made any secret of it, but told it to everybody she met. The fact that Pete felt the need to repeat it told them that he wasn't exactly the model of calm.

At the numerous local police stations there was a madhouse transcending most proportions. Red-faced constables ran back and forth like rabbits. Screaming and shouting filled the rooms to the last piece of air. At Trafalgar Square there was a clear presence of guards, but they didn't interfere, except when things got ugly. They were all over the place, but were basically totally ignored.

At New Scotland Yard there was an eerie silence. The desk sergeant on duty looked at the empty room with a certain worry clearly visible in his bloated face.

But inside an abandoned warehouse not far from there, activity flourished that night. The main hall was filled with constables. The buzz of voices made it impossible to be heard more than a few steps away. Rumors were flying and abundant. Many were pulled in from local stations and some had even been denied granted leave of absence.

– Does anyone know *anything?* One asked the guy by his side.

– Nope. Most of us have had the same experience you had. Sergeant Adams and his people picked us up at home. I asked what it was about and was quite simply told to shut up, that the explanation would come, in time.

The buzz of voices quieted as Burke Adams entered the room. He was dressed as they were used to see him, conservatively, in a long coat, wearing a tie, wearing his derby hat and polished shoes. Those who knew him or knew of him, tended to joke at his expense, but he was still the very image of reliability.

He stopped on the podium in front of them, very efficient and authoritative. He had their utter and complete attention.

– You've been called here in a very unorthodox manner, he began. – There are two main reasons for this. One is the importance of what we'll do tonight, an importance that can hardly be measured. The other is the level of corruption in our ranks, especially in connection with this case. Secrecy and us having the element of surprise on our side are paramount. What you'll be hearing from me tonight, and from witnesses will be almost beyond belief and will shock you to the depth of your being.

In another room, as Adams kept speaking, Mark and Ted had a «conversation» with Chief Inspector George Bowers. Ted held up a cage with a Canary inside. It sang so sweet, so sweet. Bowers swallowed hard.

– Tell us, they choired. They choired all the time, sounding like one person. – Tell us when it should die.

Bowers was sweating. He stared at the two as if they were the vilest of creatures, as if he couldn't quite believe what was happening, what was about to happen.

– You think I'm buying any of this? He said hoarsely. – Do you think I'm that foolish?

They had explained it to him, explained everything, all the bullshit.

– Now, NOW!

He whispered.

The Canary stopped singing, and almost before Bowers had finished speaking it fell and hit the bottom of the cage, stone cold.

He stared at it, stared at the two with insane eyes.

– One wrong step, George, Stewart said. – A single wrong step…

Bowers attempted to speak, but couldn't, attempted it again, but failed. He nodded. He made sure the two demons saw it, understood his willingness to obey them in all things.

He walked to the other room, joined the crowded assembly of his colleagues with heavy heart and the numbing fear dominating his entire perception. He thought it through, went through everything in his head a thousand times, in his attempt to find a way out.

There wasn't any. He imagined a hand around his heart, squeezing it, squeezing all life from his body. The demon eyes danced in the air before him, never taking their attention off him. There was no body, only those eyes, those demon eyes, and he realized he would never forget them, for as long as he lived.

His subordinates were on their way up from the many chairs. He nodded to them.

– Please, remain seated, he told them graciously.

He reached the dais. Adams stepped aside, nodding to him, keeping up the pretense.

– Greetings, people, he said.

– GREETINGS, CHIEF INSPECTOR, they replied.

– I merely wanted to wish you the best of luck, tonight, on this our crucial operation. It will be a dangerous night, but you're a part of the proud British police force, and I know you'll rise to the challenge and behave splendidly.

He delivered his brief, impassionate speech, filled with empty phrases and political slogans, as he always did on similar occasions, and then he left.

– This must be big, a whisper was heard. – I've never seen Bowers nervous before.

– Thanks to Chief Inspector Bowers for his unflinching support, Adams said, desperately striving to keep the sarcasm out of his voice.

He paused a bit, before continuing, drawing a breath.

– This is a large operation, one coordinated between several countries, among them France and United States. Our American coordinator is Floyd McKenzie from the FBI.

Polite applause aimed at the man entering the room, followed by stunned silence, as more of those present lost their doubts.

– Good evening, McKenzie said. – I'll be brief. I'll just emphasize that you're not alone in this, and that the value of your contribution tonight cannot be underestimated. There will be danger, more danger than most of you has ever encountered. We'll be fighting vicious, hardened criminals, but I assure you it will be worth it. If we succeed, we'll put a stop to one of the most horrible set of crimes the world has ever seen…

Adams took the place behind the dais again.

– There are a few formalities before we'll be ready, he said.

He held up a pile of papers. The men and women recognized them as personnel files. The electrifying mood in the room didn't diminish any.

It increased.

– Earl Radford, he read. – Approach.

A brief hesitation. Then Radford obeyed. He placed himself in front of Adams, in something very much resembling a military pose.

– You're under arrest.

A ruckus without peer erupted in the room. Five of Adams' most trusted men had their weapons pointing casually at the floor, quite close to Radford's position. He was handcuffed and led away. The ruckus continued as Adams read five more names. The man with the last name to be cried out, Lester Carey shouted:

– I've won the money betting on horses. I swear!

– I'm sorry, Carey, Adams shook his head. – We can't bet on that.

– You'll pay, he screamed while being overwhelmed. – PAY! All of you!

The constables holding him, and also others looked around them with doubt in their eyes. Stewart sensed their doubt easily. He was prepared for it, and he had prepared for it. He sent two more into the room.

– This is Tilla Stevens and John Jackson, Adams presented. – You've heard me speak about these two, I trust? We do this quite thoroughly, so there will be no doubt. When we throw ourselves into danger, a few hours from now, there will be no room for doubt.

– Hello, Lester, John said curtly.

– A very pleasant surprise, Tilla said. – If you insist, we may speak about your visit to the docks a few weeks ago.

– I've never seen these two before my eyes before, he screamed. – THEY'RE LYING

But the constables were convinced now, fully, if not before, when they witnessed his obvious guilt. They tied him up and locked him in the room with the others. He kept screaming. They had to gag him.

McKenzie cleared his throat. They looked at him again. He had their full and complete attention.

– Tonight, he told them sternly. – You'll have to draw fully on all your skills as fighters. Your weapons training will be of use, I can assure you of that. You will be handed your guns at the exit. Many arrests will be made. But as stated, you'll also encounter hardened criminals. Expect to kill or be killed.

Silence reigned in the room.

– That's all, ladies and gentlemen. Good luck.

Adams took the stand again.

– One last caution. There will be many innocent people in the line of fire. Do not fire, I repeat, do not fire until explicit orders have been given, and do not fire indiscriminately, or it can turn into a horrible bloodbath, and that's not what we're here for.

They made the final preparations. The characteristic hats were left behind. They were given dark coats to wear outside the uniform. Stewart was there, all the time. They looked curious, very curious at him. He was practically a legend in their circles, a ghost in the modern world, one who went wherever he wanted, independently of borders, law or forces of order, a man with no fixed allegiances or loyalties, a modern gunman just as infamous as the legendary gunmen of centuries past.

They were finally ready to leave. One of the men approached Adams with a question he burned to have answered:

– Sergeant, if I may ask…

– You may, Adams nodded.

– … is this an unofficial operation?

– It is indeed, Adams confirmed, and raised his voice, making sure everybody heard him. – No honor, no acknowledgement awaits, unless we succeed and succeed beyond expectation.

The large assembly left. Everyone grabbed one set of guns. They all left, and the building was once more empty, once more silent as death.

Chief Constable Julian Gibbs held back a little, before leaving the others, before slipping away. Once he was clear, the moment he had made sure he wasn't seen, he began running, running hard.

There were no people where he was headed, not a single soul around the row of phone booths in the quiet street. More than a bit out of breath he reached for the door.

He was grabbed from behind and turned around, staring into a familiar face.

– Carr! He gasped, recognizing him easily from their encounter at the Scotland Yard reception hall ages ago.

– Hello, Gibbs. Eric pressed the blade against the other's throat. – Did you think we weren't on to you? You would've been one of those hard to find hard evidence against. You're among the smarter, crueler and most vicious.

He cut deep into the pulsing neck, to the bone. The only sound coming from the Chief Constable was a weak gurgle. He fell against the booth and slid down it, until he sat there, as if resting. Eric dried the blade on the other's coat, and slipped silently back into the night.

George Bowers shook hard. He walked fast, constantly glancing around him, like a scared and angry kid.

– The bastards, he mumbled. – The fucking bastards. You'll pay, oh, how you'll pay. I know you, now, know what you are.

His hands were nothing but fists, tightened so hard that it hurt.

– You freaks, he cried. – You'll be freaks, more than ever before. I'll make sure of that. You're real. Everybody will know you're *real*.

He reached a public area. There were other people here, real people. He felt disengaged from them, felt dirty. There was a choke in his throat as he hurried on. A phone booth. There was a phone booth somewhere nearby, he was positive about that.

Everything else was uncertainty and disarray.

George Bowers walked through a dark passage when he saw the girl. Only a movement in the shadows at first, then full-blown reality. He reached for his gun, but it wasn't there. Of course, it wasn't. He stared at the girl. Her hair was the brightest he had ever seen. She had tied it in a ponytail, and she looked so sweet, so innocent. If it wasn't for her height she could be mistaken for a child. He had never before beheld such a sweet and innocent face.

– Another lonely soul tonight, how sad…

How tender her voice was. It didn't fit at all with the sensual subtext of her words, her smile. He realized she was intoxicated, and he felt almost aggrieved. A girl like her wasn't supposed to act like this.

She wore a white dress and carried a small bag. It was more than probable that she had recently left a party nearby, and was on her way home. The dress was so thin that he could easily see the lines of her body. When she approached him as a silhouette against the light behind her, the effect turned even more pronounced. The sudden burst of desire made it difficult for him to swallow.

– Very sad, he agreed willingly. – Where are you headed?

– Home, she said hoarsely. – I'm headed home.

She stumbled and fell against him. He almost lost his breath.

Such luck, such a rare flower, longing to be plucked.

He felt a tearing pain in his abdomen. Stared amazed at the shaft she clutched, and the blood that flowed from his insides.

– I see recognition in your eyes, she whispered. – The last time you saw me I was wearing a lot of make up, and I was tied to a bed. You saw me mostly from behind. You've killed a lot of girls that way, haven't you, in the name of the law?

Pain numbed him. The lack of sensation numbed him.

– I feel so strong, she said casually, like she was talking about the weather. – I am. I'm holding you. I'm the lifeline keeping you in this world.

The sensual smile kept blinding him.

– You will never have the chance at exposing us.

She pushed the blade upwards, through his body, tore his insides apart. Held him there, watched as life left him. She pulled it out and let him go, let him fall. By then he was already dead.

Eric approached her carefully.

– Are you alright?

There was no reply.

– Linda?

– All right? She looked incredulous and detached at him. – Of course, I am. Shouldn't I be?

She licked the blood off the knife, did so with a skill and meticulous dedication that took his breath away. The black blade flashed in the shadows.

– Where have you learned to use… that thing?

– I've been performing since I was a little girl. She shrugged. – I've always been good at it.

She looked speculatively at him.

– You're quite the curious one, you know…

He looked down at Gibbs' mangled body and swallowed hard again. He knew what the bright shimmer in her eyes meant. She enjoyed killing.

– We should get going.

He glanced nervously at their surroundings. There was no one else here. There was no sound of steps growing louder in his ears.

– I'll have to dress first, she said. – It's cold tonight.

She removed her dress and used the part of it not already bloody to clean the blade further. He witnessed the same efficiency, the same detachment. She let the dress fall to the ground, leaving the knife on top of it. Then she pulled a sweater and pants from the bag, and clothed her naked body. But all he could think of, all he could see was the knife decorating the dress, the black and all the red on all the white. She grabbed the black, the red and the white and threw it in the bag.

– Come.

She grabbed his hand and led him away.

The house, the estate at Kings Cross was about to be sealed off from all sides. It was done quietly and swiftly. The streets swarmed with people moving like shadows. They were all there, everybody destiny had gathered.

They saw the house close up from their chosen position, a bit down the road, heard people laugh, the meeting and parting of glasses inside.

A thrill of expectation shot through Linda.

– Now is the time, she told Eric. – Now, the world will begin to pay for what it has done to us.

– Eric and Linda, welcome to the ball, Caine said, meeting them at the yellow ribbon fence. – Are you sure you don't want guns?

– You don't ask Ted, I see, Linda smiled. – That's okay. He doesn't need a weapon. He is one.

– I've already lost two. Eric smiled, too.

He and Linda had found their weapon.

There were voices, a bit to the left.

– I just want to remind you not to indulge yourself, Stewart said to Ted, visibly forcing himself to remain calm. – If you don't learn to control your temper better, you risk exposing yourself.

– You're not any better, Ted replied testily. – Watch yourself, Mark.

Delayed guests were taken care of, were taken to chosen houses further down the street and incarcerated there, in spite of their incredulity and loud protests.

Then no more people appeared. The shadows and their chosen helpers in uniform began moving, began moving in, approaching the target from all sides. It was finally happening. Linda looked at Ted, looked at Tilla, looked at John, and they all looked back, and she felt the swelling pride inside.

Finally.

Chapter Twenty-one

The music sounded muted, not really very modern or updated. People filled the space, a large room looking very similar to an old dancing hall. A jazz band played from a small ledge by the eastern wall.

The Verheyen mansion had been whispered about among members of the upper class since its refurbishment had been completed last year, since the first lavish party held here for specially invited guests two months ago. And now, tonight, when more of them got to see it for themselves, they stared at the expensive materials with wet, huge eyes. People used to luxury faced luxury far beyond their ken. Even the super rich nodded in acknowledgment when they entered through the large entrance.

Limousines had been stopping outside in an even stream most of the evening. Now, most of the national and international jet set, old and new money had gathered inside. The stage was set.

Sandra appeared on the stage as the music briefly stopped.

– Thank for coming to this Gala at the Verheyen Mansion, she cried. – Know that we because of your appearance have already collected a considerable sum of money to the Verheyen fund for disabled children tonight. May it be a happy New Year.

Polite applause. People applauding themselves.

The band started up again.

Kurman Al Rashid circulated among the guests.

– This is such a fastidious party, my good Sheik. So *old fashioned,* such a departure from the horrifying and unfortunate events onboard that «luxury» liner of yours.

– I say thank you, Countess. He toasted with her, a woman around forty. – You're well informed. Not many people know we own Aphrodite.

– And that nice young bartender of yours knew how I wanted my Martini. On the drop, I'd say.

She was a shrewd old hag. Quite a few, even her worst enemies, gave her that credit.

– I especially like the presence of all the young people here tonight…

– We strive for an even representation. Al Rashid nodded. – Perhaps you would like to meet a few of them?

– Why not? They look like nice boys and girls.

The Sheik grinned as he turned away from her for a moment. He signed to one of the passing girls. She stopped in front of the two, curtseying deeply, before straightening, very attentive.

– Good evening, Iris, he greeted her.

– Good evening, sir, she replied softly. – Good evening, Countess.

– Good evening, Iris. The Countess nodded.

– Would you be so kind to find William and ask him to join us? Al Rashid told the girl.

– Certainly, sir, she replied softly. – Right away, sir.

She curtseyed again, before slipping discreetly away.

– So polite, the Countess remarked. – Contrary to most of the adolescent scum of today.

Iris was already on her way back. She slipped through the crowd towards them, followed by a dark-haired, pretty boy. Al Rashid noted pleased that the Countess' eyes lit up in expectation. He strongly suspected she would be horny as a loon in no time.

Both the boy and the girl looked good, looked so very attentive and eager to please their betters. Al Rashid shook his head in delight.

The boy was quite the charmer, exactly the kind Al Rashid knew the Countess favored.

The boy knew, of course. He had been primed to take care of the Countess for weeks. He knew her, knew her smallest, intimate secrets.

Iris stopped. Something made Al Rashid look at her. She stood there, with her head slightly cocked, as if listening. She looked at him, a look chilling his heart.

The boy seemed perfectly all right. He stumbled, and when he straightened, he was chalk white in his face, and sweating profusely. And then he looked around him with *wild* eyes.

– What's going *on* here? He shouted. – Where am I? What have you *done* to us?

Wild rage twisted his face. He grabbed a large knife from a table, and began hacking at people close to him. A man and a woman passing by fell to the floor with ghastly wounds. One moment everything had been calm, almost serene. The next chaos ruled, dominated Verheyen Mansion.

Someone finally managed to act and push a button. William screamed, as the current raged through him, but chillingly beyond words he didn't fall. He clearly felt it. Everybody could see that, see the pain twisting his features. It was as if it didn't faze him. He cut open a woman running in the wrong direction, so panicked she didn't know where she was running. The guards threw themselves at the boy. Two of them were gutted before they got him on the floor. He snarled and kept fighting, pushing out one of the guards' eyes. It fell on the floor and rolled across it, towards the guests crowding horrified by the stairs. The boy was overwhelmed only by the greatest of difficulties. He was still, even with enough tranquillizers in his system to kill him, difficult to handle, as he was dragged off.

Slowly, only slowly the situation returned to a semblance of normalcy.

Al Rashid pulled back, horror and incredulity written in his face. Sandra was there, beside him, in an instant, as the attentive aide she was.

– There's no way we can salvage this disaster, he said enraged. – No way!

– I agree. She nodded. – The best we can hope for is a modicum of crisis management.

– Have you been able to get hold of The Mask and Shuen Parker yet?

– No luck, sir. They're nowhere we can reach them.

What about Verheyen and Tremblay?

– They're on their way. I spoke to them less than ten minutes ago. They're being held up in an accident on M4.

– Find Gidman, Al Rashid spat, saliva flowing from his mouth. – Meinz, too. Tell them to come to my office. *Immediately*.

– As you wish, sir. Right away, sir.

Sandra rushed off, as the good aide she was.

The professional party host they had hired stood on the stage, holding up both hands.

– Please, calm down, Ladies and Gentlemen, he cried. – There's no need to be upset. The unfortunate situation has been taken care of. The party will go on.

Al Rashid knew people. He saw their unrest. Some were about to leave. Most decided to stay, at least for the moment, but the evening had been ruined. There was just no way things would proceed smoothly after this.

He met with Truck and four more aides at the punchbowl.

– What *happened?*

– I don't have any friggin idea, sir. The big man shook his head. – The boy, like the rest of them, hasn't shown any major irregularities for months, and he was cleared during the check up yesterday.

Al Rashid spat some more curses at the men, though he could hardly remember them afterwards.

He passed Bruce, and as he stopped, the boy stopped as well, so very attentive.

– Go to the Countess. She should be ready for you. If not, just do your best, okay.

And he left the boy, secure in his confidence that the slave would indeed do his best.

He heard a door slam in the lower office. He recognized David Gidman's heavy steps.

The Arab put a hand on the handle, and was about to open the door, when he stopped, when he froze.

He saw the girl, the revenant on the middle of the floor, parting from all the other people out there. What had he been thinking? He had forgotten her. Forgotten the scarecrow in their midst.

– They're coming, Iris cried. – I can see the shadows advance through the darkness.

And incredibly enough, so could he, and it made him cold all over.

Her voice was even, horrible.

He felt a pull, and he was drawn back to the open floor, to face the wraith out there.

– I love that, she said. – I should thank you guys, and I intend to.

Truck moved forward, whispering in his ear, clearly agitated, clearly not noticing the monster there by his side.

– Tremblay and Verheyen's group contacted us, he said. – They report that an iron ring of policemen is surrounding the estate.

Al Rashid breathed deeply. He could hardly concentrate on replying to Truck. The only thing he could see was Iris Carson's demonic face.

– Make sure the slaves are primed, he snarled. – If a group is stupid enough to attack us here, in our sanctum, they'll receive a lesson they will never forget.

Truck left.

Al Rashid saw, vividly the scene outside. He witnessed, clear as day Ted Cousin and Mark Stewart speak to two policemen.

One of them, down on one knee, operated a large machine, a radio transmitter.

– I can't say I like this very much, sir, he said. – It's like adding to their burden. I mean…

– I know what you mean, Stewart said.

– I don't like it either, Ted said. – In fact I dislike it very much.

– You know it's necessary, Stewart brushed him off. – Or we might need to kill them.

There was silence.

– Give the order, Stewart told Burke Adams.

Al Rashid took one step forward, and stopped - amazed, paralyzed. He looked down. A knife stood buried in his chest. He saw, in disbelief, how several knives rose from the table, seemingly of their own volition, and were thrown at him. They all hit him in the chest, hammered into him like bullets. Then the pain came. He fell and hit the floor. He writhed on his back, and stared up at the girl standing above him.

– You can't do this. Iris spoke, but in his choking voice. – I've got diplomatic immunity.

– I knew that, Iris said with her own, normal voice. – You won't get away. Not this time. Not like you once upon a time did.

Police officers and constables and others rushed inside the house from all sides. A voice through a bullhorn overwhelmed the music.

– THIS IS THE METROPOLITAN POLICE. PLEASE, STAND STILL. THOSE ATTEMPTING TO MOVE WILL BE SHOT WITHOUT FURTHER WARNING.

– Boys and girls… ATTACK! Truck commanded.

Many of the youths got a remote look in their eyes. They let go of everything in their hands and attacked. Suddenly they all screamed horribly and fell, fell down. They writhed helplessly on the floor.

Iris remained on her feet. What affected the others clearly didn't affect her. The man on the floor looked at the burned out and black useless metal around her neck.

I don't know what you mean. What do you mean? Please tell me. Please

Kurman Al Rashid looked at the statue above him with dead eyes.

The intruders covered the entire room with their guns and their presence. Very carefully some of them began to move through the crowd. They chained those writhing on the floor, chained them hands and feet. The horrible screams continued, and when they finally ended, the slaves moved no more.

The sounds of shots fired were heard from other parts of the Mansion. Heavy gunfire and more screams.

Adams entered through the main entrance. Behind him were McKenzie and Caine.

– Good evening, he said casually, in the sudden, deafening silence. – Let me advice you that you're all under arrest, in the name of the Queen.

The last part of the sentence he added after a brief hesitation, shaking his head.

A man, filled with centuries of inbred dignity, stepped forward.

– What in darnation are you *saying,* young man? May I ask what the reason is?

– You're here. That's reason enough.

Another man stepped forward, very self-conscious, very confident.

– I've got diplomatic immunity.

– Hello, Lefere, Caine greeted him. – Your presence here doesn't exactly surprise us.

– We'll see how much it will help you, Adams snarled. – And if you do get off, we'll make you Persona Non Grata in most countries on Earth.

The attackers met with far greater resistance on other fronts around the Mansion. It was well guarded, as expected. But its defenders were way too few to deal with the onslaught the attackers mustered. Mark and Ted penetrated the walls with blazing guns. A policeman was hit in the head, falling like a tree. Stewart was hit in the side, but kept running, kept shooting, as if only a mosquito or something had hit him. People fell in droves before his blazing guns, and those under his command. The defenders ran off in absolute panic, pulling further inside the building.

– Are you okay? Ted wondered casually.

– The roof, Stewart spat, ignoring the other's words.

The retreating gunmen were shot down like flies. Only a few succeeded in surviving the first wave of attackers.

– I SURRENDER, a man cried, throwing away his gun, raising his hands.

The cry was echoed throughout the hall, throughout the building.

The police officers and constables began cuffing those who had surrendered and pushed them at the wall, at the corner by the grand staircase. Mark and Ted had already reached the upper floor by then. They heard the sound of a chopper starting up.

They just barely managed to open the door to the roof because of the wind created by the rotor. The chopper rose like an arrow in the air. Mark emptied his guns at it. *I want it stopped,* Ted thought. The front glass broke. The machine hung suspended in the air a fateful moment… The rear rotor was torn off. Police officers and constables watched it all wide-eyed from the lawn below. Then it was like the large, main rotor was torn off. A large, dark figure threw himself out. The chopper fell to the ground and exploded. Everybody threw themselves away to avoid the flying wreckage. A few, breathless seconds passed. David Gidman, with torn and bleeding skin, and a right foot he could hardly stand on, rose with an effort, an effort of will. Ten policemen surrounded him, making sure they didn't come in each other's line of fire, directing their guns at his head. Gidman measured odds, in a few long seconds, before he slowly and painfully lifted his arms above his head.

– He's getting away, Stewart said darkly to Ted. – Getting away again. Kill him. Tear off his head and make sure he never rises again. I know you can do it. Do it, before it's too late.

Ted looked at the hateful figure, the stranger by his side.

– No, he said, shaking his head. – I don't know if I can do it, without harming the others down there. Not now. At least we know where we have him. For a while.

– You're right, Mark mumbled. – It would be too easy. I want him to know it before he dies. Know *beyond* doubt.

Ted patted the shaking figure a few times on the back, before retracting his hand.

He left the roof alone.

Eric, Linda, Tilla and John ran together, charged together, like a unit, like a seething mass of rage. Smoke rose from everywhere around them. Bullets were flying. They raged on. Tilla and John carried guns. Eric and Linda their knives. Linda let the black blade slide between her fingers, almost as if she was caressing it. Eric was point man. Linda and Tilla moved in a catlike way, while he was more wagging like an ape. John had removed his shoes in an attempt to move as silently as the other three.

They reached another darkened hall. There was no one there, not much of furniture to hide behind. On the opposite wall there was a door ajar. Eric hesitated a bit before using the military hand signals he had learned in Vietnam. He wasn't really surprised when the others reacted correctly to them, reacting without thinking, like good soldiers. They spread out, moving carefully towards the door, more than expecting bullets being fired at them.

– It goes far below… to… the torturers' room.

Tilla's voice was so low that Eric hardly heard her. No one else further away would.

They reached the wall, hitting it softly, soundlessly with their shoulders. Eric dived through the door, catching a glimpse of the stairs. There was no one there. He remained point man as they moved down, far below. They reached the first level, moved across the floor to the next stairs. Burning eyes sought potential hiding places and covers. No one fired at them. They descended further. Underground, Eric thought. There was a broad metal grid staircase ahead, not just one more of the narrow passages they had moved through. The sound of their feet hitting each step echoed in the empty rooms. They reached another level, another opening on their way down, when Eric stopped. The others, following his lead, stopped as well. Linda, impatiently, signaled she wanted to proceed. He signaled sharply to her. She relented, baring her neck to him. Then, through breathing he imagined was loud as a storm, he heard the familiar sound, the cocking of a gun. He threw himself backwards, pushing the others with him to the floor. A thought later it thundered from below. The ceiling above them was peppered with bullets.

One, Eric signaled. He signed to Tilla, and she gave him her gun.
He fired one shot down the stairs. The inspired reply came instantly. Eric saw the man as he pulled back, behind the corner, his rather poor cover, expecting a response.
Fifteen large steps, he signaled.
I see him, John signaled hesitatingly. But…
You cover me, Eric ordered. The moment following the next salvo, you fire.
– Should we do anything at all? John wondered. – There's no need, is there?
– I want to, Linda snarled silently. – I want to gut them all.
Tilla had already found her position. John joined her reluctantly.
The staircase bent slightly. Eric measured the distance, measured the odds, smelled the scent of trees and jungle, and he was certain they did as well. He returned the gun to Tilla. It slid across the floor, and she grabbed it in an elegant swing of her arm. She fired that instant. The response came spontaneously, and in the immediate silence afterwards Eric moved. He threw himself down the steep staircase, moved as he did so, moved like lighting, like a snake, like a cat, like a shadow not hampered by a body. Tilla and John fired, both simultaneously and alternately. He was astounded at how good they truly were. The enemy wasn't allowed to fire more than one, ill-directed salvo before Eric was over him. Eric struck the enemy's arm. The machinegun fell to the floor. They tumbled backwards, into the darkness.
Eric went for the man's face. He didn't miss, but it wasn't a good hit. Eric took a hit to the chest. He knew, even after a second or so that this was a worthy, more than a worthy opponent. He took a hit in the belly. Gasping he threw himself backwards, drawing his knife, cutting the air in a wide range before him, making the other man stay back. Eric went for the other's head with his right foot. The man grabbed it and twisted it around. Pain cut through Eric. Damn. The blade flashed towards the man's throat, but cut the shoulder instead. The opponent grabbed his arm and broke it by the shoulder. Eric screamed, screamed aloud. The knife slipped from his hand. He kept fighting. But the other man was better, so much better at it. Eric was thrown at the wall, all air being pushed from his lungs. The fight was done. He crouched there, shaking his head in dizziness, desperately attempting to make, to *make* his paralyzed body work, to act as the grinning man picked up his machinegun. Eric saw in glimpses a white shadow slip through the darkness. The man fired. The hail of bullets struck Eric in the chest. The white shadow, a white, strong

arm embraced the large man's neck. He choked in his attempt to scream. The large frame began shaking. The weapon fell from his powerless hands. The punctured body slipped to the floor, at Linda's feet. Eric imagined that the blood on the black blade glowed in ruby red, as the girl knelt by his side.

– This was the elite of the Abraxas Omega inner circle. He coughed. – One who has learned his lesson.

Wondering, because she didn't quite understand she signaled for him to lay still. The worried look in her eyes warmed him.

– The White Rose, he said hoarsely, he baptized her.

Tilla and John rounded the corner. They spotted a woman with a machinegun running towards them. Tilla cried out a warming. She fired at the shadow, as she threw herself and John to relative safety. She missed. Linda was hit and fell on top of Eric, clutching the black blade in her hand.

– She is completely without cover, she told John. – *Take her out.*

But he didn't seem to hear her.

– Damn you, she cried contemptuously.

Resolutely she stuck her head out and fired at the shadow rolling across the floor. She missed by far, and pulled back right before bullets chipped the corner. John pulled her back and fired one shot. It hit the shadow in the head and killed her instantly.

Tilla rose. John let his hand and his gun fall to the floor. She studied the shadow carefully, held her gun in both hands, making sure the body didn't move. Her eyes moved around the room, never resting.

– I hit her good, John said. – She's dead.

He threw up. And threw up. Between the vomiting he sat on his knees, virtually unmoving.

– Fuck, FUCK, Tilla exclaimed, as she knelt by the bloodied bodies of her friends.

Eric was at best unconscious. Linda moved, moaning. Tilla turned her around, carefully, nervously.

– It's not… serious… I think. Linda moaned again. – The shoulder and the arm, I suppose.

– Correct the first time, Tilla said softly. – Lay still, you'll be okay.

Linda opened her mouth to say something, had to strive a bit.

– Bend… closer.

Not quite understanding the redhead hesitated a bit, but when she saw the other girl's begging eyes, she relented. She felt a kiss on her cheek, light as a feather. Linda smiled as she let her head fall back. Tilla returned the smile. She understood.

She coughed. Her eyes fell on the machinegun not far away. She reached for it. Her numb fingers grabbed it and pulled it into her lap. She remained like that, on her knees, sitting on her heels, at Linda and Eric's side, clutching the lethal weapon, until Ted arrived.

– Hello, warrior, he greeted her. – Are you okay?

He had approached so silently that she knew it was him. She nodded, alleviating his fears.

– I'm okay, she said quickly, kissing him with her eyes.

She looked at the two bloodied figures on the floor.

– Can you do anything for them?

He didn't reply at first.

– I'm not like Stewart, he said. – You know that, saw that. He can give, too. I can only take.

She looked at him, sharing his anguish, his cruelty.

– You let Gidman get away? She wondered. – Not because you were afraid of harming a few cops, I gather.

– It was interesting to see Mark's reaction, he grinned.

Staring just as intensely at her.

– I'm going in there.

They both looked at the door in the shadows.

– Kurt Meinz is in there, she said.

He nodded.

– I know.

– Then I'll come with you, she said.

– I, too, John choked. – I want to.

– No, you must stay here, guard them.

Tilla understood. She had to guard the defenseless. John, as he was, now, couldn't guard a rock.

– I'll be back, Ted said.

He ran through the door, and kept running. No one attempted to stop him and he encountered no one. There wasn't a human being in sight. He slid through shadows and deserted halls and hallways, becoming a shadow himself. Meinz' office was empty, too. Empty but filled with horrible memories and his cruel instruments. Ted froze for every new item, every instrument of torture he spotted and recognized. He pressed on. Rage pushed him on. He ran into the combined training hall. There was a swimming pool covering half of the ground. Empty, with steam rising from its vast depths. Flashes of memories came to him. There was a lot of apparatus here, many places for a person to take cover behind. Ted smelled fear and he grinned. He saw no one, but he was convinced there was someone hiding in here.

Then the light was turned off, and he knew that what his instinct had told him was true.

– You've forgotten something, Meinz, he said mockingly. – I see just as well in the dark as you.

Not quite true, he ventured. It still took time for him to adjust to the darkness. He moved as he spoke, throwing himself down, behind cover. A gun was fired. A bullet struck the floor a few steps away.

He kept moving, emptying his mind, moving, sensing, stalking. Flashes of memories. Another, identical swimming pool. Meinz had made them, him, Tilla, Betty, Iris and Linda dive, dive deep, into the Abyss, and stay down there, until their lungs threatened to burst. He had been experimenting on them. He knew what they were.

Where the first few moments had been total darkness, there were now outlines, shapes, details, appearing faster this time, faster every time he experienced abrupt darkness. Another shot, unpleasantly close, but this time he glimpsed the iron gray mane. He sent a large box towards where Meinz had vanished. There was a cry of pain.

– What is it, doctor? Did something fall on you?

The reply came in the form of automatic fire. Behind him. There were two of them. *Assholes*. He threw himself down again. The large shadow frame emanating from his body, emulating his body shook in rage. The other couldn't see in the dark or he would surely have been hit, he knew that. The other had fired in the direction of his voice. He grinned.

Ted approached the place where Meinz had last fired, closing in on him step by step to where he was Now. Both Meinz and the other used exploding bullets. Ted kept grinning. This, all this just created a quivering expectation in him.

He could see well, now, very close to normal, in some ways even better. All movement registered in his mind, the slightest variation of air pressure. He saw it, sensed it in his vision beyond his vision. It felt so great, and there was recrimination, brief, but notable, over the years he had wasted, wasted on normalcy.

Time passed. He couldn't tell how much. Dust rose and fell as he stalked Kurt Meinz and the other still unidentified person around the pool. He sensed Meinz'… *energy,* now, saw him even when he wasn't in the direct line of sight. He was close.

Suddenly bright light flooded the hall. Meinz and Ted both covered their eyes. Both screamed, screamed in rage. Meinz recovered first, as

Ted knew he would, with his greater experience in this. A salvo from the automatic weapon and Meinz screamed some more. He was hit. Ted saw the older man fall to the floor. Ted screamed as well, in rage, in desperation. For the first time in his life he let it all out. Bursts of power erupted from his brain. There was another scream, a horrible noise, the sound of wood breaking, and of metal hitting the wall. His eyes cleared. The water, the tears, so prominent the moment previous to this, dried to desert sand in an *instant*.

The floor was cleared in a huge circle around him. All the material in the room had been thrown in large piles of rubble. Meinz had avoided most of the outlet's immediate results, but he was also shot to pieces by the machinegun salvo. The other, a girl Ted recognized as a Master was partly covered in the ruined equipment. She managed to free herself from most of it. She shook her head as she rose, as she desperately, in vain, scanned the surroundings for her weapon.

– Such a brave traitor, Meinz cried softly to the girl. – But you didn't quite succeed. You'll pay for that, little Sandra.

– He… destroyed me, Sandra choked, perhaps speaking to Ted, perhaps to no one in particular. – The sadist took from me my very last possibility to live a normal life.

– Come, *come to me*.

Meinz' voice turned seductive, possessive.

His eyes cut into the girl. Her chokes stopped, and she rose and walked towards the doctor. Her eyes turned vague and glassy.

– Now, you were good, little Sandra. She stopped by his feet, straightening, attentive and eagerly awaiting his next command. – The water is quite lovely tonight. Take a dive, Sandra. Show us how good you are.

She ran to the edge of the pool. There wasn't the slightest hesitation. She dived. There was a thump as she hit the bottom far below. Nothing more.

– She deserved it, Ted said, clearly fascinated. – Taking away my fun.

Two burning eyes met.

– Take a dive, you too.

Meinz' persuasive will washed over the boy.

Ted just grinned. He didn't feel the slightest compelled.

– Betty had far more success with that, and then I wasn't what I am, now.

He knelt down by his kin, Kurt Meinz. Blood kept flowing into the pool. But Ted easily saw how the wounds kept knitting themselves, kept attempting to heal.

– It's incredible, Ted said, just as fascinated. – Damn me, I would say you actually have a chance.

He concentrated slightly, and the wounds expanded in the course of seconds. Meinz screamed.

– You do have something to tell me, Kurt. Please don't believe otherwise.

Meinz coughed. He moved an arm, incredibly steady, drying blood from his jaw.

– I will tell you *something,* he acknowledged.

There was short break. Ted stood there, shaking in rage.

And this was what Kurt Meinz told Ted Warren:

– I tried everything to keep you docile. I really did, using all my considerable expertise. It worked temporarily, several times, but you kept bouncing back. I filled you with enough drugs to kill elephants. Your system purged it at an ever-faster rate. I tried everything in my power. Nothing works. You're everything they said you would be. I tell you, studying you has been an amazing experience. Amazing. Most scientists would find an absolute anomaly like you… taxing, but I've always had a certain fondness for pieces that don't fit in… don't fit in anywhere.

Ted nodded, without really knowing why.

– You know, Meinz said quietly, with a strange glare in his eyes, somehow echoing that in Ted's own. – I don't think anything is able to stop you, not even death. Delay you, perhaps, but nothing can really actually stop you, stop your flight.

Meinz giggled.

– Did you think that was what I wanted? Ted raged. – More innuendos, mere suggestions of what's happening?

He broke a finger. Then he broke a hand. Meinz screamed, not so much in pain, as in pure, crystalline rage.

– YES, that's all you get, you damn FREAK, he shouted.

Ted stepped back, not so much in fear as in acknowledgement.

– You're a pig, Kurt, and you'll die, butchered like one. Only a fool lets an enemy live. A person giving mercy to enemies is doomed to die by an enemy's hand. And you're my enemy, Kurt. You should be happy I'm a bit lazy, or I would've brought you somewhere, and made sure you suffered the worst pain imaginable, suffered for a thousand years. Do you hear me, you sick fuck?

His voice was thick with emotion, choking as he was, burning as he was.

Meinz laughed. Not loud, but hard and scornful, triumphant.

– You'll *be* there. You will also be struck down by my vengeance.

– What do you mean? WHAT THE HELL DO YOU MEAN?

But Meinz just kept laughing. Ted snarled, deep down in his throat, so uncanny, so equal to an animal.

And he felt the fury.

The torn-to-pieces body of Kurt Meinz was torn further apart as it was pulled into the air. He yelped and blood gushed from his mouth. There was a gust of wind or something to that effect, and the leaf that was his body floated towards the center of the pool.

Meinz hung suspended there for a moment, looking down.

Then the body disintegrated, and the leftovers fell into the moist darkness.

Meinz fell, and Ted fell with him, into the Abyss.

Ted stood still, looking down there, into the mist and shadow.

Silence. The shooting stopped. No one shouted or cried. The only sounds originated from the abundant silence. Francis Caine couldn't recall ever having experienced such a total, total quiet before. He had never been even remotely this sensitive before, before getting to know the Warrens.

He walked between prisoners, constables, officers, dead and wounded, knelt down between the last two in the line. Linda waved to him. He reacted to all the red in all the white. It didn't fit.

– Don't worry about me, she said, while correcting her dressing. – I'm okay. I feel fine, actually. It's Eric you should be concerned about.

– Eric will be okay, too. You concentrate on getting yourself up and running.

She nodded, woozy because of the painkillers, smiling.

Stewart held office on the upper floor, standing behind the large desk. He held a hand to his side when Caine entered the room. Caine knew there was a wound there, but it was hard to actually see anything. It was hardly bleeding. Stewart removed his hand. There was a tiny hole there, that's all.

– You need to get that bullet out, Caine felt compelled to point out.

Stewart held a small shrapnel-like bullet in his palm.

Caine strived to speak.

– Carr got hit, got hit bad.

– How bad?

– I would've said he was done for, if not for your recent miracles…

At that moment he realized he had believed what he had told Linda. He had truly believed it.

There was a sound from the hall. Caine didn't hear it, but when Stewart turned, he did, too.

Burke Adams stuck his head inside.
– Jeez, what a setup they've got here, he said. – I've never seen anything like it.
– Wall to wall state of the art technology, The Gambler nodded.
A little comic relief. He was glad Adams was here.
– The facts contained in these wonders of technology are even more impressive, Stewart said.
He held up a pile of sheets, printouts from the computer.
He gave them one sheet each.
The more Adams read the paler he turned.
– … what *is* this?
– Shards from their very thorough archives. A list of members, contacts, compatriots… Many heads will roll when this gets out, in London and all over the world. A number of oppressors will lose their hard-won positions of power. Too bad people will stand in line to fill those very positions.
– The world will shake on its foundations when this gets out.
The Gambler shook his head, shook it hard.
– There might be slight tremors, Stewart said patronizingly. – But not that much more. You know that.
– But… Adams began to regain his color. – On this list are military, politicians, businessmen, and one hell of a lot of respected people… The Superintendent will never believe this.
– He won't wish to believe it, Stewart said dryly. – He won't even wish others to believe it. But faced with the overwhelming evidence he can't ignore it. Not this time.
There was a knock on the door. Tilla stuck her fiery head inside.
– They're here, she told them.
– Excellent, Stewart grinned. – Send them in.
Tilla returned the grin. Caine caught a glimpse of the Stengun she carried over the shoulder.
Pete and Sandy entered, escorting a man and a woman in their middle or late twenties.
– Carl Palmer and Zoe Stella Espershin?
They nodded, not that nervous, but not very comfortable.
– Happy to meet you both.
Stewart stepped forward and extended his hand, enthusiastically. Caine blinked.
– I'm Mark Stewart, also known as Elmont Fontaine and a number of other names.
– Stewart, Palmer gasped. – *Fontaine?* You want me… for your defense?

– That, too, that, too, kid, if necessary, but it probably won't be. So far you haven't quite succeeded as a lawyer, have you? You want to be known as one of the best, but your idealism is keeping you from it. Like many others you've discovered it keeps you from so much. There are those crawling and bowing that are usually winning in this world. Well, until tonight that is. Before this night is done, you'll have to learn to behave on television, kid.

– But… why in… why me?

– A lot of people have asked themselves that question before you, Stewart stated cheerfully. – For lack of a better reason, call it fate.

Stewart turned towards the woman.

– You're into both clinical psychology and a broad spectrum of surgery. The way I've heard it, you're one of the most talented young physicians today. Have I heard right, Zoe?

– Why ask questions where you already know the answer? Espershin asked.

– I wanted to hear it. From you.

– You haven't heard wrong, she replied, not without a certain caustic pride.

Palmer was still like paralyzed when Stewart put an arm around his neck and led him to the desk.

– This is Caine and Adams, Carl. They'll show you everything. I'll have to show Zoe her patients. There are quite a lot of them.

– Many, you say? Where are they?

– Most of them are in chains outside. Her eyes widened. He took her hand without her reacting. – Shall we go?

Adams coughed as Stewart departed.

– I would prefer if you considered yourself under open arrest from now on, he said cautiously. – Is that okay with you?

– Quite okay, Stewart replied calmly.

The Gambler smiled as he shook his head.

The journalists arrived first. Right after that the Superintendent, accompanied by John Jackson and Floyd McKenzie. Then the first ambulances began to appear.

The Super was pissed. Not so strange, perhaps. He hadn't come voluntarily.

Fifteen minutes later he was pale as a ghost. Then he was pissed again, because the journalists had been given free reign.

– Look at it this way… Stewart chastised him. – We were fairly certain of your… uh… relative innocence, but not completely so.

The Super paled some more, and he kept his mouth shut.

– What a pigheaded bull, John said afterwards.

– Well, I feel quite confident this pigheaded bull will knock quite a few people around before he stops or is stopped. Comparatively speaking? He isn't that bad.

– CHRIST. They heard his incredulous cries some time later. – MINISTER…

Caine stood by himself, not really participating anymore. There was no need. It was over. This battle was. Everything went ahead practically unaided, now.

The newly arrived constables and soldiers walked around more than a bit pale. They had visited the basement. Seen the irrefutable evidence concerning what had been happening. And this was only the beginning. Far worse sights would greet those who entered the other Abraxas Omega headquarters around the world.

He wondered, bowing his head, how long it would take for people to forget this, like they had forgotten so many things, so many atrocities committed by public and private government.

There were sounds all over the place. Nothing or nowhere was silent.

A sound, a thought gnawed at the back of his head, one he couldn't grasp, something about water… a river.

Then, there it was.

– Has anyone seen Ted?

They replied that they hadn't. No one had, for quite a while.

He rushed into the hallway. Tilla sat there.

– Where is he?

– On the roof. She shrugged and pointed with her gun.

On the roof. Christ! He increased his speed. A few moments later he was running.

When he arrived at the windy roof, he saw no one there.

– Ted! He cried. – Ted Cousin!

A hard breath of wind. He almost fell. Then he spotted a pair of glowing points in the night, a supple figure sitting at the top of one of the many chimneys, staring wildly at the ground far below, his long, raven hair blowing in the wind.

– Ted *Warren*. It wasn't a cry, but the voice still carried far. – Not Cousin. I'll kill anyone calling me that from now on, do you *hear* me?

Caine looked back. Tilla and Mark stood in the door, in silhouette. But he saw them well enough, more than well enough. Frost rode him again, and this time he knew it would never more cease.

– I begin to understand, Tilla said. – What she meant. I really understand.

Mark didn't speak. He spoke no words. His lips were twisted in a kind of ecstatic half-smile. He looked triumphantly back at Caine.

Caine looked down a brief moment, at the policemen and women, and the other people down there, at all the normal, ordinary people. For just a moment he felt the need to throw himself off the ledge, back to reality.

To safety.

Other published and upcoming novels by **Amos Keppler** from **Midnight Fire Media**:

The Janus Clan - (ten chapters about the Wild Man in the modern world, a world balancing on a razor's edge):

The Defenseless
The Slaves
Birds Flying in the Dark
At the End of the Rainbow
Lewis of Modern York
The Werewolf of Locus Bradle
The Valley of Kings
Eye in the Sky
The Iron Cage
Phoenix Green Earth

Birds Flying the Dark

Ted and Elizabeth Warren are finally claiming their name. In the crowded city of London, in the wilderness of the American Rocky Mountains they come of Age, learning more of what and who they are.

Ted and Tilla settle in London, with many of their old friends. Their eyes are open, wide open. They see the world. They see it in every street, every house, see it for what it is, not the fairy tale they have been told, told from birth it is. And the world sees them. It reaches for them with its machinery and its dull claws. The past will not let them go, and neither will the future.

Elizabeth is growing up. She sees the falseness of it all, the reality behind the façade, the illusion. She is looking, looking for the truth of the world and also for the truth behind the mystery that is her life. And she finds it, finds the first sparks, the first exploding sparks. She is Changing, changing into something Other. Her body is changing, but most of all she is changing inside… into what she has always been.

The Janus Clan has been dormant for decades, but now it is once again, finally, asserting itself in the world, and they… and the world will never be the same.

To be published April 30, 2011

Your Own Fate

From The Book of Fate:

In the Book of Fate there is everything. Every incident, all times, everything that has been, that is, that will ever be, everything that might be, everything that could have been.

But who is writing it? Who is penning it? Who is turning page by page, too many to be counted, blowing in the wind? Does it perhaps write itself, with a pen moving across the yellow sheets? Or is it a hand moving the pen, one unseen, one stretching back into the past, back to the time before everything was created, creating itself from nothing?

Timothy Joyce is an enigma, a man without a past, appearing from nowhere, to go on a rampage in an astonished world.

Jeremy Zahn is hunting Timothy Joyce. It seems like he has always been hunting him, from old London, from the island of angels, where it is said they met for the first time, to the city of angels, California, the new world.

Here, on this shaky ground, following confrontations spanning the globe, its time and space the two will fight for the last time.

And the world is watching, its people shivering in their frozen hearts.

ISBN 978-82-91693-05-7

Night on Earth

This is said to be the age of enlightenment and reason...

A culmination of thousands of years' development and illumination.

The hunters are dying off, they say. Their day is done, in favor of the new, enlightened time of neon lights, technology and civilization.

But a hunter is stalking the streets of London, a creature without form, eyes and skin. In a city on the brink of chaos, of social and economic collapse, it is stalking cops, killing them in ever more horrible ways. Sheila Watts is a hunter. She's a cop.

Sheila is lost, losing herself further by the second. She's losing herself, finding herself, as she's closing in on the creature of the night, as it is closing in on her.

Sheila Watts can taste the sweet blood in her mouth...

To be published December 10, 2010

The Defenseless

The two rivers meet and join in the city of Denver, becoming one...

The two dark brothers, growing up with their sister Linda in a mundane, average suburb, a place well entrenched in modern United States and the world, have since their moment of birth been at odds with the world... and with each other.

Mike and Ted Cousin are not who they are. There is a mystery here, one of birth and upbringing, one of fate. Violence and death, blood and fire follow them all the days of their lives. The fire is resting somewhere inside... waiting for the Spark.

Their parents know something, but are not telling it. The policeman Mark Stewart and their aunt Trudy do, too. Everybody knows something, pieces of the whole, but nobody knows the whole truth, nobody telling it.

The ancient power is returning to the world, a world massively suffering from physical and spiritual poison, on the brink of collapse and a collective tailspin suicide run without its like in human history.

Magick is returning from its long exile. Thus begins the story of the wild beasts rising from their ashes.

The Spark is struck, horrible and terrifying.

First book of ten in the Janus Clan series: Ten stories of the wild man in the modern world, forty years of wandering, before the Phoenix is rising from its ashes.

ISBN 978-82-91693-08-8

www.ingramcontent.com/pod-product-compliance
Lightning Source LLC
Chambersburg PA
CBHW060604310726
48982CB00008B/1233/J

* 9 7 8 8 2 9 1 6 9 3 0 9 5 *